The Human Element

Apex Predator Series book 2

J.A. Faura

Barola Publishing
DALLAS, TX

J.A. Faura/Barola Publishing
5205 Brougham Lane
Plano, TX/75023
www.jafaura.com

Publisher's Note: This is a work of fiction. Names, characters, places, and incidents are a product of the author's imagination. Locales and public names are sometimes used for atmospheric purposes. Any resemblance to actual people, living or dead, or to businesses, companies, events, institutions, or locales is completely coincidental.

Cover Layout & Design ©2016 – Clary Design

Ordering Information:
Quantity sales. Special discounts are available on quantity purchases by corporations, associations, and others. For details, contact the "Special Sales Department" at the address above.

The Human Element/J.A. Faura -- 1st ed.
ISBN-13: 978-0-9908991-2-9

Para mi madre

For science, the end of the evolution struggle is simply represented by 'survival.' As for the means to that end, apparently anything goes. Darwinism leaves humanity without a moral compass.
— Bruce Lipton

We do not just fear our predators, we are transfixed by them. We are prone to weave stories and fables and chat endlessly about them.
— Peter Benchley

Prologue

The old couple sat at the same outdoor table in the same café patio they'd been sitting at for the past twelve years. Actually they'd been sitting at that spot for much longer than that, but the current owner had only built the patio when he bought the property twelve years prior. They enjoyed sitting outside and smelling the combination of azaleas and sea breeze that always came off the Narragansett Bay at this time of year. The café was actually more of a convenience store, one of two on Pertinence Island and the old couple were two of the 188 year-around residents on the island. It was virtually impossible to go unnoticed on Pertinence. Whether you were coming by way of water taxi, private boat or ferry, every individual coming onto the island was visible from the lighthouse at the top of the cliffs on the Northeast part of the island, which was precisely what the lighthouse's current resident was looking for when he'd bought the place eight years ago. When he'd come to the island all that time ago, the entire population of the island had noticed him almost immediately. He didn't look like the normal summer people and he most definitely did not act like the normal summer people. In fact, it was almost certain that nobody would see him more than three or four times during summertime on the island. During the summer the population of the island could get up to 1,000 people counting all the tour visitors and people just wanting a picture by a picturesque lighthouse, the people that rented the few available houses and the people staying at the bed and breakfast on the island. And while everyone always asked about the lighthouse at the top of the cliffs, all tour operators or guides knew that there was no way to go onto the lighthouse, in fact, they knew that they should not come within one hundred yards of the property the lighthouse sat on. Like many things known in many small towns in New England, people knew these things not because anyone said anything, but because they simply knew. It wasn't too difficult to figure out that the man who lived there was someone you most definitely did not want to have a disagreement with in any way, shape or form. He was around 50-years old, six feet four inches tall and he carried about 220 lbs. of muscle on his frame. He had greying brown hair, cut short, a hard, angular face that had more scars than wrinkles on it and, because of his natural scowl, steel blue eyes that were bright and engaging when he was content and cold and frightening when he wasn't. Every single day he would run the three miles from the lighthouse down to the docks and the convenience store where he would pick up his newspaper, nod a quick hello at the old couple sitting outside and run the three miles back. Early on, some of the people had thought he was just a summer visitor in the midst of a mid-life crisis or a self-discovery deal or whatever those kinds of people called not knowing where the hell they belonged. That opinion lasted until Stan Sullivan, he of the old couple at the café, got a good look at him. The man may have been a lot of things, a crazy, a hermit, a Martian, whatever, but someone who did not know where they belong, that was just not possible, no way. Stan Sullivan had been in the Marine Corps for thirty-two years, had fought in two wars and could almost smell the scent of war that came from the man. The look in the eye, a look that saw beyond the here and now, the easy gait that only came with the confidence of having been to hell and come back to tell the tale, the way you could tell that nothing would ever catch the guy by surprise, not ever, all let Stan know this guy was no lost summer bum. He picked up more than most people picked up when they saw the man from the lighthouse, but not too much more. The reality was that the man was a trained killer, trained by the US government first and by life and other entities, very powerful and secret entities, later. There was no conflict for him in what he was trained to do, he'd been certain very early in his life that killing was something he'd been born to do. He actually never viewed what he did as a choice, it just was what it was, what he did. That certainty of purpose and lack of moral ambiguity along with more than two decades of increasingly difficult training, made the man exceedingly good at what he did. He hadn't come to Pertinence Island to hide from anything; he had accumulated enough favors from people in very high places, not only within the US government, but also within governments in Europe and Africa, that he wouldn't *need* to hide from anyone or anything for the foreseeable future, if ever. Over the years he had come and gone with no discernable calendar or pattern. His schedule wasn't based on anyone else's calendar; being in complete and absolute control of each one of the days in his life was critical to how he wanted to live it. Whether it had been in the military or early on working for himself, he had spent over two decades living his life on someone else's clock, now he was living on his own clock, he'd earned it. The population of the island got used to seeing him at different times of the year and for various lengths of time. Sometimes he'd be gone for two weeks, other times he'd be gone for six months; once he was actually gone for a year and a half, but in the end he always came back. He didn't come to this place because he was afraid of being around people, he came to the island because he could be completely at ease, relaxed and that was not something that would ever happen in a place where he could not see the horizon in ever direction and with a larger population than that of the island. He worked out, read, wrote and worked on his models of scenes from various wars throughout history, something he was incredibly passionate about. He had scenes from feudal Japan, the Civil War, the crusades and scenes from every war in the 20th century. War was his business, so it made sense that it would also become his pastime. Some of his models had taken years to complete. Throughout his time on the island his only steady company had been his two mastiffs. When he was gone he left both of them with the Holland family, the owners of the convenience store with the patio where the Sullivans liked to sit. They had two teenage kids who absolutely loved it when the dogs came for a stay. Over the years there had been three or four women that had come to visit, none of them ever stayed longer than two weeks, none of them were the same twice in a row and none of them were the young, trophy-wife-type of women many men his age tended to go for. He'd tried the married thing early on and had discovered that neither he nor his profession were suited to be in a relationship that was supposed to last a lifetime, let alone raise a family. He spoke five languages and was always working on mastering another one, something that also consumed his time when he wasn't working. Like everything else he did, he could not just be good at something, he couldn't know a language well enough to be understood, he had to master the language, he had to be able to say everything he wanted to say in as nuanced a way as he wanted to say it in whatever language he was speaking. That kind of determination to not only know, but to master whatever it was he took on, was another reason he could simply not have the same type of relationship that other men had or that most women wanted. He'd made peace with that fact long ago and believed it to be a fair trade he'd made with life. He could forgo traditional relationships if in exchange he was able to absolutely commit to whatever it was he was interested in and be the absolute best at it. He had very few friends, something that was the case with most men like him and all of his friends knew not to reach out to him unless absolutely necessary. Most of the time, if it truly was absolutely necessary, he would be there without the need for anyone to reach out to him. All his friends knew that he preferred to be alone and that he did not like to be put in the position of telling them to stay away or telling them that it was none of their business where he was or what he was doing. This was as inviolate a rule as there could be around his life and how he ran it. It was an absolute. Outside of four people on the planet, no one knew where or how to get in touch with him, so it was pretty certain that if one of them did reach out, it was absolutely necessary. Like the rest of the world, he'd been watching the Loomis case with some interest. It wasn't really that necessary to be interested in the case in order to keep informed about it, you actually had to try pretty hard to *not* see, hear or read something relating to the case. He'd begun looking into the science the case was based on from the very beginning and now felt like he had a very clear grasp of what the science and the argument built on it were. Truth be told, he had pondered this point many times before. Were there people out there that had somehow mutated or evolved, people that had abilities and physical advantages beyond what was humanly possible and which others simply did not have? He thought there were people just like that and he thought they'd most likely been born that way. He'd come across situations over a three-decade career where there was simply no way a normal human being could do some of the things he'd seen. No way. Hitting a target with a head shot at five hundred yards in complete darkness and without optics for the gun or for the shooter; having the ability to somehow sense an IED on the side of the road with nothing to give it away and no equipment. There were many cases of guys doing that in different theaters of war, but he'd seen only two where the same individual could do it over and over again and could do it regardless of the type of trigger. He'd heard of stories of someone dragging themselves ten miles with everything but one arm either gone or completely broken and he had been a part of a squad where the same guy walked point over and over because he could see, hear, smell or somehow feel the enemy, again without equipment or training to do it. He'd seen many of these things and had come to the exact same conclusion that Steven Loomis was now using as a part of his defense: there were people out there that were simply something else, something not human or at the very least, a different kind of human.

After returning from his run to pick up the paper he turned on the television. Given that he'd basically been disconnected from the rest of the world for the past couple of days, he wanted to catch up on any important news from around the globe. Once he'd gotten what he needed to get from the TV news, he was ready to begin his workout in earnest. The second floor of the lighthouse was set up as a home gym. There were no Nautilus-type machines anywhere; there were no treadmills or elliptical machines; everything was done with free-weights. He had an open room where he had a variety of exercises set up, his own inventions to train a particular muscle group or tactical response, either hanging from the ceiling or set up on a variety of dummies used for martial arts training. He started his workout with breathing exercises from Systema, a Russian martial arts philosophy that was more than 1000 years old and was favored by the Spetnaz units. Once he finished and felt stretched out and warm enough, he went into his weight workout. He did not use very heavy weights, having too much bulk tended to slow down reaction time. After he was done with the weights he went to the cellar of the lighthouse where he'd set up a shooting range to practice while his heart rate was still elevated. Most of his practice with the handgun focused around using his left hand to do everything as well as he did it with the right hand. He knew that the left would never be as good as the right, it was almost impossible, physiologically speaking, to train the muscle memory of both the dominant and weaker hand to react at the same rate and level of performance. He exercised for an hour and a half, practiced tactics for 45 minutes and then called it a day. He never missed a workout and he never worked out for less than an hour. He'd been doing the same routine for over 20 years, which helped explain why, aside from the number of scars and wrinkles on his face, he looked better in his 50s than most 30-year-olds. As a warm-down routine he switched between Tai Chi and other traditional push-hands routines. After his workout he fed his two French mastiffs, Baron, the male, and Alabama, the female. They were five and six respectively and like everything else he did, he'd poured himself into the training of his dogs since they had both been puppies, which made them amazingly well-trained dogs. In addition to being two of the few living beings on earth he could honestly say he loved, the dogs patrolled the whole of the lighthouse and the property around it. The two massive dogs never needed to bark too much or even growl for people to be terrified. Although French mastiffs had been popularized by the movie Turner and Hooch, they were still impressive when seen in real life. Impressive for some, terrifying for others. Baron had a 25-inch neck. He had literally had to buy two collars to cobble together one that would fit his dog. The breed also lent itself to his personality; French mastiffs tended to bond to one person and one person only. They could be friendly, sociable dogs, but once they bonded with their owner that was it, there would never be another bond like it and their loyalty to their owner would be absolute. The reality was that the security and other tactical advantages of having both dogs patrolling the property didn't compare with what their companionship did for him.

With his morning and early afternoon routine finished, he went to the top of the lighthouse, sat on the small balcony he'd set up right outside where the old lighthouse used to shine on Narragansett bay and thought about what he had to get done over the next few days. He drank a cup of coffee and felt the cold chill of the early evening breeze. It was this time alone that had always served as the foundation for how he kept balance in his life. In his line of work he knew that if he did not find balance, he could lose himself very quickly. He had seen many men lost just that way. He loved to sit up here and think about the plans for his house, which he changed continuously; about whether he might want to actually have someone to share it with and what that person might be like. Looks were not particularly important to him. Like any other sentient being, he appreciated and was drawn to beauty, physical beauty, but for him intellect or the lack thereof could change that in a split second. That was the reason that he had not shared a relationship with young, trophy-wife-type women. He was of the opinion that for someone to have the type of view about life and about the world he considered thoughtful, she needed to have done some living of her own. He finished his coffee, took a shower and went to finally do some work for the project he was currently in the middle of planning for. With unrest in the Middle East and Africa and billions of dollars at stake, companies put together their own security forces. They were actually more like small armies than security forces. The number of people in them was in the thousands; they had military-style ranks and armament and equipment to rival some countries' armies. The other difference between traditional armies and these security forces was how they paid the men that made them up. Because of that they were able to recruit some of the most experienced and best-trained men available. When it came to the rank and file companies recruited from the towns in the countries where the companies had a presence, but when it came to officers and squad leaders it was a very different story. Most Special Forces soldiers found their way to these groups after serving in their own country's military. They got paid three times as much, had the same benefits and were less likely to engage in heavy combat than if they stayed in their countries' armies, so it wasn't much of a debate whether they'd stay in or go private. These days he only needed to take one or two projects each year in order to continue to live comfortably and still save for building his house. Actually he only needed one, but he kept thinking that when he decided to call it a day and walk away from the work, he might want to actually do some traveling, maybe visit some family, if he could find any to go visit. Whether he traveled or visited family or did anything else, he was absolutely committed to building his dream house. A house he'd designed himself more than twenty years ago. Architecture was one of his true passions and his house was the most perfect manifestation of what he considered to be balanced, organic architecture. It was the one project that he thought about when he was on an assignment, although he never allowed it to get in the way of his work. He had started the plans twenty years ago, but he'd worked on them constantly since then. His taste and his knowledge of architecture had evolved over time, so the house looked very different now than where it had started. He used to wonder where he was going to build the house and had gone back and forth with himself over dozens of options over the years. He hadn't made a final decision about where exactly he was going to build it, but he had at least settled on the location where he wanted to spend the rest of his days. There was a group of islands between Finland and Sweden and it would be on one of those islands that he would end his days. When he wasn't at his lighthouse in New Hampshire, he was on one of the islands in that chain, trying each one to see which one fit him best. Most of the work he did these days involved strategic planning or tactical management of efforts or initiatives already in place and almost all of it was working with the private security forces around the world, which meant that as he got older he had more time to think about his house. Any and all organizations and individuals around the world, who made their money by knowing about wars and who was fighting them, called on him and in most instances they would be calling at the same time. That meant that he could and in fact did, command a much higher payment. Not that money had ever been an issue or an impediment to him working for a client. His clients tended to operate in the billions of dollars, so asking for $250,000 for a three-month engagement with another payment of $150,000 when the job was complete, was absolutely not an issue, not ever, especially when it was for *his* services. The reason he was in such high demand and could command such fees, was that he was worth it both from a desire to be successful and a financial perspective. If you had a West African country paying two hundred million dollars to a global security firm for them to eliminate a terrorist or rebel force and there was a bonus of another $75 million if they did it within a specified period, paying two or three hundred thousand to the best in the business to make sure that happened, was chump change. On the other hand, if you made a mess of a job and not only did not deliver on suppressing the opposition in time, but completely failed tactically, you had to pay to get things cleaned up, usually to one of your competitors. No, there was absolutely no doubt that having him working on your project would always pay for itself. The reality was that there was less than a one percent chance that he would ever see any action or that his skill-set would be truly tested, but even that was too high a risk when you were working in the billions. Another reality was that sometimes his reputation was enough to give pause to those who might be contemplating a move. It was a reputation earned across a lot of land and paid for with a lot of lives. It wasn't something he was proud or ashamed of, it simply was what it was.

He was planning on leaving for his latest assignment in two days which meant he'd start making arrangements the next day and he needed to get started early doing that because the arrangements he needed to make were different than they'd been in the past. Once he was done with his arrangements he would get on his way to the project. He was planning to make a couple of stops to look in on a couple of things before leaving the country. Normally he would only make one stop before going to work; for the first time he was planning to make two or maybe three, which meant he needed to rearrange his routine. He would start by taking his two dogs to the Holland's house; they'd be expecting him. As he walked around the lighthouse and made sure things were exactly as he wanted them, he thought about his current situation and whether it might now be time to do something different. He thought it might be too late to try to be a father, but he could maybe give marriage another try, be happy. Maybe. Well, this assignment would be shorter than most and he was planning to go straight to Umea, one of the islands off the coast of Sweden, in the Gulf of Bothnia; he would think about it seriously then, right now it was a distraction and he hated distractions.

HOUSTON, TEXAS

John David Garzen looked long and hard into the mirror in the changing room and as always, he liked what he saw. He smiled, frowned, raised his eyebrows, quivered his lips; he had each and every one of those looks down cold. It was his expressive face that really endeared him to his followers. He was not a physical specimen by any stretch of the imagination. Has was almost 50 years old, just short of 5 feet 8 inches, weighed about 270 pounds with thinning hair and he had a pockmarked complexion that held flat, expressionless features and small rodent-like eyes. No, John David Garzen had never had any luck with girls as a young man, but Reverend J.D. Garzen had his pick of any number of women. Young, old, rich, poor, married or single, it didn't matter, if they were a part of his flock, he could have them. In spite of the fact that he was married and had a son, he thought of himself as available, how could he not be? The women of his flock needed him and who was he to deny them that comfort. He knew that his wife was well aware of his activities, but he also knew that she would never say anything, she enjoyed the lifestyle she had too much to make trouble. She knew she could divorce him and get half of his assets, but she also knew that his lawyers and accountants had made sure that a great majority of the assets he'd accumulated did not appear in his name. There were houses, boats, cars, even a private plane, all held by a complex set of corporate entities and offshore leasing and real estate companies. Aside from the tax consequences of having those assets under his name, it simply did not look good for a preacher, whether he was on television or not, to have houses in Vail, Big Sur, Atlanta and Connecticut, along with a fleet of classic collectors' cars and another of exotic German and Italian cars. No, if Dorothy, Dottie, Garzen wanted to keep her lifestyle without the need for divorcing J.D., she knew she'd have to turn a blind eye to his activities on the side, something she was more than happy to do. She couldn't remember the last time that she and J.D. had actually made love, over a year for sure, and if she was to be honest, even when they were doing it somewhat regularly, it was never something she cared for. J.D. was a clumsy and thoughtless lover, someone who had clearly never been schooled by a father or a brother on how to please women. J.D. fixed his tie, checked his wireless mike and finished checking his makeup. Once his show was picked up by a major network, he had insisted that he needed a makeup artist to work with him every Sunday. He said it was because the lights made him look shiny, which was true, but the real reason was that he wanted to cover his acne-scarred face. J.D. had begun his career as a preacher almost by mistake. Growing up in Los Angeles California he was an awkward and insecure child and later young man. J.D. had a difficult time making friends and an absolutely horrible time trying to find a girl who would go out with him. After he turned twenty-one, he decided that one way to make new friends and perhaps find a woman who would go out with him was to volunteer for a state senator's campaign. J.D. did not really know anything about politics or for that matter, the candidate he was volunteering for, he had no political viewpoint to speak of. As a volunteer, however, he learned about the man's politics, his viewpoints on a variety of issues and his voting record in Washington. On a rainy February evening, he had been manning the phones at campaign headquarters when he saw a group of older people come in the front door. Everyone was too busy to notice, but J.D. did notice and was curious as to who they were and what they were doing there. He had walked up and introduced himself and found out in short order that this was a group of Jewish voters from the district who had been asked to come to headquarters to hear about the candidate and his policies. Obviously someone had forgotten about the group. J.D. did not hesitate; he decided he'd cover until the campaign manager got there. So he had led the group into an empty room with some chairs in it and proceeded to explain why they *needed* to vote for the senator. It was then that the awkward and shy young man had realized what he was meant to do. The way he lit up while telling the senator's story, where he came from and what he stood for, literally transformed him into an engaging and outgoing speaker and let him know he'd found his calling. He himself had no political ambitions, so he knew politics was not for him and he just could not figure out where else he could tell stories for a living. He'd been looking for some time when he happened to walk by a storefront church that had the door open. He could hear someone in there, but not what they were saying. So he'd walked in out of curiosity more than anything else. What he'd seen had sealed his fate, he had found home. He saw a man holding his audience absolutely enraptured with what he was saying. It reminded him of how it had felt to speak to the Jewish voters, except that this audience had a look of absolute worship that the other group had not. Just like with politics, he did not have any true or sincere religious viewpoint of his own, he had never gone to church as a child and his parents had never spoken about it. Over the next few years he'd gone from denomination to denomination trying to find one where he might be able to eventually be ordained, but every denomination had requirements that would take years and he just did not have the patience to wait. He'd finally decided he would be nondenominational and had gone through an online 'divinity' program that, once he paid his $499, would grant him a master's degree in divinity. He'd begun his ministry on that day and the reverend J.D. Garzen had been born. He had moved to Texas because he understood that in order to really establish himself as a preacher with any sort of credibility, he had to go to the Bible Belt; the fact that Houston had the largest number of 'lay' preachers in the country settled what city he chose. He had grown his congregation every year since he'd started. Early on that was not very impressive since he would go from around 40 followers to 45 followers, but over the last seven years it had a growth explosion going from thousands to hundreds of thousands. He was smart enough not to think that it was his religious insights that had drawn most of his followers, he had no religious insights to impart. No, he knew they had come into his fold because over the last seven years he'd become the preacher of the ultra right wing conservatives in the GOP, someone who was completely willing to say what others shied away from saying. He had come out loud and clear against things like abortion, homosexuality and other religions, that had been no different than any number of preachers. What made him different, however, was his stance on things like women working, interracial marriages and assorted issues that seemed to pop up on a weekly basis. He had clearly tapped into a number of issues that people had strong opinions about, but were afraid to share. The reality was that he did not give a shit about any of it, politics, social justice, helping those in need, none of it. He was not religious and in fact he held religion in more contempt than he held anything else. It just happened to be the way to truly own the heart and mind of an audience, of getting more than just recognition or validation. It was the only true way to *own* their souls. He had a talent and he had learned how to use it to its full advantage, his charisma had afforded him a life of possibility and he had been wise enough to recognize that and to utilize it to build his life. It was a testament to his charisma and preaching that he had African American and Hispanic followers in spite of his positions on interracial relationships. He had always made sure to explain that 'It wasn't a race thing, it was a god thing.' That was one of his signature sayings when he couldn't figure out how to defend his arguments with logic or facts and he could make it work for anything. 'It isn't a gender thing, it's a god thing' or 'it isn't a political thing, it's a god thing' were well-worn favorites. He had perfected the viewpoint that humans were presumptuous and conceited to think that they could understand why god did the things he did. He loved to answer reporters' questions with sayings like 'I don't know why god decided to do the things he decided to do, do you?' Anyone with a scintilla of true religious belief, not to mention the mainstream media, discounted him as a charlatan and a crackpot, some even called him dangerous. The fact of the matter, however, was that his congregation had almost a million followers spread all around the world with thousands coming on every day. His team believed that the flock would be more than two million strong within the next twelve months. The growth explosion was a result of the success of his television show, soon to be network. A cable network had approached him just over a year previously and asked whether he might want to have Sunday services televised. He jumped at the chance and the Ministry of Light had been born. One of the things he'd realized early on in his televangelist role was that he had to come up with issues to have an opinion about to keep his followers giving him money and his face in the news. It didn't matter what it was, it just had to have the potential of getting media attention and he would jump on it, always with the most controversial view point. And so in short order he'd gone from thinking about his flock in the thousands to thinking of them in the millions with the money attached to those numbers, of course. As he got ready to walk on stage he thought that he had hit the mother lode of social issues, a human who had dared to make a claim in god's territory, a human who believed he was holy enough and enlightened enough to decide what was human and what wasn't, reverend J.D. Garzen smiled as he prepared to fire the first of what would be thousands of shots aimed squarely at Steven Loomis. He bounded onto the stage wearing his most engaging smile, what he called his 'moneymaker'. The audience, already standing, raised the noise up a notch as they gave him the elixir he had become so addicted to, adulation.

"How is mah flock this lovely mohnin'? Are you all readyaahh?"

He always poured on the southern accent when preaching or doing interviews. His true accent was reserved for his inner circle and only for instances when he was royally pissed off. His accent was so cartoonish that most people outside of his congregation thought he sounded either like the Looney Tunes rooster Foghorn Leghorn or another Looney Tunes favorite, Yosemite Sam, sometimes like both.

The cheering rose up into a frenzy as they all screamed the answer to his question, "Yeeeahssss!!"

He looked around giving his face to the entire crowd, "That's raght! It's time to step into the laght!"

This was the way he began every service and the title of his first book.

Stepping Into the Light went on to sell more than a million copies. "I want to start today's service by talking about one of the most abominable siahns I have evah known, a sin that is almost unforgivable."

He walked around the stage letting it soak in, hearing the 'amens!' being shouted from around the crowd, "Yes my brothahs and sistahs, we are all human, so we are all sinners. But our sins come because we break god's laws, because we cannot abaaahde by them every hour of every day!"

He kept walking the entire stage, making every segment of audience feel like he was speaking directly to them. Early on in his ministry he understood that by pausing and letting his most powerful insights soak into the crowd, he could keep them not just paying attention, but enthralled.

"Christ new that, he knew we would always be sinnahs so he gave himself up to cleeeaaanse our sins! But he also left us ways for us to atone when we sinned again."

Now that he was getting warmed up, his own tone and demeanor started to rise to match that of the crowd, "But that's not the sin I'm going to speak to you about. No sir, the sin I am going to speak to you about is one committed baaahh a man, a human, a sinnah beyond all others, a sinnah who beleeahves that he is god!"

He shouted the last sentence and the crowd responded; they booed, some hissed and some shouted 'No!'

Now he was truly in his element, "Yeahss! A man who thinks he has the rahght to decide who is human and who isn't; a man who thinks himself a godddd!. Such a man is no mere sinnah, such a man is a deeeahmonnn among us! A deeeahmon who passes himseiilf off as human, a deeeahmon who uses his disgahse to corrupt othahsss! This man, a man who kiahlled a human! A man who pretends to have a family, this man who has the world's attention has claimeahd he can decide who and what is human, who and what should liveaah and who and what should dieaahh!"

The crowd was now on its feet, shouting a confirmation of every point he made, "But even this sinnah above all sinnahs; even this deeaahmon, can be called back into god's aahhms! And that is what we must all believe, what we must all work fahh! It's up to us to redeeaahmmm his souuulll!"

He was smiling and nodding, his energy now completely entwined with the screams and cheers of his flock, completely taking in what they were willing to give him. This was a remarkable moment, his flock had never given themselves like this before. Yes indeed, reverend J.D Garzen had found the mother lode and its name was Steven Loomis.

VAIL, COLORADO

Nigel Barlow was thousands of miles away enjoying the view from his chalet. He had left New York immediately after his fact-finding session with Harvey Lynch. It had proven to be a waste of time, but it had served as a release for him, which made it not a complete waste of time. When he arrived, everything he had requested was ready. All his files had been encrypted and loaded into 22 separate jump drives, each representing one part of his work. He had then had his lawyers prepare documents to provide clear and minutely detailed instructions as to how his operations and his property were to be utilized. He had named various directors, each dedicated to a specific part of his enterprises, each one of them would be handed one of the drives on the table. None had any influence or authority over another. They were to function independently, only reporting in to the law firm to access funds, communicate with Barlow and to continue to expand their reach, his reach. He had been crafting this structure over decades and now finally felt it was time to truly implement what he had been planning all along. After a few years of doing his work, Barlow had realized that he would simply not be able to do everything himself, not if the work was to reach as far as he intended it to reach. After some more time had passed, he realized that he needed to set things up in such a way that the work would continue, regardless of what happened to him, and so for the next 13 years he had begun to set things up. Over that time, he had established distinct areas that he wanted to take his work to. Politics, entertainment, media, energy and military were among some of his principal areas of interest. Within each of them there were subareas of interest. Within entertainment, there was content development, production or talent. Talent was his guilty pleasure. He had many accomplished and quite famous performers in various areas that he was able to consult, all in the pursuit of his one original objective, of course. Likewise there were subareas within politics, foreign policy, funding, elections, etc. They were all organized this way. Sometimes the different areas of interest would overlap. Politics and finance were a perfect example, energy and military were another, and so on. He had kept meticulous records of all his work. Contacts, relationship to each, influence or financial worth, it was all in his files. He had read everything there was to read about J. Edgar Hoover. He felt a kinship with the former head of the FBI. They were both men whose lives were dedicated to locating, cataloging and using information to influence individuals they had an interest in. That had included JFK and his brother, Bobby, the Attorney General at the time. His filing system was based on his research of how Hoover had set up his confidential files. He had also become a master at using that information the way Hoover had used it when he had been alive, gathering the innermost secrets of those in power and then applying pressure. Or sending others to apply it. Hoover had almost certainly been a Prime Force, *a Homo sapiens predator,* one of the new species, Barlow was certain. Smart, ruthless, keenly aware of those with influence and how to utilize them should he ever need to. Never married, perhaps a homosexual, but that was nothing of consequence to any of his subjects. They satisfied their needs and desires as they saw fit, whether it was with a man or a woman was of no importance. Only when procreating would that play a role in their choice of partner. Barlow paused, put all the documents aside and left the drives on the desk where he had been sitting, and walked over to the massive window with the breathtaking view of the Rockies. That was an area where he really felt he had not made sufficient progress. The rise of a new species depended on the ability of that species to adapt and procreate. Without procreation, history would look upon the new species as a random mutation, something that over time became extinct because nature had not intended for them to be alive in the first place. He couldn't be too hard on himself, however, because he knew how difficult it was to find and nurture and guide one of them, let alone trying to find two of them and to get them to breed with each other. He had made some valiant efforts early on, utilizing genetic matching and a variety of other standardized tests to determine how suitable a woman was for some of his younger projects. There had even been a couple of instances where he had actually needed a suitable male. In almost every instance, though, their offspring appeared to be completely human, remarkable but human nonetheless. *Almost* every instance – there were five offspring out there that showed incredible promise. He had maintained close contact with their parents and been appraised of every step of their education. He would be taking over their education very soon. He smiled at the thought. To be able to work with them from a young age was his dream, one of the things he had really hoped to be able to do at the outset. Still, five was far too low a number for what he now knew he would have to do. He had looked into Donald Riche and what he had done because he had learned to look for certain elements in the situations he heard about and he thought that what had been happening in New York had the feel of something he might be interested in. But, before he could learn any more about Riche and what he had done, Steven Loomis had stepped in. Barlow had been initially disappointed when he had learned about what had happened to Riche, but fate had richly rewarded him for his work and persistence with Loomis. What a fascinating turn of events that had been! There was something about Loomis, something that went beyond his training and experience as a Special Forces commander that Barlow could sense in the man. A certain intellectual flow just under the surface, something Barlow had sensed before in others, but in a very different context. Still, after the Riche incident, after Loomis had done what he had done, things had changed dramatically. The true objectives of Barlow's entire body of work had been remarkably crystallized for him in the past few months. Everything he had worked for, all the risks, the ridicule he had endured from those he had once called colleagues, had been all worth it. He had built something much, much more significant than he had ever dared hope for. His reach, the level and sophistication of the understanding he had been able to acquire, were also far more than he had ever hoped for. He smiled as he looked upon the sun going down, bouncing off the snow on the mountains, and had to smile. He was thinking about the technology available when he had begun, particularly the technology that helped to map the human brain and its function. It had been almost medieval in comparison to what he had at his disposal now. Genetics, robotics, all of it had been just the lore of science fiction when he had begun his work. But, if he was forced to choose the one technology that had made most of his work possible, there was no question. The Internet had made it possible to reach beyond his own borders, to obtain information on those he was interested in, to search for instances that might lead him to find what he was looking for. If he were to chart his progress, the graph would look fairly flat over the first 16 years, especially during the time he had tried to do things their way. Those had been wasted years. Then, when the Internet had really taken off for him in the late '90s, the graph would pitch up dramatically, and when social media took hold, it would once again pitch up. As he made it back to the desk where the drives were, he wondered what the next technological advancement would be that would put another spike on the graph. Perhaps the gene sequencing work going on in the Netherlands or the stem cell work in Japan. It didn't matter, whatever it was, he would be among the first to know. He reviewed the documents that his attorneys had given him. It all looked in order. The door to his study opened and his valet led Lon Crawford, one of his attorneys, a more junior one at the firm, into the room.

Barlow stayed seated and motioned to the chair in front of his desk, "Thank you Cole." Cole nodded and left, "Mr. Crawford, I wasn't expecting you this evening."

Crawford remained standing, "I know, but we might have a problem with one of the corporations you want us to set up in Belize."

Barlow's eyebrows rose, "Oh? What problem would that be?"

Lon shifted on his feet. He was clearly uncomfortable with what he had to say, "Well, it seems that the Department of Defense has an issue with the use of some of the technology you want to use. They insist it is classified and that the kind of fabrication you are looking to do could turn it to, uh, well, they say that it's not meant for...see the thing is..."

Barlow was tired and wanted to simply to have dinner and go to bed, "Spit it out, Lon, I don't want to sit here all night while you grow some testicles."

Lon took a breath and spit it out, "They say that it can be weaponized. The man who came to the firm said that it can be used to deliver both chemical and biological weapons."

Barlow smiled. His elbows were on his desk and he was tapping the tips of the fingers of one hand against those of the other, "Hmmm. That is unexpected, indeed. I wonder who it was that spoke to the DoD about the technology. We have kept our procurement of that technology very quiet, and we've hired experts from other countries and vetted them out thoroughly about the project, so I am truly perplexed as to who it could have been."

He picked up the documents he had been reviewing and handed them to Crawford, "These are fine. Move forward with everything and leave the documents for the Belize project with me. I'll take care of it."

Crawford nodded. He knew Barlow would in fact take care of it. Lon wasn't too familiar with Barlow's business. He had been with the firm for just over a year and only knew that Barlow paid the firm hundreds of thousands of dollars each year. He didn't know why, but the old bastard gave him the willies. He took the documents Barlow handed him, turned around and walked to the door.

Before he was able to leave, Barlow called out to him from his desk, "Oh, and Lon?"

The young man turned around.

Barlow had a thin smile on his face, but his eyes were ice cold, "Tell Brian Drake the next time he has one of his underlings come to give me news like this, I will be...displeased."

Lon shuddered without knowing why, nodded and left.

1.

Felix Garcia finally had 15 minutes to run downstairs and grab a hot dog from the vendor that was always in front of the *New York Chronicle* building. Garcia, a reporter for the *Chronicle*, actually ran a tab with the guy he was there so much. He had been looking for some unique angle to cover the biggest story in the history of New York, perhaps the U.S. and maybe even the world. A criminal trial where what defines a human being would be litigated; a first-degree murder trial, no less. As he stood in the elevator, Felix thought about how it really did depend on what the audience thought about the case. If they believed the defense's argument that there was indeed another subspecies under *Homo sapiens*, then it most definitely would be the biggest story in the history of the modern human. If they thought it was just some sort of ploy or gimmick the defense was using to get their client off, then it wasn't quite that big. But it was still the biggest story New York had ever seen, for sure. It wasn't just the argument the defense was planning on using that made it a huge story. The facts of the case were simply sensational, even by New York standards: a father, who is a former Navy SEAL and whose daughter is kidnapped and murdered, decides to take out his daughter's killer. After he does it, however, he does not claim insanity, temporary or otherwise, but in fact declares that his motive for killing the man was to bring the world's attention to what he says is the most significant and real threat humanity has ever seen. It had everything, a sympathetic figure, a monster, a hugely divisive issue, and some groundbreaking scientific testimony. It did not get any more sensational than that, and it hadn't ever, anywhere. So even if it wasn't the biggest case modern humanity had ever seen, it was definitely in the running. With that kind of case, the media attention had also been unprecedented and just kept getting even more frenetic, something that Garcia and most other reporters covering the story had not thought possible. He had almost given up on getting a scoop when his local contacts at the courts building, the police department and strategically important law firms came through for him. He had made the deadline last night and knew the digital version would be published any time and the print version would command the front-page headline in their evening edition.

The elevator light showed they were on the first floor, the door opened and everyone in the elevator exited except for Felix and two other people who also worked for the *Chronicle*. They knew that the first-floor lobby was a chaotic and crowded space where reporters from all kinds of media would be parked on every square inch available. Felix and the two other people, however, knew that if they went down one more floor to the basement of the building, they could exit without having to navigate equipment and people, trip over cables or risk being seen. Felix was still the only reporter that Steven Loomis, the man accused of the murder, had spoken to, which now made Felix something of a celebrity himself. The three of them walked through some storage, past an electrical panel and out a side door, which locked once they were through. Felix pulled his coat collar up over his ears; it was still very cold, even though it was almost mid-March. As he walked to the vendor's cart, which had now morphed into three carts, all owned by the same family, he got a notice on his smartphone – the piece had hit. He stopped, stood to the side and pulled up the story on the *Chronicle*'s mobile app.

District Attorney will not pursue lesser-included charges
API-Manhattan, New York
By Felix Garcia/New York Chronicle
The district attorney's office has confirmed that there will not be lesser-included offenses used on the Steven Loomis murder trial. Loomis is charged with the first-degree murder of Donald Riche, who was suspected of the kidnapping and murder of Tracy Loomis, as well as eight other girls between the ages of 5 and 7 years old. Riche was shot while being transported from the courthouse to the holding facility in Manhattan. NYU Law School criminal procedure professor and Chronicle legal consultant Hank Weller believes not including lesser-included offenses is a very unusual step for a DA to take, especially in a murder trial of this nature, "Normally in a murder trial, you want to make sure to give the jury plenty of choices to convict, so you would include the charges of second-degree murder, voluntary manslaughter, involuntary manslaughter, whatever is appropriate. David Neill is basically saying that he believes so much in the facts of the case that he doesn't need other charges as a choice for the jury." While District Attorney Neill did not comment personally, a statement from his office seemed to confirm Weller's opinion, "The district attorney's office believes that the charges in this case fulfill the precise requirements for first-degree murder without question. This decision is not an attempt at making a statement or trying to influence the jury pool, it is a decision based on the facts of the case alone." During a telephone interview, Drew Willis, Steven Loomis's lead attorney, seemed unconcerned about the DA's decision, "That is a choice every prosecutor is entitled to make,

regardless of the facts of the case. As a defense team, we cannot concern ourselves with every choice the DA chooses to make. If we did that, we might have to change our strategy every couple of weeks." Other experts interviewed also found the DA's decision unusual. Carrie Hutton, a senior attorney with the public defender's office, disagrees that it is not a decision meant to communicate a message, "We see this kind of decision when the district attorney is absolutely convinced that the jury could not find otherwise, when the facts are so crystal clear and the evidence is so convincing that it is almost a foregone conclusion that the jury will find a defendant guilty. It is usually done to pressure a defendant into taking a deal and pleading guilty. I think this could backfire for the DA in this case. I don't think the facts are as clear as the DA thinks they are." She went on to explain that while the facts of the case are undisputed, the science and other probable evidence make it a situation where the jury could find for the defense, "Consider, the defendant shot the victim in broad daylight, confessed after the shooting and clarified that he had planned exactly what he was going to do. By all rights, that should not be in any way defensible, not unless there is a claim of insanity, which there isn't in this case." Loomis's defense team strategy has been the focus of intense international media attention. The defense strategy is based on what they claim is solid and significant scientific research that points to a previously unclassified subspecies of Homo sapiens, a subspecies they are calling Homo sapiens predaer or Homo sapiens predator. Hutton went on, "That's why the defense's argument is so fascinating from a legal perspective. The human element is not something that has ever been litigated before. Not in this context at least." Professor Weller agrees that it may be a wrong decision by David Neill, "I think he's laying his cards on the table and simply establishing just how clear-cut this case is, but it is far from clear-cut. Juries can do a lot of things, as the OJ trial showed us. I think it is a strategic move designed to give the defense an incentive to make a deal with the prosecution." Jury selection begins Monday, May 12, at 8:00 AM. The county information office confirmed that there will be a jury pool of approximately 1000 potential jurors, far more than would be called *in, even in the most visible and public cases. Weller, Hutton and other legal experts believe that jury selection may take as long as three weeks, also far longer than for any other case that has been tried in the state and perhaps the country. It is widely believed that the outcome of the case will hinge on jury selection and the strength of both sides' expert witnesses, which may be the reason jury selection would be considered more critical. Hutton stated she believes it is going to be a much more contentious process than it normally is, "I think both sides are doing some serious assessment of the type of juror they are looking for and they will go toe-to-toe to get the jury they want. They don't have to spend time litigating any of the facts other than what the defense is claiming, so they can focus on the jury they want." She explained that each side is allowed a number of preemptory challenges, challenges where neither side has to give an explanation for why they are dismissing a juror, but she believes that each side will go through those challenges in the first week and will then need to challenge for cause, where they have to provide the court with a reason for dismissing a juror. The court is not obliged to accept the reason each side presents. Although it is extremely rare, the judge may decide that a juror can stay, even though one side or the other might have provided a reason for the request to dismiss.*

Felix smiled; the story had probably hit the rest of the media like a lightning bolt. Even the most well known reporters and their teams had not been able to get that information but had definitely been looking for it. He had gotten the information before anyone else covering the trial because of his contacts and his absolutely relentless work ethic. That had also been the reason that Steven Loomis had only spoken to him. Robert Grady, the lead detective in the case, had given his name to Loomis when he had asked for an honest, balanced member of the media that he could trust with writing his story. It wasn't just his work ethic that had allowed Felix to scoop much bigger media outlets, it was also the fact that he had grown up on these streets, specifically Spanish Harlem and the Bronx. His grandfather had been a well-known hustler on those streets. Never into anything too heavy, just enough to keep his family covered, Augie Garcia had made a lot of friends in a lot of places; friendships that extended into family and that had been cultivated and maintained over the years. The 'grapevine' on the street was always the best source of information if you were really looking for the story, the true story. Any son of the streets of Spanish Harlem and the Bronx could tell you that.

Garcia, walked up to the hot dog vendor, who smiled at him, "Hungry, big Felix?"

Felix held up two fingers, "You know it, Ali. Hit me up with a couple."

Ali started preparing the hot dogs, "Everything on them?"

Garcia winked at him, "You bet."

Not too far from where Felix Garcia was enjoying his hot dogs, the District Attorney, David Neill, was in a meeting with the two deputies that would be handling the Loomis trial, Barton Logan and Melanie Farris. Bart would be lead counsel with Melanie backstopping him. She was actually more senior than Logan, more seasoned, which meant that if the trial went to hell she'd have more to lose. Both of them had been very cleverly manipulated, almost ambushed, into handling the case. Not that they really had much choice. When it was going to be a trial to convict Donald Riche, murderer of young children, Neill was going to handle the case personally with Farris as second counsel and Logan as the third-string sub. Bart would have more than likely been researching points of law and citations for them to prepare for the trial. When Loomis shot Riche the situation had gone from a 'can't lose' type case, to a 'can't win' type case. How do you prosecute a man who is an upstanding citizen, a decorated military commander serving in the military team that was literally made up of the best of the best? A man whose daughter, the victim in this case, had been kidnapped and brutally murdered along with eight other girls and who knew how many other victims. How do you prosecute such a man? Very carefully, that's how. You make sure you don't attack him or who he is and you focus on the law, on establishing the elements of the crime and that's it, no judgment of the man whatsoever. His boss had called this meeting to go over preparations for the trial, but had instead been ranting about the article that had just been published by the New York Chronicle. David Neill was not a very amiable or charismatic individual; he was a dry, focused individual who had been born to be a public servant. He believed in the absolutes of the law and expected every one of his deputies to be the same way. There were no gray areas in the law for David Neill, something was right or something was wrong, period. He had used that complete commitment to the law and to catching and convicting those who broke it to get elected twice already. Right now, however, Neill was breathing fire about the article.

He had lost it after Michael Gordon, one of the chief deputies in the office, had notified him about the article, "I want to know who the fuck is talking to that little bastard from the Chronicle! That spic has been hanging around the courthouse and our offices for years getting all kinds of information that nobody should be able to get. It hasn't really been an issue because the crap he usually covers is small-time, but this is different, this will literally make or break the careers of every single person from this office who is involved in the case directly. That includes me, in case you were wondering! So I want to know who he's talking to and I want their balls on a platter!"

Logan and Farris both smiled as they looked down, but Neill still caught the gesture, "You guys think this is funny?! We'll see how funny you think it is when the media is roasting you over an open fire after losing the case."

He turned to Gordon who had just been frozen in place since giving Neill the news.

Gordon tried to mollify his boss, "We're trying to find out precisely that as we speak. I'm confident before the end of day we'll know who it is he's been talking to, at least about this case."

Neill seemed to settle a bit, but was still angry, "You better hope so. I'm serious Michael, I want their balls when you find out who it is."

Michael nodded and left. He had wanted to ask his boss what he'd like to have on the platter if it was a woman that was talking to Garcia, but he thought better of it and just left without saying anything.

Neill got back to the business at hand, "Well, it is what it is, now they know. Melanie, where are we with our expert witnesses?"

Farris looked down at the open manila folder in front of her, "We have experts for just about every aspect of the science they are most likely to use. Anthropologists, evolutionary biologists, archaeologists, paleoneurologists, psychiatrists and at least five other disciplines."

Neill was visibly taken aback, "That's a lot of experts to prepare for, so we're going to need to have other people in the office handling some of it. Get Diaz from the human trafficking unit, Marchowski and Thompson from organized crime. All of them have had a lot of experience with expert witnesses and they can prepare ours for when the defense cross-examines them. I want the two of you to concentrate on coming up with the cross for their witnesses. By the time you are done with their experts the jury should be thinking they're just a bunch of crackpots capitalizing on a high-profile case."

Logan and Farris looked at each other as if to ask 'Do you tell him or do I'; neither one of them was looking forward to this case having Neill looking over their shoulder and they really weren't looking forward to telling him when they thought he was wrong about something.

It was Melanie Farris that finally spoke up, "Um, sir, we believe it may be risky to just discount their experts. We've looked into all of their backgrounds and they all check out as serious researchers at the top of their field. Perhaps it would be more effective to go forward with the assumption that their findings are correct and simply attacking their conclusions. We don't need for them to be crackpots to win the case, sir, we just need to show the jury that as accomplished as the expert are, they are human beings that can and have made mistakes."

Neill let her finish and then shook his head while a wry smile spread across his face as he turned and looked directly at Bart Logan, "I see, and is this point of view shared by Logan?"

Bart Logan was definitely not as bold or seasoned as Melanie Farris was, but he very much shared the point of view so he nodded and chose to just go with a simple 'yes sir'.

Neill nodded, put his hands on his waist and began to pace as he laid into his deputies, "Are you both crazy? Do I need to find two other deputies to handle this case? Anything short of taking apart their witnesses gives credence to this bullshit theory of theirs and credence is something we absolutely cannot give the defense. Not in any way."

Farris's eyes were focused on a point on the floor as she listened. Neill had a point, but it was one that both she and Bart Logan had already explored and discounted. She had told herself she wouldn't respond to Neill, not matter what he said. She wasn't able to contain herself, however, "We actually started with that strategy in mind, sir, but after going through each of the witnesses' backgrounds we realized it just wouldn't be possible."

Neill shook his head emphatically, "Nonsense, any witness can be taken apart by a good litigator, any witness. I don't care what their backgrounds are; this theory is ridiculous, so all we have to do is show the jury just how ridiculous it is. And, don't forget we also have very solid witnesses who will be testifying to that fact. So we go after the witnesses and we don't go after

Loomis himself. Public sympathy is a powerful thing, especially because of what he's been through. We stick with the law and we destroy the science and we'll be golden. This one is a slam dunk guys, it's an amazing opportunity to win the highest profile case this city, this country for god's sake, has ever seen."

Now both Melanie and Bart were now looking down at the table they were seated around. Neither one of them responded to Neill, but they were both thinking along the same lines. They were both thinking 'if it was that easy it would be you handling the case', but they knew it didn't matter whether they said something or not.

Neill's mind was made up, "You're both new at these high-profile cases, so I'll overlook your fumble this once, but one is all you get. All right let's go over our expert witness list."

Farris and Logan nodded and came around to the side of the table Neill was at to look at the list. Neither was willing to let Neill know that they both thought the decision to pursue murder one and only murder one was a huge mistake.

Ten blocks away, Steven Loomis was gathering his thoughts at the law offices of Max Zeidler and Drew Willis, his two principal defense attorneys. They had been going over expert witness testimony all day for almost two weeks, grilling every single potential expert witness in every conceivable way. They even had two litigators that had been senior prosecuting attorneys for the U.S. Attorney's office do the cross examinations. Both were brutal litigators who had well-deserved reputations for ripping expert witnesses to shreds. Steven looked out the window of the boardroom he had parked himself in. Even this high up he could see where the media was parked all over the city. They had basically erected a temporary, mobile city around the building and wherever they could find a place near the building. Initially he had wondered whether he had made the right choice by going with such a large law firm, but now he was truly thankful he had. Their resources were amazing and the legal talent was absolutely top-notch. Willis was new to the firm, but he was an experienced litigator who had established, maintained and grown his own small law firm before making the decision to take Max Zeidler up on his offer to come onboard. With offices in 10 countries, 95 partners and more than 3300 associates, the law firm of Corliss, Zeidler and Kirk was a large law firm even by New York standards. Steven had been referred to them by Art Goodman, CEO of Global Intelligence Consultants (GIC), the security assessment and consulting firm that Steven worked for as an executive vice president. He was widely believed to be the most likely successor to Goodman before all of this. General Art Goodman, Marine Corps (Ret.), was used to getting his way, and he had gotten his way in this instance as well. It had not been much of a decision for Steven to make. He had not considered what lawyer he would eventually ask to represent him, so when the General suggested Zeidler and explained that his firm was on retainer and that they billed GIC about $10 million a year, Steven agreed to call them. Of course he'd had to wait until the right time to actually reach out to the lawyers. He had to get square with his family first, to make sure they were covered, really covered. He knew he was at risk of going away for a long time, maybe for life, and before he could make that kind a decision he needed to make sure they would be okay no matter what happened to him. He was still not used to the level of media attention his case was getting. The truth was that none of them were, not even Zeidler who had litigated countless extremely high-profile trials. He could see the media stationed in just about every open spot for three square blocks around the office, five square blocks around the courthouse and two square blocks around his house. It was an uncharacteristic move by the media that they listened when Steven had asked them to take it easy and give him and his family some room to breathe. He thought that perhaps some of the people who were providing security for him had spoken to a few members of the media and suggested they might want to give Loomis some space. His children were at his in-laws' house, where media was also parked everywhere. In contrast to New York, however, Queensbury was a small town in Vermont and could be easily covered and controlled by the security teams that were covering them. One team was very obvious and public, the other team was never seen, never heard, but they were covering all the blind spots that no security detail ever covered. Both teams were made up of people that Steven and the General knew well. The boardroom he was in was a corner room, so he actually had two wall-length windows. He walked to the other window and looked over another part of the city, which was just about the same as the other side he'd been looking at because the media was also parked everywhere. Steven knew how important these strategy and preparation sessions were, how important it was to prepare every expert witness, how important it was to prepare himself for being cross-examined, and he was doing his best to do that and make sure his family was safe. But there was one thing that was getting in the way, and by now he knew it was not going to change – Doctor Nigel Barlow, neuropsychologist, profiling consultant, scientist and the single most significant threat to humanity he had ever believed there could or would be. Steven had met with Barlow after Riche's shooting because of the man's insistence and, truth be told, because Steven had been a bit stir-crazy after being confined to his house for over a week. He had also done it because he believed Barlow was a scientist looking into the same science that Steven was actually researching at the time. Thirty seconds into their conversation, Steven knew that Barlow was all the things he had believed he was and far, far more. Barlow had reached out to Steven because he had wanted more information about Riche, about what Steven had seen and experienced at the warehouse where Riche had brought all his victims, including Steven's daughter Tracy. He wasn't looking for science, he was looking for the things that could not be captured in a report, the things that made every single person, CSIs, police officers, and everyone in that warehouse first shiver and then completely nauseous. When Steven had let Barlow know that he knew what he was after, Barlow had completely dropped his sham and let Steven know exactly what he *was* after and exactly what he was. He had been doing the same research all right, except that his purposes had been quite different from those of every other scientist working on the science. Barlow had basically been alienated and excommunicated by the mainstream scientific community because he was thought to be unstable and even dangerous. He wanted to observe the subjects of the research in action, while they were on the hunt, regardless of what that meant for the persons being hunted. Now, 20 years later, Barlow had established, developed and grown a network of individuals who he believed fit into the subspecies he and the other scientists had identified, *Homo sapiens predaer* or *Homo sapiens predator*. Steven had not been the same since that meeting and what happened a few days after it. He had asked Cecil and Thurman Meeks, two operators he knew well, to look into the guy's background, where he was from, how much money he had, everything they could possibly find to help paint a full picture of the man. While Steven had been waiting for them to get back to him, Barlow had managed to knock him out with a shot of tranquilizer administered by a very skilled operative, taken him to a nondescript motel in New Jersey, and let him know under no uncertain terms that he would leave Steven and his family alone, but he would expect the same courtesy. Steven had to agree to leave Barlow alone and let him go do whatever it was he did with no interference. He had let Steven know that if he found that someone was trying to look into his business again, all bets would be off and his family would be the first to feel it. The fact that he had gotten the jump on Steven, and that he had been able to register that two very skilled operators were looking into his business, let Steven know that the man had the resources and access to the talent and technology necessary to make that threat and carry it through. So here he was, preparing for trial and leaving Barlow alone, but he was never too far from Steven's mind. He was also thinking about Diana, certainly not her real name, and what she had warned him about. If there was anyone who knew what Barlow was capable of, it was Diana. She had been the operative that Barlow had used to deliver the shot that knocked out Steven. She was clearly Special Forces, whether from the U.S. or elsewhere. He believed she was most likely Mossad. Her accent, her demeanor and the Star of David around her neck made it almost certain that she was trained by the famed Israeli agency, their version of the CIA. She had told him she was talking to him because she decided she did not want to be a part of whatever Barlow was planning. She had explained she had done a few jobs for Barlow in the past and that she did not know too much because everything the man did was compartmentalized. It made sense to Steven, that's how you had to develop effective, complex operations, by compartmentalizing and making sure each element could function independently of any other element. He wasn't sure whether he believed everything the woman had said, but it had sounded solid.

He had told his lawyers about what happened with Barlow because he believed they could also be affected by what happened from that day forward, but he had told no one about Diana. He hadn't told his lawyers, he hadn't told the General and he hadn't told his wife. Well, he had placed a couple of calls earlier today to finally remedy that, at least the part about Barlow. He still wasn't sure about what to say, if anything, about Diana. Since his encounter with Barlow, he had been really off in everything he did and he knew it was because he knew he should have told his wife what happened. She might not understand that the reason he had done that was because she was simply not ready to hear it. That had changed now. Now she was almost back to herself and they had fallen into a rhythm, as much of a rhythm as the situation allowed, so he knew it was time. He also knew it was time to tell the General. Goodman had done more for Steven and his family than anyone else in every sense. He was footing the bill for his defense, which would be well over two million dollars; he had covered the bail so Steven could wait for trial at his house instead of sitting in jail; and more important than everything else, he had been there for Steven, emotionally, like a father would have been. The General was a father figure for Steven, who had grown up without one. From the time Steven had arrived at GIC to the present, Goodman had taken a deep personal interest in Steven, his family and his career and throughout everything he had done nothing but help all of them. So, yeah, the time had come for Steven to come clean about everything; *almost* everything, in any case.

2.

On his way home from the day of preparing for trial, Steven tried to prepare for what he was about to do. He thought he knew what he wanted to say, but the truth was that, like everything else related to the past six months, he was having to figure things out as he went along. He could not have prepared for any of it. He was still introspective enough to know that part of what he was dealing with was a deep sense of guilt. It hadn't been his intention to bring his family into a world that none of them was even aware of before Tracy had gone missing, but that's exactly what had happened. Even so, there were some things that had helped him to feel better. One of the biggest ironies about that was the role the media had played in all of it. Initially, he had been incredibly mortified with all the coverage, which he saw growing every single day. Now, with some time to let things fall into a routine, he was thankful for their coverage. His lawyers had explained to him that whatever evidence they would not be able to get in for the jury to consider, the media would have no problem putting in front of almost every potential juror in New York. It made sense; he knew that there was around-the-clock coverage in multiple channels, which meant that finding a juror that had not heard anything about the case would be practically impossible. The media had also helped keep him feeling better about his family's safety. He believed that as long as the world's attention was firmly planted on his case, his family would be safe. It would be virtually impossible for anyone, regardless of their resources or their connections, to get to his family undetected. The attention would be there through the trial and most likely for some time after that, but it would not be there forever. If what Diana and Barlow himself had said about the type of individual that might have an interest in him or his family was true, they would most definitely wait until things died down and the world's attention was no longer on the Loomis family before making a move. That gave Steven a few months, at least, to decide what the best solution would be. One of the first things he knew Beth would want to know would be whether her parents were going to be in any danger once it was all over. He did not know what the answer was, but he did know that after he explained the scope of what they were facing, it would be very easy for her to make that decision on her own. Neither one of her parents had brothers or sisters. Lucy, her mother, was an only child and Tom had only two brothers who died years before. One had died in the Vietnam War and the other one had died of lung cancer after three decades of a three-pack-a-day habit.

When they arrived at Steven's building, the same trucks that had been there in the morning were there that evening, as were the reporters and photographers belonging to the trucks. Steven saw with some satisfaction that they looked exhausted and appeared to be wrapping up their coverage for the evening. He could not imagine how frustrating it would be to have to sit out in the cold, under rain, snow, waiting for something that *might* but would most likely not happen. Steven and Lou, his driver and bodyguard, got out in front of the building where another security team had already ensured that what few photographers and reporters were there did not get in their way. Benny, the building's doorman, was already holding the door open for them.

Steven was first through the door, "Thanks, Benny."

The young man smiled and shook his head, "No problem, Mr. Loomis. Man, those assholes just don't give up. Would you believe some of them actually tried to bribe me to let them up? They offered me $250 bucks to let them up. I told them to go fuck themselves. Unbelievable!"

Steven squeezed his shoulder as he walked past him to the elevator, "I appreciate it, Benny. Did Beth go out today?"

Benny knew it wasn't about Steven keeping tabs on his wife, although he had plenty of other people in the building who did in fact keep very close tabs on their spouses and bribed Benny with all kinds of swag to keep them informed.

He shook his head, "No, not while I've been here. But the older man that came by yesterday is upstairs now. He got here about a half an hour ago."

Steven stopped in his tracks, "The man who was here last night?"

Benny realized he might have made a serious mistake, "Hey, that's alright, isn't it, Mr. Loomis? I mean, I called your wife before I let him up. She said it'd be fine. I told her who it was and she said if it was the same man as last night to let him up. She didn't hesitate or nothin'."

Steven could see the man was thinking he might have made a serious mistake, "That's fine, Benny, you did the right thing. He's one of the good guys."

Clearly relieved, Benny went back to his post. Steven bid goodbye to Lou who was as tired as he looked. Another team would take over for the overnight shift and Lou would be back for him in the morning. While he was in the elevator Steven wondered what the old man needed. He wondered whether maybe Beth had called him, but decided that was not likely. The General would have called Steven to let him know. Whatever he wanted to speak to Steven about, he also wanted Beth there. He walked through the door, took the gun from his lower back and placed it in the same drawer he had put it in before. He walked into the living room where Beth and the General were sitting. The old man had his customary tumbler filled with 18-year-old Scotch and Beth had a small cup with what he thought would be Earl Grey tea. He threw his overcoat on a chair, loosened his tie and worked out of his suit jacket all as he moved further into the living room. Beth and Goodman stood up and she came over to greet him, "Hey, you. We were getting worried. I told Art you'd be here more than an hour ago."

He hugged and kissed her and walked over to shake the General's hand as he explained why he was late, "I know, babe. We're trying to narrow down our list of witnesses. I had no idea we had that many potential experts. I only spoke to two of them, but Max and Drew's staff have found almost a dozen more that could be great for us."

Steven and Goodman sat down. Beth walked over to the kitchen, "Can I get you something to drink?"

Steven turned to answer, "A glass of ice cold tea would be great."

She smiled, "Coming up."

Once she was out of earshot, he turned back to the General, "I'm surprised you're here. I'm glad as hell you are, but I'm surprised."

That caught the old man off guard, "Glad as hell? Just in general or because you needed to talk to me."

Steven paused to take the glass from Beth. As she turned to go back to the kitchen, he stopped her, "Hold on. Sit down, honey, I need to talk to you."

A puzzled expression took over her face as she complied and sat down next to him.

He turned back to the General and answered his question, "Both actually. I'm glad as hell that you're here because it always feels great to see friends, real friends, when things are tough, but I am also glad you are here because I wanted to talk to you and you saved me the call."

Now both Beth and Goodman had puzzled expressions on their faces. They waited for Steven to continue. For his part, Steven had thought they would barrage him with questions about what he needed to talk to them about. It would have made it easier for him to just dole out answers to questions, but when neither one asked anything he realized he was going to have to do this cold. He began by explaining his research, how he had come upon dozens and dozens of scientists and researchers doing work on what he now thought of as 'his' science. He explained how it had been difficult to ascertain which ones were involved in serious research and which ones were simply opportunists looking to make a buck off his case. He had never spoken to either of them in detail about the process he had followed to find the science he had found. He then went on to tell them about his admin Stephanie's call about a Dr. Barlow and how insistent the man had been on seeing him. By that point, he had been going a bit stir-crazy, he explained, and was maybe just looking for a good excuse to get out of the house. He had also thought that maybe Barlow was one of the scientists who were doing serious research and maybe he thought Steven could help his work in some way. He continued and told them about that first meeting, how he had felt something off with the man. He went on to explain how the meeting had progressed and noticed as both Beth and the General tensed up and worried expressions took over from puzzlement. Steven went on, not waiting for them to ask any questions. Now that he was rolling, he didn't want to stop. He explained about the Twins and what he had asked them to do. He had been looking directly at Goodman as he had explained that part of his story and finally felt that he needed to pause.

He had to explain to both of them why he had kept quiet, "I know I should have told you, but at that point I didn't really know much about Barlow. When I asked the Twins to look into the man, I was expecting them to come back and simply tell me the guy was some wacko involved in some creepy cases. I never expected for it to come to anything."

He meant for this explanation to be for both of them, but kept his eyes on the General, because he knew that while telling his wife *might* have been a good idea, telling the General should have been a given. No going back now.

It happened, he made a mistake and was now explaining to both why he had made it, "It's no excuse, I know. You two are the people I trust most in this world and not telling you was killing me, especially after what happened next."

Now Beth's face went from worried to scared, "What do you mean 'what happened next'? What happened next?!"

Steven looked at her and held her hand. He could tell she was getting overwhelmed with all of it and wanted to reassure her as he explained the really difficult part of his story. It wasn't lost on him that Art Goodman's expression hadn't changed. He never flinched when Steven had made reference to what had happened after he sent the Twins to look into Barlow. He wondered whether that was because he had learned to keep a poker face over decades of tough negotiations or because of something else. Steven continued his story explaining his encounter with the woman holding the packages, his being knocked out in the car and waking up in the motel room. Goodman simply listened, but Beth was clearly getting more and more upset as he went on. He squeezed her hand as he continued to signal her to let him finish. That squeeze let her know he would explain as much as she needed him to explain, but not now. The squeeze had been their private 'not now' signal to each other. They had used it countless times for more years than he could remember, and Steven had never been more appreciative of that signal than he was then as he went on with the story. There were things he needed to tell his wife and his wife only. He told both of them that he had believed Barlow when he said he would leave him and his family alone if Steven returned the courtesy. He had wanted to make that clear to Beth so she could at least know they were not in any imminent danger. He already knew that Goodman would be thinking far beyond the immediate danger. A man did not get to the rank of general without having a keen strategic mind and Goodman's was keener than most. Steven went on to explain how he had tasked security teams to keep an eye on his family in Vermont and on his place in New York. He was relieved when he saw, when he felt, Beth exhale. Once again, half a lifetime of being together allowed them to communicate some of the most important things without saying a word. He imagined it was the same with most solid marriages. Two people joined at the heart didn't need words to communicate, and with that exhale Beth had let him know she was okay. She would probably take him to the woodshed over not telling her and he would have a lot of explaining to do, but now he knew she would be okay in the end. He had gotten through the really tough part. He finished the story by explaining that he intended to do precisely as Barlow had requested. He would focus on his trial and protecting his family from it and the media coverage as much as possible. Once again, he reiterated that he believed Barlow when he had said he would leave him and his family alone. He went on to say, for Beth's benefit more than anything else, that he believed that the media's attention, the world's really, would serve to keep his family safe. Now he did stop. He wanted to let both of them catch up and process everything he had just told them and he knew each would do so at their own pace. Goodman would be much further along than Beth in that regard, but he wasn't worried about him.

Steven got up and went to put some ice in his drink, "Can I get you another drink, Art? Babe, can I get you anything?"

Both shook their heads but didn't say anything.

When Steven came back to sit down, it was Beth who spoke first, "I guess the first thing I want to know is that the kids and my parents are safe. They are, aren't they?"

It broke Steven's heart to see the pleading look on her face. It also broke his heart that she had gotten so used to the surreal quality of everything that had happened in their life in the past couple of months that she took his story in stride. She didn't break down or come unhinged, something that would have almost certainly happened before Tracy had gone missing. Steven couldn't imagine what a wife, any other wife, would say if her husband came home and told her that some sick bastard had knocked him out and taken him to a motel in New Jersey where he warned the man to stay away. Forget about what happened to Tracy or what he had done to Riche, that type of story would serve to send any other wife into a panic and almost certainly into a nervous breakdown. But now Steven understood. She had spent almost her entire adult life with him living with an almost daily uncertainty about what he was doing and where he was. She knew how dangerous his job was, how he would never be called into anything that didn't require the best and most experienced and deadly operators in the U.S. military. It was no wonder that the divorce rate among Navy SEALs was rumored to be over 80%. He couldn't imagine what it was for those who were a part of that most elite fraternity, DEVGRU or SEAL Team six, but it had to be higher than 80%. And yet here she was, through it all, through all those years and through all the missions, here she was. In a singular moment of clarity, Steven came to realize that destiny or fate or God or whatever it was that decided such things, had chosen them for this because they were equipped to handle it. He seemed to recall a saying from church about God placing problems and challenges only in front of those who were able to handle them. Wherever it was he had heard it didn't matter, what mattered was that it could not be truer than it was right then and there, with him sitting next to his wife.

He smiled at her, gave her a kiss on her forehead and answered her question, "They are, babe, they are absolutely safe. The people watching over them are serious operators. I know all of them. You've met some of them, in fact. You know the Twins, Cecil and Thurman, right?"

She nodded. She had met them a couple of times while they had served under her husband and again at some function or other while Steven was at GIC. Two very attractive black men in their late 30s or early 40s. She remembered them being very intimidating, but very professional and well mannered. Identical except that one wore a goatee and the other one did not. She seemed to remember thinking the same thing about most of the people her husband worked with. She knew what it took to become a SEAL and what it took to be chosen to be a part of Team six. You were invited to try for the team only after years of combat experience in one of the other SEAL teams. The country was only now finding out what she had known for almost two decades, that these men were truly the best of the best. She considered the irony of the fact that some of the things she had resented about her husband's chosen profession were now things that gave her great comfort. The men watching over her family were trained to see what others didn't, to anticipate what others didn't and to take out any and all threats without hesitation. Most of them spoke several languages and all had to have above average IQs. They were experts at becoming experts of whatever it was they were tasked with and if they had been tasked with watching over her family she was certain that by now they knew her parents' and her children's routines by heart. They had scouted out their lake house, the town it was in and every other potential location where they thought a threat could come from. All of it served to make her feel, as her husband did, that their family was safe.

Still, she had some questions she wanted answered, "Okay. What now? What are we supposed to do now? God, Steven, why now? Why did this happen to us now, when everything else is going on?"

Steven could have pointed out how it was all connected, how one thing had led to another, but he didn't want to do that because he knew in the end the common thread, the connection between every one of the things that had happened to them after Tracy was found, was him, his decisions. He could sense she was starting to panic and needed him to bring sense to it all, as he had done many times before.

He didn't disappoint her, "Really, nothing, nothing besides what we were doing already. I'm going to concentrate on the trial and on working with my lawyers to put the best case forward. Obviously we have to be more vigilant now, but we were already pretty cautious and aware before any of this happened. Like I said, it's ironic but having the media everywhere helps us in this case. Think about anyone trying to come or go without being noticed by the media, it would be virtually impossible. And if they did get past the media, think about them trying to get past the security teams in place, it would be *literally* impossible."

He knew that was technically not true, but she needed the reassurance. She took this last comment and mulled it over.

She got up and headed to the kitchen, "I have to get dinner going." Steven nodded, held on to her hand and pulled it to his lips before she walked away.

Once she was in the kitchen and out of earshot, he waited to hear from the General. The old man was most definitely turning things over in his head. Steven had seen the same expression of concentration countless times before.

When he finally spoke, the old man almost knocked him out of his chair, "I already knew."

He saw no expression other than deep concentration and heard no tone of recrimination.

He waited for him to explain what he meant. "I already knew about all of it, the meeting with Barlow at your office, the thing in New Jersey and I even know about your little side trip to Little Italy to talk to that woman. That's what I came here to talk to you about. I came by last night, but I couldn't wait for you to get home. I'm glad I didn't have to ask you, that you did it on your own."

Steven's mouth hung open for a half a second and then it shut. He hung his head and shook it slowly. He should have known. There had been an instant flash of resentment at the fact that Cecil and Thurman had told the General about Barlow and, he assumed, everything else that he had asked them to keep in confidence. But the feeling had quickly been replaced by a realization and acceptance of the fact that deep down inside he had always known that Art Goodman would somehow find out about everything, whether it had been the Twins or not didn't really matter, he would have found out some other way. How many times had Steven been completely baffled by the man's ability to get information that he had thought was simply impossible to get. Yeah, he should have known from the beginning.

When he finally looked up at the old man, there was a sideways grin on his face, "I should have known. Did know, actually, I think I always knew you'd find out somehow."

The General returned the grin and nodded, "Well, it is what it is. The question is what do you want to do now?"

Steven didn't need to think about it, "Nothing. Exactly what I said to Beth. I certainly can't do anything about Barlow right now."

Goodman nodded, "I understand. I noticed you didn't tell Beth about your meeting in Little Italy."

Steven shook his head, "What for? To tell her what she's already heard about Barlow? She doesn't need to be convinced about how dangerous the man is, trust me. That's what Diana, that's the woman I met with, was trying to do. She was trying to warn me about how far his reach extends and how many resources he has at his disposal."

The old man held up his hands, "Hey, I'm not saying you should have told her. Fact is, I think it was the right thing to do. What I meant was what do you want to do in the long term?"

Steven hadn't really thought about that. He was busy with his trial and with keeping his family safe for its duration. His only long-term goal was to get through it without going to prison for the rest of his life.

If he ended up going to prison, whatever plans he might have would be moot, "I have to beat this charge, there's no two ways about it. Before Barlow came along I felt that even if I lost I would have accomplished what I set out to do."

Goodman went to say something, but Steven raised his hand and kept going, "I wasn't saying I was throwing in the towel. I told you before, I'm nobody's martyr. I've always planned to defend myself with everything I have. I'm just saying that back then going to prison would have been what I imagine going to prison is for most. Losing their family, their job, their life. It would have crushed me, but I could have moved on. Now that I understand what Barlow is and how far it goes, I'm not so sure. My family's safety is above everything else, and if I went to prison I would go crazy worrying about them, but it would be doable because I have you and Beth's parents and everyone else who is behind me to protect them. What about all those other people, the ones who don't have anybody protecting them? The ones who are victimized and preyed upon every day? They have enough trying to keep safe from human predators, what about when these things come knocking? I keep thinking about the families of the other girls that Riche took. What have things been like for them? Their lives destroyed, their little girls gone."

Now the General did interrupt him, "Wait a minute, son, you can't put all of that on your shoulders, nobody can. We, humanity, know the dangers out there and we do our best to protect ourselves. It was that way when we lived in caves and it's that way now. No one man is ever going to be able to step up for humanity. Many have tried and lost their minds in the process."

Steven shook his head in frustration, "I know that, Art. I'm not diluted. But one thing that Barlow has made clear for me is that these things, these predators, have been in the shadows for a long time. They've done what they've done and preyed upon people completely unnoticed this entire time. We hear of disappearances and we put up our posters and eventually people just let it go, never knowing what happened and why. There are wars and riots and murders and we are fed what the media deems we should be fed, and they are guided and moved by those in power. Don't get me wrong, I'm sure most wars and riots and every other form of uprising are exactly what we understand it to be, but now I know that there are some that are something else. There are some that were *designed* by others with a different agenda."

The General now took on a look of open skepticism, "You're telling me that there are wars that are engineered by one of these things, these predators for their own amusement?"

Steven leaned closer, "C'mon, Art, do you really think it would be that hard? We've seen it done many times around the world. That's our business. Mad geniuses convincing people to go to war over their own personal agenda, to commit suicide for God's sake! World War II, Uganda, Rwanda, hell, North Korea, it happens all the time. You think that it couldn't, that it hasn't, been done by one of these things?"

Goodman mulled it over. It didn't take long; he had seen it with his own two eyes for more decades than he cared to think about.

Steven went on, "I'm not trying to be humanity's savior, but I would be lying to you if I said that I don't feel a sense of responsibility. Barlow let me know that with all of this, the trial, the media, all of it, they would come out from the shadows, maybe not too many of them, but some. He let me know that they've been operating in the shadows because they feel powerful, knowing what they are and having the world think they're just human gives them that power. That is how Barlow has been able to do everything he's been able to do. What do you think senators or CEOs who have grown up believing they are freaks or psychopaths do when Barlow soothes them and lets them know that they're not freaks, that they're nature's next iteration? That they were designed to be what they are? Can you imagine their relief, their sense of empowerment and purpose? It's no wonder they're willing to shell out as much as they need to for him or to give them the access to power that he has. But now that I have brought the world's attention to them, some of them are going to resent being 'outed' and they're going to come looking for the one who did it. It's not them I'm worried about, though. I told you, I know we're covered. The ones that worry me are the ones who relish the world being aware of them and who might take to doing things that are more brazen and deadly in order to own what they are."

Goodman nodded thoughtfully. Everything that Steven had said made sense and he knew it. He had the experience that only having lived through wars and watching men die because of one man's madness could bring.

He still tried to bring Steven back to his original point, however, "Okay, I get it. What do you want to do about your family? I'm talking about tactics now, not the end game."

Steven *had* thought about that, "I think Beth is fine here. She's being watched 24/7 by two rotating teams. They've got our place under electronic surveillance as well. Anyone points a parabolic mike or tries to put fiber optics in from anywhere, we'll know about it. They're all people you know."

Steven smiled before moving on, "What am I talking about, you probably helped the Twins pick the teams."

Goodman simply nodded. Steven went on, "So I don't need to tell you Beth's parents' place is also very well covered. I also wasn't making it up when I told Beth that having the media camped out everywhere is going to be helpful to us. I'm pretty comfortable with the situation right now, as comfortable as I can be anyway. That's why I am able to give my attention to preparing for the trial."

Goodman now stood up to pace, a habit that Steven had also picked up over the years, "Okay, so we're set tactically. I think it would be a good idea right now to begin planning for what happens after the trial. We need to figure out how to keep your family safe in the long term. That's priority number one. What you decide to do after that's accomplished is up to you. I agree, you have to beat these charges, no matter what. I've been doing some research and I've talked to Max. He feels, and I agree, that even if you are convicted you would almost certainly not be sentenced to life in prison. I'm not saying that to blow smoke up your ass and make you feel better, I 'm saying it to put things into perspective. Even if you lose the trial, there will be an 'after' for you. So we'll concentrate on keeping your family safe for now and figure out how to make it permanent after the trial. The rest we can play by ear."

Steven had heard that phrase countless times over the years. Whether he was talking to a president in one of the areas they operated or to his troops or to the janitor, he had the power to break things down into bits that could be digested and tackled. Everything in life came with an ever-present dose of uncertainty, however, and Goodman had the wisdom to understand that some things you just couldn't plan for until you knew more. This was the perfect illustration of that very point. Both men looked into each other's eyes. As always, some of the deepest thoughts were communicated in these looks. Steven could see how much the old man truly cared about him and his family. And he could see how worried he had been and would continue to be for some time. Goodman could see that Steven, his best executive and the closest thing to a son he would ever have, was tired and worried, but still all there. It gave him immense comfort to see that in Steven's eyes. The General had been afraid that the loss of his daughter and the subsequent pressure of what he had done and what he was facing had served to erode the spirit that had endeared Steven so much to him. He had seen many men, good men, beaten down over time, plodding along because they had been trained to never give in, but no longer with the spark in their eyes that had let him know they were different, that they might go on to be great in time. That spark was still very much alive in Steven. Of course he would worry about him, he looked not just physically tired but emotionally weary and that concerned the General. But a tired body and soul could be revived with rest, deep rest, as long as the spark was still there.

They were about to get up to join Beth when Steven reached out and pulled him back down, "Listen, General, I need you to help me with Beth. She's going to need support through this and I might not be able to give it to her when she needs it. She believes me when I tell her things will be okay, that we're safe. I've always proved it to her. But this, this is different. I know she believes me, but she's still going to worry. She respects you almost as much as she respects her father, and that's saying something. She needs to hear that we're going to be okay from someone else besides her parents and me. Someone who knows it for a fact and isn't trying to just make her feel better."

The General smiled a gentle smile, "I understand. My Kristy was the same way. Every time I'd leave on a deployment she'd get that look, a look that said exactly that: 'I believe you when you say things will be fine, but I'm still going to worry.'"

Steven saw deep sadness in the man's eyes. Goodman had lost his wife five years ago and still mourned her sometimes. They had been high school sweethearts and gotten married when they were both 20 years old. They had never had any kids. Steven had never learned why and his boss hadn't offered.

After two seconds of that faraway, sad look, Goodman looked back at him, "Of course I'll be there. You don't even have to ask. You may still not know this, Steven, but you and Beth and the kids are family to me."

Steven squeezed the man's hand, "I do know it, Art. Now, more than ever, I know it."

3.

The next day when Steven arrived at his lawyers' offices he knew it was going to be one of those days. He could hear Drew and Max arguing and Ray Gretche trying to mediate. This was no different than what happened almost every single day, it just hadn't happened at 8:00 in the morning before. He walked into the big boardroom they'd converted into their war room and saw Drew standing in front of the dry erase board where there were at least eight names written and Max sitting at his usual place with what looked to be his third cup of coffee. Ray was also sitting at his usual place, which was between Drew and Max, clearly chagrined things were getting so heated so early.

He tried to bring some perspective to the discussion, "Guys, we don't need to decide that right now, we can see which ones make good witnesses and decide then."

They both ignored Ray and kept up their argument, "We're going to confuse the jury Drew! They're already going to be stretched to understand the science we're presenting as it is, throw in more witnesses and we're going to really confuse them!"

Drew shook his head, "What difference does it make how many witnesses we put on if they all help to make the point? If we don't cover some element of what we are arguing completely, the jury might decide it's just a stunt and find for the prosecution Max, we will have done all of this for nothing and all because we didn't give the jury enough information to find for us!"

Ray was about to try to diffuse the situation again when Steven got their attention, "What's going on guys? Isn't it a little too heated for this time in the morning? I mean you guys don't really get rolling until two or three in the afternoon, so what's got you both so hot and bothered?"

Drew sat down at the table and smiled, "Yeah, we're getting heated up pretty early, but we're getting down to the wire and we need to make some decisions. My point is that we need to give the jury enough information to make them confident enough in what we're arguing to find in our favor."

Max also wanted his point to be heard, "I am totally in agreement with that, but there is a point at which jurors just start to go hazy and you lose them."

Ray tried to make his point again, "Guys, I think you're both right, but let's just see which experts make for better witnesses and then go from there."

After getting himself a cup of coffee Steven sat down and gave them his opinion, "I have to be honest and tell you guys that I've actually given a lot of thought to both of the points you're making. I've wondered if we aren't giving too much complicated information to the jury. I've also thought that if the jury does not have their questions answered they might just decide to rely on what they know. The fact is that what we're arguing is unlike anything ever argued before, so both of those points are well taken. I think Ray hit it right on the head, let's go through all of our witnesses and see which ones make better witnesses and decide after that."

Max and Drew both started to talk at the same time, Drew ceded the floor to Max, "That's fine, we can do that, but there are some witnesses that we don't have any choice about, we have to put them on because they're the only scientists doing the work we're referencing in any sort of credible way."

Drew picked it up from there, "We all agree we need to put Dr. Leonard on, that's a given and I think we all agree that we also need to put on Dr. Scoma, but everyone else is still up in the air."

Steven nodded and asked a question that he'd been thinking about for a couple of days, "Can you guys explain to me who the witnesses are and how we came to find them? I know Scoma and Leonard myself because I spoke to both of them personally, but I don't know any of the other witnesses or what they're going to be testifying to at all."

Drew looked at Max and asked, "Do you want to walk him through it or do you want me to?"

Max stood up and headed for the coffee pot, "Why don't you walk him through it, I think you probably have a better grasp of the scientific crap."

Drew smiled, "I'll be happy to. You already know what we're going to put Leonard and Scoma to prove. Both of them will testify about their work and research on the species that have evolved beyond the human species. We're bringing Dr. Allen Schultz, a physiologist from Cornell to testify about his work on the physiological changes that humans undergo when they are lying. Leonard was the one who told us about his work. The reason we're putting him on is because he's done research among tens of thousands of individuals and has found that there are some minute physiological changes that *all* human beings display when they lie, there is no way to suppress them or change them in any way. If you're human and you're lying you will undergo those physiological changes, period."

Ray interjected, "So if you are able to lie and not undergo these changes, then you're simply not human. Schultz is actually a really good witness, so he's not one of the ones we're wondering about."

Steven nodded, "Okay, Leonard did tell me about him and his work when we spoke early on. It sounds like what he'd be testifying to would be pretty straightforward stuff. Who's next?"

Drew went on, "Alright, next we have Dr. Samuel Grossman, a forensic psychiatrist from Columbia. He has done research very similar to what Leonard and Scoma have done, but he's structured it differently."

Steven nodded, "Leonard also told me something about him. Something about a scale, right? A scale that measures murder, isn't it? Doesn't he also have a TV or radio show?"

Drew nodded, "That's right, it's a scale that catalogues murders and how evil the people committing them are. There are twenty-two levels that go up as the murder becomes more and more horrifying and sadistic."

Steven shook his head, "I don't get it, how does that relate to what we're arguing if his scale catalogues twenty-two levels of murder that *humans* commit?"

Max, now back at his seat smiled his famous 'cat that ate the canary' smile and answered the question, "There's a twenty third level."

Drew continued, "His twenty third level is reserved for situations where the murder and how it's committed simply does not fit any human standard or measurement tool. His television show does not include this twenty-third level, just the first twenty-two. The network felt the twenty-third level was too much for a television audience. We only found out about it because one of the interns working for us found a white paper that mentions his twenty-third level. It makes for really scary reading, even knowing everything else we know."

Steven seemed to understand the point, "Great, it sounds like it fits really well with what we're arguing, doesn't it?"

Ray, Max and Drew exchanged a look. Steven caught it, "What? What's wrong? Am I not correct about that?"

Drew shook his head, "The problem is not the science or the theory; the problem is Grossman himself. The guy is a bona fide asshole. If we put him on without first softening up how he comes across, the jury will discount his science just because of what a dick he is."

Steven looked at all three of them, "Are you serious? How bad can he be, guys?"

Ray answered the question, "He's pretty bad Steven. He is pompous and really full of himself. He can't understand why he should have to change the way he explains anything and he comes across as though he thinks anyone who does not understand his science is just plain dumb. I'm a pretty patient guy and he even gets under my skin."

Steven smiled; he had to agree with that, if someone got under Ray's skin he had to be a real asshole, "He sounds charming. Do we need his testimony?"

Max responded, "That's what we're trying to figure out; that and whether we call all of our experts to testify. My take is that if we overwhelm the jury with science and with a whole bunch of testimony that will, for the most part, go over their heads, we will lose them."

Drew was quick to also jump in, "Yeah, and my take is that if we don't give the jury enough information they may not feel confident enough to find for us. Think about it, if you were a juror and someone was asking you to basically decide what defines a human being legally, wouldn't you want as much information as you could possibly get before you made the decision?"

Max shook his head and started to raise his voice, "They're not going to be able to decide anything if they don't understand shit! Do you think we're going to have rocket scientists on the jury? We'll be lucky if we get two or three college graduates!"

Drew's response overlapped Max's, "Jury selection is precisely where we need to spend a good deal of our time! Having the right jury is key; we can't be thinking that this is just like any other jury that has been empaneled before. We..."

Steven had heard enough arguing and was eager to just get to work again, "I get it guys, I get it! I told you, I think they're both very valid points, so we'll need to keep them in mind when we make decisions, but I think Ray has the most valid point. Why can't we work with all the witnesses, talk to the two litigators you guys have had grilling them and ask them which ones would make better witnesses and decide then?"

Ray was nodding vigorously, "That's right guys, we're losing time and we don't have time to lose. The trial is in eight days; my vote is that the three of us go through the testimony we want to get from each of the witnesses, go through Steven's testimony again to tighten it up and then decide who we put on."

All three other men were nodding thoughtfully. Ray was right; the trial was just around the corner. They'd spent months sifting through potential witnesses, working with over twenty associates, paralegals and interns to find any and all information on cases where a similar issue had been litigated, finding any reference in academic and professional white papers dealing with similar science. In short, they'd prepared the case as well as they could prepare it. Now it was time to make some tough decisions. Drew and Max looked at each other and chuckled, they both knew that the pressure was getting to them and were still wise enough to recognize it. Both, the old, wily veteran and the young, brilliant maverick knew very well what each other brought to the table and were truly thankful for it. Ray's old, wise grandfather personality was a nice complement to the other two. He was nowhere near where Max was and Drew would eventually be, but he was a good lawyer who knew how to work a jury and had done so effectively for decades. Steven stood up to refresh his coffee and asked what came next.

Drew answered, "Why don't we go over the list of the witnesses we're still trying to make a decision about. You need to know what it is we're all talking about when we are talking about how many witnesses we should call and what they bring to the table."

Steven nodded, "Fair enough."

Ray stood up, took a large sheet of paper that had been sitting face down on the table and taped it up to the whiteboard at the front of the room. Steven looked at it and now understood Max's point a bit better. There had to be twelve or thirteen witnesses on that list, most of them with a Dr. or a Phd next to their name. Steven couldn't imagine how many scientific disciplines were reflected on that list, but he was sure that it was more than six or seven. Yeah, he could see Max's point much better now.

He looked at Max and Drew, "Alright, where were we?"

Drew stood up and walked up to the dry erase board, "We left off with Dr. prick, right? Grossman?"

Steven nodded. Max joined Drew at the dry erase board. "Next we have Dr. Lindsay Vargas. She is an evolutionary biologist. We would be putting her on to testify to the fact that having more than one human species is nothing new. Human remains found back in 2005 show that *Homo sapiens* was alive and kicking more than 100,000 years ago, way before the scientific community believed *Homo sapiens* had risen and it was alive in the form of *Homo Sapiens Idaltu*, a subspecies of human."

Steven nodded, "What does that have to do with our argument?"

Drew explained, "See, if we can show that what we're arguing is not as dramatic as people think, the jury will be more willing to find for us."

Max picked it up, "Dr. Vargas is very engaging. She clearly knows her science and she has done work that feeds into Leonard's research."

Now Ray asked the question, "You have to explain to me what that means, guys. I still don't quite get it."

Drew went on, "Okay, we're arguing that there is now a separate species from us on the planet, right, a subspecies of human. Well, most people think this is something new, that we've uncovered something that is beyond anything ever found or understood before. Have you heard the damn talk shows and all of the wannabe experts weighing in on every form of media? They are all saying this is preposterous or groundbreaking or made up, but the fact is that it is simply nature. We are a species and like every other species on the planet, we have evolved. That has been the case since the dawn of time. It isn't anything new or extraordinary, scientifically speaking anyway. Thousands of years ago that evolution was driven by a changing environment; our ancestors *needed* to evolve in order to survive that change. Still, it took hundreds of thousands of years for the species to evolve, to change. Once we started to use our brain to create and develop tools, to tame animals like horses and oxen, to establish a social order, that evolution slowed down."

Ray nodded, "Because as a species we didn't need to evolve to survive then, we had tools that helped us to do that. Evolution and biology gave way to creativity and intelligence."

Max smiled, "That's exactly right Ray. See, you're not too old to learn new things."

Ray threw half a bagel at him.

Drew went on, "That's right, it did, but not completely. We have been evolving all along, but the changes are much, much, more subtle. Actually imperceptible for the past few thousands of years; imperceptible, but not gone. So it made sense that at some point those changes, that evolution, would add up to a different species or subspecies of human."

Steven nodded, "And this scientist will testify to all that? Have you already worked with her on her testimony?"

Ray answered that, "We've worked with all of them, Steven. Between Max, Drew, the two former litigators from the Attorney General's office and myself, we've worked with all of them. Those two guys have had a go at all of them, so we've gotten a good look at all the witnesses."

Steven looked at him, "So you guys are confident that these two litigators you got to work with our witnesses are as tough as the prosecution is going to be on them?"

Drew chuckled, "Steven, if the prince of darkness himself had an attorney, he wouldn't come close to being in these guys' league."

Max smiled as well, "I thought I was a tough litigator on cross examination and actually I *am* a tough litigator, but these guys are head and shoulders above me. Unless they've been hiding them somewhere, the prosecution does not have anyone who will be tougher on our witnesses. Nobody."

Steven smiled, "Okay, who's next?"

Drew went on, "Next is Dr. Francis DeVaulle from UC San Diego. He is an evolutionary anthropologist. He will testify to the fact that human evolution has shaped society and that social evolution has in turn influenced biological evolution over millennia. His testimony is different that Dr. Vargas because he focuses on human behavior across history rather than focusing on the biology or physiology. He will be able to tell the jury that once humans evolved and began to use tools and weapons they developed, they became the absolute apex predators on the face of the earth.

"No longer were the big cats, or bears or hundreds of other species apex predators. Their advantage in size, speed and strength was overcome by human ingenuity. He will also be able to explain that although the human brain became more evolved, humans still had the hunter-gatherer instinct; it is what made them supreme hunters. Finally, he'll be able to testify to the fact that evolution is not uniform across the planet. As Vargas will have explained, biological evolution comes about as a response to a changing environment. It's no surprise to anyone that environments on earth vary greatly, so evolution also varies greatly. When it comes to that response to a changing environment, you're talking about a very basic and fundamental drive to ensure the survival of the species, which may mean eliminating potential enemies, predators or anything else that could threaten their survival. Sometimes that dynamic can look brutal and cold, but it's all based on nature. What do you think happened to the Neanderthals, they just popped out of existence one day? Vargas believes, and she's not the only expert that believes it, that *Homo sapiens* eradicated Neanderthals and other hominid species that shared the planet with them. Not because of anything 'evil', but because it was basically dog eat dog at that point in our evolution."

Steven's face took on a puzzled expression, "Survival of the fittest? So he's basically going to explain that that's the same dynamic we're talking about? That this new subspecies are not engaging in 'evil' deeds in the biblical sense, but just adhering to a natural order?"

Max clapped a couple of times, "Very good Steven, you're absolutely right. See we figure some people might say 'How can this species be considered evolved when they are so incredibly brutal?' and our guy's testimony will answer that. Dr. Leonard will already have explained that evolution does not necessarily mean more civilized, enlightened or considerate. Dr. DeVaulle will clarify that this dynamic, humans evolving, but engaging in what seems to be brutal behavior, has nothing to do with their intellect or level of enlightenment. He will also explain that in close social environments, like any major city on the planet, humans tend to weaken physically with each evolutionary cycle. That is because humans have each other to help hunt, raise a family, that kind of thing. In other words they don't have to be physically tough individually because the group dynamic makes up for the physical strength. When it comes to *Homo sapiens predators* he believes that this group dynamic simply does not fit, that they will not allow their survival to be dependent on the 'group', they will ensure the species survival on their own and they can do that because they have no problem eliminating any and all competitors for system resources. He theorizes that when a *Homo sapiens predator* feels a desire to hunt it is not based on a whim; there is a strategic purpose to it. He and Dr. Leonard have worked on using that strategic purpose or view to be able to determine who is really a *Homo sapiens predator* and who is simply a psychopath."

Ray jumped in, "Do you see a pattern beginning to develop, Steven? Do you get the gist of what we're looking to present?"

Steven nodded, "I think so. You're trying to establish that what we're presenting is not as outlandish or new as everyone believes it is. You're trying to present a case that this is simply nature continuing its course, just as it always has."

Drew nodded, "Exactly. The more we are able to establish that the defining of the new species is simply natural evolution for the jury, the more likely it is that they will be at ease finding for us."

Steven still had some questions, "Okay, I get that, but you do know what the media is broadcasting and writing every single day, almost every hour, don't you? They are claiming this is a completely unexpected and frightening development, something we couldn't have seen coming. They have no interest in the science behind it or the implications as it relates to the science of evolution. They just want to get people to tune in or buy their paper or book or to listen to their radio shows, and to do that they are willing to make it as sensational, bloody and frightening as they possibly can. If it happens to be plausible, even better, but facts and science are definitely not a prerequisite."

Ray answered, "Yes, we do know that, but we can't just decide to respond to the claims and opinions of the talking heads and their experts, can we. No, we need to use the science, we need to come across as being above all that."

Steven asked, "So the science is critical, I think we all agree on that, but are we maybe giving up some of the humanity of it, the emotional element? It seems to me that juries make decisions on both things, right? The facts of the case, the hard evidence and the emotional element, or am I wrong about that?"

Drew responded, "Damn Steven, are you sure you never thought about becoming an attorney? You're absolutely right; juries do make decisions based on both things, although they're not supposed to. The judge instructs them to make their decision on the evidence presented to them and nothing more, but everyone knows that's seldom the case."

Ray interjected, "Look at OJ or Casey Anthony, the juries were willing to set aside the evidence to come up with their own answer."

Max brought them back to the original point, "But you're right, it's a lot of science and obviously it is pretty dry stuff, pretty cold if you think about it. We don't have to worry about the emotional or human aspect of the case though; we have you for that, Steven. That's the essence of the case, the heart of it. Your actions were based not only on the science you found, but the effect it had on you as a *human being*.

"Your fear, your desire to protect your family, your consideration for humanity as a whole, that's is the reason we have any chance whatsoever. The jury pool will be made up of parents, brothers, sisters, people with families. We have a chance because any of them would probably be willing to do what you did, or something like it in any case, to protect their families and what they love most. The reality, Steven, is that at the end of the day the jury will need to decide if they can be a part of the same species that Donald Riche came from. We're going to be framing the argument legally, but the story is yours and only yours to tell. That is the true heart of the case."

Steven nodded thoughtfully. He'd come to a similar conclusion on his own. Still, he needed to make something clear to his defense team, "I don't know about legal procedures and what I am allowed to testify to, but I will tell you guys, what I felt, what I experienced in the warehouse and then again when I spoke to Barlow, was evil, pure and bone-chilling evil. Trust me when I tell you that I completely understand the science and I can absolutely see where science, biology, anthropology, all of it, has been the basis for the development of this new subspecies, but there is something else there, something that cannot be explained by science. I'm convinced of that. And please, please know that I am not talking about anything related to religion or the devil or heaven or hell, I'm talking about something beyond human physiology and cognitive processes."

Max and Drew nodded thoughtfully, but it was Ray who spoke next, "And we need that to come through, Steven, but you need to understand that when you talk about it you need to contextualize it like that, something *you* experienced and felt. See, if any of the expert witnesses try to speak to that 'evil' element, their credibility will be seriously compromised. You are exactly right to stay away from religious hype. I'm not saying it exists or that it doesn't exist, but in this scenario, in the legal world, it can seriously erode scientific testimony."

Steven took on a puzzled expression, "What exactly does that mean? You're making it sound like it's all in my head, like what I am referring to is not real."

Now Drew spoke up, "No Steven, that's not what we're saying, we know it's real. In fact, every single one of the witnesses we have been preparing spoke of it, of feeling something that was not registered in their studies or reflected on their graphs, something truly evil. The problem is that when they talk about it themselves they open themselves up to some pretty brutal cross-examination. Our two litigators tore each one of them up, every single one of them. As soon as they started talking about things that are subjective, things beyond their area of expertise, things like evil or spirituality, they became fair game. A couple of them brought up a religious aspect and our guys destroyed them even more completely. No, the discussion of evil and its implications will not come from the expert witnesses, it has to come from you."

Steven nodded, "I'm ready to do it." Max, looked out the window and thought to himself 'I hope you really are kid, I truly do, because if you're not it's your life'.

To Steven, however, he just gave a warm smile and said "How 'bout we all take a piss break, I know I need it."

Melanie Farris was also going over the prosecution's expert witness list. She was in a big conference room standing in front of a whiteboard as big as the wall on one end of the conference room table. On the board were the names of seven expert witnesses she was considering. She kept erasing one and then changing her mind and writing the name back. She'd been going at it for two hours and she still hadn't gotten anywhere. She sat back down in the chair at the end of the table to go over her notes for what seemed like the hundredth time. She knew that Willis and Zeidler had more than twice the number of witnesses listed for the trial, but she also knew there was absolutely no way they would be calling them all, it would completely overwhelm the jury if they did it. She also knew exactly what each of the witnesses' area of expertise and their profession, but what she was not exactly sure about was what they would be testifying to. Someone listed as an evolutionary biologist could potentially testify to any one of the thousands, maybe hundreds of thousands, of facts, figures and conclusions that were covered in their field. Of course she had the paralegals and clerks in the office researching their principal area of focus so she could formulate some kind of plan to cross-examine them. Whatever they found, however, did not guarantee what they would testify to and that meant she basically needed to prepare not for what they would in fact be testifying to, but what they *might* be testifying to and that made it a truly daunting task. She had to admire Zeidler and Willis, they had probably known this was precisely what she'd be faced with and they'd also known that she simply would not have the resources to research every potential witness as thoroughly as she would need to in order to prepare effectively. Truth be told, she'd admired both Willis and Zeidler well before this case ever came up. Willis was young and brash and sometimes obnoxious, but he was an absolutely brilliant litigator who had an almost preternatural courtroom instinct that allowed him make changes on the fly, without preparation. She'd seen him do that more than once. He would be in the middle of a cross-examination when something the witness said opened up a completely different angle or path from what Willis had clearly prepared for. He would not hesitate or even pause in taking the chance and pursuing an angle and line of questioning and coming out on top. She would never be able to do that, never. She had to prepare, to think of everything the witness could potentially testify to and prepare for it. If another path or opportunity opened up for her during a cross, she would have to finish the cross, let the court and the defense know she might call the witness again and then go prepare to pursue the new angle. By then, of course, the defense would have also prepared and the opportunity would be lost. She also respected Willis because although he was a sole practitioner, or used to be before he joined Zeidler's firm, he never seemed to take cases where he was defending true scum of the earth, someone truly evil. He mostly defended drug dealers, burglars and other thieves. The murder trials she'd seen him in were heat of the moment or drug-related situations. Max Zeidler, on the other hand, had no problem defending anybody for any crime.

The joke around the office was that if the devil were up for the murder of trillions of souls, Zeidler would be the one defending him. And he would probably win. She had to admire the guy, though, his courtroom presence was absolutely overpowering. It was something he had mastered after decades of practicing the law, but it was most likely something he had been born with, a certain charisma and panache that had women swooning and men shaking his hand within two minutes of his opening statement. Farris thought that when he was a child in elementary school he probably never got in trouble, regardless of guilt. He was just one of those people.

She came back to her own list and went through the names again. Seven experts, that was all she would have access to for the trial. There had been another three names on the board, but Neill insisted they pare the list down. He had actually wanted to take it down to four, but both Farris and Logan had both objected strenuously and he had compromised and let them keep seven instead of four. His rationale for reducing the list so much was not unsound. He argued that if they tried to match the defense witness for witness they would always come up short. The defense had more resources, clerks, paralegals and associates that could research them to death. It would also communicate to the jury that they, the prosecution, believed that this defense had merit and that the experts all had something of value to present. No, he reasoned, they would call seven experts to refute whatever the defense's experts testified to. She saw the logic and actually agreed with it, but she also knew how good all the attorneys for the defense were, Ray Gretche – the old wise grandfather included – which meant that there was no way they would put anyone on the stand that they had not completely vetted and were absolutely confident would provide value to the defense. She knew her seven witnesses would be able to counter everything any of the experts for the defense testified to, but they'd have to do it in a general sense, not from any sort of specialized area of expertise they'd dedicated their lives to pursuing. So, if Dr. Tyrone Leonard, professor of forensic psychiatry, testified to the existence of a new human subspecies, her experts could get up and testify that they did not accept Leonard's conclusions because they were based on fringe science. They would not be testifying to the fact that they had done the same research and found something different, just that the establishment did not agree with Leonard's conclusions. That would be the case with any witness the defense called. Her witnesses included a biologist, a human physiologist, a forensic psychiatrist, a psychologist, an anthropologist and an MD specializing in cognitive processes. These disciplines were what she, Logan and Neill had agreed on. They'd decided on this list partly because they were the disciplines that would allow the most flexibility in refuting the defense's witnesses and partly because they were the most affable of all the expert witnesses on the list. And that was not very affable at all. She'd seen Tyrone Leonard on various television shows and interviews and she had to admit the man was absolutely engaging. Short in stature and with completely white hair, his dark ebony skin, his dazzling smile and his honey-colored eyes combined to paint a figure that you could simply not stop watching. As if that wasn't enough, he was also absolutely brilliant in his field and completely buttoned up when it came to his science. She sighed for what seemed like the twentieth time in the last five minutes.

As she was going over the list again, Bart Logan came into the conference room carrying two mugs of steaming coffee, "Here, you look like you need this."

She took the coffee and smiled a thank you. He turned to look at their witness list, "You're still stressing over the witness list? Forget it Melanie, it is what it is. It's not our call, so why try to make it our fault?"

Farris looked at him, back at the board and then at him again, "I know, trust me I know, but I can't let it go, Bart. Have you seen the expert witness list for the defense?"

He nodded, "It's long and distinguished, that's for sure."

She chuckled, "Yeah, I guess you could call it that. I'm sure they're not going to call all of them, it would be stupid for them to do that, but they have choices, unlike us."

Bart walked over to the whiteboard, "Yeah, that they do. But, remember that the jury will not be made up of scientific geniuses, just regular people. That means that they have to be careful to call only those witnesses that can explain their science and their conclusions in a way that a layperson can understand. And that means that their list has to shrink down quite a bit."

Now she gave him a full smile, an expression that did not often grace her face, "You're right, damn Bart, you're right. That does narrow down the list some. But you're right about the jury. I think that's where this thing will be won or lost, picking the jury. Another thing to stress about."

He returned the smile, "So we go over how we want to define our perfect witness, we can't do much more than that. We can also prepare for that shorter list of experts even better by doing some out-of-the-box legwork."

She took on a puzzled expression, "What do you mean?"

He still had the wide smile on his face, "I mean we send an investigator to the universities where they teach and to talk to their students to see what they're like. Are they engaging, boring, easy to understand? That kind of thing."

Her smile came back, "That's a great idea! I've just been thinking of having the paralegals and clerks looking up any online lectures, whitepapers, that kind of thing."

Bart sat down next to her, "That's because you've been cooped up in here staring at that list for days now. I admire your work ethic, I really do, but you need to step back and unplug sometimes. It lets you look at things from a new, fresh perspective, which means maybe coming up with new ideas."

She hung her head, looked back up and ran her hands through her hair, "I know, I just get too dialed in sometimes and you're right, I just keep thinking of the same things over and over again."

Bart took the notepad she had in front of her, "So why don't we do this? Why don't you go home and get some rest, which you really look like you need, and I will work with the paralegals to narrow down the list some. I will also get the investigators rolling to do what I just told you."

She tried to get the notepad back, but he pulled it further out of reach, "It's not really a question Mel, you *need* to go home, seriously. You are no good like this. If Neill sees you he'll throw another fit and just get in our way. Go home."

She got up, held up her hands and hung her head again, "Alright, alright, I'll go home. I need to feed my cat anyway."

Bart smiled, "There you go. Go feed the cat, plop on your sofa, turn on the TV and put on a Jerry Springer marathon or something just as mindless that you can fall asleep to."

She gave him one last, thin smile and walked out the door.

He was starting to go over her notes when the door opened back up, "Don't ever call me Mel again; got it Barton?"

He smiled and gave her a quick nod. She left again and did not come back.

4.

DALLAS, TX

He got on the tram that took travelers from the ticket counters to the actual gates their flights would leave from. He held on to the metal handle above his head and looked around the tram cart he was in. What he saw were people so engrossed in their own lives or so focused on staying connected through their phones, that they were absolutely oblivious of the world around them. He knew that a skilled thief could probably walk out with a few wallets, purses and other valuables without a single person knowing anything was missing. He had no patience for that kind of idiocy, none at all. It was one of the reasons he had opted for living a quiet, undisturbed and simple life in his New Hampshire lighthouse. His line of work and the preparation it demanded, not to mention the experiences that had brought him to his level, provided him with all the intensity that he needed. He chose the lighthouse and the quiet existence it provided because he needed balance in his life. He knew plenty of guys who lived lives like his, full of intensity, moving, traveling, always being in the thick of violence and life-or-death scenarios in distant lands for a variety of reasons. Those guys, the ones who lived a complicated, troubled life away from the action their jobs brought with them, almost always burned out. That's the balance the lighthouse provided. Some took the easy way out and killed themselves, some suffered throughout their lives and alienated everyone who loved them and still others, not knowing how to quiet their demons, turned to random violence. Most of the people that were involved in his kind of work spent their lives in prison. Some a physical prison, but others lived in a worse prison, an emotional and spiritual prison, put there by the decisions they'd made long ago. He was one of these prisoners, emotional prisoners. He would never be completely free from what he did; it just didn't come with the job description. If he was going to spend his life in a prison, however, it was going to be one of his own design. The lighthouse.

He had always had trouble identifying with what he called the 'sheep' of humanity, people who were just living a bland, unremarkable and most often inconsequential life, people who had no interest in anything going on around them or in the world they lived in, people like those in the tram he was riding. The people immediately around him looked up from their smartphones to see why the air felt different around them. They got a look at him and immediately either lowered their eyes or pretended they were looking at something or someone else. This was not an unexpected or remarkable reaction to him; he had experienced the exact same thing throughout most of his life. He thought about everything he had to do and wondered for what seemed like the thousandth time whether he really needed to make the two stops he had set out to make and for what seemed like the one thousandth time had decided that yes, he did need to make both stops. There was no real reason, none he could figure out anyway, for him to feel so much conviction about doing things that in the past he'd been able to forgo doing, but he was someone who firmly believed that some things you couldn't explain rationally, you had to go on by feel. And one of the things he needed to check in on was one of those instances.

The tram slowed down as it arrived at the next set of gates. The airport in Dallas was as big as a city with hundreds of gates and dozens of airlines using it. It was the American Airlines hub airport, which meant that if you flew American from wherever you lived you'd have to probably switch planes at DFW, which also meant that the airport was almost always teeming with people, regardless of the season. The tram had only a few seats around the outside and a metal pole and handles for everyone not seated. When the tram stopped and the doors slid open some people got off, including an older man who was sitting in one of the few seats on the tram. There was an older woman next to him who was extremely overweight and who clearly needed the seat that had just opened up. As she went to take the empty seat, a guy of about thirty stepped in front of her and took the seat. He hadn't finished getting comfortable when the lighthouse keeper shifted his weight and changed his posture to come within inches of the man now sitting in the seat. The man started to open his mouth to say something, most likely 'excuse me' or 'please step back' or 'you're crowding me', but then he looked up and saw who it was that was crowding him, immediately closed his mouth and looked down. When he saw that the guy was still standing inches from him he looked up and saw a face with not an ounce of humor nor trace of a smile on it, a face scarred by who knew what and who knew how long ago, a face that made him more uneasy and nervous than any he'd ever encountered before. He looked at the man and followed his gaze to the heavyset woman who had been watching the whole thing and then back to him. He stood up and the man stepped aside to let him pass. He then looked at the woman and gave her a slight nod. She smiled back, mouthed the words 'Thank you' and sat down in the seat that had just been vacated. He was certainly not the protector of the oppressed or a hero of the masses by any stretch, but it had really pissed him off when that guy had just plopped himself down when he could see the older heavyset woman was struggling just to keep standing. He could have still gone without doing anything, it wasn't his business, but the asshole bumped him and stepped on his foot without an 'excuse me' or an 'I'm sorry'. He could care less whether the people around him thought him a hero or protector, but there were just some things he could not let go.

When the tram got to the section where his gate was he stood up, looked back at the woman and the asshole one last time and got off the tram. The rest of his journey from the Dallas/Fort Worth airport to San Diego was uneventful. He got in late, past 11 o'clock, so all he wanted to do was check into a hotel and go to sleep. The stop was a short one, but it was the one he always needed to get done before he took on a new engagement, regardless of how long it was. Sometimes he wondered whether it was really worth it to travel all this way, spend the time and the energy to do what he had to do and every time he came to the conclusion that it was absolutely worth it. The next morning he woke up at four in the morning, his body clock wasn't adjusted and he wouldn't be in California long enough for that to happen, so he just went with it. He walked down to a 7-11 he'd seen on the drive to the hotel, got a cup of coffee, a banana, a muffin and bought the newspaper. He went back to his room and waited for the sun to come up and for the city to start its day. At 7:30 in the morning he got into his rental car and drove across the Coronado Bridge onto the island of Coronado. He had always thought that when God took a vacation, he went to Coronado. Small-town quaint, with easy access to a major city, white beaches all around and amazing weather pretty much all year around, Coronado was as close to paradise as he was willing to accept the concept of paradise. He had thought about moving to Coronado many times, but in the end he always came to the conclusion that it would not be a good idea. He drove down Orange avenue, Coronado's main drive and finally turned left as he came across a small park in front of a church and a school. He parked across the street about a block down from the entrance of the school, Sacred Heart Elementary and Middle School – the only private Catholic school on the island – pulled out a small set of binoculars, and watched all the kids getting dropped off by their parents. He spotted the two he was looking for without any trouble at all. The boy, eight-years-old as of a month ago was big for his age, had light brown hair and bright blue eyes. His face wore a natural scowl, something he'd inherited from his father. The girl, eleven, was also tall, but her hair was jet black, like her mother's. Her eyes were also bright blue, just like her brother's but with a hint of green, also like her mother. He smiled as he watched them talking with their friends, laughing, just being children. They seemed like happy normal kids, but if you looked really close, you could see there was something grown up about them, something pensive.

He looked for and found the car that had dropped them off. He had always known that both kids got their good looks from their mother, but as they got older it became more and more apparent. Still, the boy was starting to look more like his father. It had been worth the trip out here just to see that. It was *always* worth the trip out here. Their mother also looked great. She had aged wonderfully and not having the stress of dealing with a life full of uncertainty, complications and pain had done wonders for her. He was always wondering when she might show up with someone else to drop off or pick up the kids, so far it hadn't happened, but he knew that could not last forever. He smiled, his eyes softened and as it was usually the case, he got a lump in his throat. It was about as close to crying as he ever let himself get, even when he was alone. He had tried to be a husband to her and a father to his little girl and newborn baby boy, but it just wasn't in the cards for him. Like many other times in his life, he had made the logical decision at the cost of immense personal turmoil and pain. He had gone on an assignment and simply never came back home. He did it that way because he was not sure he would be able to do it if he saw her and the children. He knew that they were his only weakness and had simply decided not to test himself. She had known, however, she had known something like this was coming. When it happened it didn't surprise her. After spending four years with him she had become completely numb. It was the only way they'd ever had a hope of making it. He had always provided for them, something that allowed her to be a stay at home mom if she chose to.

Although he came before projects once or twice a year, he also came just because, for no other reason than to see the children. It took literally two full days to come from the East Coast, see them and fly back, but he didn't care. He'd done what he came to do, so he drove back to the airport to wait for his flight to his next destination. He still wasn't sure whether he should go to his next destination, but it was planned now and he never deviated from a plan. Besides, they weren't expecting him in Dubai for another five days, so he had plenty of time to go get done what he needed to get done. He returned the car to the rental agency, took their shuttle back to the airport and looked at the departures board for the information on all the flights headed to New York.

MANHATTAN, NEW YORK

"Bart it's just dumb, just stupid! If we don't give them options we're going to risk losing the biggest case in history! And it won't even be our decision!"

Bart Logan was sitting at the conference room table running both hands through his hair, "Exactly Melanie! Exactly! It's not our decision! We've already brought up the issue to Neill and he's not going to change his mind, so let's move on, please! We need to finalize our witness list and really go over the profile we are going to be looking for in the jury pool. That's where this thing is going to be decided you know, in the jury selection."

Melanie sat down in the chair closest to her and exhaled in frustration, "I know, trust me Bart I know, all of it. I've gone over the profile our jury consultant put together and to be honest I'm not sure I agree with him. He came up with that profile without really understanding the details of the case, of the science. We need to bring in an outside consultant, a real heavy hitter. How the hell can Justin determine what kind of juror we want or don't want if he doesn't know what the jury is going to be asked to consider?"

Bart shook his head, "He's not a hired gun, but he does know what they're going to be asked to consider Melanie! The whole fucking world knows what they're going to be asked to consider!"

Melanie chuckled, "You're right about that, but I'm talking about the details Bart, not what all those morons on all the cable talk shows are spewing, the real details about the real science."

Bart stood up, poured himself a cup of coffee and another one for his partner, "Listen, I think it's time for us to unplug for a couple of days. The trial starts a week from Monday and neither one of us has actually gone one twenty-four hour period without being in the office, in this conference room in fact. We've done as much as we can with what we have Melanie; it's time to have some family time away from all of this. I know I've been putting off my mother for more than three weeks; we used to have dinner once a week before all of this started. I think she's wondering whether I still live in New York by now. And there's a woman I have been seeing who thinks I'm dodging her."

Farris smiled. Bart had a point, they were both on the verge of burnout and walking into the biggest trial of their careers looking like stepped-on road kill was just no way to start things.

She held up her hands in surrender, "Alright, alright, you have a point. Call your mother, go have dinner with her. Treat her to a really nice place too, because if we lose this case I don't think either one of us is going to be buying very many nice dinners for a while for anyone, maybe not even ourselves."

They gave each other a quick hug and Melanie left the office. Bart told her he still had a couple of quick things he needed to tend to and then he'd be heading home himself. The truth, however, was that he wanted to look at the witness list and think about the case without having Melanie there to muddle the waters. She was right, of course, it was stupid to say 'either you convict him of first degree murder or you don't convict him at all' to the jury. It simply did not make good strategic sense. Bart knew why his boss, David Neill, was doing it. He wanted to show confidence and he wanted to show that when it came to the shooting of Donald Riche, only the strictest representation of the law would do. First-degree murder was written very clearly and required only a few elements. You needed to prove that a human being had killed another human being, that they had done it with premeditation and that they had done it with malice, which meant that there had been a plan to kill the individual. It was clear and looking at the letter of the law as it was written right now, Steven Loomis was absolutely, positively, guilty of first-degree murder. But the science being discussed could change all that, in fact it would most likely change everything regardless of the outcome of the trial. Bart was pretty confident in the fact that whatever happened with this case was irrelevant; other lawyers would try the defense Loomis was trying here in New York and across the country. They would use it because more often than not, there really wasn't anything else they could conceivably use as a defense. So moving forward prosecutors would need to be prepared to prove that what had been killed had in fact been a human being. The science was solid, he'd looked at all of it, had read a host of peer reviewed opinions, journals and white papers and it all looked rock solid. When it came to criminal law and murder, the human element would no longer be simply assumed, it would need to be proven and that's what made Bart and Melanie uncomfortable. It was the main reason they thought it was dumb to take other potential verdicts off the table. David Neill seemed to think that whatever was being broadcast day in and day out regarding the science and the claim Loomis was making was just a bunch of hogwash that the jury would easily be able to see through. Bart didn't know whether that was what Neill really thought or whether he was just posturing, but in the end it didn't matter which one it was, they were both huge mistakes. If he really thought it was all hogwash it meant that either he hadn't read all the materials they'd found on the scientific evidence or, even worse, he'd read it and simply did not understand it. If he was posturing then it could really backfire when the jury came to that conclusion – that he was posturing – on their own; if he didn't understand the science, then nothing Melanie or Bart could say would make any difference. Well, they were on their way now, for better or for worse, they were on their way now.

Steven Loomis had been getting home at close to midnight every day of the week before trial, so he was more than willing to go when his attorneys told him they didn't need him at 7:00 pm. He had called Beth to let her know he'd actually be home before she went to bed. When he finally made it home the first thing to hit him was the smell of homemade marinara sauce with fresh sausage, one of his favorite dishes.

He walked in, set the gun he kept in his lower back in a drawer by the front door and made his way to the kitchen where his wife was waiting for him with a glass of chardonnay, "Welcome to Café Beth, Mr. Loomis, can we offer you some chardonnay?"

He smiled, gave her a bear hug and took the glass of wine, "I see, are you the chef of this establishment?"

She smiled and gave him a kiss before going back into the kitchen, "Absolutely, I am the proprietor as well."

He smiled and sat down at the dinner table while she finished cooking dinner. For the last couple of months whenever they had time to spend with each other almost every single topic of conversation was about the trial, the case, the media covering the case and any one of other hundreds of subjects surrounding the case. So tonight Steven wanted to make it about her and not about the case. Her days were usually pretty limited given the fact that wherever either one of them went there were dozens of paparazzi and reporters wanting to get a picture or a comment. It amazed Steven that even though they were refused every day for months, they kept coming back. Some were paid to do exactly that, but others were freelancers who were only paid if they sold a story or a picture. Most days Beth would go to a bakery three blocks from their condo, each day she would get two croissants and a pastry for Steven and maybe a coffee or a tea for herself. She would then read the newspaper, actually magazines since the paper was replete with stories about the trial and the case. She would spend a couple of hours there, would talk to the owners and be on her way. They didn't really need, nor want for that matter, the carbs, but it was something she could do that was normal, that made her feel like she had her life back. The owners of the bakery were used to her coming each morning with her security team. Beth would buy each of her security guys a coffee or a latte every day. They finally got the point that she would do that and would not take no for an answer. Most days after the bakery she would head home where she would Skype with her kids and her parents at least three times a day. Steven tried to join her for the last Skype session of the day, but he'd been coming home so late that he wasn't able to make it. Two or three days a week, she would stop by a small grocery store two blocks from their house. It was one of those little sidewalk grocery stores that had fresh produce displayed out front, clean and extremely fresh. The prices reflected the size of the market and the quality of the produce, but Beth would not buy any produce from anywhere else. They'd been going to that little market since they moved to their condo five years ago. Beth would stop by and talk to the couple that owned the market for hours before everything happened. She knew their names, their kids' names, their grandkids' names and what was going on with all of them. The couple, the Morgans, would always throw in some amazing treat for the kids whenever she stopped by. They would be things like melon balls with honey and plain yogurt or strawberries and real clear with some molasses, healthy things that still had the sweet taste kids loved. They had actually had the Morgans over for some drinks a couple of times over the years, usually during the holidays when they'd invite their friends over to celebrate whatever the holiday might be. After everything happened she'd stopped going to the store for a few months, but she'd started going again a few weeks back. She told him that the Morgans had sold the place and moved to Michigan where most of their family lived. They hadn't been planning to sell at all, but a buyer had made an offer they simply could not refuse, well over what the store was actually worth. The new owner was a young guy of about 40. He was from California where he'd made a pile of money from some Internet venture or another. With almost a billion dollars at his disposal Lester Allen could afford to pay whatever it took to get the Morgans to sell. At first he'd been reserved and considerate of Beth's security concerns. He'd even told her that if she wanted he would close the store while she was there so she could shop in peace. She'd told him that would not be necessary; it was the normalcy of shopping for her produce along the other people of the neighborhood that she was looking for when she stopped in.

"He's so nice Steven and so considerate. I swear, one of the things that really gets to me is when people look at me with pity or sadness in their eyes. He didn't do that, he just walked up to me said good morning and asked if I needed anything. That was exactly what I was looking for, just someone being normal and treating me the way someone who has none of my problems would expect to be treated, normal."

Steven chuckled a bit, "I know what you mean. I really look forward to you and I spending time with the kids, reading the paper or a book or magazine, watching TV or just this, having dinner and I look forward to it all because of that, because it's what normal people do."

Of course her security team, all of whom Steven knew and had worked with personally, had checked the guy out thoroughly and found a pretty vanilla background. He'd grown up in California, had a brother somewhere in Utah and his parents were both in Arizona. They liked the hot weather. He'd been a tech geek from the time he'd been a teenager and by the time he was 35 he sold his stake in the company he co-founded for more than $750 million dollars. He told Beth he'd done the travel thing for a couple of years, then he'd volunteered for some organizations and gotten involved in some philanthropy, but he'd still been restless until he'd found the little grocery store. He'd been visiting a friend, who Beth suspected was his partner, when the two of them had come into the little store. Lester loved the neighborhood, loved New York and obviously loved the little grocery store, not to mention the guy he'd come to visit. He'd asked the Morgans about selling the store and when they'd told him it wasn't for sale, he'd simply said thank you. The next day he delivered an envelope to Fred Morgan with a letter in which he offered far more than twice what the store was worth with the only caveat being that they stay on for a couple of months to introduce him to the customers, show him the business of running a grocery store – he was a digital technology genius, but knew nothing about running a grocery store – and settle all of their affairs in New York. Even with the exorbitant offer, the Morgans had balked at selling. What had finally sealed the deal had been when Lester told them that he'd pay off the mortgages on the homes of two of their kids and the student loan for the third. After that there was simply no way that Fred and Missy Morgan were going to say no. Beth had gotten to know Lester much more within the last few weeks and really liked him. She also told Steven that his partner would work in the store from time to time, just to get away from a high stress Wall Street job. She liked him a lot as well. She also explained to Steven something a bit curious about Lester. He was not gay, not completely in any case. There had been a couple of instances where a woman came by the store and seemed quite friendly with him. Not friend kind of friendly, but *that* kind of friendly. When she'd asked him about it, he had told her that he was not going to limit himself to one gender when building a life with someone he really loved. She and Steven both gotten a smile out of that. It was most definitely a different generation, one where things were fluid and became the norm almost overnight; a generation very different to their own. Neither one of them had been overly religious or conservative, but there were some things they just could not understand. In any case, Lester and his romantic escapades had provided Beth with precisely what she was looking for, a distraction, some normalcy and a friend who understood what she was going through and was willing to not pity her for it. Steven had met the guy a couple of times and he'd seemed okay, but he was still uneasy with Beth spending so much time with him, especially with everything else going on. It was not that he was jealous in the least, but the last thing he needed was some tabloid making allegations of infidelity from Beth or some other media outlet making it another distraction. Steven had to remind himself over and over that he'd have to learn to trust people again in order for their lives to eventually get back to normal. He knew he'd have to do it eventually, but for now he was fine with being just a tad uncomfortable about anyone that he had not known *personally* for years spending time around his family. Lester had been looked into by the people taking care of his family, people who knew what they were doing and they'd found nothing. Carl Gilliam, the most senior IT and digital information executive at Global Intelligence Consultants (GIC) had done the background research on Lester and on anyone, *anyone*, who was anywhere near him or his family. Carl came from the world of black hat hackers where he'd been somewhat of a legend. If it was stored in digital form anywhere on the globe, literally, Carl could get to it. Steven had wondered many times how Carl was able to get some of the information he'd gotten, but had always opted not to ask him. The truth was that Steven knew Carl was most likely breaking some law somewhere and being in the security and intelligence world, they both knew the fewer people that new about those laws and how they were being broken, the better. It had been Carl who had gotten the information the police had obtained about his daughter's and the other girls' murderer, Donald Riche and it had been that information that had led Steven to the warehouse the girls were found in. So at the end of the day Steven was fine with Lester because he'd been checked out and it was really good to see Beth animated and talking about normal things. It let him know that there was a light at the end of the tunnel for them, that one day they would be a normal family again, even if it was years away.

Steven smiled when she explained Lester's romantic predilections, "So he's good with either a guy or a girl?"

Smiling and in between bites, Beth nodded, "Can you believe that? I mean how can you do that? How can you say you're good with either one?! I don't get it, but then again, I don't get a lot of things about this new generation."

Steven nodded, "Yeah, neither do I babe, neither do I."

Beth took a bite and said something that she wasn't sure Steven would take well, "I was thinking of having Lester and Brice, that's his partner, over for dinner and drinks, what do you think?"

She expected for Steven to hesitate and hem and hum while he thought of a way to tell her he didn't think it was a good idea.

What she got instead, however, was, "Okay. Could you do it before the trial though? I think it would be pretty difficult to do it once the trial starts, don't you think?"

That response caught Beth so off-guard that she literally could not answer for a couple of seconds.

Finally she smiled, "Yeah, of course. I'll ask him tomorrow and see if they can come on Friday. I'd like to make lobster tails and filet if you're okay with it."

He raised his eyebrows at that, "Wow, that's a pretty fancy dinner."

She returned the eyebrow raise, "And I haven't even told you what I am making on Sunday just for us. Sunday I am making Chilean Sea Bass with miso glaze."

Now Steven's eyebrows really went up, "Double wow. When did you learn to make Chilean Sea Bass with miso glaze?"

Beth chuckled, "I told you this is Café Beth and I am the chef monsieur!"

They both chuckled, "And I looked it up on Google."

He nodded, "Well, I'm still impressed."

She nodded, "Well I hope so mister. So I'll ask Lester and see what he says."

They kept eating dinner and talking and just being a couple. It was a great way for Steven to get ready for trial, relaxed, with one of the three people he cared the most about. The light at the end of the tunnel looked just a bit brighter indeed and Steven could see a life after all of this. If he was able to get through the trial of course, everything depended on that didn't it? However Steven wanted to think about their future would always depend on getting past the trial. He didn't know what 'getting past' the trial meant. It was just an idea he knew he'd have to keep front and center as he made his way through all of it; and he knew that eventually he'd have to figure out what 'getting past' meant, but it wasn't right now. Right now he wanted to have dinner with his wife and listen to her talk about her day and her friends, the couple she could actually spend any time with and talk to and about the kids and her parents. After dinner they poured themselves an after-dinner drink, Amaretto for him, Bailey's for her and sat in the living room watching old movies. They paused the movie they were watching so they could say good night to the kids over Skype. When the movie ended Beth woke from a light sleep to the sound of her husband sleeping and to the feeling of his chest rising and falling. She lay there like that, just feeling his body sleeping, relaxed, safe, for almost an hour. While she lay there in his arms she thought about Tracy. She thought of her every single day in different ways, remembering different things about her. Her smile, her laugh, her cries and tantrums, all of it broke her heart every single day. She had gone through what she could only imagine was as close to hell as someone who was still alive could come and had made it through to the other side, mainly because she remembered she had two other children who needed her and a husband that was going through his own hell. Still, Tracy made her way into her heart every single day. Today she came while Beth was in Steven's arms, listening and feeling him breathe. Tonight she would let herself feel everything that always threatened to come up whenever she thought of Tracy: guilt, defeat, loss, all the things she'd learned to keep at bay. Tonight her husband's arms gave her comfort, even if he himself was asleep. Tonight she would let it all come and she would cry silently and miss her daughter completely. As the jingle for one fast-food restaurant or another played on the television, tears ran freely down Beth's cheeks. As she let herself finally breathe deeply and fall asleep, she could not have seen her husband's own cheeks where tears had also drawn thin uneven lines of moisture as he felt his wife let go.

The next morning Steven was gone by the time Beth woke up; he was leaving earlier and earlier now that the trial was about to start. She got up, took a shower, went to the kitchen and made herself a fruit smoothie. After reading a popular lifestyle magazine for a few minutes she went to talk to the kids and her parents via Skype. It was always hard on her, but it had been getting a bit easier as time went by. What hurt her most was that her children were having to deal with their sister's death without their parents there, but it could not be helped. She had stayed with them at her parents' house in the beginning, but she'd known that she needed to be with her husband; he had nobody else that would stand next to him, it had to be her. She knew that the General would always be there for Steven, as would every single person he'd ever served or worked with, but that was different. When the sun went down and he was alone lying in bed he would have nobody there and it broke her heart. So she'd come back to New York. She would never had done that if it had been anybody else taking care of her kids, but it was her parents and both she and Steven trusted them implicitly. After drinking her smoothie she went to the bakery to get her things. People there were used to her and her security by now and did not even raise their eyes from their newspapers, tablets or computers. If there were anyone there besides the usual customers, any unwanted attention would stand out like a sore thumb and would be immediately corrected, most often by the other patrons, but also by her security. Next she went to the little market by her condo. She *loved* the place and was starting what seemed like a great friendship with the new owner. Lester was kind, funny and incredibly smart. She had been hesitant at first, opening up with someone she had not known for years was always difficult, but now even more so. Lester had somehow known exactly what to say, how to say it and most importantly, when to say it. He was never nosy or pushy and always seemed to know when she just needed a good laugh.

As she walked up to the market he saw her, smiled, and waved to her as he greeted her with a funky British accent, "Good morning me lady!"

She returned the smile, walked up to him and gave him the usual light hug and kiss on the cheek that had become their usual greeting, "Hello you! Who're you supposed to be today, Winston Churchill?"

He got an exaggerated look of outrage on his face, "Sacrilege daaling! I would never pretend to be a fat, British politician, it's so last year. If I was going to pretend to be anybody it would be Lady Gaga."

She smiled and shook her head. He never failed to make her smile, "Alright, Lady Gaga it is. Did you get the pears and pomegranates you were expecting yesterday?"

His eyes got big as he responded, "Yes! And OMG are they amazing. Here, come here, you have to try a slice."

He walked her over to a small table by the cash register cut a thin slice of the fruit and handed it to her.

She took one bite and her eyes flew wide open, "Oh my god, that is amazing! Where the hell do you get these? I have never tasted fruit as sweet as what you carry, never. Even when the Morgans owned it the fruit was not as sweet as it is now."

He smiled, "Yeah, their stuff was good, but I have some friends that live in the Napa valley and some that live in Hawaii and friends of friends that live just about anyplace where fruits or vegetables are traditionally grown. Just wait until pineapple season when my friends in Hawaii send me some stuff, you will want to cry it's so good."

She walked over to the table and got another slice of pear, "I have to have another one. I'm sorry, it must seem like I am a total freeloader. I'll be happy to pay for it."

He got the hurt look on his face again, "Sacrilege again daaaling! Are you kidding me Beth, seriously? You're my friend, anything I have in this humble little market is there for you and your family, whether you pay for it or not. And don't give me any lip back, you know if you owned the market you would feel the same way and do the same thing."

She had to admit he was absolutely right.

If she owned the market and she had someone she considered a friend come by, she would definitely share anything she had whether they paid or not, "I know, you're right. But still, it is a business Lester and you need to make some money to keep a business going."

Now the sideways smile on his face was one that simply said, 'are you kidding me here' He didn't even have to say anything. She recognized how ludicrous what she said had been. The guy was worth close to a billion dollars; he could afford to keep the market open for roughly the next 100 years, even if he never had a single customer.

They were still in the back of the market by the cash register when Beth pulled him a bit further back.

She had been thinking about the question she wanted to ask him and thought now would be the best time to ask, "Lester, I wanted to ask you a question. Are you and Bri..."

He didn't even let her finish the question and held up his hand, "You want to know how it is I can like both boys and girls, right? Your face when Robin came in the other day was priceless. Your bottom jaw about hit the ground."

She smiled and looked down, "Alright, you got me. How Lester? I mean it's got to be one or the other, doesn't it? I mean I can't even begin to imagine having some sort of romantic relationship with a woman."

He shook his head, "Why? Why can't it be that I look for someone's personality and their soul? It's actually safer to do it that way, you know."

She smiled, "I guess, but I just don't know how you can be physically attracted to both men and women. Sexual orientation is established at birth, isn't it? So didn't you have a sexual orientation early on? Believe me, I am not judging in the least. I actually think some of the most stable couples I know are same sex couples, it's the bi in the equation I am trying to understand."

He was nodding thoughtfully, "Yes, you are right, it is something you are born with and yes, I should have had some sexual inclination as an older child or as a teen, but I honestly didn't."

She could see that his youth was not an easy topic for him to talk about and felt horrible about having said anything.

But before she could say anything, he kept talking, "See I was not always the charming, handsome, disarmingly sweet individual you see before you today. I kept to myself mostly, building models and tinkering with all kinds of electronic crap. I loved taking stuff apart and figuring out what it did and how it worked. When computers came along I finally fell in love. So I guess you could sat my sexual orientation was not straight or homosexual, it was digital."

She smiled and nodded, "It seems to have served you well. Didn't you make all your money in high tech stuff?"

He nodded vigorously, "Yes, most of it and yes, you are absolutely right. As I got older I learned to reverse-engineer stuff, mostly video games. And later on having done that for so long really was the best form of training for what my company ended up doing, which was to deliver the most fun and successful digital experience for retail companies."

He got busy unloading another box of pears and setting them up on the display by the cash register, "Back to sex. So I didn't really start thinking about people in a romantic sense until much, much later, well into my adulthood. So you see, by the time that happened, I really wasn't thinking about whether I liked women or men, I was just trying to figure out what it would be like to have a relationship with someone that could love me. I know most people don't believe it, they think just like you, that I need to figure out what I like and then just go for that, but honestly Beth, sometimes you run into amazing people, people that you think you might be able to build a life with and they just happen to be the wrong gender.

"Well, I won't do that. So right now Brice is absolutely my number one, but I am not closing myself off to anything and he knows that. He knows I *want* him to be it, but he also knows if he gets too comfortable or if he starts to take things for granted, I'm open to whatever."

Beth nodded through his whole explanation, but now had to ask something, "So you're telling me Brice knows that you do not have any preference when it comes to gender and that you're open to having other people come into your life?"

He stopped unloading the box of pears, "You make it sound so horrible! The answer to your question is no and yes. No, he does not know that I do not have any gender preference and yes, he does know that until we take the plunge, the whole plunge, I am not closed to anyone. Put a ring on it, you know what I mean?"

Beth looked at him and gave him a quick nod letting him know that she understood everything. She wasn't sure she agreed with everything he'd said, but she did understand the rationale he had just given her and truth be told it really wasn't any of her business. In any case, she had also been planning on asking him and Brice over for dinner and she did not want that dinner to be the least bit awkward because she couldn't keep herself from seeming too nosy.

She changed her posture and her tone, "Well, now that we're all clear on the sex stuff, do you want to come over for dinner, you and Brice, on Friday night?"

He stopped unloading the pears again. His tone was completely serious, "Are you being serious here Beth? Or are you playing with me? Because if you're playing I don't want to get too excited and then be totally heartbroken when you laugh it off."

She shook her head, "Of course not! I would like to have both you and Brice over for dinner. Scratch that, *Steven and I* would like to have you guys over for dinner. It's not a game Lester, not when it comes to something like that."

He looked at her without saying anything for a few seconds and she could see that he was actually getting choked up, "Beth, that is the nicest thing anybody has ever done for me."

She tilted her head and smiled, "Oh c'mon Lester, you've been asked to dinner before, now it's you who is playing with me."

He shook his head and his face still had no trace of a smile, "I am absolutely not playing here Beth, not at all. Yes I have been asked over for dinner, many times and by many people. This is different though. Look at what your family has been through and what you're still going through. Look at the television Beth; it's 24/7 coverage of Steven's trial. With all of that going on I know you have probably not had anybody over to your place for a while. So, having you invite Brice and I over for dinner is absolutely the nicest thing anybody has ever done for me. Ever. Now do you understand?"

Beth had also lost all hint of a smile as well. She'd blown it. She had said the wrong thing and it had obviously really bothered Lester.

She nodded as she answered his last question, "Yes I do, I do understand Lester and I am so sorry for being lame. I swear; I have a knack for saying the dumbest things."

Lester got his smile back as he took both of her hands, "Nonsense! You are just a nosy bieatch and I love it! I'm just kidding, but no worries at all, seriously. We're friends, and on our way to being good friends, at least that's what I think, and good friends say dumb things to each other all the time. So, if the invite is still there, I would like to RSVP for my partner and I for dinner Friday night."

Beth's smile reappeared on her face, wider than it had been, "Fabulous! And yes, we *are* becoming good friends. I sweat Lester, if it wasn't for you and that little bakery a couple of blocks down, I think I would have gone insane by now. Well, maybe not insane, but I definitely would have gone back to my parents' house. I'm so glad you bought the market and that we met when we did. I think it's so interesting how destiny puts people in front of you just when you need them."

Lester pulled her into a hug, "I totally agree. Meeting you was also just the thing I needed. Being new in the city and everyone here in New York being far too good and busy to even say good morning, might have also sent me into a funk. Finding Brice and then you has been the best thing I could have ever imagined coming from my move to New York."

She returned the hug and then held him out at arm's length, "Okay, so I will be expecting you and Brice at my house for dinner Friday at six sharp, that isn't too early is it? I thought we'd unwind and have drinks before dinner. What time does Brice get home from work?"

He shook his head, "That queen? Ha, he works at home on Fridays, so no time is too early and I can close the store when I need to, so don't worry, we will be there with bells on!"

Beth gave him a last squeeze and then the two of them went around the market tasting the fruits and vegetables and talking about everyday things. When Beth left the market she had decided that yes, Lester Allen was indeed becoming a good friend.

5.

The reverend J.D. Garzen was upset and he was letting everyone in the room know it. They were in the large dinning room of his estate in the Houston suburbs. It was 13 acres, large by any standards. The property had a small man-made pond, go kart track and dog runs. The main house was 23,000 square feet and had two principal dinning rooms as well as 10 bedrooms, 6 baths a gourmet kitchen as well as a smaller kitchenette in one of the wings. The property also had a pool with a slide, a waterfall and a small cave where people could disappear. There was also a guesthouse that was just over 2000 square feet and had two bedrooms a full kitchen and two bathrooms. In addition to everything else there were flat screen televisions of various sizes all throughout the house. Overall the property was everything that could be imagined when someone had paid $23 million dollars for it.

In the dinning room where the meeting was taking place there were four people, all belonging to Garzen's inner circle. Charles 'Bubba' Jones was just past his sixtieth birthday, but looked much older. He was bald, short and on the verge of obesity. He was in essence his number two. He was the President of the Light Ministries empire and was one of two people who could contact Garzen anytime he needed to and anywhere he might be. He was the first person that Garzen had employed full-time when he had gotten started. Prior to working for the reverend Bubba had been a long-haul truck driver for thirty years. He had risen to the position he held now because from the beginning he had understood one basic rule that everything else was dependent upon: Garzen was always right, no matter the topic, no matter what anyone or evidence said, Garzen was always right. Many, many people had simply not understood that one basic rule and all of them had been let go at the first instance they had shown they didn't understand the rule. In addition to being in charge of the operation of the organization Jones was one of the reverend's close, if not closest, confidants.

Another attendee of the meeting was Homer Buck. He was the media director for the ministry, which meant he was the individual that was in charge of all media relationships across the various media channels they utilized and of deciding what channels that would be. He had a budget of $7 million dollars to use in whatever way he needed to throughout the year. Having a healthy budget meant that a host of media channels were constantly reaching out with complementary tickets, gifts and introductions to various personalities, all of which Homer took full advantage of.

Charlene 'Charlie' Simmons was Garzen's stylist as well as fashion and current events advisor. She had worked in a big time PR agency for fifteen years and looked the part. She was in her late forties, but very fit and well put together. She kept up to date on everything going on around the world and would advise Garzen on what his position needed to be in order to be most effective in his ministries and his preaching. Gay marriage, race relations, popular culture, all of it had to be considered and a position had to be established. She also advised on the right look, how Garzen needed to balance looking good, but not too good. He was, after all, a preacher. In addition to all of her official duties, Charlie had unofficial duties that were almost just as important as her official ones. She had been having an affair with Garzen for almost four years. She had come onboard just over six years previously and had risen to her current position starting just after two years of working for Garzen. Everyone in the inner circle and those closest to that inner circle knew about the affair, but also knew to never, ever, show that they knew about it. She had been following the Loomis trial and the whole situation very closely and she had been the one that had crafted Garzen's current position on the issue, which truthfully had not been utilized very much at all by the reverend. She had wondered why that was, but she, like every other person in the room, knew to not ask questions or imply disappointment or disapproval. If Garzen was not using it there must be a reason or at least that was what she had to tell herself.

Oren 'Junior' McDaniel was in charge of all security, transportation and logistical support for the ministry. Prior to coming on board Junior had worked with Bubba Jones at the trucking firm doing a lot of what he was doing now, figuring out logistics, driver logs and ensuring security when there was a sensitive load or shipment being handled. He had put together a security detail for the reverend that was made up of former military people he'd met while on the Texas National Guard reserves. Most of them had plenty of experience with weapons and with using their size and military skills to push and intimidate people, but not one of them had actual personal security experience. Not that Garzen cared very much what kind of experience they did or did not have. As long as they kept people away from the reverend and made sure that nobody could ever make it closer than whatever Garzen wanted, he was totally fine with Junior's security detail.

The last of the five in the meeting was Ross Menard. Ross did not have an official title or job like the others; he was someone that the reverend used for special projects and nothing else. There was wide speculation about what the special projects might be and what Menard did for Garzen, particularly among the other three people in the room. The fact was that Menard did jobs and handled issues that were questionable from a legal perspective. At times it wasn't questionable at all, he knew what he was doing was illegal. He was the only individual within the organization that had not had a background check done, at least not a background check that Junior's team had done. The only person that knew anything about Menard was Bubba and like everything else relating to Garzen, he knew to keep his mouth shut. Prior to coming on board six years previously, Ross Menard had done fifteen years for manslaughter in the state of Illinois. Garzen had met Menard when he had done an outreach campaign for ex-cons that wanted to get out of the life and go straight. Garzen had made a big impression on Menard and from the beginning Garzen knew that Ross Menard would do anything for him, anything. Over the six years that he'd been working with the ministry he'd handled a host of situations where none of the others could delve. Bubba knew Garzen was basically insulating the others with Menard and that if a red flag was raised by anyone or if Menard was caught doing whatever he happened to be doing for the reverend, he would take absolute and total responsibility for it and exonerate anyone else involved. People like Ross Menard were always needed in large organizations, particularly ones that were so emotionally charged and controversial, which religion always was. He was the only other person that could get in touch with Garzen whenever and wherever he was.

As the five of them sat without saying a word and waiting for Garzen to come in each of them wondered whether they would be called onto the carpet, something reverend Garzen was always ready to do and had in fact done to each of them at various times. He came into the room, quickly walked to the head of the table and just nodded while looking at all of them. It would have been amusing had they not been terrified; from the outside it would have looked like a chubby and poorly dressed man nodding and looking at each of them as though he had the goods on all of them.

Finally Garzen let them in on the news, "What is it that you guys think keeps this ministry going? Hmm? What allows you all to make six figures and fly in private jets and take care of your families? What do you think it is?"

He looked from one to the next waiting for someone to answer the question. His accent had absolutely none of the southern drawl he used when he was in public. It was a California accent with some nuances that came in the form of the singsongy way that Valley girls spoke with.

When he did not get an answer he went ahead and answered the question himself, "Well, since apparently I am surrounded by morons that do not know what makes their nice lives possible, I will answer my own question. What keeps us all in the lifestyle we are accustomed to is controversy."

He looked at each of them again and waited to see whether anyone had anything to say. They didn't. He kept going, "When there is an issue that plays on our followers' passions and very conservative opinions they are much, much more likely to open up their wallets. That is what keeps this ministry going. We've had gay marriage, abortion, 9/11 and other very polarizing events and issues to rely on for a long time, but that has changed. Does anybody know the number one issue everyone in our congregation hears about every single day multiple times a day? Hmmm? Oh c'mon now, you have to know this guys!"

Bubba spoke up tentatively, "The Steven Loomis trial and all the other stuff related to it."

Garzen smiled, "That's right, Bubba, that's exactly right. That fucking trial has taken over almost every single media outlet and it's only going to get worse. Okay, so now that we've established what our followers are hearing every day, what do you suppose is our role in this all-consuming issue? What have we done about Mr. Loomis and his crack legal team? Hmmm? Don't know? Well I'll tell you, nothing, abso-fucking-lutely nothing!"

Now they were all nodding and looking grave. Every one of them with the exception of Russ Menard who did not have any responsibilities like the others and who could sit back and just listen while the rest of them got their asses handed to them.

Garzen went on, "We've been hitting the 'only god can decide whether someone is a human being or not' angle, but it's getting old. Besides getting old, it was never too popular to begin with. People, no matter how religious, and particularly those from the south, don't have a big problem with the father of a six-year-old girl taking out the piece of shit that kidnapped and killed her. Would any of you have any problem with him taking the piece of shit out?"

He looked around the table and saw all of them shaking their heads, "Okay, now that we've established that you all might do the same thing he did, what do we do? What aspect of this issue do we clamp on to and build our messaging around? Whatever it is we better be sure about it because once we go with something we will go at it with everything. I didn't let Gary Udell come in here with me today, but he wanted to. He says our monthly numbers are down by twenty percent. Twenty fucking percent! He wanted to come in here and rip all of you a new asshole for allowing that to happen."

Gary Udell was the ministry's accountant and he only took a back seat to the reverend himself. The battles between him and Bubba were legendary, both thought they were number two and Garzen had never corrected either one because he enjoyed the conflict and the drama around it. If push came to shove Gary would probably outrank Bubba. Having control of the ministry's accounts and knowing the various ways that Garzen put money away gave him that edge.

Garzen went on, "So, does anybody have any ideas?"

He looked around the table, but nobody said anything. He shook his head, "How the hell are we supposed to come up with something if none of you have the balls to make any suggestions?"

He looked around again and this time Charlie Simmons, his lover actually raised her hand.

Garzen smiled, "You don't have to raise your hand Charlie, I'm not your fucking middle school teacher. What do you have?"

Charlie began speaking in a quiet voice, completely prepared to back off and concede the floor to anyone who thought what she had was a bad idea, "Well, I saw a story last week where some psychologist was saying that maybe the Loomis's other two kids should be taken into custody to make sure they were safe. The guy, I can't remember his name, but I can find it out easy enough, said that whether what Loomis was arguing was true or not, his kids might be some of the first targets for people that *thought* they were these predators."

Now Junior McDaniel spoke up, "That's stupid! Why would they be in any more danger where they are now than they are with their parents? The guy must have some other agenda rev, the story Charlie's talking about doesn't make any sense."

Garzen snapped at his security chief, "Shut the fuck up Oren! Go on sweetheart."

Charlie went on, now a bit more confidently, "Actually Junior is not completely wrong; it does not make any practical sense and he probably does in fact have some other agenda, but it's something we can latch on to and promote. The whole idea that the Loomis kids are in danger because of what their father has done has a lot of potential. What that guy said about these creatures coming after the kids is bullshit, but there are plenty of other things that could put the kids in danger; maybe not in physical danger, but in emotional danger and even more important, in *spiritual* danger."

Garzen raised his arms and shouted, "Hallelujah! Or should I say Eureka! That's exactly what we needed! Who gives a shit about the whole physical danger thing! Those kids are in imminent spiritual danger! Their very souls are in jeopardy through no fault of their own and there's nobody paying attention to that. You know why I like that? Because it works with what I have already been using. Their father, this Loomis mutt, has held himself as an equal to god, able to determine who is human and who is not, who should die and who should live. It's beautiful!"

With every one of them smiling Charlie was now very confident about what she had to say, "I can reach out to my freelance film crews and see whether any of them can go to Vermont to get some footage."

Junior spoke up, "I don't know how close they would be able to get, those kids and their grandparents are being watched by some real pros, guys who have no problem taking your camera and shoving it up your ass if you get too close. Is there a way that we might be able to get closer to them while they're in Vermont by maybe coming up with a school angle or something along those lines?"

Charlie shook her head, "It would be really tough to pull off. We would have to completely distance ourselves from whomever is coming up with the school angle and even then, if the security is as good as Oren is saying, that will be impossible to do."

Garzen was nodding thoughtfully, "I agree. What about using a political angle? I mean what if we got a local politician to ask to meet with the family to offer them peace of mind and cooperation from any resources they might have to offer? If they do that then we can have a photographer there to capture the whole thing."

Junior nodded, "That could work. It's not too out of the realm of possibility that a politician might reach out to the family to offer support, as long as it's the right politician that is. And it would also be completely up to the parents and grandparents whether they agree to it or not."

Bubba spoke up for the first time, "What do you mean 'the right politician'? Is there a wrong type of politician?"

Junior smiled, "Are you serious? You can't see how a politician who is loud and very prominent in the media and always yelling about one thing or another would be a 'wrong' politician?"

Bubba was known for making asinine statements like the last one. It was in moments like these that his background as a truck driver came up to haunt him. He was loyal and he could be crafty when managing the day-to-day operations, but whenever things had to do with some understanding of human nuances or something more subtle about the ways that people interacted with each other, he was clueless most of the time. He was also sadly uninformed and unconcerned about politics, business, just about anything not having to do with the immediate task of running the ministry. And while a lot of people, most of who were in the room, wondered why the hell J.D. kept him around and gave him such an important position, it was never an issue for J.D. himself. He liked the fact that Bubba was poorly educated and clueless when it came to the world around him, it meant that he was going to always be loyal and would never be looking to go out on his own and do something stupid. Bubba was absolutely clear that J.D. held his life in his hands and was therefore completely dedicated to whatever the reverend told him to be dedicated to.

He still didn't get it, "What's the right politician Junior? Huh? Tell me what makes a politician the *right* politician?"

Junior didn't flinch, "Someone with credibility you moron! If it's someone that everyone thinks is a loudmouth crackpot then having them be a part of it would actually be counterproductive, now wouldn't it?"

Bubba just sulked, but the others were actually thinking about who might fit the bill.

Finally Charlie spoke up, "What about Albert Potter, the senator from New York? He's definitely a staunch conservative and is well accustomed to speaking to the media. His positions about faith in the schools and at work almost always get him a spot on the nightly news. But he's not too kooky, he comes across as thoughtful and he is very articulate. Even if you don't agree with him, he is still respected. And he's spoken up about children in foster care and living under the poverty line. I think he would be perfect for this."

Homer Buck spoke up, "I think you maybe onto something there. Aside from the religious aspect of the whole thing we've made some pretty healthy contributions to his campaigns. I think we've probably given him two or three hundred thousand over the last three years."

The figure caught J.D.'s attention, "Whoa! Two or three hundred thousand! What the fuck Homer? You're supposed to be buying media with the money, not making campaign donations! And why did you decide to give this guy all that money in the first place? We haven't been using him for anything before now."

Homer sighed as he explained something he knew he'd have to explain again within a few months, "We didn't single him out for those donations, we make donations to every faith-based or faith-influenced politician in both houses of congress and in a variety of local races. Potter was someone we identified as a good prospect because he is a neoconservative politician from a very liberal, Democratic-leaning state. We don't give all of them that kind of money; we decide how much to give depending on what kind of return we think we can get on our investment. And lookie here, it looks like good ol' Potter is going to actually pay off!"

J.D. was nodding more emphatically the more he heard, "Alright, alright! See, I knew it was a good idea to make donations to political campaigns! I knew it! Alright, Charlie reach out to his people, Bubba you back her up. Let's let this Potter know which side his bread is buttered on!"

Everyone looked around and exchanged quizzical expressions.

Junior finally spoke up, "So now we know who it's going to be, but what the hell are we going to ask him to do?"

J.D. shook his head in frustration, "Do I have to think of everything? We're going to ask him to speak up on behalf of those poor children, the aah..."

Charlie interjected, "Loomis"

J.D. continued, "...the Loomis children! We're going to ask him to bring up the fact that these children's father has put their immortal souls in jeopardy and that someone needs to be brought in to counsel the family. But he's only going to say that *after* he's met with the family, if he says it before there's no way that the family lets him in. They might not let him in no matter what he says, but this way they're more likely to agree. Charlie, you'll make sure he understands, right?"

Charlie nodded, Bubba was busy taking notes on all of it and Homer and Junior were both rolling their eyes.

Finally Charlie jumped in, "What do we want as our end result? I mean once we get Potter to say whatever he's going to say, what then."

J.D. Garzen was caught off guard by the question, he was used to people telling him what the result of a specific campaign or another would be, not to being asked what the result would be, "Uh, well, uh, we want to see the kids! Yeah, we want to have the kids evaluated and make sure they're ok! That's fucking beautiful! Can you imagine the media around that kind of thing?"

Charlie was nodding, "I like that. It lends itself to a great media event regardless of what the family says. I like it."

Garzen was on a roll, "Homer you see who you can get some coverage from. Squeeze every one of those bastards you pay millions of dollars to. Get me on some talk shows or get them to produce a special. They've done a shitload of specials on the case and on the kids' father. I bet they're all hungry for a new angle. And it's right before the trial which will mean that everything we are able to get done will get even more play, if that is possible."

Everyone was now smiling, comfortable that their six-figure lifestyles and their traveling by private jet was once again safe. What almost all of them thought, but none of them brought up, was the fact that J.D. had not explained how exactly he was going to use all of the attention to drum up more donations. They all also thought it was a stupid idea that had almost no chance of succeeding, but once he jumped on it with both feet, nobody was willing to tell him what they really thought. The truth was, however, that they all also knew that if there was something that J.D. was an absolute genius at, it was figuring out ways to get donations from just about anything and anyone.

He looked around the table satisfied; he had kicked ass and taken names and shown all of them just how to resolve this kind of thing.

Sometimes if he wanted something right he had to do it himself, "Alright, get rolling and cracking and as always, let the light guide your steps."

They all rolled their eyes as they mouthed the last sentence. Before they could all leave J.D. called out, "Russ, stay back for a minute will you?"

Russ Menard smiled and sat back down. He'd been expecting to be asked to stay; he usually was after these kinds of meetings.

Garzen waited until they were all out of the room before he started to say something, "Russ, I know you don't need me to say so, but we need to make this here deal with the Loomis kids something that will be remembered, something that will get major play on all the networks and maybe even compete with the trial for media time."

Russ was nodding, "I agree rev, but what are you thinking? I mean that whole family has some serious security around them, *serious* security, not those rent-a-cops you see at concerts. I bet every one of those fuckers is Special Forces. If that's the case there's just no way to get closer than 10-20 feet from them as they get whisked by, if that."

J.D. slammed his fist on the table, "Godammit I pay you a shitload of money and I give you everything you want, everything! Now, you sold yourself as someone who can get things done, who can provide answers when answers are needed, it's time to prove it Russ!"

Russ had a sideways grin on his face, he'd actually proven it time and time again, but he knew it wouldn't matter right now, "That's true rev, all of it is true, but I would hope you understand that when you have that kind of security around, you can't just push yourself into their path and say 'excuse me, can we get a picture'. I said it was going to be tough, I didn't say it would be impossible. By now they have fallen into a pattern, a routine and have most likely gotten a bit lax; even spec ops studs start getting lax after a while, but these guys seem like they're something extra, so we'll assume they're still razor sharp. We will create a commotion during the time the family is being transported from one place to another. We will send in a couple of our drones to shout about damnation and everlasting hell or some other bullshit and when the security team reacts to them you can slide in and do your monologue. If we pull that op off I guarantee you you'll get play on every channel online and offline."

J.D. was now smiling, "That's the sneaky bastard I know and love! We will need to make sure Homer and Charlie get us a lot of play with the media though. The trick to having this work the way we want is going to be whipping every Christian conservative around the country up into a frenzy and getting people talking and arguing. I don't give a shit which side they take as long as they take a side. Once the issue is red hot we pull the trigger on our little event. Get your people in and have them get ready while I'm talking to our congregation about it and getting them riled up."

Russ nodded in agreement, although this one felt wrong to him for more than one reason.

Before he left he wanted to make sure Garzen understood something, "Listen rev, you have to agree that if I'm going to do this, I'm going to bring in some heavy hitters, people I know can pull this kind of thing off."

J.D. waved his hands, "Yes, yeah, whatever Russ, just don't make it those fucking troglodytes from the biker clubs you used last time. Christ, anyone with a half a brain would be able to pick them out of a line up. There wasn't a big outlaw biker community at the Christian Coalition Gathering; you know what I mean? Other than that you can bring in whomever you want Russ, just get'er done. And you need to get'er done double quick, you understand? Now that I think about it we need to do this before the trial starts, otherwise it will just get looked over and nothing will come of it. I'll light a match under everyone else's ass to get Potter to say what we want him to say today or at the latest tomorrow. We'll make it worth his while, so he'll do it and he'll do it when we want him to."

Russ went to leave and as he was leaving he said, "Okay, we'll get it done, but I'm just lettin' you know that there is a chance that some folks might be hurt. Nothing big, you understand, just a light ass whupin' or two and a shiner or two. Those reporters can get pretty rabid, so my guys will get rabid back and that's when bad things can happen."

Garzen wasn't really paying attention any more, as far as he was concerned he had given his people all the information and support they would need to go execute what he wanted them to.

He just nodded as he picked up the crossword puzzle, "Aha, yeah, you bet; you got it Russ, whatever you need buddy."

Russ smiled a sardonic smile, shook his head and left the room without saying anything else.

6.

Steven had in fact been getting to the law offices earlier and earlier, especially the past four days. Since Friday of the previous week he'd been getting there between 6:00 and 6:30. Most of the time he was there before anyone else, Drew got in next, usually at around 7:00 am. For the last three days though, Drew, Ray and Max had all gotten to the office before Steven and in fact looked like they'd been there for a couple of hours by the time Steven got there. The trial was starting the following Monday and all three attorneys knew they'd probably be putting in 16 hours leading up to it, even with the massive legal team they had working with them. They had finalized their witness list and now needed to truly go through their testimony. Each attorney would be responsible for part of the story, all of them fitting seamlessly together. They had all agreed that each of them would be versed in everyone's testimony, regardless of the witnesses they were responsible for. Steven had been getting to the office early because he wanted to be a part of the process, the whole process, of preparing for trial. Today, however, it was going to be the first time that Drew was going to be going through his testimony for real, trying to mimic what the prosecution was likely to do. Like the prosecution, Max, Ray and Drew realized that the case was going to be won or lost either on the cross-examination or the jury selection. After they were finished preparing the last witness Drew asked Steven whether he was ready.

Steven responded immediately, "I am ready, there really isn't much else to do is there?"

Drew answered him, "You're right, there isn't a lot more you can do in preparation, but the way you say it and the way that you respond to the questions the prosecution has for you are going to be critical. Remember Steven, all along you have been taking the position that your sanity was at no point compromised. You are going to have to make absolutely sure that you come across exactly like that. The jury can't see you as some delusional crackpot who lost it and decided to blow Riche away. This is probably the only murder case in which it will be essential that the shooter show that he was completely sane and that he planned his act very carefully."

Max patted Steven on the back, "Remember what we talked about Steven, it will be important that people understand that if you had wanted revenge you could have easily gotten away with it. I know I've said it before, but it truly is important for two reasons: first it gives you credibility because you are not shying away from admitting that you shot him; and second it will help to put the trial really into perspective for the jury. You are not a run-of-the-mill witness or defendant Steven, regardless of the type of case, they need to understand that."

Steven was confident that he would be able to do just that, but his lawyers explained to him that the prosecution was going to be relentless trying to prove exactly the opposite. They would try to prove that he had in fact lost it and that he had come up with this crazy idea about Riche's humanity after the fact. At the very least they would try to establish that he had decided to kill Riche immediately upon seeing his daughter and not days later, after going through all this research, as he was claiming. And to do it they would try to get him to crack, to show the anger and fury and need for revenge that was just under the surface. Ray asked to do the cross examination because Drew was too close to Steven and had come to care about him and his family. Both Max and Drew agreed. During his preparation Ray had started out nice and easy, going through direct much the way they expected that they would when he was on the stand. Once direct examination was through, he had hammered away at Steven in a way that completely took him by surprise. He questioned him about how he decided to do what he did; what he had been thinking; what he had known about the claim he was making, that Riche was not human, at the time he pulled the trigger. He had pushed and pushed until he had gotten him to admit that he had been angry, that he had in fact been incensed beyond all human reason when he saw his daughter. Ray had been graphic and callous when asking him about what he had seen. To top everything off, Ray had pulled out crime scene photos. Steven had remained cool for the most part, but once the pictures came out he had exploded at Ray, screaming at him that he couldn't know how it felt to see your daughter's head without eyes, that he didn't know what it was like to feel evil in the flesh. He had stopped at that point. Drew had called a break and told Steven to go for a walk and get fresh air. Both he and Max were taken aback at Ray's ability to turn it on just like that. Vicious and callous was simply not what either man would ever associate with Ray Gretche.

Drew was wondering whether maybe they had come at him too hard, too soon and could see that Max may have been having the same thought, "Maybe we should have warned him Ray. Maybe we should have prepared him better."

Ray looked at them incredulous, "Are you guys shitting me here? You think the prosecution is going to be looking to give him a break? To let him prepare more? Farris will be looking for the slightest crack and she will go for blood if she finds it. No guys, this was how we needed to do this, we need to get him to understand that even though he was a victim and even though he lost his daughter, the prosecution has a job to do. We've all seen the lengths to which the prosecution can go to convict someone. I'm really surprised you guys are reacting this way."

Drew knew he was right. This was exactly the reason he had asked Ray to join the defense team. As confident as Drew was in his abilities he knew he hadn't developed the trial chops that a lifetime of courtroom battles had afforded Ray and Max. The truth was that he had also gotten too close to his client and this had shown him that he needed to take a step back. Max was probably in the same boat; they'd both come to really care for their client. Ray had come in after the fact, so he was better able to step back.

Steven came back from the walk. He had also realized that he needed to understand both sides of this argument. All along he had been certain about what he had done and why and knew that he had made the right decision, but he really hadn't fully thought about the fact that there was another team of attorneys that would invest everything to try to disprove every single thing he would be testifying to.

He walked over to the bottles of water that were on the table grabbed a bottle and took three long pulls from it, "Listen guys, I'm sorry. I should have been ready for that. I feel like I let you guys down."

Ray clapped him on the back, "No worries. That's what this is about. This is the time for this to happen, not on the stand. I'm just glad that you are understanding how these people are going to come at you. I am being pretty extreme here Steven, but it's better that we approach it this way. There will be nothing beyond what we just went through to make you crack."

Max and Drew also needed to say something. Max spoke up, "We're sorry too Steven, we should have been preparing you like this all along. I think you're such a solid witness and have such a great professional background we assumed too much. We just got sidetracked with the experts, but the truth is that your testimony may be as if not more important than the experts. At the end of the day the jury is going to look at you and then decide whether they are going to lend credibility to what we are saying and they are going to decide that based on whether they like you or not, based on whether they *believe* you deep down."

Steven put the water down and sat back down in the chair they had been using as the witness stand, "Alright. Let's get going again. I'm ready."

Ray picked up his notes and asked, "Are you sure man, we can call it a day and pick it up tomorrow?"

Steven just remained in the chair, "Let's do it."

They went at it for another two hours with Ray hammering Steven every way he could think of and Steven maintaining his cool. He had been able to do that, but still show emotion. Not showing any emotion might make the jury think he is a psychopath. When they were finished both he and his lawyers were confident they could handle anything the prosecution could throw at him. Another point that Max had brought up was that while they could hammer mercilessly at him in preparation it was unlikely that the DA would be as harsh. There was a lot of public support for Steven and a lot of sympathy and the prosecution understood that hammering him too hard might seriously backfire on them. They were fine with doing their job and doing it well, but they understood the situation and that their boss, David Neill, had political aspirations beyond the DA's office. All of which meant they would tread carefully when they were cross-examining him.

They all came out of the conference room and headed in different directions, Max and Drew to their respective offices, Ray to the bathroom and Steven to the coffee room.

He was getting coffee from the single-serve machine the law firm had when he heard a well-known voice, "Mr. Loomis? Steven?"

He turned around and found Tyrone Leonard standing there with his briefcase and that disarming smile of his.

He immediately put the coffee down and went to shake the man's hand, something he did with both hands, "Dr. Leonard! It is great to see you! I've been wondering when you were going to come in to go over your testimony. The guys didn't tell me."

It had been Tyrone Leonard's work that had gotten Steven started down the journey he had chosen and the man had been as gracious after he knew about everything as he'd been when Steven had first talked to him.

Leonard returned the warm greeting, "It's good to see you too Mr. Loomis. Actually I've been working with some of the other lawyers here. We've been working a couple of floors down though; today is the first day I will be working with your actual team in earnest."

Steven walked him over to the conference room where they'd been working, offered him something to drink and sat him down, "Professor, I wanted to..."

Before Steven could finish the sentence Leonard interrupted him, "Mr. Loomis please do not say 'thank you' or 'I'm sorry', we've gone over that before. You have nothing to thank me or apologize for. Your case has brought more attention to my work and the work of others than I could have ever fathomed, so if anyone has something to be thankful for it's me."

Steven smiled, "Fair enough. I'll tell you what, I will stop trying to thank you or apologize to you if you call me Steven."

Leonard's smiled widened and Steven was reminded of just how charismatic the man was. He lit up a room with his smile and the spark that resided in his eyes. He was short in stature with a deep ebony skin and white hair and he was absolutely engaging. Add to all that a brilliant mind and you had someone that would have the jury eating out of his hand.

They sat without saying anything for a couple of seconds with Steven fidgeting and heming and huhing before Leonard finally spoke up, "What is it Steven? What do you want to ask me? I know that fidgeting and that shifting look, so out with it."

Steven smiled, "Yeah, I guess I'm not too subtle am I? Well professor I've been doing more reading and I've been thinking quite a bit. Back when we first spoke and when I spoke with Dr. Scoma the issue came up about individuals being heads of companies, politicians, famous entertainers, that kind of thing, remember?"

Leonard nodded, but didn't say anything. Steven went on, "Well I've been thinking about it and if these things really are in those positions and they are able to bring about chaos or war or tragedy, would that satisfy their predatory instincts? I mean would bringing about a genocide, for example, satisfy the man who brought it about the same way that he himself doing it could?"

Leonard nodded pensively, "It's a question I asked early on in my work and one that is being asked more and more. You see, I think that the question has two answers, not just one. If one of these things finds themselves in a competitive situation at work or in politics or in any one of thousands of arenas and he or she can gain an advantage by killing people or having people killed or bringing about destruction and pain, they will, without batting an eye, they will whether it's ten, a thousand or a million people. They will do whatever will help them to win, whatever 'win' might mean to them. But that's not the whole story, because along with that desire to win, to be in control, they also have their own desires, their own hunger to go on *their own* hunt and that is something that nothing other than them doing it with their own two hands will satisfy, nothing.

"We spoke to someone abroad who was convicted of crimes against humanity. The reason he came to our attention was because in addition to what he had done as far as crimes against humanity, he had also been charged with seven murders in his own country. The bodies of men, women and children were found under his mother's house, his own hometown in fact."

Leonard's tone had become more pensive, more somber as he remembered something that he was clearly disturbed by. The striking dichotomy between his normal, charismatic, engaging tone and this more somber, more troubled tone had caught Steven off guard when he'd first spoken to the scientist and it did so again.

Leonard went on, "He confirmed for us exactly what we were just pondering. He killed the people he killed at home because bringing about the death of tens of thousands of people did not satisfy him personally."

Steven nodded. He had thought that at the end of the day these predators would want that personal touch. Aside from whatever atrocities they might commit in other places and situations, they needed to feel like *they* had hunted and *they* had gotten their prey.

Leonard continued, "Now, if you consider that for a moment, you can also see how doing one of the things you brought up, committing genocide, might set up a very fertile ground for them to do what they want to do."

Steven looked up, "Seriously? Just when I think I've thought every angle something else comes up."

Leonard nodded, "Is that so hard to believe? Let's say that there is a racially charged situation somewhere that is not too well adjusted to accommodate such things; and let's say that a *Homo sapiens predator* who was a councilman or congressman or senator from that area pulled enough strings to bring the

National Guard down and hammer the people protesting or marching in an over-the-top and violent way. You can see the pictures, can't you? Riot-geared police shooting tear gas, using batons and tasers on anyone and everyone. Now, you and I both know that if something like that happened in a situation like that, in an area where there was racial turmoil, it would grow and grow quickly in size and in violence. You'd have riots, looters and people just being violent. Okay? Now, think about what the police in such a situation are likely to be doing. Whatever it is, they would most definitely be focused on the riots."

Steven nodded. Leonard went on, "Okay, now, is there any doubt in your mind that their ability to go on a hunt or to go do whatever they wanted would be improved dramatically? That's one scenario where they would use something to help them carry out their own personal pursuit or hunt if you will.

"Let's now imagine that one of them happens to be an arms dealer. Obviously their business would thrive in places where there was war going on, whether it was declared or not. Can you see where they might fund one or both sides of the war in order to escalate it and keep it going? Can you see how they would do it without regard for human life? Without regard for the old, women or children? Do you see how they might also pay people to actually start it by killing people from one side and then the other all the while fueling both of them."

Steven nodded at first, but then began shaking his head, "Wait a minute professor; I know there are people, very human people, that would do the exact same thing and they would not lose a minute of sleep over it and who would have no problem enjoying the fruits of their actions."

Leonard nodded. His tone was coming back to his natural delivery, "You are absolutely right Mr....Steven, you're right, but I would argue that one of two things is true if it is in fact a human doing it: either they are a sociopath or psychopath, a human sociopath or psychopath, or they will in fact be severely scarred psychologically and emotionally speaking and will eventually have a breakdown, whether others are aware of it or not. Remember, the research I have conducted over the last twenty plus years has by necessity had to include a deep understanding of human behavior, aberrant human behavior to be sure, but human in the end. Obviously if I am going to claim that there is another human species it is because I have seen individuals that go beyond the norms for even aberrant human behavior. And if I am going to do that, I have to be able to speak to the absolute limits of aberrant human behavior. So, yes, you're right, people who are driven by greed can and often do these things, but their overall long-term vision is quite different."

Steven was not clear, "I don't quite get what you mean when you say 'overall long-term vision'."

Leonard went on, "What I mean is that if you polled all of those individuals and asked them whether they would be willing to stop doing what they do if you gave them a billion dollars, they would all take you up on it. All of them. A billion dollars would ensure a lavish lifestyle for them and their progeny for some time, so money would no longer be the objective. If it is a *Homo sapiens predator* doing it, they would only stop when their objectives were accomplished, which would be something else entirely."

Steven shook his head in disbelief, "Damn professor, now that you are sharing all of this it's pretty obvious. I've just been knee deep in all of this for months and it gets blurry sometimes."

The truth was that as Leonard had finished talking Steven had immediately thought of Nigel Barlow. Barlow fit the description that Leonard had just outlined to a T. He could and most likely did pull strings, make deals, create chaos in a variety of settings and in a variety of ways without any compunction whatsoever. If it facilitated his overall plan in any way, he would absolutely throw old people, women and children into a grinder without batting an eye. Hearing Leonard talking about it had somehow made it more real for him. Steven also knew that in order for Barlow to do the things he was doing he needed vast resources, probably in the billions, which meant he had to find ways to make that money and that was exactly what Leonard had just described in one of his scenarios.

Leonard saw that he had gone somewhere else for a moment and was genuinely concerned. He knew what Steven had gone through in the past few months better than most, "Steven, are you alright? Did I say something that upset you?"

Steven snapped back and responded with a thin smile, "Sorry I spaced out there for a second doc. I have barely gotten any sleep this past week. I have just one more question for you, do you know of anybody specifically who is doing something like this? Like what you just described?

Leonard shook his head briefly, but avoided Steven's eyes, something he had never done before, "No, I can't say that I know of anyone who is actually doing these things right now. Other than the case I just described for you."

Steven's eyes narrowed and held the scientist's eyes for just a split second. In that time could see that Leonard had something he did not want to share with him.

The man had been more than generous with Steven over the time everything had been going on, so he did not push, "Fair enough. Well, I hate to say it doc, but it's back to work. Now that it's so close to the trial I find myself constantly thinking that we need to prepare more. The lawyers keep telling me that we're fine, but I can't get myself to relax. It was like that when I was in the service. We might prepare for an op for months and months and I would still think we needed more preparation. The closer the op came, the more I thought we needed to prepare."

Leonard smiled at him as he responded, "I would imagine that you're not too different from other people in high-stress situations. For you there will never be enough preparation and truthfully I don't think that's a bad thing. I would imagine it served you well when you were a SEAL, so don't be so hard on yourself and trust your instincts."

Steven nodded and held out his hand again, "Thanks doc, I really appreciate it. Sometimes I just need someone who is a bit removed from a situation to give me a little perspective; usually that is my wife, but in this instance that is just not in the cards. And thank you for testifying. I know how much it is going to inconvenience you and I know how supportive you have been, so thanks."

Leonard shook his hand smiling broadly, "Hey, what about our deal. I'm going to start calling you Mr. Loomis again if you don't cut out the 'thank yous' and the 'I'm sorrys'"

Steven nodded as he went back to the conference room, "Fair enough. I'll see you later Dr. Leonard."

Leonard had seen the man go from an anxious, worried man, to a driven and purposeful one. It had been quite amazing actually and had the circumstances been different, he might have asked Steven if he'd be willing to participate in some research. He had actually thought that he might still do that after everything was done; obviously it would depend on the outcome of the case. He had spoken to James Scoma about it and they both agreed that Steven would make for an interesting subject in their research, Scoma's more so than his. Tyrone Leonard had dedicated a long and brilliant career to understanding the edges of human behavior, the last twenty to violent and aberrant behavior and the genetics and physiology that came with it. And in all that time he had never encountered someone who had been able to do what Steven Loomis seemed to be doing. Somehow he was able to either compartmentalize his psyche in such a way that he could operate at a high level even though he and his family had gone through the most traumatic experience anyone could go through. Some might say that maybe Loomis did not really love his daughter, that maybe he just never bonded with her, others might think he is a sociopath or a psychopath, but Leonard had seen the man right after everything happened. He had looked into his eyes and seen what seemed to be an almost broken man. The truth was that for normal individuals recovering from what Loomis had gone through would take months and more likely years. In fact most people would simply not recover at all. Ever. Steven, however, seemed to have completely recovered. Leonard thought that the more likely explanation was that Steven's ability to compartmentalize his psyche had come from years of training and running operations for the military. Either that or there was something in Steven Loomis that went beyond what Leonard could see on the surface. Whatever the case might be, Leonard knew what the man had and was about to go through and if there was any way that he could make Steven's journey more bearable he was going to do it.

Back at the conference room Drew, Ray and Max were waiting for Steven. On the board he saw six names written down. These were the seven expert witnesses that they had decided on calling. The list included Leonard, Dr. Jim Scoma, Dr. Grossman, Dr. Vargas, Dr. DeVaulle and Dr. Schultz. The seventh was someone who just had a question mark next to the 'Dr.'.

Steven had heard about all of them, but he wanted to know what they deal was with the question mark.

He asked Max who smiled his famous sideways smile, "Ahh, yes, our Dr. Who. That one is left like that because there are actually about three dozen doctors that we could call for what we would like prove with their testimony."

Steven looked at him as though he'd lost it. He looked around at Drew and Ray and saw a similar expression, "What are you talking about Max? Guys? What the hell?"

Drew stepped up to respond, "See, one of the things that all of the biological and evolutionary anthropologists believe is that skull size and shape has been a pretty solid way to anticipate and eventually catalogue human evolution. The bigger the brain the more synapses and dendrites can interact.

"Remarkably the change in human brain size for millennia had shown the human brain had actually *shrunk*. The changes in the shape of the braincase came about to in a sense redistribute the additional brain cells into the areas of the brain associated with language, cognition, things that make us human. This change in the skull size and shape was obviously significant when Neanderthals and other hominids – humanoids for lack of a better word – roamed the earth. Since the appearance of *Homo sapiens* about a hundred and sixty thousand years ago, there has not been any major change in human brain shape and skull size. Some scientists believe that the shrinking came as a result of not needing certain parts of the brain, of removing the necessity to function as a hunter/gatherer."

Steven was nodding, "That makes sense; you're talking about modern humans, right? The species that emerged in that period are modern humans."

Now Max picked it up, "That's right, which is why there hasn't been any major change. But guess what about three quarters of the doctors that examined the brains of Dr. Leonard's and some of the others' research subjects have found when they take a look at their brain and skull sizes and shapes?"

Steven's eyes opened wider, "Are you serious?! Bigger brains and differently-shaped skulls?!"

Max nodded, "Yup. Don't you think it makes sense once you think about it? We're going to be claiming empirical, objective, physical and cognitive differences between *Homo sapiens sapiens* the name for modern humans and *Homo sapiens predators*. This is pretty objective and pretty empirical proof."

Steven still looked doubtful, "Why hadn't we heard anything about this before? I mean it's a pretty damn big piece of evidence not to have heard about it."

Drew explained, "We totally agree and the truth is that we hadn't thought to ask because we're pretty busy trying to figure out who is going to testify to what and who we are going to use and honestly, none of us are scientists. Leonard was the one who brought it up and he did it as an aside, while explaining some of the findings he's gotten. He said that the reason he had overlooked brain and skull size and shape was because the different pathologists that had examined each of the subjects examined only one. So, they might think that the difference in shape and size is a bit curious and interesting, but that's all. It's not until you take three dozen of those pathology reports and analyze them together that you see a completely clear pattern and the only ones that had all that data together were Scoma and Leonard."

Steven nodded, "And they were probably looking at them one at a time and for different reasons, right? So they themselves probably didn't see any pattern until they'd taken a step back or maybe talked to each other."

Ray shook his head in disbelief, "Damn Steven, I guess being around all of this has made you an expert yourself. That's exactly what happened, they talked to each other and mentioned the size and shape differences. Both of them went through the same files and found the same thing, *Homo sapiens predators* have larger brains and skulls shaped differently."

Steven looked at Ray, "I'm not an expert Ray, but remember that I have been looking into this for a while now. I have a question though; doesn't that mean that eventually we might evolve to the point where an average female's hips and birth canal won't be big enough? Wouldn't that have to evolve or increase in size as well?"

Now all three lawyers looked completely stumped. Drew spoke up, "Ahh...that is definitely not something that we really looked into at all and honestly if we had I don't think we would have understood the answer. It's a good question though. It would be interesting to ask whether that size increase to accommodate larger heads would really come about or whether the fact that we have the ability to do cesarean sections would mean that since

Homo sapiens predator females don't *have* to increase in size their bodies won't change."

Max brought them back to the business at hand, "Alright already with the Discovery channel fan club. Can we get back to work? So we've gone over the testimony of the experts we are planning to use, but now we have to make some decisions about how we are planning to conduct the trial, procedural stuff. We want you here Steven because we want your input, but please wait until we've had a chance to discuss it and we've made a decision."

Steven raised his hands, "Hey, I'm happy just being a spectator. I'm tired guys, exhausted actually and I can't imagine that you guys aren't there too. So, please, have at it."

Drew stood up, "Okay, well the first thing I'd like to discuss is whether we do our opening after the prosecution does theirs or we reserve it until we are ready to present our case. There's pros and cons to each of them, so I'd like to get your thoughts."

Max also stood up and paced in the conference room as he spoke, "The pros to waiting would be that we create a sense of anticipation and we reengage the jury after the prosecution bores them to tears. The other advantage is that we do not give them any sort of context or roadmap for where we are going to go with the science. The cons, as I see them, are that we give the prosecution center stage and have nothing to counter their claims or plans, they'll basically be grandstanding. Also, the jury might not take it well. People have seen all the movies and read all the books and they will be expecting for us to stand up and explain why whatever the prosecution just explained is simply wrong, why our client is innocent."

Ray didn't stand up, but he did chime in, "That's the one that worries me the most, not giving the jury what they are expecting. Juries are fickle, funny and a different animal altogether and they can turn on us if they are resentful. I'm not sure it's worth the risk."

Max added, "I agree, reserving the opening for later is an unorthodox tactic and one that could really backfire on us. I think I agree with Ray, I'm not sure that it's worth the risk."

Drew, now seated again, shook his head, "I think you guys are missing the point. Yes, it is risky and yes, it could backfire on us, but consider the upside. If we don't give the prosecution a context to question their experts with, what will they be left with? Nothing. They will basically be asking doctors to confirm that Donald Riche was human; why they thought Donald Riche was human and whether they think he could be something else. And what are they going to answer? See what I mean? It will be anticlimactic, dry and dull as hell. The reality is that they can't really present their case until we present ours."

Ray shook his head, "All of those things are true, but we don't need to reserve the opening to have that be the case. Their experts are going to be dull no matter what we do, they won't be able to really present a case until we've presented ours regardless of when we do our opening; see what I mean? Why take the risk of having the jury be turned off by something we do. We are already asking them to make a pretty big jump buying our argument. That's my opinion, but I'm totally open."

Max nodded, "I see your point Ray, but I also see Drew's point. Think about it, we have been talking about our theory and people in the media have been hitting it just about every way you can imagine. Some of them are saying it is genius, others are saying it's bullshit and still others are saying they don't know if it's genius or bullshit."

Ray shook his head, "I don't get what that has to do with what we're talking about."

Max responded, "Well, if we present our opening statement right after the prosecution we are going to be telling the jury why it is that Steven cannot be convicted of murder, how what the prosecution is presenting is wrong, what our experts are going to testify to and basically our roadmap for proving our case, you know, standard opening statement elements, right?"

Ray and Drew nodded. Max went on, "Alright, so we do that and then when the prosecution gets up to present their case in chief they have a context that they can use to direct their direct examination. Think about it; having Melanie Farris get up and just walk the detectives through the case, their experts through 'Was Donald Riche human', I mean can you imagine that?"

Drew and Ray were actually chuckling, Max continued, "Right?! I mean think about it 'Dr. was Donald Riche human?' the doctor says 'yes' and then Farris asks him 'and how do you know that' and he answers 'ahhh, well because he was human' or 'because he looked human, had two legs, a head, arms'. Ha, ha, ha! See where I'm going with this, it will be pretty ridiculous. The jury will be sitting there looking at their watches wondering when lunch is."

Drew and Ray were nodding and still chuckling, but Max was on a roll, "Okay, now think about her getting up there after any of us presents our theory, after we talk about the science and how Steven got to where he got. Now Farris asking about Riche and whether he was human is not so dull, now the jury has something in their head, something we gave them, that makes the prosecution's case more interesting or at least not as dry and boring as it would be otherwise. We'd be giving them something they can hang their hat on."

Ray spoke up, "I get it, I really do guys, but I'm still not sold. I still think it's an unnecessary risk in a situation where we can't really afford to have something go against us."

Drew finally spoke up, "Alright, well we can go on for a few hours on this alone, so here's what I think: if we do something like this then we all need to be onboard with it. I have no problem going with our opening after the prosecution, I thought that it would really put the prosecution in a tough situation trying to keep the jury engaged, but you're right, the prosecution will have a hard time presenting their case regardless of when we do our opening. Max, what do you think?"

Max shrugged, "I'm good either way. I can see both points, but I agree that if we're going to be doing something like this we all need to be onboard with it."

Drew went on, "Okay, that's settled. Now, what order are we going to call our witnesses?"

Ray smiled, "Now it's me who is going to propose we do something a bit unorthodox. We've all talked about it, we've just done it two at a time, never the three of us."

Max had a puzzled expression on his face, "What are you talking about Ray? Are you talking about putting Steven on first?"

Ray nodded and then Drew nodded as well, "That's right, we have all talked about it, but we never decided on anything, any of us, right?"

Ray answered, "That's right we never decided anything, but I think we need to decide on it now. I think we put Steven on first, then we put on the experts and then we close our case with Steven again."

Drew leaned back in his chair, "Okay, walk us through your rationale."

Ray moved to the front of the room and began pacing as though he was doing an opening statement, "Well, we just finished talking about the fact that the prosecution's case is going to be dull and dry and that they're going to have a hard time keeping the jury engaged, so I think it would be really powerful if we went the completely opposite way from that right from the beginning. I think we can galvanize the jury right from the start. They will go from yawning from the prosecution's case to being totally human and tragic and real right from the get go for our case."

Steven had been totally quiet throughout the discussions up until this point, but he wanted to make sure that his lawyers were straight on a couple of things, "Guys, I don't really have an opinion about when it happens, but I want to be completely clear that I am going to testify. I'm good doing it at the beginning or in the middle or at the end, but I'm doing it."

Drew nodded, he'd had this conversation with Steven before, "We're straight on that Steven and in fact we've come to be of the opinion that we can't do this *without* your testimony. I think we've all talked to you about it, but I wanted to confirm it. Remember what we talked about earlier; any of the testimony that has to do with the concept of evil from a human perspective will have to come from you and only you. Any mention of that kind of thing by the experts will really erode their credibility and open the door for the prosecution to jump on them and tear them up. Believe me, if Melanie Farris gets even a sliver of opportunity, she will slice our witnesses to ribbons, so we can't give her that chance."

Steven was clear on everything until Drew got to the point where he talked about the concept of 'evil' from a human standpoint. What other kind of concept could it be if not a human concept.

He asked Drew who understood his question and concern, "What I mean by the human concept is that the 'soft' abstract or spiritual idea of evil has to come from you. Remember that Grossman, one of our experts, has a scale of evil he's developed and will be talking about. The context of evil in that sense is different. He is using the concept of evil as a measurement tool, something to call the different levels of his scale. Even then, Farris is going to go at him no holds barred just because he uses that term. We actually asked Grossman if he could call his levels something else and he went ballistic."

Ray chuckled about that, "Boy did he ever! I thought he was going to punch you when you brought it up, Max! Ha, ha, I don't think that I've ever seen an academic that angry about anything."

Max smiled, "I know, I thought he was going to come over the table as well. If he was a dick before that happened, he was an even bigger one after. He actually said he was not going to testify. Drew talked to him and brought him back around, but you can see why we're telling you that there is only one way to talk about it in the context that most people think of 'evil' and that's going to be through your testimony."

Drew looked directly at Steven, "But, Steven, do not feel like you have to talk about it just because of what we're telling you right now. Talk about it if it feels right and it's a part of what you would say, don't be thinking about ways to get the topic of evil into your testimony."

Steven shook his head, "You don't have to worry about that, I know what I saw and felt and I'm sure it will come up naturally, I would be willing to bet on it."

They kept going moving the names of experts up and down on the list. They would come to an agreement on an order to call the witnesses and then they'd come up with an idea or an issue that would make that order not optimal. After going through the process for all of the morning and most of the afternoon, they finalized the order they thought would work best: Tyrone Leonard would be the first expert, right after Steven's first turn on the stand. He would testify about his work, how he started to go down the path of a separate species and what he's done over the past two decades to validate his work; then they were going to call Samuel Grossman because they felt he needed to testify early on given his personality issues and how Farris was likely to come at him. The logic was that they didn't want the jury to have Grossman fresh in their minds right before they went into their deliberations; then they would be calling Allen Schultz, the physiologist from Cornell who would explain his work around the physiological changes that humans undergo when they were lying or attempting to lie. He would testify to the fact that based on his years and thousands and thousands of subjects, he had developed a test to measure those physical changes happen. He would show that humans, not matter how well they were trained and no matter who they worked for, the CIA, the NSA, any of them, would display the physiological changes his test measured. Finally he would explain that when he'd come across Dr. Leonard's work and done the research he'd been doing with Dr. Leonard's subjects, his test had proved almost useless. The lawyers felt that Schultz's testimony would be key to their case. He was someone who had not set out to establish or define a new species, he had set out to come up with a measurement tool that could be used to detect lying in even the most trained and experienced liars and had in fact come up with precisely that. It had taken more than a decade and more than thirty thousand subjects to do it, but he had ultimately done it. And it had been wiped out in an afternoon of working with Leonard and some of his subjects.

Next would be Francis DeVaulle who would testify to the fact that his research into human behavior through evolutionary anthropology pointed to the fact that human evolution is not something new or novel, it's happened before and it will absolutely continue happening through history. He would also testify to the fact that the anthropological record he and others had examined had shown *Homo sapiens* to be an adept and ruthless hunter that had no issue eliminating anything that threatened their survival, including the Neanderthals.

After DeVaulle testified to the behavioral aspect around human evolution Lindsay Vargas would testify to the biological changes humans have undergone over the last two hundred thousand years and the fact that those biological changes have come about because of a shift in the environment around them. She will explain that the social structures that humans had begun to form over a hundred thousand years ago had an effect on how humans evolved physically or actually how their biological evolution slowed down significantly. A bigger more organized and educated society meant that humans would not need to rely on physical evolution to keep their species alive. Having more evolved, creative brains meant that humans relied more on intelligence than on brawn to survive. But she would also explain that did not mean that humans had stopped evolving, just slowed in their physical evolution. She would explain that having a subspecies of human defined was not something new or out of the ordinary. She would crystalize that *Homo sapiens predator* was the next step in human evolution, that it was no surprise and that it would not be the last step in human evolution by any stretch.

After Vargas they would bring in one of the pathologists that had examined Leonard's subjects' braincases and brain size. They would testify to the fact that there was a marked difference in size and in fact shape, between the braincase and brain size of the average human and the species that was being discussed.

Finally, Jim Scoma would come in and explain that he and Leonard had taken the testifying pathologist's work along with more than three dozen other pathologists and had identified a clear and consistent pattern when it came to the size and shape of humans' braincases and the size and shape of the brain and braincases of the species they had identified. He would then move on to explain his work around a different side of human evolution, a side that was not defined by dark and predatory instincts, but something different, something harder to define. To close their case they would bring Steven back in and they would walk him through his testimony to the point where he decided what he decided and how all the research played into it. It would be difficult and it would be painful, but having Steven leave the jury with the very clear and emotional sense that he truly did not believe Riche was a member of the human species, would be an incredibly powerful way to finish the case.

QUEENSBURY, VERMONT

Bethany Loomis had her nose right up against the window at her grandparents' house in Vermont. She and her brother had been here for more than five months and while Chris still had fun in the snow when it was there and playing with his grandparents, Bethany was feeling cabin fever in a big way. She could simply not go do what other nine-year-old girls could go do. No going to the movies, to an arcade, to have some pizza or ice cream, nothing. Her activities were limited to short trips to the houses of some of her grandparents' friends and to a property they had where she and Chris could roam outside without having reporters anywhere near them. She had also been watching the reporters and other people who came and went from the edge of her grandparents' property. She enjoyed reading and had gone through more than two-dozen books and who knew how many magazines on her iPad since they'd come to her grandparents' house. Bethany Loomis was mature for her age and she scored well above average on every IQ test she'd ever been given. She had skipped one grade, but her parents had decided against her skipping another one when the school had brought it up. They wanted her to have a normal social life and that would be hard if the kids in her grade were two or three years older than her, regardless of how mature she was. She had heard her mother say 'She's nine going on forty' and her grandma say 'she has an old soul' plenty of times. She didn't know about all that, but she understood very well that she did not think the same way that kids her age thought. From the time she could walk Bethany had been incredibly close to her father, although she spent much more time with her mother. She loved her mother a great deal, but she instinctively sensed that her father was more like she was, more aware, inside, like she was. She was not giggly or silly and she was always asking about the why of things. When people gave her a pat answer or simply made something up she pressed them until they admitted they did not know or they gave her a real answer. Her father had not shielded her believing that doing so would erode his credibility with his daughter. He thought that if he shielded her from things and then she found them on her own or came across them some other way she would know he had not been honest with her. In that he had been right, it was that dynamic that had affected how close she became with her mother. That maturity and intelligence also ensured she understood everything that had happened to her sister, what her father had done and what her whole family was going through now. She had known that her mother was completely destroyed early on and she had known her father was trying to find an answer, to what she did not know at the time. Now she knew and she understood exactly what it was he had done, why he had done it and what he was claiming as a defense. She also knew that if her father was found guilty of killing that man, that thing, whatever it was called, he would be going away for a long time. She had found out long ago that if she wanted grown up people to leave her alone all she needed to do was act like they believed a little girl her age should act. Not asking too many questions, no acting bored of things other kids her age thought were cool or funny. This was especially true of her grandparents, they had never understood why she was treated basically like a grown up by her parents and they took every opportunity they had to try to get her to be more like a normal little girl.

As she sat and watched the crowd in front of her grandparents' house she imagined who they were and what they did when they got home. People watching had always been a favorite thing for her to do when she was out and about with her parents. Her dad would sometimes join her and they would do the same thing she was doing now, try to imagine what people did when they were at home.

Lucy Delaney came up behind her and hugged her. She had been looking out the window for almost 45 minutes, "Bethany, honey, are you hungry? Can I fix you something to eat? Chris is having chicken noodle soup, would you like some?"

Bethany looked back and shook her head, "No thanks grandma, I'm not hungry."

Her grandmother gave her a kiss on top of her head, "Okay, but if you get hungry you'll let me know?"

She nodded and smiled. Lucy left her and went to the kitchen to give Chris his lunch. Although he was till far too young to really understand what was happening, he knew that things were not normal and that his sister was gone and was not coming back. More than once he'd asked his grandparents if Tracy was ever going to come back and while the adults had always found a way to get around the question, Bethany had explained Tracy would not be coming back when he had asked her about it. Lucy looked back at her granddaughter and felt a deep pang of sadness. She had watched her nine-year-old granddaughter literally age before her eyes and she had felt her leave her childhood behind, all before the age of ten. It broke her heart.

Bethany, back to her people watching, noticed a few new people among the crowd. By now she knew everyone that was there day in and day out. Even when people left and came back, seeing them over a period of months made it not too difficult to remember who was a 'usual' in the crowd and who was new. The other thing that Bethany noticed was that the new people looked and behaved differently than the people that had been there over the past few months. Even though she did not yet know what being a journalist or a news crew member entailed, she knew the physical type of the people who had been there up until now. If they were the reporters in front of the camera they were always dressed nice, their hair and makeup was always perfect and they kept looking at themselves in anything that gave off a reflection. The people who were in the crew that were behind the camera or that drove the vans were not dressed very nice, were for the most part just laying around or talking to each other when they were not recording the reporters on camera. While they were obviously very different jobs and very different types of people, their mannerisms and overall countenance was easy for Bethany to spot. These new people were different. For one thing they did not move very much, they stood in one spot for a long time and then moved somewhere else and stayed there for a long time before moving again. They didn't do anything, they just watched everyone else and kept looking at their watches the whole time. All of them, even the women she could see, were also different physically, more purposeful with all their movements, like they meant to do whatever it was they were doing, every tiny detail. Bethany did not understand the theory behind everything she was seeing, but like her father she was intuitively drawn to shifts, changes, even minute differences. There were about twelve of these new people and other than the differences in the way they moved and acted, some also all had earbuds going into one of their ears. She had seen the reporters with those earbuds as well, but the new people used them differently, they did not react to whatever it was they were hearing. The reporters or their crews seemed to want the people around them to know they were hearing something, that someone was talking to them. Again, Bethany did not understand the why for that, but she had a sense that for one group they were something you wore to be cool and for the other group they were something they used for their work and whatever their work was, it was not cool to walk around pretending someone was talking to them over the earphones they were wearing. As she looked through the crowd Bethany thought she saw someone that looked familiar to her. It had just been a flash and she could not remember the man specifically, but he looked familiar to her in a way that made her think she knew him or had at least met him at some point. The same thing happened when she saw people her dad worked with or friends of her mom. She saw them in other situations, knew she'd met them at some point, but could not remember where and how. The glimpse was too quick for her to really try to remember where she knew him from, but she was pretty sure she'd seen the man before.

Tom Delaney walked by his granddaughter and felt a pang similar to the one his wife had felt only moments before. It killed him to see Bethany just looking out the window, unable to go outside to play, to go to school, to go be a normal girl of nine. What made it even more difficult was the fact that she was so precocious and so smart, there just was no glossing things over with her, she had to know things, really know things.

He walked into the kitchen where he found his wife and his grandson in the middle of eating lunch, "Hey you, watcha eating?"

She kissed him and nodded towards Chris, "Just some of Chris's chicken noodle soup."

Chris smiled at his grandfather, "Yeah, grandpa, chicken doodle soup!"

Tom chuckled, "Chicken doodle huh, it sounds good kiddo! Got any for me?"

Lucy stood up, "We just ate all of it, didn't we buddy? Can I make you a sandwich? Ham and cheese?"

Tom sat down at the table next to Chris, "That sounds good. Extra mayo please."

She smacked him with a dishrag, "I will do no such thing! Thomas, you know about your cholesterol! Seriously, you're worse than a child!"

Tom chuckled, "I was just kidding, Luce, sheesh, are we a bit testy today? Just the regular amount of mayo is fine."

Lucy responded, "Light mayo, light mayo mister!"

He looked at Chris, "Can you believe nana buddy, she won't give your grandpa what he wants!"

Chris smiled at him and looked at his grandmother, "Give grandpa what he wants nana! Don't be mean!"

After Lucy made the sandwich she let Chris down from his seat and sat next to Tom to do the crossword puzzle. After taking a couple of bites and a sip of milk, Tom turned to look at his wife, "I got a call today from Pete Rollins."

Lucy didn't look up from her puzzle, "Oh yeah? And what did our trusty mayor have to say?"

Tom kept looking at her, so she finally looked up, "He got a call from Senator Albert Potter."

Lucy was puzzled, "The guy from New York, the one that's always on TV?"

Tom nodded, "Yup, that's the one. Apparently he wants to make whatever resources we might need available to us, especially as it relates to the kids."

Now Lucy was fully engaged, "What do you mean 'especially as it relates to the kids'? What does that mean?"

Tom answered in between bites, "Well, he says that he's seen that the kids are always in the house or being rushed from one place to another and he says he'd like to see them get out and do more of the things a kid should be doing."

Lucy shook her head, "What in the world does a senator from New York, not even from Vermont, have to do with helping the kids get out more? It doesn't make any sense."

Tom raised his hands, "Hold on now, Lucy, that's not exactly true. The man has brought about some really drastic changes in the child protection laws in New York."

Lucy looked at him suspiciously, "And how would you know that Tom? Hmm? You keep up with New York legislation, do you?"

Tom took another bite of sandwich and sip of milk before answering, "His chief of staff told me. It doesn't make it less true Luce, the man has a strong record of advocating for kids and kids' rights."

Lucy, now washing dishes nodded, "Okay, fine, he's a friend to the children of the world, how does any of that help our kids?"

Tom became more animated, "That's what I wanted to know. What his chief of staff told me that he just wants to help Bethany and Chris have an opportunity to just be kids and not be accosted by the media everywhere we take them. He has said he will ask the governor to engage the National Guard if necessary to keep the kids away from the media."

Lucy stopped doing what she was doing, "Oh c'mon! The National Guard? And you believed him Tom? Oh for goodness sakes! I thought you were more of a skeptic than that."

Tom smiled, "I am! Alright, so maybe that was a bit of a stretch or an exaggeration, but it doesn't mean he could not help us to keep the kids engaged in something besides watching movies and playing video games. What he can do is order a park or another site owned by the state shut down for a day or two. Who would oppose that once they know the reason? We need to do something Luce; it breaks my heart seeing the kids stuck inside all day. Have you seen Bethany? She's a thousand miles away, staring out of that window and thinking god knows what. If we don't want to take Potter up on his offer, then we need to come up with an option that we are all comfortable with, someone that could really do something to help."

Lucy sat back down, "I know, I was thinking that just today. They need to be kids, even if it's just for a little while. They need to remember what it's like to play and laugh and just be silly."

Tom nodded, "Bethany won't ever be able to completely shut off her thinking about what's going on, but being around something different and fun might make it easier for her to deal with everything going on."

Lucy nodded, "Alright, ask Potter if he might be able to do something to make talking to the guy here a bit easier. He needs to do something as mayor besides ride in the Fourth of July parade. Maybe he can use the police to let this guy's people get here easier, I don't know, something."

Tom chuckled, "Yeah, he's not much use, is he? I'm sure they will have plenty of security and that they could get here without a problem, but I'll ask him anyway. You want to call Beth and Steven? We can't do anything until they give their okay anyways, so I'll wait until after you call them."

Lucy got up to leave the kitchen, "Yes, I'll call them. I really think they won't go for this Tom, but I do agree with you that we need to do something to make things a bit better for the kids. I just hope that we can do it before they get so damaged that they will always have a scar."

Tom got up to follow her, "I'm sorry darling, but I think that's already happened, maybe not for Chris, but for Bethany. You can see she's hurting deep inside. She's my main reason for wanting to do something, whatever it is, just something."

7.

D avid Neill was pacing around in the conference room where Melanie Farris and Bart Logan were preparing for trial. The room looked like a true war room. There were pieces of paper and sticky notes plastered all around the room; there were photographs sprinkled among the walls along with the papers; there was a stack almost a foot tall sitting at the end of the table.

It was about that stack that David Neill, the district attorney, came in to talk to his deputies, "Fresh from the presses, those are questionnaires from the first four hundred people coming in for jury duty. They sent fifteen thousand of them out along with the summons. They expect for six thousand to actually be a part of the pool. They will call two hundred in the morning, have you go through voire dire and start going through people. When the remaining pool gets down to one hundred they'll call in another hundred and so on until you get down to twelve jurors and twelve alternates. As soon as someone is chosen to be a part of the jury they will be immediately pulled and will wait in a separate office until the twelve jurors and twelve alternates are chosen. The judge is planning on going through a short questionnaire of his own through which he anticipates thinning down the group as well."

Melanie and Bart were literally looking at their boss with their mouths hanging open. Normally the *entire* jury pool for a first-degree murder trial was one to two hundred people; now their boss was saying that the jury pool for this trial was thirty times that number. They had never heard of such a thing, the biggest jury pool they had ever heard about was nine thousand for the man accused of shooting all the people at a movie theater in Colorado.

Neill went on, "That means that if you go by previous high-profile trials you'll probably take about two months to pick a jury. I'm toying with the idea of being an active part of the jury selection process. I think that having a seasoned litigator for the process will ensure we are getting the people we want."

Bart finally broke from his shock, "I think that would be a mistake if you're not planning on being an active part throughout the trial. If you're there for the jury selection, but you're not a part of the trial team, people will think that you were just doing it to get media attention."

Both he and Melanie knew that was precisely why Neill was thinking about participating in the jury selection. It was the best of both worlds for him, he would get attention from the media, but he would not be blamed if something went wrong and they lost the trial.

Melanie was impressed that Bart had said something to Neill and decided to back him up, "I agree boss; I think it may not play well for us if you are not going to be a part of the team for the duration."

Neill stopped pacing and glared at both of his deputies, "There are all kinds of jury selection specialists used every single day, it's nothing new. I don't see any problem with me being a part of the selection process the same way that a jury consultant or expert participates."

Now emboldened by his colleague's support Bart pushed back again, "I understand Mr. Neill, but this situation is different for a number of reasons."

He stood up and paced a short pattern right be the chair he was sitting in as he went on using his fingers to make his points, "First of all, you are much more visible and well-known than any jury consultant or expert in the country; this case is the most visible case in US legal history, which means that people are going to be hyper-critical of anything and everything both sides do; and finally, and maybe most importantly, there is significant public sympathy for the defendant. Any one of those things would make it pretty hard for you to do that, all of them together make it impossible sir. Maybe you can do the direct for a couple of our witnesses. That could neutralize some of the opinions about why you're participating."

Neill glared at his deputy with even more intensity. He knew that Logan was right, but it still grated on him immensely to have one of his deputies throwing him a bone by suggesting he could do the direct for a couple of witnesses as though he was an inexperienced, newly licensed attorney. By putting him to the decision Logan ensured that Neill would not keep trying to come up with ways to be a part of the trial team without exposing himself to the risks that came with it. He needed to stand up and be a part of the team now, or he needed to allow his deputies to do their job. The truth was that both Logan and Farris were more than willing to let Neill take the lead, but they knew that he was much too politically savvy to put himself in that kind of situation. If he were an active part of the trial team both of them would be shielded for the most part. Bart had heard that Neill had been thinking about a large litigation team to handle the case, but he'd been talked out of it. He was told that a larger litigation team would give the defense's case more credibility right from the start. Considering that the essence of the defense's case was based on their presentation of the scientific theory about a new species, given the science, giving credibility was the last thing they wanted to do.

Neill gave Logan one last nasty look, "Alright, alright, I got it. I'm too busy to spend months on trial that for all intents and purposes should be a color-by-numbers case."

Melanie bristled at the comment, but kept her mouth closed. Logan gave her a look to ensure she didn't say something. Neill had dropped the idea about being a part of the jury selection and he didn't want him to engage again.

Neill continued, "Anyway, take a look at those questionnaires and get familiar with what some of the people are thinking about the case. I think the judge did a pretty decent job with the questionnaires, so it should be pretty easy to spot people that just will not work for us. As usual, left-wing, tree-hugging, softies should be eliminated immediately."

Now Bart did need to say something, "Mr. Neill, we only have a finite number of preemptory challenges, if we use them all up early we'll be forced to challenge for cause and I don't think being a tree-hugging, left-winged softie qualifies as a cause."

Neill shot him daggers with his look, "Logan, I don't give a shit if you use preemptory challenges, challenges for cause or a hit man to get rid of them, you just need to get rid of them."

Bart nodded and said nothing. Neill was right, they would definitely need to eliminate anyone who might be friendly to the defense on philosophical grounds, but it was just not going to be possible to get rid of all of them, especially when the jury pool was so massive. It was going to take months to pick the jury and both Bart and Melanie had agreed that they would try to keep their preemptory challenges for as long as they could, reserving them to use on people that they truly wanted to keep off the jury. Through an agreement with the judge and the defense it had been agreed that each side would be given thirty preemptory challenges, which was about twice what they would normally get. Preemptory challenges were challenges that either side could use to eliminate someone from the jury and did not require the lawyers to give a reason. Once the preemptory challenges were used, each side would need to provide a reason for removing a juror and the judge could simply decide that the reason was not good enough and ultimately keep the individual. They had never heard of something like that happening, a judge keeping a juror when one of the sides challenged, but this case was likely to have many 'first ever' instances. It hadn't even started and there was already a first ever with fifteen thousand people in the jury pool.

Neill needed to give them one more piece of information, "Oh, that jury consultant you guys wanted to hire for the case should be coming in tomorrow. She'll be using Kevin Farmer's office while she's here. She's been sent an electronic file with the questionnaires you have in that stack. I suggest you both get really familiar with that information and start to use it to fine tune the profile you have established as your idea."

They had been working on the case for four months straight and had their profile as fine-tuned as they thought it could be, but in this instance Neill was right. Having information about people's preferences, level of exposure to media about the case and other information would allow them to improve on their profile. They were both also completely surprised that Neill had decided to pay for the consultant they wanted. She was from California and cost more than ten thousand dollars a day. They later found out that Neill had negotiated her rate down. She was not stupid and knew that this case would give her more exposure than she would get at any other time in her career, ever. She could write her own ticket if the prosecution won the case. She had agreed to work with them for four thousand dollars a day, which meant she would most likely end up costing the state of

New York more than two hundred thousand dollars by the time it was all said and done. Still, her reputation was well deserved and both lawyers were thankful that their boss had stepped up.

He saw the look on their faces reflected surprise and relief and for the first time smiled the way a father might smile when he saw the thrill in his children's eyes, "You're welcome! She better be worth it is all I have to say."

Bart spoke up. He addressed Neill first and then addressed Dennis Anderson, a senior deputy in the office and one of the people that had been rumored to be Neill's choice to lead the team.

He had been the one actually carrying the files with the questionnaires, "Thanks boss, seriously! She is the best there is; it's not even close! We'll get ready with the questionnaires. By the way, thank you for bringing those Dennis."

Neill knew that Logan was saying thank you to Anderson to be a smart ass and to rub in the fact that it was he and not Anderson who was leading the team for the prosecution. While other bosses might reprimand their employees for doing something like that, Neill was of the opinion that to be a good litigator you always needed to be razor sharp and ready to pounce when the occasion arose and this was a perfect example of such an occasion.

He smiled as he left the conference room, " Okay, let's go Dennis and leave these two to prepare."

Dennis said nothing, but shot both Bart and Melanie a dirty look.

The two of them looked at each other with their mouths open and a smile forming on their face.

Bart was the first to speak up, "Can you believe that?! Can you believe he actually sprung for the consultant?! Shit, I can't even imagine how much it's going to add up to with that many people in the jury pool."

Melanie nodded, "Yeah, I have to be honest and admit that I did not think it would be that many people in the jury pool. I can understand why they made it that way, but I just did not see it coming."

Bart stood up and walked up to the dry erase board they'd been using, "Okay, so let's finish with the witness list and then let's bring in the JV team."

Farris chuckled, "I hope we're doing the right thing using these younglings. You know the defense, especially Drew Willis, will be licking their chops when they see them get up to handle direct."

A trial lasting months and under the kind of scrutiny that this case was sure to garner was exhausting for the lawyers involved. Aside from the time preparing and doing what needed to be done during the trial, there was an emotional toll that having someone's life in your hands exacted from those involved. That was especially true in this case. Because of that, Farris and Logan had agreed that they needed to bring in a few people who would do the direct examination of the prosecution's witnesses. As the defense had correctly assessed, the direct examination during the prosecution's presentation of their case in chief would be almost laughable. The question of who had done it, how they had done it and whether there had been intent had been resolved before the case had even begun since Steven confessed to all of it. These questions were what normally took time in a murder trial. The accused would deny they'd done it or they'd say it was an accident, that they'd never intended on doing it or they'd claim self defense, in many instances they challenged every single point the prosecution made, even points that were clearly proved by objective evidence. The prosecution could not in any way bring up anything that was not directly witnessed or arrived at by the witnesses they were calling. That meant that the witnesses would be asked about the things they had done and seen directly. If they were experts they would be asked about their qualifications and then they would be asked to provide expert testimony about whatever was at issue. The policemen, the first responders, the pathologist and medical examiners, all of them would be very dry and, honestly, boring as they explained what they'd learned, done or seen. It would not be until the defense presented their case that the real battle would begin; that would be when the prosecution could poke holes in the defense's case and in the testimony of their witnesses. That would be when the real fireworks would begin. Because of that, Logan and Farris had decided to bring in three more junior deputies to handle the direct examination and had been working on them for a couple of months to prepare them for any potential issue that could arise out of the direct examination, something both principal attorneys highly doubted. Still, you never knew with Max Zeidler in the mix; the guy could bring chaos and uncertainty, both huge issues for the defense, in a trial for a parking ticket. Drew Willis had built a good reputation as a litigator and it had been because of his ability to confuse and trap prosecution witnesses. The fact was that both deputy district attorneys understood very well that the defense team was a formidable one with the young brash attorney, the flashy wily veteran balanced out by a likeable and respected grandfather type in the form of Ray Gretche. Still, the three lawyers handling the direct examination weren't exactly rookies and had all proven their chops in their own trials.

Bart waved his hand, "I'm not worried about that and neither should you. The direct will be based on the police, coroner and witness reports. There really isn't much that any of them will be able to do with the direct. Their client established all of the elements of the crime when he confessed."

Farris shook her head, "Not all of them, at least based on their case."

Logan waved his hand again, "Yeah, yeah, I know the whole human element thing. Actually I think the more people think about it, the more ridiculous it is going to seem."

Farris poked him as she walked by to get some water, "Don't go down the path our distinguished boss has chosen to go down, don't underestimate their theory. I think both of us need to make sure we don't go down that path. They are good attorneys Bart and they can really charm a jury, so let's not get too comfortable."

Logan nodded, walked to the tray with the soft drinks and got a Coke, "Well, we need to have some help during the trial and you know that bringing in more seasoned or experienced people would make it way more difficult, they would want to weigh in on trial strategy, how to question the witnesses and on and on. No, having these three do our direct is the perfect solution, and don't forget, we're both going to be right there if they get in trouble."

Farris smiled as she left the conference room, "Okay, well, why don't we do this: I'll work with Linda, Will and Allie and you bone up on the stuff Neill brought in. I think the three of them are about as prepared as we could hope they'd be, but there's never being too prepared. I'll really throw some funky shit into the mix and see how they handle it."

Logan chuckled, "Did Melanie Farris, tough bitch extraordinaire just say 'funky shit'? What is the world coming to?"

Farris threw her empty Styrofoam cup at him and left the room to prepare their team. Bart looked back at their list of witnesses and the list of potential defense witnesses and got worried again. There was simply no way to prepare for the trial, no real way in any case. It was an unprecedented argument that would be based on extreme research by some pretty formidable scientists; there just was no way to prepare. Bart wanted to keep things light for the last days leading up to trial, otherwise he thought both he and Farris would start to crack up under the pressure, but he knew that underneath the pithy exchanges and lighthearted banter, both of them were tense and on a hair-trigger mode. They'd been getting ready for months now, there really wasn't much else to do besides working with the consultant on jury selection. He wished Neill had agreed to bring Margaret Hollis on board sooner than he had, but he was thankful that he had eventually given in. She was by far the best jury selection consultant in the country. Her record was simply amazing, thirty-seven trials, thirty-seven wins. The trials were both civil and criminal and ranged from contract disputes, to negligence to rape and finally to murder. In every instance experts had agreed that the selection of the jury was the key to winning the case. Well, things would be on the way in just a few days and whether they were prepared for trial or not would become a moot point. The truth was that they had really no way to anticipate how long the jury selection was going to take, some people thought it would be at least two months. Bart wasn't sure that would be the case, he thought it could be longer than that, but then again he thought that if it went on for more than two weeks, there really was no length of time that would be too long or too short and that too, was something Bart Logan had never seen.

HOUSTON, TEXAS

J.D. Garzen was rehearsing in his immense media room. He picked out the section of the bible he was going to be using, went through a mental check list of all the controversial issues that were being covered by every form of media around the globe and crafted his sermon. Whatever else might be said about reverend J.D. Garzen, nobody could deny that he was a media genius. He knew how to use it, when it would get the most play and almost as important, when to move on. He had become a master at it after his services had started to be televised and had done so organically, just by listening, watching and reading about media and its uses. He also seemed to have a preternatural ability to anticipate which on-air personality was going to get the most play. Nobody on his team could figure out how the hell he did it, but they all had seen him do it time and time again. One of the reporters he'd given an interview to just over a year prior, had gone from being an on the ground, carry-her-own-camera-to-crappy-stories reporter to a local weekend anchor, to a local anchor to a network reporter and eventually a network weekend anchor. She was rumored to be the next in line for the six o'clock news anchor job for three of the major networks. How Garzen had known that she would eventually rise to where she had was beyond what anyone on his team could come up with. Most of them had initially thought it had just been chance, although they had eventually all changed their mind when he did it again and again. The fact was that he did have a gift for picking talent, but the reporter who had risen so far so fast had in fact risen as far as she had because reverend J.D. Garzen had made it happen. He needed someone who would be friendly to him and his cause and who could provide credibility to whatever he was expounding on at any particular time. He had noticed that Gretchen Simpson was very ambitious and that she had a great ass. Initially the latter quality was of more importance than the former for the reverend, but eventually he saw other possibilities.

As he kept preparing he kept coming back to his laptop to see if he could come up with any new issue, any quote, anything he could relate to bible passages and to his ministry. He was also a master at doing that, monetizing any issue he took on. Abortion was always something he could fall back on if there was nothing else out there, but he rarely needed to do that. Stem cell research, premarital sex, same sex marriage and a slew of other issues always provided an angle he could use. Same sex marriage had been his cash cow for the past couple of years. He stopped pacing and smiled as he thought of the potential of the Steven Loomis case. He would be able to milk that for millions and for the foreseeable future. The case had so many angles that he was actually getting giddy as he thought about it. Once Russ's people did their thing and the media turned their attention to whatever the situation developed as a result, they would be off and running. It didn't matter if it was a fight between supporters and detractors of Steven Loomis, skinheads protesting the fact that white people were killing white people, whatever they came up with, anything, would get immediate and extensive play. The situation was unlike anything Garzen could have ever imagined; it was unlike anything the media themselves could have ever imagined, really. Any change, regardless how small or inconsequential it might appear, would draw huge attention and once that happened he knew he could take it and run. And that did not even take into account the variety of ways to leverage the whole thing that his team could come up. Who knew how much he might be able to raise with it, more than any of the other issues combined, that was for sure. He was looking out his massive window and running down the different ways he could begin his crusade when Russ interrupted him. Garzen knew that whatever his 'fixer' had for him was serious; he had never interrupted him like this before. The man was clearly upset and for the first time the reverend saw his man spooked. He was breathing fast and heavy and he was sweating profusely. He came in looked around and when he spotted him walked quickly, a bit too quickly, to where Garzen was standing.

Garzen raised his hands, "Whoa there, cowboy, slow down! Damn Russ, you look like shit. Have you been boozin' again?! I'm serious Russ, if you've been drinking again you better tell me the truth right now!"

Russ did not seem to even hear what Garzen had just said; he had a crumpled paper in his hand. Finally he stopped, took a deep breath and gave Garzen the news, "We have a problem, a big fucking problem."

Now Garzen went from mad to concerned, "What do you mean? What kind of problem?"

Russ, now more calm, explained, "Alright, well you know that my plan was to send some of my people to Vermont to scout the situation and then come up with a plan, right? Well they did exactly that; they went there, saw the lay of the land and came up with a plan, a really great plan, actually. These were some of my top guys, J.D., no bikers or crackheads or other losers, these guys are pros, all of them have serious military experience and all of them have done work for me before. Like I said, they are total pros. There were six of them and what they planned to do was to go recruit some people to carry picket signs supporting opposite ends of the Loomis thing, come up with fake organizations that supported each side, with websites and everything, and let them go at it over the situation. The people they recruited would be paid a daily rate at the end of each day with a small bonus for performance. You know, people that can get in front of a camera and talk."

Garzen, still puzzled was nodding all along his explanation, "Okay, that sounds great, so what's the problem?"

Russ shook his head slowly and was not able to come up with the right way to say what he needed to for a couple of seconds, something else that Garzen had never before seen from his man.

Russ started, "Well, they were getting ready last night, they'd built the websites I just told you about, they had a good number of people recruited, everything was going great."

Russ shook his head again as he paused. J.D. was losing his patience with him, "Goddammit Russ! Spit it out! You know I don't like any keep-him-in-suspense shit! Now what the fuck happened?"

Russ nodded once, more for himself than Garzen, and went on, "They got the living shit kicked out of them. Every one of them. Two of them are still in the hospital with broken ribs and a broken wrist. All of them look like crap and all of them are pulling out of the job."

Garzen's eyes narrowed as he bored into his asset, "What the fuck are you talking about Russ? Who kicked the shit out of them? Why did they kick the shit out of them? You better give me better information, this shit just will not do, so take it as slow as you need to and explain what it is you're talking about."

Russ nodded again and went on explaining as much as he was able to explain, "To answer all of your questions in three words: no fucking idea. No fucking idea why, who, how, nothing. I'm telling you J.D. I've never seen anything like it in all my life, neither had any of my guys. Not even back when we were doing jobs overseas."

He paused and when J.D. didn't say anything in response, he kept going, "They were at the hotel last night working and getting organized. They had five rooms in their name, three for them to actually stay in and two to do the web sites, work with the people they recruited and to work on the backstory and maybe engage with some media. They had all agreed to meet in one room at eight thirty. So once it got to be around nine o'clock, one of them decided to go look for the two MIAs and when the guy that went looking for them didn't come back himself, the three that were left in the same room knew something was not right. So they decide that they would *all* go look for the three missing guys. They went from room to room with no luck until they finally got to the room where they were working on the websites. When they got there the light was off and when they turned the light on they were fucking floored with what they saw. The room was totally destroyed; someone had taken a knife to the cushions on the chairs, pillows, curtains, anything they could take a knife to they took a knife to. And all the computers and printers were completely destroyed. That's not what floored them; what floored them is that their three colleagues were unconscious, bleeding from a variety of wounds. One of them had a huge scalp wound and what turned out to be broken ribs. Another one had what they knew was a broken arm. They checked on them to see if they were still breathing and while two of them were doing that and another one was calling 911, the light went off again, they heard someone moving around and glass breaking and the three of them were also knocked unconscious. When 911 finally got there all six of them were awake and all six of them had been given a serious beating. Like I said, two of them are still in the hospital."

Russ paused his explanation to gauge Garzen's reaction. He saw that Garzen was trying to process what he'd just told him. His eyes were still narrowed and his expression was one of serious doubt, Garzen did not believe a word Russ had said.

He crossed him arms and in a sarcastic tone, started to replay what he'd just heard, "So, six guys, all of whom have military experience, all of whom you say are professionals get the shit kicked out of them, they have no idea who did it or why they did it and have now pulled out of the job. Is that the gist of it Russ? Is that the story you want to go with?"

Russ bristled, "What the fuck J.D.?! When have I ever lied to you?! When?! Hmm? All the other brownnosers you surround yourself with may lie to you or just tell you what they think you want to hear, but I'm not like that, not even when I was drinking, and you fucking know it! You think this is pleasant for me? You think I want to catch the shit you're giving me? These were good assets, professionals and those are not easy to come by. Now they are out and believe me, they will make sure to look into who and why, but they all know they won't find out dick. Whoever did this were also pros, also probably ex military and most likely Special Forces. Mossad used to do this kind of shit back in the day. They would strike fast and hard, disappear into nothing and deny everything if anyone did make an accusation. They went to check the video surveillance of the hotel, but it turns out the cameras in the hallways are just for show, they don't actually record. It's a small motel in a small town, probably been there since the 50s, so they're not all updated."

Garzen backed off a bit. The fact was that Russ was absolutely right, he had never lied to J.D., he had been more than willing to say things to J.D. that he knew were going to make him furious and had always been able to back up anything he'd said. Still, the guy had had a pretty serious drug and alcohol problem a few years back and you just never knew with people like that. Add to that the unbelievable story he was hearing and he felt somewhat justified in being skeptical. But Russ had in fact never lied to him and the reverend knew that too.

He reached out and grabbed Russ's arm as he tried to calm him down, "Alright, alright buddy, relax. That's it breeeathe, good. Okay, so keep going, what happened next?"

Russ responded to Garzen's effort with a thin, sideways smile. He knew J.D. still did not believe him, but he was now more willing to listen to the story.

This was good because what Russ had to tell him next made the whole thing even more surreal and almost into the realm of science fiction, "Well, they got treated, paid the people they had recruited this morning, paid their hotel bill and went on their way. We paid them in full J.D., I'm telling you now because I don't want you coming back at me later. I had to do that to have any chance of using them again."

J.D. waved his hands as though he didn't care about the money part.

He clarified, "So they're still willing to work for us on this?"

Now Russ actually chuckled, "Fuck no! They won't touch this job with a ten-foot pole! And neither will anyone else. It's a small community that does this kind of job and they all either know what happened or will know by the end of the day."

Garzen was pacing and shaking his head, "What the hell happened? Was it robbers going for the equipment? I mean who the hell would do that and why in the world would they even try?"

Russ shuffled and looked clearly uneasy with the question.

The reverend picked up on it immediately, "What? What are you not telling me Russ?! Goddamit! You better come clean right now, I'm serious Russ! If this is just another one of your fuckups you better just own up to it and come clean here and now, your job depends on it!"

Russ was obviously put off by the reaction, "That's not fair J.D! It's been a long time since I've messed up and you know it!"

He calmed down and went on to explain what he was so uncomfortable saying, "The thing is that the guys are saying it was one guy...they all agree on that."

J.D. was confused, "What was one guy? What are you talking about?"

Russ went on, "One guy who beat the shit out of all of them. I asked each of them independently and I gave them every opportunity to change their story and none of them did, not when they told me the story separately and not when they all told me together. Believe me, these guys admitting that one guy got the jump on them and kicked the crap out of them is not something they want to admit to, but they all did."

Garzen stared at him with his mouth hanging open, "Are you freaking serious here?! You are telling me that one single, unknown man kicked the shit out of six professionals with military experience?! Is that what you're telling me Russ, seriously? That's the final story you want to go with?"

Russ looked straight at the reverend and in an even, sober tone and without blinking said, "That is exactly what I am saying to you. And not just any professionals, there wasn't one of these guys that was under six feet and under 180 pounds."

The reverend chuckled as he kept pacing, "Okay, even better! A single, unarmed, unknown guy kicked the shit out of six professionals, six heavy, wrestler-looking, professionals. Ha! It just gets better and better."

He kept pacing and shaking his head. Russ just waited for whatever was about to happen, which would most likely include him getting fired.

J.D. stopped pacing and with a wry smile on his face said, "I actually believe you, you son of a bitch. There's no way that you, even in your most fucked up state, could come up with a story like that. Still, how could a single guy do this and an even better question why would he do this?"

Russ shook his head, "I've been turning it over and over in my head and all I can figure is that he got a jump on the first two, kicked the shit out of them and then, when one of the four others came looking for them, he surprised him too. Then he waited for the other three to come looking for their friends. He would have already come up with a few likely scenarios of how and from what door they would come in, what they'd do when they saw the scene and whether they came with weapons, that kind of thing. So when they all came looking together they probably thought they were covered, I mean three of them would be hard for a whole team to take down. I would have felt pretty safe in that group.

"Anyway, they all said that from the time things started happening to the point where all three of them were on the ground it couldn't have been more than twenty seconds if that. Each of them said that the guy knew exactly where to hit someone to incapacitate them immediately and that once he'd knocked the three of them down, he just proceeded to beat them and ultimately knock each one of them out. They also said that it wasn't more than one minute from the beginning of the attack to the time they were knocked out. I have never even heard of anything like this so I called friend who was in the Special Forces and asked him about it. He wasn't too surprised at all. He said that three guys without Special Forces-type training walking into a situation they were not expecting, nor prepared for or trained for, an experienced operator could put them down in just about the time this guy did. He explained the concept of violence of action"

Russ went on, "Violence of action is basically what we commonly refer to as the element of surprise put to use in a combat situation. He said that with a kubotan and violence of action a well trained operator could put six guys like than down easy."

Garzen shook his head "What the hell is a kubotan?"

Russ explained, "Imagine a crayon made out of hard wood or more likely, metal, except this one is a giant crayon, about eight inches long and proportionately thick. You hold it like you would a knife, but since it is not sharp like a blade you don't slice or cut with it. Anyway, someone could use one of those to break bones and hit vital points without the blood loss and mess of a knife. Obviously it is also much less lethal, which seems to follow this guy's thought process. If he'd wanted to he could have killed every one of these guys without a problem.

"Think about it, the guy gets the jump on the first two guys, maybe asks them a question or for directions or whatever, then as soon as he sees them relax he puts them down and then knocks them unconscious. Then the third guy comes and the same happens. Then the three guys come looking, see the destruction and the three guys on the ground. Can you see how they would still be processing what they're seeing when the light went out on them? My friend said if it's just one guy, then he's got to be something like Delta Force or a SEAL from team six to be able to do something like that, if he was American, if he was something else he could have been Mossad like I said or Russian Spetnaz or British SAS."

Garzen nodded thoughtfully, "So, what do we do now? You're saying nobody will touch the job, so now what?"

Russ nodded, "That's right, nobody who knows what they're doing anyway. This guy told one of my guys 'I have all your cell phones' so they're all scared shitless. You can always hire a few morons for beer money, but you told me and I agree, that this job needed pros that know what they're doing. Honestly boss, I say we just regroup, rethink and re-execute. I know you wanted to do this before the trial starts, but really when I thought about it some more, I think doing this after the trial starts will actually work better for us."

Garzen looked up, "Okay, let me hear what you're thinking."

Now that he knew he was not getting fired, Russ became much more articulate and animated, "So the trial is going to last months right, maybe over a year, right? Some people say longer than the OJ trial. Do you remember that trial? Remember how after two or three months people just kind of tuned it out and updates from the trial just became a normal part of the six o'clock news?"

Garzen smiled, "Yeah, I remember that. I couldn't wait for it to finally end. By the end of it I was completely fed up with it. I honestly didn't give a rat's ass who won or lost."

Russ held up his finger, "That's exactly right! I think that after a couple of months people will be fed up with it and will be zoning out, just waiting for updates on the nightly news. What better time to shock them with something different!"

Garzen, now smiling broadly, nodded, "I like it! I like it! And it will give us time to prepare something really good. I can milk the old standbys, abortion and gay marriage, for a couple of months."

Russ responded by actually reaching out and tapping Garzen's arm with his own, "Exactly! And it will give the guys I want to use some time to forget about the whole pros-getting-their-asses-kicked thing."

Garzen, now back to pacing was on a roll, "But we need to be careful, this is *not* the OJ trial. I think it's going to take a lot longer than a couple of months for people to get tired and bored with it. Remember that the OJ trial was an American thing. I mean the whole world knew about it, but very few people outside of North America knew why it was such a big deal or cared about it as much as Americans did. Loomis's case is a no-shit, for real worldwide thing. I mean even the people on television keep saying that it is like nothing anyone's ever seen. I bet you there are people living in huts in the middle of some damned jungle previously untouched by man who know about this trial and this case."

Russ smiled, "That's okay, we don't need to rush, we can just wait until things start to hit a lull and people are getting used to it being on all the time."

He stopped pacing abruptly, excited about the idea he'd just gotten, "And I can always use the trial and everything around it during my sermons to set things up for us. I can see what the papers and the news are saying about it and Loomis and use that to make the sermons really effective getting people riled up. I like this more and more Russ. I'm glad I came up with a way to fix your fuckup."

Russ just smiled a wry, sideways smile, "Yeah boss, I am too. I am too."

MANHATTAN, NEW YORK

Steven was on his daily call with his father in law. Having spoken to both of his kids with Beth through Skype, he still preferred to speak with his father in law through a normal landline call. With all the pleasantries and the weather having been covered, Steven knew he would really talk to his father in law in a way he could not talk to anyone else. The man had been a surrogate father for Steven and since Tracy's tragedy he had been someone Steven could always count on for some strength and some perspective, he never felt like he needed to hold back when he was talking to Tom Delaney, "How are the kids really doing, Tom? No bullshit, how are they coping?"

He heard silence on the other end of the phone, which is what he expected since Tom never spoke without thinking and he never had pat answers.

This was the first time Steven had asked him about the kids this way, more often he had asked about them in a more general sense, but not today, "It's rough on them Steven, really rough. Chris is just Chris, you know, he'll make due with whatever he's got around him to play with and I swear that boy has the most amazing imagination I have ever seen. He will make empty boxes of cereal into rockets, caves, cars, whatever, but he is noticing things are not the way they should be. And he's only two and a half, which helps. Still, however, his parents aren't here, he can't play with other boys his age and he sees dozens of people following him and his family everywhere. So yeah, I think it's starting to wear on him."

He went quiet for a few moments, something Steven knew he would do again, before talking about Bethany, "How is she Tom? Do you know?"

Tom Delaney knew the reason for the question. There was how Bethany wanted you to think she was doing and how she was really doing and both men knew that if she didn't want to open up about herself to anyone, Jesus himself would not be able to get her to talk.

Finally Tom answered, "She's okay, I mean as okay as someone like her can be under the circumstances. She goes into those long thinks of hers where you can tell she's somewhere else doing something else. When her grandmother and I ask, her she usually tells us she's fine and does it in a way that seems sincere enough to believe. She doesn't fool me though and she knows she's not fooling me, but we both seem to just be willing to keep it that way. Except today, today she watched the window a lot longer than she normally does and she didn't have that lost stare when she was doing it, she seemed to really be looking at the people out there. It almost seemed as though she'd recognized someone because when I walked by she called me over like she does when she has a question and then just said never mind."

Steven wanted to know about that as well, "And how is that going? Has the media let up at all?"

Tom chuckled, "Hell no! There seems to be more people every day, although it has leveled out quite a bit. I think the networks have gotten the idea that there's just not going to be much of a story to get around here, so it's pretty much the same groups doing the same thing out there day in and day out."

They were both quiet as they both considered everything going on around where each of them was and what tidbits were worth saying something about when Tom finally broke the silence, "Oh, almost forgot to tell you, we had ourselves a bit of excitement last night."

Steven perked up, "Oh? What's that about?"

Tom had a smile on his face and sounded like it, "Seems some of the media crews got into a fight if you can believe that happy crap! Heh, heh, they beat the hell out of each other!"

Steven smiled as well. Every once in a while fate rewarded those who waited with a small gift and this felt like one such occasion.

Steven was curious, "Did it happen on air? While they were taping or broadcasting?"

Tom responded, "No, not at all. Only reason I know is because it's a small town and everyone knows just about everyone else in town. Lucy's in the same bible group as Lila Brunner, the head nurse who was working when they brought them in, six of them. Anyway, someone had beat the living crap out of them, apparently some of them had broken bones so they needed to stay in, but the rest were treated for cuts and bruises with stitches and some topical analgesic and sent on their way."

Steven shook his head, "Damn, whatever they were fighting about was obviously important enough for them to take it that far. It must have been humorous to watch them trying to actually fight. Haven't you ever seen what they fight like when they're on TV? The look like twelve year old girls, scratching, pulling hair, it's funny."

Tom was quiet for a couple of seconds, "Hhm, I don't think that's the kind of thing they got into, no, these boys had their asses beat and not by each other."

Now Steven did engage a bit more seriously, "How do you know they didn't do it to each other? Did somebody see them fighting?"

On his end of the phone Tom shook his head, "No, but Vivian Delson's son is an ambulance driver and he says that he saw them all leaving together in one van. Now, that obviously doesn't necessarily mean they're all together, but it is a pretty good indication that at the very least they weren't fighting each other, not to cause that kind of damage."

Steven ticked the information and filed it away for later use, if necessary, "Jeez, nothing can happen there without the entire town knowing about it, huh? There's just no way someone could get by undetected."

Tom smiled, although he could not see his son in law, he knew exactly what he was doing because he himself had done it many, many times before. Once the decision had been made that Bethany and Chris would come to stay with their grandparents Tom found himself thinking that with as much media as there was all over town and with everyone so keyed up to spot new or unknown people, it would be next to impossible to get past them without being seen, no matter who you were. Tom imagined that Steven himself would probably think the same exact thing a few times a day. And having something happen like these guys getting beaten, something that none of the news outlets found out about or reported, but the rest of the town found out, confirmed for both of them the reason they could both feel that the media was helping to keep the kids and the rest of the family safe.

They were about to hang up, but Steven could tell that his father in law still had something on his mind, "Listen Steven, you know we adore the kids and that as far as we are concerned they – and you and Beth – can stay here for as long as you want whenever you want. You know that."

Steven believed exactly that and let his father in law know it, "Of course Tom, the kids love it there; we all love it there. So what's on your mind?"

Tom realized Steven could sense he still had more to say, "Well, it's just Bethany, Steven. She may be starting to crack a bit."

Steven responded immediately and with more intensity than he meant to, "What? What do you mean she's 'cracking'? We were just talking about this and you said she's okay, that she is the same as she's always been, so what the hell?"

Tom could have kicked himself. He couldn't have approached it any worse than he had.

Now he needed to fix it immediately, "Steven, Steven, relax, okay? Relax, son. That was my fault, I think the older I get, the dumber I get. What I meant to say about Bethany is that you can tell she wishes she could just go outside and play and run and just be a kid. She's a brave kid and just about smarter than all of us put together, but she's a kid in the end and kids like to do those things. I'm bringing it up because Pete Rollins, the mayor of Queensbury called me. He said that Albert Potter, US senator Albert Potter, called him and asked if there was anything he could do to help. I was just going to tell him thanks but no thanks, but then I thought about it and realized that maybe there could be something he could help with."

Now more settled, Steven was curious what his father in law thought a politician might be able to help them with, "What do you mean Tom? What could someone like Potter do for us? I mean let's not forget that Potter is a senator from New York, what the hell is he calling a mayor in Vermont for?"

Tom was ready for the question, "Well you know how Potter has so many child-focused causes that he supports, his people told Pete that he would be happy to do anything in his power to help Bethany and Chris have a more normal childhood, within the situation, obviously."

Steven was still not quite sure what any of this had to do with him calling the mayor in Queensbury.

Tom started getting frustrated, "I don't know Steven, maybe because he saw the kids on television and saw they can't be outside playing in the snow like all the other kids, maybe because someone on his staff told him he should call. I don't know why he decided to call, but I think if there's something he can facilitate because of his position then why not."

Steven knew he had crossed the line a bit, "Sorry Tom, I didn't mean to be such an ass, it's just getting down to the wire and things are so tense over here you could cut them with a knife. What kinds of things were you thinking he might be able to do?"

Tom was ready with that as well, "Well, I'm assuming he has some influence over state parks and such, doesn't he? If he doesn't himself I'm sure he has access to whoever does have that kind of influence. So what if he, or whoever, were to close a park early or for just one day so that Chris and Bethany could just run around? Maybe invite a few of their friends, wouldn't that be great?"

Steven thought about it and could see what his father-in-law was talking about. Someone in that kind of position may be able to afford the kids the opportunity to have some fun in a way that nobody other than the president might be able to.

Still, the idea of more media attention and more politicians involved in his situation was something to think about, "Alright, why don't you set up a call with the mayor, Potter, you and I and let's see what he has to say. Set it up for this weekend if possible, around lunchtime. I think we're pretty much set with the preparation so I should be able to take an hour or two on Saturday to talk to him. I would imagine that you agree that if this sounds like any kind of a stunt, we're done."

Tom nodded on his end of the phone, "Of course! Are you kidding? If it even *smells* like one we're done. And I apologize if this was stepping over my bounds, Steven, it just kills me seeing Bethany looking so pensive and bored."

Steven responded immediately, "Don't ever think that Tom! You are like a father to me and Bethany is your granddaughter. I trust you implicitly, so don't ever think you're stepping over any line, okay? Let's talk tomorrow after we talk to the kids just to make sure we know what we want to say. Oh, and Tom, tell him that if he or Potter or Potter's people even breathe any of this to the media, it's over."

BERN, SWITZERLAND

Nigel Barlow walked into the formal dinning room of the stately home at precisely 9:00 PM local time. Waiting for him were twelve individuals all dressed in similar and impeccable five-thousand-dollar pinstriped suits and Piaget watches with varying numbers of complications, none less than $70,000 and all a gift from Nigel Barlow. As soon as he came in the room the din of conversation died down and after nodding at each one of them Barlow took a seat at the head of the table. In front of each individual there was a wooden box with a jump drive in a chromed casing. The reality was that all of this was for show, each of the twelve individuals knew the exact content of each jump drive and its significance to them and more importantly each of them knew the meaning of tonight's meeting. Barlow looked at all of them, taking his time to look each one in the eye and to give each one a brief nod. There were four women and eight men seated at the table, all twelve of them were some of the most powerful people across a range of industries and government organizations from around the world. The group included three Deputy Secretary-level US politicians, a Federal judge, two movie studio CEOs, two CEOs from Chinese and Indian technology companies, a senior scientist specializing in evolutionary biology from Germany and another specializing in genetics from Belgium, a CEO of a financial conglomerate based in Hong Kong and the CEO of a hospital specializing in psychiatry and cognitive neurology. The twelve individuals around the table were responsible for more than 300,000 humans losing their lives and all twelve had taken at least one life with their own hands.

Barlow smiled and got the evening on the way, "Welcome! I hope all of you have been made comfortable and that your transportation here was acceptable. I know that this was not the date that we agreed upon for this meeting, but I want to assure you that there is a very good reason for us to move it forward on our calendar."

Nobody said anything nor took their eyes from Barlow, "I am sure all of you have been following the Steven Loomis case and I am sure that each of you has perhaps pondered whether that case and what Mr. Loomis is presenting as a defense could have any consequence on what we are doing. Well, the reality is that yes, the Loomis case could have some consequences on what we are doing and what we have been working on."

He paused for effect, looked down at the table with a somber expression, after a couple of seconds he looked back up with a smile on his face, "Fortunately all the consequences I have considered have been rather positive ones."

The entire room seemed to exhale. Everyone around the table smiled, sipped their drinks and turned their attention back to Barlow who kept going, "I don't want to be reckless and say that this could be momentous for our plans, but it is difficult to think about it in any other terms."

One of the techies in the room, a man originally from Beijing, but who now made his home in Redwood Shores, California broke the group's silence, "Nigel, if you don't mind, I'd like to hear your thoughts on the matter. As you said, initially I wondered whether there might be something to be concerned about, but came to the conclusion that it would make absolutely no difference to what we are doing one way or another. Can you share with us your thoughts on this? I'm particularly interested to hear how it is that you feel this case might actually have positive consequences on what we are doing."

Barlow turned to face the questioner, "Of course Jeff, I would be happy to. I don't think anyone around this table would argue the point if I were to say this case has gotten and will get more media attention than any other case in history."

Everyone around the table nodded thoughtfully, but nobody said anything.

Barlow continued, "The attention the case has gotten has been all over the place. Some people think it is a hoax, some people think it is a brilliant legal strategy, some think it is a Hollywood stunt; it's all over the board. In any case, whatever the world might think, people who might in fact become incredible resources for us will be aware that there is another possibility for who and what they are. Imagine how each of you would have felt if while you were confused and scared and looking for answers you had something like the information this case has brought to light dropped on your lap. Would you have perhaps looked into it some more? Hmm? Maybe done some more research about it? And how would you have felt if while doing this research you found science that explained your situation, science that explained who you are? What if you came across cases exactly like yours, situations like the ones you found yourself in? How would you have felt if you heard someone saying the very things you were thinking, describing the very things you thought about and did? And finally, what if you'd found an organization, or it'd found you, dedicated to helping you bloom as what you truly are? Can you all imagine what it would have been like?"

He looked around the table as he was making the point and saw as each individual smiled remembered their own turmoil and struggle.

Barlow went on, "So do you see how finding useful resources might become far easier once everything settles down. Of course with the additional attention will also come the thousands of imbeciles who think they are something more than what they are and who want to believe they are not just depraved and broken human beings, but something designed, something *meant* to be. Something. Like. You."

He paused after each of the last three words. He looked at Jeff to see whether he still had a question and Jeff simply nodded slightly and smiled. He had no more questions.

Barlow stood up and started to walk around the table pausing for a beat at each of the chairs, "So, I wanted us to get together to formally launch our journey together. Each of you has a jump drive in the box in front of you. Each one has the accounts, the individuals, the companies and the plans to cover your component of the enterprise. I want to be perfectly clear about everything because I do not want to have any of you claiming ignorance later."

He paused and let that sink in, "There will never be more than two of the people in this room together at the same place and at same time. Never. There will never be contact between each of your organizations unless it is in the normal course of executing your plans. None of you will in any way undermine or compromise another's organizations, unless of course, something they are doing compromises the bigger enterprise. In that instance each of you will be expected to assist in any way you can to ensure that whatever the danger, whatever the threat, it is dealt with decisively.

"After tonight you and I will have *absolutely no direct contact*. Within all of the information you are being provided there are very specific instructions on how to reach out to me or to any of the other organizations that are a part of the enterprise. This, I am afraid, is an absolute and inviolate rule."

His voice had dropped low and he was very deliberate in how he was saying what he was saying. There would be no ambiguities, no misunderstandings. Each of them knew it and each of them was perfectly fine with it.

Barlow was back at his chair.

He smiled, took the glass of wine on the table and raised it, "So, let us raise our glasses and toast the beginning of an important step in the evolution of humanity."

All twelve raised their glasses and all twelve knew that it was indeed the beginning of a period in history that hundreds of years from now would be looked back upon in the same light as the Renaissance, the Age of Enlightenment, the Macedonian Period and other momentous periods in human history and evolution. The fact was that they all knew that the US was controlled to a great extent by individuals who were a part of secret cabals, the Freemasons; Skull and Bones; NWO and most likely a couple others. Before they became political leaders, they were members of these societies and the truth was that the decisions they made were more about expanding and maintaining the control and prestige of the organizations than about helping the country. The general public was not and would most likely never be prepared to accept that, but the people in the room were not only prepared for it, they were counting on it. All of them, in one form or another, were a part of a secret society already. This was different, however. Hundreds of years from now people would think of them as they thought of the other secret organizations with the only difference being that the organization they had just founded could, and most likely would, decimate all the others.

8.

The next morning Nigel Barlow was in his study having sublime coffee, a tall glass of orange juice, a small plate of pastries that he tried to eat whenever he was in Switzerland and two truffles as a small finish. He was in the process of going through newspapers from around the world. He liked to go through regular newspapers from big cities, London, New York, Rome, Beijing, etc. He also tried to keep up with the financial markets, so he would go through dailies or weeklies that covered finance. The Internet age had made this task much more manageable. He could now go through a few printed versions of newspapers – he liked the feel and the smell of the newspaper – and he could use his iPad or computer to go through the rest. It also allowed him to find scientific papers and journals on a variety of topics that were of interest to him and the rest of the enterprise. He was in the middle of this activity when his valet, Cole knocked on the door to the study. Barlow immediately became concerned. Cole had never interrupted Barlow's morning routine in the seven years he had worked for him. Barlow told him to come in and immediately was able to relax a bit. Cole was carrying an envelope and what looked like a dozen roses.

He walked up to Barlow's desk where he was going through the newspapers and held out an envelope and a vase with the roses in it.

Cole wanted to make sure he had not angered his employer, "Forgive the interruption doctor, a local courier had a couple of unusual items this morning."

Barlow took the roses and the card with an expression of puzzlement on his face, "Is that right? Thank you Cole, that will be all."

Cole withdrew and closed the door.

In the envelope there was a greeting card. The vase with the roses had a small ribbon around it that matched the decorative ribbon on the card. Both pieces were clearly related to each other. Barlow set the roses down on his desk and opened the envelope. The quizzical expression changed into a smile that widened the more he read the note handwritten card. It read:

Doc,

I sent this card to the law firm you gave me the information for and made arrangements to have it and the flowers delivered to you. I just wanted you to know that I followed your advice and have been patient, very patient in fact! Shortly after you left I undertook the most ambitious project I could possibly imagine or think of and it is about to come to fruition.

Thank you for your help and guidance, I think you were absolutely right, had I simply continued doing what I was doing I would never in a million years have accomplished what I have been able to accomplish.

Please accept these flowers as a small token of appreciation. As you will notice there is one rose missing from the bouquet of roses. I am using the twelfth one!

Your most ambitious client!

Barlow looked up after reading the card with a huge smile on his face. He knew exactly who had sent it and was fascinated by what he might be working on. He was Barlow's last project and someone who had advanced much, much faster than any of Barlow's other projects. Barlow had felt compelled to advise him to be more patient and careful. When someone was as effective – and prolific – as his client was becoming, there was a chance that he might draw unwanted interest in his activities. If that happened it might bring unwanted attention to Barlow himself and that simply could not happen, it would put in jeopardy the entire enterprise and the whole cabal. Barlow had stopped seeing his client abruptly and suggested he be patient and more prepared when he undertook his projects. This card told him his pupil had listened.

The situation with Steven Loomis in New York had finally convinced Barlow that his career as a practicing neuropsychologist was over. His work would now need to consist of staying on the cutting edge of science and leading the enterprise. That was the primary reason for getting it underway a bit early. If he was not going to be actively scouting and counseling potential resources, someone else needed to do that. The scientists and doctors that were a part of the cabal had plenty of medical and scientific resources they could recruit through. Each of them knew that they were now responsible for taking his place in each of the areas they covered. Well, he suspected that he might find out what his client's project was all about before too long. Projects like the one he was most likely occupied with were usually pretty noisy; it was part of the satisfaction for the author of the note to make sure people knew about what he was doing. Barlow had told him to be patient, so he had no problem listening to his own advice.

MANHATTAN, NEW YORK

Steven woke up with the sun and went through his morning ritual of coffee, newspaper and some fruit, but today things were going to be very different. The legal team would be reviewing the various transcripts that had been gathered from all the expert witnesses and would also be working on the profile they were going to use to select the jury. That meant that Steven could come in after lunch and still be okay. In fact he was thinking they might be longer than that and if that was the case he would gladly take the time to read, spend time at home with Beth and maybe go on a walk with her. It was going to be exceedingly difficult to do that, but he was willing to try. At the very least he would just get to disconnect for a day or two. They had brought in one of the best jury consultants in the country and were very surprised to learn that the DA David Neill had brought in another top jury selection consultant. So he was pretty sure they'd go past lunch working with the consultant. The guy looked like he was all business and wanted to get to work right away. According to Drew the city of New York did not normally spend the kind of money that type of consultant cost. That told Steven they were planning on coming at him with everything. Any sense that they would just go through the motions went out the window with that tidbit of information. If he were to be honest, he did not really understand why the DA was going after him so hard. All he could come up with was that the case was such a high-profile case. More than Manson, more than OJ, more than the Unabomber, more than any other case by far. The fact that none of those cases took place in the age of global and social media ensured that his case would be covered incessantly across the globe and would by far be the biggest trial in history. Anywhere. Ever. Still, Steven knew that public perception was decidedly in his favor, so going after him with such zeal might backfire on David Neill. Unless there was something that Steven – and the rest of the world – couldn't see. Well he, along with the rest of the world, would find out soon enough.

He sat at the table next to the kitchen window and looked over the city. There were even more media tents and support personnel to make them work. But the truth was that he was actually starting to get used to it. He truly had never thought he would, but it was happening. Within the chaos that came with that kind of media circus there was some sort of order and routine. Thinking about it as he drank his coffee and orange juice, it actually made sense. Time was money and those teams down there cost a lot of money, so any media outlet of a certain size would want reports, updates, some return on their investment. And if that was going to happen there had to be some established routine, established patterns that he and his security team would recognize and adapt to. He could hear Beth getting up and going to the bathroom to brush her teeth and rinse her eyes out. She wore contacts because she had been too scared to do Lasik surgery to correct her myopia. Sometimes she went a few days wearing her regular glasses, but most of the time she wore contacts. Steven himself loved her in her regular glasses.

She came out to the kitchen with a smile on her face, "Oh my goodness! Look who's still here! Are my eyes deceiving me or is it that hunk from the television?"

Steven returned the smile, "That's right ma'am, it is that hunk from the television. I have come to take care of you while your husband is in court."

These moments of levity were something that had very much been a part of their marriage and they had completely stopped after Tracy's disappearance, but little by little, they were coming back into their conversations.

She walked up to him, gave him a kiss, got some coffee and sat across from him, "What's the deal? How come you're not going in to the law office this morning?"

Steven explained what his legal team was up to for the day. Beth nodded while he was explaining, all the while with a smile on her face, "So you are mine for today, is that it? I can do what I please with you."

Steven reached across the table, gave her a kiss and whispered in her ear, "Absolutely madame, I am always yours, but today you can do as you please with me."

He pulled back from her seemingly struck by something.

He continued whispering in her ear, "I'm sorry Beth. I'm sorry about all of this and about not being with the kids and...I'm just sorry."

Beth pulled back and held Steven's face in her hands, "I trust you with all my heart, and I know that you would not have done this unless you knew that what you were doing was going to change something, was going to make things better somehow."

She pulled him close again and spoke in his ear, "I'm here Steven, if you go down then so be it, I think I'm ready for that. But I'm not ready to let my husband go through this alone, I'll never be ready for that."

He pulled back and looked at her, looked into her and saw that she did know; she did understand that he had done what he had done for something more than mere revenge. He paused for two beats and then kissed her passionately, deeply, almost desperately. She kissed back and welcomed his touch. Steven ran his hands all over her body wanting to somehow bring her closer. He missed this so much, this kind of touch, her warmth, the feeling of deep love that she brought to their relationship. In one swift motion he picked her up and took her to the bedroom. They made love like they had not done so for the past six months. At times it was tender and soft and at times it was aggressive, almost reckless. Both of them got lost in it. Both of them *needed* to get lost in it, needed to feel they were still husband and wife in spite of everything going on around them. The one thing that had held them together, held their family together, was the intense, true love that they felt for each other. Theirs was not a relationship most people could understand. Most people just did not believe either one when they said they loved each other more now than they had when they first got married. Every time they said that people smiled and said something like 'oh how sweet' or 'how nice' but you could see in their eyes that they simply did not believe it.

After some time with Beth laying on his chest Steven spoke, "That was incredible baby, thank you so much."

She raised her head, "Thank you?! Just thank you?! I'm not that kind of girl you know!"

Steven smiled and kissed her nose, "Duly noted. I'm serious though, Beth, and it's not about the physical thing, although that was also pretty amazing. It was about you just taking a ride with me, about being able to get lost, both of us; just you knowing that we needed this as much as I knew it, that's what I'm thanking you for honey. Really I'm thanking you for just being you."

She returned his kiss with a tender smile, "Well, in that case, you're welcome. We did need this and of course I knew we needed it. My god Steven, can you believe we've been together for twenty-six years? If you don't know when you and your husband need to connect and that you need to get lost in each other after being a part of someone for that long, I think maybe you don't belong together."

Steven took the opportunity to talk to Beth about Bethany and what her dad had spoken to Steven about. She had obviously already spoken to her father and was a bit more comfortable with the situation than Steven was because she had talked to Bethany, really talked to her. She was obviously stressed and somewhat scared, but for the most part she was fine. Being as smart as she was allowed her to understand what was going on around her and to put it into the right context. In addition to being smart she had the love, support and understanding of her parents and her grandparents, all of who were more than willing to talk to her and answer her questions about whatever she was asking about. Not based on her age, but based on her level of understanding. At first her grandparents had been hesitant to answer the questions she asked them. There were just some things that a little girl shouldn't be thinking about. But after seeing that she would get her answers anyway, even if it took her longer to get them and that when she did get her answers, she was mature beyond her years, they got with the program. Beth explained to Steven that he needed to have some alone time with Bethany, even if it was over Skype. She treasured her relationship with her father and the way they would talk for hours and finding herself without that was probably the hardest thing she was having to go through. Beth told him that if he talked to her the way they usually did, it would go a long way towards having her be okay, as much as she could be anyway, with everything going on around her. He nodded, gave her another kiss and they both went to start their day. They each took a shower got ready and before leaving called the kids.

After talking to them for a while the kids were getting ready to get up when Steven spoke to Bethany, "Honey, do you mind if you and I talk for just a little bit?"

Bethany looked at her dad like he was weird, a look she'd mastered long ago, but she just said, "Okay daddy."

While she wanted to project the image of the girl with the nerdy dad, her excitement and happiness about talking to her dad was simply too much for her to keep inside. They talked for 45 minutes. About everything; about each other; about Tracy; about everything. They laughed, they cried, they were a father and daughter trying to get through the biggest challenge of their lives. He knew she would still have questions and she would still worry and be afraid sometimes, but as had been the case before all of this, he saw his daughter take a big breath. He'd seen her take 'the big breath' a number of times before and each time he'd felt the weight fall off his shoulders. This one, however, was by far the best 'big breath' he'd ever felt. By the time they finished she had lightened up visibly, viscerally. Her eyes were coming back to that curious light they always held under her furrowed brow, and her smile came a bit more readily. When they finished their conversation he asked her to get her grandfather.

Tom sat down in front of the computer, "I don't know what you talked about, but whatever it was, it lit her back up, Steven. I think you should try to have a little father-daughter time more often. It doesn't have to be as long as this one and I know the trial starts on Monday, but if you can just take ten minutes or so to let her know how things are going and how you feel, it will sure go a long way to having her be her normal curious, interested self."

Steven smiled, "She smart isn't she. I see her smile works on you almost as well as it works on me. I have no problem with that at all. It's nice to see I'm not the only one she has wrapped around her little finger."

They both chuckled and Steven moved to something else, "Did you call the senator's people back? Do we have a call set up for this weekend?"

Tom shook his head with a sideways smile, "No, it's the weirdest thing. When I called them they totally backpedaled. They said that there were other things that were on the senator's agenda that would need to take precedent. What those would be and why they didn't know about them when they called is a mystery to me, but there it is. What do you want to do?"

It didn't surprise Steven that a politician had flaked out. In his experience that was pretty consistent when it came to politicians, regardless of party or issue. They were more concerned with getting reelected than they were with following through and representing their constituents. That was one of the reasons that Steven had known from the beginning that politics would be a fertile ground for Homo sapiens predators. How would people ever tell the difference?

Steven finally nodded, "I'll reach out to the General and see what he can do. I'm almost certain he'll be able to do something. I haven't wanted to reach out too much because he's doing so much for us already, but this one might be an easy one he can help us with."

Tom nodded, "That's a good idea. I should have thought of that before. You're tied up with the trial, I should have thought about it and reached out myself. He called, you know, and gave us his private cell phone number. He said we could call him anytime, night or day."

Steven shook his head, "Don't even get started down that road, Tom. You know that we're all affected by the trial, all of us. This is how we need to help each other, to support each other, so don't worry please. You and Lucy have been an absolute god send for us and we could not be doing any of this without both of you."

Steven got up and was finishing buttoning his shirt as he said goodbye to his father-in-law. Beth was back and ready to take on the day.

Steven smiled at her, "So what are we up to today?"

She grabbed his hand and pulled him towards the door, "Well, Mr. Loomis, you're coming with me on my errands. It's just going to the little bakery a couple of blocks down and then to Lester's market. Sometimes I stop at the little newspaper stand by the bakery. It's not much, but they're my errands, you know what I mean?"

He nodded, "I do know and it sounds like a beautiful day. Let me call Lou to have him be right in front of the door when we come out."

He knew that Beth would be disappointed about having to drive there, but she understood why it had to be this way. She was still followed and photographed every single day, so having Steven along for the day would probably drive the paparazzi into a frenzy. Steven called down to Lou and they were on their way five minutes later.

They did precisely what Beth said they would do, except that on the way home they had decided to take a detour to go to Washington Park. A call to the General had ensured that NYPD would be cooperative in getting in the way of the photographers. Steven had an opportunity to say hello to Lester and was fortunate enough that his partner Brice was also there. After talking for a few minutes Beth and Steven told them they were looking forward to having them over on Friday, something that seemed to touch Lester all over again. Steven actually felt better about them coming over. He'd met both before, but it had been just in passing. Now he could see why Beth liked Lester and Brice so much. Little did any of them know that the last weekend before the trial would be one nobody ever saw coming and nobody would ever forget.

Manhattan, New York

Felix Garcia was starting to go crazy, so he grabbed his coat mumbled something about a story to his editor and ran out the door. He had been working on a story about two of the expert witnesses that were going to testify in the

Loomis case, Dr. Tyrone Leonard and Dr. Jim Scoma. He had gotten the names from Steven Loomis when he had spoken to him for the article he wrote. That article had propelled him ahead significantly. He went from a reporter covering whatever was happening at the precincts to a full-fledged feature reporter that could decide what he was going to cover and how he was going to cover it for the New York Chronicle. It felt great to work with his editor rather than being pushed around by him. He had gotten his own office, a new computer, a substantial raise, the star treatment. His was the only interview Steven Loomis had given to date and that was worth more than gold in the current environment. The media conglomerate that owned the Chronicle had made sure that Felix would be staying exactly where he was. They had done that just in time. A slew of other media outlets had reached out to him throwing all kinds of offers just days after he had gotten all his new perks. The offers he'd gotten were hard to turn down, but the saving grace was that most of them were from newspapers and media outlets in other places. For Felix there simply was no other place where he'd like to ply his trade. New York had and would always be his mistress and being Puerto Rican he knew you never ran out on your mistress. New York was where his name actually carried some weight, even if it was just in the Bronx and Spanish Harlem, and it would be where he would either rise to the top or fall flat on his face. His interview had gotten him a chip at the big-boy table, now he had to see if he could stay there. He had set the bar very high for himself and he was feeling the sniping of more senior reporters who did not understand why he had been the one to do the Loomis interview. Well, that was when his name paid off in the rough places where his family had lived since they came to the US permanently from Puerto Rico or 'the island', so having someone targeting him was nothing he couldn't handle.

What he really couldn't handle, and the reason he was running out the door, was that the Chronicle offices were now even more packed with people from across the country, around the world actually, that worked for the Chronicle's holding company. There were now three other reporters in his office, all of them trying to come up with something good, which meant new stories and information. There was so much coverage that coming up with something new and different was almost impossible. Felix could not handle three other people working right next to him, all from somewhere else and all trying to scoop each other. He knew he would scoop every one of them just like he'd scooped every media outlet and every reporter, but he was damned if he would work on it somewhere that these losers could hear or see what he was doing. The three individuals were well-known, senior reporters and they had specifically asked to be put in his office, if possible. He knew what they were doing and it was not happening.

He got to the street using the back way he'd been using and went on his way, but not before grabbing a couple of hot dogs from the stand by the office. Leonard had agreed to talk to him after Steven Loomis had vouched for him and had given him Jim Scoma's name as someone who was working on similar science, but not in the same context that everyone else was working in. He was headed for the subway to go to Columbia, where Leonard taught forensic psychiatry and cognitive behavior. Felix Garcia did not really know all that much about the actual science involved in the forensics of the case, he just knew they could eliminate or identify suspects. And he also knew that everyone on earth was now intensely interested in it, the media most of all. He didn't know about it, but he was planning on knowing much more about the science and about the why and how of Steven Loomis's decision. He was sure that's where the next big story was, in the science. He'd seen show after show after show going over the science and explaining everything in detail, but it was all so dry and boring he just couldn't stay tuned in. Nobody had actually translated the information into something that the average person could understand and identify with. He hoped Loomis's witnesses were more engaging than what he'd seen, otherwise the jury would be asleep after the first couple of days of experts giving testimony. He knew Leonard was very engaging and imagined Scoma might be as well, but it would take more than the two scientists to keep Loomis out of prison. Whatever happened during the trial, Felix knew this was where the scoop was; he just knew it. He'd made it through the tough neighborhoods where he grew up, through high school, through college and through his profession by relying on his instincts; he was not about to stop listening now, when it counted the most. It just wasn't how a Garcia operated. He finished his dogs, smiled and walked briskly headed for the subway, ready to kick some network media ass once again.

9.

On Thursday morning Steven went into the law offices to get updated on everything that had been covered on Wednesday since he hadn't gone into the office at all. They explained everything that they had gone over with the jury consultant and, not surprisingly, told him they were still not finished with the jury profile. Part of the problem seemed to be that the three lawyers could just not agree on the optimal profile for the jury and that too was not very surprising, especially as each explained what they believed was the optimal profile for a juror. Drew wanted jurors that were highly educated, some college at least, preferably a degree and even better, an advanced degree. He wanted people who were very, very digitally savvy and who knew how much, how fast and how deep the information that could be accessed online was. Therefore, Drew's ideal juror would most likely be someone younger, less than 50 years old. Max wanted the same thing, but he was more open to having older people who might also be able to use the Internet, although perhaps not as fast or as deep as their younger counterparts.

He was also open to having people that were not necessarily digitally savvy, but who seemed smart and quick and most important of all, open to new ideas. Drew and Max had clearly argued about the point on Wednesday and it sounded like the issue was still not settled. Then there was Ray. Ray thought that they should not focus on someone's age or how digitally savvy they were, but rather on the things they did not want the jury to be. His point was that the first layer of filters needed to be to eliminate the people that were clearly just not right for the case. People who were too religious or who were law and order types or who seemed to have a chip on their shoulder when they interacted with the world. They would have to identify those people and eliminate them immediately. He also believed they needed to consider engineers or engineering-oriented professionals as an ideal profession for the jury. That had sent Max and especially Drew into a tizzy because they'd been saying that the ideal professions would be actors, PR people, advertising people, artists, people who were fine with not having extensive, detailed information before they could make a decision, people who were able and willing to make a decision based on emotion and who understood that there may be things out there that it was simply impossible to prove absolutely. The three of them had begun arguing again just explaining to Steven what had gone on the day before, so he could just imagine what it had been like at the office yesterday. He had walked by the jury consultant and had been impressed by the guy's demeanor and professional image, he seemed to be a serious professional and exactly what he was, one of the best. Even he, however, looked like he'd been put through a ringer. Steven was almost certain that he had probably played referee to the three other lawyers going on and on in support of their own ideas. Steven had to feel sorry for the guy, but he also had a thought along the lines of 'welcome to the party brother'. He'd been playing referee for months now, this guy had just gotten here, so Steven had no problem with the guy getting a taste of what he'd been getting all these months.

The plan had been to go through a dry run from soup to nuts and to include Steven in the discussion about the cross of the prosecution witnesses, what the DA was likely to throw at their own witnesses during cross-examination and their summation. Steven had gone through incredibly intense preparation for his own testimony, but had limited exposure to how his lawyers were planning to go after the prosecution's witnesses. He was not worried. All three of his lawyers were very well respected litigators who had built a reputation for being brutal when going after the opposition's witnesses and each one of them had done it in very different ways. Still, he was interested in how they were planning to do that in his case. He had an idea, but he wanted to know. It looked like that would most likely not be happening today. No, today would be spent settling the jury profile issue and finally get to work in earnest with the jury consultant. Steven had no problem just observing as they did all of it. For Steven, years and years of training and of putting your life on the line time and time again meant that there really was never anything close to the idea of being over-prepared. That concept was simply not within the realm of Special Forces operators' thought process. Taking every single opportunity to prepare an op, his men and the support personnel had kept him alive for decades and he was convinced it would do so once again. So, no, Steven Loomis had no problem being a spectator at all.

Art 'The General' Goodman, Marine Corps. Recon Retired, was in one of his 'I'm-going-to-throw-something-hard-if-you-talk-to-me' moods on the fine Thursday morning. Everyone in the company knew very well that when the General was in such a mood, going into his office could be construed as an act of war. The deals he had been looking over were going along perfectly fine, but two of them were once again mired in the shit-storm that African politics always turned into when the time came to put a signature on the dotted line.

After reading the last file on his desk he stood up, looked out the massive window he slammed the folder down and yelled, "Everyone wants to be king, but nobody wants to act like a fucking king!"

Stephanie came in a bit alarmed. She was used to his outbursts, but this one had been just a bit more angry that most, "Sir, you haven't had any lunch. Do you want me to have Jaime prepare you that shark sandwich you like so much?"

Art Goodman was in his mid 70s, but did not look it. His shoulders were still broad, his hair completely white, but thick, and his chest still held the pride earned over decades of leading men into battle, so when he whirled around to face Stephanie he looked like a man ready for war.

Once he saw who it was he chuckled and shook his head, "Do I sound senile already Steph? Tell the truth now."

She came closer, put her hand on his shoulder and said, "If going senile looks like this, sign me up right now." They both chuckled.

Stephanie was a shared administrative assistant to both Goodman and Steven Loomis. Loomis needed her more on a day-to-day basis, but Goodman would not have it any other way, it was Steph or nobody. A couple of years ago he had gone through eleven possibles before they finally got the idea that it just wasn't going to happen. So when Steven was in the office or in the middle of a deal he took priority, otherwise Steph was shared with the General. Stephanie Gennero was in her late fifties, had three grown daughters and had been a widow for twenty-two years. She was a stunning woman, five feet eight inches, had long flowing hair she refused to color, so it was a combination of brown, silver and pure white. She had been with GIC just over sixteen years. During that time she had a front row seat to see the young, rugged and (if you believed the interns, gorgeous), executive that came in and acted precisely the opposite from every one of those things. He was a hot shot, but acted like he was just one of the team, he knew more than just about everyone in the room, but he still listened to ideas, he was kind and patient, but could reduce someone to a blathering idiot if he needed to. But he could also be brooding, temperamental and extremely impatient, especially with people that were just not fast on their feet. And yes, he was very attractive, but was the last in the room to think about someone's looks. No, it had not been too difficult even back then to see that Steven Loomis would one day run GIC and Steph could not be more thrilled about it. Most people that worked for GIC in a variety of functions around the world supported their leader and knew he was always fair to them and their families, but they had no idea just to what extent Goodman, Loomis and the rest of the executive team went to in order to make sure their people were well cared for. Daycare at work, free gym memberships, tuition reimbursement for undergraduate work and fifteen scholarships for graduate school with a job guaranteed upon graduation and emergency loans when people needed them. GIC employees were unbelievably loyal to their employer, but they were also protective of each other, so from the get-go Steven had thousands of supporters around the world.

Goodman turned down the sandwich and remained at his desk going through the files he had been going through for hours. The only thing the man was accomplishing was getting more and more angry as time went by.

He finally slammed the files again, "Goddammit! I have told them time and time again that the insurance structure is different when we are dealing with the Africans! I don't know how many times I have said that!"

Stephanie stepped closer to the desk, "Sir, the insurance is being handled through London, just like it always is. Steven left very clear directions."

He seemed confused, "London? Are you sure? Well, how does he expect everyone to know what he wants if all he does is leave instructions. Dammit that's no way to lead!!"

Stephanie was now around the desk and holding both of his hands, "Mr. Goodman, General..." He kept ranting and raving.

She held his hands much more firmly, ...Art! Its' okay, he'll be okay. You have done about as much as you could and then some, now it's time for his legal team to go to war for him and they will, you know, they will go to war for him and not just because he's a client or because they're getting paid, but because like everyone else that comes into contact with Steven, they love him."

Goodman was trying to think of some other issue to throw a tantrum about, but in the end he just dropped his head and he cried softly without saying anything. Stephanie took him in her arms and allowed the man to pour out all the emotion the case had built up inside him. He had absolutely nobody aside from his most trusted and closest employees. He reached around and held her tight as his quiet sobbing intensified.

He turned sideways while still holding on to Stephanie and allowing himself to be held, "I can't do a god damn thing for him! Nothing! He's got all those jackals and talking heads and those vipers at the district attorney's office gunning for him and I can't be there!"

That sent him into a fresh round of crying. Someone who was not a part of the GIC family might wonder why in the world their CEO seemed to be coming apart for someone that at the end of the day was just an employee, a valued and esteemed employee, but an employee nonetheless. Nobody outside of a very close group within GIC understood that for the General, Steven was much, much more than an employee. Art Goodman and his wife had lost a baby boy before he reached two months of age. It had been a congenital heart defect that was far too small to catch in utero and which at 2 months had caused a catastrophic tear in the small heart. It had been the saddest day for a man who knew the meaning of sadness and loss. And now he was facing the same thing again. The fate of someone who he loved, truly loved, like a son, would be put in the hands of others who had no notion of the quality of man he is, of the sacrifices he's made for his country, of the desire to help those who could not help themselves. That quality was rare, so rare indeed and they might never know it.

Art Goodman composed himself, looked up at Stephanie and smiled, "Thanks Steph, that was one of those things you know you need, but will never ask for."

She returned the smile, "That's why it pays to have people like me around, people who more often than not know what you need and that you won't ask for it."

He stood up by his desk and stacked the files he'd been slamming around. He grabbed his notepad, something he always kept handy and wrote a few lines about the deals he'd just been going through.

When he finished he gave the files with the notes to Stephanie, but before she was able to leave he held her back for a few seconds, "He'll be okay, right? I mean those guys he's working with are the top lawyers in their field, aren't they? Someone would call us if he needed something for the trial, wouldn't they?"

Before Art Goodman was able to get another word out Stephanie took his face in her hands, quietly said "shhhh" and gave him a kiss on the lips. Not the kiss of someone about to rush off to do something else, but the kiss of someone who knew that her doing that would communicate decades of time together and her feelings at the end of those decades.

Art 'The General' Goodman had been surprised many times in the field of battle, but he had never been surprised outside of it. Never. Not once. And now he was standing like a feeble, old man, probably unable to say a single word and not because he had just been knocked on his ass, figuratively speaking of course. Try as he might he could not say a word and the look on his face with eyebrows, lips, nose, all trying mightily to form a sound without being able to do so was priceless and endearing to Stephanie.

Being the military man he was he was not about to allow someone to come in with a surprise attack and then simply turn around and walk away unscathed, no way, no how. And while he was not at all sure what the best counterattack might be to such a maneuver, he was damn sure of what he could not go wrong with. He stood up, put his arms around Stephanie's waist and kissed her passionately. At first she hesitated, but it was a half a beat only, then she put her arms around his shoulders and returned the kiss. Neither one knew how long they'd been kissing, but one of the other admins on the floor had a question and since the door was open came in to ask. Her response when she saw what she saw was immediate and unequivocal; she turned around and went to leave.

Stephanie called out to her before she could get to the door, "Zoe, what do you need?"

Stephanie still had her arms around the General and he still had his arms around her waist, both were waiting for her to say something, "Ahhh....seeee....there's...I mean there was...this thing...you know...the thing for the contract thingy"

Stephanie and Goodman looked at each other, chuckled and kissed one last time so that each of them might go back to doing what they had been in the process of doing before all this romance. Stephanie and Zoe left his office, he sat down on his desk with a goofy smile on his face trying to remember what he'd been in the middle of doing and could just not come up with it. Oh, well, he'd have to ask Stephanie to remind him what it had been. For the rest of the day he walked around with the goofy grin on his face and telling people how much he appreciated them. Yes indeed, being able to finally connect with the one you loved did wonders for a man, especially a man like him.

10.

B eth Loomis woke up like a woman on a mission. While Steven was still reading the papers and drinking his coffee, she went through all the serving dishes, plates, cups, saucers, every single of the china that had been a gift from her grandmother was carefully inspected and hand cleaned in it was found unacceptable. The same exact process had been used with the silverware, not just the elegant silverware that went with the china, no, every single knife, fork, spoon, butter knife, all of it. Steven found it a bit amusing, but he didn't want his wife to have a heart attack getting ready for her guests, her two guests. He considered saying something, but then realized it was Beth's way of coping with the situation they found themselves in. This would be the first time they would have anyone who wasn't a GIC employee over for drinks and dinner, for any event for that matter. And he knew very well that after you had gone through something like what they'd gone through, something that was so out of your control, any instance where you got control over anything, a guest list, a menu, how shiny the dishes were, anything at all, was welcome.

He walked over to her, gave her a kiss on the cheek and told her he needed to get his day started to which he received some sort of mumbled 'have a good day' and a kiss on top of his head while Beth was busy with her list. It made him smile. These were the things that couples, normal couples dealt with every day. Silly things, things that made them laugh, or maybe little arguments about whose turn it was to watch a movie on TV. For Steven it was this, this very thing, normalcy, that he wanted back for his family more than anything. The world knew what had happened to Tracy and the other girls, what he'd done and what he was about to go into court to argue. Eventually time would heal a lot of things, not all things, not ever all things, but most of them. The media 'experts' were speculating that the Loomis case might not be fully out of the public eye for years to come. He definitely did not agree with that speculation, especially as it related to his family. He could deal with it if it was just himself, but he would be damned if it would be that long before the control of the remote would once again be the most dramatic thing happening at the Loomis household. That was the reason he was going through everything he was going through, the reason they were all going through it.

Lou was waiting for him downstairs by the door, something he normally did not do. Steven looked outside and saw another three guys, including the Twins, Thurman and Cecil Meeks. They were all holding the photographers and reporters back far enough that there was a path to the back door of the SUV. Lou got into the driver's seat, Steven slid into the back seat and Thurman slid in next to him from the other side. Troy Fielding, the fourth guy on the team, closed the door behind Steven and got in an SUV behind theirs.

Now safely in the car Steven had to ask, "What gives? Why all the extra coverage? Did something happen?"

Thurman shook his head, "No, man, nothing else happened."

Steven now nodding, "Okay, so why all the extra coverage?"

Now it was Lou who answered the question, "I don't think it's extra coverage, boss. I think that now that the trial is starting it's going to be like this every day."

Steven went to respond with something but closed his mouth when he saw Thurman nodding emphatically as Lou spoke.

Lou kept going, "See, I figure that it's the same as us when we're executing an op. We scout it out, right? And then we see if there are any locals that can provide us intel or who might be friendly to our cause and might work with us or help us stash weapons, that kind of thing.

"Well, I think that's what these media mutts have been doing all this time, all the recon work we would do. And now they know the lay of the land and they know what angles they might be able to exploit. They probably have locals helping them out. So of course now the A team comes in. Now that all the grunts have done the hard work for them they come in and get on camera and sound like they know everything there is to know with not a fucking hair out of place."

Steven looked in the rearview mirror, where Lou's eyes were visible to him, "Had a tough weekend there Lou?"

Lou smiled sideways, "Nah, nothing like that boss. It's just amazing to me that these fuckers can get away with doing some of the things they do and normal, everyday people, end up getting reamed. The other day I'm parked and waiting for you and in front of me comes this big ass news truck, satellite on the roof, the whole thing. And they're from Indiana or some such bullshit. So they park in the No Parking zone, I mean right the fuck on it! And this big clumsy fuck of a cop comes by and this teenybopper-looking broad gets out of the truck and smiles and pinches his cheeks and they're there for another freaking hour. So the news truck leaves and this young kid driving a flower delivery truck parks there. He goes into the back of his truck and gets two bouquets, two fucking bouquets and this prick comes over and tells him he can't park there and that he has to move. And the kid keeps trying to explain that he'll only be a few minutes since he only has to deliver two bouquets. So the fucker goes to write him a ticket and I just can't take it, so I get out." Without pause both Steven and Thurman exchanged looks of 'oh crap'.

"So I explain to him very politely that I saw him let the big news truck park there for more than an hour and that I had also seen when he told the kid with the flowers to move it. He told me to mind my own business if I didn't want to end up with a hefty ticket myself. So I pulled out my smart phone and told him I had recorded all of it, the shapely blond giving him the pinch on the cheek, the truck parked there for over an hour, the poor kid trying to make it through college delivering flowers and being abused by the system. And you know what? He walked away and said that truck better not be there for more than ten minutes! Can you believe that shit? I'm starting to realize that the power this little device carries can outclass the biggest, baddest operator out there."

Thurman nodded approvingly, surprised by the fact that Lou was so easily able to decipher the power that the media could wield if it needed to. Like everyone else on Steven's team, Lou looked like he could definitely take care of himself, but in this case it hadn't been his size or his looks that intimidated the cop, it was the camera in his smart phone.

Lou finished the story, "And you know what the kicker of the whole thing is? I didn't record shit! I came up with that when I was on my way walking to the cop! I didn't know what the hell I was going to do when I got to where he was and then just thought about what might scare him the most. The NYPD is no bullshit, a New York City cop knows how to handle himself, so being tough or trying to intimidate one is never going to be easy. But being recorded doing something wrong, that will scare the crap out of them." Thurman chuckled when Lou delivered his punch-line. Steven just smiled.

Beth smiled because she could tell Lou had forgotten she was in the car as well and had just talked the way he talked every day with her husband in the car.

All of a sudden Lou realized it, "Oh man! Sorry Mrs. L! Sorry about the cussing, it just comes out, you know."

Beth let him off the hook, "That's alright Lou, I am married to a SEAL, you know."

Everyone in the car smiled and Lou let out a breath of relief. Thurman Meeks saw Steven go back to looking out the window, lost in his own thoughts. The trial was starting on Monday and Thurman imagined that by now there just wasn't too much to do by way of preparation. Steven's team was either ready or they weren't. There simply was nothing else that either side could do to prepare now. They had either put in the time or they hadn't and on Monday he, along with the rest of the world, would find out one way or another.

David Neill, Melanie Farris, Bart Logan and Margaret Hollis along with what they were now affectionately calling the Smurfs, Linda Fillmore, Will Jameson and Allie Perkins, all junior deputy DAs and all short in stature, were looking at the dry erase board together, all of them had their arms crossed in front of them and nobody was saying a thing. Written on the board was the ideal profile of a juror in the case of the state of New York v. Steven Loomis. The list was twenty-two items long and seemed to be completely disconnected from the facts of the case and from reality as it existed around the world. For someone to conform to the profile now written on the board someone would have had to live under a rock, no, more like on another planet altogether and then under a rock.

Hollis had wanted to get the group together to go over their strategy. More than anything, Hollis didn't want Neill to come in at the last minute thinking he's the conquering hero and screw up the work she'd done with the team. How this idiot had gotten elected as the District Attorney spoke volumes for his campaign team because it sure as shit hadn't been because of his legal expertise.

She took a couple of steps in front of the group and turned to face them, "Obviously this profile is not going to be possible for us to get. Jesus, Mohammad, god himself could not get someone with this profile to sit on this trial. So, this is a guide for us, a guide that uses the most extreme elements within each of the qualities we're looking for." This was something everyone, except for Neill, already knew.

She went on, "So clearly we're not going to get someone who believes that the law should be applied as written in any situation period, whether it is something at her kids' school or at church. We know she's going to apply common sense to how a law should be applied, correct? Are we all agreed on that? We want someone who can be tough when it comes to applying rules and laws in serious situations, maybe life and death situations. Someone who believes that whatever the law or whatever the rule being applied was written by people who know better, people whose life work is, in fact, writing rules, correct?"

Everyone nodded their heads in agreement and everyone waited for the hammer that was about to come down directly on Neill's head.

She went on, "So Mr. Neill, based on what's known about the case and on the theory the defense is planning on using would this woman make a good juror for us?"

Neill took on a pensive expression, held his chin with his thumb and forefinger as he walked closer to the list and began reading from it, "Hmm, educated, churchgoing, believes in rules and following them, believes laws were written for a good reason and that there is a purpose to having laws, believes laws and rules should be applied equally, regardless of money, position or situation."

Before he could go on Hollis jumped in, "Okay. Sounds great so far. Let's say that during voire dire the defense asked her about her son's karate class and let's say that because of a traffic accident that was blocking the highway she got there fifteen minutes late for a karate competition her son was to compete at. And because they were late her son couldn't take his test for the next belt. She explained everything to the instructor, the accident, everything, and the instructor held his ground. And let's say although she was disappointed and upset, she understood that it was just rules already established for such a situation. Do we still want her on our jury?"

Neill went back to walking holding his chin again, reviewing everything listed on the board and now thinking about what Hollis had said, the situation, everything.

Finally he turned around and with a thin smile and confidently said, "Yes, I think she would still make a fine juror for us."

Hollis crossed her arms, gave him a radiant smile, nodding as if confirming his answer, walked right up to him and said, "She'd be a fucking disaster as a juror for us. Does anybody want to tell Mr. Neill why she would be a fucking disaster? Hmm? Nobody? Okay then, I'll do it. She would be a disaster because she comes across exactly like you just described her: law and order type, follows rules type, if it's a law or a rule then it's because it was written by someone who knows better type, all of it. It sounds perfect and she would hang on to all that until the jury room door shut and then someone would start throwing whatifs into the mix and people would start to rethink things and before you know it Mrs. Law and order is now Mrs. Whoamitojudge a..."

Neill interrupted her, "Wait a minute! Someone would start throwing whatifs about what? And how do you know that anyone would start throwing whatifs at all? I mean..."

She interrupted Neill loudly this time, "Who gives a shit what the whatifs are about David?! It doesn't matter what they're about, don't you get that? What matters is that they get people reconsidering their position regardless of what that position is. And how do I know that somebody will throw a whatif into the mix? Because there is *always* someone who throws in a whatif, so the question is not whether there will be a whatif or not, the question is are people likely to react to the whatifs and that part, well, that part is what you pay me all that money to know."

She was standing close to Neill, uncomfortably close for his taste, but he still smiled when she was done. Everyone in the room knew that he was like a bubbling cauldron inside, but he would never show it, not until Hollis was not around, which meant that every single person in the room wanted to make sure they left when Hollis left and each and every person in the room began strategizing that exit immediately.

As the day wrapped up, Steven, for the fist time, felt like they were ready. Maybe it was because the room they'd been working in and covered in Post-it notes and poster boards and pages and pages of law, was now pristine; or maybe it was because he had seen all the witnesses in one place at the same time or because he'd seen all the associates packing documents, evidence, everything the team might need; or maybe it was the technology his legal team was using to defend him and present his case. Technology wasn't anything Steven had thought about for one second, but clearly his team, especially Drew, knew the power that good, engaging presentation could have in a case like this one. They were using computer animations for a lot of the science, digital images with sound and narration and reenactments that had been produced like documentaries. Steven was confident his team would know exactly when to use that technology, but he wasn't sure what the judge would allow them to use.

Drew walked over to Steven as if reading his thoughts, "It's a lot of evidence, isn't it? We're not sure what the judge will allow us to use, I'm sure it will not be all of it, but we're bringing everything and we're operating as though everything we want to do will be allowed. You are the defendant and in this system you are innocent until proven guilty and the law takes that very seriously, so we will be given some leeway, but we also know not everything we are bringing will be allowed. Let the DA and his minions make their arguments about our evidence, we have way more fire power, so their task is not going to be an easy one. And, whatever we can bring in we'll leak to one media outlet or another for them to use in their broadcasts, that's not something the prosecution can do. Trust me, morning shows will get in what we can't."

Steven nodded, but clearly he just wanted to go home.

It was the last day they would see each other until the trial so Steven walked over to Drew shook his hand and gave him a short, one-armed man hug as the were shaking hands, "Thanks for everything Drew, seriously. You were the first one to believe in what I was saying and you've been willing to go to war for me regardless of the consequences. I also know that your neck is on the line at this firm and I wish it wasn't that way."

Drew shook his head as he returned the one-armed hug, "Don't worry about that, it is all something I can deal with. And you're welcome, but never, ever forget that I was willing to do this because of who you are, the kind of man you are. I can't imagine how many times you've put your life on the line for this country, for all of us, so whatever the consequences might be, they are nothing compared to what I'm sure you've been through."

Steven nodded and once their short discussion was over, started to head for the door.

He stopped before leaving the office and turned around to say one last thing to Drew, "Please, please let the team know how much I appreciate all of their work and please let them know that regardless of the outcome, I will never forget what they're willing to do. Please let them know I am sorry I can't say all of this to them myself, but I have to get out of here Drew, I think I am getting burned out on preparation. I am just ready to get underway."

Drew nodded, "I will let all of them know, but remember that every one of them believes in what you did and in your defense because they also know who you are."

Steven Loomis smiled at his attorney, nodded and walked out the door. Next time they saw each other would be in battle.

Lester Allen was straightening out his tie on the mirror. He just wasn't sure if he liked the shade of purple of the thing. He pulled out the knot and pulled the tie out, "I just can't get past the purpleness of my tie, it's so last year! I think I'm going to go with the blue and green one, the one with the paisley pattern."

Brice was also getting ready. He was in the closet also trying to pick out a shirt in his boxers and a t-shirt. It was a much easier task for him. Although he kept some decent clothes at Lester's house, it was nothing compared to what Lester had.

He pulled out a plain blue shirt, a yellow tie with a swirl pattern, "You know I love that tie on you. It's very distinguished, especially when you wear it with a plain white shirt."

That was the last the last words Brice Walker would ever utter and the last conscious thought he would ever have. As he was buttoning up his shirt everything went black and he dropped straight down. Lester was standing over him looking at him with something that might look like pity to someone else, but what he was really doing is checking things off his mental list. Lester would of course miss the fun he had with Brice, but he'd known from the beginning that Brice would need to die in the end. He had been in a relationship with Brice for the distraction value, for entertainment, but he couldn't allow someone who knew as much as Brice knew to be walking around. Who knew who might come looking for information? Brice's fate had been sealed the day they established a romantic relationship.

Lester pulled out the long, sharp spike he'd used out from the base of Brice's skull. He had severed the brain stem and his spinal cord at the base of the skull so death had been instant, painless and most of all, clean. There was a bit of spinal fluid mixed with some blood on the carpet, but it was easily cleaned. And in the end it didn't really matter, he would never come back to this apartment. Ever.

Lester finished getting ready, walked around the apartment making sure there was nothing on and that everything was as he'd planned it. Now he would go back to using the name he'd used for most of his life. Les Martin. He had decided to use his first and middle names as his first and last name as soon as he'd begun to plan everything. Les Martin was almost a billionaire because of the technology company he'd founded, so he could use whatever resources he needed to in order to make that all happen and to make it happen discreetly and most of all, legally. He needed to be sure that whatever he did was on the up and up. He knew people would come looking for answers about him and changing his name would delay their search for more than enough time for him to be far away, using another identity and enjoying the success of his plan. He had listened to his neuropsychologist, his mentor, Nigel Barlow's advice. He'd been right, if he'd continued on his path eventually people, the police and other investigators, would have started to put together a pattern, it might take them a while, but it would eventually happen. Barlow had told him to be cautious and that there would be more than enough opportunities to challenge himself. Les had immediately thought about the Steven Loomis trial and case as the biggest challenge he could find and he'd begun his quest exactly after a month of talking to Barlow and now here he was, about to make history. There was a beautiful, single red rose on the living room table. He walked over, grabbed it and a bottle of a nice Pinot Noir he'd bought for the occasion and walked out the door. His suit impeccable, everything ready, the car he'd called ready and waiting downstairs. Now the fun would really get under way. Les Martin smiled, left his apartment and locked the door.

Beth had everything she wanted just how she wanted it. The meal was almost ready, the music was what she wanted for the event, Stevie Nicks, everything was exactly how she wanted it. She'd spent all day making sure of that. Now he was just waiting for her husband and for her friend. As she was giving everything a last one-over, the phone rang. It was Benny, the doorman, letting her know her guest was here. Beth said to let them up and wondered why Benny had said 'guest' and not 'guests'. She walked over to the front door and waited for the doorbell to ring.

Once it did she opened the door and was visibly disappointed that Brice was not there, "Lester! Come in, please. What happened to Brice? Is everything okay?"

Lester smiled as he put his coat down on the nearest dinning room table as he walked into the condo. "Oh everything is fine with us, but Brice suffers from migraines. They are crippling when he has one and he takes really strong medication for them. There was no way he'd be able to make it. He'll be fine, he always is. Here these are a couple of little 'thank yous' I wanted to give you."

Beth took the bottle of wine, the red rose and gave Lester a hug, "Oh Lester I should be the one thanking you. You have no idea how much our new friendship means to me."

Les Martin returned the hug, took the bottle back from her and walked over to the wet bar where there was a wine bottle opener, "It means a lot to me too Beth. Here, let's open this puppy up and make a toast, what do you say?"

Beth came back from the kitchen with the rose in a small, crystal base, set it on the table and went over to the wet bar as well. She did not see Les mix the powder he'd brought with him into her glass while she was in the kitchen.

He handed her the glass of wine and lifted his own, "Here you go. To a beautiful, blossoming friendship!"

Beth raised her own glass up, smiled and said, "To our friendship!"

It would be another ten minutes before Beth Loomis would be completely knocked out and at the hands of Les Martin.

Steven noticed the marked increase in the media presence that Lou had been talking about. There were now actual sets that reporters from a variety of media outlets would be filing their reports from and, as Lou said, it was clear the varsity team was here now. Steven shook his head, he was ready for it now, but damn if it didn't still shock him to see how many people were out there, media and other people just looking and gawking at the goings on. Why would anyone spend their time just watching and waiting if it was not their profession? He couldn't understand that part and probably never would, people so interested in someone else's tragedy and loss. He told Lou to go to the alley where large deliveries for the building came in. It wasn't something he'd done before, but with so much media attention, it made more sense to go the back way. There were enough black SUVs driving around, that people weren't sure which one was his. At least three were GIC vehicles, so they were identical to the one he was driven in. People still saw him going the back way and came around to try to get their shots, but the space was far smaller than on the front of the building so there were far less cameras and reporters. The SUV drove straight into the garage as the super for the building was waiting for them and trying to keep the media assholes out of the residents' way. This was not a cheap place to live and one of the main attractions, aside from the fact that is was in SOHO, was the fact that the homeowners association made sure the residents' needs were taken care of immediately.

Steven said goodbye to his team, waved at the super as he walked to the elevator and got in the elevator to go home.

He walked through the door, put his SigSauer P226, a gun he'd carried since he'd been a SEAL, in the small drawer by the front door. As he was thinking about it he smiled because he smelled the food in the kitchen, saw the candles lit and heard the music.

He was still taking his coat off when he heard his name being called, but it wasn't Beth calling it was Lester's voice, "Steven! We're in here!"

Steven, now without his coat and tie and with shirtsleeves rolled up walked into the room and stopped dead in his tracks.

There on the sofa was his wife, seemingly asleep, with Lester sitting next to her holding a hand gun to her head as he gave Steven a smile, "Come in, come in! We've been waiting for you for almost an hour! Well, I've been waiting for you for almost an hour, Beth here was out in about two minutes."

He saw's Steven's look of concern, "Oh don't worry, she's completely fine, completely out, but totally okay. I mixed two Ambien tablets in her wine. I needed her for our date tonight, yours and mine, not hers and mine, you see. It's our date I've been working on and preparing for all this time, Beth was what you would vulgarly call a 'prop'; I prefer to think of her as a beautiful side distraction I could use for my work. I have to tell you Steven, I can totally see why you're so crazy about her and, frankly, I can also see why she's, why the world, is so crazy about you."

Steven realized what Lester was before he could say anything else. The smile, the preparation, absolute calmness and lack of emotion in his demeanor and the fact he was a genius billionaire who was just over thirty years old, all fit the profile perfectly. He was standing in front of a Homo *sapiens predator*. With that now established, Steven knew there was a reason for this, there was a logical plan behind it. Lester was clearly not out of his mind and he wasn't some sort of spree or drugged up killer. So before he could do anything, he had to hear what Lester's plan was and based on that start his own plan of action.

He started to move forward, but Lester pulled the hammer on the pistol he was holding to her head before he could move two inches, "Ah, ah, ah, please do not make a single move Steven. Believe me when I tell you that I would have absolutely no problem in pulling the trigger. I think by now you've thought about who and *what* I am and you already know that I would not have a problem doing it because I've already planned every possible outcome with and without me dying, going to jail, escaping, all of it. Believe me Steven, I can think faster than other people, I've always been able to do that, but it hasn't been until this last year that my full charisma and charm, and if I'm to be honest, my looks, have shown themselves through."

Steven, still trying to process all the information coming in needed to buy himself some time and to establish a conversation, even if it was one where the predator was in control, "Alright Lester, I won't move unless you tell me to. Can I have a seat next to my wife while I hear what you have to say?"

Lester chuckled, "Nice try Steven, you're thinking that violence of action will overcome me and give you the edge, huh, which it might, but which you are not going to try at all. You see, the scenario where you do that and I have to respond accordingly is one of my least favorite ones, so I'd rather not try that one.

"So, yes you can have a seat, the two chairs right next to you have been prepared for just that occasion. No lose pillows, no small objects nearby to tempt you. You know, the standards."

Steven put his arms our where Lester could see everything he was doing and moved very slowly into the chair on his left, "Okay, you're the boss, Lester. I'm just sitting down, okay?"

Now Lester's mood and demeanor darkened visibly, his entire countenance and tone changed in a second and Steven saw a glimpse of his true adversary, a glimpse of the predator that Lester was underneath "I will advise you Mr. Loomis, to not be condescending in your tone or in your communication with me. You treat me like an equal and recognize I am not a crazy or drugged up criminal you deal with on a daily basis or I will make you suffer even more than you already have.

"Believe me Steven, I built a billion dollar company and I have hundreds of millions of dollars and hundreds of millions of dollars can get anything done in this world. Anything. Aside from the money, I have also made a few ahh...friendships let's say, these past few months. Friendships that can also get anything done, anything at all."

"But, if we can have a conversation like the two hunters we are, like equals and I can share my story with you, and you follow my instructions to a T, you and your family can go back to what you are dealing with. Beth will wake up a bit hung over in the morning and you will know exactly what happened and can either tell her or not."

His façade of the charismatic Metrosexual genius also came back in a flash, "So what do you say Steven? Can we have a conversation like two adults of intelligence and experience."

Steven now knew he needed to really think about what he was going to say and how he was going to act. He had absolutely no experience dealing with these things, not past what Barlow had shown him, and that situation had not had a direct and immediate threat to him or his family. He was going to have to figure this out on the fly and just go by instincts and what he'd learned from Leonard and Scoma. They were all he had right now.

He lowered his arms, started nodding his head and sat down in the chair, "Alright Lester, let's have a conversation on equal terms. You're right, I think I know what you are and I can see you have just about everything covered, but I can't for the life of me figure out what the fuck you are doing drugging *my* wife and sitting on *my* couch holding a gun in *my* house. You're right,

I shouldn't be condescending with you, but you need to be straight with me and explain what the fuck is going on if we're going to be equals. That was exactly how I would talk if I was dealing with a professional."

Lester's smile was back in full, as was his light-hearted and easy personality.

He gave Steven a small nod in appreciation, "Bravo Steven, bravo. Frankly I wasn't sure if this was going to happen or not because I didn't know if you would be capable of dealing with a mind like mine, like ours, our species. And you've answered that challenge admirably."

He raised his fingers, counting what he was saying while still holding the gun on Beth, "So I have to deduce a few things from that. One, your team has done an amazing job preparing you, two, you have done an amazing amount of research on this, three your experience doing what you've done for so many years spilling so much blood have collectively given you the experience necessary that you now almost think like one of us; or four you simply have a knack for this, an instinct that almost allows you to sense us the way we sense you. *Almost.* Personally I think it's the last one, but it could be more than just one. Oh man, this is going to be good! I don't think this should surprise you too much Steven, but there are a lot of us out there who underestimate you. A lot! But not me, absolutely not. I couldn't, you see. That's how I got to be here in *your* house on *your* couch with a gun pointed at *your* wife"

Steven nodded in frustration, "Yeah, whatever Lester, tell me what the fuck is going on. You said be straight and professional and now you're breaking your own rule."

Les Martin settled down, "Alright, alright, you're right. I think we need to do introductions first. Well, I have to introduce myself. You and Beth and probably your entire team by now, have known me as Lester Allen and those are in fact my names, they're on my birth certificate. But they're my first and middle names, my last name is Martin. See, I knew if I came up with a completely made up name your guys would crack it in no time, but using a variation of my real name, one that could be tracked back to my birth certificate, now, that could work. That and enough money to do a few things. Anyways, my name, the one I've always been known by is Les Martin."

Steven just looked at Martin without saying anything. He could see exactly what the guy was saying. With money to make whatever changes he needed made, Lester Allen would have come across exactly as he had, like some techie who made a ton of money. And his name would be on everything. It was probably the reason Carl hadn't found anything worrisome in the guy's background.

Steven asked the only question that seemed to matter, "You said there was a way to have my wife and I be safe, what is it? Just let me know that and we can get on our way to make that happen."

Les smiled wider, "Of course. I like your thinking, pragmatic, efficient. Well, if we're going to get going there are a few things you need to understand. For any of this to make sense I think you need to understand what my ultimate goal in doing all of this was. I already told you what my goal was. Actually it was you who said it first. My goal at the outset was to be *here* doing *this*, exactly what we're doing, with all of this going on around us." Les used his arm in an expansive flourish signifying everything going on around them.

Les went on, "I mean, could you have believed it? Someone doing this? With everything going on around you, with all the security, all the world's attention on you and your case? But I knew I could pull it off, I knew it. So I got started figuring out how I would do it. There was no way I'd get past your security as some crazy, no way."

Steven interrupted him, "But why? Why the hell would you spend all that effort, the time, the money, all of it? To what purpose? You already explained your ultimate goal, but why was that your goal?"

Les nodded, "Good question. I think I need to explain something else. I have a sort of therapist or mentor who had been helping me. He's a neuropsychologist, but he was that and then some to me. He was the one who saw who I was, what I was. He explained everything and turned me into the individual you see in front of you today."

Steven could not suppress his reaction, "Barlow. You're one of Nigel Barlow's clients or projects or whatever the hell he calls them."

Les's eyes opened wide and he couldn't suppress his reaction either, "Yes! You know him?! I mean, in person?! Oh my god I get it now! That's why he had to leave, to come look into all of this. That's why he told me he'd be gone for a while!"

Les laughed in earnest. He wasn't making fun or being cute, he truly had just put everything together. How ironic that the advice Barlow had given him during their last session had led to this. He had said for Les to be more cautious and patient and by being both he had ended up here. Ironic indeed.

He stopped laughing, but still had the huge smile on his face, "Dr. Barlow was the one responsible for explaining who I was, what I was. You see all my life had been sheer misery until then. As a kid I had all these ideas and impulses. I don't know how else to explain it. I just knew that they were not the same ideas and impulses that other kids my age had, so I thought maybe there was something wrong with me. The impulses got worse as I got older, they became more like obsessions and being older and smarter than most other people my age, I now knew there was something wrong with me.

"So I decided that I would see what it was like to give into these impulses. It was sublime. It felt like I had been reborn, like this was what I was meant to be doing. It didn't make me feel like I was fine, mind you, on the contrary, it confirmed for me that I was a defective person and that there was truly something wrong with me. So I kept to myself, became a loner and poured myself into my other passion: computers."

As he was talking about it Les became more pensive and quiet. It was obvious to Steven that the memories were painful ones for Les. He was explaining exactly what Barlow had explained to him, but from the point of view of his patient or client or project, whatever. This is how they felt growing up. Steven decided to say absolutely nothing and let Les keep going uninterrupted.

Les kept going, "Throughout my life I gave into my ideas and my impulses a few times, all of them as amazing and liberating as the first one, maybe more. I got better at it, so it was something else, besides technology, that I was good at. But with each instance that I allowed myself to give into my impulses, my conviction that there was something wrong with me, that I was a despicable and sad example of a human being, grew and grew. That's why I was a virgin into my thirties, why I didn't have any friends, why I had never even imagined being in a relationship with anybody. But now I am here, somewhere that by all rights I shouldn't be and it was through Dr. Barlow's guidance an advice I made it into your inner sanctum and I made it in the only way I could do it, Beth."

Les was serious and quiet as he explained this, but he was not letting his guard down. Steven could see that whatever little motion Les's body went through as he spoke, his gun remained pointed at Beth without fail. There would be no way on god's green earth that Steven could get the jump on him as long as he never let his guard down.

He remained quiet as Les continued talking. He seemed to read Steven's mind, "Don't even think about it, Steven, I might be blowing my head off, but I will hold this gun perfectly pointed and it doesn't take long to pull the trigger."

Steven held up his hands in a gesture that told Les he would not try anything. Les went on, "So, by the time I was in my thirties I was almost a billionaire, but had absolutely nothing else."

Steven interrupted, not for any tactical issue, but because he was truly curious, "What about family? Your parents?"

Les looked at him with something akin to annoyance, but answered the question, "You mean did they abuse me or did someone else in my family abuse me? No, nobody abused me at all. On the contrary, they were very loving and supportive and they tried to help me to open up and make some friends when I was a kid. As I got older though, they had to admit that there was just something different about me. I was an only child, so they had no child to compare me to.

"Anyways, I just worked and researched and when things got to be too much I gave into my inclinations and felt like crap and like a substandard human being. There are a lot of people I know who have the same kind of lifestyle, alone, quiet, awkward and depressed. These are people who have come to believe that there is something wrong with them, with how they think. So, one of the people I know, a CEO with a technology firm, recommended his therapist, a neuropsychologist named Nigel Barlow. Now, remember that I knew this guy before and the last time I'd seen him he was worse than me. Now he looked great, he actually looked amazing. And his whole countenance was different. He's a tall guy, but you couldn't tell because his posture was horrible, hunched over, head looking down. Now he was standing straight up, looking up, he looked five feet taller. So I give this therapist a call, Dr. Barlow, and told him I was referred by my friend and he agreed to see me and the rest, as they say, is history. It was slow at first, but he knew exactly what to say, how to say it and when to say it. He *knew* my thoughts, how I had grown up, everything before I had told him any of it. He told me he knew because he'd heard the same story before, many times. So I began to open up and he explained everything to me. He explained about the difference between species, about the science and he told me there was nothing wrong with me, my thoughts, my inclinations and my instincts were all what they were supposed to be, not for humans, but for the new species, for *Homo sapiens predator.*"

Steven was glad to be hearing everything because it gave him more information about them in a way that he had never heard it before, but his wife and he were still in danger. He didn't care about himself, he'd been in danger many times before, but he'd be damned if he'd allow harm to come to his wife, "I understand Lester or Les, whatever your name is, but what does any of that have to do with us? Why would you do all of this?"

Les made a an exaggerated sad face, "Steven! I thought you wanted to know about my life. I'm hurt that you're not interested in the details. Besides, if you'd just wait you'd learn everything eventually. But okay, have it your way. I began my own transformation and the more I transformed, the more I allowed my personal inclinations and natural instincts to take over. The same things that gave me anxiety and dread were now setting me free. I told Dr. Barlow and he told me to slow down and to be patient. See, I was finding things easier and easier, once I understood the context for everything and the reasons for it, it really made things simple. But he thought I needed to allow more maturation, more time to fully develop my persona. When I explained how easy things were for me, he told me to be patient and that there would be a way to really test myself, my new skills and my newly found confidence. That was the last time I saw him because he said he had some traveling he had to do to attend to another project. Well, I think we both know what that project was.

"Anyway, I had gotten to where I was by listening to him and by following his advice, so, as hard as it was, I decided I'd be patient and that eventually something would come up that would really test me, challenge me. And we both now know what that was, don't we?"

Steven nodded and was about to say something but Les held up his hand, "I know what you're going to ask and if you keep you shorts on, I'm about to get to it. What I wanted to test was whether I could penetrate your circle of protection. You'd have to be pretty dense and blind not to see that you were surrounded by some of the best security in the world, Special Forces operators most likely. And it wasn't just your team that had an eye on you, it was the *whole world* that was watching everything related to your case. You rival the president or heads of state when it comes to how much attention you have on you. So it was obvious to me what the most difficult challenge for anyone would be. So I started to plan and to move pieces around and here we are."

Steven nodded and listened to everything Les was saying and what he'd been thinking was confirmed for him. Whatever Les was saying as far as Beth and he just waking up with hangovers was a lie. His challenge involved killing him and now that she was in the mix, Beth. He knew that to simply penetrate his security would not satisfy Les, the juice for him was in the hunt and at the end of the hunt there was always a kill. Now that he understood exactly what was going on and what the outcome would be if Les had his way, he needed to figure something out. I would be impossible to do anything from the distance he was currently at from Les. There was just no way he could react fast enough to beat the trigger on the gun, no way. He'd have to see if an opening materialized as things progressed. He was thinking about a couple of things he might to do if nothing opened up.

Les came to the end of his story, "So, like I told you, if you behave, then you and Beth will simply go to sleep, I will be on my way and you both will wake up tomorrow. You can decide if you tell Beth or not, I myself would recommend against it, you know she is still pretty fragile."

Steven had to keep him comfortable, "Yes she is. I was already thinking that way. I'm not sure she'd be able to pull out of this if she knew the truth."

Les smiled tenderly, "Yeah, she talked to me quite a bit and I'd have to agree with you there. So here's what we're going to do, you and I are going to trade places, but I am going to leave this glass of wine here. When you come sit down next to Beth, you're going to drink the glass of wine. I'm going to wait for you to be completely asleep and I will leave the way I came in, sound good?"

Steven nodded, but didn't say anything. He had to come up with something, but he was not sure what that would be. He could see that as he came around the coffee table to the left, Les would move around it to the right, all the while keeping his eyes square on him, gun perfectly trained on Beth. The distance between he and Les was just too great for anything he did to be in any way a surprise. Reaction time was reaction time and the more distance between the two the less quick Les needed to be to do what he needed to. He started to move to the left of the coffee table and as he did he saw the blinds shuddering a little bit. That meant that the sliding glass door to the balcony was open, which never happened. If they went outside they'd close the door behind them, same thing if they came inside. But tonight was a different situation, it was a special night and they had guests coming. Some guests. Still, he kept moving to the left and Les moved to the right.

He smiled at Steven, "Well done. Now don't do anything stupid and we'll be done here before no time."

As he kept coming around Steven kept checking on Beth. He hadn't had a chance to check on her since he came in, he just took it on faith that Les had not killed her, so the first thing he wanted to check was that she was alive and well. As he came around one way, Les moved the other way. Each of them was moving at around the same pace. The next five seconds seemed to go by in slow motion. It was just the human body's natural reaction when there was an overload of stimuli and input. The brain slowed everything down to a speed that it could make sense of everything. For the vast majority of people that meant having enough time to do whatever would save their lives. Like the mom who, while driving, sees a car in the last split second before crashing and is able to stretch out her arm to hold her child back before the airbag deploys. Almost everyone alive had had an instance where mere seconds seemed to stretch into minutes. For someone like Steven, someone who operated in very tense, dangerous theaters of conflict, that had been something that happened numerous times a day. So even though the dynamic was the same, Steven's training and experience allowed him to see what was happening and at the same time make sure that Beth was covered. As Steven continued to the left and Les continued right, the blind trembled as a result of a breeze. It was just an innocuous, natural thing that happened in hundreds of homes and although Les was something different from the norm, he did not have the kind of training that would have kept his attention focused on Steven and Beth. It also had to do with the distance between he and Steven. There was simply no way that Steven was going to get the jump on him. So, when he heard the blinds trembling, he turned his eyes in the direction of the blinds just in time to see a figure getting bigger and bigger. As it was about to hit the screen and the blinds. Steven started to turn as the figure hit the screen, came through it and through the blinds and knocked Les on his back. When he got hit Les squeezed the trigger, but the shot from his gun went halfway up the wall behind the sofa. The gun had a very effective suppressor on it, so it there was just a metallic sound as he squeezed the trigger. As he saw the same thing that Les saw, Steven reacted immediately and dove towards Beth to cover her with his body. Years and years of training allowed Steven to discern each element of the scene as he made each decision about what he needed to do first, what came after that and so on. As he dove towards Beth he kept his eye on Les and on whatever was coming through the screen and blinds. He landed on Beth, felt the shot hit halfway up the wall and immediately began checking on Beth to see if she was hit. Whatever was coming was not coming for him, at least not at first. As he was checking on Beth and through his peripheral vision, he saw what he knew now was a man, dressed in black from top to bottom, disarm Les. Almost at the same time that Steven saw the gun drop he heard what he knew was a neck snapping. Les began wheezing and then convulsing. The stranger rolled off of Les and went to pick up the gun. Steven checked on Beth, making sure she was alive and unhurt. Her pulse was nice and strong and she was in a deep, restful sleep. Now that he knew Beth was fine, Steven got up and was preparing for whatever the guy had planned. He was definitely trained, bigger than Steven and now he had Les's gun. Steven started to get up and saw that the guy was completely unconcerned with him. Was there somebody new on his security team that he didn't know about? It wasn't out of the realm of possibility. If he was new on the team, whoever had picked him had done well. The guy was a total pro, smooth, efficient, no bullshit. He was checking Les's pulse, going through his pockets and pulling out his wallet and what looked like a small calendar booklet. Seeing that the guy was not worried about him in the least put Steven at ease, especially because Steven saw the guy had put Lester's gun on the chair he was next to. The guy finished what he was doing and started to stand up. Steven was waiting for the guy to say something and when he didn't Steven finally spoke up, "Hey, who the fuck you are?"

The stranger looked up and came as close to smiling as he ever came, which still looked more like a wince than it looked like a smile.

When Steven saw him his mouth fell open and his eyes went wide, "Zlk?! Zlk is that you?! What the fuck are you doing here??"

Zlk answered simply with an accent that sounded maybe Western European, maybe Russian, maybe Scandinavian, "I'm watching your six, Steven, just watching your six, like always."

Steven came around the coffee table and gave him a bear hug. Zlk had been a part of the team Steven had commanded and had worked with Steven and his teams at GIC even after he'd left. He also did his own thing. They'd been together in Africa, the Middle East, South Asia, Eastern Europe, too many places, way too many places, to be in the middle of a conflict. Each was one of the only individuals that the other trusted and that trust had been won over many wars, battles, deaths and successes. Each one was also one of the only men that would ever hug the other. It wasn't a macho thing, it was a trust thing. Steven had not seen Zlk for almost five years and had no idea where he might be or what he might be doing. After Zlk returned Steven's hug with a quick 'man' hug, Steven pulled out his cell phone and called Cecil to tell him exactly what happened. He told him to come up with Thurman and Lou and to call the General and have him come as well. He told Cecil to come in normally, without running or looking like there was something wrong. He also told him to come into the building one by one and when the three of them were inside to come up. Benny was going to come up with them, it was standard protocol, so he told them to not give him a hard time, he himself would let Benny know everything was fine so he could get back to his desk. While they waited for Steven's security team, he picked Beth up and took her to their bedroom. He was debating whether to take her to a hospital, but the more time he spent with her the better he felt about her physical condition. There was really no reason for Lester to have lied about what he'd given her; she hadn't really been what he was targeting.

11.

Mikhail Yevgeny Rozlkovich or Zlk (pronounced silk), the lighthouse keeper and guardian of Steven's six, was a legend in just about every place he had ever plied his trade. There were stories from across the globe, most of them true, some wrong and none that came from Zlk himself. Most people called him Chief because his rank while in the SEALs had been Chief Warrant Officer; his friends, his close friends, called him Zlk. The difference between his close friends and the rest of the world was that his close friends called him that to his face; the rest of the world used the name when they shared stories about him, but never to his face, not if they wanted to keep their teeth. After spending 12 years in the US Navy, Zlk became a freelancer. The friendships he had made ensured that he got invitations everywhere, Europe, Asia and from the best Special Forces teams in the world. The Special Air Service (SAS), considered by many to be the best Special Forces team in the world, the GROM from Poland, the GSG9 from Germany, the Spetsnaz from his home country and Eko Cobra from Austria. He had even spent time with the Maori of New Zealand learning their ways. That was about as close to a long-term vacation as he would ever come. Zlk was known for his cold, detached manner, for his efficiency and for his absolute and unquestioned courage. More than anything, Zlk inspired fear in just about anyone he met. Some people thought he was going to rob them, others thought he was going to kidnap them and even the people that knew he was there to protect them, wanted no part of anything he was near because something told them that if there was action, if someone made a move, it would be Zlk who would be there first. He had killed a lot of people and he was in fact cold and efficient in the way he did it. He'd done some things that he was not necessarily proud of, but which he knew needed to get done. As he went on assignments or took on projects, he kept an eye on both Steven and the General and on their families. He did it from afar, without them knowing it. He was in fact covering their six and doing it in a way that only he could.

Steven came back from putting Beth down, "She's going to be out until tomorrow. If she takes anything for sleep, she takes half a pill and this fucker gave her two. She's going to have a massive headache. I can't say thank you enough Zlk, seriously. I was trying to think of a way to take the guy, but I was not having any luck. He was too far for me to make a move."

Zlk gave a quick nod, "No problem. I was also trying to figure out a way to take the guy down alive. I imagined he might have some interesting things to say. He was just planning to walk as soon as you also passed out after drinking the wine with the Ambien?

Steven shook his head, "No, that's what he said, but that's not what he was planning to do. I am certain he was planning on killing us once I passed out, quiet, no mess. At least he was planning on killing me, maybe not Beth, but definitely me."

Zlk nodded, "Okay, then I don't feel as bad."

Steven's face took on a curious expression, "Oh, has something changed that you now feel bad when you take someone out?"

Zlk gave him a thin smile.

On his face it actually looked more intimidating, like a wolf showing its teeth, "Not the way you think. I don't give a shit about the guy's life, not even a little bit. I was talking about killing him without getting info, I was kind of feeling bad that we didn't get to talk to him, but now that you told me what he had planned, I don't feel that bad. Who the hell is this guy and more importantly, how the hell did he get into your house and how the hell does Beth know him?"

Steven explained about Barlow, who he was, how they came into contact with each other and how Les fit into Barlow's world. He started to explain about the little market and how Les and Beth had become friends when the doorbell rang. He paused his explanation and went to open the door. Zlk just stayed seated in the living room. Steven opened the door and saw three intense faces and one scared one. Cecil, Thurman and Lou were standing there ready, even though he'd already told Cecil everything was fine. Benny the doorman was also there and his face was literally white from fear. Steven came out into the hallway and told Benny that there was someone that had come in through the delivery bay, but that he'd done it just to test his security team, something that wasn't entirely untrue. He also told him there might be a couple more guys coming by and that they would also be coming through the delivery entrance just so they wouldn't call the media's attention. He asked Benny if his partner downstairs could wait for them there to let them in. He explained they were just coming to a small impromptu get-together they were having after the exercise was over. Steven saw Benny literally exhale a huge breath of relief and he saw the color come back to his face. He told Steven he'd see to everything. The three security team members were already inside by the time Steven came back inside, Cecil and Thurman were talking to Zlk, Lou was standing off to the side with a look of absolute awe. It would have been kind of cute if the situation were different. Zlk was talking about how things had gone down and letting Steven's security team know where the crack he made it through had been. The reality was that his security team was doing a great job of keeping everything covered, Lester made it into his inner circle the only way anyone could have done it: by being invited into it. Steven thought that he would have to call Carl Gilliam and find out what happened, why he didn't find anything on this guy. Lester had basically explained that already. He used his given name, just a different permutation of it. He had no criminal record and he most likely used an incredible amount of money to change whatever needed to be changed in order to make sure any search would reflect the name he was using. Even then, Carl would still have been able to find a trail without any problem, but again, he didn't change his name, he just changed the order of the names and how he was using them. Zlk was walking the guys through his own actions and as was patently clear, the only vulnerability to their operational security or Op Sec was Steven's personal security Per Sec, in other words, for someone to make it past his security, they'd have to be invited in.

Steven walked back in inside and bumped into Lou on his way to the living room, "Close your mouth Lou, you're letting flies in."

Lou snapped his mouth closed and got intensely flushed, if circumstances weren't what they were it would have been funny. Steven walked into the living room where Zlk, Cecil and Thurman were all seated now and talking about what happened. They all got up to speed on what everyone else knew and by the time the next knock at the door came, everyone knew the same things that everyone else knew. Steven, hands still shaking, went to answer the door, but Lou held his hand out and went to answer the door himself. It was Troy Fielding, the fourth and newest member of Steven's security team. Now that he knew the perimeter security team was engaged, Lou let him inside and

Steven told both he and, Lou to make themselves at home and to feel free to get something to eat or drink in the kitchen. Both men took him up on it.

Once in the kitchen Lou explained everything to Fielding who froze while putting ice into his Coke, "Wait, wait, wait, did you just say that guy in there is Zlk? The Zlk? Are you freaking kidding me?!"

Lou held a finger up to his lips telling Fielding to keep it down, "Isn't it surreal? I've been hearing stories about the guy since I was going through BUDS."

Fielding nodded, "Same here. The guy is a fucking legend, man; I was thinking that maybe he was something the instructors made up to scare us, you know, kind of like the boogeyman."

Steven came over to both of them and let them know what was going on, "Guys, I need one of you to go with Cecil to pick up the General and I need the other one to go with Thurman to pick up Carl Gilliam."

Fielding protested, "I don't know Mr. Loomis, that would leave you completely without cover. Can't one of the twins go by themselves?"

Before Steven could answer, Lou stepped in, "We're the Op Sec team, the Per Sec team is still there and they need to stay out of sight. That's why the commander called us instead of them when everything happened. I imagine you probably called them back too, right boss? To make sure they didn't break cover?"

The kid was learning. Steven gave him a quick nod, "That's exactly right Lou. Besides, even if they were not there I think I'm pretty well covered"

Steve said the last phrase while nodding towards Zlk who was standing by the window, "So please go with the twins and pick them up, will you? I don't care which one goes with whom, but please get rolling."

That's all either man needed to hear. They each went to go get the cars and told the twins they would be downstairs in five minutes and to come down whenever they were ready to go. After about ten minutes, Cecil and Thurman came out of the building. Cecil went with Lou and Thurman went with Fielding.

Once on the way Lou just couldn't keep himself from asking, "Hey C, you did some work with Zlk, didn't you? What was he like? Are all those stories about him true?"

Cecil thought long and hard about whether he wanted to answer the kid's question. Given that Zlk was now in point of fact working with them, it made sense for Lou to know who and what he was talking about when he talked about Zlk.

Cecil nodded, "Alright, I'll tell you what I know, but kid, if you share any of this with anyone I will never trust you again. You've been doing really well and you have an amazing future if you keep it up, but burn me and I guarantee you it will not happen at GIC or spec ops."

Lou looked properly somber and a bit startled by the stern warning. He thought it was just going to be one pro telling another pro a story of the 'this one time' type, but it was clear it would be something more.

Cecil nodded and began, "Yeah, I worked with Zlk twice and I don't know about all the stories about him out there, but I can tell you about what I saw with my own two eyes. The first time we worked together we were on the two teams that were put together for an assignment in Africa. I was on the blue team at that time and Zlk was on the black team."

By telling Lou that both he and Zlk were on SEAL teams identified by colors and not numbers he was telling him they were both members of SEAL team six. Specifically the blue team was an assault team and the black team was a reconnaissance and surveillance team. Cecil explained that by that time Zlk had already worked his way through most of the other teams.

He went on with his story, "Anyway we'd been in Africa for just over two months. Now, you need to know that before we got there two warring factions had called a truce, something that allowed us to set up our forward operating base right where we needed it to be. Otherwise it would have been a hike for us every time we needed to set up an op. We knew that the truce had been bought, that both sides had taken payments of millions of dollars to agree to the truce. But we were late leaving and the two warring factions were ready to get back to killing each other, so we would have to blow up some stuff on the ground instead of taking it with us. What you have to understand is that each side was just about three miles from our FOB or six miles from each other. Between us and one of the sides, there was a small village. All the men from that village had gone off to fight with the faction they belonged to and they had decided to take the fight to their mortal enemies. Anyway, Zlk, the pilot, myself and one other guy were on a Blackhawk on our way back from having finished blowing everything that needed to get blown, when we look down and see that the faction, let's call it team A, that the village was a part of, has been completely overrun. The other faction, team B, about 500 heavily armed men, is now on their way over to the other, team A's, township and in between them and the township is the little village. So we look down a bit later and we see that there are just about thirteen women down in the little village, they couldn't have been younger than seventy years old. They had obviously been left to take care of the babies and small kids, too small to run off or defend themselves."

Lou could sense and hear that the story was actually having an effect on Cecil who was himself a seasoned and well-respected operator. Lou wasn't sure he wanted to hear a story that made Cecil get uncomfortable and sound uneasy. Still, he knew not to interrupt.

Cecil went on, "What you also need to understand is that before we ever got there, these two factions had been going at each other for years, decades and any time either side was able to take prisoners they did not remain prisoners for long. The men were tortured horribly and killed, the women were raped and then killed in a variety of ways meant to entertain the men that held them and the small children and babies were used in some of the most heinous ways you could possibly imagine. Sick stuff you would never believe a human being could do to a small child. They experimented on them, used them for target practice, horrible, horrible stuff. So when we see them down there, we know exactly what's going to happen to them. Remember, the fact that we were in Africa at all was not for public consumption, it had to be an in and out op. So Zlk tells the chopper pilot to land on the backside of the village and to keep the rotor going, that he's only going to be a few minutes. The chopper pilot tells him he's on a tight schedule and that he can't put down. Well, you probably know what happened then. Zlk told the guy if he did not put down where he'd just asked him to put down, when we got back to the base he was going to maim him and make it so he would never fly anything with wings or rotors, not even one of those kiddie rides that take a quarter to ride. And the guy had heard the stories you've heard and knew without a shadow of a doubt that Zlk would absolutely do exactly what he said he was going to do. So the guy puts down and Zlk jumps down with his MP5 and his P226 and tells the rest of us to stay on the chopper. He's the tactical ranking officer, so we all know not to question him or try to ignore him. Then, after a few seconds we start to hear the pop of the MP5, but it's the only thing we hear, there's nobody firing back, it's just the MP5. So after a couple of minutes of hearing the MP5 we started to hear the P226 and then, almost at the exact same time, we all realized what he was doing. He went into the village and put a bullet into the head of the three women and every child and baby there. We all knew why he was doing it and we all knew that none of us, not one, would have been able to do what he was doing. We'd all be too tormented and we'd all be asking too many 'what ifs' to be able to do it. And if we *were* able to do it, we would need counseling for the rest of our lives."

Lou's eyes flew open, "How could he do that?! C, how the hell could he do that!"

Cecil nodded, "I know how it sounds, man, I really do and if someone back home heard about that, Zlk might have been in some deep shit. But you have to remember what would have happened to those kids if he hadn't done that. Notice I'm not saying what 'might' have happened to those kids, because it was a certainty. I was *there* when we first got to Africa and I walked through another village like this one, except for the other side and what I saw there will never, ever leave me. The interpreter we were using told us that what we were seeing was nothing special, that each side tried to outdo each other when it came to cruelty and inflicting as much pain to any member of the other tribe. I had nightmares for years after that."

Lou could just not let it go, "I understand C, but seriously how can someone walk up to a child, a baby and just shoot them in the head? How does somebody fucking do that? You have to be colder than cold to be able to do that."

Cecil was quiet for a while after Lou had finished, but eventually he continued, "You know what kid, the cold ones were the ones who stayed on the chopper, all of us. We were the ones who knew, *knew* with absolute certainty, what was going to happen to them and didn't care enough to do the same thing he did. That has haunted me more than anything else. I felt like I was heartless and like a coward. I almost left the service after that. I've talked to the other guys on that chopper and to a one, they all had the same nightmares, the same instances where they wish they could go back."

Lou was now nodding, he understood what he'd been told much better, but he was still in awe that someone would be able to do that, regardless of what the reason was. Still, he knew that if the same situation came up and he decided to stay on the chopper he would have the same nightmares.

He wanted to know one other thing, however, "Why couldn't you have engaged them or called in air strikes?"

Cecil looked at him like he was dumb, "I just told you that we couldn't break cover, that we weren't supposed to be there at all. And even if we had tried to engage there were 500 heavily armed men against the four of us. We would have made it interesting, but no way to hold them back. We didn't have around the clock air cover to call in strikes either. And before you ask we couldn't have taken them with us because of the Blackhawk's weight limit. It was a fucked up situation all the way around."

Cecil went on clearly still very emotional over the incident, "So Zlk comes back, he has a...a....a bit of blood splatter on the front of his camos. He just jumps back on the chopper, gives the pilot the signal to take off and we take off. He didn't say a word on our way back to the base and we all knew not to say anything to him. When we got back he got off, went to change his shirt and came right back into the preparations for us to leave the place. I went over to talk to him; of all the people that were on that chopper I was closest to him. I started to say something like 'Hey man, I know that had to be hard' or something like that. He stopped in his tracks put down what he was carrying and squared up on me. Now, I'm a SEAL too and like him I'm a member of team six or as it was called back then, DEVGRU, so I'm no slouch when it comes to combat and I will tell you kid, he looked like he actually got *bigger*. I mean *literally*, he looked taller and wider or maybe it was just me and the fact that I felt small in comparison because of what he'd been able to do. Anyway, he looks at me square in the eye and in a really low voice he says, I'll never forget it, he says, 'Cecil, you are my friend and my teammate and I would lay my life down for you, but if you ever talk to me about that again we won't be friends anymore and I will rip your fucking throat out."

Lou was back to being incredulous. Cecil was right, he was by no stretch of the imagination a slouch. Lou knew him to be tough as nails, well trained in close combat and completely fearless, so to hear him now talk about how another man had instilled the fear of god into him was not just unbelievable, it was surreal.

Cecil could tell that was exactly what Lou was thinking, "I know, you'd never imagine it, trust me, I know. I would have never imagined it either, but I will tell you Lou, he would have done it. I have absolutely no doubt that he would have kicked the living shit out of me, 'get out of the Navy for medical reasons' kind of shit. You know how I know he would have done it? Because he *did* do it, not to me, but to someone else on the chopper that day. The guy was one of those nurturing types, always wanting to analyze his feelings or someone else's feelings, always trying to come up with some Buddhist principle to talk about, that kind of guy. Anyway, you could tell that other guys had said something similar to what I'd said and that he'd told them some variation of the same thing he'd said to me. And unfortunately this guy was somewhat new and didn't know about Zlk, well, not everything in any case. So a couple of days later when we're about to take off from the FOB to go back to an airbase Thurman tells me that Pickens, that's the guy I'm talking about, was taken to Germany to get surgery on one of his arms and one of his legs. He also tells me that his face is all fucked up, broken nose, teeth knocked out, detached retina, fucked up royally. The official story was that it was an accident, but everybody knew exactly what had happened. When this guy decided to go on another chopper ride the next morning, Zlk went on the same ride and when they came back Pickens was all fucked up."

Lou was wondering something, "How do you know that it really wasn't an accident? I mean, you know they happen and that they can do that and worse."

Cecil gave him a wry smile, "The only 'accident' that hurt Pickens was his big mouth and the fact that he couldn't just leave things alone. He'd done the same thing before, pestered people until they wanted to kick the shit out of him. Zlk isn't about *wanting* to do anything; if he thinks something needs doing he's going to do it, period. And the reason I know it wasn't an accident is because it was supposedly a helicopter accident, a hard landing to be precise. The only thing was that when the mechanics went to look the chopper over, the pilot shook his head and waved them off and nobody else was hurt, not even a scratch. No, nobody saw it happen, but we all knew. A while later the Naval investigative service team came to talk to us and to do an investigation of the incident. Nobody knew if it was because Pickens had talked or because of something else, but nobody talked to them. When they went up the chain of command, the leader of the op, lieutenant commander Steven Loomis, told them to go fuck themselves and that was that."

Lou whistled under his breath. This was the kind of story that made Zlk a legend and those who had been there almost legends as well. It was the same basic premise in every story people told about him. He was so cold and efficient that people would often wonder if the guy was a psychopath. Most of those that had been there to witness the story in person didn't wonder if he was a psychopath, they *knew* he was that or something else, something there was no name for. That, along with skills that every one of them aspired to have, to *really* have, skills used in action exactly how they were meant to be used. Zlk seemed to be the perfect soldier, the prototype for SEAL team six in any case. There were stories about him and his supposed counterpart on the Army's Delta force facing each other for bragging rights. Well, they might have been bragging rights for the Delta guy, for Zlk it was just a way to test himself through just about the harshest test the US military held for him. The Delta guy had ended up with far less teeth than he'd started with and his thumb and forefinger broken. When people had asked why he'd broken the guy's thumb and forefinger, one of the people who knew about the rivalry and about the coming fight said that every time that the Delta guy had seen Zlk, he'd given him the universal sign for 'OK' with his finger and forefinger. Zlk made sure that he wouldn't be using that particular sign with that particular hand in quite some time. He had not gotten away from that fight without a scratch, however, he got stitched for a gash over his eye, another one on his cheekbone and another one under the other eye, you can still see the scars. There was also the story of how Zlk had taken an M16 into a crowded alley in Ramadi and come out the other side with empty magazines and 19 confirmed kills. People didn't even know he was in there until they heard the gunfire and by the time they'd figured out where it was coming from, it was over. Nobody knew how many medals the guy had and most people theorized that he himself probably didn't know how many he had either. People knew that he'd gotten the silver cross, four purple hearts and two bronze stars and the only reason they knew that was because those were actually reported on the base's newspaper.

After a while Cecil kept going, "My other Zlk story happened when I was in Coronado as a part of the green team and on a training rotation. There were three of us there as trainers, Zlk, Thurman and myself. The other trainers were permanent trainers or they came from the other teams."

Lou smiled and Cecil knew what he was going to say, "I know, right? You'd think at least the military would separate us every once in a while, but nope, they just didn't split us up. Anyway, Zlk had been meeting with the CO of the base and one of the instructors thought it would be a good idea to tell the candidates that whoever won out on the personal defense and close combat exercises they were practicing, would get to face Zlk. I don't think the guy meant it to be anything disrespectful to Zlk and I don't think he wanted to hurt the guy, Zlk himself had made the same offer to previous classes 'win out your close combat exercises and you get to face me'. He didn't mean to hurt the guy or disrespect Zlk but it did both things. There was this big, corn-fed bastard from like Iowa or Wyoming or some such place. He must have been six three or six four, maybe 240 pounds of rock solid muscle. He had obviously had some previous training in the martial arts and he'd been kicking everyone's ass, but once this instructor brought Zlk into it, he became positively obnoxious. So, Zlk comes back from talking to the CO and this big fucker keeps pointing at him and yelling 'I'm coming for you Zlk! I'm coming for you man!'"

Lou winced at what Cecil had just said. He couldn't imagine someone using his nickname in public and in that way.

Cecil smiled, "I know. Some of the guys around him literally put more space between themselves and this guy. They knew he was pretty fucked now, but they didn't know how fucked. None of us did. He finally makes his way through everybody and Zlk gets up, takes his shirt off so he's only in a t-shirt, gets on the mat with him and they begin. This guy was incredibly strong, so it's not like Zlk just put him down right off the bat, he lasted a good five or six minutes, but once he had him in an arm bar, he was done. So the guy taps out, but Zlk doesn't just let him up. He holds him low, raises his fist and cracks him on the side of the face, then he does it again and again and again. By the time he was done with him the guy had four less teeth in his mouth, his eyebrow was split open, his cheekbone was split open, his eye was completely swollen shut and he had a concussion. Bottom line, he kicked the living shit out of the guy even though the guy had already tapped out."

Lou was shaking his head, he had never gotten the shit kicked out of him like that, but he'd seen others beaten down like that, "Why? Why would he do that to the guy?! He probably had to drop and wait for the next class because of his injuries."

Cecil was nodding, "That's exactly what he had to do. After he got helped out and taken to the hospital, Zlk gets in front of the whole class and says something like, 'He got hurt because he was thinking of himself only, not the team and in this business when you are thinking of yourself only, you make mistakes and when you make mistakes you die. Having someone like that be a part of your team puts you and more importantly, the mission, in jeopardy.' Then he goes on to tell them all that no matter what the mission, you need to always remember that you are just a part of a whole, a team. When you need to step up, you step up, but until then you are just a part of a whole."

Lou nodded in agreement and in understanding. The two of them sat without saying anything as they waited for the traffic to move.

Cecil was the first one to say something, "Listen, Lou, I told you all of this because you need to know what you're a part of. That guy is no bullshit. He's got no patience for people who say they can do something they can't or that they know something they don't know. He will slap someone like that down as hard as he possibly can, metaphorically and literally. He will have infinite patience if you simply say 'I don't know' or 'can you teach me'. I don't know all the stories, kid, but of the ones I know most of them are true. For Zlk the Loomis family is his family, so I knew I'd see him sooner or later. As far as I know Steven Loomis is the only officer he held any true respect for and the only one he established a lifelong friendship with. He really is that cold, he really is that good."

Lou smiled, "Yeah C, I got that. He made it past all of us and he saw something none of us had seen, so yeah, I think he is pretty fucking good. I'd never heard the story about Africa, but I have to tell you, that's going to haunt me for a long time, man. Mainly because I know that I could not have done that myself."

Cecil nodded, "Yeah, it haunted me for a long time. It still haunts me sometimes."

By the time they got back with Carl Gilliam, Thurman and Troy were already there with the General. Troy and Lou were posted outside the door to the condo while the five men talked.

As was normally the case, as much focus was given to what came next as to what had happened. Art Goodman was already speculating that Barlow had something to do with it.

Steven wanted to make sure that there was absolutely no doubt as to what had happened and why, "He was Barlow's patient, just like all the other people Barlow made reference to when we spoke last. But Barlow did not put him up to it and I want to make sure that we are all *absolutely* clear about that."

The General wasn't willing to let it go that easily, "How do you know Steven, I mean seriously how could you be so sure."

Steven nodded his head as he listened to Goodman ask the question, "I'll tell you how I know General, because Barlow told me he would leave me alone if I left him alone and now having a better idea about the scope and size of what he's talking about, what his 'work' is, there's no way in hell he would have jeopardized that just to get to me. The other thing that lets me know he had nothing to do with it is because Lester himself told me so and he told me so at a point in time where he didn't have to lie. Barlow told him to slow down and be patient because he was going too far to fast. I bet if Carl does a search out in California where Lester was from he's going to find a whole bunch of people going missing in a short period of time and with something in common, I'm not sure what they would have in common, though. Anyway, there is no way that Barlow would risk whatever it is he's doing on someone like Lester, he had not been counseling him for very long. It's just like we've been speculating, he counsels people who are outcasts, misfits who are often marginalized because of their intellect or, more significantly, their inclinations and predilections."

Cecil interjected before Steven kept going, "I hate to be the one to bring it up, but how are we getting this guy out of here?"

Steven and Zlk had already been talking about it, so Zlk responded, "We're going to have to put him in a container and then take him out through the loading docks."

Steven spoke next, "What kind of container can we use? He's what, about five nine, five ten, so we need a trunk or maybe a recycling bin like the ones they keep for weekly pickups."

Cecil went out the door, "I'm taking the two youngsters to look and see what the building has downstairs."

The General was next, "Alright, if there's nothing downstairs do you have a trunk or a big suitcase Steven?"

Steven thought about it, "We have a pretty huge suitcase he might fit in. We'll have to fold him though. That would be the easiest thing for us to use. We can walk right out the front door with that. Art, do you think we can please call someone and have them go by this mutt's place?"

After getting the address from Steven, Goodman made a call and gave very specific instructions on what to do once the men got there. He sent Travis Pruitt and Victor Demers, the two operators that had gotten inside Donald Riche's rented warehouse and found Tracy Loomis and the rest of the girls and who were also a part of Steven's security team. They were rumored to be able to get into and out of any place, any time and they'd proven they could do it time and time again. Steven had told Goodman that they would probably find Lester's boyfriend and that he'd probably be dead. About 20 minutes later the got the call confirming precisely that. Goodman told the two men to find a trunk or suitcase to remove the man from Lester's place. They found an extra large suitcase that seemed to have been set aside by Lester for precisely that purpose given that it was lined in plastic. Goodman gave them a few more directions and hung up. He told the group what they'd found and about the suitcase.

Steven needed to speak up, "I'm not sure how we do it, but we need to find Brice's, that was his boyfriend, we need to find his family and let them know he's gone. He's not involved in any of this, aside from having hooked up with this asshole."

Carl nodded, "Done. I will figure something out. Maybe I'll plant a missing persons report in the police and FBI database.

Don't worry about it Steven, I will make sure that if he has any family, they know what happened to him."

Now that the cleanup was figured out they needed to get to the more pressing and important question, they all knew it, but it was the General who spoke up, "Now that we have that taken care of, what are you going to do about security Steven? I mean obviously this guy made it in the only way he possibly could have, so the security is and has been top notch."

Zlk needed to interject, "It really is Steven. I probed a few points and they were all covered. If this guy doesn't get invited in, he simply would not have had access. The fact that he knew that and that he was able to come up with an effective plan and to have that plan executed is surprising and I think it speaks to what these individuals seem to be able to do."

Steven was nodding, "I agree, there's really nothing else to be done security-wise. I will not allow Beth or anyone else in the family to 'make friends' with anyone they come across. I don't think it will be an issue for my in-laws; they're pretty private people and keep a close counsel. Their friends have been their friends for a long time. No, it's Beth I'm going to have to worry about on that score.

Zlk interjected, "For starters you're going to have to decide what you're going to tell her about all of this. As far as she knows Lester was her friend and he came over, that's it. She's probably not going to know anything else."

Steven seemed caught off-guard by the question, "I hadn't thought of that. You're probably right, she probably fell asleep before she could figure out there was anything wrong. I guess I'll have to tell her after she wakes up."

Zlk shook his head once, "Why? I don't think that's a good idea. If you are able to just tell her that she drank a bit too much or that she passed out, I think that's what you should tell her, Steven. She's probably pretty shredded right now, right?"

Steven nodded, Zlk went on, "And if you tell her the truth you might send her into a depression. That's not the kind of distraction you need right before your trial."

Goodman also spoke up, "He's right Steven. There's absolutely no additional value to having her know what happened. Her security now is going to be as tight as possible and this monster is gone. The reality is that it depends on whether you believe Barlow, Steven. If you think he had nothing to do with this and you think he'll keep his word then there really is no reason to tell Beth about any of this."

Steven thought about it and ultimately agreed with Zlk and the General. The truth was that he had been thinking the same thing. The only thing he needed to figure out was what he was going to tell Beth when she woke up, most likely tomorrow.

He nodded and looked at the four men around him, "Okay, so let's get this garbage out of here. I don't know where Travis and..."

Goodman interrupted him, "Don't worry about that we'll take care of it. Is there a large suitcase or trunk or box they can use?"

Steven thought about it and shook his head as he could not think of anything when he suddenly looked up, left the room and came back with a large trunk, "This should be more than big enough to fit him into. Beth keeps the kids' baby clothes, a lot of her old sweaters and clothes from her high school days in it. It sits under the bed because after Tracy, it's the only place big enough to hide it."

The trunk was about four feet by three feet by two feet tall, it was huge. Zlk shook his head, "Damn, that is a big trunk to keep old clothes in."

Steven nodded, "Don't I know it. I've been telling Beth we can take it clothes to storage, but she won't do it. She says she needs to have access to them. But I think she just feels better having the stuff under her constant watch."

He cast his eyes down and lowered his voice as he continued, "It has Tracy's clothes, cheerleader uniform, costumes, that kind of thing. She will never let it out of her sight now. I put the clothes in three big suitcases and under the bed, so take this thing and make it disappear."

Cecil and Thurman took the trunk and dragged Lester over to the foyer.

As the two of them watched this happen, Goodman lowered his voice and spoke to Steven and Steven only, "Steven, I will take it from here. You don't need to be worrying about this right now. Take the weekend with Beth, go see a movie or have brunch or whatever you want. You need to be clear for what's coming, son, you really do."

Steven nodded, "I know I do, believe me I do. And I don't have any problem doing it Art, seriously, but you can't ask me to just forget about this. You know that because you trained me that way. Besides, I want to talk to Zlk. But I promise I'll do it over brunch or breakfast and I promise I'll try to disconnect as much as possible."

Zlk was over by the window, drinking a glass of water, looking down at the media circus and across the street at Steven's security team and shaking his head at all the clowns with microphones. The team was optimally positioned to cover the house, had parabolic mikes and night vision optics. They also had what looked like a CheyTac sniper rifle. It was about as good as security got. He hadn't been bullshitting, if Steven hadn't invited the son of a bitch into his life and into his house, there's just no way he makes it in, no way in hell. Well, he'd done what he came to do and he needed to get on his way. He did not like to rush into a new assignment, although the current job was an established client and scenario.

He walked over to where Steven and Goodman were talking and once they were done talking went to say goodbye, "Well,

I've done what I came here to do, gentlemen. I will be on my way now, I have a project I'm starting."

Steven shook his head vigorously, "No way. You're staying here, at least for the weekend. These guys are going to be busy for a while and I need backup."

Zlk went to say something, but Goodman interrupted him, "You can take the company's plane to wherever you are going. No stops, no changing planes and you can go anytime day or night. And I can call your employer Kwait Energy, correct?"

Zlk was always impressed at the information the General had access to. He could have told the General that his client had a fleet of planes and would make as many as he needed available to him, but he kept his mouth shut. The truth was that he felt good being wanted, not for his unique skills, but because of a friendship. Steven had more than enough people to back him up if he were to need it; Goodman had more than 20,000 employees around the world in various assignments. If he wanted to he could put a hundred men around this building. No, what Steven wanted was a friend, something that was probably very rare given the circumstances, someone he could trust without question and in the security field that boiled down to four people the Twins, Art Goodman and most of all Zlk. And the dangers of allowing people into your life that you had not known for years and years became dangerously apparent tonight.

Zlk smiled, "Well, I suppose I could hang around a couple of days if you're willing to lend me one of your planes General."

Goodman smiled, "Anywhere you want to go. Just call me directly and I'll have one fueled and ready an hour after."

Zlk turned to Steven, "Well, I guess I'm staying. I need to find a hotel though, I checked out of mine already."

Steven was once again shaking his head, "Hotel? You're staying here, man. We have two rooms not being used right now. Here, follow me, I'll put you in Chris's room; just like you, he loves models."

Zlk walked into the room and noticed that there were in fact about two dozen models around Chris's room. They were obviously not put together by Chris alone; they were painted with an air brush and put together expertly.

Zlk was impressed, "Looks like Chris and I are not the only ones who enjoy models."

Steven nodded, "Alright, I confess, I enjoy putting them together enormously. They allow me to get away for a bit, I don't know how else to describe it. They calm me down."

Zlk's smile widened, "You don't need to describe it at all, I know exactly what you're talking about. They calm me too. Do you suppose there's something about what we do that primes us for it? Something that makes us vulnerable to models?"

Steven shook his head slowly, "I don't know, honestly, but I just met a professor in forensic psychiatry. We could ask him."

They stayed up and drank beer and caught up with each other's lives. They had not seen each other for five years and each of them had no friends outside of the people they worked with. In fact Zlk had no other friends aside from Steven and Art Goodman, they were the only two people he would be willing to trust implicitly. Cecil and Thurman Meeks were not quite friends, but they were people he'd worked with and trusted, the other two guys, Lou and Troy, he didn't know at all. He'd have to do some research and find out who they were. They finally went to bed at three o'clock in the morning.

12.

The next day Steven opened his eyes at exactly six thirty. He had been programmed to wake up at that time for years and his body simply followed the way it had been programmed. Beth was not next to him and he could hear dishes in the kitchen. He hurried out of bed, put a robe on and went to find his wife. When he did he felt horrible for her. She looked like hell. She had bags under her eyes, her make up was all ruined and her hair was completely disheveled.

When she saw Steven her expression reflected the massive hangover she was probably feeling, "What in the hell happened last night, Steven?!"

Steven had thought about it and believed that Beth was strong enough to hear the truth; he just needed to figure out a way to tell it to her, "Well, Beth we..."

Beth interrupted him, "No, you don't have to tell me. I know exactly what happened. I drank too much, didn't I? I knew when I served myself the second glass of wine, red wine no less, that I would be sorry because I hadn't eaten all day and oh god, am

I sorry. That and...Oh my god! What happened to Lester?! I am sooo embarrassed Steven. What happened to him?"

Steven did something he did not do often at all: he changed his plan. Hearing Beth talk like there was absolutely nothing wrong, nothing aside from the embarrassment of passing out while her friend was over, was all he needed to hear.

He still tried to be as honest as he could, "Well, when I got home he was sitting on the couch and you were passed out. He explained things and we talked for a little while. Then he had to leave."

Beth ran both hands through her hair, "Oh my god, Steven, I have to go by the store and apologize. Shit, the first invitation to come to dinner and I act like some sort of lush!"

Steven kissed her head, "Well, you're going to have to wait for a while, he and Brice left this morning. They're going on a trip together."

Beth smiled for the first time, "That's really great! He didn't tell me at all, maybe he thought I'd slip and say something to Brice. Maybe Lester will pop the big question while they're traveling. And maybe he'll give me another chance and come over for dinner. Where did they go?"

Steven shook his head, "I don't know. I think they're just going to do some wandering around in Europe, maybe Asia. Lester didn't say exactly, just that they'd be gone for a while."

Beth smiled again, this time after taking three Advil with a glass of water, "Well, good for them. I bet they want to get away from this place with everything going on and all those vultures chasing us all over the place. And god knows Lester can afford traveling for as long as he wants, he has his own private plane you know."

As they were sitting at the kitchenette table drinking the coffee that Steven had made, Zlk came wandering down the hall.

When Beth saw him her eyes flew open and she actually yelled, "Mikki?!?! Oh my god, what are you doing here?!"

She went over to him and gave him a tight hug, which he returned. As much as he wanted to deny it, it really did feel good to be around friends and to feel welcomed by them. If he ever found a woman, which was doubtful, he wanted one like this one: strong, faithful, committed.

Beth walked over to Steven pulled on his earlobe, "What the hell?! Are you trying to give me a heart attack or what? He didn't say anything about you being here Mikki. What are you doing here? How long are you going to be here? Where are you staying?"

Zlk held his hands up, "Whoa there, I'll answer your questions if you let me. I'm here on my way to a project and wanted to check in on you guys. I've been watching all this mess on the TV and thought you might need a friend. I'm only here today and tomorrow, I leave tomorrow night; and I'm currently staying in Christopher's room, but I'm thinking of leaving this morning."

Beth shook her head, "Ugh, what is it with you men? Always wanting to run off. No, you will stay here Mikki and you will let me make you some breakfast."

She did and they all three ate and talked until almost noon.

They Skyped to talk to the kids and to Beth's parents and when Bethany saw who was there she almost went through the screen, "Uncle Mikki! Oh my gosh, I can't believe you're really there!"

Bethany had been almost four, when she had seen Zlk last, but her intelligence was far above that of a four year old and for some reason the little girl had bonded with the bear-sized man.

He smiled as wide as he ever did, "Hey pretty B! How are you baby girl! I missed you a lot you know."

Bethany smiled when she heard that, her uncle Mikki was the only one that called her 'pretty B' and she loved it, "I missed you a lot too! I got your birthday cards and your presents. Thank you."

And with that they were off and running. They talked for thirty minutes about all kinds of things, where Zlk had been, what countries, what Bethany had read, everything that was important to each of them. She reminded him about when he went to her soccer game and how her soccer coach had been yelling really mean things at the girls that didn't play well and how her uncle Zlk had walked over to the coach and said something in his ear and the coach was so sweet and encouraging after that. Steven had not told told her that Zlk had assured the coach if he kept yelling at the girls that way it would be him yelling like a little girl instead of at little girls after the game. One look at Zlk and the coach understood it wasn't a threat, it was a fact. He was voted most encouraging coach at the end of the year. Bethany wished her uncle Zlk had been there. He told her about his dogs and showed her a picture of them. Steven sat and watched and listened and loved hearing his daughter so ready to move on, to remember she was still a little girl. He also loved the fact that she had bonded with a good man, a man that watched out for her family and who would lay his life down for her and her brother if their father was not there for some reason. It gave him considerable comfort to know his family was being watched over by what he considered to be one of the three most skilled operators in the world. And he only included the other two to have a margin of error, but what he really believed was that there was no better spec ops operator in the world. None.

Steven got up, went to serve himself a cup of coffee and was reminded of the size of what he was dealing with when he saw a pair of helicopters, trying to peer into their condo. He closed the curtains and placed a call to the General, who then placed a call to the police commissioner. Within fifteen minutes, there was a police chopper telling the other two choppers to move along or set down or spend the weekend in jail. Steven took a shower and while he was under the water he thought about the last 24 hours and marveled at the fact that even though he'd seen what he'd seen, that his wife and he had almost been murdered, it looked like it might turn out to be a decent weekend. That more than anything else amazed him, what the human mind was able to assimilate and incorporate into its normalcy was truly beyond measure. He wondered whether his mind was going to need to adjust to a new normalcy for the rest of his life and hoped against hope that it would not be the case.

Each of the lawyers trying the case did something different over the weekend before the trial. All of them knew that, regardless of the outcome and what happened during the trial every one of them would be changed by it. And without thinking about it each of the attorneys trying the case spent the weekend making plans with loved ones, thinking of places they'd go after the trial or bared their soul to someone, their families, a special someone. Every one of them did what they did just in case, none of them would acknowledge it if asked, but all of them spent their last weekend before the trial doing the things they thought they might not be able to do after the trial. As much as they, the Loomis and the Delaney families, Beth's parents, wanted to ignore them, the media had risen to a fever pitch. Every outlet, online and offline, was represented and they all wanted to out-position each other and get an angle, a shot, anything that was different than the other channels. It got to the point of being obnoxious. Add to that the level of police coverage the mayor had deployed for the beginning of the trial and you had the makings of a truly never-before-seen level of chaos and that was saying something given that it was New York City. Detectives Robert Grady and Mark Mullins of the NYPD homicide squad and the two detectives that had been in charge of the Donald Riche case and had been there at the warehouse to process the crime scene after the girls had been found, knew they would be the first witnesses that the prosecution was going to call. They needed to establish the chronology of everything that happened and how Steven had followed the case, had seen his daughter, all of it. And while it would not change their lives as much as the lives of the attorneys trying the case, their lives had most definitely changed. They'd both received commendations and promotions. Grady had finally made sergeant of detectives and Mullins had been put in charge of the vice squad, so yes, their lives had definitely changed. They both also had book deals waiting for them after the trial.

BERN, SWITZERLAND

Nigel Barlow had just gotten off the phone and he was in a foul mood. The promise of one of his clients doing something momentous had turned into a true fiasco. Well, the client would not need to be dealt with as that had been done by Loomis's security team. But he had been close and that, thought Barlow, would have been disastrous. Although he would never articulate it as such, Barlow considered Loomis to represent the only version of humanity that could pose *Homo sapiens predator* any sort of challenge or risk. And he needed that because as things unfolded they would need to stay sharp and not get too complacent, which is what tended to happen if the other side was completely outmatched. Barlow needed Steven Loomis to keep his enterprise sharp and while Loomis did not yet acknowledge, nor would he for some time, that his life had now taken a very different path than he had ever imagined, Barlow knew that would be the case. He knew Loomis would simply not be able to know about what was going on, people dying or worse at the hands of a *Homo predator* and simply turn a blind eye. It was not how the man was built and Barlow had said as much when the two of them had spoken last. For the time being, however, Barlow needed to get word to Steven Loomis that he had had nothing to do with the unfortunate events of this weekend. Barlow needed to make sure that Loomis knew his word was sacrosanct, whatever else might be true, his word was rock solid. He was thinking of a way to get a message to Loomis when an idea finally struck with the unexpected force that the simplest ideas seemed to pack. He would send Loomis a message by courier. Before cell phones and smart phones and email and the rest of it, this was how high powered people messaged each other. Ironically it seemed to be the only way they could now use if they wanted to ensure that the message would not be intercepted. Barlow was feeling a bit better about things, not only had he thought about a way to get the message to Loomis, he had also come to realize that Loomis would most likely already know that Barlow had nothing to do with his client's escapades, otherwise he was certain that some of his assets would have already detected someone probing their network. There was nobody probing the network because Loomis was keeping to his word and he knew Barlow had not broken his. In this instance, however, there just wasn't any room for speculation or ambiguity. Nigel Barlow needed Steven to *know* he hadn't been involved. He called his assistant Cole and got the process of sending a message via courier under way.

After giving Cole instructions Barlow turned on the television and changed the channel to CNN. He wanted to see whether there was any coverage of a disturbance at the building where Loomis's condo was located. There was nothing, just the same coverage that had been going on since the beginning. He was about to turn the television off when the picture changed and a new story came up. The story was about how a televangelist had galvanized the public to protest and stand up against what he thought to be sinful and dangerous behavior. Barlow decided to leave the television on for a bit longer. The story went on to say that the reverend J.D. Garzen had a massive following with his Ministry of Light church. Barlow watched with some amusement as the man delivered an impassioned sermon where he asked his followers for money to help combat the evil that lurked in the heart of Steven Loomis and those like him. Even though Barlow had absolutely no patience for organized religion and even less for Christian fundamentalists, he could not pull himself away from the television. He could see very clearly that the man was no more a follower of Christianity or any other religion for that matter, than Barlow was himself. Even so, the man had something that commanded attention, a certain magnetism or charisma. He was fat and he was ugly and clearly had no sense of fashion, but his audience, every member of his congregation was absolutely enthralled with him; they were hanging on every word he said. If he could have that effect on Barlow who knew about such men and the weaknesses they tapped into, imagine what effect he could have on other audiences, audiences beyond the pulpit, beyond the creepy and strange world of televangelists. Barlow suddenly had a new project he could sink his teeth into. He would find out everything he could about this reverend Garzen and then perhaps come up with a way to use his talents. Barlow knew that eventually the enterprise would need a public face; someone that could speak for the entire organization in a captivating way and that could engender support from a wide variety of audiences. It was the type of assignment that would have been perfect for a publicist or PR consultant, had theirs been a normal organization. But it wasn't, was it, theirs was an enterprise that required a different skill set, one that Barlow knew was going to be difficult to find. At least he'd thought it would be difficult to find before he heard reverend J.D. Garzen breathing fire and brimstone down on his congregation. Yes indeed, reverend Garzen could be very useful indeed.

SUNDAY

On Sunday evening Beth, Steven and Zlk had a dinner of filet and lobster, a last treat before the trial got underway. After dinner each of them had a small glass of liqueur, Bailey's for Steven, Amaretto for Beth and Midori for

Zlk. The stereo was playing soft jazz and the three of them were talking about common experiences, current events, sports, light conversation. They all knew what was coming and wanted to keep it light the night before the trial. The phone rang and Beth and Steven immediately looked at each other. It was the landline, so they knew it had to be Benny calling from downstairs and that was completely unexpected for both of them.

Steven stood and answered the phone, "Yeah Benny."

Benny responded, "Mr. Loomis, there's a guy down here that says he's a courier. He has an envelope."

Steven thought about it, "Thank you Benny, can you please sign for it. And if you could be good enough to bring it up I would really appreciate it."

Benny agreed on both counts and was at their door five minutes later. Steven gave him a nice tip and close the door, but did not go back to Zlk and Beth. Instead he opened the letter by the front door. It was what he'd assumed it was and from the person he assumed would send it:

Steven,

I wanted to send you a note to say that I am sorry for your troubles this past Friday. I also wanted to let you know I have kept to my end of our bargain and that the individual who gave you such problems was not sent by me, not intentionally in any case. Young Les was a client of mine and misunderstood my advice to be patient and look for a project that challenged him more meaningfully. Fortunately it appears you and your security have dealt with Mr. Martin very efficiently indeed. I wanted to make sure we were both clear that our agreement is still in effect. Good luck with your trial.

Kind Regards, Nigel Barlow

Steven finished reading the letter, crumpled it up and put it in the bottom of the garbage in the kitchen. He would have to find a moment to tell Zlk about it when Beth wasn't around and he'd have to come up with a story about who had written and sent the note via courier. When he got back outside to the balcony where they were sitting he got the chance to tell Zlk who had sent the note, Beth was in the restroom.

Zlk was about to say something about it when Beth came back from the bathroom, "So, what was that all about?"

Steven smiled, "Just some of the guys at work sending me a note to say good luck. They used some pretty foul language in it, though, that's why I didn't save it."

Beth shook her head, "Damn, you can take the men out of the SEALs, but you can't take the SEALs out of the men."

They all chuckled and went back to talking about mundane things. About an hour later Beth stood, gave Zlk a hug, said goodbye and went to bed.

Once she was out of earshot Zlk finally got the chance to say what he'd wanted to say to Steven, "You know Steven, you're going to need to decide what your plan is for after the trial. I mean security-wise. I don't think you want to make living like you are now something permanent, do you?"

Steven shook his head, "No, I don't. Honestly Mik, I'm hoping that after a while people will just get tired of the whole thing and go on to something else. There are other things happening in the world you know."

Zlk shook his head, "You're the biggest game in town brother. Maybe you forget because you are so involved, but this is something that will affect humanity, not just here, but around the world."

Steven shook his head at that, "Oh c'mon man, seriously? I thought you hadn't bought into all the hype."

Zlk responded, "See, that's how I know you're so close to it that you've lost perspective. Steven, we are in the United States of America, you are defending yourself by claiming that there is another species of human sharing the planet with us. Regardless of the outcome of the trial, the conversation has gotten started. There are people talking about this and arguing and doing work on the science all over the world. Like it or not what you've done has and will definitely affect how human beings see each other and will establish the reality that there is another subspecies."

Steven was quiet for a couple of seconds, Zlk was right, he had lost some perspective on how big his case actually was, "So you're saying that I will never be able to get back to a normal life? That my family and I are screwed?"

Zlk shook his head, "No, that's not what I'm saying at all. I actually think that once the other people doing work on the science come up with different findings and other people begin to use the science in their trials, which you know they definitely will, I think people will move on. I'm just saying that until they do that, you need to think about security and how you want to handle it, that's all."

Steven hung his head, "Sorry about that, I'm just on edge man, I thought I had it under control, but I guess not."

Zlk smiled as he stood up getting ready to leave, "Are you joking with me? I am amazed you are not bald by now. I would have lost all my hair by now."

Steven smiled as he stood to say goodbye to his friend, "Yeah, right, you, lose your hair? Mik, I think you could do a tour of hell itself and not bat an eye. Sheesh, lose you hair...!"

Zlk nodded, "You are right, I could do a tour in hell, I actually have done a tour in hell. But that's different than having everyone on the planet looking at me and my case. That, I think, is more than hell, I think it takes more balls, yes?"

Steven nodded, "I guess. Zlk, I can't tell you how good it is to see you and how much I appreciate you watching my six, man. I think it is funny how things work out. You're the only person I ever fully trusted to watch my six and here you are again, watching my six. I wouldn't be here if it wasn't for you, Beth wouldn't be here, so thanks man."

Zlk shook his head as they hugged, "Do not even say it, Steven, we are brothers, all of us, and that's what we do.

Steven walked him to the door, "Where are you off to?"

Zlk rolled his eyes, "Africa, again."

Steven smiled, "Somalia?"

Zlk gave him a wry smile, "You know I can't say, but yeah, something like that."

The two men hugged one more time and Zlk got on his way downstairs where Lou was waiting in the SUV. He was pleased to see that the other guy, Troy, was stationed in the lobby and was all eyes and ears. Before Zlk got in the truck he looked up at his friend who was in the balcony looking down at him. He hoped he was doing the right thing leaving Steven and Beth. Their security team really was the best he'd seen, but as he'd found out, even they could be penetrated. Well, not much he could do about it now, he would have to trust that their security team would keep them safe. For his part he was planning to go to the project he had, make sure that everything the client was paying for got on the way exactly as planned and then he would come back to help his friend if he still needed it and Mikhail Yevgeny Rozlkovich was almost certain that he would.

On their way to the airport Lou and Troy did not say much, they didn't know quite what to say.

Finally Lou spoke up, "Uh, Chief, I can't tell you how awesome it is to be sitting here with you, even if it's just taking you to the airport. A lot of the guys I know think you don't really exist, that you were made up to scare the younger guys."

Zlk did not respond right away, he wasn't being an asshole, he just simply tried to limit conversation with people he didn't know to pleasantries like the weather or a good movie. Still, the kid seemed to know what he was doing and, even more significantly, Steven had trusted him with his own life. Even so,

Zlk would try to limit the extent of the conversation and would take advantage of it to communicate a point of his own.

He looked at the kid's eyes in the rearview mirror as he answered, "Well, it was good to see my old friend and to help him with this. I've seen how you conduct yourself while on the job and I'm impressed, but you still have some things to learn, things nobody can teach you, things you have to learn through experience. What's your name again?"

Lou was smiling; if he could have his smile would have been from ear to ear. He had just been told by the most accomplished and feared operator in the world that he was impressed with Lou's work.

He nodded as he responded to the question, "I'm Lou Werner Chief."

Zlk looked at Troy directly since he did not have a rear view mirror, "And you, what's your name?"

Not quite as in awe as Lou was, Troy's response was less eager, "My name is Troy Fielding Chief, it's nice to meet you."

Zlk nodded, "It's nice to meet both of you and as I said just now, I'm impressed with the work you are doing as security for the Loomis family. That said, however, I want you both to know a couple of things. First of all, the reason instructors use me to scare new candidates is because I have no patience whatsoever for incompetence or showboating or acting like you are a one-man show. And when I say I have no patience, I don't mean I will scold you or reprimand you or just not work with you, I mean I will beat the living shit out of you without batting an eye. I've done it, more than once. Second and most important of all, Steven Loomis and his family, Beth and the kids, are among the only people on the face of the earth for whom I have feelings of friendship and care, they are in fact family to me. That means, gentlemen, that when it comes to their wellbeing I have even less patience for all the things I just mentioned. I want you to know that if any harm comes to Steven Loomis or anyone in his family as a result of your incompetence or showboating, I will hunt you down and I will hurt you in a way that you won't come back from. I'm not talking about something like what happened this weekend, you guys were not responsible for that, you did your job as well as it could be done. I'm talking about a situation where you let something by or you fall asleep at the switch. Believe me when I tell you that I will hunt you down to the gates of hell if I have to, but I will eventually find you. I will make it my life's work to find you. Now, do you both understand what I just said?"

Both Lou's and Troy's eyes were open wide and their faces now had a somber expression. Yes, it would be safe to say that they both understood the implications of what the man had just said and yes, they both knew that he would indeed find them wherever they went if they failed to protect what was in essence his family.

Zlk saw that his warning had had the desired effect.

He wanted to make sure, however, that if these guys had any concerns or needed anything, they wouldn't be too scared to contact him, "If you do your job though, I will also not forget it."

He passed a small piece of paper to Troy, "Here, that is an email address where you can send a message. It is not encrypted or secure, so watch what you send on it. If you need anything to help do your job here better, just send a number I can call you at. If it can be a secure line, all the better, but even if you can't find a secure line let me know where to call you. I'm sure GIC has plenty of secure lines you can get a call on, probably some encrypted cell phones too. And just like I told you I have no patience for incompetence, I have infinite patience for people who acknowledge they don't know something and ask for help. People like that I will help as long as I need to and in every way that I can. Better to ask a lot of questions if you're not sure of something, even if they seem dumb or redundant. You know what the alternative is, so if you have a question ask it."

The smile was back on Lou's face, although not quite as effusively as it had been and now Troy himself had a grin on his face. Both men knew that the list of people who could reach out to Zlk was probably in the single digits and now they were part of that list. It was not something they could put on their resumes, but it definitely was something they could mention in an interview and in the world of international security and intelligence, being one of the very few people that could get a hold of him would most definitely make an impression on whoever was interviewing them.

Lou simply nodded and said, "Thanks Chief. Will do."

13.

On Monday, May 12th at 8:00 am two hundred and fifty potential jurors filed into judge Newman's courtroom. Chairs had been made available for those who did not get a seat on one of the benches, nobody outside of those people directly involved in the case was allowed in the courtroom. Judge Newman had allowed a few of the more prominent media outlets to have a camera set up, but only the cameraman would be in the courtroom and he would stand behind his camera. Other than those few individuals, the prosecution and defense teams, Beth was the only other person not involved in the case allowed in the courtroom. Even with the chairs set up, however, approximately 50 people had to sit on the benches outside and would take a seat inside as soon as someone was eliminated.

Judge Newman got down to business without much preamble.

He began by having his clerk call the case to order "On the matter of the State versus Steven Loomis, case number NY-2438765, appearances."

The prosecution team stood, "Bart Logan and Melanie Farris for the people."

Next the defense stood, "Andrew Willis, Max Zeidler and Raymond Gretche for the defense your honor."

Newman now addressed the courtroom, "Ladies and gentlemen let me begin by thanking you for being here. Your service in the matter at hand will be absolutely invaluable. In this case, the defendant has been charged with first-degree murder. The prosecution will explain the elements of that crime during their opening statement. I think we can all agree that the case that is before this court today is most unusual. It is clear that the circumstances that bring the defendant and the prosecution before this court are tragic and that the approach that the defense has chosen to take is also most unusual and unconventional. I think it proper at this point to bring up the issue of the media coverage. I am well aware that this case, as well as other cases which may have some bearing on this case, have been covered extensively by all forms of media. Those of you that are selected to serve on this jury will be admonished as to how to consider this as you deliberate. Until then, however, I am going to ask that while you are part of the jury pool you avoid talking with any member of the media at all. We will begin this process by asking that twenty-four of you take the seats here to my right in the jury box. These twenty-four individuals will be questioned by both the prosecution and the defense. This questioning is meant to allow both sides to select those jurors that they believe will best serve in this case. The reason we need twenty-four jurors is because we will need twelve for the jury and twelve to be alternates. Normally we only need between two and four alternates, but because of the high profile of this case and the fact that calling a mistrial because we don't have sufficient alternates to fill the jury would cost tax payers millions of dollars, we're going with twelve alternates.

"Whether you are selected or not does not reflect on you personally. Each side has their own idea of what their ideal juror will be and will select the jury accordingly. Twelve of you will be selected for the jury and twelve will be selected as alternates."

Newman turned to address the attorneys, "Counsel I think that perhaps we could streamline the process if we can agree on some general questions for the entire jury pool."

All attorneys were in agreement with the judge's suggestion because unlike in most instances where potential jurors would try to get out of serving on a jury, most of the people on this jury pool would love to be selected. After a brief sidebar meeting between the judge and all the attorneys the judge proceeded to ask the questions they had agreed upon. The first question the judge asked was whether they had heard about the Donald Riche case. Every hand in the courtroom went up. The judge then asked whether after hearing about the case they had formed an opinion regarding Mr. Riche. Seven hands went up. All seven individuals were dismissed by the judge after listening to them explain in various ways that Riche was a depraved psychopath that had gotten what he deserved. The judge then asked the same question about the case that they had been called to serve in. This time twenty-two hands went up. The judge also asked them if they had formed an opinion regarding Mr. Loomis as a result of what they had heard or read about in the news or online. Six hands went up. Five of them were dismissed after explaining that Loomis had done what he did out of revenge or that Loomis had lost his mind because of what happened to his daughter. One individual was allowed to stay. She had explained that she believed that Mr. Loomis was just a regular guy that had been put in an extraordinary situation, but that he seemed to be in his right mind. The judge knew she would most likely end up being dismissed by one of the sides, but her answer was not enough to have the judge dismiss her on his own. The questions were repeated as new people came in to replace the ones that had left. This process continued through the morning. After the judge's questioning forty-seven people were eliminated from the jury pool. The voire dire process then began in earnest.

After the initial voire dire by both sides it became clear what each side was looking for. Each side had exercised two preemptory challenges for that very reason, to see what the other side was looking for. Both the defense and prosecuting attorneys knew that to be the case and were fine with using two preemptory challenges for the purpose, it was a part of the brinksmanship of high-profile trials. The defense was clearly looking for educated individuals, preferably with graduate degrees and preferably in the science or technology fields. They were also looking for individuals with families, preferably with young children. The prosecution was looking for god-fearing, middle class types who led simple lives. They were okay with individuals with young children as long as religion was a part of their lives. The prosecution also seemed to be angling for individuals with jobs in the public sector, nurses, toll booth attendants, etc.

The jury selection went on for the next three weeks, much less than had been speculated, but far longer than any other trial for the same crime. Both sides had exhausted their preemptory challenges by the middle of the second week, which meant that any challenge to a juror would have to be for cause, which then meant arguing for what could be hours over one juror. The first week and a half was contentious and both sides seemed to be looking to land the first blow, by the end of the third week, however, both sides were content to get some of their jurors on the primary panel. Judge Newman helped that along when he stopped allowing either side to object to a juror without first having established how having that juror on the panel would be factually prejudicial to their side. By raising the standard Judge Newman hoped to speed things along and by most accounts he did precisely that.

In the end the jury was composed of seven women and five men. The men were a construction foreman, a seminary student, a gas station owner, a vice president of marketing for an automotive firm and a structural engineer for the city. The women were a nurse, an accountant, a homemaker, a café owner, a software analyst, an art director for an ad agency and a veterinarian. The youngest juror, the seminary student was 28 and the oldest, the nurse was 56. The alternate panel was similarly composed except that instead of a seminary student there was a young engineer. There were also no jurors in the public sector, the closest was a nurse.

FRIDAY, MAY 30TH

For the first time since the trial began, Beth and Steven Loomis were having a nice, homemade dinner. Wedge salad with warm bacon dressing, roasted chicken with a béchamel sauce, fettuccini al dente and for desert Beth's own recipe for flan. Before this evening, Beth and Steven had food delivered or made something easy. They spent their weekends watching old movies, putting puzzles together and talking to the kids and Tom and Lucy Delaney. The fact was that until earlier in the day, when the jury was empaneled, both Steven and Beth felt like nothing more than spectators. They had both been very engaged for the first two days, but after the repetitive questions and answers and the legal brinksmanship had put even the judge into a bit of a stupor. The only thing that kept him awake were the knock-down-drag-out fights the prosecution and the defense engaged in. From what Steven could see and understand, his team was as good as advertised, in fact they were much better than he imagined. Each had a role to fill and each one of them did it flawlessly and with perfect timing. Steven knew they'd practiced for hours and hours leading up to the trial, but that was never the same as doing it when it really counted. They actually seemed to get better, sharper. Max Zeidler had to be one of the top three attorneys in the country and rightly so. He was able to shift his line of questioning on the fly, without preamble or hesitation. Drew, who was clearly on his way to that very elite list of top attorneys, was also able to adjust and adapt depending on what the prosecution objected to or what they'd try to accept as their perfect juror. Ray was less able to shift his strategy on the fly, but he knew the controlling law verbatim and came across as a kindly gentleman trying to make the best of a nasty situation. The three of them together were absolutely brilliant as they incorporated the information the jury consultant into their questions and objections. Brilliant. While both sides ended up with some jurors with the profile they wanted, it was clear to Steven and everyone else watching that the defense had gotten more jurors they wanted on the panel than the prosecution.

When they spoke to the kids Bethany wanted to talk to her father for a few minutes by herself.

Steven was thrilled she wanted to do that and after they were done talking with Christopher and her grandparents, her dad stayed on to talk to her, "Okay sweetie, it's just me on this side."

Bethany looked skeptical, "Are you sure dad? Are you sure mom isn't sitting off to the side where I can't see her, but she can hear me?"

Steven smiled as Beth, who was in fact doing precisely that, moved away, "No honey, it's just me. What's on your mind?

Bethany knew exactly what she wanted to ask, "How come uncle Mikki was here? Are you going to work right now, with the trial going on?"

Steven shook his head; he could understand why she might think that.

Bethany had only known Zlk when they were both on the job, "Well, he just wanted to check on your mom and I. Uncle Mikki heard about what is going on with us and with the trial and wanted to make sure we're okay. You know the whole world is watching this, right honey?"

Bethany looked exasperated, "Duh! Of course dad, there are a whole bunch of people with cameras here and when I turn on the TV to watch a show or so Chris can watch his cartoons, your case is on a whole bunch of channels."

Steven nodded, but did not say anything.

Bethany asked her next question, "Dad, now the real trial will start, right? Now that there are twelve people that will decide things?"

Steven explained, "Yes baby, that's right, but there are actually twenty-four people that were chosen to listen to the case. The other twelve people are just in case the someone has to leave or is just not able to be in the trial."

Bethany listened carefully and nodded pensively, "Yeah, I wondered how come they selected those other twelve people. Dad, your lawyers will win, right? I mean they are like the best there is, right?"

Steven wanted to make sure his daughter understood everything going on, "Yes baby, they are the best there is, but there is no way to tell whether we will win or lose. See those twelve people we were just talking about are the only ones who can decide who wins and who loses. They will listen to both sides and then make their decision, so it's really up to us to convince them. Where's this question coming from, baby?

Bethany lowered her voice and Steven could see she was upset, "Well, Sandra Moore says that it doesn't matter how smart your lawyers are because what you are saying is crazy. She says everyone knows that it's crazy so you're going to lose and they're going to put you in prison for a long time."

Steven felt his face flush with anger, but he realized that one way or another his daughter would hear precisely what she was saying her friend had said, "Well honey, it's true that some people think what we're saying is crazy, but they think that because we have not explained *why* we are saying what we are saying. When the trial really starts next week, there are going to be a whole bunch of scientists that have done a lot of work to discover some new things. So after they tell everyone what they have found, what we're saying won't sound so crazy."

Bethany nodded in understanding. Steven knew that she was not just nodding for show, he knew she really did understand and now that she did, she could better defend herself when others said similar things.

She smiled as she internalized what her father had explained, "Okay. I also read some things on the Internet that say the same thing you just told me. I told Sandra she didn't know what she was talking about because she is just a little girl with a little girl brain. I just wanted to make sure I was right and I was, so thanks dad. I know you're going to win. Christopher is in my room dad, got to go! Love you tons!"

Steven smiled, "Love you tons too baby."

After ending the Skype connection Steven went into the kitchen and told Beth about the conversation he had just had with Bethany. They both shook their heads in amazement. She had been amazing them since she was a year and a half old and was able to speak in full sentences. That level of intelligence ensured that she would be able to understand precisely what was going on in full, not with the limited scope of view of a typical girl her age. And while they understood that had its advantages, it also had some drawbacks because she would truly understand the implications if he lost. Well, they both agreed, he would just have to win, period.

14.

On Monday following the week the jury had been empaneled the media reached a new level of intensity and pushiness. In just about every media outlet they began their coverage with some permutation of 'Round 1' or 'Let's get ready to rumble' and as cheesy and trite as it might have been, the audience was eating it up.

In the courtroom, however, Judge Newman was clearly anxious to get the trial going, "Now that you have been selected for the jury I am going to once again ask that you avoid speaking with the media, with your spouse or with your fellow jurors about the case. You are to limit your discussions of the case to the jury room and the jury room only. You are also not to visit any place that may be associated with the case and you should not conduct any experiment or test regarding the case on your own. Ladies and gentlemen I would like to emphasize that from this point forward you need to avoid anything that could potentially influence your deliberations in this case. This also includes the alternate jurors, your instructions are the exact same as those of the primary panel. You will be in the courtroom to hear all the testimony, the arguments, the summation, everything. Therefore, you will be held to the same standards as the primary panel."

Newman decided that he needed to clarify just how important it was for them to avoid outside influences, "If this court finds that the jury is being influenced by outside coverage and the media, I will be forced to sequester the jury. Believe me that is something that I do not want to do, but which I will be more than willing to do if I deem it to be necessary."

The judge let that hang in the air for effect. Ray was surprised by the judge's admonition and by the look that both Logan and Farris had on their faces, so were they. More than anything, Ray was surprised by the fact that neither he nor Max nor Drew had thought about the jury being sequestered. Not that it would really do anything from a practical standpoint, but it would almost certainly ramp up what was already a ridiculous amount of media coverage.

Newman explained what would happen after lunch, "When we reconvene after the lunch break the prosecution will proceed to present their case. After making an opening argument, they will go on to present their evidence. The defense will then go on to do the same. After the defense is finished the prosecution will have one last opportunity to present a rebuttal of what the defense presented. I will be going over certain instructions to you on how to consider the evidence that was presented to you. Now have a good lunch break and I will see all parties at 1:30."

Drew, Max, Ray, Beth and Steven went to the cafeteria to grab a sandwich. To get there they had to navigate a maze of reporters all shouting question, taking pictures and following along. His security team was able to move most of them aside, but the space was too small so even then, there was some bumping around along the way.

Ray was the first to give his opinion, "All in all I think we did well. Obviously we weren't going to get every juror to go our way, but I honestly think that they got some bad advice on the type of juror they needed to be looking for. They may have had the high-powered jury consultant, but I don't think she got it right. I think them going for people in the public sector is going to backfire on them. I think people like that are going to be more open to our argument than the prosecution thinks."

Drew nodded, "I agree, although I could see their reasoning. I also think we did well. I think going for higher education was a good call."

Max interjected, "I don't only think the consultant got it wrong with the advice she gave them about the jurors they want, I think she missed the boat as far as what our ideal juror would be."

Beth didn't understand why, "I don't understand, why do we want people with higher education?"

Steven cut in, he thought he knew why, "People with higher education are more likely to understand the science that our experts are going to be presenting. They are also probably more familiar with some of the studies that the experts are going to be presenting. Likewise, people with more middle of the road educational backgrounds are more apt to dismiss what they can't understand and if they come from a religious household then they will fall back on what they have learned from their religion about what is human and what isn't. Am I somewhat right?"

Ray smiled, "You are exactly right."

Beth wanted to know more about the jury they had selected, "I was watching some of the jurors answer the questions you and the prosecution were asking over the past couple of weeks and it was totally clear to me that they were giving whatever answers they thought might get them on. You guys can't tell me that you didn't see that."

Max responded, "No, you're right, they were. In a case like this Beth, most people want to serve on the jury so they will in fact answer what they think might get them on. That's why it's important for us to ask questions that seem innocuous during the voire dire, but that will let us know something about how they truly feel."

Ray jumped in, "I've got twenty bucks that says the CPA ends up as foreman."

Drew took him up on it, "You're on. My money is on the construction foreman to end up as foreman."

Beth was uncomfortable with the whole conversation. Max, Ray and Drew, and Steven, for that matter, seemed to be taking this whole thing too lightly. Steven was about to go on trial for his life.

Ray saw that Beth was having a hard time with the whole thing, "Listen, Beth, I know it might seem out of place for us to be joking and chatting lightly about this, but we have to, if we don't we'll burn out before the trial is over. Trust me, everyone involved knows how serious and how tragic all of this is, but if we don't take a moment here and there to lighten up it will show. The jury will see that we are constantly tense and out of sorts and believe it or not they will draw some conclusion from it. We need to come across as being confident, as knowing the seriousness of everything, but being certain of our position. Remember, we are asking them to believe something that is completely new to them. If we are asking them to believe, we need to come across as believing without question ourselves."

Beth could see what he was saying. More than anything she could see that he was right, if she was going to last through the trial with her wits about her she would need to learn to relax now and then.

They finished their lunch and headed back to the courtroom. As they walked by the windows facing the street they could see the sea of news trucks and cameras that were stationed in front of the courthouse. It was then that Beth understood just what they were in for. She thought that once the trial came to a conclusion the media attention would begin to go away, now that she saw the extent of the coverage and the sheer numbers she finally understood that it was going to be much longer than she imagined before the attention of the world moved on to something else.

Everyone was promptly back in the courtroom by 1:30. Now that the jury pool was gone the courtroom was filled with reporters as well as family members of Donald Riche's victims, all of whom sat behind Steven. Steven looked back and met the gazes of the other girls' families. In every instance there was a supportive smile and a nod. Although Steven had not set out to be anybody's hero, he had to admit that having these people behind him, having their support made him feel good and reminded him why he'd done what he'd done.

Once everyone was seated the judge Newman called the court to order and nodded at the prosecution, "Counsel, proceed with your opening statement."

Melanie Farris stood and turned to face the jury, "Thank your honor. Good afternoon ladies and gentlemen, my name is Melanie Farris and I am one of two attorneys that are here to represent the people of the state of New York in the case against Steven Loomis. As the judge stated earlier, Mr. Loomis is being charged with the first-degree murder of Donald Riche. To be convicted of first degree murder the state must prove that a human being killed another human being with malice and with premeditation. That is the law as it is written in New York's penal code. In this case we need to prove that Steven Loomis killed Donald Riche, that he intended to do so and that he planned on doing it with full knowledge of what he was doing and ladies and gentlemen, that is precisely what the state will do. We will present evidence that will prove beyond a reasonable doubt that Steven Loomis killed Donald Riche, that he planned on doing it and that he was in his right mind when he did it."

Farris paced in front of the jury box as she went on with her opening statement.

She was calm and controlled and used a very clear tone, a tone that said 'this is going to be so obvious that you won't have a choice but to find him guilty', "But, there are two sides to every story and our legal system is based on ensuring that the accused have an opportunity to present as vigorous a defense as is available to him.

"You will hear from experts on both sides, experts that will give you their expert opinion supporting the argument from each side. As you can see, our argument is simple. It is based on objective fact and our experts will provide you with their opinion supporting what may seem to you to be obvious and trust me ladies and gentlemen, it is indeed obvious. You will hear expert testimony regarding matters that may appear to be in contention, but which in reality are settled. You will hear testimony about what makes a human being human, about the science of it and about the history of human evolution. Don't be confused by all of that. Listen to it carefully, you have made the commitment to do that and the defendant is entitled to it, listen to it carefully, but don't let it cloud your own common sense. You have made the commitment to both sides to use your best judgment and your own life experience when considering the evidence presented to you. Your own life experience, don't forget that ladies and gentlemen, don't forget what you have always operated under, the beliefs and the reality that you have always known. You will hear about the horrible circumstances that have surrounded this case, about the tragedy that we all know is connected to this case and you will hear about how those horrible circumstances had an effect on Steven Loomis. But in the end this case is about him, about Steven Loomis, shooting another man, the man he believed to be his daughter's killer,

Donald Riche, with malice and premeditation. He was a father full of rage because of what happened to his daughter, a father that now knew who had been accused of her murder.

"You will hear from the investigating officers that took Steven Loomis's confession. I ask you now that you keep the essence of this case front and center as you hear what the defense's witnesses have to say. Remember that this case is about a human being killing another out of revenge, period."

She paused for effect and started back to the prosecution side. She used her arm for emphasis of her next point, "There is a sea of media out there, there are all kinds of stories, all kinds of versions. There are a lot of things attached to this case, but this trial is not about any of them, the trial is meant to answer the question to 'Did Steven Loomis kill Donald Riche with malice and premeditation. Sometimes us lawyers get hung up on legalese, but malice means did he mean to do it and if he did mean to do it, did he plan it. My job is to give you enough information for you to be able to answer yes to all of those questions without leaving a reasonable doubt as to the answer.

"The defense is entitled to your careful consideration of the evidence, but so is the state and once you hear everything that will be presented to you, the state is also entitled to have you decide what is true and what is right and in this case, ladies and gentlemen that decision should be to convict Steven Loomis of first degree murder. Thank you very much for your attention."

Newman turned to the defense, "Thank you counsel. Mr. Willis, Mr. Zeidler, Mr. Gretche, if you please."

Farris walked around the table and sat back down in her chair. There was none of the fire and brimstone that prosecutors usually brought to the opening statement in a murder trial, none of the finger-pointing and raised voices. She had done a masterful job of explaining what the case was about and not getting into the specifics of the defense's argument. Max knew that by doing so she had essentially discounted anything their experts had to say as something extraneous to the real case, the murder case. She didn't attack it directly or specifically because that would have lent it credibility right from the start. She glossed over what they would most likely hear about Donald Riche, again referring to it as something that was tragic and horrible, but not in any way relevant to this case. Melanie Farris had indeed done a masterful job of leaving the jury thinking what the defense dreaded most, 'why are we even here?'

Drew was about to stand to deliver the defense's opening statement when Ray put his hand on his leg and stood beating him to it, "If it please the court you honor, the defense would like to defer the opening statement."

Drew sat back down speechless, Max was trying to keep his mouth shut, but having a hard time doing it and Ray was waiting to hear what the judge had to say.

He leaned down and whispered to Drew and Max, "It just feels right to do it this way, what can I say guys, you were right."

The judge was somewhat taken aback, but finally turned to the jury, "Very well. Ladies and gentlemen of the jury, traditionally the defense makes their opening statement after the prosecution presents their opening statement. In this instance the defense has selected to defer making their opening statement until after the prosecution presents their entire case. This should in no way affect how you consider any of the evidence. You should not give any more or any less consideration to either side as a result of it. It is a well-established legal trial tactic, so it should not influence whatever credibility you assign to the expert testimony for either side. Ms. Farris, your first witness."

Melanie stood, if she was surprised by the defense's decision to defer she didn't show it, "The people call detective Robert Grady."

Detective Grady stood and came around to the court clerk's desk where he was sworn in. Farris asked all the questions establishing his position in the department, his experience and his role as lead detective in the investigation of the Donald Riche and Steven Loomis cases. She walked him through the shooting at the courthouse, where he had been and what he had done immediately after the shooting.

She was very precise and deliberate in her direct examination of Grady, "After the shooting at the courthouse, what was your next move?"

"I went about trying to develop a list of possible suspects and I made sure that we had all the evidence we could gather from the site of the shooting."

"Who else worked on the case with you?"

"Detective Mark Mullins was the second detective on the case. There were also uniformed officers that were assigned to the case. I have a list if you need it."

Farris shook her head, "Not just now detective. And Detective Mullins also worked with you to develop the list of possible suspects?"

Grady went on, "Yes he did. Mostly, though, he worked with the forensic team to make sure the evidence was collected properly and he followed up on anonymous tips we received."

Farris was now standing in front of the witness stand, "Did any of those tips work out?"

"No, most of them were pranks or people that were clearly not in a position to know anything."

"How long did you spend on the case before you were able to ascertain who the shooter was?

"Three days. From the time the shooting occurred to the time we had information about who had done it, it was three days."

"And what happened, how did you get the information about who was responsible?"

"I received a call from Steven Loomis telling me that he wanted to speak with me."

Farris now moved aside, "Do you see Steven Loomis in the courtroom detective?"

Grady nodded, "Yes I do."

Farris went on, "Can you point him out please."

In what had to be the least surprising identification in the history of legal proceedings detective Robert Grady pointed at Steven Loomis.

Farris went on, "What happened then detective?"

Grady explained the process whereby he and Steven Loomis had a couple of telephone conversations in which Loomis initially denied any involvement in the shooting and provided evidence of an alibi only to then reach out to Grady again, "Mr. Loomis explained that he needed to speak with some people and that he would come to the precinct after that."

"And were you surprised by the call?"

"No, I can't say that I was. It made sense."

"Why do you say that?"

"Because he was one of the parents of the girls that Donald Riche had been accused of killing. When the shooting occurred he was one of the people I thought might have done it."

"And did he come to the precinct?"

"Yes he did. He came to the precinct accompanied by Mr. Willis and by Max Zeidler."

Melanie walked over to the prosecution table and picked up a DVD as she asked the next question. "What happened then detective?"

Grady saw the DVD and knew what was coming, "We all went to our conference room and sat down. Mr. Loomis said that he wanted to give us information about the shooting at the courthouse."

Farris walked over to the witness stand and showed the detective the DVD, "Did you record Mr. Loomis's statement?"

"Yes I did. I first asked him if he was willing to let me record it and he stated that he was fine with it."

She held up the DVD, "And is this a DVD of that statement?"
"Yes it is."

Melanie held the DVD up and asked that it be admitted into evidence. Once the judge admitted the disc into evidence Melanie asked for a television and a DVD player, which the bailiff brought from the jury room. She inserted the disc into the player and turned the volume up. The courtroom was completely quiet while the disc played Steven's statement. When Steven was heard saying that he had shot Donald Riche a murmur spread through the courtroom and whispering could be heard, it was loud enough that the judge called the court to order by banging his gavel and admonished everyone in the courtroom that he would have anyone found whispering or talking removed from the courtroom. Melanie hit the rewind button and allowed the disc to play again.

She was about to do it a third time, but Ray objected, "Your honor I believe that we have gotten the gist of what is contained on the disc. Anything beyond that would be repetitive. Additionally, your honor, we would be willing to stipulate that Mr. Loomis admitted to having shot Donald Riche, so there is no need to play the DVD again."

Newman agreed, "Sustained. Move along Ms. Farris."

Melanie went through the confession with Grady, asking him whether Steven had seemed out of it or in any way impaired. Grady had responded that he seemed to be perfectly fine, in fact completely calm while he made his statement. Grady had also explained that Zeidler had tried to stop Loomis from going on with his statement.

Melanie wanted to make sure the jury understood the implication, "And did Mr. Loomis listen to Mr. Zeidler?"

Grady shook his head and looked at the jury, "No he did not. He said that he knew what he wanted to say and that he was going to say it."

Melanie asked him whether Grady had tried to question Loomis and Grady had explained that Loomis had said that he was not going to answer any questions about anything other than what he had done. He explained that Loomis had made it clear that he would not speak about the reasons he had done what he did. Once the questioning about Loomis's statement was concluded Farris went about asking how the detective had made sure that it had been Loomis that had shot Riche. She led him though the process of authenticating Loomis's testimony, going to retrieve the gun from the place that Loomis had stashed it and checking the information he had given them about caliber and the make of the weapon. Bart Logan stood up next and called Mark Mullins to the stand. He walked him through essentially the same testimony that Grady had just gone over. Confirming Loomis's demeanor, the information about the rifle and the way in which he had set up the shot. It was very straightforward testimony, factual and without any spin to it. It was simply the detectives in charge of the case letting the jury know how Steven Loomis had come to be the defendant in this case. There had not been any cross-examination of Grady because there really wasn't anything to clarify or to try to trip the detective up on. With Mullins on the stand Drew had decided that this might be a good point at which to bring in the concept of motive.

Once Logan was finished with his direct examination of Mullins Drew stood up, "Detective Mullins, prior to Mr. Loomis calling to say that he was coming in to make a statement, did you and detective Grady have any discussions about who could have possibly done this?"

Mullins remained calm, "Yes we did."

"And what conclusions, if any, did you come to?"

Mullins looked like he was puzzled by the line of questioning, "Well that there were plenty of people who had a motive to do it…"

Drew pressed on, "What do you mean by that detective?"

"I mean that we thought there were probably a lot of people out there who would want to do this."

Drew closed the line of questioning, "Why would there be a lot of people who would want to do this?"

Logan objected, "You honor the detective already answered the question about what conclusions they came to without Mr. Loomis's call. Mr. Willis is trying to get in evidence that the court has already ruled is inadmissible."

Drew responded, "How am I trying to get evidence ruled inadmissible?"

Logan responded, "By having the detective talk about the reason that there were many people who wanted the deceased dead. You already ruled on the evidence that can be referenced and this seems like an attempt to get around that ruling."

Drew was ready, "Judge we are trying to establish that Mr. Loomis was on the list of possible suspects before Mr. Loomis made the call."

The judge thought for a moment, "Overruled Mr. Logan. Next time Mr. Willis, just ask the question."

Drew looked back at Mullins, "Understood your honor. Detective please go on..."

Mullins nodded and went on, "Well we thought that there would be a lot of people that would want to kill him because of what he did to those girls."

Before he could go on Farris and Logan both stood, "Objection your honor! There is no evidence about Mr. Riche doing anything. Please admonish the witness."

This clearly had an effect on Mullins. He became a bit fidgety on the stand.

The judge turned to him, "Detective you can testify only to what has been established as fact or you can give your opinion if it is called for. You can make reference of what Mr. Riche was accused of doing, but you can't say that he did it as though he'd already been convicted"

Mullins still looked a bit confused, "Sorry about that. What I mean is that we thought that because of all of the news coverage of the murders and because Mr. Riche had been accused of them there would be a lot of people that would want him dead."

"Was Mr. Loomis a part of that list of people?"

"Well, yes, just like all of the families of the other girls were."

"Were you a part of the investigative team in the case of the missing girls?"

"Yes I was."

Drew wanted to bring it to a close, "And you were a part of the team that found the evidence that caused Mr. Riche to be indicted for those murders?"

Both Farris and Logan were paying very close attention to this line of questioning as both of them could see that Willis was trying to lead Mullins down a path that was going to bring the murders fully into the mix.

Mullins nodded, "Yes I was."

Drew pushed on, "How did your team come to find that evidence detective?"

Now Mullins really got nervous. This was a line of questioning he had hoped to avoid altogether.

Before he could answer Logan was up. "Your honor this line of questioning has completely moved away from the original direct examination."

The judge agreed. "Where are you going with this counsel?"

Willis knew the objections were going to come and he knew that the judge would probably sustain them, but by asking the question he brought the girls into the equation, "Judge, I am trying to ascertain how the evidence they found affected their discussions after the shooting."

It was a lame response and Drew knew it, but he had done what he wanted to do.

The judge had had enough, "Counsel that is tenuous at best. The objection is sustained. Move on."

Drew went on. "Very well. Before you received the call from Mr. Loomis did you, detective Grady or any other member of the investigative team identify Mr. Loomis specifically as a potential shooter?"

Mullins was glad to be talking about something other than how they'd found the warehouse, "No, not specifically. He was just a part of the group of people I mentioned, the families of the victims, that's all."

Drew went on, "Had you spoken to Donald Riche about the missing girls during your investigation?"

Logan stood, "Objection. You honor where are we going here?"

Newman agreed, "Where are you going with this counsel?"

Drew responded, "Your honor I am trying to find out whether Mr. Loomis had spoken to Donald Riche at all before this happened."

The judge gave him some room, "I am going to give you some latitude here counsel, very little latitude, but I want you to move it along now. Go ahead detective."

Mullins answered the question, "Yes we spoke to Mr. Riche as part of that investigation."

Drew went back to the original question, "And during that questioning did you find out whether Mr. Loomis had had any contact with Mr. Riche?"

"No he had not. He was the father of one of the missing girls, but he had not spoken to Mr. Riche."

Drew finished his cross examination of Mullins by reviewing his testimony about the rifle, where it was found, the caliber and the details that Loomis had given them to authenticate his confession. Once Willis finished with the detective Logan called their next witness, Dr. Albert Wilson the representative for the medical examiner's office who had conducted the autopsy of Donald Riche. Logan directed him through the details of the autopsy, beginning with the external examination and moving on through the trauma and the cause of death. During the questioning Logan brought out two photographs of Donald Riche's body one a top view of the body and a side view, both of which showed the enormous exit wound that the bullet had left, virtually exploding the back quarter of his head.

Logan did not want to make it an overly graphic presentation, "Doctor, based on your experience do you have any opinion regarding the kind of weapon that must have caused Donald Riche's death?"

Wilson nodded, "That kind of injury is caused by a high caliber, high velocity round."

Logan went on, "And can that kind of round be fired from a hand gun?"

"No, that kind of round is fired from military grade weaponry. Sniper rifles, assault rifles, that kind of thing."

Now Logan was going to go through the process of preemptively eroding the credibility of the defense's claim, "Doctor, during your examination of Donald Riche, did you see anything out of the ordinary about his physical state?"

The doctor made a face that let the jury know he thought this line of questioning was ridiculous, "No, there was nothing out of the ordinary, other than the hole in his head."

The sarcasm was unmistakable, but Logan wanted him to articulate it, "And when you went through the process of cataloguing his organs did you find anything out of the ordinary?"

Again very emphatically, "No, there was nothing out of the ordinary in his body."

Logan didn't want the jury to get exasperated with what was the very obvious point he was trying to make, "Doctor, based on your examination of Mr. Riche did you come to any conclusions as to whether he was a member of the human race?"

Dr. Wilson knew he was going to be asked the question and had been prepared for it, but he still had a visible, visceral reaction, "I came to that conclusion upon seeing the body coming into the morgue. I didn't have to do a full examination to know that I was going to be doing the autopsy of a human being. If it hadn't been a human being I would not have been the person doing the autopsy."

Logan finished up, "Thank you doctor. No further questions your honor."

The judge looked to the defense, "Mr. Willis?"

Max Zeidler stood up this time, "Yes your honor. Doctor your statement is that you did not have to conduct an examination to determine that Mr. Riche was a human being, is that correct?"

Wilson nodded, "Yes, that's right."

Max went on, "So would it be fair to say that you came to that conclusion based strictly on what you saw?"

"Yes, that's right?"

"You never examined Mr. Riche while he was alive did you?"

"No I did not."

"You never did a psychological examination or any form of forensic analysis of Mr. Riche's behavior prior to his death, correct?"

Wilson shook his head and was not sure where this was all going, "No I did not. That's not my job counselor."

Logan had had enough, "Judge the doctor has already stated that his conclusion was based on his physical examination of the body."

Newman also thought the point had been made, "Mr. Zeidler, we get the point. Let's move it along."

Zeidler thought he had made the point, but he wanted to make sure the jury was completely clear, "Doctor per your testimony, your job was to determine the cause of death and that's all, correct?"

"Yes, that's correct."

Max had one last clarification he wanted to make, "And as a part of that determination did you examine the DNA of Mr. Riche?"

The witness shifted before answering, he could sense where Zeidler was about to go, "No, I did not."

Zeidler stopped pacing and now faced the doctor, "And did you take any measurements of Mr. Riche's cranial cavity?"

Now the witness sneered, "That would have been difficult to do given that a full quarter of his cranial cavity was missing."

Zeidler smiled, "I see your point, but you could have taken measurements of what was there, couldn't you?"

Dr. Wilson hesitated, but finally said, "Well, yes I could have measured what was there, but that is not..."

Zeidler had made his point, "That's all doctor. Thank you, no further questions your honor."

The doctor was dismissed from the stand. The rest of the prosecution's case was painfully anticlimactic. They called a physiologist to the stand to establish the physiological make up of a human being, going through rather boring testimony about the body's organs, the brain's cognitive capabilities and the skeletal system. Ray cross-examined him to establish that once again, the assessment as to whether Riche was a human being or not was based solely on the physical condition of the body. Dr. Walden, the physiologist, was a difficult witness; he responded with some sarcasm and added on his own brand of hostility to every answer.

When Ray asked the final question about his assessment of Donald Riche as a human being he responded, "Yes, counselor, my conclusion is based on a physical assessment and on the fact that the victim was walking and talking like a human being prior to being shot in the head."

Ray was not going to engage with the man because there was no upside to it. He simply smiled at the answer, looked at the judge and concluded his cross-examination.

Max wasn't done with Walden, "Doctor Walden, one last question please. Do you think that a human subspecies, if it existed, might talk like, look like and behave like a human being?"

Walden wasn't sure how to answer the question, but before he was able to Farris stood up, "Objection your honor, speculation. That is not doctor Walden's area of expertise."

Max actually chuckled, "What? Your honor we just went through doctor Walden's qualifications as a physiologist, how is a physiologist not able to provide an opinion on what a human subspecies might look like?"

The judge agreed, "Overruled. Go ahead doctor."

Walden had nowhere else to go, "Well, if it was a human subspecies, yes, it is possible that they would look like, act like and sound like a human being. But I want to emphasize the word 'possible' here, because there's just no way to know what that species looks like because it simply does not exist."

Zeidler was going to sit down before Walden made the last statement, but now he couldn't let that stand, "I see. Have you ever conducted research into that possibility? That there is a human subspecies not previously defined?"

Walden shook his head, "Well, no, but..."

This time Max didn't let him get in a last statement, "That's all doctor, thank you. I'm done your honor."

The state called an anthropologist, a neurologist, a forensic psychiatrist and an evolutionary biologist. They qualified each of them as an expert. The defense did not object to their qualifications because there was simply nothing to object to. The prosecution walked each of them through a line of questioning that ended with each of them declaring that Donald Riche was in fact a human being. And after each of them concluded that, Max, Drew or Ray asked similar questions to what Max had asked Walden: did they come to their conclusions by comparing Donald Riche's physiology, neurology, psychiatric records and in each instance their answers established that yes, their conclusions came as a result of a physical comparison of Donald Riche with their established norms for a human being and in each instance the experts responded that, yes, that was the primary way they had come to their conclusions. The direct, cross and redirect examination of the witnesses had taken two weeks. In each instance the expert witness gave their testimony very carefully in order not to step into some sort of trap. Max, Drew and Ray had done some of the cross-examination of the prosecution's witnesses without getting into the science of the defense. All they had wanted to do was to ensure that each witness committed to what they were testifying.

The only expert witness from the prosecution with something different and directly related to the case they would be presenting was the evolutionary biologist. After qualifying her as an expert Melanie Farris wanted to be very clear in what their expert, Dr. Susan Wright, had to say about what the defense was about to present. Farris was not allowed to make reference to something that was not yet a part of the evidence, but she could once again preemptively erode the credibility of what the defense was going to present. The true value of the experts would come once the defense had put their experts on. Once that happened then the prosecution could call their witnesses back to the stand and directly poke holes into the expert testimony, their direct testimony now was not where they would really do some damage. Still, the evolutionary biologist could in fact poke some holes in their defense right now.

After all the questions about her qualifications Farris went into the terms that the jury would be hearing. She walked Dr. Wright to each of the terms. She explained that modern humans were actually called Homo sapiens sapiens. She looked at the jury as she explained that Homo was the genus, sapiens was the species and sapiens was the subspecies.

Farris then got to heart of the matter, "Dr. Wright, have human beings evolved from the beginning of life on earth to now?"

Wright smiled, "Well yes, although if we're talking about the beginning of life, our predecessors, they were not human beings for some time. Homo sapiens, we now know, emerged approximately 100,000 years ago. Since that time there have been some minor changes in human physiology, but big changes in cognitive capacity."

Farris followed up, "What kind of changes?"

Wright explained, "Creativity, imagination, ingenuity, that kind of thing. The humanoids that preceded humans also had these abilities, but in a much more limited capacity. Then there was a huge leap where our cognitive capacity, our imagination and our ingenuity evolved significantly. This is where we see the development of complex patterns, tools, social order. There is no way for us to know why that happened with a hundred percent certainty. Some people believe that there was a random mutation and once that happened there was that huge leap in cognitive capacity, others believe that it was a gradual change as we transitioned from humanoids to actual humans, but there is simply no way to know."

Farris needed to wrap it up, the jury was looking sleepy, "Dr. Wright, do you believe that modern human beings, *Homo sapiens sapiens*, have evolved so much as a species that there is now another subspecies of human, one that shares the planet with us?"

Dr. Wright looked directly at the jury as he answered the question, "No, I don't believe so. Based on our evolutionary record, the rate of evolution we've observed, we would need another 50,000 years to see the evolution of another human subspecies."

Farris wanted to hammer the point home, "So if you were told that there is now a human subspecies sharing the planet with us what would you respond?"

Wright delivered, "I would respond that is highly, highly unlikely, next to impossible really. Science has set out a roadmap for us to follow and if we follow it we'll see another subspecies in another 50,000 years."

Farris smiled, "Thank you Dr. Wright, no further questions."

Judge Harris looked at the defense table, "Defense?"

Drew stood up, "Thank you your honor, just a few questions. Dr. Wright, have you ever heard of Homo sapiens idaltu?"

Wright nodded smiling, "Of course. You can't be in the field of evolution and not have heard about Homo sapiens idaltu."

Drew moved in, "So, if I understood your testimony correctly, Homo is the genus, sapiens is the species and idaltu is the subspecies, is that correct?"

Wright nodded, "That is correct."

Drew pushed on, "And the fact that the genus is Homo, the species is sapiens means that they were in fact human, correct?"

Again Wright nodded, "Yes, that is correct. They were humans, but a part of a different subspecies."

Drew went to make the point, "And Dr. Wright, when was the evidence of Homo sapiens idaltu discovered?"

Now Wright wasn't smiling, she knew where Drew was headed, "Well, the evidence of Homo sapiens idaltu was discovered in 2003."

For the first time there was a murmur and some shifting from the jury box because they now also knew where Drew was headed.

He delivered, "So if someone had asked you in 2002 whether it was possible that there was a human subspecies not previously defined you would have said that it was very, very unlikely, next to impossible, is that correct?"

Farris stood up, "Objection your honor, Mr. Willis is testifying for the witness."

Drew turned to respond, "I was just summarizing what the witness already responded when she was asked about another subspecies. I didn't add anything to that testimony."

Newman nodded, "Overruled. But let's move it along Mr. Willis."

The doctor simply answered, "Yes, that's correct."

After hearing the answer Drew held his hands up with a smile on his face, "I'm done judge, no further questions."

The judge looked at Farris, "Do you care to redirect counselor?"

Melanie considered the question and ultimately shook her head, "No your honor. We can move on."

The prosecution wrapped up their case on the sixth week of trial by calling the two guards that had been escorting Riche. They wanted to finish with memorable testimony and the two guards were asked about the shooting in minute detail. Grady had gone over the scene after the shooting, but the guards provided a blow by blow of escorting Riche getting out of the elevator, hearing the shot and seeing the back of his head come apart. The forensic psychologist had not been called up yet because no testimony had been presented about Riche's psychological makeup. She was engaged by the prosecution to rebut the defense's witnesses. The entirety of the state's case had been to basically establish a timeline, confirm what Loomis had already confessed to and to establish what they considered to be the outrageous nature of what the defense was going to be claiming. They couldn't attack what hadn't been presented yet. The reality was that the entire courtroom, the entire country was waiting for the defense to present their case, that's when the fireworks would fly. This part of the trial had seemed like little more than a warm up for the real case to begin. This hadn't been lost on the prosecution, which was the reason that they had not engaged in any histrionics when presenting their case.

For the most part, the media covering the trial thought that the prosecution had done very well. They had presented the case as nonchalantly as they could afford to and Max, Drew and Ray had to admit that they had made a good impression on the jury without seeming pompous or cold, they had come across as professional and to the point.

At the end of Thursday on the sixth week of the trial and once the prosecution had wrapped up their case, Drew conferred with Max, Steven and with Ray and stood to address the court, "You honor, we would like to ask for a half a day before we present our case. Would it be possible to reconvene tomorrow at 1:30?"

The judge thought about it for a moment. He was reluctant to extend the trial or at least he wanted to appear reluctant.

Like everyone else he knew that the real case was going to be presented the next day so he agreed, "I'm going to grant the defense's request, but let's not make this a habit Mr. Willis."

The clerk called the court to order and the day was convened. The media had been like sharks sniffing around blood trying to come up with a sensational angle to report on the trial, but there just wasn't one. Everything presented and cross-examined thus far had been everything that had already been reported. The media, like the rest of the world, was waiting for the defense to begin presenting their case. Max, Drew and Ray had decided that they needed to review everything that had been presented until now. There had been nothing unexpected presented, nothing that the prosecution had thrown at them that they hadn't already planned for, but the way the prosecution had presented the case had been masterful, something that none of the defense attorneys had foreseen. All of them thought that Logan would come across as a stiff, unfeeling attorney and that Farris would come across as a cut-throat, win-at-all-costs bitch. Instead both came across as professional and efficient, well aware of the circumstances that surrounded the case and sensitive to them, but still able to sidestep those tragic circumstances to do their job.

The DVD with Steven's confession had also been a bit more damaging than what the defense had initially thought. He was clear and unflinching when he explained how he had shot Donald Riche. He didn't come across as a grieving father or a tormented victim, he came across as cold and worse of all, he came across as someone that had done this before. Even though the jury most likely already knew about his military experience, hearing him speak the way he did on that disc about killing still gave the defense some concerns. At the end of the day what the prosecution had done was to put the complete onus on the defense to prove their case. In the American legal system the prosecution has the burden to prove the defendant guilty, but in this case the tables had been turned from the beginning, their client had done it, had admitted to doing it and had set out to challenge the very essence of the crime of murder. They knew they were going to be rowing upstream, but now that the moment was here they felt they needed to make completely sure that their witnesses understood just what their testimony meant to this case. The prosecution's witnesses had been very dry and had really not provided anything other than confirmation of what anyone with a pulse already knew. Their witnesses, particularly Dr. Leonard, needed to understand that the reality was that the case hung squarely on their work and how convincing they could be in explaining it. Most of the witnesses were solid and should come across as very engaging, but Grossman might get rattled if Farris went at him and his conclusions. The concept of developing a scale that measured how 'evil' someone could be and at what point that scale measured something beyond human parameters, was going to be difficult to defend in a murder trial. The defense team, Steven and the witnesses went directly to Zeidler and Drew's office to prepare. Beth wanted to be a part of it, but Steven had convinced her that the witnesses really needed to concentrate and that she might be somewhat of a distraction. The truth was that Steven himself needed to concentrate and while he loved having Beth with him, he was having a difficult time staying completely focused. This had been the reason he wanted her to go back to her parents, but now he was committed to having her here for the duration. Max, Drew and Ray went over the order of their witnesses again and what they would be testifying to. All of them had been prepped already, but now they knew what they were facing on the other side.

Max went to address the group, "Dr. Leonard, we're going to begin with you. Remember that you can't testify to anything relating to Riche beyond what you have reviewed in the files. You can go over the findings of the psychological autopsy you conducted and you can relate those findings to your work."

Now he addressed the whole group, "That goes for all of you, you can refer to the analysis you conducted of his file and all the information we provided to you, but all of it has to be weaved into the work you have done. You've all heard about what we are up against and you've seen the people that will be coming at you. Believe me, they will come at you hard, they're going to do their best to make you doubt your work, just stay grounded in what you know, go through your work confidently, but try to remember that the jurors don't have your background and your education and they need you to explain what you know in a way they can understand."

Grossman spoke up, "That may be difficult Mr. Zeidler, some of the work we have done involves concepts that they may not be familiar with."

Max thought it would be Grossman that would have the hardest time with doing just that, explaining things in a way a layman could understand them, "That's ok doctor, just walk them through those concepts in a way they understand. Look, they have all been watching the news, they know what Riche did, even thought he wasn't convicted of anything. They all saw the warehouse pictures and they have all heard the stories. They all know what we are going to be arguing and believe it or not they want to believe, they want to believe that someone that could do things like that is not like them, so just give them that, a reason to believe."

They decided that Leonard would begin by laying out the science their defense was based on; the rest of the witnesses would follow in the order they had already established. There was nothing for them to testify to yet, the defense hadn't brought up their theory. They would end with Steven himself on the stand. Now that they had seen the prosecution present their case they knew just how important it was going to be for Steven to take the stand. In almost every case of murder, actually almost any serious crime it was a bad idea to put the defendant on the stand. Having a seasoned prosecutor cross-examining someone who was almost always guilty of the crime they were being accused of was the kiss of death for the defense. In this case there was no way to proceed *without* having Steven testify. Only he could explain why he had done what he did, how he had made the decision, how he had been affected by the information the experts were going to be presenting. Steven sat through the final preparation of the expert witnesses without any reaction. Ray noticed that he seemed to be a bit absent, almost like he had been daydreaming through the preparation of the experts.

When they called a break to let everyone go to the bathroom Ray went to talk to Steven, "How're you holding up?"

Steven seemed a bit surprised by the question, "I'm good. It's been a long day, but it think it's gone pretty well how I expected so far."

Ray agreed, "Yeah, they did a better job than I thought they were going to do. I thought they would be a little more reckless to be honest with you. I thought they would be more showy, more dramatic. That would have worked to our advantage."

Steven took that in stride, he smiled, "Well, I think we'll be ok, don't you?"

Ray found him strangely serene, especially for someone on trial for his life, "I do, I do. Hey, Steven, I have to tell you man, you look incredibly calm for someone being accused of murder."

Steven looked at him. They hadn't known each other for as long as he had known Drew and Max and he hadn't had a chance to really hear why all of this had happened in the first place.

He explained it to him, "I know we haven't really had a chance to speak other than preparing for the case, but let me tell you Ray, I am calm because to my way of thinking I have already accomplished a big part of what I set out to accomplish when I did this. I believe, with every fiber of my being, in what we are presenting, I truly do, but my goal wasn't to have everyone agree with me. Actually, I was pretty sure that it would be almost impossible for anyone to agree with me."

Ray was curious, "So why go through all of this? Why put yourself and your family through this?"

Steven answered him, "Because I wanted, I want, the world to know that these creatures exist, that they have existed for some time now and that they are out there hunting us. I believed that the only way that would happen would be if something like this trial happened. I wanted Tracy's death to mean something. Trust me Ray, it wasn't revenge, it really wasn't. If I wanted revenge I would have done it some other way and I wouldn't have turned myself in."

Ray listened. He had figured out that he hadn't been looking for revenge almost from the beginning, but he really hadn't heard the why from Steven until now.

Steven went on, "I'm calm because the world is now talking about it. Have you heard all the stories out there? Have you seen all the interviews with experts and all the debate on the merit of my argument? I had gotten caught up in the whole process of going to trial, of presenting my defense and winning the case and the truth is that seeing all the press and all the reaction from people reminded me of the original, the real reason I did this."

Ray understood, but he also became concerned, "So you don't care about what happens in the trial?"

Steven smiled, "Don't worry, of course I care what happens. Don't get me wrong, I don't want to spend the rest of my life in prison and I will fight for that with my everything I have, that's why I have the best team that could possibly handle the case, but I would be lying to you if I didn't tell you that I am prepared to do that, to spend the rest of my life in prison. It is out of my control whether that's the case or not and now I know my family will be okay. As far as the rest of the world, well, they've been warned, now they know who's out there, *what's* out there."

Ray stood, "Good enough. I'm glad we had a chance to chat because now I can see why this whole thing happened much more clearly."

When they began prepping again, everyone seemed refreshed. After going through everyone's testimony Ray explained to the witnesses that Steven would open up their case. As with many of the decisions they had made regarding this case this was an unconventional approach, so the witnesses raised their eyebrows. Max, Drew and Ray agreed that they would recall him to end their case, but it was going to be important to have him testify first and give the jury someone to root for. It was almost midnight when they called it a day.

At the prosecutor's office things had been much less intense. Farris and Logan were satisfied with their presentation of the case and Neill seemed to also be satisfied with their performance. Now they could only speculate about what the defense was planning to do.

Neill wanted to make sure that things would remain on track, "Keep the same tone when you cross-examine their witnesses, efficient and almost disinterested, but not condescending."

He said this as he paced around the conference room they were meeting in, "Right now the jury is probably wondering why the hell they are sitting through this and that's exactly how we want them to be thinking."

They also reviewed the order of the witnesses they would call to rebut the defense's case. The order would be determined by the order of the defense witnesses, but they wanted to be ready for whatever the defense threw at them. While Logan and Neill were going over the witness list and what they expected from the defense, Farris was leafing through a file she had put together during their initial preparations for trial. The file addressed the legal elements of first-degree murder and the legal elements of lesser included offenses, second degree murder, manslaughter and so on. Although Neill had already decided that they would pursue a conviction of first-degree murder and only that, Farris wanted to have the file ready just in case. Neill believed that by also pursuing lesser-included offenses like second-degree murder and manslaughter they would be showing doubt about the first-degree murder case. He was right, in theory. Usually when a case was a clear case of first-degree murder, the prosecution pursued only first-degree murder. Farris was very confident in their case, more so now than before the trial started, and their approach to the defense, but the whole idea of public opinion still bugged her. Setting aside the trial, the truth was that everyone involved, including those in the district attorney's office, was relieved that Riche was dead. He was a monster and the media had made sure that the world knew he was a monster. Melanie had been considering the possibility that the jury might be influenced by that public sentiment more than the prosecution team had expected and she still believed it was a good strategic decision to include those lesser-included offenses. Had they done so, they might have provided the jury with an option of convicting him of something less than murder. Technically they could still add the lesser included charges and request that the judge provide the jury instructions accordingly, technically. Melanie knew, however, that Neill would never go for it.

Still, it was bugging her enough that she had to try one more time "Mr. Neill, I think we should consider adding lesser included offenses to the charges. We should give the jury options and hedge against the influence that public opinion might have on them."

Neill stood up from the conference table and walked over to the end where Melanie was sitting, he had a smile on his face, "Farris, is that doubt I hear in your voice? You know that if we did that every legal hack in this town would see it as us doubting the strength of our case. You both did an excellent job of coming across as confident and certain about your argument and you've established a good presence in the courtroom. I don't want to undermine any of that, so we're going to stay the course. I have a dinner with the mayor tonight and he's going to want to know how everything is going, so keep up the good work."

Farris had expected his response, but she still had to try. In the end it would be her and Logan on the hook if the trial went sideways so she wanted to put all of her thoughts on the record.

Once Neill left Logan came over, "He's right you know, if we do it now it will look like we're not confident about a conviction for first degree murder. If we were going to do it, we should have done it already. Besides, what could we argue to convict him of other than first-degree murder? How do we go for second-degree? How do we argue that what he did was spontaneous, that he killed Riche on a spur of the moment? Or manslaughter? Do you see the problem? Loomis himself kind of shut the door to us doing any of that."

Farris had in fact thought about all of it, but she still thought it was a safer approach, "I do see the problem, trust me. But do you see how if we don't give them an option of convicting him of anything other than first-degree murder we are taking the risk that if they sympathize with him and want to find a way to follow the law, but not convict him of first-degree murder we are shutting the door for *them*?

"I get what you are saying and legally you are right, but you also know that juries are guided by human emotion Bart. Do you really think that they will put aside everything they heard and saw about what Riche did? No way, trust me, they're going to be looking for something to believe what Loomis is claiming and I think we need to give them an option so that when they decide they might agree with him, but that they still need to convict him of something, we give them that something to convict him of."

Bart listened and thought about it for a few seconds, he agreed, but like Farris he knew it just wasn't going to happen, "No sense beating ourselves up about it, what's done is done. Let's get out of here and go grab a bite."

15.

The next day the defense spent the morning organizing and cataloguing their exhibits, the photographs they would utilize, the graphs the studies that had been done, the computer animations. They also decided that it would be a good idea to sit down and discuss what had been going on in the media. Although the judge had admonished the jury, both sides knew that they would be exposed to what was being said in the media one way or another.

Overall the consensus was that the prosecution had done a good job of presenting the case. Most legal experts were quick to note, however, that it was basically color by numbers for the prosecution, there was just no way for them to do anything but present the case exactly how they had done it. It was also clear that every single news outlet, legal pundit and commentator was waiting for the defense's case. There had also been quite a bit of discussion and debate about whether Loomis would be testifying. The consensus was that he probably would testify, but many experts were of the opinion that having him testify and be cross-examined by a seasoned prosecutor would be a mistake. Beth, having stayed at home with nothing to do other than to watch the coverage, was on edge. It was almost impossible not to get some exposure to the coverage. Even HGTV interrupted their regular program to cover the trial. She had seen the media leading up to the trial and she'd been followed by them everywhere she went, but that felt different than watching the coverage full on. As much as she didn't want to, she was nervous and scared for her husband.

HOUSTON, TEXAS

Reverend J.D. Garzen had done exactly what he'd told his 'fixer' Russ Menard that he would do. He had been talking about topics around the trial without going full on after Steven Loomis. He talked about killing another human being, putting your family at risk, suffering for living a life away from god, everything but what Steven's actual defense was going to be presenting. All of that that lead to this sermon, the one he was delivering as, if not more, masterfully as he'd delivered all the others. He was truly pleased with himself because having held back on going after Loomis had created a tense and charged congregation, a congregation that was ready for Garzen to finally pull the trigger on what they all knew was coming. His special Friday service let the congregation know that this one was going to be truly special.

He had been talking about every one of the topics he'd touched on leading to today in his sermon and he had his southern accent fully deployed, "Do you all see what all of this is resulting eahnnn? How speahndinnnggg yohh lifeah away from the loooahrd leads to sieehann, to thinking you are goahdd, to placing yoah famileh in mohatall dangeahhh? This man, Steven Loomis, is traahing to take the place of our loaahrd. He claims that heahh and onleh heahh can determeahnn who is a humaaaahn and who is not. Do weah agreeah with heahmmm?"

Garzen paused to give the congregation time to absorb what he had been saying and to react to it and react they did. There were dozens of shouts saying things like 'sinner!!' and 'blasphemer!!' and 'satan's imp' among others. Everyone, it seemed, wanted to get their poke in and Garzen could not be happier. His face, however, looked as somber and serious as they had ever seen him.

When he continued with his sermon he turned down the histrionics and the southern drawl and instead went on in a calm and reasoned voice, a voice that told his congregation that he had wisdom that others did not because he was close to god, "Now brothers and sistahs, we need to desaahde if we will simply allow this heathen, this blasphemer to march on and think he is god. We need to desaahde if weeah are going to sit by and watch as his childeeahn are put in mooohrtal danger of going to hellhlll!"

Now that he had put the question to them, 'are you just going to sit idle while all this happens', he wanted to give them enough time to answer and this time, in unison, the congregation answered, "Nooo!!"

Garzen knew they were going to answer this way and immediately capitalized on it, "That's right! We will nooot sit idleh by while this imp from satan does whatever he wants!! That is noooaaht the kind of congregation we are! We will step forward and we will bring light to where there is only darkness; we will bring the looaahrd's light to thisss famehleh!"

Another pause as they internalized that, "But we need your help, we need your support to step up for these poor misguided souls. We need you to step up as well and we need you to do it now, today!"

His inner circle always got a kick out of watching when he finally asked for the money. His southern accent went out the window, the whole televangelist vibe went out the window and in its place was a very businesslike, clear voice, a voice that without articulating it said 'either put up or shut up' and the congregation always put up and they would put up in record numbers after this sermon. His inner circle never failed to be amazed by the man's ability to raise money and get the congregation doing what he wanted them to do. It never got old.

After the telecast was over Garzen had Charlie and Bubba back to his dressing room. Everyone else in his inner circle was waiting for him back at his compound. Bubba could not wait to say something to Garzen who saw his dancing around and knew exactly what it meant, "What is it Bubba? Shit, you look like you've been holding your bladder for three hours."

Charlie smiled, but didn't say anything. Bubba, now finally able to speak took a big breath to calm himself down and finally opened his mouth to say what he'd been waiting to say, "J.D. you won't freaking believe this! We have gotten more than three million dollars in donation over the last week just from the telecast! That's almost three times what we normally raise in one week from the telecast! But hold on, that's not the only news! We had a single donation of two million dollars from Maggido Enterprises!"

Garzen froze and his head whipped around at the last bit of news, "Did you just say we got a donation of two million dollars?"

Bubba simply smiled and nodded his head briskly.

Garzen still wasn't completely clear, "What was the name of the company again?"

Charlie answered his question instead of Bubba, "Maggido Enterprises."

Garzen smiled and shook his head.

He could see that Charlie and Bubba did not know what he was smiling about, "You don't get it? Seriously guys, if you're going to work for a ministry you might want to brush up on your bible. Maggido is the name of the mountain where the final battle in the book of revelations is supposed to take place. Armageddon, get it?"

Bubba responded with a smile, "I don't care if their name was ShitForBrains, LLC, if they make a donation of two million dollars they are a great company in my book."

Everybody got a chuckle out of the comment, but Garzen was also curious. In his experience anyone making that kind of donation expected something in return. Oh, they might say they were just doing it to support the cause and help those in need, but Garzen knew better, he just wondered who was behind the company and what they would want in return.

MANHATTAN, NEW YORK

It was very difficult for Felix Garcia not to feel like he was missing out on something. Until now he had not written a single thing. With everyone writing about the trial and telling the story of what was going on blow by blow it just didn't feel like one more writing the exact same thing would mean anything to anybody. There were no less than five reporters from the company that owned the Chronicle, Felix's paper, who were all doing precisely that. Felix had been incredibly patient and had been rewarded for it with the most amazing interview anyone could have gotten. He preferred to wait and see if he could come up with another interview like the one that Steven Loomis had granted him. He had gotten that interview because detective Robert Grady had vouched for him when Steven Loomis had looked for a journalist that could tell his story without spinning it one way or another. He had spoken to Loomis for over three hours and after he wrote the article Loomis had let him know he was very pleased with how he had written it.

Robert Grady had been a great resource before, it was worth for Felix trying him again, he called him on his cell phone, "Detective Grady, how are you?"

On his end Grady had to smile. The kid was nothing if not persistent, "What's up Garcia? Are you at the courthouse with the other 20,000 reporters there?"

Garcia smiled as well, "No, I think they have it covered with the 20,000 there, don't you? What do you have for me detective? Actually it is detective sergeant, isn't it?"

Grady shook his head. The kid had good sources, "Yes, yes it is. And I have nothing for you, nothing at all. I really don't Felix, I'm not just bullshitting you. But I will give you a lead on something. If you have someone at the DA's office reach out to them and ask them about the trial team and why they're upset at the DA himself. If I knew I would tell you, but I don't. I just know that Farris and Logan are pissed with the DA about something."

Felix was writing furiously what Grady was telling him. Once finished he smiled a broad smile as he said goodbye, "Much obliged sergeant, much obliged."

Before he could cut the connection Grady needed to say one last thing, "And Felix you..."

Felix finished up for him, "...never heard it from you."

Grady was pleased to hear the kid still knew the value of protecting sources, "Good man"

Both men ended the connection at the same time.

After all the preparations and all the discussions it was time for them to go to court and to present their case. They made their way to the courthouse and rushed past the sea of cameras and reporters stationed in front of the courthouse with the security team and additional policemen holding them back. With the courtroom closed to cameras every talking head and camera crew was jockeying for position in front of the building. Once inside the attorneys, Steven, Beth and the experts made their way to the courtroom directly. The experts stayed outside waiting to be called and the rest of them went inside. The prosecution team was already inside and seated. Once again the courtroom was filled primarily by reporters, sketch artists and the teams for the defense and prosecution. At 1:30 on the dot the judge took the bench, the clerk called the case to order and after the attorneys stated their appearances, the moment everyone had been waiting for was finally at hand.

Drew stood from the defense table came around into the well, the area between the defense table and the judge's bench and turned to face the jury, "Ladies and gentlemen, I want to begin by also thanking you for being here. I can't imagine it's been easy on you and your families, but as the judge said, we couldn't do this without you. I want to begin by addressing the obvious, the reason we are here today. The prosecution is absolutely right, this case is about a charge of first-degree murder, the crime my client has been charged with. The state has been very thorough in explaining to you that in order for my client to be convicted they have to prove that a human being shot another human being with malice and premeditation. I think that it has been established by the media coverage in this case and by the prosecution during the presentation of their case that my client did indeed shoot Donald Riche, that he intended to do so and that he was in his right mind when he did it. On the DVD the prosecution played you have all heard from my client precisely that, that he intended to do it and that he planned how he would do it. So, of all the elements that make up the crime, what's missing? The prosecution would have you believe that no element is missing, that my client's statements and what you have seen in the media should tell you that no element is missing. But I'm here to tell you that it is our contention that one element is missing. It is perhaps the most critical element of the crime, the human element. It is our contention that Mr. Loomis should not, cannot, be convicted of first degree murder because the individual he shot was not in fact human."

At this point Drew paused for effect and the courtroom stirred enough that the judge had to call the court to order, "Ladies and gentlemen please remain quiet."

Drew walked over to the jury box, put one hand on it and one in his pocket and continued with his opening statement, "Now this may seem like an outrageous claim and the prosecution presented testimony from various experts that established that in their opinion Donald Riche was in fact a human being. It all seems very straightforward and clear, but let me tell you that the issue is much more involved and let me explain how. Let's imagine that there was an individual, Mr. Smith, who was in a hospital and had been there for two years hooked up to a machine having been declared brain dead for those two years. What made him Mr. Smith, his intellect, his sense of humor his cognitive ability was gone, completely gone. Let us then imagine that I decide to shoot Mr. Smith, that I buy a gun to do it and that I walk into the hospital and shoot him dead. There would be a shooting, it would be clear that I was the person that shot Mr. Smith and that I intended and planned on doing it, but as in this case, the question would be: was Mr. Smith a human being? Could I in fact be convicted of first-degree murder? Based on the elements presented by the prosecution the answer is yes, he was a human being, but there are other experts you will hear from ladies and gentlemen, experts that research was makes a human being human. That is the essence of what we are going to be presenting in this case. The question of Mr. Smith's humanity in my example had to do with deciding whether a body with a beating heart and breathing on its own, once brain dead, is a human being. The question regarding Donald Riche doesn't have to do with him being brain dead, it has to do with his behavior, his psychological makeup, his physiological and genetic makeup and whether that makeup places him outside of human parameters.

"We have heard from the prosecution's witnesses that based on their physical examination of Mr. Riche he was a human being, but we can also see from my example that it is possible for an individual to fit the physical requirements established by some scientists to be a human being and perhaps not in fact be a human being based on other science also established by brilliant scientists. So, the point of the example was that humanity requires something more than two arms and two legs and a beating heart with a brain. The question of humanity and what constitutes it has been discussed and debated in many contexts over many years. Some cultures believe that to be human you must have a soul; others believe that simply having a body with two arms, two legs and a head is enough to be human. You may be thinking that these situations are quite different from the situation we are dealing with here and you would be correct. The point is that being human is not as simple as the prosecution would have you believe.

"You will hear from Steven Loomis himself. He will explain to you the reasons he did what he did, he will tell you about the information that he used to make his decision and he will tell you about what he experienced after the death of his daughter Tracy. We have all heard about the circumstances that surround this case, it is virtually impossible to not have seen or heard something about the case Mr. Riche was involved in when the shooting occurred. The judge has explained that he will give you instructions on how to consider that information, the media coverage and anything else you might have heard about the case. It is also clear that the circumstances in that case had a direct effect on my client and he will tell you about that as well.

"You will hear from experts, people that have dedicated their professional careers to exploring the parameters that we as a society have set to define human behavior and how there are individuals that fall outside of those parameters. You will hear about their research and how that research has led to them coming to their conclusions. Each of these witnesses will weave their work with the information that has been developed after conducting a psychological autopsy of Donald Riche. You see, an autopsy, the kind of autopsy that the prosecution walked you through, deals with the physical body, the psychological autopsy deals with the psychological makeup of Donald Riche. I should make it clear, and the experts will as well, that none of them treated or examined Donald Riche while he was alive. The psychological autopsy was developed by doing an analysis of his behavior leading up to the moment that he was shot, of the behavior and the actions he was accused of which led to him being indicted. Unlike in a criminal trial, the doctors can utilize that information even though Mr. Riche had not yet been convicted of anything. So while they cannot detail his behavior for you, they can and will let you know what their analysis of behavior that has been documented has led them to conclude. The experts will give you the details of what a psychological autopsy comprises but, in short, it is based on interviews of his co-workers, analysis of his history growing up, reading the materials that he left behind that opened a window into his mind, basically anything that could have contributed to becoming what he eventually became."

Drew walked from the jury box to the middle of the well and continued with his opening, "The prosecution was correct in asking that any testimony or evidence relating to whether Mr. Riche did what he was accused of doing be excluded from your consideration, but it is incumbent upon our witnesses to consider the fact that he was accused of these crimes. The prosecution has already asked that you use your common sense and your experience when deciding the case and having been exposed to the stories about Donald Riche and the opinions of various experts on different forms of media before you were called to be a juror are all a part of the experience, that common sense..."

Farris stood at this point with an objection.

Objecting during the opposition's opening statement was something that most attorneys tried to avoid, but in this instance Farris felt she needed to speak up because Drew was treading in the area of Riche's crimes, "Your honor counsel is basically telling the jury to ignore the court's instructions about avoiding being influenced by the media and he is making reference to evidence the court has ruled inadmissible."

Drew was exasperated with Farris, he believed that she had done it to disrupt his rhythm, "Your honor we are clear on what is not being admitted into evidence and I believe we have made it clear to the jury that Mr. Riche was not convicted of anything, but he was in fact accused of various crimes and he was in fact indicted. The jury is allowed to consider all information relating to the case. The charges against Mr. Riche are part of that information your honor. Hearing about this case and the case against Mr. Riche from various forms of media is in fact part of the life experience and common sense that the prosecution have so ably asked them to use."

The judge was actually also upset by the objection, he tended to be a stickler on litigation etiquette, but even more than that he was annoyed by what he also considered to be an objection designed to break Willis's rhythm, "Counsel I am well aware of what I ruled relating to the evidence that is or isn't allowed. I think we can all agree that based on the responses we got during the voire dire process the jury has in fact heard about the charges against Mr. Riche and the coverage that that situation generated. Indeed I think that a juror who claimed not to have heard about Mr. Riche and what he was accused of doing would have some serious credibility issues. Overruled."

Drew turned walked back in front of the jury box and continued, "The question we are posing with this case is clearly a complex one, particularly in this context. In fact it has never been litigated before in a criminal trial, so we are dealing with something we do not have a guide for. The reality is that what makes us human is more complex and at the same time more subtle than anything else that we might ever consider. Our physical makeup is but one of the components of being human. There is our social structure, our history, our empathy towards one another, our sense of self-preservation, these and many other considerations go into the recipe that makes up a human being. Besides the experts dealing with the psychology of being human, you will hear from experts in social anthropology and evolutionary biology who will walk you through what we as a civilization, as a species have, over time, determined are the norms for human social structure, evolution and procreation.

"The good thing, the thing that will let you ultimately make a decision, about what we will be presenting to you, besides the expert testimony, is that there is history, there is clear evidence of what we as a society have determined to be humanity, what we have determined makes someone a part of our species. Please be clear ladies and gentlemen, we are not looking for you to decide what Donald Riche was, not even our experts can make that determination. What we want you to do, what we are asking from you, is that you listen to the testimony and that you consider the possibility that while you may not know, while none of us may know, what Donald Riche was, we can all come to a conclusion about what he wasn't, *Homo sapiens sapiens*. In fact, you don't need to come to the conclusion about what Donald Riche was or what he wasn't. In reality all you need to decide is that there exists the possibility, based on the evidence, that Donald Riche was not human. And if you can come to the conclusion that based on the evidence Donald Riche does not fit into the definition we as a society have established for being a part of the human species then you must, by law, find my client Steven Loomis not guilty of first degree murder.

"Now, it's time to hear from the most important of all witnesses, Steven Loomis. Only he can answer the why. Thank you very much for your attention."

Drew walked over to the defense table and addressed the judge, "The defense calls Steven Loomis your honor."

The courtroom stirred and the judge once again called it to order. He turned to Steven and asked that he step forward. Steven stepped to the witness stand and stood as he was sworn in. He walked around and took the stand. Drew stood and began to guide him through the basics of his testimony, his age, his education, marital status, professional experience, military experience and education. Drew asked Steven more specific questions about his military experience, the jobs he had held, the places he had served in and the missions he had undertaken. He placed particular emphasis on his experiences with the SEAL Special Warfare Development Group (DEVGRU) or what was also known as SEAL Team six. Steven answered as many questions as he could, but he was also careful to point out to Drew that there were details he could not speak about since they were top secret in nature. Drew knew that to be the case, but it was important for the jury to hear that he still carried a sense of duty and that he was still bound by that sense of duty and honor. It let the jury know that beyond his taking an oath in court, he was a man of honor. Drew carefully guided him through testimony about instances when Steven had had to kill as part of his duty in the service. This was an extremely sensitive part of the testimony because the jury had already heard Steven talking about killing with cold efficiency.

They needed to understand Steven's training and the way in which he had been trained to consider killing, "Mr. Loomis as part of your training with the SEALs, were you trained to apply deadly force in certain situations?"

Steven nodded, "Yes I was. Actually I was trained on using deadly force during my basic training initially. Everyone who goes into the service is trained to use deadly force if the situation calls for it."

Drew needed to make sure the jury understood the difference between what regular military personnel were trained to do and what SEALs were trained to do, "But was your SEAL training more intensive than your basic training in that regard?"

Steven answered, "Yes, my SEAL training was much more intensive, it had to be. The DEVGRU unit, Team 6, was even more intensive because it was only called when the situation had reached a boiling point."

Drew walked him through the types of situations that would call for the DEVGRU unit. Next Drew asked Steven how he had felt when he was called upon to use deadly force.

Steven's answer to this question was crucial because it would form the basis for his testimony about Donald Riche, "Mr. Loomis, on those occasions when you had to use deadly force, how did you feel afterwards?"

Steven shifted in his chair and thought carefully about what he wanted to say, "It was always difficult. I knew it was necessary and I knew that I had signed up for doing whatever was necessary to complete our mission and to defend our country, but it was still hard. The first few times I had nightmares and flashbacks, something that I had been told might be the case."

Steven paused as he considered what he would say next. His testimony so far had made clear that he had killed more than once and that it had been hard every time, "Each time it happened I tried to really understand the reasons that it had been necessary to use deadly force."

Drew had to make sure that the jury understood who it was Steven had been forced to kill, "Without divulging any information that might violate your oath to the Navy, can you tell us the type of individual that was on the other end of the deadly force your were forced to apply?"

Steven listened carefully, he wanted to make sure he understood the question, "If I understand your question you want to know who it was that I was forced to kill?"

Drew walked over to the stand, "That's correct."

Steven responded, "It depended on the mission. In many instances it was terrorists, people who had been identified as having intentions to harm Americans, military or civilians. In other instances it was insurgents, people who had sworn to protect those who would harm the US or its allies."

Now Drew had to elicit the answer to the key question, "And at any time before or after engaging with these individuals did you ever consider their motives or the reasons they were considered threats?"

Steven answered, "Yes I did. It wasn't something that was necessarily a part of our missions, but it was something I had to understand. I had to understand the why of the things they did. Some of the things I was exposed to, some of the things they did, seemed to be so brutal, so beyond what I understood that I couldn't just let it go."

Drew wanted to clarify, "What do you mean you couldn't let it go?"

Steven explained, "I had to understand the why. I knew I had a mandate, a duty, and I wanted to know if they had the same mandate or the same sense of duty in their mind, if that's why they did what they did. SEALs by nature, Mr. Willis, are trained to look into a situation, not just obey blindly without understanding the why of things. There are military forces that holds true for, forces that know they need to obey an order no matter what, but that's not the SEALs."

Drew went on, "And what did you find about that?"

Farris stood to object. She could see that Loomis was scoring with the jury, they all had a soft look and warm smiles on their faces as they listened to him testify.

She had to break the rhythm between Loomis and Willis, "Your honor where are we going here? I believe we have been patient with Mr. Willis, but we would like to know where this line of questioning is headed."

The judge was once again bothered by the objection, he could see the real reason she was objecting, but he could also see the point she was making.

Before he could rule on the objection Drew interjected, "Your honor we are trying to establish the fact that Mr. Loomis has a history of analyzing instances when he has had to use deadly force. We are trying to show the jury that this wasn't something that he began doing when he came across Donald Riche, it was something he had a history of doing, something he had been trained to do."

The judge ruled, "Overruled. I can see what you are trying to do Mr. Willis, but move it along please."

Drew nodded, "Very well your honor. Mr. Loomis?"

Steven went on, "I found that in every single instance these people had a sense of duty. In most cases their sense of duty would seem insane to us here in the States, in our culture, but to them, based on their religious or political beliefs, the things they did they did in pursuit of a bigger objective. Most of them were religious zealots and martyrs, individuals who have been brainwashed since they were children to hate all Westerners, infidels."

Drew went on to guide him through the rest of his testimony, "To your knowledge, did any of the people that you encountered in your missions do the things they did, the terrorist acts they engaged in, simply because they felt like it?"

Steven chuckled and smiled a wry smile, "No, I never encountered a terrorist that did what they did simply because. By definition they did what they did because they had a greater purpose, to create terror and fear, to disrupt trade or to start wars. I don't claim to understand the reasons they did what they did, I just know they never did it for no reason. In almost every instance they wanted for the world to know why they did the things they did."

Drew spent the rest of the afternoon walking Steven through Tracy's disappearance, the investigation and the moment when he found out that they had found something.

He wrapped up his examination for the day with Steven explaining how it was that he was able to get the information about the case, "As I explained earlier, I am an executive with a global security firm and I have resources at my disposal that allowed me to track the progress that was being made in this case. On the night that I went to the warehouse they found Tracy in, I got the information the simplest way possible, through monitoring a police scanner. I had been doing it throughout the investigation so I heard when the call went out and I headed down there immediately."

Drew knew they were about to get into some critical testimony and it was late in the day so he asked the court to conclude for the day. The judge was agreeable and the day was concluded. The judge admonished the jury about listening to coverage of the trial and about talking to their families about the case. After admonishing the jury judge Newman called the court adjourned and once he walked out of the courtroom all the members of the media shot out of their seats to go file their stories.

The media now had plenty of information to develop their stories. It really wasn't anything new, but the fact that Steven Loomis had gotten on the stand and had spoken about his past and his missions in the Navy made for great stories. It was more of the hero profile that the media had been building all along. There were interviews with former members of his SEAL unit, people that had served under him and even though the entire media corps tried to find something controversial about his service, there was simply nothing to find. Everyone that had something to say about Steven spoke very highly of him as a SEAL and as a commanding officer. Some of the stories that the media outlets were able to find were so outlandish that they decided not to use them because they felt the audience would think is was all fiction. Stories like that of Steven going into a dark alley by himself to retrieve injured soldiers with nothing but a pistol and a knife and coming out the other end with two or three fallen comrades without the aid of night optics. Or the story where Steven stopped an entire convoy, all fifty-seven vehicles and guided them around a point in the road where a pickup truck was blow to bits by an IED after the convoy went through. None of the people that worked at the company he was employed by now would speak with the media. The only individual that said anything was Art Goodman, the General, and the only thing he said was that the company and he himself personally were behind Steven completely. He never responded to the question whether that meant he was in agreement with what Steven had done, simply repeating what he had said about being behind him one hundred percent.

When Steven got home Beth was waiting for him since he had gone to Drew's office after the courthouse to review his testimony. Beth was taking her role monitoring the media very seriously since she knew how important media influence could be in the trial, "Every single media outlet is talking about how you are a war hero. They have gotten information that I have no idea how they were able to get about your record and the missions you went on. It's pretty ridiculous."

Steven knew it would be bad after he testified, but he never expected that they would be able to get details of some of the Top Secret missions he went on. He had also not expected the whole hero thing to take, but it had and now Steven was worried that the judge would see it as being too influential on the jury, something the prosecution was almost certain to argue. There

329 The Human Element

was nothing to be done now. It was what it was and the media coverage was almost certain to get much worse before it got better. Steven hadn't seen Felix Garcia in the courtroom and wondered why. The kid had done a good job with the interview, but, Steven supposed, he might still be too junior to edge out someone more seasoned writing for the paper he worked for. Little did he know that Felix Garcia would scoop the other big name reporters once again and that this time, it would actually have an effect on the trial and its outcome.

At the prosecutor's office Logan and Farris were reviewing Steven's testimony much the way Drew and Ray had done when they were going over the DVD. It was clear that Loomis had scored some points with the jury. He had come across as vulnerable and his entire history was impeccable. It was clearly going to be a big challenge to cross-examine the guy and try to trip him up. Tomorrow he would be testifying about his daughter and the things he had seen at that warehouse, both Farris and Logan would need to tread very carefully when making sure that his testimony was limited to his daughter only and that it not make any reference to any of the other girls. There would be no way to avoid having what Riche did have an effect on the jury, what they would have to do is to make sure the jury kept the law front and center. They would also have to ask Loomis to admit he was angry and that he wished Donald Riche dead. They were still both thinking that they should add the lesser-included charges, but the reality was that the DA, David Neill, had been doing the rounds with all the morning shows explaining that the trial was going according to plan. There was no way he was going to allow them to add the other charges. Judging by how the jury was reacting to Loomis, it was looking more and more like they really should hedge their position. The other thing that the prosecution team realized was just how much influence the media was likely to have on the jury. The stories about Loomis being a hero, the interviews with the people that had served under him, and the incessant positioning of Loomis as an all-American boy next door were sure to influence the jury. The judge had already stated that he was willing to sequester the jury and considering what the media was doing, it would be madness not to ask him to do just that. Unlike the OJ trial, this trial would most likely not go beyond five or six months, in reality Farris thought it probably wouldn't go more than three or four months longer. Tonight both deputy district attorneys decided to go home and be with their families and to enjoy some time away from the case. The next few days were going to be extremely intense. Both Farris and Logan relished doing their job and doing it well, but they were both human beings and both had been affected by the Donald Riche case like every other citizen had been affected. Neither one of them was under the delusion that the man had been anything other than a brutal predator who had done unspeakable things to the girls he had targeted. So tonight both of them just wanted to enjoy the company of their family.

The next morning every single morning show had experts on discussing what they believed would be the testimony from this point forward. All of them speculated on the type of witnesses the defense was likely to put on. They had Dr. Leonard's, Dr. Scoma's and Dr. Grossman's names and were dissecting their qualifications. Grossman was already somewhat of a public figure since he had a show on the Discovery channel about his work and the levels of his scale of 'evil'. The show, however, only dealt with the first twenty two levels of his scale, the highest level, the level that dealt with individuals whose behavior placed them on a level beyond that of a human being were not addressed in the program. It had actually been the network that had decided to leave the last level out, as they believed that to have it be a part of the show would take away from the credibility of the rest of his work. He had balked at the idea initially. The highest level of the scale was the true essence of his work; they represented the cutting edge of forensic psychiatry. Still, Grossman had agreed, as he wanted at least the majority of his work out there. Leonard was not quite as well known as Grossman, he didn't have a television program, but among those within his discipline he was well known and although many researchers did not agree with his findings, they all respected him. Both Grossman and Leonard had testified for the prosecution on a number of occasions over the past few years, neither expert was critical in the cases that they had been asked to testify in, they had been asked to present some aspect of their work, but the most important testimony in the cases they testified in had been presented by another expert and the prosecutor. That Friday morning there had been at least thirty additional cameras and even more reporters, most of whom sounded foreign.

16.

After a weekend of countless stories about Steven, the SEALs, hunting Osama Bin Laden and dozens of talk shows providing analysis of the case, the two teams made their way to the courtroom where Steven went directly to the witness stand and everyone took their seats. The judge reminded Steven that he was still under oath; he acknowledged he was under oath and took the chair.

Drew began by reviewing some of the testimony from the day the testimony that they had ended on. He walked Steven up to the point where he heard the call go out about the warehouse. He asked Steven about his arrival at the scene and engaging the police officers that were there. Steven had gone into this resolute to not lie at all, but he had to be careful with what he was going to say about how he got into the scene. He knew it was Mullins and Grady on the line for it. As resolved as he was to not lie, he was even more resolved to not bring Mullins and Grady down.

Drew asked him how he was able to get into the scene and Steven didn't quite lie, but he certainly didn't tell the whole truth, "When I got there they had set up a perimeter and there were a couple of uniformed officers guarding it so that no one would get by."

Drew continued, "And how did you manage to get past the officers?"

Steven responded, "Well, I acted the part. I didn't need to act actually, I was a worried father and I was scared and angry and I wanted to see my daughter so I told them I had to see her."

Drew went on, "And how did they respond?"

Steven explained, "They did their jobs, they kept me from going through for a bit."

Drew asked, "What do you mean for a bit?"

Steven clarified, "Well, I explained to them that if my daughter was there I could make a positive identification which would then give them what would be a critical piece of information on the biggest case in New York."

Drew asked, "And did they let you pass after that?"

Steven went on, "Yes they did. On my way to the warehouse I ran into detective Grady who was already there and had told them to let me pass. They had probably called him when I first got there. I had been in communication with him during the investigation of the case so I was very familiar with him and he with me. I told him the same thing I told the two officers about providing positive identification if it was my daughter. He had already gone in the warehouse and knew that it was Tracy in there, but he also knew that I could in fact provide the first positive identification for the case he had been working for the past three weeks."

Both Mullins and Grady who were sitting in the audience breathed an almost audible sigh of relief. Steven had done a great job of skirting the truth without out and out lying. Both the officers knew they were really in the clear now.

Drew asked, "And did he let you go in then?"

Steven now got visibly upset. He straightened out his tie, shifted in his seat and swallowed hard. He started to say something and then stopped and looked down trying to compose himself.

His voice broke just a bit when he finally started speaking, "He tried talking me out of it. He knew what he had seen and he knew she was my daughter. Detective Grady is a father also and he knew what my reaction would be to seeing my daughter like that."

Steven had to stop. He had to compose himself again before going on. He knew where this direct examination was headed and he needed to steel himself for it. He looked down for a minute before continuing.

Drew was concerned, "Are you okay Mr. Loomis? Would you like to take a break?"

Steven shook his head, "No, I'm fine. We can go on."

Drew continued, "So after you met detective Grady at the scene, what happened?"

Steven explained, "I went into the warehouse and saw the setup in there, that and the conversation I had with detective Grady let me know that what I was about to see was going to be bad."

Drew continued carefully, "What happened then?"

Steven steeled himself to what he was about to go through, "While detective Grady was explaining something about the equipment I walked over to two freezers that were next to each other on the back wall of the warehouse. I don't know why, they just stuck out, but really, I don't know why I went there first or why I looked in the particular refrigerator that I looked in."

Farris could see that Loomis was once again scoring with the jury. Most of them were in tears and Loomis himself was also about to lose it. Moreover, the back and forth between him and his lawyer, Drew Willis, had fallen into a nice rhythm and that too was scoring points. Both of them had been holding back because they didn't want to come across as insensitive, but at this point they both felt they needed to intercede if only to disrupt the smooth rhythm of the direct examination.

Bart Logan finally stood up, "Objection your honor. As the court has previously ruled, we are here to try Mr. Loomis not Donald Riche."

Willis snapped his head around; he couldn't believe they had actually gotten up to object, "Your honor, we are trying to establish Mr. Loomis's state of mind and the court has ruled that Donald Riche's alleged crimes against Tracy Loomis are admissible."

The judge had also looked disapprovingly at Logan and he let him know just how much he disapproved, "Overruled. Mr. Logan I don't appreciate what I consider to be frivolous objections and I will tell you that the next time you feel the need to do it, I will hold you in contempt. Do we understand each other?"

Logan looked down at the floor, "Yes your honor."

More importantly than what the judge or Steven's defense team thought of the objection, the jury shot Bart Logan the nastiest look they had used since the trial began. Farris had to admit that objecting at that point had been a mistake, not by Logan, but by both of them since had he not objected Farris would have objected herself.

Drew Willis turned back to Steven. The objection had at least given Steven a few seconds to prepare for the questions that he was about to be asked.

Willis moved on, "Please continue Mr. Loomis."

Steven complied, "Like I was saying I don't know why I decided to go to that particular freezer, but I went over to it and I just opened the lid. Detective Grady tried to stop me from doing it, but he was too late. By the time he turned around and saw where I was I was already opening the lid to the refrigerator."

Drew lowered his voice as he asked the next question, "And what did you see?"

Steven took a few seconds to answer, he looked down at his chair, he looked up at the ceiling, then quickly at the jury and finally back at Drew, "I saw my daughter's severed head. Her eyes had been removed."

There was an audible gasp in the courtroom and people in the audience stirred in their seats. The jury was horrified, but also enthralled. All of them had tears in their eyes and most of them were shaking their heads at what they were hearing. Some of the female jurors covered their mouths with one hand, horrified. Drew had been dreading doing what was coming next, but it was critical to the case. One thing was to hear about what Steven had seen and another thing was to see it. Ray placed the exhibit they were about to introduce on the defense table.

Drew walked over and picked up three boards that were about two feet by four feet, "Your honor we would like to introduce exhibits 3a, 3b and 3c into evidence."

The judge allowed the exhibits to be introduced into the record. Farris felt they had wasted the objection they should be raising now earlier. There was no way to stand up and object now, lest the judge really slam them from this point forward. The truth was that he had already ruled on whether these things could be admitted, any objection would have to be about the fact that Donald Riche had never been convicted of any crime and up until now the defense had stayed away from any assumptions that he had in fact done these things. They really didn't have to get into it, the world had been exposed to what Donald Riche was accused of doing and to the evidence of it, so there was no need for the defense to do it. This was exactly what they had been afraid of, the fact that the media had basically introduced all of the evidence of his alleged crimes for the defense.

Drew walked from the judge's bench where he had gone to ask to introduce the photographs over to an easel that had been placed at an angle in front of the jury box. He placed the pictures covered with a thin sheet on the easel, then walked over to the witness chair. What was coming next was hard and Drew wanted to be very careful about how he went over it with Steven.

The volume of his voice went down further, his manner became gentle and soft as he asked Steven what he needed to ask, "Steven, I know how hard this is for you, trust me I do, but it's necessary. Is this what you saw when you opened the freezer?"

At this point Drew removed the cover from the first picture and this time there were people that actually cried out and people who got up and left the courtroom, seasoned reporters got up and left the courtroom. The judge banged his gavel a couple of times, but he was also visibly shaken. He had just glanced at the pictures before, but now he had to look at them, really look at them and like any normal human being he was deeply affected by the gruesome images.

Steven looked at the picture quickly, he didn't need to stare at it to know exactly what it was and he answered simply, "Yes, that's what I saw."

Drew left the photograph on the easel for a few moments to let the jury see it. He left it uncovered and then moved on to the next question, "What happened next?"

Steven was glad to move on, "After the initial shock wore off I noticed the rest of the contents of the freezer. There were other heads, little girls' heads, other body parts, arms, legs, they were dressed in little girls' clothes... some of them."

He was struggling to speak. He was halting and he was beginning to really cry now.

He continued, "I could tell that one of the arms was Tracy's because she had jus painted her fingernails and put little flowers on them. One of the hands in that freezer had those flowers on it."

He did have to stop now, really stop because he was openly weeping with his head in his hands.

At this point the judge wasn't going to leave it up to Steven, he'd had enough, "Why don't we take a ten minute break at this time?"

He stood, everyone in the courtroom stood and he left the bench. Steven stayed in the witness chair as the jury filed out, his head still in his hands.

Once the judge left almost everyone in the courtroom also left. Most went to file their reports of this morning's testimony, by far the most impactful until now. There were plenty of digital journalists and some had cards for their computers to get online wherever they were, those that didn't were not going to leave and risk not getting back in time to resume the trial. With everyone out of the courtroom it became the best place for the defense team to take the break. Drew went over to Steven and walked him over to the defense table. There really wasn't anything that Drew, Ray, Max, the investigator there and the two clerks they were using in court could or needed to say about what had just been presented.

Each of them was processing it in their own way. It was very different to just glance at something to make sure it had been mounted properly than looking at it in the context of what had happened. For most of them this had been the first time they'd seen what Riche had done to the little girls. If they were ambiguous about what their client had done and why, seeing those pictures settled it. Steven poured himself a glass of water and sipped it in silence during the break. The prosecution team had adjourned to a conference room on down the hall from the courtroom.

David Neill was already there by the time Farris and Logan walked in.

He was not pleased, "What the hell is going on out there? It's like a Steven Loomis tribute out there! We need to make sure that we keep the real case in front of the jury. Right now they are about as far away from remembering what this case is about as they could be."

Farris was frustrated, frustrated about the position they were in; frustrated by the fact that they had not included lesser offenses on the indictment; and frustrated that Neill had no idea what he was talking about.

She couldn't hold it in any more, "Mr. Neill, the judge already ruled on the admissibility of the material, we already objected and he was not pleased. There is just no getting around the impact of what this man went through getting to the jury. We talked about this, about the fact that the media basically established the case of Donald Riche's alleged crimes. I don't understand what it is you think we can do about any of this."

Neill paced around the conference room. He could tell his deputy was frustrated bordering on angry and he recognized that he had come down on them when they really couldn't do anything about what was going on.

He took a few breaths before speaking again, "You're right, I know you can't do anything about it, but it's still frustrating. The damn media has done a great job of trying Donald Riche on air and in print. Still, we need to keep the eye on the ball and bring the jury back to the central issue of the case. You've done well, just keep bringing them back to what's important, the shooting of Donald Riche. Eventually you'll be able to use all of this to establish motive."

Farris wanted to thank Neill for pointing out the obvious, but she held her tongue, "We'll begin to establish that when we cross-examine him. It's going to be tricky because we'll need to be sensitive to what he went through while still treating him like the defendant. Once we get into the expert testimony and our cross-examination of them I'm sure the momentum will shift again. I think you can now see that this is going to be closer than we thought it would be. Maybe we should consider filing the lesser included offenses so the jury can consider options."

Neill actually took a couple of seconds before answering, "I know it seems like we should hedge our position, but if we do it now it really will look like we're not confident in our own case. If we were going to do it we should have done it at the beginning...I should have done it at the beginning."

Both Logan and Farris almost fell out of their chairs. Neill had actually conceded he made a mistake and there weren't any microphones or cameras around for him to score points with! Neither one said anything. They wanted to leave the situation just like it was, with Neill's admission hanging in the air.

Farris stood up, "We need to get back to the courtroom."

Once everyone had taken their places and the people in the courtroom were seated, the direct examination continued.

Drew went over to Steven who was now seated in the witness chair once again and asked the next question, "Steven, when we left you were talking about the other things you saw, do you recall?"

Steven nodded, "Yes I do."

Now Drew walked over to the easel again and showed the next photograph, a photograph of the same freezer where the camera had zoomed out a bit in order to show more of the freezer's contents. Once again the courtroom stirred, although not as dramatically as it had with the first picture, partly because everyone had been desensitized to an extent and partly because this picture was from a bit further away and wasn't a blow up of the face of a little girl. It still had a significant impact on the jury and it showed.

Drew went on, "And is this what you saw, what you are describing?"

Steven looked at the picture and nodded, "Yes it is. That's what I saw."

Drew moved on, "What happened next?"

Steven actually looked out at the gallery where Robert Grady was seated and gave him a slight nod as he answered the question, "Detective Grady guided me out of the warehouse. He could see that I was in shock."

Drew was almost finished with the more difficult line of questioning, "And did you see anything else before you left the warehouse?"

Steven, now a bit more composed, nodded, "Yes, when I was walking out I turned and saw two stand-up freezers. There were some people from the crime scene investigation team going over them, but I could see what was in them."

Drew walked over to the easel and showed the last photograph. The picture showed the two standup freezers and the mannequins made of real body parts that Riche had been making, "And is this what you saw in the freezers?"

Steven nodded once, "Yes, that's what I saw. I saw what looked like two dolls in there, but then I noticed some things and I knew they were not dolls."

Drew went on with the questions, "What was it that you noticed?"

Steven responded, "I saw stitch marks around their wrists and stitch marks around their necks. I knew what they were then, they were the other girls that had been taken."

Farris stood up, "Objection your honor. The court ruled that this evidence is inadmissible."

The judge had known this objection was coming, "Mr. Willis, what do you have to say?"

Drew walked over to the judge's bench, "Can we have a sidebar your honor?"

The judge agreed, "Very well. Mr. Logan, Ms. Farris."

All five attorneys walked over to the side of the judge's bench. They were going to discuss something that was not going into the record.

Drew began, "Your honor we know what the court ruled. That photograph contains one of Tracy Loomis's arms. You agreed that we could bring in evidence relative to Mr. Loomis and his daughter and this clearly qualifies as that."

Max also had another response, "And even if that was not the case, your honor, the questions and the photographs show the other girls taken, but there has not been a single question or comment relating the pictures or anything else to Donald Riche:

The judge turned to the prosecution, "Counsel, the objection is overruled. I understand why you objected, but given Mr. Loomis's testimony about the physical condition of his daughter's hand and the fact that the picture in fact shows a hand with fingernails as he described, I have no choice but to overrule the objection."

Everyone went back to their places and the judge put the case back on the record.

Drew walked over to the witness chair, "So you were escorted out of the warehouse. Did you leave the scene after that?"

Steven shook his head, "I sat down in a police car for a few minutes and composed myself. Then l left the scene."

Drew was glad to be done with the warehouse, "Where did you go?"

Steven was also glad they were done with those questions and those pictures, "I went back home. I knew I had to tell my wife because cameras were already there and I didn't want her to find out that way."

Drew took Steven through his testimony about what he had done for three days after having gone to the warehouse. He asked about his state of mind and about what the news had done to his wife. Steven went over his mental condition, how he was angry and confused. He admitted to the fact that those first few days were hazy for him, that he had a hard time remembering what he had done and that time seemed to stand still. They spent a good deal of time discussing the mental state of his wife and his children, how his mother-in-law had to come in to help him with his wife and his two other children.

Finally they got to the point where Steven had begun to process the whole situation, where he began to form his ideas, "Mr. Loomis, we have been talking about those first few days after the discovery at the warehouse. At what point did you begin to come out of it, out of your stupor?"

Steven explained, "As I've been saying, it is a bit fuzzy for me, but I do remember when I began to come out of it because it's when I began to do some reading."

Drew went on, "What kind of reading are you talking about?"

Steven clarified, "I wanted to understand. I wanted to understand why; I think I had to. Maybe it was because I had to occupy my mind or because I just didn't want to face my little girl was gone. Since my time in the service I have always wanted to understand the why of a mission. In war it helps to understand your enemy's motivation, his way of thinking and that's what I wanted here, I wanted to know why because what I had seen was so far out of anything I'd ever come across or even thought about."

Drew continued, "And what did you find out?"

Steven was quick to respond, "I went online and I found some research on this type of behavior. I read quite a bit of it and I got pulled in. It did what I wanted, it explained the why and it did it with quantifiable research."

Drew was now back by the jury, "And once you thought you understood the why, what did you do?"

Steven explained, "I tried to keep busy. We had just had a service for Tracy and had family in town so I tried to engage with them, but I didn't have much luck. The reality is that I was conflicted about what to do."

Drew continued, "What to do about what Mr. Loomis?"

And Steven clarified, "About what I found out, about the conclusions I had come to after reading all that research."

Now that they were past the really difficult testimony, the two of them really did get into a rhythm, "And what conclusions were those?"

Steven answered, "The first conclusion I came to was that Donald Riche was not a human being and that whatever he was and wherever he was, he would always be a predator. Remember, I had been following the investigation and I had a great deal of information about him. The next conclusion I came to was that he wasn't clinically insane, he wasn't an individual in the grip of a psychotic break, everything had been well planned, researched even."

Drew asked the next question looking at the jury as he did so, "And you came to this last conclusion from the research you had been reading?"

Steven nodded, "Partly, but the biggest contributor to it was Riche himself. The way he looked when I saw him on television, how lucid and calm he looked. It wasn't a look of insanity, not the way we understand it anyway."

The day was coming to a close and Drew didn't want to have Steven go over as important and element of the trial as this was with the jury thinking that it was time to go home."

He turned to the judge, "Judge, we are coming to the end of the day and we are about to get into a critical part of the testimony, can we continue first thing tomorrow morning?"

The judge had been thinking about this himself so he granted the request. He asked that everyone be back next day at 8:00 am sharp and wished everyone a good evening.

Before he got up, the prosecution also stood with a request. Logan was the one to stand, "Your honor, I understand the burden this trial places on the jury we have selected and on their families, but we believe it has become patently clear that the media surrounding this trial has clearly had an effect and is most likely still having an impact. The number of reporters in the courtroom and the number of cameras outside indicates that media coverage is most likely going to do nothing but increase. We would therefore respectfully request that the jury be sequestered for the remainder of the trial."

Some of those that were on their way out of the courtroom stopped in their tracks and sat down in the nearest aisle. The judge sat back down in his chair to consider the request. It was unusual for either side to request that a jury be sequestered, but certainly not unheard of.

The judge had already been considering sequestering the jury and the prosecution's request just confirmed his first instinct, "Mr. Willis, I am inclined to agree with Mr. Logan, any thoughts?"

Willis knew that the media coverage would benefit their case, but he also knew that the prosecution's argument had merit. In the end he looked at the jury and saw the consternation in their faces. Who wouldn't be exasperated at the prospect of being held in a hotel for who knew how long?

Drew responded, "Your honor we believe that they jury is fully capable of filtering whatever information they might come across and of keeping the interests of this court front and center."

The judge had already made up his mind, "I can appreciate that Mr. Willis and normally I would tend to agree with you, but the prosecution makes a compelling argument and I have myself seen the extent of the media coverage. It is enough to overcome even the most resolute of jurors. I hereby order that the jury be sequestered for the remained of the trial. If there are any special requests from the jury, medical requests or family requests please let the bailiff know and we will take them under advisement. I want to make sure that the experience, as difficult as I know it to be, is made tolerable for the jury. This order of course includes the alternate jurors. Court is adjourned."

The look of consternation on the jurors' faces could not be more obvious. Being sequestered meant being completely isolated, kept away from their families and kept away from anything that might bias their deliberations, which in this case was virtually any form of news media.

Once the jury was gone from the courtroom the lawyers for both sides gathered their files and went to leave. All of the media had also left the courtroom, most hurrying to file the story about the jury being sequestered. All in all both sides were satisfied with how the beginning of the week had gone. Drew, Max and Ray thought Steven's testimony had been a lot more impactful than they had anticipated. They knew it would be critical to the case, but the level of raw emotion, sheer brutality of the images they introduced and the reaction of the jury had dialed it up a notch. Drew had opted for taking his time, letting Steven work through his emotions on the stand rather than trying to put on a brave and stoic face. His strategy had clearly worked, regardless of where the jury was relative to the case, they clearly had felt some deep emotion, deep sympathy towards Steven. And it had become clear that the prosecution had noticed it because they had objected when it was clearly not warranted, just for the sake of breaking the rhythm that Steven and Drew had developed. Drew didn't want to over-think this and he didn't want Steven trying to modulate how he came across, because he was coming across perfectly.

Still, Max wanted to get a sense of where their client was at, "Okay Steven, how do you feel?"

Steven was exhausted, but he was satisfied with how the trial was going, "I'm tired to be honest, not physically, but emotionally. I can't believe how much that took out of me."

Ray put his arm around him as they worked towards the courtroom doors, "Well, you came across perfectly. Honest, real, like a human being and like a father. That's critical Steven. You saw what that DVD they showed looked like. You saw what it, what you, sounded like on it. You sounded like an operator, like someone who has a lot of experience with this type of thing."

Steven looked at Ray, "Ray, I do have experience with this. There's no way to get around it."

Drew jumped in, "That's true Steven and you are in fact right, there is no way to get around it, we will absolutely deal with it, but we have to do it in the context of everything else. That's what we're going to be getting into when we get back. What you did and how you came to the decision to do it. Before we got into that, we had to have the jury see you as a human being, as a dad and not just as an operator, and we have accomplished that in spades."

They were about to get to the doors leading out of the courthouse and the media was already four deep waiting for them.

Before they got to the doors Drew had one last bit for Steven, "Go home Steven. Beth told me she has a nice dinner planned, a quiet dinner at home. Enjoy it. Start thinking about life after this. I think that's going to be the most useful thing you can do right now."

Steven listened to the advice. He did have to start thinking about what life would be like after this, whatever the jury's decision was. As he was thinking about it, they ran straight into the mob of reporters and cameras surrounding the courthouse exit. Some of them were interviewing the attorneys for the prosecution who had come out through the doors before them and had chosen to speak to the press. Drew raised his hands to let everyone know that for the first time the defense would actually have something to say and that it would be he talking for the defense team.

He hoped that it would deflect the attention from Steven, "We are satisfied with how the case is going. It was a bit more difficult than we had anticipated, a lot of raw emotions that everyone had to go through. This has been a tragedy all around and until this is finished it will continue to affect the Loomis family and probably the families of all of the victims. We hope we can get through this without hurting any of the families any further."

There were questions being shouted by ever reporter there. Drew, Max and Ray listened to all of them and decided to answer two or three of them, but decided to answer all of them at one time rather than answer each reporter asking the question.

Max took the lead, "Yes, we plan on putting Mr. Loomis back on after the experts. We are supremely confident in the testimony of our experts. Obviously their work is controversial and we are prepared for the prosecution to try to discredit them. At the end of the day it will be up to the jury. Thank you for your questions. I'm sure you will have more questions in the next few weeks.

Questions were also shouted out at Steven. The entire group surrounded him and followed him all the way to the car. He kept his head down and went without answering a single question.

Every reporter was asking basically the same questions: "How do you feel about the trial?" "What was the hardest part of testifying?" "Do you think you'll be acquitted with this defense?" "Are you doing this just for the publicity?" and countless varieties of those same questions.

Steven had no intention of answering any of their questions. He had sat down with Felix Garcia and given him the interview he had given him because he knew he wasn't planning on answering a single question from any of the reporters hanging around the courthouse. He was glad about having done the interview because he could easily see where, if he hadn't done that interview, he might be tempted to answer a question or two and he knew that once he did that it would be like blood in the water with the media.

Steven had Lou go directly home where there were more reporters waiting for him once again to ask all of the same questions that the reporters at the courthouse were asking. For the most part, it was only media that surrounded almost every single place that Steven and his family and his defense team went. But the group that surrounded his house today also included people with placards that denounced his argument, called him a blasphemer for thinking that he was god and could decide who was human and who wasn't. There were people that held placards calling him a hero, claiming he had done what humanity needed to have done and other signs touting what he had done. It was clear that before he got there the two groups had been shouting at each other and things were getting heated. As much as the media wanted to get a story from Steven, they did not physically get in his way when he tried to leave the courthouse or when he tried to get to his front door. The protestors, however, had no qualms about getting in his way and letting him know what they thought. Steven's security team didn't care whether they were supporters or detractors, they weren't going to stop or slow down for anyone and when people went to block their way they utilized leverage and very discreet holds on people's wrists and arms to move them out of the way without pushing them. The last thing they needed was to have video of someone of the team pushing people around.

After he made it through the pack he walked straight through the door of his building and to the door of the elevator. His security team stayed downstairs. Beth had stayed home for the testimony that she knew Steven would have to go through. She was not as strong and knew if she saw any of those images she would crumble. She had already unlocked and opened the front door for him. He walked through the door and went straight to her. They hugged for what seemed like hours. He felt so welcome, so warm, like he was in the only place where he could get some respite from what was happening at the courthouse.

He picked her up, "Man this feels so good."

Beth smiled, "I know, it does doesn't it? Can you believe those people out there? I'm not talking about the reporters; that's their job, but what about all the other people. Don't they have jobs? How do they sustain themselves is what I want to know?"

Steven grinned, "I don't know honey, I'm thinking that most of them don't really give it much thought. They probably go from one of these kinds of events to another. I'm sure some of them get support from their churches."

Beth's eyes flew open, "Oh my gosh! Can you believe how many religious nuts are out there? Have you seen all the signs with quotes from the bible and the ones dressed up like Jesus? Talk about over the top."

Steven kissed her, "Yeah that it is, but we were already expecting some of this, weren't we?"

She smiled, "I was expecting the media and maybe a few people shouting things, but I was definitely not expecting the people dressed up and I wasn't expecting that many people carrying signs. I think it's that weird, televangelist guy who's on all the time talking about you and the trial. There are obviously lots of people listening to him.

A few seconds later Beth got quiet and pulled away from Steven. She walked over to the kitchen, "Are you hungry? Do you want something to eat?"

Steven noticed the change, "Beth, what's wrong? What's the matter?"

She went over to the refrigerator and opened it, "What do you mean? There's nothing wrong. Why would there be something wrong."

Her voice was a bit shaky and she wouldn't look at Steven. He walked over to her, closed the refrigerator door and turned her around so she would be facing him, "What's wrong? Obviously something is wrong, what is it?"

She looked at Steven with tears in her eyes, "I'm sorry. It's just that I'm glad I wasn't there the last couple of days. I know I need to be there supporting you and letting people see me there supporting you and I just couldn't Steven, I couldn't do it, I couldn't see our little girl like that, I just couldn't."

She said all of it in a rapid fire, nervous tone. She actually seemed a little manic to Steven.

He pulled her close and just stroked her hair and just whispered in her ear, "It's ok, shhh, it's ok."

He knew what she was talking about; she really couldn't have been in the courtroom to see the evidence, the pictures that had been introduced.

She would have absolutely lost it and completely fallen apart; Steven continued, "Beth, it's okay. You know how much it means to have you here, at home taking, care of things. It gives me comfort so please, please don't be upset."

They hugged once again. I the middle of their hug, the kids finally came out from their parents' bedroom and ran to their father, "Daddy! You're home!"

Steven's mouth fell open and he looked at Beth who was smiling a satisfied smile, "Surprise!"

Bethany was the first to reach him. She jumped into his arms and wrapped both her arms and her legs around her father. He was so happy to be with his daughter. She had been deeply affected by all of this and if he was to be honest, he had wondered whether it might not be better for her to be here, with her parents. Now, having her here and hugging her and feeling her heart beating hard against his own chest, she was back to being his little girl. Christopher was the same bundle of energy and happiness he had always been and when Steven picked him up to hug him, he realized just how much he had absolutely missed him, missed his smiles and his silly noises.

He held him up with both arms and looked at his face, "Hey champ! How's my pilot?"

Christopher had always loved it when his father spun him around in the air and pretended he was a pilot, "Do it Daddy! Do it! Pleeease!"

Steven complied and spun Christopher around a few times before putting him down, "Boy, you have really gotten big buddy!"

Christopher flexed his arms like a body builder, "I am big dad and I'm really strong like Iron Man!"

Steven ruffled his hair and smiled. He hadn't felt this way since before Tracy's disappearance. He felt happy and content, glad to have his family around him. There was no way that they would be able to go anywhere during the week, but he was looking forward to spending time together playing board games, putting puzzles together, eating popcorn and watching pay-per-view movies. He was looking forward to being normal even if it was just while he was at home. His in-laws had gone to visit some friends they had in New York while the Loomis family just spent time together.

17.

On Tuesday morning the defense team met briefly at Ray's office and then headed to the courthouse. There were even more cameras and reporters than there had been the day before. They were joined by a very loud and vocal mob of both supporters and detractors yelling at Steven and at each other. The spectators now included a gaggle of people holding up religious signs condemning Steven in just about every possible way that could be imagined. And it wasn't just a couple of signs here and there, there were dozens of signs and the people holding them were louder and more intense than any of the people that had been outside of the courthouse until now. The media absolutely loved it; they had something new to report. Some of the media outlets were even interviewing some of the protestors. It was a bit overwhelming for everyone on the team. The security teams, both the one that was visible and the one that was hidden, had every one of their senses on full alert. The defense team didn't have anything new to say so they avoided every question and just walked inside.

When they went into the courtroom they found the prosecution already sitting there. There was someone else sitting at the table. The district attorney himself was sitting at the prosecution table, apparently ready to actively participate in the trial, as crazy as that sounded. The jury filed in and then the judge walked in and everyone stood. He turned to the jury and asked how their evening had gone and whether any of them needed anything. Having gotten no answer he sat down.

Once he sat and called the court to order he directed Steven to take the witness chair once again, "Mr. Loomis, do you understand that you are still under oath?"

Steven nodded simply, "Yes your honor. I understand."

The judge handed it over to Drew, "Very well, please proceed Mr. Willis."

Drew walked over to the witness chair and picked up where he had left off the day before, "Mr. Loomis, we left off with you telling us about how you were feeling after having witnessed what you did at the warehouse, do you remember that?"

Steven nodded, "Yes I do. Actually I believe we were about to talk about the research I found."

Drew nodded, "You're right, we convened right before you were able to tell us about that. I would like to back up a little bit though and go over the testimony before that point."

Steven responded, "Okay, I don't mind"

Drew continued, "Okay, so tell us again how you felt after witnessing that horrible scene."

Steven shook his head slightly and his face became harder, darker, "I was angry, devastated and somewhat confused. I knew my little girl was gone, I knew it before they ever found the warehouse, but seeing her there just destroyed me."

Drew went on, "And what did you do after you left the scene?"

Steven, still with that dark expression, answered the question, "I went directly home to tell my wife what had happened. I didn't want her to find out about it from the television or the radio."

Drew now lowered his voice knowing what was coming, "And what was her reaction?"

Steven responded, "She was already very fragile and this just sent her over the edge. She was in the midst of a breakdown. I had to get her help and I needed to get my children out of the city, so I called my in-laws to come and help me. They came and helped me with my wife and helped to make arrangements for burying Tracy."

Drew was as gentle as he could asking the questions, but he needed to ask them, "How was it that you were able to do all of this if you were so upset about what you had seen?"

Steven answered immediately, "I was on autopilot. I was allowing my mind to concentrate on something, something other than Riche and what he had done to all those girls."

The prosecution couldn't let that go, Logan stood this time, "Objection your honor, this assumes facts not in evidence and the court has already ruled on this."

The judge turned to Steven, "Sustained. Mr. Loomis, Mr. Riche was not convicted of the crimes he was accused of by the time he died, so you can't give testimony about what he did or didn't do, you can only give your testimony about what he was accused of doing."

Steven nodded, "I'm sorry your honor. I wanted to keep my mind away from what Donald Riche was accused of doing."

Drew was now using the well walking to the witness stand and then to the handrail by the jury seating, "And why did you want to keep yourself from thinking about it?"

Steven answered, "Because I couldn't understand it. I think I told you before that all through my career I always tried to understand my enemy, always tried to understand the why for the missions I went on and the why for what the people we were ordered to fight were doing. I just couldn't understand this, I couldn't understand the why."

Drew asked, "So what did you do?"

Steven nodded and for the first time looked straight at the jurors, "I kept myself as busy as I could, but eventually I ran out of things to use to occupy myself. I had to face what had happened; it was all over the news so there was no way to avoid it. There was only speculation and questions on the television, so I started to do some research on the Internet."

Drew was back by the jury, "What exactly were you researching?"

Steven looked at Drew quickly and then back at the jury, "I was researching other situations like this one, where someone had committed murders like the ones Donald Riche was accused of. I researched what had ultimately been decided, what the juries had come up with. In the middle of researching all of that I came across the name of Dr. Tyrone Leonard. He had been interviewed about a particularly brutal case in Indiana."

Drew went on, "And what about his interview caught your attention?"

Steven's expression and demeanor was back to normal, "During the interview he was talking about the why and he was trying to answer the question that I had about my daughter's murder. I went online and found everything that he had published about his work and his research. When I did that I was floored, I couldn't believe how much information I found about the same kind of work that Dr. Leonard was doing. I came across Dr. Scoma and a whole bunch of others."

Drew asked the next question, "And what was it that you found doing all of your research?"

Steven explained, "The research I found and the doctors that conducted it developed the hypothesis that there are individuals who do not fit into the definition of what a human being is. They had spent a great deal of their careers doing this research, had interviewed thousands of people and came to the same hypothesis independently."

Now they were back in a rhythm, Drew went on, "Is this something you were looking for specifically?"

Steven stalled, "I don't exactly get your question. What do you mean was I looking for it specifically?"

Drew clarified, "I mean when you started your research were you looking for someone who had come to this conclusion. Were you already thinking about it before you found the research you found?"

Steven shook his head, "No I wasn't thinking about it at all. Like I said I was confused, I didn't really know what I was looking for. I suppose I was just looking for anything that could explain the why. What I saw at that warehouse just didn't make any sense to me, as much as I tried to understand it. I needed to understand how someone can do that kind of thing to anyone, let alone to little girls."

Drew came back to the witness stand, "What happened after you had read all of the research papers? What did you do?"

At this point Steven shifted in his chair and prepared to let the world know why he had done what he had done. He wanted to come across calm and credible, but not too cold.

He had connected with the jury and he didn't want to lose that, "I thought about it for a couple of days and then I went to my office, I checked out a sniper rifle from our armory. I went to scout out an office building by the courthouse and when I found one I went inside to find an empty office that I could use."

Drew was also trying to make sure the connection with the jury was not ruined.

He looked at them and then at Steven, "That you could use for what?"

Steven answered the question, "That I could use to take the shot."

The courtroom stirred and the judge banged his gavel to call the room to order. Drew let the noise die down before going on. He too was concerned about how Steven was going to come across.

He decided to bring him back a few steps. "Let's go back a bit. What made you come to the decision that taking a shot and killing Donald Riche was the right thing to do?"

Steven thought a bit before answering, "I didn't come to the decision that way. Honestly, I didn't really know what finding all of this research meant. And then I went on a walk. It occurred to me that we, society as a whole, have come to the conclusion that many of these killers, many of the people who have butchered others are not human. We say it and we speculate about it, but we never deal with it straight on, we have never analyzed it using scientific data. People, experts even, say things like 'he's an animal' or 'he's not a human, he's a monster", but they say it in an offhand way. Well, the science I found showed that often they are correct when they speculate like that."

Drew went on, "And what does that have to do with deciding that you had to shoot Donald Riche?"

Steven explained, "After reading what I read and witnessing what I did at that warehouse, I came to the conclusion that Donald Riche was one of these individuals. I came to believe that Donald Riche was not a human being."

The courtroom stirred once again and this time the judge was angry, he banged his gavel harder than before, "Ladies and gentlemen I am going to ask you to refrain from reacting to the testimony. I am instructing the bailiff to remove anyone in the courtroom who speaks or reacts to any testimony."

The courtroom quieted down once again and Drew continued, "Mr. Loomis, please continue. You were telling us why you made the decision you did."

Steven gave a quick nod, "Yes, I decided that Donald Riche was not human and I also came to the conclusion that he would continue to be a predator, no matter where he was."

Drew wanted to clarify something, "So you came to the conclusion that Donald Riche was some kind of monster?"

Steven shook his head emphatically, "No, not at all. The research I found was based in science, not science fiction. What I came to understand was that there is another kind of human species on the planet and that Donald Riche was a part of that other species."

Drew went on, "So you made the decision to do this because you wanted to spare the world from Donald Riche? He was already in custody, he only posed a threat to other prisoners, so who were you trying to protect?"

Steven looked a bit flustered, "I guess it came out wrong. I wasn't trying to protect anyone; I wasn't thinking that he was still a threat. I thought about what he did, excuse me, what he was accused of doing and I thought about my walk in the park. I knew he would be a threat no matter where he went and I thought it was important that the world know what he was. I thought it was important that the world learn about this research and about the possibility that there are more of these individuals out there. In the service I was trained to come up with the most efficient tactical solution, with a solution that got the job done but didn't risk any more than it needed to and taking the shot was the best solution I could come up with."

Drew was in well-traveled territory, they had gone over this testimony countless times, "Why did you think that killing Donald Riche was the best solution?"

Steven took on a somber expression as he answered, "The killing part was difficult, I thought long and hard about it, but in the end he was what he was, a predator, a brutal predator that had been accused of killing and dismembering little girls. The world would be a better place without Donald Riche. Killing him would raise awareness, would get people talking."

Steven was getting flustered. Drew thought about giving him a break, but this made him more human, more vulnerable and he needed that during this testimony, he let him go on, "I... listen I wanted my daughter's death to mean something. I just couldn't come to the conclusion that she died for nothing, that he took her away and that our family was just left with the pieces to pick up."

Drew listened to his answer and walked over to the jury box before asking the next question, "Mr. Loomis, you've just given us the reason that you decided to do this, all the reasons, actually, and you didn't mention anger or revenge. Do you think that any of this had to do with a desire for revenge? That it didn't have anything to do with anger?"

Steven ran both hands through his hair and lowered his head before answering, "I wasn't sure at first, so I held off on doing it. I didn't want it to be about revenge, although it was easy to go there whenever I thought about it. If I wanted it to be about revenge, about avenging my daughter, I wouldn't have been thinking about turning myself in. I could have done it and not been caught."

Even though the judge had warned the gallery not to react, a low murmur came from the courtroom. Drew let that hang for a second, "So you're saying that you could have gotten away with this, with shooting Donald Riche? How could you be so sure?"

Steven was now more confident, not as flustered as he'd been before, he was looking straight at each or the jurors, "I was trained to lead black ops in some of the most hostile environments known to man. I have been a part of tactical operations where we needed to be in and out without anyone knowing we were there. I am a qualified sniper and I am trained to put together an explosive device with everyday household items. I have sixty-two confirmed kills in combat. Yes, I believe that I could have killed Donald Riche without being caught."

It was a difficult thing to have him testify to because there just wasn't a good way for the jury to hear it, but it had to be said and if he testified to it himself, then he would diffuse the prosecution putting it on the table first, "So when was it that you decided that you would turn yourself in?"

Steven thought about the question for a few seconds, "I decided that I would turn myself in at the same time that I decided to shoot him."

Drew continued, "And why did you decide to do that?"

Steven nodded, "Because the only way this would be brought up the right way would be if I did what I decided to do, turned myself in and then built my defense around the argument that we are here presenting today."

Drew walked over to the defense table and looked back at Steven, "So you're saying that you decided to do what you did in anticipation of going to trial and making the argument that you are making? You thought about all of that before shooting Donald Riche?"

Steven nodded, "That's correct."

Drew asked the question he knew most people would be asking, "And Mr. Loomis, why do it this way? Why couldn't you just have gotten the word out, told the world about this science and what it meant? I mean doing it this way put your own life on the line, your freedom."

Steven listened carefully and nodded in understanding, "Before I made the decision, I went to see Dr. Leonard and I asked him something similar. See, all of this seemed like just incredible information that the entire world would want to know, should know. So I asked Dr. Leonard why he hadn't publicized his findings, why he hadn't put the word out about this subspecies he'd found. He told me that he had, in fact, put the word out and tried to let the world know about his research and what he'd found. He also told me about other research from around the world, amazing things that you would think the entire world would want to know."

Drew interrupted him, "Like what? Can you give us an example?"

Steven gave a quick nod, "Yes I can. He said that researchers were now able to turn any cell on the human body into a complete map that could be used to clone someone. The example he gave me was that it could be that someone took Brad Pitt's drinking glass and from the cells left on it, they could develop a clone."

For the first time there was some levity as the courtroom gallery suppressed a giggle. The judge let it go; even he knew that having a lighter courtroom would make the experience for everybody a little better.

Drew also smiled, "Please go on Mr. Loomis."

Steven continued, "He also explained that stem cell research had now yielded people who are able to walk after being paralyzed from the neck down. He also told me other things and as he was telling me all of it I couldn't believe I hadn't heard about any of it. I mean none. I'm a fairly well read individual, Mr. Willis, I have to be, given my work, and I had never heard any of it, just like I had never heard of Dr. Leonard's work."

Drew wanted to keep the testimony clear for the jury, "Okay, and what did all of that mean to you? What did the fact that people had not heard of all this science have to do with your situation."

Steven answered looking at the jury again, "Well, you asked me why I hadn't just opted for putting the word out, so I am explaining why. If I and most of the world did not know about Dr. Leonard's work or about some of the other amazing scientific findings, why would they pay any more attention to this science?"

Drew moved on, "So, if I understand your testimony, Mr. Loomis, you felt that just putting the word out would do nothing, that you had to do something that would ensure that the world would know about all of this new science you had found, Dr. Leonard's and others, is that correct?"

Steven nodded, "Yes, that's correct, that's the conclusion I came to."

Drew now threw Steven a curve ball, he asked a question they had not gone over in their preparations, "And why did you feel that it was your responsibility to make sure the world knew about what you'd found?"

Steven reacted exactly how Drew had calculated he would, he got a bit upset, "I began answering your question by explaining to you that I wanted my daughter's death to mean something, that's why. Maybe others can discover something like this and just worry about themselves, but I'm not made that way. I saw, Mr. Willis, the carnage that one of these individuals can cause; I saw the other families that lost their little girls and how destroyed they were. If there was a way that I could make sure other families weren't torn apart, I could not just stand by. I'm just not made that way."

Drew nodded and continued, "But when you thought about doing what you did and the consequences, weren't you concerned that if you used the defense you are using you would be convicted?"

Steven paused for a moment and thought about the question.

He knew what was going to happen when he answered the question, but he thought it was worth the risk, "Yes, I knew it would be a risk that would happen. But I also knew that by using this defense there was absolutely no way that the world would remain oblivious. Look outside, Mr. Willis, the whole world is watching and listening to what is going on in this courtroom. There are people talking about it in just about every form of media. So, to answer your question, yes, of course I was concerned, I prize my freedom, just like anyone else would, but this was bigger than me."

Drew was going to wrap it up, so he walked back to the defense table, but before he could say anything else, Steven beat him to it, "I was worried, sure, but I truly couldn't imagine a jury, anybody really, coming to the conclusion that someone that could kidnap and mutilate six and seven-year-old little girls was a member of the human race, a member..."

Both Logan and Farris shot up, "Objection your honor! This is clearly an attempt to convict Donald Riche without a trial and moreover it is an attempt to make this about what Donald Riche was accused of. You already ruled on this, so this seems like a blatant attempt by Mr. Willis to get in testimony that you have already disallowed."

The judge turned to Steven, not Drew to give his admonishment, "Mr. Loomis, I have already told you that you cannot testify to something that is not in evidence. If you do it again I will be forced to find you in contempt sir. Mr. Willis I would think long and hard about the questions you pose to your client from this point forward. The jury will disregard anything that Mr. Loomis has said regarding the crimes Donald Riche was charged with. As I have made clear before, Donald Riche was accused of various crimes, but was never convicted. Anything that Mr. Loomis has said in that regard is his opinion and not evidence of fact."

Steven was nodding as the judge was speaking. He had a look of regret on his face, a look that let the jury and everyone in the courtroom believe that he realized he had let his temper get the better of him, when in reality it had been a well-choreographed adjustment by he and Drew.

Still he needed to show contrition, "I'm sorry your honor. It won't happen again."

Drew went back to his direct examination. He continued by asking Steven the specifics of the shooting, how he had gone into the office, how he had calculated for the police coverage, gotten an attorney and finally turned himself in. They had come full circle, back to where the two detectives had testified, back to what they have testified to.

Drew was satisfied with the way the direct examination had gone, "Thank you Mr. Loomis, no further questions."

The judge turned to the prosecution, "Mr. Logan, Ms Farris."

Bart stood up and walked over to the witness stand. Until now there had been no animosity between the two sides, they were certainly adversarial, but they had both managed to come across as professionals doing their job and Bart Logan wanted to keep it that way, "Would you like to take a break Mr. Loomis? I imagine that it must have been hard to see those images and remember what happened."

Steven looked directly at Logan when he answered, "Yes, Mr. Logan, it was hard and no, I don't need a break."

Logan went back over the testimony regarding Steven's background, just to verify the information he had already given on direct. He went back over the testimony about how Steven had found out about the warehouse and how he had ended up there, going past the perimeter that had been set up by the police. He wanted to take his time with this and be thorough, but he decided against using the pictures. There was no way that he would be able to put them up during the cross without the jury frowning and truth be told he didn't need the picture for what he was planning to do.

He went on, "Mr. Loomis, we have all seen the horrible pictures of what you witnessed and you have testified to the grief and the helplessness that you felt as a father. Is it your testimony that in spite of all of that you didn't feel absolute fury towards Donald Riche? That you didn't want him dead because of what you believed he had done to your daughter?"

Steven looked at Logan, then at his defense team and finally at the jury, "Of course I felt fury and yes, when I left that warehouse I wished him dead, I wished he was gone from the face of the earth, the same way I imagine any father would. But if you are referring to when I made the decision to shoot him then the answer is no, I didn't make that decision out of fury, not even anger. I mentioned my service before and believe it or not, Mr. Logan, the training stays with you, it pretty much governs how you think and how you react to things like this for the rest of your life. I don't make decisions out of anger, not even this decision."

Logan wasn't going to back off that easily, "So if you didn't decide this out of anger or a desire for revenge then I am assuming that you made the decision out of a sense of altruism?"

He meant for the question to come out without sarcasm or a condescending tone, but there was just no way for it to come out clean.

Steven listened to the question and kept his cool, "I don't know if I would call it altruism. I did it because I wanted to give meaning to my daughter's death, I wanted to give it meaning, it was personal. I wasn't thinking about humanity or how others would benefit. But I also didn't think of the rest of the world when I became a SEAL or when I put my life on the line in the most horrible and dangerous places on earth. I knew that our missions and what we did would benefit others, maybe even the rest of the world, but you don't think about that when you are deciding you're willing to risk yourself. You do it because it's a part of your DNA, the way you've been raised. If they did benefit, then great, all the better, but I didn't do it to be anyone's hero. No SEAL does what he does to be a hero, if that's what drives a man, then he will never make it as a SEAL."

Logan listened to the response and decided to move on, there was simply no upside to pursuing this line of questioning. He walked Steven through the days after being at the warehouse and through the time he was depressed and angry. He walked him through making arrangements for Tracy and through making arrangements for Beth and for his other two kids. Throughout all of it Logan was professional and direct. There was no sarcasm or condescension in any of his questions. He didn't press on the anger angle because it had become clear that Steven wasn't going to let himself be goaded that way. Instead Logan focused in on the research he had found and how it had affected him.

He was going to go for a more sensitive angle now, "So, Mr. Loomis, it's your testimony that based on what you read and on the research you found, you decided that Donald Riche wasn't a human being, is that correct?"

Steven nodded, "Yes, that's correct?"

Logan went on, "And you came to that conclusion before you made the decision to shoot him?

Again a nod, "Yes, that's correct."

It was time for Logan to pull the trigger, "Isn't it true Mr. Loomis, that you decided to kill Donald Riche when you saw what you believed to be his victims, when you saw your daughter?"

Steven remained impassive, "No, that's not correct."

Logan pressed on, "And isn't it true that you planned and executed the shooting and only after you had done so did you come up with the defense that you are presenting here today?"

Steven shook his head emphatically, "No, that's not true."

Logan walked over to the jury box and leaned against the banister in front of it, "You made the decision to confess after the murder of Donald Riche and at no point did you mention any of this, the research, how you felt, any of it, to any of the detectives you spoke with?"

Steven nodded, "Yes that's correct. I didn't speak about any of this with anyone."

Now Logan had to infuse his tone with doubt if the line of questioning was going to work, "Something so meaningful, something that had in fact driven you to shoot another man and you don't mention it during a confession you gave willingly. Does that make sense to you?"

Steven gave a wry, thin smile that made Logan uncomfortable, "Yes, actually it does make sense to me. It was my intention to take ownership of what I had done and that's exactly what I did. I was not going to present my defense at that time so that you or for that matter the media could tear it apart. It just wasn't the right venue to talk about it."

Logan kept on the pressure, "Let's go back to the research. You testified that you read these studies and that based on that you made the decision to shoot Donald Riche, correct."

Steven answered, "That's correct."

Logan pushed on, "But none of these studies were about Donald Riche, correct?"

Another quick nod, "That's correct."

Logan continued, "And none of these researchers had at any point examined Donald Riche, is that correct?"

Drew stood up; he was getting tired of Logan beating around the bush, "Objection your honor. There was no way Mr. Loomis could know if they examined Donald Riche or not. Where exactly is the prosecution going with this?"

The judge turned to Logan, "Mr. Logan, get to it please."

Logan nodded and got back to business, "Yes your honor. Mr. Loomis, you don't have training in forensic psychiatry do you?"

Steven shook his head, "No, I do not."

Logan needed to make the point clearly, "And you don't have any training in psychology, physiology or anthropology, do you?"

Steven remained resolute, "No, I never claimed that I did."

Logan pushed on, "I realize. But yet you felt that you had enough knowledge to take this research and decide that Donald Riche was in fact one of the individuals the research mentioned."

Steven knew where Logan was going and he was ready, "I wasn't making a clinical diagnosis Mr. Logan. I know I'm a layman and I realize that the jury and the world in general may find what I did repulsive, but I think I've made it pretty clear by now that I made the decision for myself and for what I believed to be compelling and powerful reasons. I also already told you that I am not claiming to have the answers for why people like Riche do what they do, it will be up to the jury to decide if I have come up with something that could be the answer. The jury and the world will decide about this relative to the law and the way the law treats cases like these in the future, but as far as I am concerned I have already accomplished what I set out to accomplish. I have engendered discussion, I have brought this research to people's attention and I have perhaps given a modicum of peace to others who may have also been thinking and wondering why their loved one was butchered or raped or beaten. As far as I am concerned what happens to me now is the price to pay for all the things I just mentioned."

Logan's tone now did become a bit sarcastic, "So you are saying that you don't care if you are convicted? That you don't care if you go to prison for the rest of your life?"

Almost as soon as the question had left his lips Bart Logan was regretting asking it.

He walked right into the answer that Steven gave him, "No, that's not what I am saying at all. I would be crazy not to care if I go to prison, if I am taken away from my family. Of course I care. I care enough to hire the best defense team I could find and I care enough to be up here testifying, going through everything all over again and not just pleading guilty and signing a paper. I care very much Mr. Logan, I said I'm nobody's hero and I'm certainly nobody's martyr."

Logan wanted to move on immediately. He knew he was going to get an answer along these lines, which was the reason that he regretted having asked the question almost as soon as it left his lips, "I'd like to go back to what you testified to earlier. You have stated a few times now that the reason you shot Donald Riche had nothing to do with revenge or anger, that it had to do with coming to the conclusion that he was not a human being. Is that correct?"

Steven nodded, "Yes, that's correct."

Logan pressed on, "So it would be safe to assume that had you not come to that conclusion, that he was not a human being, you would not have shot him, is that correct?"

Steven responded, he wasn't sure where Logan was going, "Yes, I think that would be safe to assume."

Logan pulled the trigger, "Well, don't you find that a bit convenient?"

Steven's face took on a puzzled expression as he answered, "I don't get you. What do you mean convenient?"

Logan clarified it for him, "You shoot a man and then claim that the reason you shot him was because you found research which led you to the conclusion that the man was not a human being. Don't you think that, based on what you've said here today, finding research that basically gave you a free pass on murdering someone that you felt had caused you and your family incredible pain, was convenient?"

Steven finally understood what he was asking, "No Mr. Logan, as a matter of fact I find it to be quite inconvenient since had I not found the research, I would not have decided to shoot Donald Riche and I imagine that the fact that I am sitting here answering your questions and that I turned myself in and was arrested should be a pretty good indication that I most definitely did not get a free pass."

Logan was not flustered in the least, "All of this assuming of course that you found the research first and decided to shoot after."

Steven said, "Of course. That's what I've testified to already."

Logan moved on, "Right. I want to go back over your testimony about the research. You stated that you came to your conclusion about Donald Riche after reading the research. Didn't that research also include information about the tens of thousands of subjects that were interviewed after committing all sorts of heinous crimes, but who were found to be humans with psychiatric conditions?"

Steven agreed, "Yes, it did."

Logan continued, "And you also stated that you have no training in forensic psychiatry correct?"

Steven nodded, "Yes, I said that."

Logan began to tighten the net, "And yet you thought that you had enough information to make the distinction between an individual that could be someone with a psychiatric condition and someone who according to you does not fit the definition of human?"

Steven pondered the question for a few seconds. He understood what Logan was asking, he just wasn't sure how to answer it. It was in fact what Logan was looking to do, to raise doubts about the basis for his decision and his reasoning process.

He needed to be careful about his response, "Yes, I felt I understood the research well enough to make that determination, even though I am not a doctor. I guess that a part of this has to do with feeling it in person, being confronted with these things in real life, not just reading about them."

Logan pushed on, "So going by your logic, you now have the ability to decide whether an individual whom you believe to be the perpetrator of some form of horrible crime is a human or not and you then have the justification to eradicate them, is that correct?"

Max stood up, "Objection your honor! Assumes facts not in evidence. Mr. Loomis has never said anything of the kind, the prosecution is basically testifying."

Logan responded, "I am simply clarifying the basis for Mr. Loomis making the decision he made, your honor."

The judge considered it, "Overruled. But if there is a point to be made you need to make it Mr. Logan."

Logan nodded, "Very well your honor. Continue Mr. Loomis."

Steven shook his head with some frustration now, "No, I'm not claiming to have any ability and I'm not claiming to have come up with the answer, in fact I stated precisely the opposite, that I did not come up with any universal answers and that I do not claim to have any final knowledge about anything."

Logan continued, "Except for in the case of Donald Riche."

Steven did not blink, "Except in the case of Donald Riche."

Logan smiled, "And you don't find that convenient?"

Drew stood to object, but before he could get the objection out, Logan was already addressing the court, "Withdrawn your honor. No further questions."

18.

Logan had definitely scored some points with the last part of his cross-examination. He had gotten Steven to admit to some things that definitely painted their argument with uncertainty. Although he did his best to deflect the most damaging aspects of the questions, he still came across as though he might have come up with this defense retroactively, after he had decided to shoot Donald Riche and if that was the case then this would turn into a basic case of vigilante justice, a father that was enraged because of his daughter's murder and acted on it. It was a very subtle and effective way of undermining their defense and Drew was actually impressed with Logan, he had not believed that he had it in him. They needed to put Leonard on now, Steven had been on the stand far longer than Drew had intended and the brunt of the case was now at hand, it was time to provide the jury with something to hang their hats on. Dr. Tyrone Leonard

Before Drew could call Dr. Leonard to the stand Logan addressed the court, "Your honor can we have a hearing outside the presence of the jury?"

The judge was caught off guard, "What's this about Mr. Logan?"

Logan answered, "Your honor, I believe that Dr. Leonard is the defense's next witness and I think we need to discuss the purview of his testimony in light of what we have heard from Mr. Loomis."

The judge turned to Drew, "Mr. Willis, what about it?"

Drew stood up, "I don't really see a need your honor, Dr. Leonard has been briefed on what he can and can't testify to, but if the prosecution believes we need to discuss it yet again we won't object."

The judge addressed the jury, "Ladies and gentlemen we are going to have a brief hearing to discuss Dr. Leonard and how he will be testifying as well as any other witness that will be providing expert testimony. It should take no more than an hour. Counsel we will start the hearing directly, no breaks."

Once the jury left the courtroom and the bailiffs emptied the rest of the benches of media and other observers Bart Logan sat down and Melanie Farris addressed the court, "Your honor, Dr. Leonard never examined Donald Riche while he was alive, he conducted a psychological autopsy the same as the other experts. We believe that his testimony should reflect the difference between having examined an individual and coming to a scientific or medical opinion as a result of that examination and the expert's education and experience and an opinion based on an examination of the individual's psychological state prior to him dying. It's a subtle distinction your honor, but we believe it's one that needs to be made for the jury. The people do not want the jury to take away from the experts that the two are the same."

It was a fair point and the judge knew it, "Mr. Willis, I'm inclined to agree. Any thoughts?"

This time Ray stood to respond, "Your honor, as an expert in his field, we believe that Dr. Leonard and every other expert we will be presenting, is capable of making that distinction when testifying. Obviously there is a difference between examining an individual while they are alive and after they are dead."

He said the last part with a smile and there was snickering from the gallery. Farris responded, "Very well your honor, we just want to make sure that the distinction is made regardless of whether the witnesses make it during their testimony and we believe it needs to be made by your honor."

The judge brought the meeting to a close, "Very well. Bring the jury back in."

The bailiff left to get the jury from the jury room. The other officers of the court let the people in the hallway back in.

Once the jury was seated the judge addressed them, "Ladies and gentlemen of the jury, as you will hear, the experts that have yet to testify conducted a psychological autopsy of Donald Riche. The experts for the defense will be testifying about research they conducted in which they came to certain conclusions about the individuals included in their research. They will also be testifying about conclusions they came to after conducting the psychological autopsy of Donald Riche. It is important that you understand the difference between testimony about research where individuals were interviewed directly and testimony about opinions formed after doing an examination of an individual's psychological state after they are deceased. All testimony presented regarding Donald Riche will in fact be opinion and is not in any way based on an actual examination or interview with Mr. Riche prior to his death.

"You are to treat the testimony accordingly. The credence that you lend to any of the testimony provided by any of the witnesses is entirely up to you, so unless otherwise admonished you and you alone will be the arbiters of what weight to place on any of the testimony."

The members of the media in the courtroom were scribbling furiously, careful to not react to the judge's admonition. The prosecution appeared satisfied with the judge's instructions and Drew, Max and Ray didn't really think that any of it would make a bit of difference. The jury would either find the witnesses believable and listen to them, or they would decide that their work was a bunch of crap and the defense would be over. Either way, the world was about to find out.

Ray stood up, "Your honor, the defense calls Dr. Tyrone Leonard."

The bailiff went out to the hallway where the witnesses had been waiting for their turn to testify. Dr. Leonard walked in the courtroom and immediately made an impact. He had been sitting quietly in the hallway behind a newspaper up until now, but walking into the courtroom his charisma, his bright honey and hazel eyes, dark ebony skin and impeccable appearance gave him an air of quiet authority and confidence. Logan and Farris could now see how this guy's work could prove to be very persuasive. Credibility was about the work, yes, but it was also about the man that had conducted the work. He was just someone who looked incredibly believable precisely because he appeared to not give a rat's ass about whether anyone believed him or not. He seemed supremely confident about the work he had conducted and the conclusions he had come to. He walked over to the court clerk raised his right hand and was sworn in.

Ray walked over to the witness chair and greeted the doctor. He was slow and deliberate when walking him through his initial testimony, his credentials including his education, the posts he had held over his career and all his accreditations. It was necessary to do this in order to establish him as a witness. Although the prosecution had already stipulated to his status as an expert, the defense wanted to establish him as such with the jury.

After going over his bona fides Ray began to lead Leonard into his testimony about the principal subject of his work and the very basis for their defense, "Dr. Leonard when did you begin to do work on the subject of psychopathic behavior and the related fields that came along with that?"

Leonard smiled, "I actually began to study it during my graduate work. My dissertation included some work I had done with a forensic psychiatrist that was analyzing psychopathic behavior and what defined it. His work was about instances where individuals had not shown classic signs of psychopathic behavior, but had gone on to commit extremely brutal crimes, crimes associated with psychopaths."

Ray continued, "Is that when you began to formulate your hypothesis?"

Leonard shook his head, "No, not exactly. He had just postulated the questions, but had never really provided any thoughts on the reasons for this discrepancy. His work simply outlined that there were instances where individuals who showed no evidence of a psychiatric illness or a personality disorder had engaged in behavior that we had previously reserved almost exclusively for psychopaths. My work initially also simply set out to confirm his findings."

Ray moved along, "How then did you begin your work in this area?"

Leonard went on, "While doing the research I just described to you, I also began to do some work with a colleague about how humans had evolved over time. How we as human beings had developed certain behaviors and even physical traits to better allow our survival. I'm talking about hundreds of thousands of years of evolution now, not just a few years. We also began to study the same process with other species. The evolutionary process that is."

Ray had prepared with Leonard and it showed, "Can you give us an example?"

Leonard continued, "Certainly. Sharks are a fine example of what I am speaking about. Over hundreds of thousands of years sharks evolved different capabilities to match their environment. There are more than 400 species of sharks. They are all of the same family and the same genus, but each species has adapted for things like shallow water or deep water there are even sharks that can survive in both fresh and salt water. We have all seen hammerheads and great whites, tiger and bull sharks, each of those species developed their own survival mechanism to ensure the survival of the species. Man has done the same. We have evolved into what we are today, also over hundreds and hundreds of thousands of years."

Ray needed to Leonard to clarify, "Are you speaking of evolution of our physical being?"

Leonard obliged, "Yes, we have evolved to walk completely upright. Some of us have dark skin, which, for those of us with African or Asian descent, protects us from the sun. Those of us from other regions have fair skin and thin hair, again to better adapt. But we have clearly also evolved as a civilization and a society. Our education, our systems of government, our social norms have clearly evolved over time. Look at where technology is today, that's an example of social evolution. Evolution has sped up"

The testimony was coming across as a reasoned and logical explanation for where man was today. Leonard was confident, but also clear and cognizant that he was speaking to laymen on the subject. The jury was, as expected, completely engaged by Leonard.

Still, Ray had to get him back to the issue at hand, "So how does all of this tie back to your work?"

Leonard shifted in his chair to face the jury a bit more, "Well, it occurred to me that perhaps in those instances where we observed individuals engaging in horrific, murderous behavior, but who did not fit the psychological definition for psychopathic or sociopathic behavior, we were observing a new species within the Homo genus. We are all part of the Homo genus and the species sapiens, hence Homo sapiens. Since approximately 100,000 years ago we have been recognized as the only species under the Homo genus. We, modern humans that is, are defined as Homo sapiens sapiens. So Homo is the genus, sapiens is the species and sapiens is the subspecies."

Leonard came across as incredibly knowledgeable about the science he was talking about and very passionate about it, but they needed for it to support their defense.

Ray got him back on track, "How was it that you ultimately came to your hypothesis about a new species?"

Leonard responded, "In our work with psychopathic behavior, what defines it, how it manifests depending on how an individual is raised, whether environment plays into the equation or whether it is all genetic, we interviewed thousands of individuals. We catalogued our work very carefully and we sought to validate any conclusion that we drew from our interviews. Over the span of twenty years we interviewed individuals who were in fact diagnosed psychopaths and sociopaths and we also interviewed thousands of individuals that had engaged in psychopathic behavior but never been diagnosed, very brutal and callous behavior and we compared the findings of our interviews. We found incredibly strong correlation between diagnosis of psychopathy and murderous behavior, all our findings were very much along the lines of what other researchers had found. But there were also hundreds of individuals that had engaged in psychopathic behavior, committing horrific and sadistic murders, torturing of people and other behavior, but who had until then been reserved exclusively for psychopaths. They simply were not anywhere near what we'd defined as indicative of psychopathic behavior."

Ray and Leonard were playing their parts to perfection. Ray the reasonable old pro, Leonard the genius scientist. Farris and

Logan could not do anything but watch and hope that they could erode Leonard's credibility enough to make a dent.

Ray went on, "So, doctor, just to clarify, you found people who behaved like psychopaths and even worse, but who were not diagnosed psychopaths, correct?"

Leonard flashed his amazing smile and nodded, "That is correct, that's what we found."

Ray went on, "But isn't it true doctor that it is common to find individuals who do commit horrible crimes, but are not diagnosed psychopaths? Individuals that commit crimes because of greed or jealousy or some other reason? You wouldn't claim they're a part of another species would you?"

Leonard's smiled widened and Bart Logan and Melanie Farris saw that it was going to be a tough road to try to erode Leonard's credibility, a tough road indeed.

Smile still on his face, he responded, "Yes, obviously we all know that there are murders every day that are fueled by many of these reasons, but we took that into account and discarded any such instances. What we focused on were individuals that had carried out these brutal murders through very well thought out, detailed plans that did not involve any motivation other than the desire to hunt a human being. They were rare, but they were there."

Leonard was clearly still fascinated by his work and the science that went with it. Even though he was no longer smiling, he was leaning forward in the witness chair, using his hands to explain, "We began to find that there were individuals who presented none of the behaviors that we as professionals had outlined for a diagnosis of psychopathy, but who were still guilty of horrendous behavior. They were well adjusted as they grew up, loved by their families. They tended to have very high IQs, some were in fact in the genius range. They never tortured or killed small animals and in fact many had pets, hamsters, dogs, cats while they were growing up. They formed bonds with friends and family, real bonds now, not the types of insincere connection psychopaths feign in order to manipulate others. They pursued traditional interests, sports and the like as children and youngsters and engaged in normal social behaviors, Boy Scouts, fraternities, that kind of thing, but they all communicated a very strong desire to harm or 'hunt' human beings.

"The interesting thing was that they did not view it as odd or unusual, even though they were able to articulate the knowledge that society would indeed find their desires and actions as something horrible and unacceptable. They knew that to be the case, but they did not care. They were also able to discern between having a psychiatric or psychological condition and their own situations."

Ray, now standing by the witness stand asked the next question, "These individuals sound like they tended to be more educated as well, is that correct?"

"Yes, that would be a fair statement. Most of these individuals were extremely intelligent. As I believe I stated, a full 72% had above average IQs and about 35% had IQs in the genius range. This is a much higher percentage than the at large population. In any case, during our work it was these individuals, most of all, that provided us with a clear view of the evolved being we were pondering."

Ray wanted to make sure the jury was clear on what Dr. Leonard was about to say, so he walked him through the testimony, "When you say evolved professor, I think most people think of advanced or forward progress. Or enlightenment, that they're more enlightened. Are you saying that your hypothesis is that these individuals are more advanced than human beings? That this new species is more advanced?"

Leonard thought for a couple of seconds trying to come up with the best way to explain things so that laypeople could understand them, "Yes and no. Let me explain. Clearly, we as a society find violence against one another for pleasure to be an abhorrent behavior, something we must avoid at all costs and for which we need to punish those who perpetrate it. This has not always been so. It is something we have evolved to as a civilization and a society. The behavior we are speaking about, the hunting of humans, is clearly not what we as a civilization would call evolved from a social and philosophical standpoint, in fact we would call it to be devolved behavior. However, when we think about it purely from a survival of the fittest standpoint, from an animalistic standpoint, these individuals are in fact very evolved because they are best equipped to ensure the survival of their species. Their intelligence and their ability to reason clearly, unencumbered by mental disease, give them the ability to blend in. Couple that with significant cognitive advantages and you have something quite dangerous. You see, those are predatory mechanisms, the same way a leopard uses its spots to blend in. Human beings, because of our intelligence and our access to technology and information, are apex predators, we're at the top of the food chain. This new species now takes the place of Homo sapiens sapiens as apex predators in our world. Please understand that was not an easy point to get to and that every researcher who has undertaken similar research has and continues to be vilified for doing so."

Ray nodded, "And what is this new species called?"

"I have come up with the name *Homo sapiens predaer* or *Homo sapiens predator*. For ease of use we simply call them *Homo predators*."

Ray let that hang in the air. There was a murmur in the gallery and then the sounds of dozens of pens and pencils writing on notepads given that the judge would not allow any electronic devices in the courtroom.

After a few seconds he continued with the direct examination, "Dr. Leonard, does this new species have physiological differences as well? Are they different from us physically?"

Leonard nodded, "Yes they are, their cognitive capacity as I said, the performance limits and sensory abilities they have are far above ours."

Ray needed to clarify for the jury the type of individuals that Leonard was speaking about, "So are you talking about some of these individuals or all of them?"

Leonard went on, "I'm talking about every one of the individuals we tested, every single one. Now, remember that we had not set out to prove this or any other theory, we were testing these things because we wanted to establish a baseline for these performance measures. What we discovered very quickly was that their baseline was far above that of an average human being. Actually it was far above every human that we tested, but I say average because we did not test professional athletes or trained soldiers. We were fairly certain, however, that even those humans would not match the performance we were seeing from these individuals."

Ray knew that the jury was probably wondering about the difference between a psychopath and Homo sapiens predator. They'd been dancing around it for a while now, but he needed to ask that very specific question.

He did precisely that, "Dr. Leonard, just so everyone on the jury understands it perfectly, what is the difference between a psychopath and a Homo sapiens predator? And, doctor, can you also tell us how that relates to someone who is psychotic?"

Leonard gave two examples of individuals that had committed atrocious crimes, crimes that involved mutilation, sadism and even cannibalism. He then explained how one of the individuals that had been interviewed had shown clear signs of psychopathic behavior from an early age. He explained how a psychopath is born, how it is not something that can be learned. He described the type of behavior that defined a psychopath: Early desire to mutilate or torture animals, a desire to cause pain for their own satisfaction, a complete inability to show empathy or remorse, an uncanny ability to manipulate others for their purposes but without forming real attachment. He then went on to explain what it meant for someone to be psychotic. He explained that while it was possible for someone to begin to have psychotic episodes from childhood, it was also possible that they might not have any episodes until well into their adulthood. He went on to say that psychosis could be caused by a variety of triggers which included drug use, lack of sleep, brain injury, another mental condition like schizophrenia. Psychopaths and *Homo sapiens predators* were simply born as they were. He also explained psychotics often had a complete and dramatic break from reality. And that they did not use their cognitive abilities the same way that psychopaths or *Homo predators* did. He explained that many psychopaths had issues with their amygdala, the gland in the brain that controlled and managed someone's risk-taking for themselves and those around them. Finally he clarified that the primary and absolute difference between both psychotics and psychopaths and *Homo sapiens predator* was that they were members of two different species. When Tyrone Leonard explained the last point a murmur came from the gallery and it was loud enough that the judge had to bang his gavel.

After the courtroom was quiet once again, Ray needed to ensure that Leonard went over some of the ground that the prosecution was likely to cover.

He knew he needed to just ask the question directly, "Doctor Leonard, you've explained the various differences between psychotics, psychopaths and Homo sapiens predators and it seems as though there are a variety of ways and reasons that someone can be thought of as a psychopath and or as a Homo sapiens predator and it is pretty complex stuff, isn't it possible that the two are one in the same? That there isn't any new species, but simply varying degrees of psychopathic behavior?"

Leonard was nodding as Ray was asking the question. He was impressed, this would clearly be a question the prosecution would raise and by doing it now the impact of the question would be diffused.

He just needed to make sure that he explained it in a way that was understandable for the jury, "You are absolutely correct, it is possible that there is no new species and that in fact there are only varying degrees of psychopathic behavior. As a scientist I would be remiss in not acknowledging that possibility, but it is something we took very much into consideration as we were completing our work. Believe me Mr. Gretche, if you are going to be claiming that you have found a new human subspecies you need to make sure you've asked and answered just about any and every question someone might raise. You don't want that kind of thing coming up after you've made the claim, it's just not something you can just say 'oops, hadn't thought of that' about."

There was a short and soft giggle from the gallery and even the jurors smiled.

Leonard went on, "Aside from the physical differences, the differences in cognition, sensory capabilities, we also looked closely at the behaviors that define a psychopath and compared them to the behaviors of a Homo sapiens predator. Throughout our work we found more than thirty points of difference between one and the other."

Ray then walked over to the defense table and pulled a large poster board, he asked that it be admitted into evidence and once it was he walked over to the easel and put up a list with thirty points of difference. Leonard went over the list and explained some of the more significant differences: no early desire to hurt animals, an ability to truly empathize and feel remorse, the ability to discern between behavior that should engender empathy and remorse; the ability to grow naturally and receive care from a normal family as children; the ability to have actual feelings, to form bonds of love and friendship.

Ray needed him to clarify, "So Dr. Leonard you are saying that these individuals felt empathy and remorse when it came to their crimes and that psychopaths did not feel either, is that correct?"

Leonard smiled, "Yes and no. Yes they were able to show these emotions while psychopaths were not, but no, they did not feel the emotions when it came to their victims. They could discern between their victims and those they had a family or loving connection with. So they could actually choose to allow themselves to truly feel empathy and regret or to simply look at a situation as the natural order of things. Psychopaths cannot feel empathy, love or other emotions, they are simply not able to. They can mimic those emotions, but because they don't truly feel them they sometimes seem awkward or false when they are mimicking them. That's not true of Homo sapiens predators."

Ray needed to make sure the jury was perfectly clear about this point, "So you're saying that if someone was particularly observant or educated in human behavior they might be able to spot when a psychopath is simply pretending to feel something, is that correct?

Leonard nodded, "That's exactly right. That's the reason that in many of the instances the cases we looked at with psychopaths, the police officers involved were able to spot something about the individual that just didn't ring true. Homo sapiens predators do not have that same problem, they can and do in fact feel those emotions, so even someone trained like a police officer or psychologist cannot spot them."

Ray now needed to translate all of this into the crimes that each of these types of murderer were involved in, "We've heard about the types of crimes involved with pure psychopaths, what types of crimes are we talking about with Homo sapiens predators?"

Leonard gave several examples that sounded very similar to the crimes that psychopaths committed. He described crimes that involved torture, sadomasochism, mutilation and cannibalism. "So the crimes of both are essentially the same, is that correct doctor Leonard?"

Leonard leaned forward a bit more, "Yes, they are very similar, but there are important differences. Homo sapiens predators are deliberate and they tend to plan for the long term. In every single instance their crimes had multiple victims, they were serial killers and they knew they would be hunting more than one victim. This is an important distinction because although there are clearly psychopaths that could be described as serial killers, their crimes tended not to be as carefully planned and it was rare when they knew with certainty that there would be more than one victim at the beginning of their crimes.

"Usually psychopaths committed their crime, got intense gratification from it, sexual or otherwise, and then proceeded to plan their next crime in order to attain that gratification again and again. Homo predators worked just like an apex predator would in nature, they knew they were going on a hunt, knew what prey they were looking for and proceeded to go after them, methodically and efficiently, with as little wasted effort as possible. And from the beginning they would know that there would be more than one victim and they planned as such."

Ray now had to ask what most of the people in the courtroom were probably wondering, "Dr. Leonard, if these individuals, these Homo predators are intelligent, geniuses some of them, calculating and well planned, how is it that they get caught for their crimes? How is it that they find themselves locked up talking to you?"

Leonard's nodded with a wry smile on his face, but his response sent a chill over every person in the courtroom.

Ray could not have planned it better if he'd tried, "Well, the ones that were caught and incarcerated had for the most part been turned in by a family member or close friend and once caught, it was the individuals themselves who had confessed to the crimes they'd committed. Actually it would be incorrect to say they confessed to the crimes, they actually bragged about their crimes, they were so proud of what they had done that they wanted to share the information with someone they knew they could trust, family mostly. Remember that for these individuals their behavior, their 'hunts' felt totally natural, like it was the natural order of things that they should feel and what they did. In most instances they were confused and scared for having those strong feelings of hunting being so natural, but the confusion was about the why not whether it felt natural, whether it felt 'right'. And in such instances many believed it must be genetic so who would better understand than their family?

"Mr. Gretche, we identified one hundred and twenty four of these individuals over a period of twenty years, one hundred and twenty four out of more than ten thousand individuals interviewed. Ten thousand is a miniscule number when compared to the population of the United States, which is three hundred million more or less. One hundred and twenty four out of ten thousand is roughly one point two percent. Using the same math, assuming that one percent of the entire population is in fact Homo sapiens predators, gives us a number of three million more or less. Based on our numbers there are potentially three million Homo sapiens predators in the United States. I submit to you that one hundred and twenty four, the number that has been caught and spoken to, or about .005% of three million, is an incredibly small number, which means that whatever the rest of them are doing, they certainly aren't being caught for it.

"Please understand that the difference between psychopaths and Homo predators is very subtle but significant. Psychopaths often use normal humans for their purposes; they manipulate using their charm and intelligence. They are narcissistic, impulsive and self-absorbed and most of the time they can be extremely charming. They have a complete inability to feel anything like sadness, empathy and love. Homo sapiens predators can be all of those things, but generally they plan for the long term and they try to be self-sufficient when executing their crimes, even at the cost of coming across as odd or aloof. They also have the capacity to feel empathy, love, sadness, all feelings psychopaths just don't feel. This makes them particularly dangerous because when they say they're feeling a certain way, they are being genuine, which makes them more believable."

Ray needed to make sure the numbers that had been given by Leonard were crystal clear for the jury, "Dr. Leonard, so are you saying that there are three million Homo sapiens predators still out there?"

Leonard nodded, "That is correct. We hypothesize that the percentage is most likely higher, but we have no way of knowing because it is unlikely that they will be caught at the same rate that psychopaths are caught. We do, however, need to keep in mind that the one percent I am speaking of included psychopaths. Once we look deeper, it will be more likely that there are just about one million Homo sapiens predators out there. I submit to you, however, that the damage those predators can cause is well past the damage the entire group of psychopaths, psychotics and sociopaths could cause, combined. The number of victims, the depth of their crimes, their ability to go undetected are all reasons that Homo sapiens predators are by far the most significant threat to humanity I can think of."

Ray let that hang in the air, the audience and the jury seemed to be holding their breath, it could not be going better as far as Ray was concerned. Still he needed to get some testimony in that spoke to the differences between psychopaths and Homo predators; that was what the case hinged on.

He asked Leonard about that, "Dr. Leonard, you just told us that one of the differences between psychopaths and Homo predators is that Homo predators can in fact feel emotion, empathy, love, that kind of thing and psychopaths are not in fact able to do that. Why is that important?

Leonard responded, "The reason that is important is because there is a school of thought, one we agree with, that says that psychopaths do what they do because they can't feel anything, empathy, regret, nothing, but if that they could feel something they wouldn't do the things they do. Homo sapiens predators are different, they are in fact able to feel emotion and can move that emotion aside when it fits their needs. This is one of the most significant differences because it lets us know that even though they feel the emotions, sadness, regret and empathy for their victims, their core being, their prime motivation allows them to move past that to execute their crimes.

"We do not know with any certainty whether psychopaths would commit any of their crimes if they were indeed able to feel any emotions about their behavior or the pain it causes their victims. There have been some studies that suggest that if psychopaths were indeed able to feel these emotions they would most likely not move forward with their crimes, which would by definition mean they are not psychopaths. This difference is the reason that individuals that we have defined as Homo sapiens predators are also more likely to be released early when they do get caught and they're not sentenced to death or life without parole. Their emotions are real, emotions like empathy and regret and they are therefore able to communicate these feeling in their parole hearings. There have been several studies that show that psychopaths are 2.5 times more likely to get released than other criminals. Homo sapiens predators are more than six times more likely to get released. Other researchers have labeled psychopaths as intra-species predators and they are. Homo predators are inter-species predators, they are predators that are a separate species from us. This last is also true of apex predators of other species. When a pride of lions goes on a hunt, Mr. Gretche, other nearby prides of lions do not feel same fear and need to escape that antelopes or zebras feel. Other lions simply move on or stand aside or if they want to contest the pride for the prey they will fight, but they do not fear."

Ray let that hang in the air while he walked over to the defense table and pulled another board, which he asked be admitted and then placed on the easel. The board had the numbers that Leonard had just gone over and included a graphic with dots to illustrate the numbers they were talking about. People in the courtroom did their best to not react to this testimony as did the jury, but there was clearly an air of unease throughout. The jurors looked at each other and then back at the board. The thought that these individuals were potentially out there hunting humans in those numbers, sent a chill up everyone's back. It was time to tie this to the case and to the shooting of Donald Riche. Ray walked Leonard though his testimony about Steven Loomis. He explained he had never met him before and had not spoken to him until after the girls had gone missing.

He walked Leonard through his testimony about Donald Riche, about conducting a psychological autopsy on him and he was careful to get Leonard to explain that he had never examined Riche while he was alive, "Doctor Leonard, having conducted the psychological autopsy of Donald Riche and having examined the evidence that was presented at his arraignment did you form an opinion about whether Donald Riche was a *Homo sapiens predator?*"

The prosecution couldn't let it go. It was a question the prosecution knew would be asked by the defense and which the defense knew the prosecution would object to.

Logan stood up, "Objection your honor. Foundation. I don't believe we have established what Dr. Leonard's findings were relative to the psychological autopsy, so we don't believe that he can render an opinion about whether Donald Riche fits his definition for this new species he has hypothesized about."

Ray knew the objection would come, but he had actually expected it to be much more forceful than how it had actually come. The judge sustained the objection.

He moved on without arguing. "Dr. Leonard let's go back to the psychological autopsy of Donald Riche that you conducted. What were your findings relative to that autopsy?"

Leonard took his time. He leaned back in his chair and folded his hands on his lap while he considered the question and when he moved on he looked right at the jury as he explained what he needed to. Again the prosecution was impressed with the man, with his presence and the way he came across as much as they were impressed with his testimony.

Leonard was patient and methodical. It was clear that was the reason the man was a great instructor, "Part of the psychological autopsy involves understanding what he went through as a child, how he was raised, the genetic component that may have been contributed by his parents and how he developed within an educational environment. Mr. Riche's childhood was not ideal, but was by no means abusive. His family gave him love and validation, although his mother left when he was a small child. He was not bullied and in fact his cousins took on a protective role with him when he was a young child. His adolescence appeared to be normal, no events that we would consider to be out of the ordinary. He was a part of social clubs in school and engaged in the types of activities that other boys his age engaged in. His college professors wrote excellent reviews and letters of recommendation. One thing we did notice was that he took courses in physiology and anatomy in college when none of these courses would contribute to his degree or to his chosen field of study. He had not yet begun to keep a journal of his thoughts and his ideas, so it was difficult to determine his actual intentions with regards to these courses. His subsequent journal entries and the activities that he allegedly engaged in would tend to point to the fact that he was undertaking activities that would facilitate what he would eventually come to do."

Ray knew he'd be bringing up the journal at some point, "Tell us about the journal."

Leonard complied, "The fact that he kept a journal was what allowed us to actually do a significant psychological autopsy. He began chronicling his thoughts and his ideas shortly after college. He was living in Wisconsin at the time and he decided to keep a detailed journal."

Ray walked over to the jury box before asking Leonard to walk them through what he found in Donald Riche's journal. Leonard began going through the journal from the first entries. They spent the rest of the afternoon going through these initial entries. Leonard described how Riche had begun to chronicle his thoughts and his desire to hunt other humans and could not understand why he had those inclinations. He explained that Riche had pondered many possibilities for his situation. He had wondered whether perhaps it was a genetic condition or whether it was a mental condition. Leonard went on to explain that once Riche killed his first victim, his reaction was powerful and immediate. He said that Riche felt for the first time that he knew what he was meant to do, what he was born to do. Still, however, Leonard said that he continued to ponder the reason that hunting humans and killing them felt so incredibly natural to him. Finally, he stated, Donald Riche came to develop the delusion that he felt that his inclinations and instincts were so powerful because he was meant to correct what was imperfect in human beings. That he, Donald Riche, had somehow been chosen to do precisely that. He walked the jury through Riche's first attempts at doing just that, correcting what he believed nature had gotten wrong. He made reference to entries where Riche had written that he had attempted to do it by killing and mutilating two homeless men. He was careful not to refer to the entries as points of fact; he kept them as journal entries.

Leonard went on, "There were entries in the journal that described what he believed was wrong with humans and the things he did to correct what he saw as nature's mistakes. He would remove the arms from one body and use the arms from another body to replace them. He saw this as his destiny, as his mission. There were other entries relating to his actions in this regard with various types of people, some men some women, some younger and some older."

Ray needed to make sure the testimony Leonard was about to go over would not go over the line for the prosecution, "Doctor Leonard how many entries did you find in which Donald Riche spoke about making an attempt at correcting what he saw as nature's mistakes? How many entries were there where he made reference to killing someone?"

Farris shot up, "Objection your honor! This is just another way for the defense to make reference to evidence the court has already ruled as inadmissible."

The judge turned to Gretche without speaking. Ray responded immediately, "Your honor, I believe we have been very careful to explain that these are entries in a journal. We haven't claimed them as fact or evidence of fact, but we have kept them in context. It is a key element of the doctor's psychological autopsy. It speaks to Donald Riche's state of mind, which is pertinent given the doctor's research and the defense's position."

The judge looked back at Farris, "I agree. There has been no reference to any of this being fact. The doctor has consistently maintained his testimony is about the journal entries and I believe the jury will take it as such. Overruled."

Ray turned back to Leonard, "Doctor you were about to tell us how many instances you found where Donald Riche made reference to having killed someone."

"Yes. We found seventeen instances not counting the references to the nine girls that were abducted. Thirteen were in Wisconsin and four were here in New York, two men and two women. He referred to the women as his dates and he made reference to Internet dating sites. He never referred to any of these individuals by a name, his entries just gave gender, age, physical characteristics and the elements he would be fixing."

Ray looked at his notes, nodded and asked the doctor one last question, "Thank you doctor. What conclusion did you come to after reviewing all of the material on the Homo sapiens predators and Donald Riche?"

Leonard smiled a wry smile, but the smile did not extend to his eyes, instead what showed was deep concern and almost fear, "Well, Mr. Gretche, we all go to the movies and read novels about scary things, the boogey man, the devil, witches, and we do it because we enjoy a good scare every now and again, but only because we know it isn't real, we know we won't find any of it every day. This, this is based on science, on natural selection and evolution. I'm not afraid because what I found is evil, something evil could still find redemption if it understood it was evil, this is nature, these are individuals who are simply what they were meant to be, what they've *evolved* to be. They do what they do because nature engineered them to do it. That's the reason I'm truly frightened for humanity's future."

The courtroom stirred, reporters scribbled, but none of it loud enough for the judge to call the court to order.

Ray sat down, "No further questions your honor."

The day was coming to an end and there had been some significant testimony offered by Doctor Leonard so the judge decided to call it a day, "Ladies and gentlemen we have all absorbed a lot of information today. We will adjourn until tomorrow morning. As always ladies and gentlemen of the jury, it is critical that you avoid any coverage of the case."

Every single person in the courtroom knew that in spite of the judge's admonition the jury would most likely hear some of the coverage, even while they were being sequestered. Once the judge was off the bench the jury filed out and the courtroom emptied.

Felix Garcia had finally decided he needed to be in the courtroom. He had already spoken to Tyrone Leonard and heard a great deal of the testimony he'd just given. He went immediately back to his office to begin doing research on everything he had heard today that Leonard had not told him about when they'd spoken. It was amazing stuff and the guy came across as a true expert. He smiled as he remembered how he had thought that Dr. Leonard would be riveting when he gave his testimony. He had been right; the short, brilliant and incredibly charismatic black professor had held the courtroom's attention from the moment he sat down to the end of the day. Felix had watched as the jury nodded during certain parts of his testimony and he could understand why. Leonard was patient and made sure that whatever he said could be understood by everyone, not just other scientists. That was something that usually plagued experts, especially when they were presenting scientific material. It had been the case when the prosecution's experts testified. Even though they were simply explaining why and how they concluded that Donald Riche was a human being their testimony came off stiff and difficult to digest. They got the point across, but there was no real investment by the jury. Leonard's testimony had to do with something new, a new species and yet it came off very clear and understandable. Now Felix was planning on reviewing as much of the guy's research as he could get his hands on and he hoped to be able to interview him after he was finished testifying. He would probably have to wait until the trial was over, but it wouldn't hurt to try before then. Dr. Leonard would probably be bombarded by every media outlet covering the trial. Felix hoped that Steven Loomis might in fact put in a good word, but it was a stretch given that the guy was fighting for his life. Felix was also upset about the fact that he had not been able to get a hold of that journal. The information contained in it was explosive and Felix would not have had to abide by evidentiary rules when writing about Donald Riche. His only consolation was that no other journalist had gotten a hold of it either. He understood why that had been the case. If the journal had in fact gotten out, it would have probably been found inadmissible in the trial. He got up and went to the kitchen to get himself a cup of the dark sludge that passed for coffee at the paper. He knew he would need it for the all-nighter he might be about to pull. He finally decided that he could no longer put off what he was about to do. He picked up the phone and dialed the number for the district attorney's office.

Once someone picked up the phone, Felix got down to business, "Hey, how are you doing? I know, I know, I should have called and I meant to, but you know how busy it's been around here with the trial and everything else going on."

He listened to the litany of expletives that were coming through the phone and rolled his eyes as he continued, "I'm sorry, okay? I'm really sorry. As soon as the trial is over we'll do something, dinner, movies, the works, okay? Yeah, listen, I need your help for a story I'm working on. Is there something going on at your office with the DA and the deputies handling the Loomis case? No, I don't know what it would be, but I hear there may be some issue with how they're handling the trial... that Logan and Farris are pissed at the DA..."

Once again Felix rolled his eyes and waited for the person at the other end of the line to finish ripping him a new one for not having called. It was definitely going to be an all-nighter.

19.

The trial reconvened right on time the next morning. Dr. Leonard took his place back on the witness stand where the judge reminded him he was still under oath. Ray reminded him that they were discussing the number of references to murder he had found in Donald Riche's journal. He then asked him to describe the methods that Riche had allegedly utilized to kill his victims, always making sure to maintain the testimony as a reference to what Riche had written and not as testimony of something that had actually happened. They had been tempted to call detectives from the jurisdictions where individuals had been reported missing at around the same time that Riche made mention to having killed someone, but it would be almost impossible to get their testimony in as the judge would most likely find their testimony to be far too prejudicial to be allowed in. The testimony showed the mind of a true predator, someone who had turned a delusion into his life's work. It was precisely the delusion that would prove difficult for the defense because it was indicative of mental illness.

Ray would have to ask Leonard to explain it to the jury because he knew that if he didn't, the prosecution would almost certainly do it, "What do you mean when you say that Mr. Riche came up with a delusion to explain his inclinations and predilections?"

Leonard explained, "He believed that he and he alone had the ability to correct what Mother Nature had gotten wrong. He believed that all humans were imperfect, that they were born imperfect and in order to correct them he had to get to them before they were too old. He came up with this delusion as a way to explain what he wanted to do, hunt and kill humans. You see, he had read about psychopaths and sociopaths and he knew with *absolute certainty* that he was not a psychopath or a sociopath. This explanation, what eventually became his delusion, was the only logical answer he could come up with."

Ray went on, "How was it that he came to that conclusion Dr. Leonard, if he didn't have any training in psychology or psychiatry?"

Leonard responded, "If you recall we've already discussed the differences between psychopaths and Homo sapiens predators when it comes to having the ability to have true feelings and emotions. Well, Donald Riche knew he was not a psychopath or a sociopath because he knew they did not have feelings or emotions and that he himself *did* in fact, have feelings and emotions. Once he made that determination he had nothing to explain his behavior and his instincts, so he came up with an explanation that made sense for him. This is actually very common among Homo sapiens predators. Those that can't come up with some plausible explanation often suffer from deep clinical depressions or even nervous breakdowns. Consider how any of us would feel if something that felt so natural, so good that we knew it was we were meant to do was as abhorred as their behavior is, we would all also have some significant psychological and emotional issues."

Ray moved on, "And Dr. Leonard, what else were you able to glean from his journal?"

Leonard changed his tone a bit because he knew what he was about to testify to, "He believed that he was something beyond human, that he had been created for the purpose of correcting what needed to be corrected. He found himself to be an effective predator who planned his every move extremely carefully. He believed that he had heightened senses. He wrote about being able to smell children from blocks away and being able to see in almost complete darkness."

Ray needed him to make this point crystal clear, so he walked him through the testimony, "And what conclusion did you come to in regards to these abilities he claimed to have?"

Leonard answered, "I obviously did not have an opportunity to speak with or examine Mr. Riche, so all I have is the journal he kept and my own research on the subject. During my research into this new species, Homo sapiens predaer, we found that many, if not most of the subjects, claimed to have senses beyond those of a human being. We tested their sense of smell, their eyesight, their hearing and interestingly enough, we found that about 92% of these individuals actually did have hyper developed senses or senses beyond those of a normal human being."

There was no outward reaction in the courtroom other than shifting in their seats, but there was clearly an undertow of feelings that everyone in the courtroom felt. People looked at each other with mouths open and reporters were scribbling furiously wanting to get every word down. Ray asked Leonard about the methods he and his team had used to come to these findings.

He walked him through each test and the results that lead to their conclusions, "Doctor Leonard, how did these findings fit into the work you had been doing relative to the new species?"

"These findings pointed to significant physical differences between Homo sapiens predaer and Homo sapiens sapiens or modern humans, us. As I said previously, however, it was not in every case that we found these conditions so we could not come to the absolute conclusion that if you are a *Homo sapiens predator* you *will* have hyper developed senses. We could only come to the conclusion that if you were *Homo sapiens predator* you had a 92% likelihood to have those abilities."

Logan had been waiting to hear what Leonard's answer would be to the question Ray had asked about Donald Riche being a *Homo sapiens predator*. The direct examination had gotten sidetracked, however, and Leonard had never actually gotten to answer the question.

Logan pushed to get the testimony back on track, "Objection your honor. Foundation. I don't believe Doctor Leonard ever answered the question about whether Mr. Riche fit the definition of this new species."

The judge had also been waiting for the defense to come back to that and so he agreed with the prosecution, "Sustained. Mr. Gretche I believe that Doctor Leonard needs to proffer an opinion about whether Mr. Riche does in fact fit his definition for this new species if you are planning to ask questions that make reference to physical characteristics that are present in individuals that fit the definition of this new species."

Ray complied, "Very well your honor. Dr. Leonard, in your opinion, after having examined Donald Riche's journal and after having conducted the psychological autopsy of Donald Riche, in your opinion was Donald Riche a *Homo* sapiens predator?"

"That is a difficult question to answer Mr. Gretche. Based on a number of characteristics I would say that it is very likely that he was, given his alleged crimes and other behaviors, but as a scientist I would not be able to say with absolute certainty that he was indeed a Homo sapiens predator. I was not able to interview him and he was not incarcerated, which means that he was not under the care of a psychiatrist."

Ray needed Leonard to make sure the jury understood what he was saying, "Why does that make a difference?"

Leonard responded, "Several of the individuals that we defined as Homo sapiens predators had been executed by the time we looked into their cases, but we were able to get very complete histories because they were under psychiatric care while they were incarcerated which in most instances meant years of detailed records, many of them having been videotaped. Obviously that was not the case with Mr. Riche, therefore I would not be able to make the determination that he was a *Homo sapiens predaer* with one hundred percent certainty. As I said before, in my opinion, given many of the indicators we found, it is very likely, almost certain, that he was a *Homo sapiens predator*. We certainly found that he was self-defined as something other than human."

Ray continued, "And is that an indicator that points to him being a Homo predator?"

Leonard responded, "Not in and of itself. Mr. Riche, however, defined himself as something other than human because of what he deemed to be abilities beyond those of human beings, as I stated earlier, an ability to smell, hear and see things that a normal human was unable to sense. There is no way for us to confirm any of that so like everything else we have to keep it in context. While we could not confirm whether those journal entries were about such abilities, we were able to compare his entries with our own research findings about hypersensitivity among Homo predators. What he was describing in his journal was almost identical, I mean almost verbatim, to what we had heard from individuals that we were in fact able to confirm were in fact Homo sapiens predators."

Ray felt that he had accomplished what he needed with Leonard. Now it would be up to the doctor to field the prosecution's questions and weather their attack on his work, "Thank you doctor. No further questions your honor."

Melanie Farris stood up. Drew had been right; it would be Farris that would come at their witnesses. She was able to come off as incredulous without seeming condescending or mocking. Leonard had clearly made a positive impact on the jury. The back and forth between him and Ray had worked exactly as Drew had thought it would: the seasoned, old lawyer asking a world-renowned scientist to explain his research. Even the prosecution had to admit that Leonard's testimony had a deep effect on the jury and moreover had a clear effect on everyone in the courtroom, which meant that the media coverage was going to echo exactly what Leonard testified to. It made for an incredible story and both Farris and Logan knew that there would be a thousand and one stories that would be cooked up by various media outlets, legitimate news organizations and crackpot tabloids alike. All they could do now was to methodically unhinge the core of Leonard's work and to try to bring doubt to the basis of their defense. The judge decided to take the lunch break before the prosecution began their cross-examination.

Felix Garcia was running on fumes, but what he had found out from his source at the district attorney's office was incredible. He needed to do some research ASAP in order to get the story out also as soon as possible. This would be the second time that he had scooped the major networks and publications. His stock had risen meteorically after the Steven Loomis interview, but it was about to go into the stratosphere with this story. He was not sure about many things, but the one thing he was absolutely certain about was that after this story, he would be able to write his own ticket anywhere to do anything he wanted. Before he could write his own ticket, however, he needed to write the story, so even though he could barely stand up, he got down to business with the research.

Farris wasted no time going after the expert, "Doctor Leonard are you a member of the Society of Forensic Psychiatry?"

Leonard answered simply, "Yes I am."

Farris continued, "In fact have you ever served on the board of that organization?"

Leonard nodded, "Yes, I had the privilege of serving on their board from nineteen eighty nine to nineteen ninety five."

Farris, now standing by the jury box went on, "And what brought your participation on the board to an end?"

Leonard smiled a thin, wry smile, "There was a disagreement between myself and the rest of the board and it was decided that it would be better for the organization if I stepped down."

Farris decided to bring down the hammer on this first point, "Isn't it true doctor that the reason you were actually asked to leave was that you presented a paper that the board believed to be complete fiction?"

Leonard remained impassive, "I wouldn't say that, no. It was agreed by all involved that my service might prove detrimental to the organization and yes it was because of my work, but I do not recall anyone referring to it as fiction."

Farris now started to walk in the well, "I see. Let's move on shall we. If I understood your testimony correctly Dr. Leonard, you came up with the concept of this new species, this, what did you call it...Homo sapiens predator, is that correct?"

Leonard nodded, "Yes that's correct."

Farris continued, "And everyone else that has used the term and the definition for the new species did so after you had published several papers in which you first hypothesize the existence of this new species and then provided the definition for qualifying as a Homo predator, is that correct?"

Leonard responded, "Yes Ms. Farris that's correct."

Farris got ready to pull the trigger, "So if for whatever reason your research was to prove invalid then the work of everyone who based their findings on the existence of such species would also be invalid, is that correct?"

Drew could see where she was going with this and had to step in, "Objection your honor. What exactly is the relevance of the question? We have been going over Dr. Leonard's work, not other scientists' work."

Farris was ready, "Your honor if the science that supports what I think we can all agree is a radical hypothesis is basically founded on Dr. Leonard's work and his work is found to be invalid then by extension so is the science."

The judge considered this for a moment, "I'm going to overrule the objection Ms. Farris, but please limit your cross to Doctor Leonard's work and try and make your point."

Farris agreed, "I will. Thank you your honor. Dr. Leonard, please go on."

Leonard answered, "I suppose if someone's work was based on my work and my work was found to be invalid then yes, their work would also be invalid. If their work was based on their own findings about the new species, however, then their work would still be valid even if mine was found to be invalid. And by now, Ms. Farris, there are a lot of researchers doing the same type of work, people who have come to their own conclusions based on their research alone. I believe we will hear from some of them in this trial."

Farris nodded, "I understand that doctor, but I believe that the defense has clearly established that you are the leading researcher in this field. Your own testimony has also backed that position, so the probability that someone's work in this field is based at least partly on your work is pretty high wouldn't you say?"

Leonard had to agree, "Yes I suppose that would be correct."

Melanie Farris was now ready to take apart the science that Leonard's work was based upon.

She spent almost the entire afternoon confirming each and every conclusion the doctor had postulated during direct examination and she did it by reviewing the work he had laid out as the foundation for his conclusions, "And you stated that of all the people you included in your research there were about one hundred and twenty that according to you qualified as one of these predators, correct?"

Leonard answered, "Yes that's correct."

Farris continued, "And if I interpreted your testimony correctly, the difference between a psychopath and one of these predators is very subtle, is that right?"

Leonard nodded, "Yes the differences between the two are subtle. As I mentioned before there is a list of thirty differences between them and yes each of them is very subtle."

Farris was now back at the jury box, "Isn't it true doctor that each of the thirty differences you listed can also be displayed by psychopaths? And isn't it true that these predators you came up with can also fail to display these differences?"

Leonard took his time. He could see what Melanie Farris was getting at and wanted to answer her question without undermining his previous testimony, "Yes Ms. Farris, it's true, psychopaths can display any or all of the thirty qualifiers we developed and yes Homo predators can fail to manifest some or all of these qualifiers."

Farris made a face like she was troubled by something Leonard said. She asked the next question with a tone that said she was confused, "I don't understand doctor, if psychopaths can show some or all of these behaviors and your new species can fail to show some or all of these behaviors then how can you possibly come to any sort of real conclusion about either one?"

Leonard needed to tread carefully now, his entire testimony was under attack, "Well Ms. Farris, if I were to conduct an interview with you or with the judge or with Mr. Logan, it is possible that you all display some of these behaviors and characteristics, but without context it does not mean that you are psychopaths or *Homo predators*. The list of differences is always applied in context with the behaviors of each of the people we measured, always measured along with the crimes they committed or the behaviors they manifested. The physical differences are real and tangible."

Farris would not give an inch, "I see, but if what you are saying is true, if the differences are so slight, then isn't it possible that this new species is just a different type of psychopath? Isn't the most simple answer that there is no new species, but rather that it is a different type of psychopath?"

Leonard nodded slowly as he responded to the question, "I suppose that would indeed be the simplest answer, but not necessarily the correct answer. The simplest hypothesis is not always the correct one. Sometimes we have to go further and we have to be willing to come to conclusions that lie beyond the established norms. We have to be willing to accept when our findings do not fit into established models. Believe me Ms. Farris, it would have been *far* easier and convenient to find they were simply a different type of psychopath."

Neither Drew nor Ray had any reaction to Leonard's answer, but both knew that Farris had scored a couple of significant points. By getting Leonard to admit that he had gone beyond what was accepted science and that he had come up with his definitions on his own to explain something he felt couldn't be explained any other way she brought immediate doubt into the basis of his work.

Farris continued her line of questioning, "So Dr. Leonard, would it be fair to say that the very existence of this new species is based on your conclusions, and only your conclusions, that there must be something besides what has been established as the definition of a psychopath? That it was your decision and your decision alone that this new species must exist because some of the people you interviewed didn't fit the definition of a psychopath as neatly as you wanted them to?"

Leonard smiled. This was a question that he had been asked by the detractors of his work from the beginning. There was no way to get around the fact that he was the father of the new species, that the conclusions he had come to were based on his thinking and his thinking alone.

Leonard responded, "Yes, Ms. Farris, you are correct in saying that the reason for the existence of this new species is based on my research and my conclusions, but there are other researchers, other scientists that have also conducted research and come to similar conclusions. Their findings may have brought them to the conclusion that there are individuals that fall outside of human norms, but they might call those individuals something else. They might not define them as another species, but their work recognizes that there are individuals that we have not defined previously. In the end it is true that, as far as I know, I was the first researcher to conduct this research in any sort of meaningful way."

Farris was back to pacing in the well, "That may be so doctor, but the difference between whatever their findings are and whatever they call those individuals and your new species is that their conclusions end up with a different kind of human psychopath and yours end up with something beyond a human. That's a big difference don't you think?"

Leonard smiled, "Yes it is a big difference. Anytime research develops a new horizon, a new boundary, it is a big deal. There are always detractors, people that have a hard time thinking beyond what is established science."

Farris continued, "Don't you think Dr. Leonard that these scientists that have a hard time thinking beyond what is accepted science are being responsible? Don't you think it is their responsibility to call out a theory that is based on one man's thinking?"

Leonard nodded in agreement, "Scientists always have the responsibility of speaking out when they disagree with research findings because the research is flawed or when they believe that there is a better answer. To discount a theory or a scientific conclusion because it is based only on one man's thinking would be unfortunate indeed. Some time ago there was one individual who came up with several theories on his own, Albert Einstein. Einstein was willing to have his work ridiculed and called into question because he was certain in his thinking, in his findings. All of his findings have now been validated because we now have the science that allows us to do so. I would never have come out with my hypothesis if I weren't certain of its validity. I am sure that as science and technology continue to progress we will have other methods of validating the existence of the species, but just because we don't have the science to go further in our validation right now does not mean that the species does not exist."

Farris was not expecting the response she got and felt a bit flustered, she needed to get back to making her point, "Let's assume for a moment that this species does in fact exist, that Homo sapiens has in fact evolved. There is no way you can say whether Donald Riche was one of these Homo sapiens predators is there?"

Leonard responded, "No, as I believe I stated before, there is no way I could possibly say whether Mr. Riche was a Homo sapiens predator or a pure psychopath with absolute certainty. I can only conclude that he could have and almost certainly was a Homo predator."

"And there is no way, therefore, that you could ascertain whether Donald Riche would pose any more threat than a psychopath would, is that correct?"

"No Ms. Farris there is no way I would be able to say what threat he would be either as a Homo predator or as a psychopath. Not beyond what we were able to develop from the psychological autopsy. I think the kind of threat he was would be pretty self-evident given the crimes he was accused of. But I can tell you that if he was in fact a Homo sapiens predator he would have done much, much more damage than a psychopath."

Farris went back to the defense table, "Thank you doctor. We have no further questions for Dr. Leonard your honor."

Drew had to admit that the prosecution had scored some points with the jury. Having Leonard accept that this science was based purely on his thinking and that even if Homo sapiens predator did exist there was no way for him to know whether Donald Riche was one, hit at the very core of the basis for their defense. It basically told the jury that there was as much chance that Homo sapiens predator did exist as a species than there was that it didn't. In essence it pretty much hung their entire case on how the jury considered Leonard, and while Drew knew that he made a great witness, there was just no way to predict what the jury would think in the end.

The judge turned to Leonard, "Thank you doctor Leonard, you may step down. Mr. Willis, Mr. Gretche would you call your next witness please."

Drew stood up. He would take over the direct of Grossman. He was going to prove to be a challenge even though Drew had prepared him thoroughly, "Yes your honor. The defense calls doctor Michael Grossman."

Grossman stood up from the gallery. It was clear that he was a very different personality than Leonard. He had all the traits of a stereotypical academic from an Ivy League school. He dressed impeccably, he was bald, the hair he had going prematurely white, he was tall and skinny with a Patrician nose that betrayed his New England roots and most of all he seemed to carry himself with a bit of resentment towards those that he thought to be intellectually inferior, which was most people. He walked over to the clerk who was holding the bible, he placed his hand on it and took his oath. He sat down ramrod straight in the witness chair and held his nose up a bit as if he was getting ready to smell something bad. Drew planned on going through the direct exactly as they had prepared.

He knew the man couldn't improvise if he needed to, "Good afternoon Doctor Grossman. Could you please tell us about the experience and education that qualify you as an expert in the field in question?"

Grossman started by listing all of his degrees. Multiple undergraduate degrees in biology, chemistry and physics. An MD with a specialty in psychiatry and a Phd. in physiology. He also went on to list all of the certifications on forensic analysis that he had completed throughout his career. As far as his experience he recited every position he had held since leaving high school at age fourteen. Internships at some of the most advanced institutions with forensic psychiatry programs, a stint at the FBI criminal profiling division, doing the kind of work made famous by the movie The Silence of the Lambs. Finally he went into his own research into the makeup of pure or extreme psychopaths. The work was basically the same as Leonard's, but he framed it differently. He explained that he had conducted his research with the idea of establishing, through empirical data, what society considers to be true 'evil.' He went on to say that he had not started his research with the idea or expectation that he would find something beyond human 'evil', something that was beyond the boundaries or definitions already established by humans as a society and civilization. He explained how he had developed his scale of 'evil', how he had done it with the intention of allowing any layman to understand the behaviors that composed each level of his scale. He then went on to explain how his work had caught the attention of a television producer who had approached him with the idea of a television show, a show in which he would profile some of the best-known murderers. He would utilize his research to explain how and why each fell into a particular level on the scale. This last bit of testimony he gave with a bit of an air of superiority.

It was clear, the biggest difference between him and Leonard was that Grossman was going to be hard to like for anyone, let alone the jury.

Still, Drew needed him to knock it out of the park, "And Doctor Grossman did you in fact do the show?"

Grossman offered a curt nod and response, "Yes, yes I did. We have been on for two seasons now."

Drew smiled, "That's great. On the show you go over twenty-two levels of your scale of evil, but you have developed another level, correct? Why not use all twenty three levels on the show?"

Drew had to ask the question because he knew the jury would be wondering about that. Grossman started to get more engaged.

It was obvious that the further they delved into his work, the more engaged and passionate he became, "We didn't use all twenty-three scales because the producer felt that the crimes that were involved would be too graphic, too brutal for a show on prime time television. They also felt that the work on the last level was relatively new and unproven compared with the first twenty-two levels."

Drew needed to get him started on the core of his testimony, "Can you explain what that additional level involves?"

Grossman responded, "Each of the levels of my scale is defined by specific behavior, specific elements of the crimes that people commit. All of the levels involve one human being killing another or many others, but as we all know, murder can have many forms. For example, level one is basically killing another in self-defense. It is obviously very low on a scale of evil. The type of killing moves on from there. Level two is killing by negligence or lack of care and so on."

Drew walked the doctor through the rest of the first twenty-two levels using a board that he had admitted into evidence to help Grossman.

Now it was time to deal with the last level, level twenty-three, the level that had to do with this case, "Doctor Grossman, can you tell us about level twenty three please?"

"Of course. After working with the twenty-two levels I developed initially, we believed that human evil could be defined by these twenty-two levels. After three years, however, we realized that we were coming up with a significant number of individuals that did not fit into even the highest levels of the scale. As I just explained, the highest levels of the scale involve torture, mutilation and sadism. All of these are elements of the most heinous murders on record, but all of them could be traced back to psychopathy, to a human condition."

As he got into the testimony Grossman became even more lively and more human. He was clearly excited by his work and he was happy about sharing it. Drew was just glad that it gave him a warmer tone, a tone the jury could relate to.

Grossman, now leaning forward in his share, continued, "We then began to find individuals who were committing savage murders, multiple murders of men, women and children, individuals that gave a new meaning to the word horror. When we began to analyze them we found that they did not fit the definition of a psychopath at all. They had normal childhoods for the most part; no physical or psychological trauma, no abuse. They grew up with love and care, most of them had siblings and extended family that supported them and loved them. Unlike psychopaths, they did not need to use others for their purposes, they were quiet and deliberate, it was almost as if the more horrific the murder the calmer they became. They were able to actually feel regret and love and other emotions, most of the time for their families, but capable of feelings for others who were close to them. We conducted many interviews with each individual, trying to get at the motivations for their crimes, their mindset. We were able to develop an additional level. We determined that this level would be reserved for those individuals for whom the original scale of evil was not enough, individuals who were in fact the embodiment of 'evil' as we'd come to understand it. Level twenty three deals with individuals that have executed crimes as horrific as those of level twenty three, but who are actually able to feel emotion. Level twenty-two is made up of human beings that have executed heinous murders, but who are incapable of feeling or emotion. I submit to you that the former is far more dangerous than the latter. I suppose that would be the biggest difference between the first twenty two levels and the last level, the first twenty two deal with humans' evil behavior, the last one deals with evil itself."

This last part of the testimony was masterfully delivered by Grossman. Drew let it hang in the air and it had the desired effect, the courtroom went completely quiet and the members of the jury looked at each other.

Farris couldn't let the defense score points with the jury. She was fifty-fifty on whether it would get sustained or overruled, but she raised it anyway, "Objection. Judge, as dramatic as this testimony may be it doesn't have any foundation."

Drew replied, "Your honor the witness described the way in which he developed his scale and what the levels meant. What other foundation should there be?"

It was Farris's turn to respond, "Well, for starters we haven't been told what the last level is or how one would qualify to land there."

The judge considered the objection, "Overruled. Mr. Willis can you please ask the witness to elaborate on what the level is and how to land on it?"

Drew nodded, "Of course your honor. Dr. Grossman?"

Grossman was glad to explain further, he turned so he could include the judge in his answer, "Certainly. Level twenty-three involves multiple murders with torture, sadism and mutilation. The individuals in this level are methodical and precise. They believe that killing other humans is actually what they were meant to do from birth. They have absolutely no regret, no feelings of guilt about the murders they commit even though they are very capable of having feelings and of feeling emotion. Interestingly they might feel guilty about the trouble they put their families through or about stealing $20 from their father's wallet as children, but they did not feel any of that about the murders. They appear completely normal otherwise and like most individuals who fall in this category, they have an IQ in the genius level. They don't do it for pleasure, per se, they look at it like nature simply taking its course. Most of them explained that prior to committing their first murder they felt awkward and incomplete and that they felt that way since they could remember. Some of these individuals committed their first murder when they were children of ten or eleven years old."

Drew interrupted him. He knew that he would be testifying to what he'd just said, but it was still incredible to hear. As much as they tried, the entire gallery gasped in unison and even the judge didn't use his gavel, his mouth was wide open.

Drew knew if he'd found it incredible the jury would find it unthinkable, "Excuse me Dr. Grossman, did you just say that some of these individuals committed their first murder when they were children?"

Grossman smiled a thin, knowing smile, "That's correct Mr. Willis. None of them had any issue whatsoever with telling us precisely when they committed their first murder. In fact, they were happy to get it off their chest, not because they felt guilty about it, but because it had felt so natural and it had brought them so much relief and stability in the rest of their lives, that they felt they needed to share it with someone."

Drew let that hang for a few seconds and then continued, "Did that also occur in the original twenty-two levels? Did any of those individuals confess to having murdered someone as a child?"

Grossman answered, "No, none of those individuals confessed to killing as children. They explained that they always knew they were different, that their thoughts and ideas were not like those of other children, but unlike level twenty-three individuals, none of them articulated the desire to kill humans as children, much less having done it."

Drew needed to keep him engaged, it made him more human and more likeable, "And Dr. Grossman, had any of these individuals who told you they had killed as children been caught for their crimes."

Grossman answered, "No, none of them were ever caught or even suspected of having done anything as children. It was one of the most chilling aspects of our work, if I'm to be honest."

Drew didn't know he'd be testifying to this, but thought it might help the case, "What do you mean Dr. Grossman?"

Grossman nodded, "What I meant was that we had not been expecting to hear this at all from our subjects, it wasn't something we had asked them about. They shared it with us because they felt that us knowing about it would help us to understand that they were what they were from birth, that this was not something that had happened over time or as a result of anything their parents or family did. They wanted us to know that they were normal, even though they obviously knew how outrageous their acts were."

Drew let that hang in their air, as he'd done with any other testimony that had a likelihood of affecting the jury emotionally.

He needed to get back to Grossman's actual work because he knew that Farris was going to be coming at him with everything she had, "Dr. Grossman, you stated earlier that your scale intended to use 'evil' as an objective measure, can you tell us a bit more about that?"

Grossman nodded, "Certainly. You see, as we began our work we knew that eventually we would be coming up with a way that could be utilized to indicate the gravity of the crimes and the overall likelihood that the same individual might commit the crime again. We needed to come up with something that people, even laypeople, could look at and understand as a measure of that gravity. So we came up with the concept of evil as an objective measure, as a measure that was based on the facts of the cases and the behavior of the people that committed these crimes."

Drew went on, "Forgive me Dr. Grossman, I'm trying to understand the difference between the 'evil' behaviors you described for the original twenty-two levels and the 'evil' you are referring to when it comes to the twenty-third level and I can't say I see much of a difference. Can you help us understand the difference between the two?"

Grossman smiled, he knew what was coming and he'd enjoyed it immensely when they'd prepared with it, "Of course Mr. Willis. Could we please get the photographs I provided?"

Farris and Logan looked at each other with puzzled expressions. They conferred with the other deputies that had worked on the case with them and all of them were shaking their heads.

Finally, Bart Logan stood up, "Ah, your honor, can we approach."

Judge Newman sighed and nodded. Drew approached the bench along with Farris and Logan. It was Logan that addressed the judge, "Your honor, we have not had the opportunity to see these photographs in order to understand their probative value. We would request a continuance so that we may have an opportunity to analyze and then form an opinion about them."

The judge looked at Drew and didn't have to say anything for Drew to know he was up.

Drew could barely contain the smile that kept wanting to form on his face, he needed to keep it professional, "Your honor, the prosecution was provided these photographs along with every other exhibit we have utilized or are planning to utilize. We have a receipt from the DA's office showing that these photographs along with the other exhibits were in fact received. We would oppose any continuance in order to accommodate the prosecution's inability to keep track of what exhibits have or have not been received by their office."

The judge now turned to look at the two lead prosecutors with what could only be described as a look of true disappointment and disbelief, something akin to what a parent showed their child when they brought home a bad grade.

What he said, however, was more measured, "Mr. Logan, Ms. Farris, I am not going to allow for any continuance to examine something you have apparently had access to for months. And I'd like to warn you now that any further requests of this nature, requests to have the court or the defense or even worse, the jury, allow for shortcomings in your team or your process will be looked upon most harshly, am I making myself clear?"

Both lawyers were looking down at the ground and both said the same thing at the same time, "Yes your honor."

Before they went back to their table, Bart spoke up, "If the court please, the sheer number of exhibits, documents and motions the defense has generated would completely occupy the entire staff at our office."

The judge was not persuaded, "The court pleases very much, Mr. Logan, but it's not the defense's or the defendant's fall that the DAs office is understaffed. You'll have to take that up with your fearless leader, Mr. Neill. Now step back."

Drew knew that the pictures had been sent with four massive boxes of other materials and documents, each picture in a separate box and in between hundreds and hundreds of documents, photographs and exhibits. Max was a master at coming up with that kind of tactic. He'd done it dozens of times when he'd been defending mafia dons back in the 80s.

Back on the record Drew pulled up the boards with the pictures Dr. Grossman wanted to use from the defense table,

"Your honor, for the record this has been previously admitted and is exhibit 32 for the defense."

Drew walked over to the easel where other exhibits had been shown brought it over to the witness stand and positioned it in such a way that the jury could easily see what was in the pictures. When the jury and the gallery saw the picture on the board there was a sound like the air was sucked out of the room.

Drew knew that was going to happen, but it was still difficult to look at the pictures, "Dr. Grossman, what is this a picture of?"

Grossman nodded, "Those are pictures of a crime committed by Franklin Carmody, a 30-year-old man from Michigan. Franklin had an obsession with his next door neighbor, Moira Parker. On the night of September 20th, 1996, Franklin went into Moira's home where she lived with her husband and two young children under the pretense that he needed to borrow some bleach. Moira went to get the bleach and while she did that Franklin hit her husband in the back of the head with a small mallet killing him instantly. He then hid behind a door and did the same thing to Moira when she came back into the room and saw her husband on the ground. It took three blows to finally kill Moira. When the children, three and four years old, came into the kitchen he did the same thing to them. After he knew there was nobody else coming he had sexual relations with Moira's corpse. He then cut the other bodies up and placed them around the house. The pictures on the easel now show what that home looked like once Franklin was finished with his activities."

Drew moved completely out of the way and brought the easel a bit closer for the jury. He didn't really need to do that in order for the jury to understand what they were looking at. Three jurors had a hand over their mouth and four others looked white enough to make Drew think they might actually pass out.

He needed to keep this in context, however, "And what were you able to ultimately learn about the murderer?"

Grossman now had a more appropriate expression, an expression that conveyed the disturbing nature of the pictures and the case, "Well, police were able to connect Mr. Carmody to the crime almost immediately. He tried to deny having any knowledge of the crime, but ultimately there was simply too much evidence. Mr. Carmody described a childhood that was almost a textbook breeding ground for a psychopath. He explained he'd been molested repeatedly by his mother's live-in boyfriend starting when he was seven years old and lasting until he was thirteen and could finally leave home. He also explained that even before that abuse had started he had known he was different. He knew other kids did not have the uncontrollable desire to burn things, nor the desire to kill small animals from around the neighborhood. When we talked about the crime itself it was patently clear that he had not planned the crime beyond just going over to Moira's house and somehow getting control of her and her husband. He also shared he simply went 'crazy' after he had engaged in sexual acts with Moira and that that was the reason he had cut the other bodies up the way he did. There was no plan to do so before it actually happened. Upon further conversation it became absolutely clear to us that try as he may, Franklin simply could not relate to any feelings about the crime that might have been expressed by the victims' families or by his own family."

Drew pulled the easel back to the witness stand and kept Grossman going, "And did you draw any conclusions from your analysis of the crime and of Mr. Carmody?"

Grossman nodded, "Yes, yes I did. I should make clear that by the time I was able to speak with Mr. Carmody he had already spoken to four court-appointed psychiatrists, as well as one defense expert who was a psychologist, and all of them were in absolute agreement that Franklin Carmody was a violent psychopath who would most likely commit another murder if just given the chance. We came across this case because when we were doing our comparisons between psychopathy and something else entirely we asked for mental health professionals to share their most clearly defined cases with us. This case was one of the ones that was shared as being a perfect example of the most disturbing levels of psychopathy. Our intention for it was to do precisely what we aim to do here, right now."

Drew continued to set him up, "And Dr. Grossman would you say that when it comes to what defines psychopathic behavior this case would be a good example?"

Grossman responded, "Yes, obviously each crime is different in its nature, hence the twenty-two levels, but the overall reasoning behind the crime is well-planted in psychopathy."

Drew needed to get a couple of things clarified before turning the witness over to the prosecution, "And Dr. Grossman you mentioned that in most instances psychopaths are triggered by something before they actually turn into murderers, is that correct?"

Grossman nodded, "Yes, that is correct. The trigger can be many things, but in most instances it is some form of abuse either physical or emotional. It can also be triggered by drug abuse or by physical trauma cause by an injury, however."

Drew was getting the next exhibit ready as he finished the current line of questioning, "So simply being born with the gene for psychopathy, the warrior gene we've heard about, is not enough, a trigger is needed for someone to actually turn into a criminal."

Grossman nodded once, "That is correct."

Drew picked up the board from the defense table and put it on the easel, still covered with a single sheet of easel board paper. He walked back to the witness stand, "Dr. Grossman, here is the other photograph that you requested, could you please explain what it shows?"

On the easel was a three-foot by four-foot board with a series of photographs. Unlike the previous set of pictures, there was no blood splashed everywhere on the walls and there was no sense of chaos to them. In fact, they almost looked staged and the remains pictured seemed to be pieces of some sort physiologically correct mannequins. Each photograph showed a different setting, one was a living room, one what looked to be a cabin, another what had to be a car and so on. In each of the photographs there was what were clearly human remains. The bodies had been dismembered and the limbs had been placed neatly in front of the rest of the body. The most striking thing about all of the photographs was precisely the opposite of what had been so impactful about the previous set of photographs, it was the absolute absence of blood from every one of the settings pictured. The whole thing had a clinical feel to it, like it had all been done precisely and according to some sort of grotesque set of rules."

Grossman had the presence of mind to allow the jury to inspect the photographs before he began his explanation, it wasn't something that Drew or any of the defense attorneys had talked to him about, it was something he understood from watching the jury as they looked the board over. Drew was actually impressed by Grossman's decision.

Grossman began to finally explain what was depicted on the photographs, "These are pictures from the eight murders that Gary Preston was convicted of committing. Mr. Preston was arrested after his brother called police and told them that his brother Gary had killed eight people. Prior to Ned Preston's call the police had absolutely no clues for any of the murders. In fact, they only knew of four murders that they believed to be linked to one another, the other four came only after they heard what Mr. Preston had to say."

Drew was now leaning on the rail in front of the jury box seemingly as enthralled by the testimony as the jury was. He needed to move Grossman along, however, the jury was starting to get tired. It had been a long day.

Drew walked over to the defense table and continued with the direct examination, "And Dr. Grossman, was Gary Preston a suspect in any of those murders?"

Grossman shook his head, "No, he was not. He only came into consideration after his brother called the police. Gary Preston had told his brother that he needed to speak with him. When his brother was finally able to talk to him, Gary explained that he had some things he needed to store on his brother's property. When his brother asked him what they were, Gary explained that they were a variety of weapons he had used for some projects. When his brother pushed him and asked what kind of weapons he was talking about and what projects he had used them for, Gary walked him through each of the eight murders. I spoke to Ned Preston prior to my interview with Gary Preston in order to get a sense of Gary's motivations, reasoning and to see whether someone who knew him as intimately as his brother had seen anything in his behavior that could explain what he had done."

Drew went on, "And what exactly did Ned Preston say about his brother's confession?"

Grossman shook his head lightly and seemed to still have trouble believing he had heard what he had heard, "He explained that Gary had not been angry or out of control when he told his brother about his activities, that he had been in complete control and that he had not shown any semblance of remorse or conflict about what he had done. I asked him whether his brother's activities surprised him to which he responded that they had indeed surprised him. I believe that he said he had thought Gary was joking at first. He went on to explain that his brother had never hurt anyone or anything growing up. He had been a huge dog lover throughout his life. In fact, he had three dogs he had rescued when he was arrested. Ned also told us that Gary was incredibly popular not only when they were younger, but among their current friends."

Drew needed to try and get to the point quicker. Although the jury was clearly interested, they were simply overloaded with information, "And Dr. Grossman, how did your interview and conversation with Ned Preston compare with your interviews and conversations with the family of Franklin Carmody, the individual we discussed earlier?"

Grossman responded, "It was as different of an experience as I can possibly explain. Mr. Carmody's family had been upset and saddened by Franklin's behavior and they had a sense of responsibility because they had suspected that Franklin would eventually do what he did, that he would eventually kill people. They explained in graphic detail the types of activities that Franklin had engaged in with small animals from the time he had been a child. They explained that Franklin had been a strange child and that his odd behavior had gotten more and more frightening as he got older. Family friends explained to me that the Carmody kids had all been severely abused by their biological father and then by their foster parents when they were removed from home. The Carmodys were from a low socioeconomic background and had limited formal education.

"Ned Preston was also incredibly sorry about what his brother had done, but in contrast to the Carmody case, he explained there was absolutely no way he could have predicted that his brother would do what he did. In fact, he said he still had trouble believing it even after he'd seen the evidence. It was the exact same thing when I spoke to family and friends. Gary was popular, successful, active in community events and incredibly engaging regardless of the audience. Nobody at all could have predicted he'd end up killing eight people."

Drew continued, "What are these pictures of?"

Grossman leaned forward and explained the photographs one by one, "They are pictures of each of the murder scenes in the Preston case. As you can see, there is no loss of control, no knocked over furniture or blood splashed everywhere. Each of the victims was killed, dismembered and stacked with ultimate care and precision. When I asked Gray Preston why he had dismembered the bodies, he explained that he looked at it as a hunter might look at his kill. He knew he could not possibly mount a human as a prize, but he could go through the process of preparing a body the same way he prepared a buck when he went hunting. He also explained that it made it easier to either store or transport the bodies."

Drew let the testimony hang in the air. The faces of the jurors as Grossman went through his explanation of Gary Preston dismembering the bodies told Drew he was getting exactly what he wanted from Grossman.

He needed to make sure the jury completely got the difference between the two cases they had seen, "What else were you able to learn from Gary Preston, Dr. Grossman?"

Grossman shifted in his chair and for the first time since taking the stand, looked uncomfortable, "When I interviewed Gary Preston my understanding of aberrant human behavior was completely recalibrated. I thought I had a good understanding of the types of killers out there and what made them do the things they do, but this let me know there was another type of killer out there, a killer who was in fact the most dangerous kind of predator I had ever come across."

Before he could continue Melanie Farris stood up, "Objection your honor, foundation. We have not heard anything from Dr. Grossman that explains how he defines how one killer is more dangerous than another."

Drew smiled and chuckled, "Are you serious? Your honor, Dr. Grossman began his testimony by explaining the levels on his scale. There is plenty of foundation for him to make his assessment."

Farris was not letting it go, "No, he testified about levels of 'evil', not levels of danger. Based on what Dr. Grossman explained, the two are different."

The judge stepped in, "Sustained. Mr. Willis can we please establish the basis for Dr. Grossman coming to the conclusion that one killer is more dangerous than another or as he explained, 'the most dangerous type of predator he's come across?'"

Drew nodded, "Very well your honor. Dr. Grossman, can you explain to the jury what the judge has asked for?"

Grossman seemed put off by the prosecution's question and by the need to explain his assessment, still he responded, "As I shared with this court earlier, I have significant credentials in both forensic and traditional psychiatry, as well as significant experience researching and analyzing the most extreme of human aberrant behavior. Throughout my career I have come across dozens of murderers from a wide variety of backgrounds. Some have been pure psychopaths, others have been afflicted with mental defects like schizophrenia or psychosis and others still, have simply been addicts or greed-driven killers. And over that career I have come to form a professional opinion regarding the various types of murderers I have come across. Prior to coming across Gary Preston I believed that I had come across just about every type of murderer within the realm of humanity and in fact I still believe that.

"All the killers I had come across prior to Gary Preston were obviously dangerous for a variety of reasons. Some did not have any self-control and could explode at any time, others had such mental deterioration that they did not know how to adhere to any rules or laws and others still were quiet and passive and would simply bide their time until they were able to strike their victims. In every single instance, however, I was able to find someone who knew that there was something off about the killer. Whether it was their family, friends, teachers, therapists, in every single case we researched there was an element of awareness. Now, that did not necessarily mean that people knew their relative or student or patient was going to turn into a serial killer, but it did mean that when that did in fact happen, nobody was too surprised. Additionally, in most of the cases we researched, the victims themselves had ignored warnings, either by the killers' families, or by their friends or simply warning signs the victims themselves had been able to pick up. A wife that had suffered years of spousal abuse stayed with her husband who ultimately killed her and their children, that kind of thing.

"When I came across the case of Gary Preston I must confess that I started out coming up with my own conclusions even though I had not spoken to anyone involved in the case. Sometimes researchers see so many cases that follow a specific pattern that they begin to predict and see the pattern in all the cases they research. It is something we all know and we all try to avoid, but we are all human and in this case I made that mistake."

Drew wanted to bring the testimony and the day to a conclusion, "So you had already formed an opinion of the type of murderer Gary Preston was before you talked to anyone?"

Grossman nodded, "That's correct, having run into cases that were very similar to his case I believed that this would be a case where the individual had embarked on some sort of mission that called for him to dismember his victims. In addition to being dismembered, all the victims had been tortured. It was not easy to spot because the torture was of a very specific and subtle nature, but incredibly painful nonetheless. So, I believed I would be faced with a sadist with some sort of psychotic element, perhaps schizophrenia. What I got was very different, however. Gary Preston was genius-level smart, he was articulate and clear in his statements and he was completely at ease with what he had done and why he had done it. After spending a total of eighteen hours speaking with him over three days I came to the conclusion that Gary Preston did not fit into any of the previously established norms for psychopathy. His family history, his behavior, his understanding of what he had done and the reasons that he had done it, made him different from any other individual I had ever come across. There was also something else that I had only come across in two previous instances, both of which involved individuals with severe mental disorders. You see, Gary Preston explained that he was also different physically. When I asked him how he was different he explained that he was able to hear things others could not hear, see things others could not see and feel things others could not feel. When I asked him about it he explained that he had been able to do those things since he was a child. He was also quick to explain that it wasn't like x-ray vision or super hearing, but that the differences between his senses and the senses of everyone else he had ever come across were enough to get him to believe that he was simply different from the rest of the world. He said that he had been very troubled by this as a child, but that over time he came to understand it and embrace it."

Drew went on, "And was this something you heard in other cases besides Gary Preston's?"

Grossman nodded, "That's correct. Gary Preston's case was the catalyst for us to do the research we have been doing and the reason for the twenty-third level on the scale of evil."

Drew needed to wrap it up, "And Dr. Grossman why did you say that you believed Gary Preston to be the most dangerous type of predator that the world has ever seen?"

Grossman's expression took on an expression of concern, "Because I believe Gary Preston could have gone on killing at will for years, perhaps decades and he would have never come to the attention of authorities. He had killed, tortured and dismembered eight people and none of the law enforcement agencies associated with any of the murders had even heard of Gary Preston. He was able to engage, manipulate and engender trust in every single one of his victims. He knew police procedure, how to avoid leaving a trail and how to avoid security cameras. He was careful to establish alibis for every single one of the cases even though he never thought he would need them. Finally, Gary Preston killed his victims because he happened to be hunting for their particular personality type or physical features or a variety of other things he hunted for, but not because they had in any way been connected or associated with him or any of his family or friends. I absolutely believe that Gary Preston and all the individuals I have come across since his case are in fact the most dangerous and deadly type of predators on the face of the earth. By the way, Gary Preston confessed to seventy-seven other murders, but law enforcement was skeptical of his claim and already had him sentenced to the death penalty. He didn't provide any evidence to any of the seventy seven murders he said he committed."

Drew was now back behind the defense table, "And did you believe Gary Preston killed those seventy seven people?"

Grossman nodded solemnly and for the first time in all his testimony, he looked haunted, "I believe that Gary Preston committed more than three hundred murders prior to being caught. I don't have evidence of that except for doing a correlation between people disappearing at significant rates wherever Gary Preston and his family lived. His father was a pilot and they traveled and lived all over the country and wherever they lived, people began disappearing."

Drew let that hang in the air before moving on, "Thank you very much Dr. Grossman. No further questions your honor."

The judge looked at his watch before speaking, "I see it's almost the end of the day and it was a day with a lot of information being shared, so let's adjourn until tomorrow, shall we? Tomorrow, eight thirty sharp, folks. Ladies and gentlemen of the jury I will once again admonish you not to speak about the case outside of the jury room. Thank you and have a great evening."

20.

The lawyers and the audience stood up as the judge left. Once he was gone almost everyone in the audience pulled out a cell phone or a pad and began filling their stories. Grossman had made for a much better witness than the defense team thought he would make, much more engaging. The prosecution team did not hang around to talk or go over any evidence of information; they all stood up and left immediately.

Steven and his defense team stayed seated at the defense table and discussed the day's proceedings. Overall things were going extremely well, maybe too well. Drew and Max wondered whether Farris and Logan were laying a trap or whether they were planning to attack using some angle they had not thought of. Ray on the other hand thought that they simply did not believe that the jury would buy anything the defense experts had to say. Steven was tired and did not understand legal strategy the way his attorneys did, but he did think the case was going well.

Max brought up something Drew was very much thinking about himself, "Well, Farris hasn't gotten a crack at Grossman yet, so let's not count our chickens. I think his testimony was great, but I think she's going to tear it to shreds when she gets the chance. She scored some serious points with Dr. Leonard's testimony and he was likeable. Grossman is an ass and comes across like one. I have to admit though, he did a better job than I gave him credit for."

Drew nodded, "Yeah, I was thinking about that as he was talking. He went longer than I thought he would, but he had the jury on the edge of their chairs."

Steven spoke up, "And it wasn't just the jury, the judge was more engaged that I have seen him in a while. Maybe it was because of the photographs."

Ray nodded, "That's exactly what I think. The pictures raised their blood pressure so Grossman just needed to keep their attention as he explained the pictures."

As the four of them were sitting there a clerk from their office that was working on the case came in; she was barely able to contain herself. Drew saw her and raised his hands, "Whoa there, what's going on Amber?"

Amber turned her iPad around so they could see it, "You have to read the article that was published this afternoon in the New York Chronicle. You won't believe it."

They all gathered around the device to read the article that had gotten their clerk all flustered. It read:

Prosecution team unhappy about DA's decision not to pursue lesser-included offenses

API-Manhattan, New York By Felix Garcia/New York Chronicle

As the first-degree murder trial of Steven Loomis moves on, there is significant concern within the prosecution team about District Attorney David Neill's decision to forgo including charges for lesser-included offenses. Sources within the District Attorney's office who spoke only on the condition of remaining anonymous stated that prosecution attorneys Bart Logan and Melanie Farris were both distressed and extremely concerned about Mr. Neill's decision to only pursue charges for first-degree murder. Steven Loomis is accused with the first-degree murder of Donald Riche who was shot with a sniper rifle as he was being transported from the courthouse to jail. New York Chronicle contributor and NYU Law School professor Hank Weller agrees, 'As a prosecutor you want to give the jury as many options as you can for them to convict the defendant, it's standard practice, especially in high-profile cases where public sentiment may weigh on the jury's decision about whether the defendant is guilty or not. This is as charged a case as there could be and public opinion is significant, so Mr. Neill's decision was definitely not going to make his team happy.'

Other experts believe that concerns have most likely increased now that the prosecution has had an opportunity to hear and see the defense's experts, and the defendant himself, testify. Randy Zucherman, a professor of criminal law at Columbia Law School believes that it was Steven Loomis's testimony that has the prosecution team concerned about Mr. Neill's decision, 'Steven Loomis was articulate, clear and truly heartfelt in the testimony he gave. The prosecution most likely saw the effect his testimony and the testimony of the witnesses that came after him had on the jury and are now thinking that they should have included the lesser-included offenses.' Other experts have also speculated that as the trial has gone on and the prosecution has begun to realize that the defense's case may not sound as far-fetched or ridiculous to the jury as they thought it would, the prosecution team has become more and more concerned with the lack of options for the jury. The District Attorney's office has declined to comment and calls to the prosecution team attorneys have gone unanswered. Most experts believe that the trial will most likely wrap up within the next eight weeks, assuming there will be another seven expert witnesses that will be testifying for the defense. In addition to the cross-examination of the defense's experts, trial procedure allows the prosecution to recall their own experts to rebut the testimony provided during the defense's case.

Drew, Max and Ray looked at each other and smiled. All three of them had thought of the same thing at the same time. Max was the first one to speak, "Could it be that someone in the DA's office is pissed about not charging the lesser-included offenses?"

Drew nodded, "I think that is an incredibly likely possibility. I know that Farris and Logan are definitely upset about it and I would imagine there are others who feel the same.

Ray was next, "But why leak it? I mean what would be the strategic value of doing that?"

Drew answered, "Now that this is out, Neill will feel a lot of pressure to amend the complaint to add the lesser-included offenses. It will be up to the judge to decide whether he will allow that or not."

Max chimed in, "It could be that it was a clerk or one of the paralegals. I agree with Ray, I don't think the lawyers would have wanted this to come out this way."

Ray was nodding, "My take is that he will allow it. I don't know if the rest of you are sensing this, but the judge is definitely tired of this case and seems like he's ready to boil over."

Steven nodded, "I feel the same thing. Dr. Leonard and Dr. Grossman's testimony got him engaged again, but he does look tired. I see him sighing when he's getting impatient. I know the guy that wrote the article, do you want me to reach out to him and see what he will tell me?"

Drew shook his head, "No, don't do that, you will be putting the kid in a difficult situation. He will want to answer your questions because he owes you big, but he will also want to protect his sources until the end."

Steven nodded, "Got it. You're right of course, he would definitely protect his sources before answering my questions."

Max started picking up his things, "Well the plot thickens. We'll have to see if this has any effect on the trial. See you all tomorrow. Steven, get some rest."

Drew got one last comment in before they all left the courtroom, "Well, if it was in fact leaked on purpose, we need to consider the implications. Let's all sleep on it and talk tomorrow, I'm totally beat."

At the District Attorney's office the day was just getting longer and longer for Melanie Farris and Bart Logan. As soon as they arrived at the office David Neill pulled them into a conference room where they were joined by the public information officer for the DA's office.

David Neill was in rare form, he assumed that it had been one of the lawyers trying the case, "Which one of you fuckers did this? Hmm? Which one was it? If you tell me the truth you will still have a job after this. Lie to me and you will find yourself shit-canned before the end of the day."

Farris and Logan looked at each other with expressions that said 'what the hell is he talking about'. Neither lawyer knew of the article yet since they had both been in court the entire day.

It was Farris that asked the question, "Which one of us did what, Mr. Neill?"

Neill looked at Farris with a sudden realization, "Of course, it was you! You were pissed off from the beginning about not charging the lesser-included offenses! You told anyone who would listen that it was a bad idea not to include them!"

Farris was now even more confused, "Mr. Neill I have absolutely no idea what you are talking about. I have been in court all day, so if something happened today someone needs to fill us in."

Paula Detmer, the public information officer, answered her question, "There was an article in the New York Chronicle today that said that you are both very upset about the decision not to include the lesser charges. It does not say who in our office gave the reporter the information, but obviously it had to be someone who was close enough to the two of you that they would have heard you being upset about it. Can either of you think of anyone who may have spoken to the reporter?"

Bart answered her question, "No, I can't think of anyone. And it wasn't just the two of us that thought it was a bad idea, you know. There were a lot of people in the office that also thought so and they talked to people as well. It will be impossible to determine who it was that spoke to the reporter."

Neill, now calmer, went on, "Okay, alright, sorry Farris, it's been a rough afternoon and you were pissed of about the charges. In any case, the thing now is to figure what we do from here. Of course we will issue a statement denying any such information and stating that the DA's office is together on the decision. We can't have people thinking that there are factions within the office and that those factions are in conflict with each other."

Paula nodded, "I agree, but we can't put out a statement that says that the entire office is in agreement with the decision because people will know it's not true. There's nothing wrong with people disagreeing with a decision you made regarding the trial, it just can't be the two people in this room. We can put out something that says that the lawyers directly involved with the case are in total agreement with the decision and that the individual or individuals in the DA's office who disagree with the decision are not involved in the case in any way."

Both Farris and Logan looked down at the carper as she was saying the statement would say they were in complete agreement with the decision. It wasn't that they would be saying that they agreed with a decision the DA had made even though it was a complete lie, they'd both done that many times before, it was the only way to stay afloat in the DA's office. What bothered both of them was that the statement would be going into a press release. Part of their hesitation was that something the DA knew to be a lie would be printed in a newspaper, but a bigger part was that they both felt that doing that would limit their options in the actual trial. Both Farris and Logan understood that in a high-profile trial like this one, the trial team needed to have as many options and paths available to them as humanly possible. The press release would limit those options and those paths for both of them. They both also understood that to voice any dissent at this point would not only be professional suicide, but it would open up a whole other front for them to worry about and just about now neither of them had any bandwidth to take on more than one front at a time. They both remained quiet while Neill and Paula finalized the statement. Both just wanted to get home, take a shower and sleep twelve hours.

HOUSTON, TEXAS

J.D. Garzen was enjoying a rare quiet night at home. His team had reached out to the company that made the huge donation and had learned that the CEO of the company wanted a private meeting with Garzen. The reverend had gotten requests like this before, especially from prominent businesspeople and celebrities. Most of the time they just wanted to unburden their souls of the various and sundry sins they had accumulated over a life of debauchery. J.D. was only too happy to listen to them, nod gravely and declare their sins forgiven at the end, but the reality was that what J.D. felt most of all was envy. He envied their prominence and their freedom to do whatever they wanted to do whenever they wanted to do it. So if this asshole, Nigel whateverthefuck, wanted to unburden himself, J.D. was willing to grant forgiveness. Hell, for two hundred thousand dollars he was willing to forgive just about anything. The meeting had been arranged to take place at the reverend's home and would be attended by the CEO and the reverend and nobody else. Even the security would be light during the meeting. There would be the mandatory guard at the door, but none of the other people that normally patrolled the grounds and the residence. At precisely nine in the evening the intercom buzzed and a Bentley was allowed to go through the gates and up the driveway. J.D. was looking out his study window, he wanted to see what who he would be meeting in just a minute. The man was completely unremarkable. He was tall, thin and bald and he looked like he had a stick up his ass. He was probably one of these guys with a wall full of diplomas from top universities who thought his shit didn't stink. The reverend had run into that type of individual plenty of times before and he knew exactly how to handle them.

He straightened out his lounge jacket and his slacks and waited for the door to open. Once it did he went to meet his visitor immediately, "Welcome! Welcome! Please come in my friend! It is so wonderful to have you here tonight. Can I get you anything to drink? Water? Soda? Something stronger perhaps?"

Nigel Barlow shook his head and smiled, "No thank you Mr. Garzen, I'm quite alright."

J.D. was congratulating himself on the inside. He had the guy pegged perfectly, down to the uppity British accent.

He motioned to a big leather chair, "Please make yourself comfortable. As you can see I have asked most of my staff and my security team to take the night off, per your request. I have to tell you that it made me a bit nervous. I hope you can understand I mean no disrespect, but I also don't know you at all and there are a lot of wackos out there."

Nigel shook his head, "No offense taken, I completely understand. I would like to get down to business if you don't mind."

J.D.'s curiosity was peaked now, but he simply shook his head, "Not at all. I like a man who can get down to the business at hand without a whole bunch of small talk. It is a waste of time if you asked me."

Barlow ignored his comment and simply got on with his task, "Mr. Garzen I am the CEO of a multinational conglomerate. We have operations around the world and we control better than a hundred billion dollars in assets."

J.D. whistled, but then caught himself, "Wait, did you just say a hundred billion dollars."

Barlow nodded, "That's correct. In addition to having operations across the globe we also wield significant influence and we have assets placed in the most important governments and government agencies in the world."

Garzen's curiosity was almost too much for him to hold back, "I see, that is a powerful organization indeed. How can I be of assistance to you?"

Barlow went on, "This organization is made up of a number of very select individuals, individuals who have the resources, influence and ability to do whatever the organization needs them to do in order to achieve our goals. I believe that you are such an individual."

J.D.'s heart was now beating a mile a minute. He kept hearing 'a hundred billion dollars' and 'significant influence' in his head. Outwardly, however, he pretended to look puzzled, "Oh, how's that? I don't have the type of influence and access to power that your organization has and I definitely don't have the kind of money you are talking about, so I'm not sure what you are referring to."

Barlow smiled a different kind of smile, a smile that made Garzen nervous, a knowing smile, "You would be surprised Mr. Garzen. Before we continue let me share some information with you. I know exactly who you are, reverend, exactly what you are."

J.D.'s disposition changed completely, "Hey listen, I don't know who you think I am or where you got your information, but I would appreciate it if you could get to your point so we can conclude our business."

Barlow's smile remained on his face as he did exactly as Garzen had requested, "Very well. When you were young you felt you were different than the kids around you, not just different, but better than them. You could see better, hear better, think faster than everyone around you, but you pretended that you didn't because you wanted to fit in and be popular. As you got older you started to feel certain inclinations and desires. You didn't know why you felt them, you just knew they were so powerful that you had to ultimately fulfill them. When you were twelve years old a girl in your neighborhood disappeared. She was never found and the case was never closed. Your family moved to Chicago and once again, a neighborhood boy eight years old disappeared, was never found and his killer was never caught. Over the years you perfected your craft and began to kill people away from where you lived. By the time you were eighteen years old there were at least sixteen people that you had made disappear. None of them were ever found and none of the cases was ever solved. We know all of this, Mr. Garzen, because our sources and influence can reach everywhere and anywhere and we can and do get as much information on any one on earth as we might need."

J.D. was sweating profusely and shaking his head almost imperceptibly as he listened to Barlow, "No, that's not...no, how could you know? How the fuck could you know any of that? I am...it's just...who the fuck are you? What do you want?"

Barlow continued, "Relax Mr. Garzen, I am not here to judge you and I am not planning on telling anyone about your secrets. I am here to offer you something I believe you have wanted since you were a child. Freedom. Freedom from pretending you are inferior, freedom from trying to quell the natural desires and instincts you were born with. You've been watching the Loomis trial, your sermons let me know you have been watching it with keen interest. Well Mr. Garzen, I am here because I believe you are a Homo sapiens predator, the subspecies of human they are arguing about in the trial. What you went through during your childhood and teen years is by no means unique. Our organization is made up of individuals that felt the same things, did the same things and tried to understand all of it just like you tried to understand it."

Garzen could not keep his mouth from opening with incredulity as he listened to Barlow talk. He was right about everything he had said, everything. How the fuck could he know all of that? Had they been watching him all along? It couldn't be, it just couldn't be.

Barlow watched as Garzen went through his mental process trying to figure out how anyone could know so much about him.

Barlow decided to let him off the hook, "We established what you've done through a computer program that looks for certain information. It pulled all the disappearances around the places you lived and a lot more information. Listen, I don't want to take up a lot of your time, we need someone like you in our organization, someone with a gift for talking to large groups of people and getting them excited about what you have to say."

Garzen finally found his voice, "I don't need anything from you, I have as much money as I could possibly need, my congregation worships me, my family loves me, I'm set. If this is some backhanded attempt at blackmailing me you can forget it. Everything you just talked about is your speculation; you have no proof of anything, so I think you need to go and not come back. If you leave now I will not call the police."

Barlow shook his head and smiled wider, "Mr. Garzen, reverend, do you really think I would come here and that I would say everything I just said to you if I didn't have some rock solid evidence? Let me ask you something, would you have believed someone if they told you that someone was able to put together what we've put together? Or would you have called them crazy? It's true, you have money and you have bought into the whole televangelist lifestyle, but the hunger you feel, that you've felt your whole life, is still there. Do you want me to bring up the three individuals who after interning for your organization disappeared without a trace? Listen, J.D., I am offering you an opportunity to be a part of the group that will basically run things in the not too distant future."

J.D. was now a bit more settled, "Run what things? Where will your organization be 'running things' and why would I be at all interested in whether you are in charge of anything."

Barlow looked Garzen in the eyes as he explained things to him, "What things are we going to be running? Everything J.D. Everything. Everywhere. The people who are a part of our organization include judges, doctors, politicians, captains of industry; each and every one of those individuals is just like you. Each and every one of them went through the same process you did and each and every one of them had the same doubts you have, but they all came to understand that if you are not a part of our organization you will just be one of them, one of the sheep who are being hunted and just don't know it yet. That's not you, is it J.D.? You've gotten where you've gotten because of drive and the ability to move people. Now it's time to use the gifts you were given the way they are meant to be used. Now, we have influence and resources across the globe, but after this trial and the media attention it has garnered we will need someone who can speak on our behalf, who knows how to convince people to believe whatever he's saying and that J.D. is you."

J.D. was now listening. The fact was that the man was right, he still had those urges and he was now not able to pursue his interests the way he had done it before he became a celebrity. Still, he had money, a big house, just about anything anyone could want, "And what exactly is in it for me? I mean if I am a part of your organization I will need to shut down my operation, correct? Look around you, this house, the servants, the cars, everything I have came from that operation, so whatever it is you're offering needs to beat that, can you do that? Can you beat that?"

Barlow smiled broadly and nodded, "Oh yes, J.D., we can most definitely beat that. For starters you will be able to reach to the highest levels of power in the most powerful companies and governments on earth. You will have as much money as you could possibly want. Our people have so much money that it has stopped being something they care about. And, most importantly, you will be able to pursue projects of your own, projects that allow you to satisfy the urges you feel, but can do nothing about."

J.D.'s face took on a far away look as he thought about being able to do the things he had been wanting to do for years, but had simply not been able to.

Still, that was only one side of the equation, he needed to learn about the other side of the equation, "And what exactly is it you need me to do? What do I have to convince people about?"

Barlow shifted in his chair and lowered his voice, "After this trial, those who are a part of the subspecies being discussed will be persecuted by society. People will be looking for us and thinking that we are monsters going around taking children in the night and chopping up people left and right. We need you to present our case, a case we have not been allowed to present in court the way the other side has. Our organization is engaged in projects around the world that help those in need. We have several community clinics in Africa, we are planting fields in South America so the farmers can stop farming coca leaves and we have a hospital in Germany that provides intensive care and plastic surgery to those in need. We have also been providing vaccines to people around the world, people who would never have access to them if it weren't for us. And those are only some of the projects we are engaged in, but will people hear about them? Will they even care? You see, that is why you are perfect for this reverend, you can present our case in a way that will have people believing in and most of all caring about what we are doing."

J.D. was impressed, it was clear that whatever this organization was it had the juice that the man claimed it had, "How am I supposed to do that and shut down my ministry? I don't even know how I would go about getting people to believe what you are talking about."

Barlow stood up and began pacing a short circle in front of Garzen, "You won't shut it down right away. In fact, you will start your new endeavor with your congregation. You will start preaching about all god's creatures being worthy of love, not judging before you know the whole story, god putting those who can provide in front of those who need, that kind of thing. You will also start talking about some physical malady and not feeling well. It doesn't matter what it is, heart, lungs, whatever and eventually you will announce that due to health reasons you need to step down. What you do with your ministry is up to you. You can shut it down or you can hand it over to another preacher, it doesn't matter to us. Perhaps you will do that so if things don't work out with us you can come back to it. If you agree to this, an account will be set up in your name in a Swiss bank. This account is beyond the reach of anyone in the US and will be set up to cover your expenses without touching the money of the ministry, it would look funny if you were taking money from the ministry to cover expenses that have nothing to do with it. You will keep your staff while you transition out of your situation.   We can go over details for everything as we get closer to the day you step down. Can I count on you then J.D.?"

J.D. looked at the man, hung his head and nodded, "Yeah, yeah you can count on me. But if things don't work out I will come back to my ministry, got it? I'm willing to try this thing out, but if for some reason it doesn't work out I will be coming back."

Barlow had stopped pacing and now stood in front of Garzen with his hand outstretched, "Of course, you can just come back if things don't work out. Believe me, you will not want to come back, I am certain of it. Once you get a sense of the power we wield and the kinds of perks that comes with, you will not want to come back.

Garzen shook Barlow's hand and had a thought that he would come to have many, many times after this meeting, he was agreeing to what Barlow was presenting because not agreeing did not seem like an option he really had. For better of worse, the reverend J.D. Garzen was now part of something bigger than what he could have imagined, something that would allow him to be who he was and to do the things he wanted to do. As for Barlow, he was thinking that this had gone easier than he had expected. Garzen was dirtier or stupider than he had thought, most likely both. Well, he was on board now and if believing that he could simply decide to come back to his ministry if things didn't work out made him more comfortable, Barlow was fine with confirming the fiction.

21.

As the defense team along with Steven walked into the courthouse, they could tell there was something off. The reporters outside of the courthouse were all doing live updates and everyone in side was writing or talking on a cell phone. Drew tried to hear what they were saying, but he just could not make anything out given all the voices talking and the acoustics in the courthouse. When they got to the courtroom they saw one of the things the reporters were talking or writing about. The courtroom door was closed and locked. The door had been open since seven in the morning every day until now, so they all knew something was going on. Just as he was about to ask someone whether the prosecution was already inside, Max saw the prosecution team coming down the hall displaying the same look of confusion that the defense team had on their faces.

Farris looked at all of them and tried the door. Once she saw it was locked she turned to Drew, "What's the deal? Did the judge say anything?"

Drew shook his head, "We don't know. The door was locked when we got here. We were wondering whether you guys were already inside. We didn't knock on the door, though, let's do that and see what's going on."

Drew knocked hard on the door, its size and the level of noise meant he needed to really pound on it for someone inside to hear. After a few seconds the bailiff opened the door, looked at the defense team, the prosecution team and motioned to them, "Please come inside gentlemen – and lady – the judge would like to speak with you."

Each team went to their respective tables and set down their briefcases and started for the judge's chambers.

Drew looked at his colleagues, at the prosecution team and shrugged his shoulders to indicate he had no idea what the judge wanted to talk to them about. Melanie Farris and Bart Logan both returned the same gesture at the same time.

Steven went to follow his lawyers to the judge's chambers, but the bailiff stopped him, "I'm sorry, but It's just the lawyers he wants to speak to right now, Mr. Loomis. I'm sure you lawyers will let you know what they talk about."

Drew was about to protest, but he thought better of it, "It's okay Steven, we'll definitely fill you in on everything we discuss in there."

Steven nodded and went to sit down at the defense table.

The five lawyers filed back to the judge's office where they found him going over some files. Drew noticed with no small amount of relief that he was indeed wearing pants under the robe. Maybe the rumors weren't true after all. His pants were way too short, however and he wore white socks with his black shoes, which only enhanced the effect. He looked up at all of them, opened the drawer to his left and pulled out a paper bag. The lawyers watched him with some amusement and Max actually wondered if old judge Newman was about to pull a fifth of Whisky out of that bag.

The judge actually pulled out a croissant and an old banana and placed them on his desk, "You don't mind if I eat while we talk do you? My wife insists on me eating breakfast."

He addressed the question to all of them and all of them simply mumbled in the negative.

He went on talking through a mouthful of croissant, "Mr. Logan, Ms. Farris, I know we haven't brought this up before now, but have there been any discussions with Mr. Neill about the possibility of a plea deal?"

It was clear that all of the lawyers were completely taken aback by the question. It was also clear that Logan and Farris had probably had a conversation about precisely that because they both hesitated and looked at each other before answering, not quite sure whether to let everyone in on their conversations.

Finally Logan spoke up, "No judge, we have not really engaged in any discussions about a plea deal. Mr. Neill felt we had a strong enough case for first degree murder."

The judge kept eating, but responded nonetheless, "I see, I see. Well, maybe you do, but the defense has done a more than adequate job of presenting the jury with an alternative theory."

Now Farris spoke up, "They have your honor, but it is a theory that truly pushes the boundaries of accepted science. Truth be told, it borders on being science fiction more than real science."

Drew took exception to that, "Whether you like it or not the theory is based on accepted scientific methodologies. We still have our experts about the biology and evolutionary science around the theory."

The judge stepped in before the lawyers could get into it, "Alright, I think we are all clear on the fact that both sides believe fervently in the arguments they are making. You wouldn't be the lawyers you all are if it was otherwise. I also know that both sides understand that a jury is capable of doing anything for any reason. Witness the O.J. Simpson case. I think that case will forever live as an example of what a jury is capable of doing, regardless of the evidence. Mr. Willis, Mr. Zeidler and Mr. Gretche you all have to admit that you are asking the jury to set aside the world they have been living in for the entirety of their lives and to accept a new world where they are sharing the planet with a species that is the next evolutionary step from humans and that's a pretty big leap to ask them to take. Mr. Logan and Ms. Farris, you have to also acknowledge that the public sentiment overwhelmingly favors Mr. Loomis and let's be honest, regardless of the legal reality of what Mr. Riche did, most people believe he is absolutely guilty of all of it and like it or not it has definitely had an effect on the jury."

The lawyers didn't respond and just looked at the judge surprised. He peeled his banana and chuckled at their reaction, "Oh come now, I know what you all have to say when the cameras are rolling, but it's just us here and we know that the reality of the situation is far from what we would like it to be. So let's dispense with the clichés and the official lines and let's get down to where the rubber meets the road. Mr. Willis and company, do you think that Mr. Loomis would consider a plea deal if one were offered?"

Drew thought about it and responded as truthfully as he could, "I honestly do not know your honor. It isn't something we explored at all given that it has been first-degree murder from the beginning."

The judge nodded, "Do you think he might consider entering a plea if the offer is the right one."

Drew responded, "Again judge, I don't really know. I think that he may consider a plea if the charge is the right one. He has stated from the beginning that his goal was to bring attention to this science and I think he has more than accomplished that."

Before anyone else could speak up Max spoke up, "I can tell you after having spoken with Steven that he would not even consider a plea if it entails a significant amount of custody. I think he would be willing to gamble and risk it all before agreeing to a significant amount of prison time."

Now Farris spoke up, "I can pretty much guarantee you judge that if Mr. Neill was to consider a plea it would definitely come with time in custody."

Max responded, "I believe Steven is reasonable and that he understands that he would have to serve time in prison for what he did, but I am just letting you know that if it is any substantial time he will more than likely roll the dice and let the jury decide."

Judge Newman was finished with his breakfast and he was also finished saying what he had asked them back here to say, "Well, I assume that you all understand that I am asking that you all go back to your respective corners and consider the option of bringing this case to a conclusion by way of a deal that is satisfactory to everyone. Mr. Logan, Ms. Farris I am fully aware that your task is the more difficult one and if you feel that it would be productive we can have a hearing outside of the presence of the jury where we can have Mr. Neill join us and discuss the possibility of a deal. I am more than willing to do anything in my power to facilitate that, so you let me know."

Logan responded, "We'll let you know your honor. I think we should address this option with Mr. Neill initially and see how he feels about it."

The judge nodded, "Very well. Have a good afternoon. Let's agree to meet here in my chambers tomorrow morning to discuss where we are relative to a possible deal, shall we?"

All the lawyers agreed with the judge and took their leave. The defense lawyers went back to their table in the courtroom. Logan and Farris walked out of the courtroom. Steven was clearly anxious about the proceedings.

Drew sat right next to him to let him know what was going on. "We just met with the judge and the prosecution and there are some things we need to talk about. Let's go to the office and order some breakfast in and talk."

Steven was not sure about what Drew was saying, "What about this afternoon? Are we going to have enough time to come back this afternoon?"

Max explained, "The judge has postponed the trial until tomorrow morning so that we and the prosecution have an opportunity to talk about what the judge is asking. We will explain it all to you when we get to the office. I don't want any of the media vultures to get ideas and start printing stories that may end up coming back to bite us in the ass."

With that they all stood up and walked out of the courtroom. The reporters who were hanging out in the hallway outside of the courtroom reacted by asking the obvious questions, "What was the meeting about Drew" or "Is your witness not ready to testify" and so on. The group walked through the reporters and headed for the SUV that was waiting for them outside of the courthouse. They headed to Drew and Max's office where they in fact ordered breakfast and ate with gusto.

Drew went on to explain what was going on to Steven, "The judge asked us into his chambers because he wanted to know if we had ever engaged in any discussions with the prosecution about a possible deal."

Steven responded, "What exactly do you mean a possible deal?"

Drew stood up and paced as he explained things to Steven, "Well sometimes when a case has possibilities for both sides the lawyers for the defense and the prosecution come to an agreement about a charge that is satisfactory to both sides. Most of the time it is a reduced charge in exchange for having the defendant plea guilty. I have to tell you that in most instances the deals favor the prosecution."

Steven didn't understand, "Why do they favor the prosecution? If that's the case why would anybody take the deal?"

It was a fair question. Now Ray spoke up, "It usually favors the prosecution because most of the time the prosecution has the defendant over a barrel. In most instances there is basically nothing for the defendant to argue. There is more than ample evidence for the prosecution to win and the defense knows it, so if the prosecution does make an offer, defense lawyers are likely to jump at it. Sometimes the only thing the prosecution offers is that the defendant won't be sentenced to death."

Steven was still a bit puzzled, "Well isn't that what the prosecution says in this case? That they have everything they need for a conviction?"

Ray explained, "Yeah, that's what they've been saying, but it's posturing, they have to say it. Now that the trial is underway both sides have gotten to see each other's strategy and ammunition and the judge wants to bring this to a close so both sides are being asked to consider a deal. The question for you is whether you would consider a plea deal at all. You need to think about everything, the possibility that the jury would convict you, the possibility that you would get life in prison, the possibility that your family will have to keep enduring the trial and all the attention that comes along with that, which I don't have to tell you is beyond anything I have seen in my career. You need to think about all of it when you are considering this."

Steven took on a thoughtful, faraway look. He was most certainly thinking about all of it. All of a sudden he thought about the most important part of this whole thing.

He turned to Ray immediately to ask his question, "What about jail time? When...if I were to take any deal would there be jail time?"

Max answered, he knew that would be the first question he would ask, "Yes, there would most likely be jail time involved. How much, I can't tell you until we know what the offer is. In some instances when a judge wants for a deal to be worked out, such as in this case, he will make certain commitments regarding how much jail time he would impose if a defendant were to take the deal."

Steven wanted to make sure he understood everything correctly, "So you're saying that this judge would tell us ahead of time how much jail time I would get if I pled guilty?"

Max nodded, "Most likely yes, that would be the case, but again I wouldn't be able to say with any certainty until we know what they are offering. I take it from your questions that you might consider taking a plea?"

Steven turned to face his lawyers and looked at the three of them long and hard before responding, "Yes I suppose I would consider it. I believe with all my being in what we are arguing, but I would be lying if I said the possibility of spending my life in jail didn't give me some serious pause. I am also thinking about my family and what they're having to go through while the trial is going on. I guess it would all depend on what they would ask me to plead guilty to. I can tell you right off the bat that if they ask for me to stand up and say that I shot and killed another human being intentionally I would not take the deal. I simply can't stand up and basically say that I take everything back, that I didn't really mean it. If I were to do that it would basically negate everything that the experts have testified to, it would set the entirety of the science back to before they started and I can't do that."

Drew nodded thoughtfully and responded to Steven's statement, "Well, there is something called an Alford plea, which means that you are taking the deal because of the advantages of taking a deal. If you use an Alford plea you will not have to admit to anything."

Steven stood up and walked over to Drew. He put his hand on Drew's shoulder and turned to look at Ray and Max, "I know and I appreciate everything you have done for me. I know how hard this has been for all of you and I know what it could potentially do to your careers and your practices. You need to know that I didn't do this, I didn't make this argument, just as some sort of ploy. I didn't shoot Donald Riche out of revenge, you have to know that too."

Ray smiled at him, "I know kid, I know. I don't think any of us would have gone into this if we thought that you were just some vigilante looking for revenge. This is groundbreaking stuff Steven and I for one am damn proud to be a part of it. So if we have to take this to the end, then so be it. I don't want you thinking about taking any deal because you think we might not have the stomach for it."

Now it was Steven's turn to smile. He walked over to Ray and put an arm around his shoulder and patted his belly, "Trust me Ray, the last thing I would think is that you don't have the stomach for it."

Bart Logan and Melanie Farris were sitting in a conference room at the district attorney's office downtown. They both had half eaten fruit salads in front of them. They had avoided talking too much about what the judge had asked them to do opting instead to wait for Neill to show up. Logan had called him immediately after they left Judge Newman's courtroom. He had been surprised by Neill's reaction. He had acted as though he might have been waiting for someone to make an overture about a deal all along. Logan expected that Neill probably thought it would be the defense asking about a plea deal, but he appeared to be just fine with the judge making the first inquiry. It made Bart wonder whether it really had been Neill that leaked the story about them being upset about the lesser included offenses not being charged.

Neill finally showed up at the conference room, full of energy and apparently brimming with confidence, "So, old Judge

Newman wants us to make a deal. The defense was probably ecstatic about it, weren't they?"

Logan and Farris looked at each other and Logan responded, "No, I wouldn't say that. They were just as cautious about it as we were. To be honest they seemed to think that their client would probably not be willing to take any deal, but they were willing to put it before him just like the judge asked."

Neill finally sat down at the head of the table, "Why would Newman want us to make a deal now? As far as I am concerned the case is going perfectly for us. You and Farris here have done a first rate job at undermining this whole bogus theory of theirs without looking like bullies and without being too condescending, so if anyone should be looking for a deal it should be the defense."

Now it was Farris's turn to respond and she planned on responding very vigorously indeed, "I have to disagree with you sir. I mean I don't disagree with the fact that the trial is going well for us, but I do have to strongly disagree that the outcome is in any way certain. I don't mean to point out the obvious Mr. Neill, but have you seen the public's response to all of this? Have you heard the talk shows and the so-called experts giving their opinion to anyone who will listen? I'm sorry Mr. Neill but this trial is anything but settled. The court of public opinion stands firmly with the defense sir and I can guarantee you that in spite of all of the admonishments in the world, the jurors are most definitely being influenced by all of the media coverage. We all know what a jury is capable of doing and that's not taking into consideration the victim and what he did."

Neill protested somewhat feebly, "What he was accused of doing! He was not convicted before he died!"

Now Logan had to speak up, "Come now sir, we all know that Riche did it and so does the public. Melanie is right, if this trial were to be decided in the court of public opinion it wouldn't even be close."

Now Neill really objected, "But it's not being decided in the court of public opinion, it is being decided in a court of law, damn it! It's your job to make sure that the law is what prevails!"

Logan backed off just in time to avoid having Neill throw a full tantrum, "I know sir. I didn't mean to suggest that we would do anything other than to uphold the law, but we have to be realistic and understand that this is a case where there is just no good angle when it comes to how the public perceives the case. He is a father whose daughter was brutally murdered and butchered by a predator who, by the way, took and murdered and butchered eight other little girls before he was caught and he did it with careful consideration and planning. Loomis has basically given life to something the entire world considers time and again when a case like this surfaces. We have to remember that what he is arguing is most definitely a stretch of accepted science and completely unheard of in a court of law, but he is right that the issue has been considered in other contexts."

Farris was actually impressed. Logan had been unfazed and he had made an excellent case for making an offer to the defense. Neill's outburst had not intimidated him in the least. Neill ran his hands through his hair and looked up at the ceiling as he considered what Logan had explained.

He finally exhaled and in a much more controlled voice he asked, "Well, what would you suggest that we offer Mr. Loomis?"

Logan considered the question, but it was Farris who answered it, "Realistically we can't offer second degree murder, they won't even consider that. I think in order to make an offer they actually consider we need to think about some form of manslaughter charge."

Neill was nodding, "I would agree, but what are you thinking about specifically?"

Farris moved to sit closer to Neill in order to explain something that she had clearly been thinking about, "I think we could offer something along the lines of voluntary manslaughter.

We would pursue the charge under the reasoning that the intent to kill another human being was not there. We would argue that Steven Loomis engaged in a dangerous activity that was likely to cause harm, but he did not believe that he was shooting a human being and therefore does not have the mens rea, the mindset, to be convicted of murder."

Neill rubbed his chin as he thought about it. He addressed Farris's idea, "You are suggesting that the intent to kill another human being was not there because he believed he was shooting something other than human. We would not be in fact saying that we agree that Riche was not a human being, we would basically be willing to accept that Loomis genuinely believed that he was shooting something other than a human and that he did it in a manner that put others at risk. I think I like it. It lets us come across as enforcing the law, but doing it with compassion, understanding everything the families have gone through. I do, I like it."

With that he stood up straightened his tie while looking at his reflection in the wide window of the conference room, "Okay let's get on this. Get Michael Gordon working on potential sentencing scenarios. No use coming up with a great deal only to have it fall apart because of sentencing guidelines. Melanie why don't you get with our public information folks and let's start to put together a statement along the lines of what you said, 'We feel confident in our case, but we feel that we don't want the families to continue going through the trauma of the trial and all the public attention and on and on. If there was justice to be had, the deal the prosecution is bringing to the table would offer some justice to all those that justice was owed to' or something along those lines. Paula Detmer knows her stuff, she'll know how to put it together."

Bart Logan was starting to get annoyed at the fact that Neill was basically handing the process of putting together the deal to people that had until now not been a part of the case at all.

Before he could get really spun up Neill turned to address him, "Bart walk Gordon through the case so far and make sure he understands that we need something that will be almost impossible to turn down. You have veto power, so if he can't come up with something you think we can work with, just put it together yourself."

He stood up to leave the conference room and both Farris and Logan were so tired they didn't even make an attempt to stand up.

As he was about to leave the room Neill stopped in the doorway and looked back at both lawyers, "You have both done an incredible job with this, I have to be completely truthful in saying that I thought you both would have a difficult time with this, but I couldn't have been more wrong. We have some changes coming in the office. We are putting together a new federal narcotics task force in partnership with the US Attorney's office and I would like for you to head it up from our end Bart. Farris, I know that you have wanted into the financial crimes unit for some time now. I think you would make an excellent part of the team, I was going to have Gordon head it up, but if you feel up for it I'd like you to consider it."

Both Melanie and Bart looked at each other and in spite of the supreme effort they were putting into not smiling they failed miserably. Wide smiles spread across both of their faces.

Neill nodded and smiled himself, "I take it both of you are up to the challenges I just mentioned. Let's not get too far ahead of ourselves though. Let's wrap this up nice and neat and put this in the files in the basement where it belongs."

He went to leave and just before stepping through the door he looked back to both of them, "Oh yeah, and let's make sure that we work a non-appeal clause in the deal. The last thing I want is for us to put this away only to have some gung ho appellate hack think that he can come up with something to save the day for Steven Loomis."

Logan spoke up, "Not a problem. I have a feeling that if Loomis decides to go for the deal he won't be wanting to keep it going by filing appeal after appeal."

Both Melanie Farris and Bart Logan were absolutely ecstatic. Not only had their initial assessment about considering a lower included offense been right, but their work had been recognized and in a case where it was almost impossible to find an angle for the prosecution, they had done a good job of handling the witnesses, they had worked well together and impressed the people that needed to be impressed. When Neill left the room, Logan looked over at Melanie and raised his hand to give her a high five. Melanie blew him away by actually walking over to him and giving him a hug. They let go and composed themselves.

Farris was the first to speak up, "Alright, now let's make sure we get this sewn up tight. We need to make him an offer he can't refuse, Godfather style."

Logan chuckled as he was nodding, "Agreed, agreed. Do you think Gordon is going to have a problem working under my direction?"

Farris gave him a mischievous grin, "Are you kidding? He's going to be swallowing Tums for months. Remember what a pompous ass he was at the beginning when we they were telling us we would be trying the case? I don't know how he got on Neill's shit list, but yeah, I think he's going to be blowing a gasket."

The smile he gave her let her know that he was going to be enjoying this thoroughly. They both picked up their things and went off to carry out their mandates.

Steven decided to head home directly after their meeting. He sat in the back of the SUV and thought about everything. This was most definitely not a place where he'd thought he'd find himeslf. Throughout all of this and especially after he had begun to work with Max, Drew and Ray in earnest, he had made peace with the fact that his fate would be decided by the jury. He had come to terms with the fact that he had been charged and was being tried for first-degree murder and everything that entailed. He had not considered at all the possibility that at some point the charges against him might change. Drew and Ray had explained to him that the most likely scenario would be that the District Attorney, if he made an offer at all, would make an offer for some form of manslaughter. He had explained to both of his lawyers that he would not, could not, stand up and accept that he had shot a human being with the full intent to kill him. Now that they knew that he would consider the right deal, they could go about the process of negotiating with the district attorney's office. They had made a call to Bart Logan and had agreed to meet that evening at their office to discuss a possible deal. That's when Steven had decided to go home instead. He had to talk to Beth about this. This was not something that they had ever discussed and Steven had no idea how she might take this. She, like him, had and still considered the possibility of having Steven be found guilty and having to spend a significant amount of time in prison. She had to deal with all the attention that the trial was generating every single day and it wasn't just her having to put up with the throngs of reporters hanging around outside the house, she was having to shield their children from it and she knew that no matter what the outcome of the trial was, their lives would be disrupted. She was putting on a brave face for him, but he knew that she was having a hard time with all of it, especially the idea that in the end he might be going away for the rest of his life.

The car was pulling up to their home when Steven spoke to his driver, "Hey Lou, do you mind going down into the parking garage for deliveries today? I don't want to deal with them today."

Lou looked at him through the rearview mirror, "Sure thing Mr. Loomis."

He went down into the parking lot where Steven could get into the elevator without cameras snapping pictures along the way. He was getting home earlier than usual and Beth was waiting for him when he got off the elevator.

She hugged him, "Hey you. I heard that court was cancelled this afternoon. What's going on?"

Steven went off to the coat rack by the front closet and hung his jacket, "I'll tell you if you will pour me a Scotch on the rocks."

She walked over to the wet bar and did as he asked. She walked over with his drink, grabbed his hand and led him over to the couch.

She sat down and patted the seat next to her, "Alright, what's going on. I finally gave in and turned the TV on and heard here and there that court had been postponed. Most people thought that there was some sort of problem with the experts that your team was planning to call this afternoon."

Steven took a sip of his drink and answered Beth, "There was no problem with any of the witnesses, everything was going as it was supposed to. The judge called the lawyers back into his chambers and asked both sides that they think about coming up with a deal."

She didn't get what he meant, "What do you mean he asked them to come up with a deal? A deal for what?"

Steven put down his glass, "A deal where I would plead guilty to a different charge."

Now Beth became visibly concerned, "What do you mean plead guilty? Why would you do that? I thought that you were fighting the charges, why would they think that you would be willing to plead guilty?"

Steven put an arm around Beth and calmed her down, "Relax honey, relax. Sometimes when the case is complicated or when both sides are really close the judge asks the defense and the prosecution to talk about making some kind of deal. What that means is that the prosecution would change the charge to something less serious and in exchange I would stop fighting and plead guilty."

Beth was still upset, "But if you plead guilty then that means that you would have to go to prison! You would have to go away!"

Steven held Beth's hands and looked at her intently, "Yes, that is true, if I plead guilty to a charge I would probably get some prison time. But Beth, you understand that if I fight this case like I am and I lose the case, if the jury finds me guilty of first degree murder I would be going to prison for the rest of my life."

Beth pulled her hands away from him and stood up to pace, "I know Steven, I know! That's what makes trying to understand why you did this so difficult! I know what your intention was, but the fact is that now you have put yourself at risk for going to prison forever! What about the kids and me?! Do you know how hard that would be on all of us?"

Now Steven stood up himself, he walked over to the window, "I know Beth, trust me, I know. You don't think I have agonized over that? There is nothing I could possibly say that can explain to you how sorry I am. But I can't change it now Beth, I am in it now and I have to deal with it the best way I can think of."

She looked at him with tears in her eyes. He walked over to her and put his arms around her, "Hey, listen, that's what I was trying to talk to you about, trying to resolve this in a better way. If the prosecution makes some sort of offer it will have to be a lesser charge than first-degree murder and my team said that sometimes when the judge really wants to resolve the case through a deal, like this one does, he will let us know how much jail time I would get if I were to plead guilty."

She looked up at him, "Really? They can do that? Tell you how much jail you are going to get before you decide?"

Steven smiled, "Apparently yes, when judges want to motivate a defendant to plead guilty they will let them know how much time they would get. Also, remember that it's just an offer and that I can just decline to take it and just continue to fight my case."

She pulled him close and hugged him hard, "I'm sorry. It's just that I try to pretend that everything is going to be okay, that when it's all over we're just going to go back to our life. I do know that you going to prison is a possibility, I have known it all along, but I have to pretend that it's not, because otherwise I will go crazy."

He smiled at her and kissed her forehead, "Well, let's see what happens. Drew told me he would call me once he heard from the district attorney."

She sat back down, "So you would consider pleading guilty? After all you have gone though, after all that you've done you would actually consider pleading guilty?"

Steven kept pacing as he answered her, "I told Max, Drew and Ray that if I have to stand up and admit that I shot a human being with premeditation I would simply just keep fighting. You're right, after everything I have gone through I cannot possibly do that. It would make a mockery of all the work that Dr. Leonard, Dr. Grossman and all the other experts have done. Can you imagine, I make this completely unorthodox argument that stretches the boundaries of the law and the definition of humanity and then I just basically say 'I take it all back, I'm really guilty'? No way, I can't do it. Anyway, no sense trying to guess what the prosecution is going to do or what they are going to offer. Drew said he'd call so we can just wait for his call. How about some dinner?"

Beth smiled and got up to go to the kitchen, "Tonight we're going to have to do leftovers. I spent all day making origami swans and other birds with Christopher so I didn't get a chance to make anything. Well, that's not really true, I did make a salad with greens, candied walnuts, grapes and crumbled blue cheese with a strawberry vinaigrette."

Steven went to the table to sit down and chuckled at what Beth had just said, "Only you would think that putting together a gourmet salad is not making anything for dinner. Man, these are sweet grapes. Where are the kids?"

Beth put a plate in front of him, "Well, I miss Lester, he always picked the freshest stuff. Christopher is taking a nap. He was pretty pooped this afternoon and I think he might actually be coming down with a bit of a cold, he was a little warm."

Steven went to dig into his plate, "This salad is awesome, I am having seconds for sure. What about Bethany, where is she?"

Beth sat down at the dinner table with him. She loved watching Steven enjoying the food that she made for him, "She's over at Mrs. Niebolt's place making batches of chocolate chip cookies for the kids down at St. Mary's."

Steven looked up at that, "Oh? How did she get to Mrs. Niebolt's?"

Beth responded, "Relax, Mrs. Niebolt lives on the fourth floor. I just walked her over there. She jumped at the chance to make the cookies when we ran into Mrs. Niebolt in the elevator."

Steven continued eating his salad as he spoke, "Good, that's good. If there's one thing I really appreciate it's anything that helps us to get back to normalcy, back to just being us. Especially Bethany. I know how hard this has all been on her and I worry that she might not be able to get back to just being a little girl."

Beth picked up his empty plate and went to give him more of the salad, "They are young and they are loved immensely, they will be alright. Bethany went to an excellent therapist while they were at my parents' house. She has learned to deal with her feelings and she has learned to deal with her fears. She still has nightmares and sometimes she has anxiety attacks. The doctor she was seeing wanted to put her on a pediatric dose of Xanax, but I've really tried to stay away from using any medicines with her."

Steven was nodding, "I agree. I don't want to see either of our children depending on a medicine in order to be calm or to be able to go to sleep, especially that kind of medicine, but I also don't want to have Bethany missing sleep and being tired all the time. I'll defer to you, but I just want to make sure that you are willing to give her the medication if her sleep patterns get significantly disrupted."

She nodded as she got his plate again, "Deal. Hey, slow down, you are going to give yourself heartburn if you keep eating that fast. So what's it going to be for dinner? We have some of the baked ziti left or we have a couple of the breaded fish you liked so much. I can give you either with some creamed spinach."

He gave her a wide smile that warmed her heart, "I will take all of it."

She laughed, "No way! I don't care what else is going on I am not going to let you get fat and lazy mister! I'm going to give you the fish, its' better for you."

He gave up, "I guess I can make do with the fish. I want you to know that you are leaving me hungry!"

She walked over with the fish, "Yeah, right. Starving."

22.

Felix Garcia was basking in renewed accolades for his reporting. He knew that the story about the DA's office was another scoop he'd gotten over the big network assholes, but he had never imagined that it would play out the way it did. After the article was published many experts speculated that perhaps the DA's office had leaked the story on purpose in order to start a conversation about a deal. Most of them believed that David Neill needed a way to save face and not look like he was backtracking and they agreed that a story such as the one that Felix had written could be just the thing to get a conversation about a plea deal. After this morning's events, however, most experts went from the story might have been leaked by the DA's office to the story was definitely leaked by the DA's office. Having the judge call for a meeting with the attorneys after his story was published ensured that he had another massive win under his belt. The publisher of the paper was now talking about promoting him to editor and he had calls from at least three major networks that he needed to consider. Felix knew that this business was not only about the story itself, but about everything that surrounded the story, everything that gave it a context. He had not seen how the story would have a direct effect on the trial itself. He didn't need to let anyone in on that detail, however, he could simply be modest and hint at the fact that he had seen it playing out exactly as it had. Aside from hard work, journalism was about being at the right place, at the right time and with the right angle. Most reporters knew that all of those things lining up exactly happened once, maybe twice in a career. They had lined up for Felix Garcia twice in the past few months. He wondered whether that was it, whether he had basically used up his magic for the rest of his career. He had wondered whether that had been the case when he had gotten the Steven Loomis interview and had come to the conclusion that if he had indeed used up all his magic, it had been worth it. Now he no longer wondered anything like that, now he knew that the magic was not in the story or the events around the story, the magic was in him and it would only become more powerful as he moved forward in his career. Felix Garcia leaned back in his recliner at home, put his hands behind his head and smiled.

Drew and Ray had pretty much kept to themselves on the way back to Ray's office, where they had agreed to meet after court. Both of them were trying to figure out, in their own way, why and how Judge Newman had decided to ask both sides to consider making a deal. Drew thought that their case was going well and that the judge wanted to avoid a mistrial because the jury could not make a decision to convict, something that was actually a strong possibility. Drew also thought that because the judge knew that public opinion favored Steven Loomis significantly and that he knew how much the jury was being affected by it, they were likely to try to come up with some other outcome and with first degree murder as the only outcome available to them, they might just not be able to make a decision. A hung jury. For their part Max and Ray believed that no matter how this ended there would probably be an appeal and old Judge Newman was only human and was not looking forward to having his work reviewed and maybe overturned by a higher court. They also thought that there was probably going to be significant testimony on rebuttal and then the defense would have to go back and try to rehabilitate their witnesses, which did not bode well for bringing the trial to a close as soon as the judge had hoped to. Both sides had so far presented a good case and both sides had definitely given the jury plenty to be able to make a decision with, which is why Ray and Max thought the judge was vying for a resolution through a deal. Had either side been overwhelming in their presentation of the evidence Ray thought the judge would probably have held out to have the jury decide the outcome. All three lawyers, however, believed that the article that had come out the day before had something with prompting the judge to make inquiries. It gave the DA an opportunity to save face because it wouldn't be his office asking about a deal, it was the judge.

When they finally got to the office Drew finally broke the silence, "So I've been thinking about it and I think that if they're going to be serious about putting an offer in front of Steven, it's going to have to be along the lines of manslaughter. It just wouldn't make any sense for them to just knock it down to second degree murder because that would basically be no offer at all."

Max was looking through his desk for something. When he finally found it Drew realized it was a bag of sunflower seeds. He had noticed that whenever he was engaged in anything that required significant consideration he would pull out his sunflower seeds.

He responded to Drew's thoughts, "Yeah, mmm, I agree, mmmh, I've just been wondering how they would word the charge. They've heard Steven say that he did all of this to bring attention to the fact that there are scientists out there that believe there is a new species and they've heard Steven say that he believes with every fiber of his being that Donald Riche was not human, so if we are going to have any chance of having Steven take the deal, they are going to have to word it in such a way that it won't require to have Steven admit that he shot a human being when he shot Donald Riche."

Ray was nodding, "That's a good point. We need to take a look at the wording in the law when it comes to manslaughter. I have to be honest, I don't really know the law on manslaughter that deeply. Besides, he could take an Alford Plea, that would resolve that issue completely."

Max was still putting seeds into his mouth as he spoke, "Well, there's obviously voluntary and involuntary manslaughter. Voluntary usually has to do with someone doing something that they know is likely to result in death, although there is no intent to murder. Involuntary has to do with gross negligence, someone being criminally negligent and causing someone else's death because of it. That's how it is usually charged by the prosecution, but there are other options, like imperfect defense, where someone claims self-defense, but the facts don't come up to really define self-defense."

Drew listened and thought about what Max was saying, he shook his head slightly, "If that's the case I don't really see how we're going to make this work, but stranger things have happened as they say."

Ray answered, "Yup, we're just going to have to wait to see what they put in front of him. We also need to be thinking about a sentence. I think, at least as far as the last time I spoke with him, that Steven is prepared to do some jail time, but I am also pretty clear on the fact that if he is looking at significant prison time as a result of the plea deal he will just take his chances with the jury."

Drew nodded, "I agree, I know he will just take his chances with the jury, but I have to tell you I don't really agree with it.

I just don't think it has completely dawned on Steven that if he is convicted he is looking at significant time in custody. Much more, I believe, than any custody he is given as part of a deal."

Max stood up and began slowly pacing, still eating seeds, which he now kept in his jacket pocket, "I think we have good leverage with the judge on that score and to be honest I think old judge Newman is living up to his reputation as a defendant's judge and I also think he will probably give us a very positive indication about custody time."

All three lawyers were committed to their client, but all of them could see how tired everyone who was working on the case was and all of them would have been lying of they didn't agree that a plea deal would be welcomed.

As they sat engrossed in their thoughts, Max's assistant came into his office, "Mr. Zeidler, I've got Bart Logan on the phone for you or for Drew."

Max motioned for Drew to take the call, "Go ahead and send the call through, please."

Drew went around the desk and sat down in Max's chair. The phone rang once and he picked it up on the second ring, "Drew Willis. Hey Bart, what's the word? Yeah, I picked up his phone, he's right here, so is Ray. So, do you have something for us to consider?"

Max and Ray watched as Drew listened intently and were relieved when they saw a smile spreading across Drew's face, "So, voluntary manslaughter and you won't pursue any specific sentence. You'll leave it up to the judge, is that basically it?"

Drew listened and nodded while he was on the phone. Ray had taken a seat on the other side of the desk and Max was sitting on the edge of the desk waiting for him to get off the phone.

Drew finally brought the conversation to a close, "Alright, well, let me talk to Steven and to Max and Ray about it and we'll get back to you later on this evening."

Drew hung the phone up and looked at his two colleagues with a smile on his face, "Well, I think they've made as good an offer as we could have possibly hoped for. You were right, they are offering voluntary manslaughter and they are willing to let the judge impose whatever sentence he feels is appropriate, they won't argue for any specific amount of time in custody."

Now Ray and Max also smiled. Ray spoke up first, "That is as good as it could possibly get. For a charge of voluntary manslaughter for a defendant like Steven I think we are looking at five to seven years and I don't need to tell you that with credit for good time and other programs he would probably end up doing just over two years. I don't know how Steven will take this, but I couldn't imagine a better outcome, other than an acquittal, obviously. I mean, guys, he shot Donald Riche in the head with a high-powered rifle from two blocks away. I know the circumstances are extraordinary and I know all about public opinion, but legally speaking this is better than I would have ever thought possible. This lets me know that the prosecution wants this thing to go away as much as we do and they are not looking to slam Steven. I hope he really considers this."

Drew was nodding as Ray was speaking. He was still sitting in Max's chair, "You know how they are planning to sell this to the judge and to the public? It's actually pretty smart; they are saying that they agree that Steven believed he was shooting something other than human. They are willing to say that he did not have the intent necessary to convict him of first-degree murder. In essence they are saying that in Steven's mind he was not shooting a human being, he was shooting something else, so the mindset necessary to form intent was simply not there. The way Logan explained it is the same as if someone had been wearing a jacket with fur on it and gone out running in the woods during hunting season. If that person got shot, the shooter would have done it under the belief that he was shooting a deer, so there is no way they could possibly get convicted of any murder charge. That's what they are basically saying, they are willing to say believe that Steven believed he was shooting something other than human. At the end of the day they will be able to say they still do not agree with Steven's defense, but they do agree that he believed it. I am absolutely blown away that Neill is willing to go along with this, but if we look at it purely from a legal standpoint it is a good proposition for them as well. Think about it, they are enforcing the law, they charged him with murder, as they were required to and if he takes the deal they are walking away with a conviction. All of it, by the way, among public opinion which strongly favors the defendant. Neill can claim that his office did its job, but did it with compassion. Can't you just hear him at the press conference?"

Max chuckled, he actually could see Neill at the press conference claiming victory and being able to avoid doing it at the expense of convicting Steven Loomis of manslaughter, "So, we need to let Steven know about what they are offering, how they are planning to argue it and what it will mean to him from the standpoint of custody. I think we should do it in person and I think we should do it with Beth there. If I'm right she will be the key to whether Steven takes the deal or not."

Drew stood up and came around the desk, "Let's go over there and talk to them. I need to get back to Logan later on this evening."

He got his coat and walked out with Ray and Max following him. All of them knew that Steven's kids were home with him, but agreed that if they tried to set up a meeting with just Steven and Beth somewhere else, the press would sniff something out and they would have to plow through throngs of reporters. They went directly to the Loomis home and made their way through the media that had been stationed there from the beginning. To everyone there it would just be Loomis meeting with his attorneys. No one knew why the afternoon session had been postponed until tomorrow morning, but there were plenty of opinions about why the judge had postponed court. Most seemed to believe that one of the two sides had objected to one of the experts that were going to be called to testify. Many of them actually got it right and speculated that a possible plea deal was probably being discussed between the two sides.

The lawyers made it through without answering any of the questions they were being asked. Steven was expecting them and let them in before they could even knock on the door. Both the kids were in their parents' bedroom and Beth was in the living room. Steven went over to the couch to sit next to his wife while he listened to Drew explain the offer.

Drew got right down to it, "The prosecution called. They are willing to make an offer of voluntary manslaughter and they are willing to let the judge make the decision about how much time in custody you should get. They will agree to not pursue additional time in prison. Whatever the judge decides, they are willing to go along with."

Beth and Steven looked at each other without saying anything. Steven was the one to ask, "What exactly does that mean for us?"

Drew was glad he was bringing these things up now because it gave him an opportunity to deal with them and to explain them to Steven and Beth, "Manslaughter has a lot of different requirements, a lot of different legal points that have to be met. Voluntary or involuntary depends on many things, but usually voluntary involves doing something willingly and involuntary usually involves an accident or another set of circumstances where the defendant does not have the intent to kill."

Steven asked for clarification, "So the charge they are offering me is the one that is usually given to people who engaged in a dangerous activity, but didn't have the intention of killing anyone?"

Drew nodded, "That's right. The way they are planning to justify it and to explain it to the public is by stating that they agree that you believed that you were shooting something other than human. They are not saying that they agree with your theory that Donald Riche was something other than human, in fact they are going to make sure that everyone understands that they believe firmly that Donald Riche was a human being and not another species."

Beth didn't understand, "So if the prosecution is saying that they believe that he was a human being how is it that they are looking to convict Steven of shooting someone who was not human?"

Drew answered, "That's the thing, the prosecution is saying that they believe that in his mind, Steven was operating on the belief that he was shooting something other than human. They are saying they believe him when he says that's what he believed then and believes now, since he did not believe he was shooting a human being, he could not have formed the intent required to be convicted of first-degree murder. I have to be honest with you Steven, this is about as good as it could possibly get. The prosecution is basically saying that they are willing to put aside the argument about whether he was human or not and they are willing to just move forward on the basis of your belief. They are doing this because they were never thrilled about bringing you up on charges of murder in the first place and this would let them walk away with a conviction under their belt, but it would also reflect the sympathy element that the entire world is also operating under."

Steven stood up and started pacing as he thought about what Drew was telling him. Beth wanted to know more about what the prosecution was offering, "Okay, so let's say that Steven decided to take the deal and he decided to plead guilty to this charge, what then? What would happen to him after that? Would he do jail time?"

Drew sat next to her where Steven had been sitting just a moment ago, "Yes, if he decided to plead guilty it is almost certain that he would get some jail time. Based on the charge the judge would most likely give him five to seven years to be served in a medium security facility, a facility where the inmates have been convicted of white collar crimes, crimes that involved no violence."

Beth put her head in her hands, "Five to seven years in prison?! That is so long! What would I tell Bethany and Chris when he is old enough to ask?!"

Drew didn't know what to answer to that and truth be told what he was really waiting for and what really mattered in the end is what Steven thought of all of this and so far he hadn't said anything. He finally walked over to the window with his arms crossed in front of him and a faraway look on his face.

He talked to Beth without turning around, "You tell him what I did and why. Bethany already knows, but I'm not sure she fully understands. Chris doesn't know about anything yet, but when he asks you just tell him exactly what I did and the reason I did it. I hate that they have to know about this at all, but that's the hand we've been dealt and I don't want the kids to grow up with shame about what their father did. I'm not proud of what I did, but I don't regret it either and I certainly don't want them to think I have any regrets."

Steven looked at Beth when he said this last part.

Beth looked at him and was clearly surprised, "I guess you've decided that you are going to take their offer without talking about it."

He came over and sat down on the other side of her. He held her hands as he responded to what she said, "No, I haven't decided what I'm going to do Beth, you know I wouldn't do that without talking about it, but I will tell you that except for the jury finding me not guilty, I think this is about as good a result as we could have hoped for."

Beth had tears rolling down her face, "Seven years, Steven, seven years without you. Do you understand how hard that is for me to grasp? Seven years where Christopher won't have a father there to be with him, seven years where Bethany won't have a dad to take pictures for prom, where she will be in high school without a dad to talk to whenever she needs to."

Drew interceded, "Whatever jail time he gets Beth, he will end up actually serving less than half of that time with credit for good time and other programs they have for early release."

Beth turned to look at him with hope in her eyes, "So you're saying he would end up actually serving less than three and a half years?"

Drew smiled at her, "That's right and that's if he actually gets seven years, we don't know yet what the judge would sentence him to if he took the deal, but if we read the judge correctly he will most likely give us a strong indication of what he would sentence him to before he actually takes the deal."

Beth now relaxed a bit, "So Steven would wait until the judge tells him how much time he would give him before he takes the deal?"

Ray nodded, "That's right. If the judge decides he is going to make an example of him or decides he is going to give him excessive time then Steven can simply just say no to the deal and we would just keep going with the trial. So you see why it's likely that the judge will give us a strong indication and why it's likely that he will decide to give Steven less rather than more time? It's he who asked for us to consider a deal so it's clear he is motivated to bring this case to a close."

Beth turned to Steven who had stood up and started pacing again, "What do you think Steven? It's you going to be you that has to be in there. I can't begin to imagine what that will be like."

He sat back down and took her hands again, "I think this is the best way honey, this is a way to end this the best way I can think of ending it. Being locked up for two or three years, that's going to be the easy part. The really hard part will be for you to raise the kids without me. Being in there for that long will basically be like being back in the Navy, where they tell you what to do and what time you can do it."

Max added, "That's right. Actually it might be easier than that. Those facilities are actually run by corporations and are pretty new. The minimum-security facilities also have a whole bunch of programs designed to shorten the time people have to serve. If Steven were to teach classes to people wanting to get their GEDs or if he were to take on a job that helps the state in some way, then he would get extra time credits which would cut his sentence even further."

Beth turned to speak to Steven and for the first time she had a smile on her face, "I guess that's it then. It's finally going to be over. Finally over."

Steven returned the smile, "That's right babe, it will be over. We can begin the process of getting back to our life, getting back to just living our life."

Beth hugged him. She knew how hard it was going to be without him, but she also knew how much worse it could have been, how he could have effectively lost his life. She let out a big sob and just broke down out of exhaustion, out of grief from losing her daughter and out of simple relief that all of this was finally going to be over. Steven hugged her back and mirrored all the feelings she was letting out. Max, Drew and Ray stood looking at each other not quite knowing what to do. Drew wiped at his eyes as he had gotten teary eyed as well, but pretended he just had something in his eye. Ray smiled and walked over with his hand outstretched. Drew ignored his hand and pulled him into a big hug.

Ray chuckled as he returned the hug, "Well done counselor, well done."

Max walked over as well and clapped both lawyers on the back, "Gentlemen, I do believe we have made history. I've been at this for longer than I care to remember and in all that time

I have never heard of a case where the defendant confessed to a fist-degree murder and was later convicted of manslaughter."

Drew stepped back and now did shake Ray and Max's hands. Ray was enjoying every bit of the moment, given the clients he most often defended, he had long ago taken for granted that he would probably not enjoy any moments like these, moments where he knew that his work as a lawyer, as a defense litigator had saved someone who deserved saving. He knew that this would be the case that his career would be defined by, the case that would define the career of every attorney involved in it and after more than thirty years of practice it wasn't a bad one to have as his main legacy. Johnny Cochran and Robert Shapiro would forever be linked to the OJ Simpson case, as would the careers of Marsha Clark and Christopher Darden. He couldn't imagine the nightmares that Shapiro must have wrestled with on more than one evening and he couldn't imagine the frustration that Darden and Clark must have felt when he was acquitted. So, no, all and all this was an awesome case to have your career defined by. Max, on the other hand, was thinking that his and Drew's firm was about to go into the stratosphere with their criminal law practice. He was also thinking that after this Drew would have to be made a junior partner and he couldn't think of a single partner in the firm having any problem with it.

Drew walked over to the door and was followed by Max and Ray, "We're going to head back to the office and call Logan back. We told him we would get back to him tonight."

The three lawyers said their goodbyes and headed out the door. They went directly back to the office and called Logan immediately. They let him know that they had themselves a deal, if the judge did the right thing with the sentence. Like the defense team, the prosecution was fairly certain that the judge was going to be very favorable to the defense when it came to sentencing. After they spoke, both sides agreed that Logan would call the judge to let him know.

23.

Everyone was in judge Newman's chambers promptly at eight o'clock the next morning. The courthouse was packed and there was an air of expectation in the halls. Most people had come to believe that the meetings with the judge probably meant that a deal was in the works, but nobody was willing to state it officially, so all the stories offered up a number of possibilities, one of which was that there was a deal in the works. The members of the media wanted to hedge their position just in case the meetings were about something else.

The judge was sitting behind his desk drinking a cup of coffee and eating a Danish. Drew noted that he seemed to always be eating when he was in his office. Looking around it was clear that this was the judge's second home. Both sides sat down in front of the judge's desk.

He smiled as he wiped his mouth and picked up the case file, "So, counselors, I believe we have come to an agreement in this case, is that correct?"

Drew answered, "That's right judge, pending a discussion with you about sentencing. The prosecution has agreed to leave it up to your honor's discretion and we would like an indication of what our client would be looking at as far as custody time."

The judge was nodding as he was going through the case file. He also had a legal text in front of him, which he was reviewing to make sure he understood the language of manslaughter and the sentencing guidelines in the state of New York. The judge had handled enough manslaughter cases to know what the law was, but this was going to be a situation where the plea deal, the language of the charge, the language of the plea itself and the sentence imposed would be scrutinized by the entire legal community and judge Newman did not want to be caught with his pants down.

He listened to Drew finish his answer and once he did, he answered the question all of the lawyers were waiting for him to answer, "Three to five years in a minimum-security facility. I can't get more specific than that, but I can tell you I am inclined to lean towards three rather than five. With good time your client is likely to do no more than about fifteen months."

Drew looked at Ray and then at the prosecution attorneys, who were sitting without any reaction to the judge's indication.

He smiled at all of them and let the judge know what the decision was, "Well your honor, I think we have a deal then."

The judge let a broad smile take over his face showing just how pleased he was with this outcome, "Excellent! Let's go ahead and get this on the record and get it done."

Logan spoke up, "Your honor, the people would like to have an opportunity to call a press conference in order to announce the deal. Mr. Neill feels that the case is significant enough and the charges serious enough that the people should have an opportunity to explain the rationale behind making the offer at this stage of the trial."

The judge thought about it and responded, "I can go along with that Mr. Logan, as long as we are not talking about taking too long to call this press conference. I think we all know that the media is going to be all over this as soon as we step back into the courtroom. We will all agree that absolutely nothing about this will be said to the media, not until we have the court hearing. I don't need to say anything about what will happen if I find someone has violated my order."

Logan answered the judge's initial concern, "Mr. Neill would like to do it this morning, if you are okay with that."

Max also spoke up, "We would also like the opportunity to speak with our witnesses and with our staff to let them know what is going on and why we have decided to do what we are doing. These people have dedicated their lives to this case since the beginning and I think we owe it to them to let them know what their efforts have garnered. And of course we need to let our client know."

The judge was nodding. He was fine with all of it, as long as a hearing could be set for the afternoon where Steven Loomis would plead guilty to the charge agreed upon.

There was one final issue that needed to be addressed and Ray brought it up, "We also need to discuss sentencing your honor. If the prosecution and the court are amenable to it we would request immediate sentencing and we would request that Mr. Loomis be allowed to report for custody two weeks from today."

The judge considered this and then looked at the prosecution, "Mr. Logan, Ms. Farris, any thoughts?"

Farris spoke up, "I don't believe that Mr. Neill would have any problem with the defense's requests, but we would have to confirm that once we get back to the office."

Max, Drew and Ray could live with that and they could live with the press conference later the same day. Everyone left the judge's chambers and went back to their offices. The media was now camped out at every single location that the legal teams could or would be going to. The number of media outlets had almost doubled at every one of the locations and most major channels had an anchor in the field. The media knew something big was happening and they wanted to make sure every base was covered. The speculation had reached a fever pitch with most of the legal experts now firmly of the opinion that a deal was likely in the works with some wild speculation about what the charge could possibly be. Steven went straight to Max and Drew's office, since his lawyers had let him know that he wouldn't need to do anything this morning. He walked around with a cup of coffee in his hand waiting for his lawyers to get back.

When they did, they let him know how things had gone with the judge, Drew went to the most important piece of information for Steven, "The judge let us know that he would give you a sentence of three to five years in prison and he also gave us a strong indication that he would probably lean towards the three year sentence, all of it served in a minimum-security prison. With credit for good time and some other early release programs, it's likely that you would actually serve just over a year in prison."

Steven listened carefully and like everyone else this morning he let a smile spread across his face. "That's great news, isn't it? I mean it's less time than you thought I would get, am I right?"

Drew returned the smile, "That's right, it is better than what we ever expected. If you just take a step back and think about it, we are looking at you actually serving just over a year after having confessed to shooting someone after planning it and with specific intent. I honestly can't think of a better outcome other than the jury acquitting you and I don't know about you, but that's a pretty heavy risk to take. The prosecution believes, and we agree, that his is a deal where everybody wins.

"I want to make sure you understand what will be happening this afternoon. The judge will call the case, make a statement saying that a plea agreement has been reached for the record and will then turn to you. He will ask you if you are doing this willingly and whether everything has been explained to you. Then, as I explained to you before, he will ask whether you are pleading guilty under an Alford Plea agreement. That means that you are not admitting guilt for any charge, so you will be saying you are taking the deal because the prosecution has enough evidence to possibly have a jury find you guilty of the charges. You will not be making any statements about admitting you shot Riche or you murdering anyone. The judge will ask if you understand everything that is going on and when you let him know that you do, he'll move forward with the plea."

Max explained about the prosecution's request and about how things were going to proceed, "You're going to be pleading guilty this afternoon."

Steven asked another question, "What about sentencing, when does that happen?"

Drew responded, "We asked for immediate sentencing. There is no probation report for the judge to consider and you have an exemplary record in every single thing you have done and he knows it, so he has everything he needs to impose a sentence, he will give you your sentence when he takes your plea. You won't be going into custody immediately though. We requested and the judge agreed to allow you to report into custody two weeks from today."

Steven was obviously surprised, "That's great. You can do that? Sorry for the dumb questions guys, but this is all foreign to me."

Ray clapped Steven on the back, "No worries kid, we'd be surprised if you didn't ask the questions you're asking."

Drew smiled, "Sure we can ask for a delay in having you report for custody. Again, everyone is comfortable with you being out of custody, everyone knows about you and your record so it wasn't a big deal for the judge to grant our request."

He sat down at the table in the conference room they had casually drifted into. He was satisfied with everything and as much of a cliché as it was, he actually felt the weight fall off his back. He had to call Beth. She was waiting to hear from him, ready to come down to the courthouse immediately if she needed to. Steven had enjoyed the deepest sleep he could remember and he knew that Beth had also just gotten the best sleep since this whole nightmare began. Thinking back to the beginning, to how things had started and where they progressed to, Steven was amazed. He was amazed by the fact that there had been so much death in so short a period of time, so much brutality including what he had done. He was amazed that as a result of all of it the world now had to consider, had to deal with, front and center, the fact that a new species was out there, a species that preyed on humans, a species that possessed above-average intelligence, incredible interpersonal skills and what seemed to be hyper acute sensory capabilities. It was a species designed to ensure its survival above everything else, a species with no compunction or moral dilemma to deal with; In short, a species that was now the apex predator above every other creature on earth, including human beings. More than anything, it was this that amazed Steven and it was also the only thing that had allowed him to make sense of any of it. Realizing that everything had happened for a reason, something that he believed had actually changed the way the world considered these predators. He sat in the conference room thinking about the case, Riche and what he had done, the trial and his family and he was satisfied, actually gratified, by the way things had gone because it all meant that in the end, the world agreed with him. Once he got past his own case and everything that came along with that, he thought about all of the predators that had come before and, most chilling for him, all of the other predators that were out there right now, as he sat in the conference room. It was this last thought that really occupied his mind. Everything else in his life had been settled, but this was something he had briefly thought about during the trial and which he knew he would have to confront at some point in the future. Right now he wanted to enjoy the moment, he wanted to enjoy the fact that his family was now free of this, would finally be free from all the attention. All he could think about the other predators was that he had no control over what happened. They had existed before and they existed now, the difference now was that the world knew that they existed. It was also out of his control whether the authorities would follow up on his theory, would utilize the science that the experts had presented.

From the few conversations that Steven had overheard, both Leonard and Grossman were booked absolutely solid. They had been asked to testify in numerous murder trials, in every instance they were being asked to testify for the defense.

He was sure that some, if not most of the cases that they were being asked to testify for were nothing like his case. Most were probably nowhere near qualifying as a *Homo sapiens predaer*, but Steven had known that would be a possibility from the beginning. He knew that it was possible that the theory would be abused, that individuals who were guilty as sin would try to make use of it. Again, he had come to the realization that all of this was out of his control. There was just nothing he could possibly do about it and so he put it out of his mind as well. He called Beth and told her about everything, all the details as they had been explained to him. He told her she didn't have to be there for the actual plea because he would not be taken into custody immediately. If she could have come through the phone to slap him she would have done it. She told him to stop being stupid and to tell her the time that they would be going back to court. Once he finished speaking with Beth he called Art Goodman, the General, in his office. Max, Drew and Ray had been quietly appraising him of the situation as the trial went on.

After all, it was his money that was paying for the defense and it had been his money that had kept him out of jail up until now. The General picked up at once, ecstatic to be hearing from him.

He had obviously already spoken to either one of his lawyers, "Steven! This is a truly great surprise! I wasn't expecting to talk to you for a while."

Steven responded, "I know and I know I shouldn't be reaching out to you, but there is no way I could go one more day without saying thank you. The case is coming to an end and none of it would have been possible without your help. I told you I don't know how I could possibly thank you."

He could almost hear him smiling on the other end of the line, "That's right! I just heard! I couldn't be more pleased about all of it. I have to be honest and tell you that I wasn't too sure how things were going to turn out. Your legal team is everything they were cracked up to be."

Steven agreed, "They are indeed. I had all confidence in them from the start of this whole thing and they did nothing but validate my confidence in them every single day. Again, it wouldn't have been possible to retain them or Ray Gretche without your help, so thanks."

He could almost see the General shaking his head with a slight wince on his face, "Damn it Steven! You need to stop with the 'I don't know how to thank you' crap! I'll tell you what, if you really want to thank me just stop thanking me every time we speak."

Steven chuckled into the phone. The old man had him. What was he going to say to that, 'I don't care what you want, I'm just going to keep saying thank you even though you have asked me to stop'

Steven smiled, "Alright, I'll knock off the 'Thank you' crap, but thank you!"

He laughed after he said it. The General just laughed and swore, "You son of a bitch!"

Both men composed themselves and continued their conversation, "How are Beth and the kids?"

Steven responded, "They're doing much better. Beth has really bounced back better than I could have hoped. Bethany still has some problems with nightmares, but we're working through them"

The General had another question he hadn't asked before, but was really concerned about, "And the business with this Lester Martin character?"

Steven sighed, "Done. Zlk made sure the guy's place, business, nothing led back to us. He supervised Lou in getting rid of the body and made sue nobody would ever consider whispering anything about Les Martin or anything related to him. I'm pretty sure we have nothing to worry about on that score."

Both men nodded in their own way on their end of the phone. They each knew that whatever Zlk had done to make sure that the guys who had been there and seen anything were absolutely crystal clear on the consequences of sharing anything they had seen, heard, smelled with anyone. And they both knew that there was absolutely no doubt that Zlk would follow through with whatever threat he had made. No doubt at all.

Finally Steven spoke, "Be honest Art, did you call him?"

Goodman looked sideways at the phone in his hand with a mixture of being bothered by Steven asking the question at all and amusement that he himself had wondered if it had been Stephen that called Zlk. The fact that they were two of four people on the planet who could actually reach out to Zlk made it almost certain that in this situation it had been one of them that had called. The fact that Steven had just asked this of the General meant he himself hadn't done it and since Goodman himself hadn't done it, they would need to chalk it up to one of those mythical stories where Zlk just knew where to be, when to be there and what to do. In the end they just shook their heads with a smile, realizing another legend about Zlk had been born.

Goodman sighed, "No, I didn't, but you knew that. Things must be so hard on Bethany. She understands more than many adults, so I would think she's had a harder time and any girl her age might have. This deal Steven, what does it mean as far as jail time?"

Steven responded, "That's the only thing about taking the deal, I'm signing up for three to five years in prison."

The General reacted, "Three to five years! Christ that's a long time! There is no way to make it any better, huh?"

Steven answered, "I wish. No, actually my lawyers think this is a much better outcome than what I could have hoped for. They tell me that I will probably actually only serve just over a year in prison with credit for good time and other programs they have to get people out as soon as possible. I have to tell you sir that being able to bring this to a close pleading guilty to voluntary manslaughter and just over a year in jail is perfectly acceptable to me. I *did* commit a crime, just not the crime they were charging me with and I do deserve to do some jail time. Besides, that time will give me an opportunity to spend some time by myself, winding down and it will give Beth and the kids a chance to try to get back to a normal life. They've been basically holed up at home or at my in-laws' house during this whole thing, avoiding the media which I don't need to tell you is everywhere."

The General grumbled, "Fucking vultures, they're all vultures. Now that you bring it up Steven, how are you in all of this? Is it what you thought it would be? Was it worth doing it?"

Steven knew he was not asking to be judgmental, he was asking because he really wanted to know. Steven found it interesting that in all of his dealings, it was always Art Goodman that seemed to cut through and get right to the heart of whatever was going on with him. He could always do it when it came to business and he could do it now, when it was personal. Nobody else, no one he had any contact with, had asked him how he was feeling about all of it. In all fairness his lawyers and his wife saw him every day so they probably thought they knew how he was feeling about all of it, but the truth was that they really didn't know how he was feeling.

He knew that because he himself didn't know how he felt about all of it either, "You know, I can tell you with complete honesty that I do not regret doing it and I believe that this whole horrible situation will end up helping some people to not be victims. I'm thankful that my family is safe, that they are on their way back. I'm not sure about anything else though. I suppose that's what I will be doing while I'm sitting behind bars, figuring things out."

The General simply listened while Steven spoke, when he was done he finally got down to talking to Steven about what he really wanted to talk to him about, "What are you thinking as far as coming back?"

Steven winced just a bit, he hadn't wanted to get into really considering his long-term future just yet, but he owed it to the old man to answer his question and to answer it truthfully, "I'd be lying to you if I said that I have thought about it in any significant way. I mean I think I've been operating under the assumption that I would come back when this was all over."

Goodman wanted to know where his head was and what Steven was thinking, "And now? You were operating under the assumption you would come back and now? What assumption are you operating under now?"

Steven knew what he was looking for, "Now I am not operating under any assumptions. I am pretty sure that I will be coming back when this is all over, but I don't want to do it because I feel like it's what's expected of me or because I can't think of something else I could do. I want to come back to the company because I feel it, because I can't think of myself doing something else."

The General sounded a bit surprised, "And right now you can think of yourself doing something else?"

Steven responded, "No, I don't see myself doing anything else, but right now I don't see myself doing anything...I don't know what it is, but I'm not feeling that burning, almost obsessive need to get back to work...not the way I'm used to. I don't know, it feels like I have been to hell and back and like I need to take some time to figure out everything I saw. It feels like there could be more for me to learn from this. I can't tell you what that is or how long I'll take to learn it, but I wanted to be completely honest with you about all of it."

There was silence on the other end of the phone, finally Goodman spoke, "I'd be lying to you if I didn't tell you that I'm disappointed. You know how valuable you are to the company."

Steven hung his head as he responded, "I know and I am so sorry about this, about all of it. I know it was all my doing and that now the company is suffering for it, but I have to be honest with you and I have to be honest with myself. I can't come back until I can give myself to the job all the way, I can't be half-assed about it."

The General responded immediately, "I understand, I do. You did what you had to do and like I told you, I don't blame you for doing it. We'll be fine, you also know we have good people, but you will be missed and you know that too. Your job will be waiting for you when you are ready to come back."

Steven was thankful, but it still hurt, "Thank you, I appreciate it and you know that I will come back as soon as I am ready. I also wanted to talk to you about Beth and the kids and my 401K plan..."

The General interrupted him, "Don't worry about that. We'll keep taking care of it the way we have until now."

Steven was close to tearing up, "I can't let you keep doing that sir, it doesn't feel right."

The old man chuckled, "Come now Steven, it is a good investment for us. Our finance people have structured it in such a way that it benefits us from a tax standpoint and more importantly, I *want* to do it. Even if it wasn't structured the way it is, I want to do it, you know that if you were in my position, if we switched places, you would do exactly the same thing, you would make sure my family is taken care of. And if I am to be totally honest, you and Beth and the kids are my family as well and you know I will do anything for my family."

And with that The General had him. He had nothing he could come back with because the old man was absolutely right, if it was Steven in his place he would in fact have done exactly the same thing, he would make sure his family is taken care of financially.

He couldn't argue the point anymore, "You are family Art, Beth thinks so as well and you know how much the kids love you. Okay, you can take care of us, but you have to let me say thank you."

Goodman laughed, "Alright just this once! Do you know where you are going to be serving your time?"

Steven answered him, "No, I don't. All I know is that it's going to be a minimum security prison somewhere in New York."

The General was relieved, "That's good. Some of those places are like day spas. That's where they send crooked lawyers and judges and politicians. There's no violent inmates looking to shank you over a pack of cigarettes."

Steven smiled on his end of the phone, "Yeah, I was worried about that. Anyway, you can see why I think this time might actually be something I can use. I have to be honest with you, I am exhausted. I hadn't really thought about anything other than the trial until now. I didn't realize how incredibly tired I am until we finalized the deal. I have two weeks to report into custody and I am going to take advantage of that time to just rest, catch up on my reading and get plenty of time with my family."

The General had an idea, "Hey, why don't you, Beth and the kids go to my cabin in California. It's quiet, it has a private area by the lake and, most of all, it's outside the reach of the media."

Steven thought about it, "I don't know sir. I was actually thinking about also spending time with my in-laws."

The old man wasn't having any of it, "Bring them along, the place is over ten thousand square feet and has five bedrooms. I am pretty sure it will accommodate you and your in-laws."

Steven was going to protest again, but he thought better of it. He was right, of course, his cabin was perfect for them to go and just disconnect for the time that he had before having to report for custody. The weather in California at this time of year was perfect, not snowy, but not too hot either.

Bethany and Chris would enjoy playing by the lake and Beth would enjoy the time to read and relax, "Alright, I'll take you up on that."

The General was delighted, "Good man! You can all take the jet to California when you are ready."

Now Steven did object, "That's too much Art."

He was ready with an answer, "Steven, come on, are you really telling me that you and your family are going to fly a commercial airline? Are you kidding? You know what the media is going to be like after this is through."

Again Steven couldn't argue with him. There really was no way they would be able to go anywhere without a sea of reporters and news vans around them, "You got me there. Okay, I will let you know when we are ready to leave. I hate to do this, but I have to go. Drew and Ray are signaling me that they're ready to go and I have to call Beth."

The General said few words before saying goodbye, "Good luck Steven. We're behind you and your family is taken care of."

Steven also said good bye, "I know sir and..."

The old man interrupted him, "Don't say it! Just say good bye will you?"

Steven chuckled, "Alright then, good bye Art."

Drew came into the conference room where he was on the phone, "Was that the General?"

Steven nodded, "Yeah, I had to call him to say thank you for everything."

Drew nodded, "He called almost every single day to check on the case you know. The old man really cares for you and your family and it's not just about your working for him, obviously. So, we are just waiting for Neill to hold his press conference and we'll be on our way. They actually asked us to participate, but I thought you would probably want to skip that."

Steven stood up, "You were right. I absolutely want to skip that whole thing. We're going to be accosted by the media no matter what and I would rather deal with them the least amount of time possible."

Drew nodded, "Understandable. You know Steven, at some point you should talk to someone in the media. There are a hundred stories out there about the trial, about Donald Riche, about your theory and most of them are just utter bullshit. You obviously don't have to talk to anybody, but I would suggest that you share the real story, your story with someone that will tell it to the world. That kid that you did the piece with, Garcia, seems like a pretty straight forward guy. I haven't read or heard anything sensational from his paper and what he wrote was pretty good. It's been the story that most reputable outlets have quoted from when it comes to what your story is."

Steven had thought about it and had already thought that he would eventually speak with Felix Garcia again. Drew was right, the kid had done a good job of telling his story in a straight forward manner, without any hype of sensationalistic spin to it. "I probably will talk to him, eventually. Right now I want to finish this and get back to my life."

Drew understood, "Fair enough. Why don't you call Beth and have her come down now. As soon as the DA is done with his media sideshow we'll be on our way." Steven did just that.

The main conference room at the District Attorney's office was standing room only. The only people allowed in, other than the reporters that had been following this from the beginning, were other media heavy weights. Anchors for Court TV and the Investigation Channel were all there. Many programs had actually set up mobile sets just outside of the courthouse. It really had become a media circus. The technology available now to anyone with a smart phone or a laptop ensured that the coverage of this trial around the world completely dwarfed the OJ trial. Finally, David Neill showed up followed by Melanie Farris and Bart Logan.

He looked over the room, went over to the podium and started, "Good morning. I want to thank you all for being here and I appreciate how much work this has been for everybody involved, including the media, so I'll get right to the point. As you are all aware this office filed first-degree murder charges against Steven Loomis as a result of his statements admitting the shooting of Donald Riche. You have all also been aware of the tragic and horrific set of circumstances that have surrounded this case going back to before Donald Riche was shot. From the beginning we all realized that this was a no win situation no matter who won the case. We proceeded with the charges and Steven Loomis chose to move forward with a jury trial. Bart Logan and Melanie Farris, senior prosecutors from our office, did a superb job of presenting the evidence in the case and of examining the defense's witnesses. It has been clear from the beginning that the theory presented by the defense stretches the boundary of accepted legal defenses for a charge of first-degree murder. While this office continues to believe that the core of the defense's case is founded on unproven science and that there is no such thing as a different species of human, we concede the point that Steven Loomis was operating under the *complete and total belief* that Donald Riche was in fact something other than human. Therefore, it is clear that Steven Loomis did not have the intent required to be convicted of first degree murder."

Neill paused at this point to let it sink in. The room was abuzz with cameras shooting away and people shifting in their seats.

Neill continued, "After consultation with the trial team, this office concluded that justice would best be served by offering the defendant the option to plead guilty to a lesser charge, which is a lesser included offense to the charge of murder. We would therefore like to announce that we have reached an agreement with Steven Loomis and his defense team, Max Zeidler, Drew Willis and Ray Gretche. The agreement was presented and agreed to by the judge presiding over the case, Judge Newman. Steven Loomis has agreed to plead guilty to voluntary manslaughter and one count of endangering the public as a result of the shooting of Donald Riche. I will let Bart Logan, the lead prosecutor in the case take it from here."

Logan buttoned his coat and stepped to the podium to continue, "The facts, as they became clear during the trial, made it clear that Steven Loomis was operating under the complete belief that he was shooting something other than a human being. It also became clear that Mr. Loomis's belief did not come from a mental deficiency or diminished mental state, but rather from his own research into criminal behavior. As misguided as we believe that research to be, it became the basis for Mr. Loomis's belief and therefore the basis for his defense. We believe, therefore, that the charge of voluntary manslaughter fits the facts of the case. Mr. Loomis caused the death of another human being, but without the intent to murder. He endangered the public by firing a high-powered rifle in mid-town Manhattan and will therefore also plead guilty to endangering the public. We have also agreed that the district attorney's office will not be seeking any specific sentence and will leave that part of it completely up to the judge. As Mr. Neill has previously stated, there are simply no winners in this whole tragic episode. The Loomis family has suffered a tragic loss, as have many other families and the prosecution had the duty to enforce the law as prescribed by the state of New York. We, Ms. Farris and I, believe that this agreement is the closest thing to a win-win situation that could have possibly evolved from this set of facts. We believe and Mr. Neill agrees, that this ensures that the people of New York will know that no matter who the defendant is and no matter what the circumstances are, no matter how horrific they may be, the law will be enforced. Mr. Loomis will be pleading guilty to a serious felony, but he will still have a life to share with his family at the end of it. We are not and have not been unaware of, or insensitive to the circumstances that led us all to this place and we believe that we have made a clear statement that while we are aware of all of it, we cannot and will not overlook the rule of law. Mr. Loomis is scheduled to appear before judge Newman at three this afternoon. We have agreed with the defense to immediate sentencing, which the judge will impose on Mr. Loomis this afternoon. I believe that concludes our statement."

He looked over at Neill, who nodded slightly and moved to take the podium again, "We will not be taking questions at this time as we would like to conclude the case and have a final disposition before we make any further statements and we hope that the media will understand that and respect all parties and will not overwhelm any of the parties involved. Again, thank you all for being here."

After Neill concluded the room exploded with questions, regardless of what Neill and his team had stated. Multiple reporters fired a myriad questions at every single person in the prosecution team. Neill, Logan and Farris filed out of the conference room without answering a single question. Once in the hallway Logan took a deep breath and relaxed.

Neill slapped his back, "Not as easy as it looks is it? Good job Logan, you continue to impress. Are we set for this afternoon?"

Farris responded, "We're set. I believe Bart already conferred with Michael Gordon about the sentence. It doesn't really matter though, the judge has already given strong indication he will go with a sentence of three to five years in a minimum security prison."

Neill looked at them as they got to his office, "You two were okay with that? It is a violent offense after all."

Logan spoke up, "Yes, but we're saying he didn't have the intent, so the violent component was not there. Not only that, but can you imagine Loomis in a supermax prison? Can you imagine what would happen the first time some white supremacist or Aryan brotherhood punk tried to recruit him? I think before all was said and done Steven Loomis would probably put several people in the hospital and this office just doesn't need to be dealing with Mr. Loomis any further."

They all walked into Neill's office. He sat down behind his desk and immediately reached for a blood pressure cuff, "Damn doctor says I have to keep track of my ticker, can you believe that shit? Anyway, yes, I agree, we don't need to be dealing with any more charges as it relates to Steven Loomis. I'm good with minimum security as long as you two thought about it."

Farris and Logan nodded. Farris spoke up, "We did think about it. We'll be leaving for the courthouse at about two thirty."

Neill was already dialing his phone, "Good. I'm already going to be there at that time, I have another case I'm dealing with, so I will see you both there."

Both Logan and Farris knew he didn't have any cases pending and was probably going to be chatting with judges and high-powered defense attorneys getting ready for the election.

As they were walking down the hall, Farris looked over at Logan, "Good call on the minimum security thing, we hadn't even talked about it."

He answered as he walked into his office, "I know, but *I* had thought about it."

She kept walking to her office and called back to him, "It was a good call anyway. I'll see you at two thirty." And with that both lawyers began the process of thinking about something besides the Steven Loomis trial.

24.

As expected, the media had exploded when the announcement was made. Every network interrupted their regular programming to cover the story, most of them live. In addition to the big networks, there were a number of smaller special interest networks that were providing special coverage. They had experts on both sides speculating the reason that a deal had been made in the case. Some believed that the prosecution didn't want to risk an acquittal and that the evidence presented by the defense had been strong enough to give the jury a reason to acquit him, which everyone agreed the jury went into the case wanting to do. Others believed that it had been the defense that had made the overture because they felt that their expert witnesses were simply not believable enough to carry the defense. Most of the most serious and experienced legal experts, however, were of the opinion that once the prosecution had a chance to hear Steven Loomis and a couple of expert witnesses testify, to see the jury reacting to the testimony and realized that this outlandish defense actually had some legs, they were probably looking to make a deal. They all agreed that the case would have gone forward if Loomis's experts had come across as quacks and Loomis himself had come across like an out of control vigilante. There were body language experts speculating about what Steven Loomis was thinking, about what the defense lawyers' next strategy would be, about what the judge would do in sentencing, there were literally dozens of angles being covered though all mediums. The Internet was a veritable lab where experts from around the world were discussing the merits of the defense's case, as they had been doing from the beginning. Many of them saw the plea as a huge win for their theory. They pointed out, correctly, that although the prosecution had stated that they believed that the defense's theory was a stretch of accepted science, they had ultimately made an offer that allowed for the possibility that such a species might exist. Many of them pointed to the fact that Steven Loomis had shot Donald Riche in the head with full intention and that the fact that the prosecutor had made the offer meant that no matter what they thought, there was a possibility that the jury would find Loomis not guilty. Others pointed out that the deal simply meant that the prosecution had finally acknowledged the enormous influence that public opinion was likely to have on the case and did not want to risk an unfavorable verdict. They pointed out that this did not mean that the theory had any more merit than before any of this occurred. Experts in the legal community were speculating that the defense's scientific experts in this case would become hot commodities with defense attorneys around the country looking to secure their testimony in murder trials of their own. These same people wondered whether the experts would simply take the money or whether they would adhere to the science and choose not to testify if the case did not fall into the category of the Loomis trial. There were tens of thousands of online discussion groups and blogs all dedicating their entire bandwidth to discussion about the case.

As the time of the court hearing approached the courthouse was completely overcome with news vans, mobile sets and all the teams that went along with that. Finally, there just was simply no more room for any more news vans and no amount of cajoling by high-profile journalists or anchors was going to move the NYPD. Having had to put up with the media coverage throughout the trial they simply would have none of it. Both sides arrived at the courthouse within three minutes of each other with the prosecution arriving first at two thirty on the dot. Both sides had to navigate through the throng of journalists from all forms or media in order to make it into the courtroom. Once they finally made it into the courtroom both sides took their respective places behind the tables in front of the judge's bench. David Neill, the district attorney for the city of New York was present along with Bart Logan and Melanie Farris. On the side of the defense were Steven Loomis and his lawyers, Max Zeidler, Drew Willis and Ray Gretche. The overall feel of the courtroom had changed drastically. Instead of a charged, adversarial feel there was a palpable sense of relief. All parties were visibly relaxed and both Steven and Beth could be seen chatting with the defense team, and for the first time in public, smiling. As soon as both sides were settled David Neill walked over to Max, Drew and Ray and said hello. He knew all of them and just wanted to acknowledge that in front of the media. It was clear that Neill wanted to give a sense of cooperation between both sides. For the sake of propriety he made his greeting short and to the point. He did not look at Steven Loomis as Loomis watched the exchange. Finally, the judge arrived behind the bench at three o'clock on the nose.

Both sides had agreed that the first order of business should be properly dismissing the jury and so the judge's first words were directed at the jury, "Ladies and gentlemen of the jury, as you have no doubt heard, an agreement has been reached by both parties to bring this case to a conclusion. On behalf of the state of New York, I want to thank you very much for your service in this case. I know how hard it must have been for you to be away from your families and how hard it has been to listen to some of the testimony presented about both this case and the other circumstances surrounding it. At this point you are free to leave, but you are also free to remain in the courtroom for the remainder of the hearing. I believe that given the time you have invested into the case you should be able to see it through to its conclusion. Counsel, I trust you do not object?"

Everybody on both sides looked at each other. What the judge had done was incredibly rare, allowing the jury members to remain in the courtroom to witness the closure, the end of the case.

Drew Willis and Bart Logan spoke up at the same time, "No your honor."

The judge proceeded to move forward. He outlined the charges that had been filed against Steven, he then went on to outline the charges that Steven would be pleading guilty to. There was absolutely no sound in the courtroom other than the judge speaking, "Mr. Loomis do you understand the charge of voluntary manslaughter as I have explained it to you?"

Steven nodded, "I do your honor"

Newman continued, "And is it your intent sir to accept the deal relating to the charge of voluntary manslaughter as outlined by the prosecution and your lawyers under an Alford agreement?"

Steven responded, "Yes your honor."

The judge went on, "Is it also your intent Mr. Loomis to do the same as it relates to the charge of endangering the public by way of a dangerous activity?"

Steven answered, "Yes it is your honor."

The judge nodded and proceeded, "And are you entering into this agreement with full knowledge and voluntarily?"

Steven nodded, "Yes, I am."

The judge kept going, "Has anyone made any promise, other than that included in the plea agreement?"

Steven shook his head, "No your honor."

The judge nodded and went on to read the specific charge of voluntary manslaughter and asked Steven Loomis whether he wished to enter a plea of guilty under the Alford agreement, to which Loomis replied simply, "Yes I do."

The judge moved on to the next charge and once again Steven simply responded with, "Yes I do."

The judge looked up to address both groups again, "The court finds that the decision to enter into the agreement was made freely and voluntarily and therefore accepts your plea of guilty to the charges under the Alford doctrine. Your attorneys have stated that you are willing to be sentenced immediately, is that correct?"

Steven nodded, "Yes your honor."

The judge went on, "Very well, Mr. Loomis after having taken into consideration the totality of the circumstances surrounding this case, your prior record and your exemplary service for this country, the court sentences you to three years in the custody of the New York department of corrections for the charge of voluntary manslaughter and to six months in the custody of the New York department of corrections for the charge of endangering the public. This sentence to be served concurrently with the three years previously imposed. The court recommends that time in custody be served in a minimum-security facility and allows for all early release credits available. Mr. Loomis can qualify for good time credits as well as other programs designed to give you additional credit for the time you have served. Your attorneys have also indicated to the court that you would like to set a date to report for custody, is this correct?"

Steven nodded once again, "Yes it is your honor."

The judge went on, "You are hereby ordered to report for custody on Wednesday, July 12th, 2014 at eight o'clock in the morning at the central jail in Manhattan. I realize it is actually more than the two weeks the defense requested, but I figured none of you would object."

He paused to give anyone who might want to the opportunity to object. When nobody said anything he continued, "You will be transferred to the facility where you will serve the rest of your sentence at the discretion of the department of corrections."

Steven nodded and finally looked up at the judge, "Thank you your honor and I am sorry that my actions encumbered the system as much as they did."

The judge took his reading glasses off, put them on the bench and addressed Steven, "You do not need to apologize Mr. Loomis. As corny or antiquated as it may sound, our legal system was designed in order to bring justice when it is called for. Now that the case is over, I will share with you my point of view. You are precisely the type of individual that the system is designed to protect. You found yourself in a situation more horrible than I could possibly imagine. You made certain decisions as a result of that and found yourself charged with first-degree murder, but in the end the system, as it most often does, brought out the truth and resolved the situation in a manner that imposed the appropriate punishment. I am gratified that a resolution was agreed upon and that both sides were able to put aside the desire to win in order to do the right thing. Your record speaks for itself and I for one wish you and your family the best and I hope that once you can put this case behind you, you and yours can heal from all of this."

Steven smiled when the judge said what he said. He hadn't expected it, nobody had expected it and when it happened almost every single reporter in the courtroom put their head down to write their notes down. None of the lawyers had expected it either, although they were all aware of his reputation as an unorthodox jurist. The judge brought the court to order and got up from the bench one last time, "Ladies and gentlemen, it has been a pleasure and I hope we can work together again." And with that he left the courtroom.

Steven shook his lawyers' hands and turned to find his wife. When he did, they came together and gave each other a huge bear hug. The prosecution team was also visibly relaxed, both Farris and Logan went over to shake Max, Drew and Ray's hands. They both nodded at the Loomis family and made their way out of the courtroom. David Neill had engaged with a couple of senior reporters and was giving them his own personal take on the case, something he had done a few times already, almost certainly claiming that it was an exclusive every time. Finally he came over to also shake the defense team's hands. Unlike Farris and Logan, however, Neill went over to Steven and offered him his hand.

When Steven shook his hand, Neill was heard saying, "Good luck to you Mr. Loomis."

Once they were done Neill also made his way out of the courtroom.

Drew went over to Steven, "It's finally over."

When Steven looked at him Drew's face lit up in a big smile, there was just no way that Steven and Beth could help but to also smile.

It was Beth that spoke up first, "Yes, it is. Listen Drew, I know I haven't necessarily been the easiest person to work with, but I hope you understand that it was just because of how much I love this man. Can you understand that?"

Drew's smile widened, "Absolutely. We expected nothing else." Beth let go of Steven and took Drew by surprise when she came over and put her arms around him.

She whispered as she gave him a big hug, "Thank you Drew. Thank you for saving my family."

Drew had held his emotions completely in check during the entirety of the case. Now he finally lost control of his emotions.

His eyes watered and his voice cracked as he responded, "It was my pleasure Beth. I consider myself lucky to have met your husband and I felt honored to be one of the lawyers he trusted to defend him."

Beth let go and held him at arm's length by his shoulders, "Good, you should feel honored and lucky. We feel honored and lucky too."

She went over to Max and Ray and also gave them a hug and a kiss on the cheek, "Thank you, thank you very much."

Ray chuckled and hugged her back, "You are most welcome, my lady."

Max was also a bit teary-eyed so he didn't say anything, he just wiped the tears from his eyes.

Drew addressed the group, "Hey guys, let's make our way back to the office. The media is absolutely buzzing with the news and there are reporters everywhere trying to get a scoop. Let's see if there is a way for us to get out of here without attracting too much attention."

It turned out that it didn't matter what they did, there were reporters absolutely everywhere. Even though everyone in the group had made it clear that they were not going to be answering any questions, every single reporter shouted questions at the group, "Drew, are you relieved?" and "Steven, do you think you got away with murder?"

Once they finally got back to the office Drew finally said something, "Alright, we need to call a press conference and put a lot of these stupid questions to bed. You don't have to be a part of it Steven, but we do need to give them something to write about the defense, otherwise they will make up their own stories."

Steven, sitting next to Beth in Ray's office, agreed on both counts, "Go for it. It's about time. We are going to be leaving for Lake Tahoe, California tomorrow afternoon. We are so looking forward to just disconnecting from everything."

Ray asked, "Where are you guys going to be staying?"

Beth answered, "We're going to be staying at Art Goodman's lake house."

Drew whistled, "I imagine it is probably a high luxury fortress on the lake."

Steven smiled, "Something like that. If either of you needs to get a hold of us just use my cell number, I'll get back to you within twenty four hours."

Drew had one final piece of business to discuss, "The only thing we still need to talk about is you reporting for custody. The judge gave you sixteen days until you have to report. Why don't we get together at my office on the third, a couple of days before you have to actually report for custody? Nothing big, we just need to chat about what you should expect. We should have a better indication of where you will be serving your time."

Beth responded to that, "That will be really useful. Please do call us whenever you find out where he's going to be. Where do you think he's going to end up?"

Max had quite a bit of knowledge of the various prisons around the state, "I think the place he is most likely to end up at is the Buffalo Correctional Center."

Beth and Steven were surprised. Steven asked, "Buffalo? Really? There isn't a place closer than that?"

Max answered, "Yes there are places that are closer, but they are medium and maximum security places. Not the kind of place you would ever want to end up. I know it will be a drive to visit him, but trust me Beth, that is the best place he could end up at."

Steven turned to address Beth, "Don't worry Beth, I honestly wasn't expecting that you would be coming every week."

Beth was frustrated, "There you go saying dumb things again, Steven. Why don't you get it? I'm going to be there every opportunity I get."

Steven shook his head, "I don't want to argue with you. I just want you to understand that I need some time to just recharge.

Let's not get into it right now. I just want to get the kids and get on our way."

Beth gave him a peck on the cheek, "Alright. Let's not argue about it now, but know I am not going to drop it."

Steven chuckled as he got his coat to get on the way, "Oh believe me, I know!"

Max, Drew and Ray went to say goodbye. Steven pulled Drew into a tight hug and told him what he was thinking, "Thank you Drew. Thank you so much for believing. Thank you for understanding and for giving it your all."

Drew returned the hug, "No Steven, thank you. Thank you for reminding me of the reason I became a defense attorney in the first place. Thank you for trusting me to present this to the world. No matter what happens now, the world knows Steven, they know they exist and that will never change."

Steven moved on to Ray, "Ray, thank you for everything. I don't know how I could possibly thank you enough."

Ray shook his hand, "You're welcome kid. Actually I should be thanking you for breathing some life into the career of a tired, old defense attorney. It feels great to push the limits of the law. You guys be careful and try not to worry about anything. We'll handle whatever needs to be handled until you get back."

Finally he got to Max, "Max, thank you for standing by Drew and by this case, I will never forget it."

Max smiled, "You need to know that we stood by Drew because of the lawyer he is and once Ray signed on, we were even more firmly onboard."

Before Steven and Beth were able to leave the office, Drew called after Steven, "Hey Steven, don't forget what I told you about talking to someone in the media."

Steven waved, "I won't. You two need to also take a break!" Drew and Ray waved at them and with that Steven and Beth went on their way.

Max called a press conference for that evening. The press conference would take place at his and Drew's office. There was not too much room, so it was standing room only, and only senior reporters were present.

All three attorneys shared an element of their defense, but it was Drew who kept the pace of the press conference. They acknowledged that their defense had really pushed boundaries in criminal law and litigation, but they were confident in the science. They explained that the experts that had not had an opportunity to testify would have testified about the biological and anthropological elements of the defense. All three answered the same question – whether this meant there was not a legal determination that there was in fact another human subspecies on earth – the same way. They all said there was no finding as to the scientific validity of their defense, but all of them spoke to the fact that the prosecution was willing to accept this deal meant that they believed the science and the experts explaining had enough credibility for a jury to find Steven not guilty. Finally they all praised the prosecution for their professionalism, their willingness to discuss a plea and the fairness in their position on sentencing. All three attorneys were used to making similar statements at the conclusion of a criminal case, but for the first time in all of their careers, they believed every word of it.

Once every one of the reporters left, the three of them went into the kitchen and grabbed an ice-cold beer. They then went to Drew's office and each plopped down on the nearest chair. Ray had his feet up on the small table in between his and Max's chairs, Drew was almost lying down in his chair from behind the desk.

Drew was the first to speak, "Ray, I can't say enough, man. You were everything advertised and more. It has been an absolute honor and, honestly, you also made it a hell of a lot of fun."

Max raised his beer, "Hear, hear. You still got it, old man, don't let anyone tell you different. You can still kick ass and take names."

Ray tilted the beer bottle he had in his hand toward Drew and Max, "The pleasure was all mine, counselors. Drew, you are one hell of a lawyer, maybe one of the best I've ever seen. Max, you are one of the best lawyers I've ever seen, but I doubt I needed to say that! Thank you both for giving an old man a renewed faith in the law."

Drew chuckled and took a sip of beer. Ray went on more seriously, "I mean it, guys. I feel new life after this. It was incredible to feel the rush again. I hope we are able to work together again, because you are right, it was a hell of a lot of fun working with both of you."

Now it was Drew who raised his beer, "Here's to a new species and to a good man going back to his life!"

Max and Ray raised their beers, "Cheers to that!"

All of the lawyers got into their respective town cars an hour later, feeling very happy.

25.

The Loomis family left for California at 10 o'clock the next morning. They made it through the throng of reporters parked in front of their home and the ones that followed along to the airport. They could not follow them into the private terminal. Once on the plane, both Steven and Beth took a deep breath and exhaled, finally able to relax completely, knowing that nobody could get to them here. It was a feeling that was unparalleled by anything else. Steven was actually surprised that he had been so tense, so anxious. It wasn't until the tension was gone that he realized how much had been there. Bethany and Christopher were absolutely ecstatic. Chris was thrilled to be in a plane all to himself and Bethany was very much looking forward to spending time with her daddy, something she had not been able to do in a long time and missed very much. Beth had a soft smile on her face as she looked out the window. Steven thought he saw a touch of sadness in that smile. It was okay, she was entitled to feel some sadness. She missed her daughter. For his part, Steven was enjoying watching his son making noises and pointing to everything he could make out from the window of the plane, oblivious to everything that had happened all around him. Steven was glad his son would be able to move on

around him. Steven was glad his son would be able to move on without knowing what had happened to his sister.

It had been incredibly hard to see Chris pausing all of a sudden and looking back at his dad to ask a question, "Dad, where's Tracy? Where is she?"

Chris had seen something that reminded him of his sister and he wanted to know where she was. Steven had responded with the same thing Beth had told him when he had asked before. Tracy had gone to heaven to be with God and to look out for Chris and for Bethany and her parents. Chris had looked long and hard at his parents when they gave him that explanation. He did not have a grasp on the idea of death, but he knew his sister would not be coming back, ever. They landed in Los Angeles at 1:00 in the afternoon Pacific Standard Time. They boarded the suburban that was waiting for them at the airport and got on their way to the General's small fortress by late afternoon. It was a two-and-a-half-hour drive, but it seemed to go by in minutes. The first thing everyone did upon arrival was to take their shoes off and go down to the shore to put their feet in the water. Steven kicked water on his whole family and ran away laughing. Bethany and Beth screamed and went chasing after him with Chris closely behind. Bethany was the one to catch up to him, and he allowed himself to be tackled and to fall into the water with his daughter, both still dressed. It was at that moment, precisely, that Steven Loomis knew his family would really be okay, that in spite of her issues, his daughter was stronger than he had imagined and would be able to move on. Beth's parents, Tom and Lucy, had shown up the day after the family had arrived. They were absolutely thrilled to be there. Steven was also incredibly happy and thankful that his father-in-law was there. The man had been a rock for Beth and the kids and a great counselor to Steven. This was the least he could do for the people that had been there throughout this nightmare. The rest of the week was exactly what both Steven and Beth had hoped it would be. The cabin, if it could be called a cabin, had every comfort imaginable including two hot tubs, a swimming pool, a wading pool, a sauna and at least five giant flat-screen televisions. When they arrived, they had found an Xbox, a PS3, a Nintendo Wii and a stack of games appropriate for the kids, compliments of Art Goodman. Steven and Beth made love almost every night after the kids went to bed. They would go out to the bedroom's private terrace, enjoy a glass of wine and look at the stars, which appeared to be within arm's reach. They talked about the kids, about Beth's family, about Steven going into custody and about what he would do after he got out. The one thing they didn't talk about was the case or Donald Riche. The third night at the cabin, while sitting out on the terrace, Beth had brought up Tracy for the first and only time in their time there. She remembered Tracy and her silly faces and how much she had enjoyed when her parents read her a book in bed. Steven remembered how she had liked to come and sleep in their bed whenever she had a bad dream, always dragging her old bunny with her. That bunny had found a new permanent home with Bethany, who apparently saw it as a way to remain connected to her sister. For her part, Bethany seemed to be having a blast. She went swimming every day and went down to the shore with her grandparents to gather shells and glass. One bright morning, Steven had asked her if he could go to gather shells with her. He claimed to have seen some great specimens. Bethany had jumped at the chance. In their previous life, she had loved spending alone time with her father and she had not gotten to do it at all while they were going through their nightmare.

This was also the first and only time that Bethany had asked her father about the case and what happened to Tracy. It had not been an easy conversation, and Steven had to decide how much he wanted to share with his daughter. Bethany had been putting shells in her bucket for about 20 minutes and had not said a word, which let Steven know that something was on her mind. She finally looked up and asked her father about what happened, "Hey, dad, what happened to Tracy? I mean, I know that man took her and that he killed her, but what happened to her?"

Steven kept picking up shells and came over to be next to his daughter so he could answer her question, "That man killed a lot of other people, honey."

Bethany also kept picking up shells, "I know, but what did he do to Tracy?"

Steven knew he would have to keep the truth from his daughter although he knew she was asking because of what other people had told her about what the man had done to her sister, "I don't know exactly what he did, baby, nobody really knows what he did to her or to the other girls."

He hadn't lied, but obviously he had held back. He hoped she would understand when she was older and learned what happened.

She was a smart girl and had clearly been trying to understand what had happened to her family, "Why did that man take them, dad, why did he take them in the first place?"

Now Steven had to measure what he was going to share with her. He did not want to outright lie, "Well, baby, that man was actually a different kind of human being, which means that he looked like us and acted like us, but he was something different, a different species from us. We don't know a lot about that species right now, but what we do know is that they hunt and kill humans. They don't do it because there is something wrong with them; they do it because that's what they feel they are supposed to do. Just like lions hunt gazelles or other animals. They don't do it because they're bad, they do it because it's in their nature."

Now Bethany stopped picking up shells, "Is that why you killed him? Because he was a different species from humans?"

This was a tough question to answer, but he had to do it. She needed to hear it from him, because she was going to be hearing many stories from many people and she needed to know what the truth was, "Yes, I guess that's why I did it. I also did it because I knew he would do it again if he got the chance. I don't want you to think that what I did was heroic or a great thing. What I did was illegal and I am going to be punished for it."

Bethany went back to picking up shells, "So then why did you do it? If it's illegal and it's not the right thing to do?"

Steven answered as truthfully as he could, "I did it because what happened to Tracy really affected me. I wanted to make sure that everybody had been warned that these other species are hunting us. And after I killed him, I told the world exactly that, that there was now another species hunting humans. You've seen all the reporters and vans doing the news about the case, right? So now people know and that is a big part of what I wanted to do."

She seemed to take this in stride. She had always considered her father to be a hero, someone who fought injustice and criminals all around the world.

She also thought about it for a while before letting her father know she would truly be alright, "You keep picking up broken ones. You can't make necklaces with broken ones."

Steven smiled at her and kicked water to splash her, "Excuse me, your majesty!"

Bethany laughed and kicked water back at him. She ran and he picked her up and threw her in the water. And just like that, Steven Loomis knew his family would be okay.

Max and Drew went back to trying to run their respective offices and found that it was going to be impossible without some help. Even with the size of their firm, Drew and Max's staff was absolutely swamped, not only with existing clients but with a flood of new clients, all looking for a criminal defense attorney. Most of the new clients were high-profile individuals with the resources to hire the best, and right now there were no more prominent names in the country. Drew had spent three days straight putting in 14 hours a day. Between interviewing new associates and trying to catch up with old cases, Max was also burning the candle at both ends. He had his pick of Harvard, Michigan and Yale graduates, all looking to be a part of a growing firm. Actually, it had been a young black attorney from Rochester that had impressed him the most, as well as an experienced public defender, Fiona Sanders, who he was familiar with and had been impressed with ever since he met her. The truth was that he would probably need to hire three more attorneys before it was all said and done. Right now, he and Drew walked on water and the partners went along with anything they wanted or needed to do.

Ray's situation was different. He too had a line of new potential clients, but he was winding down what had been an incredible career. He too brought a couple of attorneys onboard, but the attorneys he brought on were attorneys he had worked with before and who had been overlooked for partnership at their respective firms. He brought them on with the idea of eventually turning the firm over to them.

The Friday before Steven was to return, Drew's legal assistant came into his office, "We just got a fax from the department of corrections. Steven will need to report in at the central jail and will then be transported to Dillon."

Dillon was a minimum security facility in Purchase, New York. It was one of the newest facilities in the state. Not brand-new, but newly remodeled and under new management. The state of New York had contracted SafeCo International to run all of the state's minimum security facilities.

Drew took the fax, walked into Max's office and put it on his desk, "That's good news. It's only about an hour away, so it should be easy for Beth and the kids to visit. On the downside, it's also close to the media, and we all know what they've been up to since the deal."

Max picked up the phone, "I'll call Steven and Beth. They wanted to know as soon as we know."

The prosecution lawyers were also starting new aspects of their careers. Melanie Farris had been chosen to lead the financial crimes unit at the District Attorney's Office. Bart Logan had been tapped to head the capital murder unit. Never one to shy away from the media, David Neill, the district attorney, had called a press conference to announce both promotions and his bid for reelection.

The week went by much too fast for Steven, as he knew it would. They flew back to New York the Saturday before Steven was to turn himself in. The press was still parked in front of their home, at the central intake and at Dillon. There had been more than 300 inquiries by different media to get an interview with any of the Loomis family members. The General had also taken care of that by assigning the company's director of public information the task of fielding all of the inquiries. Steven had already made the decision to grant an interview to Felix Garcia, but he had decided to do that after he was already in custody.

On the Monday Steven was to turn himself in, Beth found him sipping a cup of coffee and looking out the window at 5:30 in the morning. She actually held back from going right to him and just watched him from the kitchen. He looked calm, more at peace than she had seen him in months, even before all of this happened. He always seemed to have the weight of the world on his shoulders. Not now. She still wondered at the quality of man she had married. He was strong, the strongest man she knew, he was intelligent, faithful, kind and an amazing father. He was also sexy as hell, especially when she saw him like this, without anything to distract from the man himself. She walked over and put her arms around him from behind.

He smiled and held her arms close. She asked "How long have you been awake?"

He answered, "I've been up for about an hour."

She was a bit concerned, "Did you have a hard time sleeping?" He shook his head, "Not at all. In fact, I have been sleeping wonderfully for the past couple of weeks. I guess I just want to get this out of the way."

She rested her head on his back, "It's time, isn't it? Time for you to go away."

He turned to face her, "Don't think of it as me going away, think of it as the last part of this journey, the first step to getting back to our lives."

She just rested her head on his back for another few minutes and then went to the kitchen to get some coffee for herself. They had agreed to be at Drew's offices at 7:30 to get together for the drive over to intake. They were there 10 minutes early. Ray had a deposition for another case later that morning and could not be there and Max was taking some vacation with his family, but Drew was there to welcome them. Steven went over to his lawyer and said hello with a hug.

After the hellos, Drew had to comment on how they looked, "I have to say, I am blown away. You guys look like a couple of kids back from a honeymoon."

Beth smiled, "It kind of felt like that. I don't think we've had so much quality time in quite a long while."

Steven just wanted to get this over with, "Are we ready to go?"

Drew gestured to a side exit, "Lou's waiting in the alley. You probably had to wade through the media out front. It won't get any better wherever you go today."

Steven started walking, "I know. I am hoping sooner or later they'll get the idea that I am not speaking to anybody and go away. Hoping, but really doubtful that they'll go away. Maybe after I give the Garcia kid the interview they'll finally get it."

Drew raised his eyebrows as he followed, "So you decided to talk to the media after all. It's a good move. I agree with you, though, that it should be once things cool down a bit."

They all got in the Suburban without having to deal with any press, since nobody had figured out to go to the side exit and the group had never used that particular exit before in any case. The drive over to the intake facility was without incident. Beth and Steven held hands and looked out the window the whole ride over. When they got there, they realized the media was still very much hungry for a story. There were more news vans and remote teams than there had been at the Loomis's house, and they were being extremely aggressive in trying to reach Beth and Steven. Far more than they had been throughout the trial. Steven thought it was probably because this was basically their last shot at getting any kind of a statement from him. They were able to drive through without a problem and the car pulled into the loading and unloading area within the facility.

When the time came to say goodbye, Steven went up to his lawyer and shook his hand first and then hugged him, "Drew, I want to thank you for believing me, for risking your career. My family and I will never be able to say thank you enough."

He then went to his wife who took his face in her hands and spoke directly to him. To them, there was no one else there. "I love you. Your family loves you and we are behind you. Remember that when you are feeling lonely or having a hard day. I will come to visit you as soon as they allow it."

He brought her in close for a big hug and whispered in her ear, "I am so sorry. Thank you for sticking with me through this. Take care of the kids and let them know how much I love them."

She kissed him firmly on the lips and gave him a rueful smile, "Sometimes it is hard to hold things together, but sticking with you has never been hard for me. I love you."

Steven turned to finally begin the process. The whole procedure went smoothly. He was given a jumpsuit before they fingerprinted him, took several photographs and conducted an interview to assess his psychological condition and emotional stability. Everything checked out as everyone knew it would. He was given a lunch of two sandwiches with some sort of cold cut of unknown origin, a small serving of pathetic-looking peas, a piece of hard cornbread and a square of green Jell-O for dessert. Guards had always gotten a kick out of seeing the faces of all the high-powered insider traders and crooked lawyers who looked at their trays in disgust, appalled that someone dared to put such garbage in front of them. Steven, however, had eaten much worse in much nastier places, so when he got his tray he ate it with gusto. The truth was that almost every officer Steven had come across throughout this entire ordeal had gone out of their way to let him know that they approved. It was no different now that he was in custody. Steven noticed that none of his cellmates had gotten the two chocolate chip cookies he got with his lunch and he noticed that the television had been turned so that it faced his cell. So far, every guard he had dealt with referred to him as Mr. Loomis.

At just before 5 o'clock that evening, a group of seven inmates had been put in a transport vehicle. The group took up seats and settled in for the ride. They were all nonviolent offenders, so they were able to sit without being handcuffed. There were two guards besides the driver. The driver and one guard were in the front, protected by a cage with a slit big enough for the rifle the guard was carrying and one in the back also protected by a metal cage. Every one of the prisoners had been admonished that should they make any move or try to escape the guards had the authority to use deadly force. The warning was always taken seriously, especially by the white-collar criminals who were for the most part first-timers. Steven watched with some amusement as the eyes of his fellow inmates got big and round when they heard the warning. Once they got on their way, there was a sea of cameras and flashbulbs going off all around the bus. They had to drive carefully in order to make sure they didn't run over somebody. The ride to Dillon was uneventful. Everyone pretty much kept to themselves for the entire ride over. Once they arrived, the bus went through a smaller group of reporters. Most of the guards were used to the media attention since so many of the inmates at Dillon were high-profile figures that had gotten caught embezzling or trading on insider information in some way. None of them had ever seen the number of reporters that were there when that bus arrived. They pulled into the offloading area of the facility and marched off the bus in the same order they had gotten in. Steven looked around. This was far from the scenes in the movies where all the hardcore criminals were taunting the new arrivals and calling out to them. They were met by a well-dressed man in his late 50s with hair gone completely white and a heavy build complete with a big potbelly. He looked like anybody's grandfather, wise and all-knowing. The effect was broken when he spoke. He had a heavy Brooklyn accent, which only got more pronounced when he spoke loudly. Patrick McMahon, the warden, welcomed everybody and began introducing the three names that most of them would be dealing with day in and day out. The first was Associate Warden Luis Mendez, a young guy of about 35 who wore a suit and had a tie tack in the middle of what Steven knew to be a Hermes tie.

McMahon introduced him, "Associate Warden Mendez is my eyes and ears here. He lets me know how things are going at the facility and he will be the individual that you will see around most often day to day. Mr. Mendez, they're all yours."

Mendez stepped forward. He had just a hint of an accent, very slight. It actually gave him an air of European lineage as he sounded a bit like Antonio Banderas, "Gentlemen, welcome to Dillon. Let's start out by agreeing that you are all here because you have to be here. I know none of you would be here if you had any choice in the matter. The fact is that you do not. You have been placed here because you have been convicted of a serious crime. I can promise you three things, gentlemen. You will be treated fairly by the entire staff. Each and every one of you will be treated the same, regardless of what your crime was. Your time here will go as easy as you make it, and finally, I will find out if you are in any way, shape or form trying to break the rules. Trust me, there is always someone who thinks they are more clever, and maybe they are, out there, but in here, I will find out. I'd now like to introduce Captain Zach Driver, the head of the security staff. You will see him every single day, so get used to him."

Zach Driver looked like he belonged more in a maximum security prison than watching hedge fund crooks. He was well north of six feet and at least 220 pounds of solid muscle. He had a closely cropped buzz cut, going gray at the sides. He wore mirrored aviator sunglasses, lending the scene its only stereotype. He was one of those people that no matter what they were wearing you knew they were in law enforcement.

He stepped up and looked at the group made up of the last seven inmates plus about 20 others that had gotten there before Steven's group, "Alright, men, I don't like to talk any more than I absolutely have to, not now and not while I am doing my job. The rules here will be made clear to you. If there is something that is in any way unclear, you need to let somebody know because I expect you to adhere to the rules here, and I will do what is necessary to make sure things run smoothly. Be clear on one thing, you are all criminals, you have all been convicted of a felony, and my staff and I will treat you as such if the situation calls for it. We will not hesitate to use physical force if it is called for, not for one second. I am telling you that now so you are not surprised when you get taken down for not following orders.

This is a correctional facility, my house, and I will not tolerate any bullshit in my house."

Steven listened and looked around at the group of men with him. Not one looked like they would ever try to break the rules, especially once they got a look at the guards manning the doors and at the control room. People like Driver were nothing new to Steven. He had gone through enough boot camps and hell weeks to know what he was in for. The guy looked tough and like he would rip you a new one if you tried anything, but he also seemed fair. Once the welcome speeches were finished, the group went into a classroom where they were told exactly what they could expect and what would be expected of them. They were handed a handbook with the rules and regulations. Steven decided to read it as soon as he got the chance. Once he was clear on the rules, he was sure he would have no problems. Everyone was assigned a dorm room, given two towels, three pairs of khaki pants and one pair of white sneakers. A set of sheets, a wool blanket and a peacoat were also a part of what was given to every prisoner, along with five pairs of white socks, five boxers and five t-shirts. All in all, Steven thought, it was pretty decent accommodations. It was certainly better than what Steven had expected. There were no bars anywhere. Everyone was assigned a roommate to share their dorm room with. Each room had one television, two desks, two nightstands and two twin beds. Each room had a window that looked out at the grounds. The only sign that it was a detention facility was a chain-link fence with razor wire on top. There was a common room for every eight rooms. The common room had dozens of board games, a library of popular fiction and reference materials. It was pretty complete. The law library was as complete as that of any top law firm. There were vending machines in each common room where prisoners could buy snacks, sodas and microwaveable food. There were two microwaves and two pots of regular coffee in each common area. Once a day, everyone was allowed into the yard for exercise. There were handball courts, soccer goals and three basketball courts. There were tables available for anyone to play chess or backgammon. The only thing that was not allowed was playing cards. The administration knew that if cards were available, high-stakes games were likely to sprout up now and then. Steven was one of four people from his group who did not have a roommate. During the interview, they explained that he had been convicted of a crime involving violence and it was the facility's policy to keep what were defined as violent offenders in a room by themselves until they were able to assess the risk of putting someone in with them. The counselor had told Steven it was strictly policy and that most likely he would be assigned a roommate by the end of the week. Steven was told of two programs he could participate in and get credit for. One was a reading comprehension and communication program. It was explained to him basically as a book club where inmates agreed to read a book or poetry and got together to comment and analyze what they read, with the more well-read inmates helping those with lower reading comprehension skills. The other program was a dog-training program in which the inmates would be assigned a dog that they would then have to train as a service dog for injured veterans. Steven had voiced interest in both programs. He was particularly intrigued by the training program for the dogs. He had always had a dog growing up and missed it. His family had a small dachshund, Gizmo, who died of old age when Bethany was five. Beth had gone through a bleak period following his death. They had owned the dog for 12 years. After that, Steven had decided their lives were just too busy to take care of a dog. The first time he went out into the main yard was the first time he realized that everyone around him was either talking about him or just plain staring at him. He should have noticed it sooner, but he was too focused on simply settling in. He had brought a Tom Clancy novel out to the yard and was sitting at a table reading when the first inmate to engage him in any sort of real conversation walked up. His name was Carlos Molina. He was in his early 60s, but looked younger. He wore a wool beanie and thick eyeglasses and he reminded Steven of an old and battered version on Andy Garcia, the actor.

Molina walked up to Steven with his hand outstretched, "Welcome to Dillon. I'm Carlos Molina. I see you have a following. Don't pay any attention, they always get like this when someone who has been on television comes in. Nobody comes to introduce themselves, they just stare like idiots."

Steven smiled and shook the man's hand, "Thank you. I am sure you can understand if I don't say I am happy to be here."

Carlos chuckled, "No one is happy to be here, no one who has not been to a super-max facility, that is. This place is Club Med in comparison."

With that, Carlos let Steven know that he himself had been a guest of the type of facility he was referring to, "Do you mind if I sit down with you?"

Steven had no problem with the man sitting down. He was still in wait-and-see mode, though.

He wanted to see if Charlie had some agenda, "Not at all, please have a seat."

Carlos sat down and pulled out a pipe. He lit it and went on, "Sorry I don't offer, but it's not looked kindly upon. Everyone is supposed to bring their own."

Steven smiled and motioned with his hand, "Don't worry about it, I don't smoke."

Carlos got to the point of his visit, "I actually lead the reading group in here and I am always looking for new blood."

Steven relaxed a notch and apologized, "I'm sorry if I seem a bit closed off, but I'm sure you can understand that most everyone approaching me lately wants a story."

Carlos nodded, "Yeah, we're used to that here. There are at least four or five ponzi scheme wizards who took people to the tune of billions of dollars, and every one of them was being chased by the media when they came in. There are six judges who got popped for taking bribes who had media trailing them. I have to say, though, you definitely blow all of them away. I have never seen that much coverage since I have been here, and that's been six years."

Steven wanted to trust the guy, but first he needed to know what he was in for, "Six years, that's a long time. How long do you have to go?"

Carlos answered, "I have three more years with credit for good time served."

Steven wanted to be honest with the guy, "What did you do to get so much time?"

Carlos chuckled, "You get right down to it, don't you? It's usually not good etiquette to ask someone why they are here. You didn't know, so no big deal. I was caught with 12 pounds of high-grade cocaine and 2,000 ecstasy hits."

Steven still didn't get why so much time, however, "If you are going to be doing nine years, that means you got about 20, right? Twenty years for cocaine and ecstasy? It sounds kind of steep."

Carlos nodded, "You think? The truth is that I was on probation for a prior offense when I got caught again. I served five years for manslaughter. I did it in a super-max up in Buffalo. Before you ask, I owned a bar in Staten Island and I had a customer who was high on crack and drunk. He refused to leave and began to grope one of my waitresses. I lost it, came around from behind the bar and broke his neck. The law thought it was too much force and that I wasn't in imminent danger, so it started out as second-degree murder. When they found out about this guy's background, they made the offer for manslaughter and I jumped on it. It was fair. Anyway, I met some people in super-max and I started dealing drugs wholesale. I dealt in pounds, never dealt with individual consumers of my products. I was making about $200,000 a week when I got caught."

Steven whistled, that much money was enough for anybody to be seduced, "Damn. Well, it's nice to meet you, Carlos. I'm definitely going to sign up for the group."

Carlos got the hint that although Steven was open to meeting people, he wanted to be alone right now.

He got up and before he left he gave Steven a great piece of advice, "Good enough. Listen, Steven, there is no one here who doesn't know about what happened and why you did what you did. You'd have to be dead to not know about it. People don't know how to deal with someone in your situation. Most people here have some education and are aware of the details of the case. If I were you, I would make the first move and walk up to whomever you want to meet and just say hello. The quicker you do that and just become another one of us, the quicker people will stop thinking about you in the context of your case. It's just what I've seen before. You need to take the mystery out of being you. When you do, everyone else will too."

Steven shook the man's hand and nodded, "That sounds like good advice, Carlos. I'm just settling in right now, but I will definitely take your advice into account."

Carlos went to leave, "Good. I will see you on Wednesday. We are reading A Million Little Pieces. Read what you can before then. You can participate as much or as little as you want to."

Steven got up and went over to the coffeepot. He got a cup of coffee and went to sit down to read his book. He had read only three pages when another guy came up to talk, then two others joined him. Steven could see that he was not going to be able to simply keep his head down and just read his book. Not initially anyway. He met about 10 other guys that evening. For the most part, they were just reaching out to the new, high-profile guest of Dillon. Some wanted to let Steven know how much they approved of what he had done, some wanted to share their own stories, and others were just curious to hear from the man himself. After watching him and hearing about his case for months, they were clearly intrigued. Steven accommodated them as best he could. He thanked everyone who wished him well, listened to those that wanted to share and tried as best he could to be pleasant.

Toward the end of the evening, Zach Driver came over to where the group of men were and broke up the party, "Alright, men, we need to wrap it up and get going back to the dorms."

Everyone stood up and went on their way.

Driver addressed Steven directly, "Loomis, hold on."

Steven stayed back when the other men went on their way, "I know about your case and I know about the attention you have been getting because of it. That kind of attention may be okay for the outside, but it's not something we like in here. If I were you, I would try to just blend in as soon as you can, because attention from the others in here will only bring attention from me and you don't want to draw attention from me."

Steven thought it was fair for the guy to make sure he didn't have some sort of prima donna on his hands, but he also needed to make a couple of things clear to him, "Trust me, Mr. Driver, I want nothing more than to blend in and simply do my time. I am sure you can understand that is easier said than done. You can be sure that I am going to do nothing to draw any more attention to myself than is absolutely necessary."

Driver nodded, "Good deal, then we will have no problems. I will make sure the staff is aware and that they make sure they don't crowd up on you."

Steven didn't want that kind of attention either, "Listen, I don't want any special treatment or attention in here. I think that would make things worse, don't you? I'm totally able to deal with whatever issue comes up myself."

Driver nodded, but had a response ready, "I understand that, Loomis, but like it or not your case is anything but usual. We won't give you any special advantages and treatment, but we definitely need to keep big crowds down to a minimum and we need to make sure there are no misunderstandings. There are people in here who can be pushy and who are used to having things done their way. I am sure you are a reasonable guy, but like any normal man you will push back if someone steps over the line. That's the kind of thing I am paid to anticipate and prevent, which is the reason we are having this conversation."

Steven listened and considered what the man was saying. It made sense and actually gave Steven a measure of relief. He had thought about what he would do if someone was just too pushy.

Now he understood that the administration had also been thinking about it and was thankful for it, "I understand and you are right, I might have an issue if someone was too pushy. I will cooperate with whatever the staff needs for me to do."

Driver turned on his heel and went to walk away, "Good enough. Now go get ready for chow. It's on in 15 in the mess hall."

Steven went directly to his room. He was actually feeling pretty good. The place was far better than he had expected and the people were far from the types of criminals that could be found in most maximum security prisons. The facility was run as a business and used technology as much as they used staff. He expected that he would have no problems with completing his time.

He settled into a routine that had him cleaning and maintaining the weight room and the exercise equipment during the day. He participated in the book club and he tried to spend at least two hours reading just after lunch. In the evenings, he wrote in a journal and letters to his family. He had also been using the computer in the evenings, but with all the attention the trial garnered, it was difficult to be online and not come across something. He focused his attention on research being done and scholarly papers on the subject of Homo sapiens predaer. It was absolutely amazing the amount of new information being added all over the world. Some was clearly crap posted by wackos on hundreds of blogs and social media sites, but there was also serious work being done with forensic psychiatry, forensic genomics, genetics and a host of other fields ranging from anthropology to sociology. There was also plenty of chatter on TV regarding the trial and its outcome. He worked out every evening for an hour, from 7 to 8 o'clock. He did two miles around the track outside and two miles on a rowing machine as a warm-up. He then moved on to the weights. He did a combination of heavy weights and low repetitions and light weights and high repetitions. If it had been clear to everyone that it would not be a good idea to mess with him before, it became absolutely clear once they watched him work out. He was in incredible shape already, and the way he pushed the weights around and the intensity of his workout only made it more obvious. On the third night, he was working out when a large black guy came over to where he was. Steven had seen him at the gym the past two nights working out on his own.

The man approached with an outstretched hand, "Hey, man, I'm Brandon Harris, but everyone here calls me the Judge."

Steven shook the man's hand and took a good look at him, he was about six feet two inches tall and weighed at least 240 forty pounds, most of it solid muscle.

He could see why they would call him the judge. "Nice to meet you, Brandon. The Judge, huh? Do you hold court in here or what?"

Without pausing, the man responded, "No, I used to hold court out there, though. I was a presiding judge in Brooklyn when I got caught. I was convicted of taking bribes and of possession with intent to distribute."

Steven was surprised by the fact he had actually been a judge and that he had been convicted of a drug-related offense, "Drugs? Really?"

Harris responded, he was clearly used to the question, "Yeah, the irony is that they were investigating me for the bribes and had no idea about the drugs. It wasn't until they began to put cameras in my office and recording my conversations that they learned about the drugs."

He told the story as casually as talking about a parking ticket he had gotten.

There was a short pause and then he let Steven know why he had approached him, "Listen, man, I've seen you lifting and you're about the only person I can ask to spot me. I just need a spot on the bench press."

He was completely uninterested in Steven's story or what had gone on in his case. He simply wanted a spot. Steven agreed to spot him and walked over to the bench press area. The man was attempting to lift 320 pounds.

Steven spotted him and he completed his workout, "Jesus, that was impressive. I can't get anywhere near that. The most I've done is 290 pounds and that was a while back."

Harris nodded, "That's not bad. We can work on it if you want to."

He still did not show any interest in Steven other than lifting weights. As a former judge, it was extremely likely that he knew everything about the case. As a former judge, however, he probably understood better than most what Steven had faced dealing with his case and wanted to show Steven he had no ulterior motives. Steven thanked him, shook his hand and went to continue working out. Brandon Harris seemed like a guy Steven might actually develop a friendship with.

Beth came with Bethany and Christopher every week initially. Sometimes she came by herself because the kids were at her parents' house. His in-laws had come a few times to say hello and play board games, which is what the family usually did when they came to visit. Sometimes Bethany brought her homework and worked on it with her dad. Drew had come to visit twice during Steven's first six weeks in custody. They had talked about the media and the fact that they were both very surprised that so many media outlets were still trying to get a story. They chatted about the fact that Steven had also had two movie producers make a request to see him to pitch a movie deal. On the last visit, Steven had told Drew that he was going to give Garcia the interview. He actually called Felix the following day. They sat down to speak four different times. Steven gave him a history of himself, his time in the service and his time as an executive. They talked about the family and how they were just like any other family with the same hopes and dreams and problems. He told him how much he loved his children and how much he loved his wife. He shared with him what it had been like when Tracy disappeared, how much it had hurt his family, especially his wife. He shared with Felix his own hell, the way he had evolved in his thinking. He walked him through the shooting, the trial and his time here. All in all, it was a complete account of everything that had happened from Steven's point of view. He knew the kid would do the story justice and was rewarded when he finally read the piece two weeks later. It was complete, fair and showed a level of insight that surprised Steven. The Garcia kid was on his way to being a great journalist, and this story would make his journey to greatness that much shorter. He was also gratified that the interview had in fact done what he expected it would – drive the media to give up trying to get the story. The story was out now, told by Steven himself. Anybody else who wrote anything would be second and nobody wanted to do that.

After he did the interview with Felix Garcia, Steven found himself thinking about his daughter more and more often. Late at night, after lights out, he thought about Tracy, remembered her laugh and how she had loved making silly faces. Every day he remembered a little bit from his time with her, which he now realized had been much too short. As he thought about her every day, he also found himself falling deeper into grief. He realized that he had never fully grieved for his daughter. He had not grieved properly because he had needed to be there for his family and then he'd had to deal with Riche. Now, with time to spare, he was feeling what he should have felt months before. He went through the process, denial, sadness, loss, anger and finally acceptance. It was hard because during this time, he didn't want Beth to worry, so he had to put on a happy face during visits. Beth knew him too well, however. She knew something was up but decided to let him deal with it himself. If he wanted help she knew he would eventually ask. One thing that helped to keep his spirits up were letters he got every single week from the General. He wrote to keep him abreast of how things were going at the office, to complain about one executive or another, and just to share with Steven some of his own thoughts about everything. It helped Steven keep his mind sharp. He had also allowed himself to open some of the thousands of letters he had gotten while in jail. Beth told him about all the mail she had received for him since he'd gone into custody. Most were cards saying good luck and thank you. A few were from Christian wackos who wrote to tell him he was on his way to hell because only God could determine when someone was human. There were more than a few that were just rambling nonsense from what were clearly unbalanced people. Still, it was a way for Steven to entertain himself. After about two weeks of mourning, Steven found himself thinking more and more often about Nigel Barlow. Whatever else was true, Barlow kept his word about leaving Steven and his family alone. But now that the case was over, Steven needed to decide what he was going to do regarding Barlow and what he had said to Steven when he'd kidnapped him. He had told himself that he couldn't take it upon himself to figure out what to do about others that were out there preying on people. He was just one man and there were thousands, maybe millions, of predators out there. He knew that he would not be able to do much as just one individual. He thought about how maybe now some law enforcement agencies would develop task forces to hunt them, to use the science and the research on them to catch them. In the end, though, he knew it would be an exercise in futility. Most law enforcement agencies had a hard time incorporating new approaches to law enforcement. It had taken forever to get most of them to buy into the big databases and profiling programs. And social media had positively baffled most law enforcement agencies for a couple of years. They would simply look at this as so much mumbo-jumbo and would discount it. There were hundreds, thousands of cases across the country that went unsolved every year. Steven knew the cases that were prosecuted and made public were usually cases where someone had killed because of greed or jealousy or revenge and they had practically left a note letting law enforcement know who it had been that committed the crime. He also knew there were crimes, murders that were brutal and sudden and were most likely related to other murders, but would never be solved. He knew these predators were usually only caught when they themselves took ownership and told their families or close friends. Steven also wondered what these individuals thought about the case, he wondered whether some of them had recognized themselves in what his defense had presented. He was struggling with these thoughts when he got a request for a visit from an officer Galloway. He had no idea who the man was and he declined the request thinking that it was probably a member of the media trying to get an interview. He had declined 11 such requests prior to this one. He was starting to get past his thoughts and past his grief when he got a second and then a third request from the same man. He declined both requests, but started to wonder if maybe this guy was really an officer in a law enforcement agency. Over the next two weeks he got six more requests from the man, the last one came with an assurance that he was not a member of the media and that he would not take more than 15 minutes of Steven's time. He also began to wonder whether this might be an overeager supporter wanting to thank him. He had gotten thousands of letters thanking him and it was possible that this guy was one of the people that had sent them. Steven finally decided to grant the man a visit. If he was indeed a law enforcement officer, he might be looking for some help in a murder case. Steven did not know how he might be able to help anyone to solve a murder, but he was willing to talk to the man.

On the day of the meeting, Steven was put in an interview room like the one he used when he met with Drew. There was a single round table with four chairs around it and a water pitcher in the middle. There were four cameras in the room and there was a speaker on one of the walls through which an officer could speak to Steven. He was in the room for five minutes before they brought the man in. He looked to be in his early 50s and like he kept in decent shape. He was wearing an off-the-rack sports coat and slacks, basically the standard uniform for plain-clothes policemen. He had thinning blond hair and bright blue eyes.

He walked over to where Steven was standing and immediately went to shake his hand, "Mr. Loomis, what a pleasure it is to finally meet you!"

Steven motioned to a chair, "It's nice to meet you, officer Galloway?"

The man smiled, "Yes, Galloway, Daniel Galloway. I am a detective with the Georgia Bureau of Investigation."

Steven sat down and motioned for him to sit down as well, "What can I help you with, detective?"

Steven fully expected that the man was going to pull out a big file and tell Steven he was working on solving a murder case or cases.

Instead, the man sat down and began to explain to Steven why he had wanted to see him, "Mr. Loomis, forgive my persistence in wanting to see you, but I had to thank you personally for what you have done for me."

Steven held his hand up before the man could go on, "Listen, detective, I appreciate what you are saying and what you are trying to do, but I did not do anything to be thanked for, I didn't do this to be anybody's hero or savior..."

Galloway listened, but smiled and shook his head before Steven could finish his thought, "No, I don't think you understand my situation. You see, for years, decades actually, I have suffered from deep depressions. They have plagued me for my whole life. I became a police officer because I thought perhaps it would help me figure out why I was always depressed. I know, I know, it doesn't make much sense, but when you're desperate you will try anything. Then your case came along and presented me with the answer I had been looking for all that time. When you spend your life trying to understand something and the answer never comes and all of a sudden it presents itself to you, trust me, Mr. Loomis, you want to thank the man responsible for making it happen."

Steven was not clear on what the man was saying, but a dark thought began to form in the back of his mind, "I am not quite sure what it is you are saying, detective Galloway, but whatever it is, you don't have to thank me for anything."

Galloway's smile widened and his countenance changed, he seemed to be truly enjoying the conversation, "On the contrary, Mr. Loomis, I definitely have to thank you. My family is Catholic and I went to Catholic schools through high school. So as you can imagine, everything happens because Jesus or God or some saint wanted it to happen. I realized early on in my life that I enjoyed the things I was doing, even though I knew how repulsive people thought my actions might be. All along I felt I was just a mistake, that my brain simply did not work properly and it made me depressed."

Steven listened to the man with a growing sense of horror. He began to realize the feeling he had, the visceral reaction that welled up in him before Galloway even began to speak, was very much like the feeling he had gotten when he had spoken to Nigel Barlow. As he listened to the man, he could see the things he had probably done, the lives he had probably destroyed. He thought about the damage he had probably been able to cause as a law enforcement officer, the way he probably manipulated the investigations of his murders to make sure they were never solved. He was trying to decide what to do as the man kept speaking. It was obvious he was not going to be able to do anything from inside prison, but he wanted to better understand how these individuals operated.

He remained completely calm as he asked a question of his own, "Don't you feel guilty? Can't you see the damage you cause? You're a police officer for God's sake, how can you not feel anything?"

Galloway smiled wider and nodded, "That's what you'd think, right? That investigating murders would allow me to see the aftermath and that it would make me feel like crap, but that just wasn't the case. The only thing I felt was depression because my projects made me feel so good, so incredibly alive. I had always thought to myself 'how can something that feels so natural and like it was something I was born to do be so bad, so wrong?' I had lived under the belief that I was a deficient human, a genetic mistake. When your case came along, I looked into the research immediately and I finally had my answer."

Steven was completely dumbfounded, he had never imagined he would run into another Homo predator, especially here. Now that he thought about it, however, it was not so farfetched. Everyone knew where he was and could reach out to him any time they wanted to.

Still, he wanted to understand as much as he could while he had the opportunity, "Haven't you considered the possibility that you are in fact just a human psychopath? That there's nothing different about you or what you do? That you're like Bundy or Dahmer or any one of thousands of psychos out there?"

Galloway's expression lost its lightness and the smile disappeared completely, and for just a split second Steven could see the danger that lurked just under the surface. As quickly as the expression changed, it changed back almost immediately.

The smile was back on his face, "Oh, believe me, Mr. Loomis, I absolutely thought exactly that. In fact, I was convinced I was exactly what you just said, just another psychopath. That's why the research you did and the science you found were so incredible for me. The physical differences, the absolute and complete predatory instinct from childhood, the lack of any sort of childhood or psychological trauma, the overwhelming feeling that you are meant to do precisely what you are doing, all of it finally showed me what I am. So you see why saying thank you was so important to me."

Steven was not sure how to proceed, but he was absolutely certain of what he wanted Galloway to understand, "Well, detective, I just want to get back to my family and my life. This wasn't something I set out to do nor is it something I plan on doing again. I have nothing else to say to you."

Galloway shook his head, "Of course, I can imagine how difficult it's been for you and your family. I won't take up any more of your time. I just need to say one more thing. When I was planning on having this conversation, I wondered whether after our conversation you might decide to reach out to someone in the GBI or some other law enforcement agency. It was a possibility, of course, but then I realized something. If you make any such call, you and your family will once again be the center of attention for the media. And you can imagine what some may think, maybe something along the lines of 'this guy really *is* off his rocker and is seeing monsters everywhere.' See what I'm getting at? So when you say you just want to get back to your family and your life, it is music to my ears."

Steven was beginning to form thoughts he did not want to have and to feel like he needed to end this, he needed to get out of the room. He stood up without saying anything, walked over to the door and pressed the button to call the guard.

Galloway also stood, but did not follow him, "I am sorry if I have upset you, but I think you can understand that it was a watershed moment for me. Thank you for seeing me and good luck with everything."

Steven did not react at all to what he was saying. He simply stood by the door and waited for the guard to get there. After about 30 seconds the guard came and opened the door. Steven walked out immediately. He went straight back to his room and closed the door. He didn't have a roommate yet, so it was just him. He wasn't sure about what he was planning on doing about Galloway. What could he do? Galloway was right, he couldn't say anything if he wanted to get back to a normal life. He would sound like he was seeing these things around every corner, like everyone he came across was something other than human to him. It was an impossible situation. He sat on his bed and put his head in his hands trying to figure out what to do. There simply wasn't anything he could do, nothing. He became angry because he felt powerless, but he became even more upset with himself because this was precisely the type of thing that he knew would happen if he thought about this anymore. He had to make peace with the fact that he just couldn't do anything about Galloway, or about anyone else for that matter. He knew he couldn't do anything about it, but he needed to clear his chest, he needed to tell somebody. He thought about telling Beth, but almost immediately discounted the idea. He knew that if he told her she would worry and might start to think about the whole thing herself. He just couldn't do it. He decided to write Art Goodman to tell him about it. He actually felt better after writing the old man. The General wrote him back and told him to let it go, to concentrate on his family, on getting back to them. It was good advice and it helped Steven to focus. He began to sleep well again and he got into his routine in earnest over the next four weeks. His family visited him, Goodman wrote him and he participated in the book club, it all helped him pass the time.

He kept himself busy with his job at the gym, working out with Brandon Harris and writing in his journal. He called his family every day. Sometimes they were able to speak for a little while, sometimes they could just say good night and send him a kiss.

After he had served just over six months, Steven finally got a roommate. He had wondered why it was that he had not been assigned a roommate until now, he eventually realized that the administration was being extremely careful with whoever they picked to be his roommate. They finally found the right combination. He was a 33-year-old doctoral student who had been convicted of manufacturing ecstasy. He had been found with more than $2 million dollars worth of the drug. He had kept an intensely low profile and had done all of his dealing through his old roommate, a twitchy business major who had branded his particular recipe for ecstasy. He was five seven or five eight and thin as a rail with a mop of unruly reddish hair. He also had a measured IQ of over 170, something that made him as different as could be, not only from the people in Dillon, but most of the population on earth.

The day he had been assigned, he simply walked in with his duffle bag, walked over to Steven and put his hand out as he introduced himself, "Milo Baskin. I believe you are my roommate, Steven, right?"

Steven stood up and shook his hand, "That's right. Nice to meet you, Milo."

Milo walked over to his bed and put his bag on top of it. He dug into the bag and pulled out a rolled up chessboard and a plastic baggie containing all the pieces, "They had to put these through the x-ray. Do you play?"

Steven nodded, "Yes, yes, I do."

Milo smiled a crooked smile, "Do you really play or do you just push the pieces around?"

Steven sat down on his own bed, "I have a rating of 1650. But I have not played in some time."

Milo's smile broadened, "1650, huh? Well, I can always give you the queen to make things interesting."

Steven liked the kid. He was confident, but not loud, which in Steven's book made him better than most people. Steven took him to the main dining hall for dinner. He introduced him to Carlos Molina and Brandon Harris, the only two people he actually spent any time with. Carlos Molina was actually a big chess fan and immediately engaged Milo when he learned of his chess skills. Still, every once in a while, in the evenings, once the lights went out, he thought about Galloway, about what he had probably done over the course of his life. He thought about all the others that were out there, and once again he began feeling powerless, angry.

One evening, Milo could sense he was still awake long after lights out, "Still awake?"

Steven answered him, "Yeah, I can't get to sleep."

Milo let him know he knew it wasn't the first time, "Happens a lot. I hear you awake most nights."

Steven turned to face him, "I'm sorry, I don't mean to keep you awake."

Milo chuckled, "Don't sweat it, man, I never get more than three or four hours of sleep a night."

Steven was surprised, "Really. Why is that? I am up a lot, but not that late."

Milo, his head resting on his hands and looking up at the ceiling, shrugged and responded, "I can't shut my brain down. I am usually working on three or four problems at any one time and I can't stop thinking about them, so I just lie here thinking."

Steven was curious, "What kind of problems? Family stuff?"

Milo chuckled again, "No, man, nothing like that. I'm writing some stuff on the Higgs boson, the God particle, and on chaos theory, bounded harmonic functions, finite math, stuff like that."

Now it was Steven's turn to smile, "Well, that's nothing like what keeps me awake."

For the first and only time, Milo let him know he knew exactly who Steven was and why he was in prison, "I know. I can't imagine the types of things you see at night, man. I'm sorry about your daughter. It had to be hard, doing what you did and then claiming what you claimed. I've read most of the research, man, especially the stuff on genetics, and let me tell you, it gave me the freaking chills. It stands to reason, you know, scientifically speaking, that evolution has produced something different from humans, the next evolutionary step. It's fascinating shit, but scary as hell. The guy, Richt or Richie or whatever his name was, was definitely something different."

Steven was quiet for a bit, he didn't know how to respond to his roommate, "Thank you. Yeah, it was hard, actually it still is hard. I guess that's why I can't sleep, but to be honest, I am trying to forget all of it."

Milo knew he didn't want to talk about it and so he let it go, "Well, if you ever feel like just shooting the shit, you know, about whatever, just start talking. I'm usually awake."

Steven smiled, "Thanks, Milo, I might take you up on that. Some of the stuff you were talking about seems fascinating."

Milo smiled in the dark, "Yeah, it is, that's the problem, it's too fascinating."

Both of the men fell quiet and Steven was finally able to get to sleep 45 minutes later.

He had enjoyed the Fourth of July with his family, including his in-laws, and was looking forward to Thanksgiving, but none of it would be the same until he was able to enjoy it as a free man. He was able to sign up for the dog-training program. His dog's name was Boone, a German Shepherd. His time was actually going by faster now. His routine and his family had helped to make the time go by much easier. In the evenings, after dinner and before his workout, he would sit in the yard and have quiet little conversations with Boone. With the credits for participating in the dog-training program, his time now really did go by a lot faster. On his first year anniversary, Steven enjoyed a small celebration with some of the guys he spent time with, Milo, the Judge and Carlos, other guys he worked out with and others who were a part of the reading program. Beth had brought homemade cupcakes, and once the administration ran them through the x-ray and past the drug-sniffing dogs, the men had dived in eating three each. Even now, with only four months to go on his sentence, Steven thought about Galloway at least three times a week. Most of the time it was fleeting thoughts, but at least once a week he caught himself wondering about the man. He thought about finding out where he came from and tracking him down, about telling the authorities about their conversation and asking them to investigate the man. None of it made much sense, however, none of it was going to bring him any closure or satisfaction, so he tried to put any thoughts about Galloway out of his mind. As he drew closer to his release date, Steven was thinking more and more often about going back to work. He had started to ask the General to bring him up to speed on some of the deals the company had going. The old man was only too happy to send Steven information on everything going on. Nobody else needed to know about any of it, as long as Art Goodman and Steven were on the same page. It was when he had six weeks to go on his sentence that Steven finally told him that he was planning to come back to work at GIC. The old man had taken the news like he had just found out he was going to be a father. Without Steven knowing, he went about redecorating his office completely. He wanted to make it a brand-new space for Steven. Beth had been glad that he had made the decision to go back to work. It meant another milestone, another step toward going back to their normal life.

26.

Steven finished his time in custody with no problems at all. When he was finally released, he was gratified to see only three cameras there and no one pushing to get a statement.

On his way out, every guard he came across either shook his hand or gave him a fist bump, including Zach Driver, "I'll see you around, Loomis. I never told you this and if you repeat it I'll deny it. I'm glad you took that piece of shit out."

Steven simply smiled and shook his hand. He was so happy to be out that he actually answered one of the questions thrown at him by the reporters there asking him how it felt to get out.

Steven paused and responded, "It feels great. I'm ready to go back to a normal life."

And that was it, the only statement he made to any media after the interview with Felix Garcia. Beth was outside the gates to receive him along with his children, Max Zeidler and Drew Willis. He had spoken with the General the night before and they had agreed to meet at the office in two days, on the Monday following his release. Steven went directly to Beth and gave her a long overdue and romantic hug and kiss. He then hugged his children, lifting both of them off the ground.

Drew also welcomed him with a hug, "Glad you're out, brother. Ray wanted to be here, but he is out of town."

Steven hugged him back, "I know, he called. I'm glad to be out. You have no idea how incredibly glad I am to be out. I can't believe it's over, man. I'm finally done with all of this."

He then went to Max, who also hugged him but had something very different to say, "Did these guys toughen you up or what? I've heard some scary stories about the Hedge Fund mafia."

Steven chuckled, "Yeah, they tried to recruit me, but I fought my way out of it."

The group walked over to the Suburban that had been waiting for them. Steven recognized it as a company car and saw that Lou, his bodyguard, was driving. He smiled and nodded when Steven caught his eye. The kid had been rock solid throughout everything. Art Goodman had sent the car to pick up Beth and the kids and then Steven.

Once in the car, Beth explained to Steven what was waiting for him at home, "The General is at the house, along with a few people from your office, my parents and that reporter, Felix Garcia."

Steven looked at her surprised, "A reporter? Why would you invite a reporter?"

Beth let him know, "I really liked the way he wrote that last piece on you. He was fair and he kept his word about trying to maintain our privacy. And you don't know this, but he helped me when I tried to get the reporters out in front of the house moved back."

Steven looked confused as she went on, "Oh, I didn't want to tell you and worry you. They were just getting in the way of the kids and me going to school and I called the paper where Felix works to ask them to tell their reporters to move back, along with every other paper and station I could think of. He called me back and told me they didn't have any reporters out in front of our house. There were a couple of freelancers claiming to be from the paper, though. Finally, he called me back and told me not to worry about them anymore. The next day there were a few less than the day before, and the ones that were there looked like they were there because they had to be, not because they thought they were going to actually get a story. Felix later told me he had just told the people in the group out in front of our house that he had another exclusive interview lined up with you. That's all it took. And don't give me that look. He knows tonight will be no work, no story, nothing but celebration."

Steven looked at his wife with renewed confidence. She was more and more like the old Beth, ready to take on anyone that messed with her family. During his time in prison, Steven and Beth had spent many visits talking about Tracy, about how much they missed her. Some had gone better than others and Steven had worried about her a couple of times. She had seemed fragile and depressed now and again. But now, she seemed much more stable, stronger, getting back to the old Beth.

She read the look on his face and smiled, "I'm okay. There are good days and bad ones, but I think that's probably true for you too. I thought we could go to her grave tomorrow. You haven't been since we buried her."

He gave her a slight, sad smile and nodded his head without saying anything. The truth was he was tired and what he wanted most of all was to sleep in his own bed, enjoy his family and his freedom. He understood why his wife had done what she did. There were a lot of people that cared a lot about him and who had been there for the family throughout this ordeal. When they got home, he was surprised to find as many reporters as there were waiting outside. Most had mobile sets and were actually broadcasting as they pulled up, reporting on his release and his arrival home. Some tried to ask questions, but most already knew the drill and just reported what was going on. The family,

Max and Drew went directly from the car to the front door without pausing. Once inside, there was a huge 'Welcome Home!' banner and everyone was smiling and engaged in conversation. When they came in, everyone turned and yelled. Some yelled, "Welcome home!" Others clapped, others cried.

Art Goodman went directly to him, brought him in for a huge hug and as he spoke in his ear, his voice cracked, "Welcome home, kid, it's damn good to see you."

Steven returned the hug and his sentiment, "It's good to be home, sir."

In the time he had spent in custody, Steven had come to understand very clearly that Art Goodman, retired general, Marine Corps, looked upon him as much more than just an employee. He came to understand that the General had always thought of him as the son he never had. He remembered how tough he had been on him when he started, how he had taken him under his wing and showed him how the business world worked, shared his experience with him. Over the years, he had assigned the hardest deals to Steven and had guided him through their completion, all the while pressing him for his best and immediately calling him out when he could not deliver it. The old man had been grooming him, preparing him for the disappointments and the politics that were a part of the business world and which Steven had never had to encounter in his time in the service. It had taken all of this, all of these circumstances and the time away, for Steven to see what he now and had always meant to Art Goodman. Steven walked into the living room and greeted his in-laws first. He also saw Victor Demers and Travis Pruitt, who lifted their glasses by way of a greeting. He smiled and nodded in their direction. He assumed that they had asked the General to be here and he could understand why they had done it. It had been their work breaking into the warehouse where Tracy was found that had caused Riche's downfall.

He also saw and went directly to Stephanie Dillon, his executive assistant, "Steph, it is so good to see you."

She gave him a big hug and had tears in her eyes, "I am so happy to see you are okay. I worried about you."

Steven smiled. He knew how much she probably did worry and he knew she had done everything in her power to keep his office running even when he was not there, answering questions herself or referring people to others who could answer their questions. She was not only his administrative assistant, she was the head of all the admins in the company, and she knew about almost every single deal going on in the company. The General had never had and still didn't have an official assistant, but when he needed something he knew who to go to. Steven was gratified to see she was still herself and that she was going to do her best to help him get back to where his life had been.

She smiled, "Are you ready for Monday? You know that Joe Stillman has been absolutely itching for you to get back. He wants to fill you in on the Kenya deal and he wants to ask you to look at something he is doing for a Swiss intelligence agency."

Steven raised his eyebrows, "Swiss? Wow, I have been gone for a while. He is handling his own deals now?"

Stephanie smiled a knowing smile, "I told you the kid was ready. Although he is still smart enough to have Art and Ben Anderson in logistics look over his deals. He still says you are better than both at handling the business and logistical ends combined."

Steven chuckled, "I guess you are right, he was ready to move on."

Stephanie put her glass down on the table, "Well, I wanted to welcome you and give you a hug and now I've done both so I am on my way. This should be time with your family, you don't need all the other people here."

He hugged her and appreciated that she had gone back to her role of protecting him. She went over to Demers and Pruitt and whispered something to them. They both drained their glass, waved at him and bid their goodbyes. Steven was absolutely blown away and delighted to see Stephanie walk over to Art Goodman, say something in his ear and give him a kiss on the corner of his mouth, a kiss that was definitely not a 'just friends' kiss. She glanced back and smiled at Steven to confirm what he thought he'd seen.

Felix Garcia was the next to come up to him. "Steven, thank you for the invite. I feel a bit out of place, but I appreciate it."

Steven smiled and shook his hand, "Don't thank me. It was my wife who invited you. She told me what you did to help her out and I appreciate it, so I am also glad to have you here."

Felix smiled, "It was actually entertaining telling everyone I had another exclusive. They are all assholes for the most part and they were incredibly frustrated and pissed. I took a chance, I thought you might be upset that I lied about something like that, but I figured under the circumstances you would probably be okay with it."

Steven smiled and raised his glass, "To upsetting the assholes. You figured right. I would be more than okay with anything that made my family's time easier."

Felix raised his glass and toasted with Steven. He finished his drink and put down the glass, "I am going to get going. Congratulations, Steven, I am really glad you are back home."

Steven shook his hand and said goodbye. Beth's parents came over to him. They had not gotten a chance to speak after their initial greeting.

Lucy was first to speak. As usual, she reached for his hand when she was going to say something important, "Steven, I am so happy you are back. Beth and the kids have been doing great, but it's not the same without you, I can tell. She would get these long-lost looks, like she was somewhere else, somewhere with you."

Steven held her hand, "I am so happy to be back, Lucy. I missed you all so much and I also missed my life."

His father in-law had always been a role model for Steven. The man was and had always been a rock for his family and now for his daughter's family as well. Tom was a man who would not say a single word without thought and without knowing exactly why he was saying it.

Now it was he who spoke to his son-in-law as he put a hand on his shoulder, "Beth is better, Steven, but she still hurts. She still blames herself sometimes. I know she doesn't do it in public anymore and I know she never says so, but I know she still blames herself sometimes. I am telling you that because I think it's something you will need to let her work out for herself. She knows how much you love her and she knows you will try to convince her it was not her fault, just like we have, but in the end it will come down to her. Letting her work it out will be harder than trying to help her, trust me, I know."

Steven looked at his father-in-law and understood what the man was saying. He saw in his eyes that he had himself been through this process and didn't want to see him going through it himself. Steven looked at him and understood that this was for him only and that Lucy did not necessarily agree with her husband. He was right, of course. It would be harder to hold himself back, to let Beth work some things out for herself. She had put up a strong front and seemed fine during the trial because she knew her husband needed her and would worry if she showed she was still fragile. Once he went to prison, she was able to let it all out and go about the business of really being fine and recovering. Lucy didn't want to get into an argument with Tom. It became clear that she and Tom had had many arguments about this.

She pulled him close and gave him a kiss, "We're going to go back to the hotel, now that you are home."

Steven didn't like the sound of that, "What? No way, you guys are staying here, with us. Come on, you are my family too."

Tom took Steven's hand to say goodbye, "We know that, but this time is for you and for your wife and for your children and to heal. Besides, we don't often get to stay in a presidential suite at The Palace."

Tom looked over in the direction of the General by way of an explanation.

Steven looked over and the old man raised a glass. Steven smiled and shook his head, "Well, then, you have to come for breakfast tomorrow morning. I won't take no for an answer."

Lucy smiled, "Why don't we talk in the morning and decide then?"

Steven was content to leave it at that. He said goodbye to his in-laws, who then went to say goodbye to the rest of the family. He went over to their last guest, Art Goodman.

He smiled, "I should have known you'd set my in-laws up somewhere."

The General nodded, "Absolutely. Those people are solid gold. They have been a steadying influence on your family while you've been gone, Steven, especially your father-in-law. He has been a great influence on Christopher. I know how young he is, but he has questions, and Tom has been there every step of the way. I wish he was still working. I'd have him on board so fast it would make his head spin. Lucy is also wonderful. You are a lucky man in many ways."

Steven knew he was right, of course. He didn't know and didn't want to imagine what would have happened if he did not have his in-laws, "I know, trust me, I know. I am looking forward to coming back to the office on Monday. I want to get back into the swing of things and to get my life back."

Goodman smiled, "Don't worry, you are going to have more than enough to sink your teeth into when you get back. I hope you like your new office."

Steven looked stunned, "What do you mean, my new office?!"

The General laughed, "Don't worry. I didn't put up curtains or gold leaf. I think you will like it. You needed a new space, Steven. You know you did. Your old office was packed to the ceiling with files and old cabinets."

Steven looked at him a bit guiltily, "Alright, alright, I know. You know how it is, you get into your work and you just forget about stuff like that."

The old man nodded, "I know, if it hadn't been for Steph, that office would have spilled over a long time ago. She's missed you, you know."

Steven nodded, "I know. I don't know what I would have done without all the help my family and I have gotten. I don't even know where to begin thanking people. And, by the way, I saw how Stephanie kissed you, Art, it was definitely not a 'friend' kiss."

Goodman smiled and for the first time in their entrie relationship, blushed, "Ahh...well, you know I...I'm..."

Steven let the old man off the hook, "I think it's amazing, Art. You two are people who absolutely fit together and deserve each other, who deserve to be happy again. I can't tell you how happy I am. I hope things progress well for you."

Goodman smiled sheepishly, "Ahh, well, actually it has developed into something more. We were waiting for you to get back to announce it. We're getting married."

Steven's eyes flew wide open and a huge smile spread across his face and teared up for the first time since coming home.

Before he could say anything, Goodman held up his hand and shushed him, "Please don't make a big deal. Please. Nobody knows but you. We want to announce it together, so please, hush up."

Steven looked around, smiling at the empty room, but still immediately closed his mouth and held up his hands to show that he understood.

Now the old man switched gears and spoke firmly, no more cuddling, "You keep saying how much you appreciate the people that helped you. Well, you know how you thank people, the people that really love you? By getting back to your life, by showing you are worthy of all the help and love that people showed you. Why do you think people helped you, Steven? Why do you think you had so much support? Because you are a good man, a good father and husband, and a good boss. People helped because they believe in you and in what you stand for, and you can't thank them if you don't show them you deserve their help."

Art Goodman said this with authority. Steven knew he was an orphan and that he had made it through the ranks of the marines during a time of war and turmoil with a lot of help from a lot of important people and from his late wife. The General had never remarried. The only time he had ever spoken to Steven about it, he told him he believed people should be married once and once only, that once you found someone to share your life with, you stuck with them, you were loving and a friend, and above everything loyal to the woman you married. They had a stillborn baby boy early on in their marriage and never tried again. When his wife had become ill, he had spent three years next to her fighting the cancer that was eating her alive with every ounce of his being. He had spent the last year of her life fighting death and pain the way old warriors defied what they believed to be unjust gods. He had buried her six years ago and had spent six months away from the office. No one saw him at all. No one. The speculation in the business was that the old man had hung it up, that he was finished. Competitors started to speculate how to best break GIC and how to poach the best executives. Steven had gotten two offers during that time. And all the while, the old man stayed away. Until one evening when Steven was at the office until late and noticed the old man's light was on. He went to his office and found him behind his desk looking at a file. He was floored, he hadn't spoken to the man in six months and here he was.

Before Steven could say anything, the old man looked up at him, "Hey, are you in on this Belgium thing? Someone needs to get this shit in order right quick. And who is talking to those buzzards on the appropriations committee? I swear that relic from Utah, what's his name? Pollard, that's it! That guy has to look at everything 20 times over and he still can't make a decision."

Steven had not known how to answer. All he could manage was, "I didn't know you were back. Are you okay?"

The old man had looked at him like he was feeble, "Am I okay? Of course I am. Why would you ask that?"

Steven had walked into his office, "Well, for starters, nobody has seen or spoken with you for six months."

The General smiled and motioned for Steven to sit down. He did so and Goodman explained things to him, "There is a time for grief, Steven, and a time to heal, and I needed both. My company has more than enough senior executives and plenty of up-and-comers like yourself who can keep it running successfully, so why would I worry about the company?"

When he said it like that, it seemed completely reasonable. Still, Steven was concerned with what was going on with their competition, with the things he'd heard, "General, I don't know if you know or not, but there are sharks circling GIC. I've had two offers since you left."

The General looked at him somewhat amused, "You really don't think I know? You really don't think I know what they are doing or trying to do and who they are trying to poach? You've only gotten two offers because people think they can get you cheaper once I announce I am stepping down. You want to know how orcas kill great white sharks, Steven? They simply turn them over on their backs and then eat them. No dramatic battle, no fight to the death. One predator is simply smarter than the other and knows exactly how to kill its opponent. Somehow the orca knows that when it turns the shark over on its back, serotonin floods its brain and puts it in a trance. Nobody knows how the orca knows that, but it does, and once it has the shark turned over it's done. Well, I am luring the sharks in, and when I am ready, I am going to turn them over and I am going to eat them one by one."

Steven had learned an incredible lesson about the man in that moment. He had grieved and he had healed. He had known that predators would come out and circle his company and he had known exactly what he would do when that happened. Who knew how long he had grieved and how long he had planned and schemed behind the scenes, but what was clear was that the man played at a level far beyond his competitors' capabilities. At a level that Steven himself hoped to be able to play at someday. The old man kept talking to him while looking at the file in front of him, "The orcas have to be careful, though. If they kill a shark too quickly, the smell of the death of one of their own drives the other sharks completely away, they will stop a feeding frenzy to get away. So, if the orcas want to feed on more than one shark or they want to teach a young one what or how to kill..."

When he said this last part he raised his eyes and looked straight at Steven, "...they have to keep multiple sharks on their backs."

Steven had gotten the message loud and clear. He now knew why this company was the global leader and how its chief executive had gotten it there. A combination of brutal tactical awareness, strategic skills that rivaled that of a chess master and pure business intelligence applied at just the right moment to all the right places.

He simply nodded and as he turned to walk out of the office, "I understand, sir. It's good to have you back."

As he was leaving, Steven had noticed the painting of a killer whale that hung above the far wall of the old man's office. Steven had never forgotten that day or the lesson that was imparted. Shortly after that GIC had taken deals out from under three of their largest competitors. Some had gotten hung up in the wheels of government and had to let go until GIC came in and saved the day, others had lost because of intelligence leaks that had sunk their proposals. Steven never asked and the old man never offered, but he knew he had been behind all of it. On the night of their celebration dinner the man had ordered a shark steak sandwich and had thrown Steven a quick wink across the long table. Yeah, the old man had been behind all of it and Steven had gone on to be a star pupil. He understood the old man so much better now that he'd had a chance to look at all of their history together. He wasn't telling Steven to deserve what he had been given, the help, the love, the opportunity because he believed Steven would do anything other than that, but because he wanted him to remember that the best way to move on would be to just go back to be the man he had always been.

The message was not lost on Steven. "You're right. I'm not just saying it to appease you either, you know that. It's hard though, because I know how much people did for me, for us."

The General was not going to let it go, "That's right and the best way to thank them is to go back to being exactly who you were, who you have always been."

He was tired. He nodded at what the old man had said. Art Goodman smiled and put a hand on his shoulder and also said good night.

Finally Steven was at home with his wife and his children, who were both in their parents' bedroom watching a movie while the adults chatted and welcomed their father home. Now it was just Steven and Beth. They were both doing some light housekeeping, picking up glasses and napkins and putting them in the kitchen and in the garbage.

Beth looked over at Steven, "Hey, honey, don't do that. I'll take care of it."

He smiled, "That's alright. It feels good doing everyday, normal things, you know. These are the kinds of things I couldn't do inside. I missed it."

Beth smiled at him. He continued picking up, "Besides, the quicker we get this done the quicker we can just spend time together and I am dying for the chance to just sit and watch television with you and split a bottle of wine."

She came over and gave him a hug and kiss, "Well, then, we're going to have to put the kids to bed pretty soon."

Steven nodded, "Why don't I go do that and you finish up here?"

She went to the kitchen and he headed to their bedroom. It was about 8:30, a little early for Bethany, but he knew she would be tired and ready for bed. Chris was already asleep on their bed. He watched his daughter from the door and smiled. She was growing up so fast. He could now see how much she had grown up during his time in custody. He saw with some satisfaction that she had her mother's beautiful hair and strong features. She looked like her mother more and more. He noticed this with some sadness. Tracy had looked like her father, Bethany looked like her mother and Chris was a happy medium. Tracy had had her mother's temperament. She was strong, but very much a lady, a girly girl who cared about everyone around her and who took on the role of caretaker when she played with other boys and girls her age. Bethany was the opposite. She looked like her mother, but she had her father's quiet introspection. She spent a lot of time trying to understand herself and she was incredibly analytical and intelligent. She had grown out of Santa Claus at three years old, when she had solemnly told her father that she knew he was Santa Claus. When Steven had tried to convince her that he was not, that Santa Claus was real, Bethany simply looked at him and asked him four or five questions she had already pondered and figured out the answers to. Things like 'How come Santa Claus did not give toys to every boy or girl?'

When he had told her that he did, she had come back with, 'Then how come there are some kids where I go to school that don't get toys?' Steven had looked over to Beth for help and she had smiled and shrugged her shoulders. Bethany had obviously already had the talk with her mother. She had always been very logical and analytical, just like her father, wanting to know the why for everything. It was the same with the Easter bunny and the tooth fairy, Bethany grew out of them by three as well.

Now she turned to see her father standing by the door looking at her and she smiled at him, "Is everybody gone?"

Steven nodded as he came into the bedroom. She asked, "Even grandma and grandpa?"

Steven nodded, "Yup, even grandma and grandpa."

She sat on the edge of the bed, "Chris didn't even see half of the movie. I swear, he falls asleep like in five minutes all the time."

Her father sat next to her and smiled, "He's younger than you and he is bouncing around when he is awake, so he gets tired."

She smiled back, "He does bounce around all the time. Sometimes he's funny. He makes these noises like he's fighting and falls to the ground."

Steven chuckled. He knew exactly what she was referring to. Now, as was almost always the case, a serious look came over her face and she seemed to age by a decade.

She looked at him and asked, "Are you back home for good, dad?"

He smiled, but the sadness the question caused could not be hidden. He was sad about the fact that his daughter had to deal with questions like that.

He put his arm around her and reassured her, "Yes, honey, I am home for good."

She considered that and smiled, but went back to a stern look almost immediately, "Dad, what was jail like? Brenda Davis says there are murderers in jail and they kill people when they are put in jail. Were there murderers? Did they try to kill you? I told Brenda she was full of sh...boloney. I read all about prison and jail. But I want to know from you."

He smiled at her, "Well, there are a lot of people in jail who are murderers, but they were not in the jail I was in. I met some really nice people when I was in jail and none of them wanted to hurt anyone."

She looked at him thoughtfully, "So the jail you were at was for people who didn't commit violent crimes? What about food, dad? Brenda says the food is really bad and they give the prisoners green ham and nasty juice that tastes like pee. I told her she needs to stop watching crappy movies, but is that true, dad?"

He smiled and brought the conversation gently to a stop, "Actually, Brenda is not too wrong about that. No green ham or nasty juices, but definitely not your mom's cooking. Alright, young lady, time for lights out."

She gave him a token protest, "But it's still early..."

Steven knew she was going to say that, "Okay, then you can read in your room for a little while."

Reading had always been a treat for the girls. Their parents had always positioned reading as something you get to do when you are good, a treat, "Okay. Mom finally let me read the vampire/werewolf series books and I'm on the third one."

He kissed her on the forehead and picked up her brother from the bed. She went into her room and her father took her brother to his room and put him in bed. Steven stuck his head in her room. She was already in bed and with the book open.

He smiled when she looked up from the book, "Good night, honey."

She returned the smile, "Good night, dad."

And so went the first night back at home. Other than having to entertain the people that came to welcome him, his first night home had been exactly what he wanted, just everyday stuff. Dad stuff, husband stuff, just going back to normal life was what he was looking forward to the most. Beth had known he would want to spend some time with Bethany so she stayed in the living room while he put the kids to bed. When he came out, she was already curled up on the couch with the remote control in one hand and a glass of wine in the other. There was a cutting board with cheeses and some apple slices.

It was the best thing Steven had seen in a long time, and he let her know with the smile that spread across his face, "Now we're talking."

He came over to the couch and she poured him a glass of wine. He was hungry and ate almost all of the cheese and the apples while he sipped on his wine. They ordered a pay-per-view movie and just enjoyed each other's company. They talked about menial, everyday things. Beth caught Steven up on what was going on with popular culture. What movies were out that she wanted to see, random interesting news, something other than their case, things like that. Steven had basically tried to keep up with things, but Beth had always been the one to catch him up on things beyond his world and she was doing so again. They had watched about 20 minutes of the movie when Beth started to feel the deep rise and fall of his chest and hear his soft snoring. She smiled and ran a hand through his hair as he slept. She just wanted to be here, now, with her husband and her family and to feel safe. When the movie ended, she gave him a kiss to wake him. The wine he drank made it a bit difficult, but he finally got up and groggily walked from the living room to the bedroom. While he changed and brushed his teeth, Beth cleaned up their glasses and plates. By the time she came into the bedroom, he was fast asleep again. She smiled, changed and got into bed with him. She cuddled up next to him and was deep asleep five minutes later.

They spent the weekend watching movies, playing games and ordering in pizza and Chinese food. On Saturday night, while they were putting a puzzle together, Chris asked him a question that let him know his son was more aware about what happened than he had imagined.

Steven was sifting through the pieces of the puzzle when Chris looked up at him, "Are you going away, daddy? Are you going away to the jail again?"

Steven was so surprised by the question he didn't know how to answer him right away. He took a couple of seconds and reassured his son, "No, buddy, I'm not going away to the jail again. I'm going to be here with you and your sister and your mother. Hey, I think you have a piece I'm looking for."

Christopher smiled wide and raised his hand where he was holding three pieces, "Which one?"

Steven reached out and made like he was going to reach for the puzzle pieces, but instead grabbed his son and tickled him. Bethany laughed and joined in the tickling. It was precisely the thing Steven needed to do with his family, something simple and loving and reassuring.

They did not meet with his in-laws until Sunday morning when they had brunch at The Palace. The one good thing about New York was that no matter how prominent you were, how famous, people seldom did anything more than look with casual curiosity, and that was the case with the Loomis family. Paparazzi, photographers and reporters were a dime a dozen in this town, so when they found themselves followed by a couple of persistent reporters nobody paid much attention. Lou was more than capable of moving any reporters out of the way and the covert security team would immediately engage. It was not as large as it had been when the trial was going on, but both Steven and the General thought it would be a good idea to have a couple of people as covert security. They had brunch at the hotel and then went up to his in-laws' suite, which was ridiculously large, as was to be expected. The kids ordered pay-per-view movies while the adults chatted. Steven shared with them how much he was looking forward to going back to work and getting back into the swing of things. Beth was rather quiet, but visibly happy, content.

Later that evening, while the kids stayed with their grandparents, Beth and Steven went to Tracy's gravesite. Beth was concerned about how it might affect Steven. Once there, she stood back and let her husband share some time with their daughter. Steven shed some tears. He was standing next to her gravestone with one hand on it. He got down and rubbed the stone and spoke quietly to his daughter, sharing his thoughts and memories of them together, but most of all just telling her how much he missed her. They were there for just under an hour, and on their way back to the hotel Steven let Beth know he was fine. She looked in his eyes and could tell that he meant it. He was fine. They picked up the kids and went home. That night, Steven sat down at the computer for the first time since his release. The first thing he did was a search on the topic of human evolution and forensic psychiatry. He was absolutely blown away by the number of articles and posts that made reference to his case. There were now literally millions of posts, which included articles, white papers by experts, columnists giving their opinion and blog entries that numbered in the millions. He was gratified to see that for the most part people agreed with his position, not only as it related to Donald Riche but as it related to the science of Homo predators in general. He noticed there were now other experts that had been researching the matter for years and were now publishing their work and there were experts in Europe that were also publishing their work in the States. He was surprised by the scope and reach of the research that had been conducted, particularly in Germany, where they had already established the existence of these predators and were in the process of passing legislation to deal with them. He was also deeply concerned by the fact that there were a few groups that claimed to be Homo sapiens predator groups and who claimed they deserved the same protections as any other protected class in the United States. African Americans, Hispanics, gay and lesbian people were all protected classes under the U.S. constitution because who they were was not their choice but simply what they were from birth. It was something that had taken gay and lesbian groups decades to get the courts to understand. He didn't know the legal implications, but there were definitely a lot more considerations than he had ever imagined. He could now also see there were also social and financial considerations and consequences that would need to be dealt with as these purported Homo predator groups popped up and flourished. After about two hours, just before he turned the computer off, he did something he had promised himself he would not do. He looked up Daniel Galloway. He found several entries with his information, his school records, Facebook page, but the entry that caught his attention most, actually the one that almost floored him, was the one that described him as a consultant and profiler for the Atlanta police department in addition to being an officer in the GBI. He didn't read the entire post, but it was clear that Officer Galloway was very active with criminal profiling with the police department. This was exactly the reason Steven did not want to even look him up. He shut the computer down and went to bed, trying and not succeeding to put Daniel Galloway out of his mind. It took him a full hour of lying in the dark to finally fall asleep and he did it by remembering what was important, his family, going back to work, getting back to a normal life.

The next morning, he went to work and finally got to see his office. He was blown away. The décor was perfect – a minimalist approach with some highlights here and there, but all very efficient and subdued. His mementos were tastefully placed around the office and his diplomas and certificates were also carefully arranged behind his desk. What he liked most was that the wall to his right was basically a family wall. Pictures of him and Beth and the kids were arranged chronologically, which meant Steph had to have done it. There were also three pictures on his desk. One of him and his family, one of Beth and the kids, and one of Tracy. He also noticed that the painting of the killer whale that had hung in the General's office now hung on his wall. He smiled as he looked around. The old man had been right, he liked it very much, and with the added 300 square feet it came with, they were able to put in a filing system for all of his files. Stephanie would have to walk him through the new system, but that was no big deal. He had been keeping up with all of the files that Goodman had shared with him while he was inside, so he was familiar with every significant deal that was being handled through his division. What he noticed last, and almost by accident, was his new title. He did a double take when he saw the placard outside his office. It read Steven Loomis, Executive Vice President, International Operations. He was already reporting directly to the General when he left and he was responsible for the International Operations division, so in essence he was already working at the EVP level, but he had still held the title of Senior Vice President. He wasn't going to pretend or lie, it felt damn good. GIC was now being run by Goodman and three EVPs. The company's structure had always been very straightforward and streamlined, but now the General had simplified it even further, which pleased Steven to no end, as simplicity had always been a part of their selling proposition. The three EVPs handled International Operations, Domestic Operations and Technology. Each division held its own operational functions, tactical development, technology, hardware, etc., which allowed them to keep operations sealed within each division. It guaranteed that if something came up in International, Domestic would not even blink. Once he was settled in and had arranged the files in the order he wanted to deal with them, and of course once he had gotten his coffee, he went to the General's office.

He knocked on the door, even though it was completely open. Stephanie was in with the old man, obviously having a private conversation. Goodman looked up and saw him, "Steven! Come in, come in. So how do you like your new digs?"

He smiled, "I have to say, you were right, it looks great and the extra space is awesome. I can actually see the top of the table in my office now that the files are in file cabinets. Stephanie, thank you so much for the pictures, they look great."

She turned around to face him and smiled at him, "Thank your wife, too, she helped me a lot with putting the office together."

He replied, "Well, it looks like both of you know exactly what my taste is."

She shook her head, "It's not that hard, Steven, you like your furniture to be like you: solid, simple and efficient."

Steven chuckled and nodded.

She left the two men to catch up. Goodman sat down behind his desk, "How does it feel to be back?"

Steven smiled a sideways smile, "It feels great, especially the new title."

The old man smiled wider, "About time. You were already functioning in that capacity, so it just made sense to put the title to it."

Steven came in and sat down in front of the General's desk, "I noticed you also collapsed the other divisions into the core three. It makes a lot of sense to me. I think it's going to make us even more solid while still nimble enough to move when we need to."

The chief executive allowed himself a satisfied grin, "I knew you'd approve. In this market and with everything going on around the world, people are looking for simple, efficient and effective. We have made some important investments to bring top-notch talent into the company. We've brought in a couple of top linguists, we've beefed up the cryptology function across all of the divisions, and we've acquired some of the latest technology for both field operations and information technology. So we are rock solid and prepped to make a serious move."

Steven nodded as he listened and talked to himself under his breath, "Jeez, we are set for bear."

The General then went through the most important and urgent deal in play. It became clear to Steven that in his new role he was going to have to delegate more and lead from the top rather than being so hands-on. The number of deals and the complexity of them were going to make it impossible for him to be as hands-on as he had been, especially given the fact that the other divisions had been collapsed into the remaining three. It also became apparent to Steven that the General was planning not only on keeping their current pace but also on making inroads within the industry and that getting Steven back was the last piece of the puzzle. Steven was a bit taken aback by the intensity so early on, but truth be told, he needed it.

He thanked Goodman for all of it and let him know he was on top of it. Goodman stood, "I expected nothing less. It's good to have you back, son, I mean that."

Steven got up to leave and just before he went through the door the General stopped him, "And Steven, it's time to turn the sharks over..."

Steven smiled a knowing smile, remembering the killer whale painting hanging in his office. His tactical and competitive juices were starting to flow and he was starting to engage completely. It felt great to be back.

Steven absolutely poured himself into his work and his family. When he was not with Beth and the kids, he was at the office or traveling. The novelty of his celebrity wore out very quickly once he started pulling deals out from under their competitors. The biggest change people noticed in him was the absolute ruthlessness with which he went after the deals the company had in the pipeline. He did not do anything illegal, nor did he do anything that could in any way be considered unethical, but in the past Steven had been more humane when it came to taking a client or a deal from a competitor. Calls would be made to smooth things over, certain considerations would be offered. Not anymore. When Steven got the calls he knew would inevitably come, his response was always the same and Godfather-like: it's not personal, it's business. But it was personal and he knew it. Some of the deals GIC landed were deals that other companies had been working on for months, sometimes years. Some of those losses cost some companies entire divisions and hundreds of jobs. Between the General's connections in Washington and internationally and Steven's strategic vision, it was almost an unfair fight. At home he did the same things he had done before, spent time with the kids at bedtime, talked with Beth after dinner while sipping wine, visiting his in-laws, just family stuff. But throughout all, he always kept one eye out for trouble, both at home and at work.

Beth had soon gone back to her routine, taking care of their home, doing things with the kids, picking them up from school and taking them out on walks and to different venues. She was thankful for Lou and for the other people she knew were watching over her and her children. She had not said anything about those covert people, but she did, however, say something to him when he came home early from the office on a Friday afternoon. She wasn't angry at all, she just wanted to let him know she knew they were there.

He had smiled a guilty smile, "Oh, yeah, I'm sorry, I forgot to tell you. I can't be there all the time, hon, and I wanted to make sure there was someone making sure you and the kids were safe. I knew you would never carry a gun, so this was it."

Next, Beth almost floored him when he shared something with him, "I carry a Glock in my purse."

Steven's jaw dropped, he could not believe it, "What?! Since when? Who got it for...never mind, I know who! He probably arranged for someone to show you how to shoot it, too, didn't he?"

Now it was her turn to smile a guilty smile. She didn't say anything, and he came over and gave her a hug.

He was proud of her, but he was also sad that she felt so unsafe that she felt she had to carry a gun.

She smiled a coquettish smile, "I think we're even in the 'sorry, I didn't tell you' category."

He chuckled and gave her a kiss on her forehead.

For the next three months, both of them tried to resume their lives. As time went by, things got better and their routine became more and more normal. The media slowly dissipated and soon it was just the odd paparazzi that turned up now and then. The kids, in particular, fell back into their normal routines. It had taken a long time, but the Loomis family was indeed getting their life back. After about nine months with Steven back home, Beth began to notice that Steven was becoming more distant, more distracted as time went by. It was literally like he was not there, like he had checked out and was completely focused on something other than what was in front of him. It happened more and more often in a variety of settings. At first she chalked it up to thinking about Tracy or work. Steven's new role meant he had more responsibilities and he had to stay on top of everything that was going on, but when it happened on Christopher's fourth birthday she finally had to say something.

He had been apologetic, but he didn't recognize there was any problem, "I'm just a bit distracted, Beth. There's a lot going on at work right now and we are shorthanded. I'll try to be more present. I love you and I love the kids, and I don't want to miss important moments, so believe me, I will pay more attention."

He hugged her and kissed her forehead, basically putting the problem away, but Beth knew better. She knew her husband better than he knew himself and she knew he had never, ever checked out from an outing with his family, not even when the company had emergencies going on. She was positive whatever it was that was pulling his attention away had nothing to do with GIC. She had almost decided to reach out to GIC's CEO to share her concerns but had thought better of it and held back. Had she had a word with the General about it, she would have learned that he was also getting concerned about Steven. The same things that were going on at home were going on at the office. Steven would check out at meetings that he wasn't leading and he would sometimes be late for meetings, which had never happened in all the years Steven had been at GIC. Even when he was actually in the meetings, he was sometimes absent, not there. He would be looking out the window or just at a point on the wall. People had let it go because of what he had been through and because once someone snapped him out of it he seemed to have heard everything that had been said, but Art Goodman noticed it and made note of it, even though he hadn't said anything. Of everyone in his life, Stephanie, his assistant, had noticed it most of all. She would walk in his office in the middle of the day and find him standing by the wall-length window with his hands in his pockets and his eyes focused on something that seemed to be a thousand miles away. At first, like everybody else, she chalked it up to his thinking about Tracy so she never said anything, but eventually it happened often enough and he seemed so far away that she began to get concerned. Had anybody been around Steven on a rainy Tuesday morning the prior February, they would have understood exactly what was on his mind. Always tuned into CNN, CNBC and the BBC, he liked to keep on top of economic and business news, as well as coverage of places of unrest around the world, since unrest, intelligence and security was precisely what his company dealt with. On that day, he was going over all the news wires and international news coverage on the three screens in his office when a domestic headline caught his attention and what drew his attention chilled his spine. It was a headline about three more women missing in Atlanta and the profiler with the Georgia Bureau of Investigation, Daniel Galloway, warned there were probably going to be more victims. Steven was certain there would be more victims, but he could do nothing about it. What could he possibly do? Call in one of thousands of anonymous tips accusing the head profiler for the police of exactly what, he didn't know. But he did know that Galloway was on the loose and in hunt mode and he knew exactly which way the police were moving, so there was no way he was going to get caught. Once again, Steven found himself thinking about him every day and every day realizing there was simply no one to tell. He also remembered this guy had nothing to do with him or his family, and as long as he kept it that way, Steven needed to focus on what was important. And he tried, but as was clear from what the people around him were able to notice, he was failing miserably. About two weeks after reading the headline, he had Carl Gilliam develop a file on the case in Atlanta. Carl had delivered it the next day. There was a blank file folder on his desk filled with 14 pages of all the inside information Carl could get on short notice. It let Steven know there were now 17 women that were considered missing under related circumstances. There might have been more, but these were the ones the police, with Galloway's guidance, could associate to each other. There appeared to be no specific pattern to who had been taken. Some of them were wives and mothers and others were college students and young professional women. There was no ethnic preference to speak of. Some were white, some were black and some were Latinas. The one thing police did recognize, again with Galloway's input, was that none of the women were prostitutes or drug addicts. Carl hadn't asked why Steven wanted the information, although given what Steven and his family had gone through, he could guess.

Finally, Beth decided to confront him, "Steven, I need to talk to you, but I need you to really pay attention and listen to me, really listen."

Steven sat down in the living room next to her, worried about what she was going to say.

Beth looked directly at him, "You and I have been together basically since we were kids. We have gone through everything, and I mean everything, together. The years with you away in God-knew-where, the years where you started at the firm and were trying to learn about life after the navy, the kids, Tracy, everything. I think I know you better than anybody knows you, and I know you know me better than anybody knows me, better than I know myself in many ways. I also think I know you better than you know yourself sometimes. Actually, I think I know you better than you think I know you, and it surprises you when I am right about something."

She wasn't angry and she wasn't losing control or composure nor was she crying, so Steven wondered what it was she was talking about, "For the past three months, you have been somewhere else, Steven. Not all the time, but enough that I know there is something up. You have never been absent during a family event, especially one with the kids. You are there, your eyes are there, and the kids absolutely love that, but right now you are barely there. If you weren't there physically, you wouldn't be there at all."

Steven smiled a sideways, guilty smile and shook his head as if to say 'You got me,' "I'm sorry, honey, I know I've been a little distracted and I'm sorry. The new job is intense and I am constantly trying to deal with three or four things at the same time. I'm so sorry and I will definitely fix it."

Beth smiled at him with a look on her face that said 'Seriously?' "Steven, that's why I asked you to listen to me and I asked you to really listen. That's why I reminded you of everything we have gone through and when we went through it. You know better than that. Did you really think you were going to just say 'Aw shucks, honey, I'm sorry and I'll try to do better' and I was just going to smile lovingly and just say 'Okay'?"

Steven went to say something and she held her hand up to shut him up, "Ah, ah, don't. If you are not ready to talk to me, that's fine, but don't take me for an idiot because it will make me mad."

And that did shut him up. He hung his head, letting Beth know he was ready to really talk, "Alright, then. What is it you want to know?"

Beth got closer to him, "What is it? Is it Tracy? I know better than to think I can just tell you it will be alright and make it all better. I just want you to talk to me, let me in. We have never kept each other out of anything, not even during the worst of the time about Tracy, so it scares me that you are doing it now."

Steven thought about everything she was saying and knew exactly what she was talking about. More than anything else, their marriage had always been one of open communication, of trust and honesty. They had never kept things from each other, even at times when maybe they should have. Now Steven had to consider whether he wanted to adhere to that, to what they had always done, which was share everything that occupied their minds, or whether he was going to protect his wife and family. If he told her about Galloway, about what he had found out and what he was thinking about, there was absolutely no doubt in his mind that she would have a serious reaction and she might even have a breakdown. It wasn't only that Steven was thinking about it, it was that it was still going on, how it reminded him of Riche and what he had done to Tracy, and it was the worry about what he might do about it. It wouldn't be only Steven who was distracted or even absent, the kids might find themselves with two parents that were just not there.

Still, he could not bring himself to lie to her, so he was going to have to be selective in what he shared with her, "I've just been thinking about Tracy. Sometimes there are things that go on that remind me of her even more or there are things I read that remind me about the case and I just start to go down a road that I can't pull out of."

Apparently that was enough of the truth to get Beth to at least think he was really sharing everything with her.

She took his head in her hands and pulled him close, "I know. Seriously, I really do know because it happens to me also. I think about her, about what happened, about how much I miss her. But you know what always brings me back, what always gets me through the worst of it? Bethany and Chris and you. You are my family and we are here, now, trying to move forward, and you know what, doing a damn good job. So I always think about you guys and I remind myself that there will always be moments for Tracy, moments when I cry, when I miss her. It's part of moving forward, of getting our life back."

Steven kept his mouth closed. He was afraid about what he might say, about letting it out without thinking about it. He kept it simple, "I will try to be better about it and I will definitely try to process it better. It's just hard."

She held his head in front of her face and smiled at him, "I know, babe, I know. But at least now I understand. You see the difference? Talking like this actually makes it better because it keeps things clear, the way they have always been."

He pulled her close and gave her a hug that she thought said 'I am so happy we did this' but in fact he was feeling horrible. He was powerless, he was feeling angry and trapped, and he could not talk to the one person on the face of the earth that he could trust with anything. He just held her close to him for a couple of minutes. That was the only exchange Beth and Steven had about the matter until much, much later.

27.

In mid-June, Steven scheduled a business trip to Miami. He was going there to have an initial sit-down with the CEO of a company that provided onboard airline security, a sort of privatized air marshal service. GIC was looking to buy the company and Steven was going to feel out senior management and see how the company's morale was. The meetings were to take place on the Friday of the weekend he was going to be traveling to Florida. Steven could have done the meeting, a walkthrough of the facilities and been back in New York just after dinner on Friday. Instead, he decided to drive back. He told Beth, the General and his assistant, Stephanie, that he needed the time to think, to disconnect for a little while and recharge his batteries. Nobody questioned it. In fact, they thought he might actually benefit from the time away, so they were very supportive. Indeed, when Steven finally made it home on Sunday night, he seemed actually more relaxed, more present and more expressive. Beth thought it might be a bit early to think it was a total change, but she was hopeful. That following morning, Steven came back to work with gusto. He was apparently refreshed from his time away and ready to dive back into the deals they had in the pipeline. He was razor sharp and completely into everything that was up in the air with the deals. Stephanie, like Beth, thought it might be too early to tell, but he certainly seemed to be better after his little respite. The General was out for the first three days of the week, but on Thursday he left word with Stephanie that he wanted to meet with Steven whenever he had a moment. Steven had back-to-back meetings for much of the day and two interviews that he ended the day with. He had not had a chance to meet with Art Goodman during the day, but he headed to the old man's office immediately after the second interview was over. He knocked lightly on the open door.

The General looked up and smiled and waved him in, "Steven! Come, come. I am just going over that business with the Dutch. Damn difficult position, but I think we can win the business."

Steven came in and sat down in the chair in front of the General's desk. He brought him up to date on all of the current deals in process and he told him about the interviews he had just finished. Both had been the next-to-final interviews for the men to be hired into the operations organization. Both were former Delta and both had significant operational experience in Iraq, Afghanistan and the Horn of Africa. The good thing about hiring Deltas and SEALs was that they knew before the men even got to GIC that they had above-average IQs. It was a requirement to join Special Forces and particularly when they were going into the sensitive side of the engagements. The General listened to all of it, nodding and asking questions at the right time. Steven knew this wasn't the reason he had asked him to come by, but he played dumb and just approached the meeting as a work-related thing.

Once he was finished, Goodman smiled and asked him what he had been waiting to ask him, "Great, thank you for the updates. Now, is there something else you need to give me an update on?"

Steven made a show of thinking about it, shook his head and told him, "No, I can't think of anything..."

The General pressed him, "Really? Nothing to update from your trip to Miami?"

Steven reacted immediately. He knew what the old man was getting at but still kept up the façade of this being a meeting related to work and the deals they had going, "Oh, yeah. I didn't want to say anything until I had a chance to talk to some other people about their company and about the work they have done..."

The General was beginning to get aggravated and Steven knew it.

He was an incredibly generous boss and he had been like a father to Steven, but he still was not a man to be trifled with, "Steven, you know that the one thing I absolutely will not do is abide bullshit, and right now I am starting to lose my patience."

He pulled out three printed pages from a folder on his desk and slid them to him on the other side, "You want to give me an update on this?"

It was pages from an online edition of one the newspapers in Atlanta. Steven got the papers and turned them so he could read them. At the top of the first one in big capital letters, the headline read 'Police profiler found murdered in his home. Missing women's remains found in his freezer.' The rest of the papers outlined how the man had been helping in the investigation of the case of the missing women in Atlanta, how body parts from some of the missing women had been found in his freezer, and videos of the women in their final moments had been found on several DVDs and on his computer, and the fact that police were uncovering even more evidence and feared there were many more victims than those that had been identified. The article stated that he had been found with his spinal cord severed through a single entry wound on the back of his neck, and while some of the women's family members were being questioned, police had absolutely no evidence to speak of. They were asking the public for any information not only about the man's murder but about any woman that had gone missing in Atlanta for the past two years. Steven read the article without any reaction and without looking up at him. Once he finished, he let the pages fall on the desk and turned to look out the window. He stared out into the city for several seconds, but finally he turned back to look at Goodman. The look on his face let the old man know everything he needed to know.

It confirmed what he already knew and it told him that Steven would now really talk to him, "What do you want to know?"

The General stood up from behind his desk and came around to sit on the desk in front of Steven, "Why wouldn't you tell me about this? After what you told me when you were inside, didn't you think I would figure it out?"

Steven shook his head, "I suppose I knew you would, I just hoped that maybe it would go by under your radar. I know, it was a stupid thing to think, but I didn't want to involve you or the company or anybody else. I just couldn't let it go, he was hunting those women and he was getting information on the investigation from the police. Who knows how long he had been doing this, how many women, how many families he destroyed over the years."

The General nodded, "I understand why you did it. In fact, I could have told you some time back that you were going to do this. Did you think your out-of-body experiences were going unnoticed?"

Steven was a bit surprised. The old man was not angry or upset about the fact that he had done this at all, he was upset about the fact that Steven hadn't let him in on it ahead of time, "Like I said, I think I knew you would know, but I was hoping. Can you understand that I just could not involve anybody else again? Art, out of everything that happened, I think one of the things that bothered me most, that gave me pause and made me almost regret what I did, was how it affected the people around me, the feeling that I was putting people in a difficult position. I didn't want that again, not again. I finally made the decision to do it and I thought I could do it clean, without anybody close to me finding out or getting hurt."

The General chuckled, "Come on, you thought I wouldn't think anything when they found this guy dead, the victim of what was clearly a professional hit? Did you think I would believe that a family member would know how to sever a man's brain stem and kill him immediately, no sound, no blood, no evidence?"

Steven walked to the window, "No, I told you, I think I knew all along you would know exactly what happened, what I did, but I didn't want to involve you. Now you know, yes, but it's done. He's done and won't hunt anyone ever again, he won't destroy anyone's life again."

The old man stood up from the desk, walked to the door and closed it, and then went over to where Steven was standing in front of the window. They both stood there for some time without speaking a word to each other. It was the General who broke the silence, "To be honest with you, I wondered how long it would take. I thought it would happen much sooner than this."

Steven turned to look at him, "What, going after Galloway?"

The General shook his head, "No, not going after Galloway. Realizing you haven't let go of this, that you have gone past a line you can't come back from."

Steven's eyebrows came together in a frown that gave away his growing unease and the beginning of annoyance, "What exactly do you mean by I've gone past a line that I can't come back from? You're the one who told me to move forward, to think about my family and let go and to focus on what's important. That's why I came back to work."

The General also turned to look at him, wearing his own frown and clinched jaw. He too was getting annoyed, "I meant every word, Steven, don't ever forget that. I never say anything just to make people, especially you, feel better. I don't blow smoke up your ass and you know that, I meant what I said. But I also know you, I've been here to watch you grow, I've gone over your record, your complete record, many times and I know the kind of leader you were, what your men thought of you, what your COs thought of you. I think you know that I know you maybe even better than you know yourself. Steven, once you learned about Riche, once you saw what he did to your daughter and the other children and you understood why he did it, there was no going back. You found the bogeyman and you found out he is real, that he is out there and that you can't 'unknow' something. I know the kind of man you are, I know there is an order in the universe that you answer to and it has nothing to do with God or with religion. I wasn't around then, but I would bet my left nut that it was the same way when you were a kid, you have always known what is right and what is wrong, and you have always believed that good wins. Even now, with everything that happened, you saw it as good winning over evil, as a monster being taken off the face of the earth. When you saw that our system was not going to deal with this monster, with Riche, the way he needed to be dealt with, you did it. You dealt with it."

Steven looked back out the window, "That's right, I dealt with it, but that's it. I did it because I knew, I know, what he was. There's nothing we have developed or established as a society to deal with these things and I needed to at least bring attention to the fact they exist."

The General turned to face him completely, "And you did that. You took care of Riche and you brought attention to the fact that they exist. And Galloway? What was the purpose of that? What was the goal, Steven, because I don't see the connection? I don't see the connection between him and your family and I don't see how he fits into any of this."

Steven was quiet. He knew the General was right, of course. There was nothing to connect Galloway to anything close to Steven, nothing to do with his family's safety. He had done what he did because he knew Galloway would keep hunting. He knew he had probably been hunting for a long time, much longer than the disappearances in Atlanta. He knew this and what Galloway was and that he would probably never be caught, and Steven couldn't let that happen. That was the truth of all of it, he couldn't let that happen. He was removed and absent from his family, from his work, from his life because part of him was thinking about Galloway, and if he was going to be really honest, he was also thinking about others like him. Nigel Barlow had said it when he came to see Steven, that there were others, others that also came to the realization of who they really are, why they do the things they do. Steven thought about them, too, and the lives they were destroying every day, how the system of police and forensic science as it existed was not ready, not in any way ready, to handle these beings. He knew this and he tried to get past all of it, he tried to unring the bell he had rung when he learned what he learned about Riche. The old man was right, it was something he couldn't 'unknow,' something he could not let go of or pretend wasn't there. The fact was that Steven did believe in right over wrong, in good triumphing over evil. He had always believed it, with every fiber of his being. He had stepped in as a kid when someone was picking on somebody else, even if he didn't know the kid being picked on. As a young man he had volunteered for civic organizations he believed were making a difference, and while in the Navy, especially while in the SEALs, he had always conducted himself with the absolute certainty that what he was doing was the right thing, not just politically, but fundamentally, morally. He believed he was successful in what he did because it went along with what was right. It was wrong to kill, unless killing someone meant that hundreds, thousands, maybe millions would be saved. It was wrong to destroy, unless by doing so you ensured the rebirth of a nation, the genesis of a new generation. It was these universal truths, these fundamental laws, that guided him then and were guiding him now.

The General stepped closer to him and spoke to him in a low, intense voice, "Steven, I am not here judging you, I'm just making sure you acknowledge why you are doing what you are doing, because it's going to happen again, son. What you did with Riche was triggered by what happened to your daughter and the other little girls, but once you discovered these things were real, once you discovered something very real is out there hunting humans, you began to function driven by your sense of right and wrong."

Steven listened, but didn't say anything. There were things he was saying that Steven had thought about, but was maybe too afraid or simply unwilling to accept. He had come to the conclusion that he just simply would not be able to put Galloway out of his mind.

Goodman continued, "When you decided to do this with Galloway, you took a huge risk. You had no backup, no operational intelligence. It wasn't the way I know you normally run ops. I know Carl got the info for you and I know you have been monitoring patrol patterns in Atlanta, but it was still sloppy and you know it."

Steven still did not respond. He knew Carl hadn't said anything and that the old man had found out about it on his own, the way he seemed to always find out about it.

Finally he broke his silence. Without looking at him, Steven finally responded, "So now what?"

The General was standing next to him, also looking out the window. He let Steven know he had also been thinking about this, "Well, it depends on you. You know I am more than willing to just move forward. Hell, that's exactly what we've been doing and goddamn if we haven't been kicking some serious ass. But I have a feeling you won't be able to just move on. It was Galloway this time, who is it going to be next? How long until you run across something that catches your attention? You know I won't lose any sleep over Galloway. He was a sick bastard and he would have kept going."

Steven looked at Goodman when he made that comment and Goodman smiled at him, "What, did you think I didn't know about him aside from what you told me? Did you think I wouldn't look into him after you told me about him? Steven, I had confirmed exactly what he was by the time you were released. I didn't know whether you would do anything about it, but I knew you wouldn't be able to just let it go."

Steven wasn't surprised. Now that he was saying it, he had known the old man would find out about it and maybe had even counted on it.

The General continued, "I told you when the Riche thing came up, I had always known there were things out there that were not human, things that really do go bump in the night. We are in the business of bringing order to chaos, bringing security where there is doubt, so this is not something so far removed from what we do that I wouldn't suspect predators are out there and hunting. I had never researched and I had never speculated on what they were, but when this happened and you researched it and found what you found, it made all the sense in the world to me. So to answer your question, I have another question, what do you want to do?"

Steven thought about it. Before he was able to answer, Goodman held up his hand, "Before you answer that question, you have to accept what you are probably likely to do."

Steven crossed his arms and hung his head, the man knew him as well as anyone and he knew what was in Steven's future.

Steven asked him for help, "What do you think? What do you think I should do? I have to tell you that for the first time in all of this, I am not sure about what to do, Art. You're right, I don't think I can let it go. I think about it all the time, I know they are out there, hunting, and I just can't, like you said, 'unknow' that. I thought I could just get past it, get back into my life, engage with work, with my family, and just keep it in the back of my mind, but I just can't."

The General stepped closer to him, "How is Beth dealing with this?"

Steven shifted in his place and looked at the old man, "She noticed something was up. I knew there was no way I could keep it from her. I don't mean what I've been thinking, I mean that I've been absent, distracted. We had a talk and I told her I have just been thinking about Tracy and having a hard time dealing with it, which is not a lie, but you know it's not the whole truth. I hate it. I've shared everything with Beth since we met and I feel like shit that I can't do that now. She let it go, but I know she still thinks something's up."

The General was nodding, "Yeah, it's going to be difficult for you to pull off. She's too sharp, and like you said, she knows you and knows something is going on. I think the only choice you have is to tell her and get through it together or to keep trying to just move past it. If you ask me, I don't think you're going to be able to keep it from her."

Steven nodded, "I know, I don't think so, either. She just knows me too well. I just don't know what to tell her, I don't know how to tell her without worrying her. She's already gone through so much and she's doing so well. I just can't bear the thought of bringing that down, of reminding her about what happened and having her collapse again. I can't do it, I just can't."

Art Goodman thought about what Steven was saying. Finally, he told him what he thought, "What you tell her will depend on what you decide to do. If you decide to just try to bury all of this and move on, you'll tell her one thing. If you decide to do something else then you'll probably have to tell her what's been on your mind and what you've decided to do about it."

Steven put his hands in his pockets and with a puzzled expression asked, "What exactly would 'something else' mean?"

The old man took on a faraway look, "You've seen these things, been in their presence, suffered the most horrible consequences of what they're capable of and you now know what to look for and you know the science. I have wondered about them for a long time and I have always thought that one day, in some way, I would help to find them and bring them down, whatever they might be. It was always a vague idea, something I just thought from time to time, but something I never did anything about. And every time I heard about a mass murder or a serial killer, I was reminded of it, but there's just never been an answer, I've never thought of anything specific to do about it until now. When the Riche thing happened, you couldn't let it go, you had to do something about it and you did. We worked and committed our lives to bringing an end to tyrants and genocidal extremists through our work in the military, but I've always known that not all of them are tyrants or crazy dictators. In the civilian world they do what they do under the radar, without calling attention to who they are or what they do."

Steven was still not clear, "I still don't get it. What is it you're suggesting?"

He looked at him intently, "I'm not suggesting anything, Steven, I am stating it. We both know they are there and we both know they are hunting. You just need to decide if you are going to let it go, and I think we've determined it is going to be next to impossible to pretend they aren't out there and to pretend you are just going to let it go."

Steven was beginning to understand what the old man was saying, and he was surprised, "So you're saying we could do something about this, that we are going to do something ourselves to bring these things down?! What about the police, the FBI, they're the law here, Art! We've never operated outside the law! We have always adhered to a code of honor! This is something in which we need to involve law enforcement."

The General reacted, "And how is it you see this as something outside that code of honor? We know law enforcement is not set up to deal with these things, not even close. We know they have the capacity to bring horror and destruction to many, many people, and we know they have absolutely no hesitation killing and mutilating even the most innocent and youngest of victims. So how are we breaking the code of honor? We just talked about it, Steven. We are guided by a much deeper code of honor, a code of right and wrong, a code that somehow compels us to try and protect those who can't protect themselves, to do something when nobody else can or will. It's the reason I didn't say anything until you decided to take Galloway out. You chose to do something about it, even though there was no threat to you or to your family. You did it because it had to be done. He had to be stopped and you knew if you didn't do it nobody else would."

Steven was pacing slowly around the old man's office, trying to process what he was hearing and having a hard time doing it. The General was talking about pursuing these predators actively, outside of established laws and outside of the purview and reach of law enforcement. There was no other way of doing it. If they were operating in the U.S. and it was related to crimes committed in the U.S. and they did not involve law enforcement, they would be breaking the law, plain and simple. Not to mention everywhere else around the world.

Steven paused to look at Goodman, "How do you suggest we do this?"

The General smiled a sideways smile, "I'm still working on that. I do know a couple of things. We can't do it half-assed. If we decide to do this, we will need to do it up to our standards or not at all. I'm still considering it. Why don't you give it some thought, too, and we can get together in a few days to talk about it. Before that, though, you need to decide how you are going to deal with it as far as Beth and your family are concerned. You can't lie to Beth, you know that, and you know she'll know there's something up with you, so you need to decide how you are going to deal with it. Let's just get together in a few days and talk. I'll think about it some more, but I think I have a pretty good sense of how to do this. A lot of it will depend on you, so just think about it."

Steven nodded, looked at him and walked out of the office. He had always known the General would find out about what he had done. Maybe he had even relied on that fact because he knew he wouldn't just simply tell the old man. This was unfamiliar territory for Steven, trying to figure out how or if to tell Beth about what was going on with him. He had always been up front and honest and completely open with her, and anything other than that was foreign to him.

Thousands of miles away, in his apartment in Dubai, Mikhail Rozlkovich, Zlk, was looking at his computer screen and for the first time he could ever remember was left speechless by what it said. Once he took a moment to think about it, it made more sense. Really, it was pretty logical once you thought about the situation back in the U.S. Now he had to make a decision. There really was nothing to decide, the decision was made for him decades ago. He immediately began planning how he would hand off the current project he was working on to his second in command. The man was a boorish, arrogant ass from Yemen, but he was a competent military officer, so Zlk was willing to turn the reins over to him. Had it been any other way, he would have simply gone around the man and found someone he thought would be able to do the job. The man was sure to appreciate the extra income. It was more than $130,000, after all. More than the money, however, the man was going to revel in being number one, in having the entire organization reporting to him. Zlk knew there were a few young officers who were ambitious, very well trained and more than willing to stand up for themselves and for their men. He knew the Yemeni would most likely run afoul of one or more of these officers and when that happened he would have to stand firm and justify his position or to yield it to one of them. That was not his problem. If the man wanted to be number one and the money and responsibility that came with that, he would have to earn it and keep it. Once he had gone through the process of handing off the position, he needed to make arrangements to fly back to the U.S. The good thing was that he had a few options when it came to his transportation. He just needed to make a few calls. As he left his apartment, a smile spread across his face. His life was about to get more interesting, and for Zlk that was worth more than carloads of gold. He had given up expecting life would throw something at him that made his existence more interesting, so the smile on his face was a long time coming.

When he got home, Steven went directly into the bedroom, something that caught Beth's attention. Normally he would put his things down, go into the kitchen to get something to drink and turn on the news. It was his pattern when he got home and it was incredibly consistent. He sat on the end of the bed and looked out the window. She walked into the bedroom and he turned toward her and smiled.

She came over and sat down next to him and put her arm around his shoulders and rubbed his back, "Hey, are you okay? You blew right past the kitchen, I didn't even get to say hello."

He chuckled, "Sorry about that. I am absolutely wiped honey, I'm trying to keep some deals going that have been looking pretty dicey."

He kissed her and put his arms around her, "What are we having for dinner?" Beth stood up and gave him a big smile, "I have whipped up an incredibly quiche. Looked up the recipe on the Internet and I have to say, it is awesome. I also grilled some asparagus and made some jasmine rice."

Steven smiled, "Wow, a quiche. It sounds absolutely wonderful."

She went to go back to the kitchen, "Clean up and change and come to dinner. Bethany is doing homework and Chris is watching cartoons. I'll get them to the table by the time you're ready."

Steven went into the bathroom, splashed water on his face and looked at himself in the mirror. This was going to be harder than he ever imagined. He finally made it to the table. The kids were already there and waiting. He kissed both of them on the head and took his seat. They had dinner and talked and laughed and he enjoyed every bit of it. For the time being, he was sitting at the table with his family. He completely forgot about the rest of it, he was just a dad and a husband and he was happy. Everyone had ice cream with some chocolate syrup and whipped cream. Bethany and Chris started a minor food fight with the cherries their mother had put on the table for the ice cream. Steven joined in for a few seconds before Beth put an end to it.

Steven helped her with the dishes after dinner and while they cleaned he got lost in thought. Beth noticed he had become distant, "What's on your mind? You're quiet tonight."

Steven kept washing dishes as he answered, "I'm just swamped at work, honey. I'm really having a hard time with some of the new people."

His wife saw that he really was tired. It wasn't like him to complain or to seem so run down, but he was working with a lot of new people, getting deals closed, trying to get the new structure to work, so she understood. That evening after reading with Chris and helping Bethany finish her homework, Steven went into his office and closed the door, something he never did.

Beth came in after about an hour, "Are you okay? Is there anything I can do to help?"

She came around his desk and sat on his lap and noticed it wasn't work he was looking at and paging through, it was family albums and a box full of pictures. There were pictures of the kids, of her parents, of his parents, of all of them together. He had hundreds of pictures out on the desk.

Something was up, this was not like Steven at all and they both knew it, "What's going on, Steven? And don't you dare say something about work and how hard it is, because you and I both know that has nothing to do with it. What's going on?"

Steven looked at her and smiled a sideways smile, the kind of smile that let her know she had him, "I don't know, Beth, I can't get past it, I can't forget."

Beth held his hands, "Is it Tracy? Is that what is eating at you?"

Steven shook his head slightly, "No, it's not that, not really. What happened to us was horrible and it was something we didn't ask for, but it opened my eyes to these creatures, to what they are and to the damage they cause and I can't forget that. I can't seem to just move on and act like they don't exist. I keep dreaming, having nightmares actually. I keep wondering who is being hunted and how many lives are being destroyed."

Now it was Beth's turn to smile and look out the window, "I knew once you made the decision to do something about Riche you would never be able to just let it go. I hoped you would and I think I convinced myself that you had been able to do it, but I knew, I knew the kind of man you are."

Steven looked at her, "And what kind of man is that?"

Beth responded, "The kind of man that can't just stand by when he knows others are hurting, the kind of man that is governed by a deep sense of right and wrong and who feels compelled to set things right."

He brought her close and kissed the top of her head, "Yeah, you do know me. I don't know what to do, Beth. I don't know how to deal with this. I don't want to hurt my family anymore, Beth. I don't want to hurt you guys anymore."

She cocked her head and took his face into her hands, "Steven, the only way you are going to hurt your family is by betraying yourself. Did you really think I just chalked everything up to you thinking about Tracy? That I just ignored all those blank stares? I knew there was something deep inside and I knew that you would eventually share whatever it was with me. I didn't know when and I didn't know what it was, but I know you and I knew you couldn't hold it inside forever."

Steven nodded, "You're right, I can't hold it in anymore, but I don't know what to do about it, Beth, I really don't. I just know I can't wake up every day and think that people are dying because of these creatures and I am not doing anything about it, but I don't know what to do."

Beth looked at him, a bit puzzled, "I don't understand, Steven, you just said it. You can't just stand by and let this happen, you have to do something about it, so do something about it."

He looked at her, honestly surprised. He had not expected this answer, "Are you serious? What if doing this means that I am away from you, from the kids?"

She smiled a tender smile, "Steven, you are away from us right now. Oh, I know you are here in body, but you and I both know you are not here in spirit and we can feel it, I can feel it. So what do you do? I don't know, sweetheart, I don't know, but you have to do something."

Steven picked her up and put her down as he stood up from his chair, "Art has something in mind. He hasn't told me what it is, though. He knew something was up too."

Beth blew him away with her response, "He finally decided to talk to you after Miami?"

He looked at her, completely blown away, "What about Miami? What do you mean he finally talked to me?"

She chuckled, "Come on, Steven, I know you don't think I am stupid, I know it. You know I would figure out you were up to something on that trip. It doesn't take three days to do what you went to Miami to do. You only packed for one day and you didn't take your roll-about. I knew something was up. I just didn't, still don't, know what it was you were up to and I don't want to know. Whatever it was, I know you wouldn't do it unless you thought it was absolutely necessary."

He nodded, "Yeah, it was. I guess you're right, I've always known you would figure something out. I guess sometimes it's easier to pretend and to think eventually it will just blow away. I don't know what it is that the old man has in mind, but he asked me to think about it and we'll get together in a few days."

Beth smiled, "So think about it. But don't hide from me, Steven. You know that's not how we work, and you know in the end it will just make everything more muddled. I am not asking you to tell me everything you are thinking. I just don't want you to pretend you are not thinking at all and that you are all here with us."

He walked over and held both her hands, "I will, I promise. But Beth, what if this means I have to go away? What if what I have to do isn't something I can do here?"

Beth, just starting to tear up, responded, "Then we'll wait for you to do what you need to do, however long that takes. I would rather wait for you, Steven, all of you, than to settle for just a part of you, and I want the children to know their father is really here, not pretending to be here."

He gave her a passionate hug and whispered in her ear, "No matter what, Beth, I love you. Please don't forget that. Please don't forget that I love you and the kids more than I love life itself and that I would never do anything to hurt you."

Beth returned the hug and pulled her head back to show him a tender smile, "Silly, silly man. Of course I know it. We would never have made it if I didn't know how much you love me, how much you love all of us. Do what you need to do, Steven. Be honest with yourself and do what you feel is right. That's what made me fall in love with you and that's what makes you the best man I know."

Steven did think about it for the next three days. He went into the office and did his work and held his meetings, but more than anything he thought about his conversations with Beth and the General. He realized very quickly that they were basically the same conversation. Both were people that knew him better than he knew himself. Both were people that realized that whatever was drawing his attention away from his life was deep and was something he was carrying with him and would probably carry with him for some time, if not forever. Both had said the same thing, do something about it. But what? What could he do about the things he was thinking? Riche and Galloway had been specific instances that had come into his life without him looking for them. They were part of the hand that life had dealt him and he had done what he needed to do with that hand. Now there was nothing, just his life, just his family, so whatever he was going to do wasn't something that was thrown at him. Now it was going to be something he had to go out and find. He tried thinking about the science, about what he had learned about them, about the experts, but in the end it always came down to going out and finding what he knew was out there. On Wednesday night, he called the General to set up a time for them to meet. They agreed to meet on Friday in the old man's office after work. When Steven got there, the chief executive had laid out some drinks and some sandwiches on the table in his office. He motioned for Steven to sit down and then sat down himself. He had the look Steven had seen many times before, a look of purpose and ideas, like a man on a mission. Steven grabbed a sandwich and a Sam Adams and drank it from the bottle.

He was going to let Goodman lead the meeting, "So have you given it any thought? Have you figured some things out?"

Steven, in the middle of taking a bite, nodded, but didn't say anything.

The old man didn't need him to say anything, he had something to say and he was going to say it now, "I think we both know that what needs to be done can't be done within the purview of law enforcement. What needs to be done is to find these things and deal with them efficiently and with extreme prejudice."

Steven nodded, but he brought up one of the points he had been thinking about, "What do you mean by these things? We're not thinking about doing some sort of vigilante operation where we do the police's job, are we?"

The General came over to sit on the edge of the table in front of Steven, "Of course not. We have more than enough information to make the right call. We are not after psychos, we are not after thieves or drugged-out killers or anybody for that matter who is clearly a human with a psychiatric condition or motivated by greed or drugs. We have actually been working with Dr. Leonard, believe it or not, to develop a profile of the cases we are interested in. Here is what he developed. That man is a genius in his field, by the way. I have made him an offer to come onboard full time at GIC."

Steven suddenly looked scared, "You're not planning on involving him in any of this, are you? He won't do it, and more importantly, I won't let him do it. His work is important and it needs to continue."

The old man made motions with his hands that told Steven he needed to calm down, "No, he won't be involved directly. He is going to be coming in to continue his research, except now he will have unlimited resources, the latest technology, access to the best international talent and science, statistical programs, resources to find subjects and a more than generous grant to do his work with a healthy stipend for him personally."

Probably north of a million dollars, Steven thought. It was a perfect setup for a scientist that needed as many resources as he could get. Steven could see the use of Leonard's work. They would have the latest information on how these things worked, what made them tick.

The old man continued, "He's already come up with a list of elements that separate a human murderer and the possibility that it is one of these things in the middle of hunting. He established it was likely that the crimes would not be discovered until there were several victims. There will be no apparent pattern, unless one is worked up to throw authorities off. It will be rare that the predator is related to their victims in any way, so husbands and brothers or cases where they are primary suspects would probably not be anything to do with our targets. In most instances, there will be absolutely no single thread of evidence left at the scene. If the police do develop an interest in one of these individuals, there is a high likelihood they will disappear. Most of them will be highly intelligent and highly educated. There would be no drifters. All instances where a psychiatric condition is identified would be out since at that point they will most likely have been caught. It is very unlikely that the police will have established a connection between any of the murders. Leonard believes we will need to use the geomapping technology to help. He has committed to work with Carl to develop an algorithm we can also utilize to establish whether it is a situation we need to get involved in at all."

Steven nodded, "That's pretty impressive. There's no way to be completely sure, though, you know that."

The General shook his head, "No, I don't know that. You told me you could feel something, something different about Riche, something different about Galloway. With everything Leonard has developed, Steven, all we really need is for you to confirm.

We have also reached out to Jim Scoma to bring him onboard, same terms as Leonard, but we have not heard back from him. Some of the work he's doing could be incredibly useful. If he and Leonard work together, the algorithms Carl puts together will get better as we go along."

Steven stood and walked over to the window where they'd had their conversation some days ago. He was thinking about the reason he was able to do precisely that, confirm what these monsters were. He was thinking about it, but he was not going to talk about it. Not now, maybe not ever.

He turned to listen to what the old man had to say next, "I've thought about it, Steven, and I think I've come up with something. You will be moved to a new assignment, in-house, Special Operations. This division will have its own technology support, its own ops contingent, its own hardware and transportation element, and its own Housekeeping component. We have a CRAY-TX3 on order now, and before you ask, it's an NSA-level super computer that Carl can make sing. Our computers will search out key phrases, thousands of variables and other key criteria, will crunch the data, will look for patters, even the most innocuous things, and based on a score will spit out the cases around the country that are likely being driven by these predators. Once the computers spit out a case, you will take the lead and confirm the assessment or call an abort. The programs Carl created are pretty tight and already incorporate the data from Leonard's work, and Scoma's when he comes onboard, so if they spit something out we are going to take it seriously. Once you confirm, we bring in a tactical ops team to take care of the problem and the housekeeping to clean up after. In and out before anybody begins to ask questions."

Steven was already shaking his head, "No go. I won't do this with a tactical ops team. First of all, I don't want anybody else to get hurt or end up in jail. I know they are good, but still. Second of all, I don't know if they are committed to this or if it's just a paycheck, and I think that makes a difference. And third, you said it yourself, I felt what being in the presence of one of them is like, I felt it. We also need to keep this whole thing as lean as possible. The less moving parts, the less likely the op runs into a problem."

The General stood up and put both hands flat on the table, "Are you saying you would be the only operative? That it would be you and not a tactical team?"

Steven nodded, "Yeah, that's what I'm saying and it's exactly what you knew I would say. You just wanted to hear it come from me and you never expected this to be executed by anybody else."

The General hung his head defeated and smiled. Steven also knew him as well as he knew himself, "You're right, kid, you're right. I am guilty. I did want to hear it from you. I wanted to see if you had thought about it and you obviously have. It will be an extremely lean organization. Special projects will be dedicated 110 percent to this initiative. We have done a top-rate job of sanitizing anything that would in any way tie back to you, and we have also done a superb job of gathering the top black hat hackers and provided them with the latest equipment. That team is headed up by a friend of yours."

Steven frowned, "I don't know any black hat hackers."

The Goodman smiled, 'Oh yes you do. In fact, you know the black hat hacker."

Smiled thought about it and then it hit him and he grinned, "Milo Baskin."

The old man smiled, "Bingo! Have you looked into the kid at all? He's done some shit that the NSA, the Geospatial Agency and the CIA are trying to figure out. The info says he's in the 170 IQ range, but Carl and his IT people say that's a conservative number. He says he's never seen the like in 30 years of doing this. So you will always go in backed by every resource the company has at its disposal."

Steven was thinking about it as he looked over the roster of people that Goodman handed him. There were seven people designated as full-time employees of the Special Projects division, including him. He also noticed that every single document, list, roster was Executive Eyes Only, the highest level of security in the firm.

There was one name on the list he was absolutely blown away to see and needed to ask Goodman about, "You have Brice Hatcher here. Is he coming onboard full time? What does Carl think about that?"

The old man shook his head, "No, he's not coming onboard full time, he's coming onboard on a contract basis for the time being, and yes, Carl knows about it and supports it."

Steven shook his head in amazement. He still had some questions, although for the most part he thought he knew what the answers were, "So what happens to my deals? What happens to my people?"

The General responded, "I will take them over personally. If we can find someone who has what it takes to help, then great, but for the time being I will take them myself. I am up to speed on everything and we won't have an issue with anyone questioning authority."

Steven was nodding, it was what he had expected. There was nobody else within the company that could take over Steven's duties.

He still had a lot of questions and knew he'd probably have even more as this idea moved forward, but for right now he just wanted to know the fundamentals of the General's ideas, "How are we going to determine what we are going to go after? I know we are going to use the computers and the algorithms Carl developed using Leonard's work, but there has to be something else to determine what we go after. And I don't mean my gut feeling. I know that's important and that it will help to confirm, but if we are going to go in full-bore and we are going to take these things out, we need more than that."

The General nodded, "Agreed. We're not planning on taking these guys in, we're not going to be turning them over to the police, so yeah, we need more and we will have it. Aside from the programs Carl put together that look for certain criteria, we have satellite support and it will be routed to allow our hackers to be able to get into any law enforcement computer in the country. And remember, we will have Brice Hatcher to head that up. We will look at the evidence, we will look for anything that can attach any of the intelligence we develop to individuals we find. Make no mistake, Steven, most of these cases will not have a suspect developed, not one that fits our profile anyway. Remember, there could be instances where the police have a suspect and it may not be the same suspect we come up with. We fully expect that many of the cases and scenarios we assess will simply be the work of psychopaths."

Steven understood and he wanted to make something perfectly clear to his boss, "We agree then that we won't move on anybody in any way until we are absolutely sure they are what we think they are."

The old man nodded, "Agreed. That will be where our resources will really come into play. Just like it happened in your situation, we don't have to adhere to the law, which means we don't need warrants and we don't have to take evidentiary rules into consideration. We will be completely straight up about what we get, but the way we get it is up to us. I promise we will not make a move on anyone if we are not sure."

Steven nodded, he was used to the level and amount of resources the company could bring to bear, but even he had to be impressed by what Goodman was willing to use to make this idea happen.

The old man had a question, "You are right to be concerned about making sure we get things right. How is it that you went after Galloway? I know what happened as far as him coming to see you, but still, you couldn't be sure before you did something."

Steven walked over to the table and took a seat, the General followed, "You don't understand. When he came to see me, he was so excited. He let me know he had done things, things he had been ashamed of before, but things he now understood better. He knew then what he was. I had Carl look him up, education, childhood, prior crimes, all of it. He was an all-American kid from a well-to-do family in Atlanta. He had two sisters, both married. His parents are both professors, he was never abused and, at least as far as we could find, he never engaged in any sort of deviant behavior and he had no incidents involving the police. When I found out about the missing women in Atlanta, I knew. To answer your question, I drove from Miami to Atlanta. I already had his address, so I waited him out, and with Carl's help, I got into his house. He had a sort of false bottom in his refrigerator where he kept his victims' limbs. I wasn't sure I was going to find anything at his house, so I guess you could say I was lucky. Would I have taken him out if I didn't find anything? I don't know, I'd like to think I wouldn't have done it, but if I'm being totally honest, I think I probably would have taken him out anyway. It's different, though, and you know it."

Goodman put his hands up, "Hey, you don't have to convince me. I was just wondering how it was that you confirmed things with Galloway. It was a risky deal, Steven. It could have gone wrong easily. Why did you choose a Ka-Bar? Why not take him out from a distance?"

Steven answered and with his answer let the old man know that his operational chops were as razor sharp as ever, "I needed the time to get out of Dodge. I didn't have a suppressor, which meant I would have made noise and alerted the neighbors. I didn't have a backup team, so there was nobody to run interference or to warn me when the police were notified. That way, they didn't start missing him for eight hours and I was far away by then. He didn't have any sort of heavy tactical background or martial arts experience, so I wasn't expecting any trouble, and I didn't get any. It was done and over within less than a minute, no noise, no blood, and nothing at all to put me there."

The General had known Steven had used a knife to sever the man's brain stem. The strike was usually placed at the base of the skull where the backbone ends and the skull begins. It is at that point in the body where every single physical function is controlled. Once the brain stem was severed, death came almost immediately. There was almost no blood, just some spinal fluid that trickled out from around the knife. It was not something that could be done by an inexperienced operator. Although the police had not speculated about who had done it, they had made the determination that whoever it was had to have had training in military tactics, most likely Special Forces. Once the bodies were found in the refrigerator, finding out who had killed Galloway took a back seat. They had a lot of work ahead of them trying to figure out whether all the women could be traced to Galloway and whether there were other victims somewhere on the property. Carl had brought Steven up to date on the investigation and had told him that speculation was that one of the women's family members had figured out it was Galloway that had taken their loved one and had come looking for revenge. They were currently looking at every woman's family and interviewing anybody that had any military experience or martial arts training. Steven realized the General still had one thing to talk to him about and he knew it was not going to be easy. It was something Steven had thought about himself and it had proven difficult then.

Goodman finally brought it up, "You know you can't do this as yourself, don't you? You are too well known, and even if you weren't, there's no way we can risk this coming back to your family."

Steven had thought as much, he just hadn't taken it any further than that, "I know, I thought about it. It's one of the things that has really been giving me pause."

The older man replied, "It's up to you how you want to handle this, but if we are going to be completely invested in this, if we are going full-bore, there can't be any hesitation, there can't be any delay or doubt."

Steven nodded. He knew all of this, he had the tactical experience to know an operation like this depended completely on the ability to go in, do the job and leave with no delays and no trepidation. He also knew he could not do this within the construct of his family. He knew he would have to commit to this fully and would have to leave his family behind, for however long it took. This was an operation that had no specific end, it was an operation that would go on until he was ready to move forward, to truly put all of this behind him, and there was just no way to know when that would be. Maybe the time would come when someone else might take over, there was just no way to know. He had thought about being away from his family for years and had been reminded of the story of Donnie Brasco, better known as Special Agent Joe Pistone. He was a special agent for the FBI who had gone undercover for over two years and had brought down more mafia heavyweights than had ever been brought down. Pistone had completely immersed himself in the mafia culture – he had to, because had he had even one minor misstep, he would have ended up dead. This was going to be the same. Steven would have to leave his family behind and completely dedicate himself to this effort. He would keep in touch with Beth through channels provided by the company and he would see his family when and if there was an opportunity to do so, again with the company facilitating the visits. The General didn't have to say any of this. Steven knew that's how it had to be and he knew the old man had probably already made arrangements to provide a new identity, complete with a detailed backstory including employment, education, anything that someone might look up doing research on him. They would need to agree on all of it before anything could be created, but the old man had probably already begun working on it. His biggest and most difficult test was still ahead of him. He had to speak with his wife. Even though they had already spoken, he had to explain to her why it was he was going to have to go away again. She knew something was happening with him, but he was almost sure she didn't quite get the extent of it. She had told him she would wait for him for as long as it took, but he didn't know if she would be willing to do that if he was really gone, if he needed to be gone for years, not months.

He wrapped up the conversation with the old man, "Well, I know what I have to do now and you know how hard it is going to be with Beth. I assume you have already gotten started with the details, IDs, weapons, backstory, all of that?"

The General nodded, "It's been taken care of. I will brief you on your backstory, new identity, logistics, all of it, once you make the final decision. Why don't you go home and take care of what you have to take care of and we can discuss the details when you come back. Call me when you are ready and we can set up a day and time for you to come in. When you do it, leave everything behind, clothes, IDs, everything."

Steven nodded. He knew how to disappear, although he had never been involved in an undercover tactical operation of this scope and length of time. He would have to consult with someone who had experience, someone who had gone deep undercover. He would have Carl search for someone within the company that had that kind of experience.

He was looking at himself in the mirror and he could barely recognize himself. J.D. Garzen had always had a healthy ego, helped along by his ability to manipulate people and situations according to his whims, but he was not delusional, he knew he was far from handsome. His flabby, almost always oily face, his small rat-like eyes and porkish mouth along with thinning hair and an out-of-shape body ensured that even the most kind of assessments would never find him far from outright repulsive. But after a haircut done by a true top stylist, a facial to clean his pores and trim his eyebrows, and a fitting at a Savile Row tailor, J.D. Garzen looked like another person. Nigel Barlow stood with his arms crossed and smiled at his newest creation. He had seen hundreds of people blossom and become who they were meant to become, but none of them, not a single one, could compare to the physical transformation that Garzen had gone through. Now the work to refine his manners, use the proper diction, and develop his intellectual ability could commence in earnest. Garzen was a brilliant mind when it came to manipulation, understanding the human psyche and engender true faith, but when it came to culture, history, geography, philosophy, anything that made an individual a truly educated person, he was a complete disaster. Barlow had not realized that until they had been at a five-star restaurant and Garzen had asked if they had barbeque sauce for his fish. He'd been joking, of course, but the way he'd made the joke, coupled with his overall look and demeanor, had made Barlow cringe. It had been then that Barlow let Garzen know he'd be going through some changes. He had been concerned that perhaps he'd made a mistake, perhaps Garzen was so far from ever becoming what Barlow needed him to become that he would just not be able to transform him, no matter what he did. Now looking at his latest project, he felt much better.

Garzen turned from the mirror, "Damn, Barlow, I gotta give it to you and your people. I've never looked this good before. Do you know the kind of tail I could score looking like this?"

Barlow smiled, but not with good humor, "You will not be 'scoring' any 'tail,' John. The whole point of transforming you is not to help you seduce women. The audience we need you to seduce is much, much bigger. But I assure you, it will be far more satisfying than simply bedding women."

Garzen frowned, "What happened to me finally becoming who I really am? To allowing me to follow my desires, my needs?"

Now Barlow's smile did turn into a real smile, "Oh, believe me, you will be able to satisfy all of your desires, and you will be able to pursue your own projects, but all in good time, John, all in good time. First there is work to do. You have to put in the effort and prepare. Things have come far too easy for you, that's part of your gift, but this is a whole other level and things won't just happen, you have to work to make it happen."

Garzen nodded thoughtfully and then, as though he just realized something, tilted his head, "And what gives with the whole 'John' bullshit? I'm J.D. Garzen, goddammit."

Barlow unfolded his arms and took two steps forward so he was standing inches from Garzen, "No, John, you were J.D. Garzen, an uncultured and uneducated reverend, bore and asshole, you are now John David Garzen. And you will now be an educated, refined and incredibly charismatic gentleman of the world. That's what you will be because that's what we need you to be."

Garzen once again nodded thoughtfully and actually smiled at the idea of being a refined man of the world, he liked the sound of that. The smile didn't last too long on his face, however, because for the first time since he'd embarked on this whole odyssey, he realized he would be all those things because he had to be all those things. He realized Barlow would make certain that he would be that or nothing at all.

When Steven got home, Beth could tell there was something on his mind, and based on their previous conversations she thought she knew what it was, "Do you want to eat dinner?"

He came over to her and kissed her, "Sure. Where are the kids?"

She told him Chris was in their room playing and Bethany was in her room, probably on the computer. They had put restrictions on her computer, in spite of her protests, to avoid her coming across information she had no business seeing.

Steven held on to Beth, "Do you mind if we talk after dinner?"

Beth kissed him back, "Of course. Did you talk to the General?"

He nodded, "I did. You were right, he also knew something was up and in fact he had already thought of what I might do."

He wasn't going to tell her about Galloway, but he had to let her know the old man was really aware of what he was thinking.

Beth went about setting the table, "So is that what you have to talk to me about? What he came up with?"

He nodded again, but he didn't say anything. He might be completely wrong, but he had a feeling Beth somehow knew what it was that he had to tell her and it made the wait all that more difficult. For her part, Beth seemed unfazed. She was calm throughout dinner and she tried her best to get him to also relax a bit. The three glasses of chardonnay she had poured him during dinner had helped that along. After dinner, the kids had been told they were allowed to order a pay-per-view movie, and Bethany had bolted from the table as soon as her parents had said it was okay. Chris, as usual, was a beat behind and yelling at his sister to wait for him. Beth had poured herself an amaretto and Steven one of his favorite dessert drinks, Baileys Irish cream. They moved to the living room and sat down right next to each other. As much as she had tried to get Steven to relax, he still seemed tense. Whatever it was he had to talk to her about, he was struggling with it.

She tried to make it better by starting the conversation, "So, tell me about the conversation with the General."

Steven looked down and had both hands on his glass, "I told him what I was thinking about, what I had been thinking about. To be honest with you, he actually told me what I had been thinking about and he was right. Just like you, the man knows me really well, maybe even better than I know myself."

She smiled at him, "It's not hard to see why that would be the case. He has mentored you since you left the service, and he cares about you as something much more than just an employee and you know it. He's been here for us during our toughest moments, so yeah, I could see how he might know exactly what was on your mind. Believe it or not, to the people who love you, the people who know you, you have a hard time hiding yourself, hiding what you are thinking."

He smiled, "I am finding that out. I know you will understand. I know you of all people understand what I am going through and I am still having a hard time talking to you."

Beth took his hands in hers, "If you are having such a hard time telling me what's on your mind, it must be that you are going to be leaving. There is nothing else I can think of that you would have such a hard time saying to me. Out of everything that happened, everything we went through, the thing that seemed to really hit you the hardest, to really affect you, was the fact you were going to have to leave your family. So, I imagine whatever it is you talked to him about and whatever you have to tell me has to do with you leaving us."

Steven didn't know how to respond, he tightened his hands around hers as he prepared to talk to her.

He couldn't help but give her a smile, she knew him so well and she was such a strong woman, "You got me. You are right. There is just nothing I can keep from you. In the end, you always see right through me and I wouldn't have it any other way. Yeah, I have to leave, honey. What I have to do, what needs to get done, is not something I can bring home. There is just no way I could possibly do this and think that any of it could possibly touch you or the kids."

She listened and nodded and looked into his eyes, "I understand, Steven, believe it or not, I do understand, and although I don't know what it is you will be doing, I know it is important enough to have you leave your family. I told you I love you and I will wait for you and that is still how things are, it is how things will always be. I want you, I want my husband, all of my husband, and if I have to wait to get that then I will wait. You are my soul mate, Steven, you have always been, and you are the best man I know, in every way, so I am going to wait for you as long as it takes. Whatever it is you have to do, I want you to do it and I want you to do it the way you have always done everything, giving it your all and not having any regrets. This is different, now you will be leaving on your terms, our terms, not because you are forced to."

He looked at her and he couldn't help but to tear up, this was his wife, strong and smart and above all full of love for him. She knew him better than anyone else and she knew he needed to do this.

There was nothing else for him to really say to her, "I love you so much and I am so sorry that I have to leave again. I just can't get past it, Beth. I can't think about these things hunting and killing and destroying lives. I know, we know, what that feels like. We know how it makes it so that you can never get your life back, not really. It's just in my DNA, I guess. I can't let something like this, something so wrong and evil, go on when I know it is happening and I can do something about it."

And that was as much as he was going to tell her about what he was doing.

It was also as much as she wanted to know, "I told you, I don't need to know what it is you are going to be doing. I know it is important."

Steven had to let her know some of the details, though, "The company will give me a new identity and I will probably have to change my appearance. They will put me up somewhere, probably somewhere from where it is easy to travel. I will be able to contact you from time to time. I can't tell you how often or how, but the company will arrange for it. I will also be able to see you every once in a while, and if there is any emergency, I will come home immediately."

Now the full weight of what he was saying really hit her and she began crying softly.

It killed Steven to see her like that, and what made it even more difficult was that it was because of him that she was crying, "I'm so sorry, Beth. I wish it was different. I wish I could just let it go."

She turned to look at him and took his face in her hands, "Don't do that, Steven, don't you do that! Do not apologize for being who you are, I told you that is the man I fell in love with and, I don't know, maybe if you could let it go, something would change and I would see it and I would feel it, and it would change who you are, so don't do that. I'm crying just because I will miss you, because the kids will miss you, but I would be crying if you were still in the Navy and you were going on an 18-month tour on a ship or on some assignment with the SEALs, so please don't kill the romance for me!"

Steven chuckled, "Fair enough. I guess I didn't think of it that way. I didn't think of it as just another assignment, another job, but you are right, that is what it is."

She pulled him close and kissed his lips, "As far as your wife is concerned, and as far as your children are concerned, that is exactly what it is. A job their father has to go do that is going to take a long time."

Steven smiled at her and hugged her tight. She was an absolutely amazing woman, she was his soul mate.

She wiped her eyes, "When will you be going?"

He stood up and paced, "I don't know. He told me to think about it and when I was ready to call him, but I don't know."

Beth got up and went to pour each of them a little Baileys.

She came back with both glasses in hand, "What do you say we have a wonderful weekend and come Monday you can start your assignment?"

He looked at her for a long time, with a smile on his face. What a wonderful, strong, amazing woman and she was his woman, "Deal."

She handed him his glass and, with tears still in her eyes, raised hers, "Here's to your new assignment."

He didn't say anything, he simply raised his glass and toasted with her. They both took sips from each of their glasses.

Steven turned to put his glass down at the wet bar. Before he could turn completely, Beth grabbed his arm hard and brought him close to her and with a look that he could not ever remember seeing on her face before, she said to him in a low tone, "Get them, Steven, kill every single one of those motherfuckers."

And just as suddenly as she had grabbed him, she let go of his arm and went to find the kids. It was done. She knew, not how, not who, but she knew and she understood. With that realization, every bit of hesitation that Steven Loomis had held onto vanished. He was once again driven, driven the way he was used to being driven, by his internal compass and by the passion that drove him. He could now transition into an operational mode, into becoming the razor-sharp weapon he had been while in the SEALs. Beth came back with the kids and they watched a movie and made popcorn and were just a family for one more weekend. On Sunday night, Steven called the General to let him know he was ready. They agreed to meet at a safe house the company had on the Upper East Side. Steven got up at 5:00 in the morning. Beth got up with him and made coffee. They had a cup of coffee together, but in silence. When the time came for him to leave, he simply hugged her close, kissed her long and hard, and said goodbye.

She pulled him close and whispered in his ear, "We'll be here when you get back."

They had agreed that she would explain to the kids what their father was doing and would let them know their dad was going to be doing a job that was very important, but he had to be traveling to do it. The process reminded him a lot of when he would leave on deployment with the SEALs. They both had gotten it down to a simple process that did not allow either of them to dwell too much on the fact that he was leaving. Now there were more preparations to be done and not a lot of time to make them. The General had started the preparations, but until they were on the way, there was always a bit of anxiety. Each of them would think about it and have a difficult time with it on their own, but the moment for saying goodbye was not it.

Felix Garcia was now chief crime beat reporter for not only the New York Chronicle, but for two other papers also owned by the holding company that owned the Chronicle. This meant that he oversaw the assignments and writing for seven junior and associate reporters. The position came with an editor-size office, a company car and per diem, and perhaps most important, reserved parking 20 feet from the elevator. Not only had he gotten the job he wanted with a ridiculous raise, he had negotiated his next three jobs into his contract, something the paper had never done, not even for big-hitters they brought onboard. Aside from that he had the absolute and sincere respect and admiration from everyone in the paper, everyone. All of them knew without a doubt that Felix Garcia's stories had raised their paper to a whole other level and thus had made their jobs just a little safer. Even the other young reporters at the other papers had to take their hat off to him. He'd proved that it wasn't just about how long you've been doing it or whether you're a big shot on network TV, it was about making connections, doing the legwork and absolutely, positively never backing off a story when you smell one there. Life was good for Felix and he now had to help other young journalists like himself to do the things he'd done and to pursue his own stories. But he would always have an eye out for the Loomis story, not only because it had taken his career to another level, but because he could smell more story there. He didn't know what or how or why, but he felt there was more to that story, much more. He would always keep that with him and look in from time to time, but for now he had to kick one of his young protégé's ass. The kid basically wrote what another guy had written with no additional insights or information. Damn it, kids, sheesh, who could put up with them.

28.

When Steven got to the safe house, he was surprised to see Brice Hatcher and two other men he had seen from time to time but didn't know. The General was waiting for him and led him to a table with juices, fruit and bagels. Steven had to smile, this had the feel of a standard small office meeting. He passed on everything but the coffee.

Once he sat down, the old man took over. "Alright, so I wanted to have the core of the new organization here so you could all formally meet and get acquainted. Steven, you know Brice Hatcher."

Hatcher also had a measured IQ of 167 and was one of perhaps two people on the face of the planet that could outdo Carl Gilliam when it came to hacking. Actually, now he was one of two people who could come close to Milo Baskin. He was also a legendary ladies man. People said Hatch could meet a woman anywhere in the world and have her in his room by the end of the evening. He was a multimillionaire but it never came into play with the women because he simply never told them. He was a decent looking guy and he was a dwarf. Steven raised his cup and Hatch lifted his glass of orange juice.

Steven had to ask, "So you're ready to settle down, Hatch? Or are you still doing your own thing?"

Hatch smiled, "I'm always running my own thing, you know that. But as far as coming onboard, yes, I'm in. You had to find the one thing on earth that piqued my curiosity and my interest. The old man said that to participate I had to be in all the way, so here I am. How's the company cafeteria, by the way?"

Goodman answered his question, "It's excellent, but you won't get to see it or eat in it. Hatch is going to run the IT function and he will control all of the electronics used in all of the ops. Milo will strictly be hacking. All information will funnel through him. This is Avery Chambers and he will run cleanup when you need it. It will always be your call, though."

Steven nodded at Avery. He was a tall African American man with light green eyes and was built rock solid. His head was clean-shaven and he had the look of a seasoned operative. Steven's guess would be former Delta Force or Army Rangers.

The General answered the question, "Avery is a former MI6 man by way of the SAS."

He then turned to face the other man in the room. The man was definitely familiar to Steven, although only by sight. "This is Marcus Donahue and he will be handling all of the hardware, surveillance equipment and weapons. He will get Hatch whatever he needs and will coordinate transportation whenever and wherever you need it."

Steven looked at the men. It was a lean team indeed, but an incredibly professional team with people that had years of field experience and had more knowledge of hardware and technology than any 10 people put together. Steven remembered Donahue now. The old man had poached him from an MIT graduate program. The man had two doctorates, one in electrical engineering and one in applied physics both completed by the time he was 22. There was an ongoing joke at the company that they had their own little MacGyver at the tactical directorate.

Goodman went on, "You all know why you are here, you know what our mandate is and you have all been selected because of your belief in what we are doing, as well as your expertise. This is a completely voluntary program, if you decide it is not for you then you can simply go back to your job, no questions asked. You will be dealing with things that most of you have never seen. You all know what Steven went through and you all know how he defended himself. That science, that discovery engendered the genesis of this group. Steven will be in charge. He will make the ultimate call on how, when and even if the group moves on anybody or anything. You will all be briefed on each situation as needed and as determined by Steven. Publicly, you are no longer a part of GIC. You are not on the payroll and your benefits have been moved into a private fund. You, gentlemen, are the corporate equivalent of a nonofficial covert operative. Hatch and Avery, you both know what it is like to operate as NOCs. Steven, talk to them about it, get some insight into what it is like. There will always be at least 10 potential situations in the pipeline at any one time. Hatch's programs coupled with Dr. Leonard's research have already spit out more than two dozen potential situations. Steven will review them and will decide which ones need to be moved on. It will be his decision as to whether he brings you into that process or not. My official involvement with the group ends here and now. We will see each other only in extreme circumstances. All of you and your families will be taken care of through private channels, and I think you all know that your families will always be okay."

They all nodded. Whatever else might be true, that certainly was and they all knew it, "Alright, this building belongs to an offshore corporation and will be your base of operations. There is a private plane at a hangar at JFK which belongs to the same corporation and which will be used for all travel related to this group. Finally, Steven Loomis does not exist any longer as far as you are concerned. You will know the official story in the next 48 hours."

They were all operatives and all had experience with alternate identities and with people disappearing off the face of the earth. They all nodded and said nothing, they had all been briefed and other than what the General had shared with them they saw no need to ask any questions. Before Goodman could say anything else, there was a knock at the door. Goodman smiled, "Late, as always."

Steven could not imagine who it was. They had everything covered with the team they'd put together. As he looked expectantly at the foyer, a big smile spread across his face.

Goodman brought the visitor in. Only Hatch knew him personally, everyone else just knew him by reputation.

He slapped Zlk's back and addressed the group, "Gentlemen, I believe you know this guy, this is Mikhail Rozlkovich, Zlk. He will be backing Steven up on every operation. Steven will have tactical command, but I think we all know that when you spend as much time doing what each of you does, no command is ever needed."

Marcus Donahue and Avery Chambers' eyes flew open, but they simply nodded his way.

Brice Hatcher smiled actually put his orange juice down and headed over to Zlk, "Damn, Mikki, they hooked you too? Well, at least now we know this gig is not going to be boring."

Zlk actually smiled, walked over and picked up Hatch and gave him a hug, "Hatch, you crazy bastard. Don't even think about setting me up with anyone, Brazilian model or not."

Back down on the ground, Hatch shook his head, "You're never going to let that go, are you? Did she not look like a freaking supermodel?"

Zlk made a shooing motion with his hands, "I think it's funny that you keep calling him a 'her.' Yes, he did fool me and the only reason you are alive is that his friend fooled you."

The group chuckled at the exchange. It was actually kind of surreal that two of the most experienced and legendary operators looked so vastly different from each other. It had always been a source of amusement for Steven that Hatch and Zlk got along so incredibly well. Zlk didn't get along with more than three people in the entire world and they were all in the room. Steven looked at the group. They were all intense and serious professionals and they had all been vetted for this operation. Whatever their emotional commitment was, Steven would eventually find out, but he was sure none of them were in it for the paycheck alone. Having Zlk as a part of the team changed things. They could be very lean and not suffer for it. Zlk would take the place of a team of four to five men and that, in a situation like this one, was invaluable.

He addressed them for the first time as a team, "Gentlemen, we all know what we need to accomplish and we will all figure out how to do it together. This is new for all of us and we are going to have to be willing to learn as we go along, we all have to be willing to reset our way of thinking. I imagine you all have things you want to establish before we engage our first situation, so set things up the way you want and we will all get together in a couple of days to get this thing going."

Again, they all nodded. Steven got up from the table and nodded to the General, "If you gentlemen will excuse us, we have a couple of things to discuss."

They both left and headed for a small sitting room at the front of the house.

Goodman spoke first, "They are all good men, dedicated and professional."

Steven nodded, "I have no doubt whatsoever. We need to discuss one more thing, you and I. We need to agree on what we will engage and what we won't. We will go after those cases where we know it's a Homo predator hunting, nothing else. We will not be vigilantes going after psychopaths. They're dangerous and also hard to spot, but they will be for the police to deal with. Barlow explained, and I've read, that Homo sapiens predators can be anywhere and be anyone, so they will be hard to spot."

The General nodded, "You said it, psychopaths are for the police. It is my intention for this group to go after those that are something else, something not human, and as depraved and sick as psychopaths are, they are still human. Carl and Hatch have been working with Dr. Leonard on the programs you'll be using to establish potential situations we need to consider. Once Scoma and Milo get online, it will be an even tighter filter. Some situations will warrant more close examination because they are immediately suspect. So any instance where there is a clear sexual or economic element will be flagged as probably not what we're looking for. Instances where the relationship between each murder is clear and obvious will also be flagged as suspect. There are other situational elements that will also be flagged as suspect. Believe me, if there is any doubt as to who and what is hunting humans, we'll flag it, consider it and, if necessary, discard it."

Steven was looking out the window, wondering if this was crazy, if he had started something that made no sense. As quickly as the thought developed, however, it went away, aided by the memories of that warehouse, memories of his daughter and memories of all of the pictures and journals he had found at Galloway's house and office. No, whatever else was true, these things existed, had existed for many, many years, generations perhaps, and they were hunting.

He looked at Art Goodman, "Why are you doing this? Why go to all these lengths? I know it isn't just because of what happened to me and to my family. There's something personal here, what is it?"

Now it was the old man's turn to stand and walk over to the window and look out at New York. He turned to face Steven with his hands in his pockets, "You're right, it's not just because of

Riche or what he did. I have seen these things too, Steven, many, many years ago. In a place where death and horror were a part of everyday life, I found pure evil. I don't want to talk about it just yet, I don't think I am ready to do it, but I knew the second you made the decision to take Riche out, that you had also seen it, felt it.

"Now it's your job to bring your team along, to share with them the things you have experienced, the things they need to be ready for. They believe in you, Steven, and they believe in the science of your decision, in the science of a new species. They each have a story to tell, and they will tell it when they are ready, I'm sure. Hatch actually asked to be on the team. Avery and Marcus have their own demons to exorcise. And you know Zlk, you know what he's done and how he's done it. He is incredibly complicated, but it's clear there is something about this that deeply touched him."

Steven nodded. Zlk was in fact the only individual on the planet that Steven would allow to back him up on something like this.

Steven gave him a thin smile, "So you're not ready to talk about it, then?"

Goodman took a deep breath and sighed. He looked out the window for a few seconds and then back at Steven, "No, I'm not ready just yet. Someday I will talk to you about it, but not now."

He decided it was time to get on with the briefing, "So what is my identity going to be? Who am I?"

The General smiled and pulled out a thick envelope from his coat pocket.

He handed it to Steven and began to explain, "You are an academic researcher and freelance writer, a PhD. Your subject of expertise is forensic psychiatry and neuropsychology, and you have the credentials to back it. We wanted to make you a researcher and academic because for the most part people will talk to you far easier than they would a reporter or an investigator. It is also an inconspicuous persona when it comes to law enforcement. A private eye always catches the cops' attention, if only because they think you might get in the way, so we decided to pursue the scientific and academic angles."

Steven took the papers and leafed through them. It was a life, complete with childhood, education, early professional career, everything. Steven was certain that if anybody were to check out even the most innocuous fact they would find it to be completely true. The company was meticulous when it came to their backstories, but he was certain that this one was beyond airtight.

Steven looked up at the General, "What about my name?" The General nodded and smiled, "Your first name is the name we chose for our son before, well, before he passed."

Steven was touched, but he only said, "It's pretty, Art. I'm honored."

Goodman nodded, "Your last name is obvious. You know how much I love irony."

Steven looked at what was to be his name and smiled. It was no better or worse than some others he'd known. It was short and easy to pronounce and write.

The General went on, "You are going to have to change your appearance. Nothing drastic or dramatic, but enough to match the ID. You'll have to lower your bulk, you look like a linebacker right now."

Steven nodded, working out at as much as he had had put on a solid 20 pounds, most of it muscle around his shoulders and chest. He saw his photo on the California ID and on the passport he'd been given, his hair was dark brown with just enough gray to give it a silver hue and cut in a modern, layered style. He had wire-framed glasses on and a goatee to match his hair. The old man was right, it wasn't anything dramatic or substantial, the genius of it was its subtlety. He was certain that once he had undergone the changes, he could pass by anybody that knew him on the street without being recognized, unless they stopped and stared, and even then it might be difficult. They went back into the room where everybody was. The General bid farewell without saying anything further. After spending a few minutes talking about the hardware that should always be available and getting a more detailed explanation from Hatch about the programs he had running and the algorithms he used to go through information and identify possible engagements, the group relaxed and began to gel. He explained to Steven and the group that the 10 folders that were ready for his review had been developed over the past week. After they all had a chance to share their points of view about what they would be doing, they all said goodbye and went about fulfilling each of their roles.

Steven was alone in the safe house. When he went upstairs to one of the rooms, he found a full wardrobe. The clothes were expensive and stylish, very much in line with a successful academic and researcher. There were three pairs of wire-framed glasses with no prescription on them. Steven smiled. He could see Beth's hand in the selection of the clothes. He had no doubt that the old man had recruited her to choose a wardrobe. He went back downstairs and walked over to the wet bar, which looked to be well stocked. He poured himself a shot of Johnnie Walker Blue, went to the front room where he and the General had spoken and sat down at the small table by the window. He enjoyed looking out the window, watching the city go by. He was deep in thought, thinking about his journey here. Now that he was actually here, he could look back at the path he had taken, the things that had been put in front of him and the things he had chosen to do himself. As he sipped his drink and looked out the window, he decided the time had finally come for him to come to terms with the real reason he was here, a reason that not the General, not even Beth, knew about. Throughout this whole ordeal, everyone around him had been completely convinced that the reason he knew with such certainty that Donald Riche had been something different, something other than human, was because of the research he had conducted. Nobody, not one person, had questioned the reasons for his complete faith in what he was claiming. Given what he had been through, what he had witnessed, nobody was going to doubt him. Drew Willis had been the only person around him that had seemed to question the reasons for his absolute certainty, but he had never asked the question. Steven had just seen the question come across his face a couple of times while he listened to Steven explain why he was so certain. He didn't know that Dr. Leonard had also thought about a different possibility after they spoke at the law office right before the trial. Now, on the eve of a new life, on the eve of the start of something bigger, it was time for him to face the truth and to accept it and then let it go, forever. He couldn't blame anybody for the total faith they had in him and what he had done, what he had decided. There was no way they could have known the real reason for his certainty about Riche, about the new species, no way to know what he really was. As a boy, he had known early on that he was different, that there were some things about him that were, well, just different. He had learned to walk when he was 10 months old and had learned to speak in clear, full sentences at 18 months old. His parents had known their only son was gifted early on. Steven had gone on to school when he was three years old and had quickly shown his intelligence. His games and his work were far beyond that of his classmates. Reading came in his first year in school. His teachers had always tried to keep him stimulated, interested. Eventually they basically let him learn at his own pace, although he never skipped a grade. He had realized he was different, really different, in the first grade. He had engaged in play that kids his age engaged in, space travel, cowboys and Indians, cops and robbers, all of it. But he had to pretend to play the same way the other boys did, because if he had played the way he could play, the games would have been over quickly. He was able to hear things his friends couldn't, smell things his friends couldn't, see things his friends couldn't. It wasn't that he had x-ray vision or any such thing, it was that he noticed things, minute details that went unnoticed by everyone, the way they were arranged, the way they fit into the big picture and the way they fit into whatever it was they were playing. When he started to figure out that his friends simply could not physically hear some of the things that he heard or smell the things that he smelled or notice things the way he noticed them, he got scared. Over time, he became aware of how often he would ask 'Can't you hear that?' or 'Can't you see that?' So he stopped asking. He was a kid and finding out things about himself that a child his age shouldn't have to deal with made him mature emotionally as well. So he grew up knowing there was something different about himself, but he was willing to accept it and make the compromises he needed to in order to be accepted by his friends. And accepted he was. After his parents died, he went to live with a second cousin of his mother's. A decent family willing to raise him, but with no desire to form any sort of significant emotional bond. He was a great athlete in middle school and high school. Whatever the sport was, he seemed to have an absolutely preternatural sense of where the play was going and was therefore able to anticipate it. That, combined with a lean, muscular frame, made him a formidable athlete. All of his coaches adored him and all stated, without question, that Steven Loomis had a future in professional sports if he wanted one. He had chosen the military instead. By the time he had graduated high school, Steven understood the full weight of his differences, the impact that he could have in whatever he decided to do. He had also known he was different because of his almost rabid pursuit of the right thing, the fair thing, sometimes at the expense of direct orders or other people's concerns. As a child, he had gotten in more than one fight over someone being bullied, even protecting and stepping in for kids he didn't know. He never hesitated, even when the bully was much bigger. He never lost a fight.

As he grew up, he volunteered with several organizations that helped those in need. His friends knew this zealous side of him and would roll their eyes every time Steven took on another cause. As he grew and matured, he realized there were things he could do to set things right and there were other things he simply couldn't reach at his age. He pondered joining the police department, but instead opted for an education and a life in the Navy. He knew if he was able to find the right job, he could really make a difference, not only in the U.S. but abroad. And he had done just that. During his years in the sensitive investigations group, he had helped to solve some crimes that had gone unsolved for years. He had put away men who had murdered and raped and betrayed their country, and he had found all of it immensely satisfying. He had developed a reputation for going after everyone, regardless of rank or influence, with the same dogged intensity. Eventually, though, he realized he could perhaps make an even bigger difference in an environment where his physical gifts could be utilized, so he had gone on to join the SEALs. In every mission, he had gotten further confirmation of the differences between him and everybody he met. He had honed his senses to the point that they were razor sharp. SEALs functioned differently than others anyway, but his were innate gifts and, with the training, went much further than what he knew to be normal. His men trusted him implicitly. He always seemed to make the right call and he had no problem rearranging their orders to do the right thing. For his part, Steven became focused, almost obsessed, with the pursuit of those he considered to be evil, madmen that were willing to sacrifice lives to further their own political and religious objectives. His years in the SEAL team had helped him to learn how to utilize his senses, his awareness, his strategic vision in the most effective and efficient way. He had never shared his knowledge with anybody, had never tried to quantify it or understand it. Not until Donald Riche. When Riche was arrested and Steven did the research on these creatures, he was immediately engaged by the part of the research that showed that almost every one of the individuals that were a part of the research reported higher than normal sensory capacity. They claimed to be able to smell better, hear better, see better than other human beings. He learned that these individuals had known from very early in life that they were different, that they were something other than human. These individuals most of the time had been classified as psychopaths or schizophrenics. It wasn't until Leonard, Scoma, Grossman and other experts had begun to find the presence of something else that things had changed. This was the part of the research that had drawn him in, that had made him think about himself and the things he knew to be true about his life, about his own being. And it was then he had come to a simple and fateful conclusion, he too was something other than human, the same as Donald Riche and others like him. He had the same physical attributes they spoke about, but he had never developed the predatory sense the way they had, his was a different sense of pursuit, a pursuit for the feeling of satisfaction he felt when he set things right. It was the feeling he had always been on the hunt for, it was the feeling that was his prey. He knew these creatures were hunting humans, not because they wanted the physical body of the victim for some particular purpose, but because they were getting a feeling of supreme power, of being almost godlike and they were getting it from the suffering and despair they caused. Initially he had been convinced he was not, could not, be a part of Homo sapiens predator. He wasn't sure what he was, but he wasn't that and he wasn't human.

The conversations with Dr. Jim Scoma had provided the answer. And in one moment of clarity, he saw everything come together. His childhood, his abilities, his dogged obsession with the pursuit of fairness and doing the right thing. When he saw that warehouse and read the research, he understood he was not alone and that those others who were also something else were true predators, and he knew, he felt, that they could hunt their prey in a way that no human could. He knew the kind of damage they could do. He had felt it with his own family. It was damage he had inflicted on countless terrorist cells, insurgent positions and enemy combatants. Although not publicized or claimed, Steven's record officially reflected that the operations he had led had had the highest net yield in the Navy. That meant that every mission he had led had produced the most efficient yield of enemy lives. He had lost two men in ten years of operations and his unit was responsible for over 7,400 confirmed enemy deaths, by far the best net yield in the history of the SEALs. He had completely unleashed his predatory instinct during those missions and after 10 years was ready to move on. Until Tracy had been taken, he had never gone back, never engaged in any sort of predatory behavior nor had he felt the need to use his senses to further his cause. He had turned into an executive who made sure his deals were fair and that somehow they made the situations they were meant to address better. And so here he was, now fully invested in what he knew he was, another subspecies of the Homo genus, a species at the other end of the spectrum from Donald Riche, fully invested in the opportunity to make a difference. It was the reason he knew he would never simply get past it. He knew if he and his team did run into one of these creatures, it would be up to him to lead them in bringing an end to the mayhem. He knew they wouldn't be able to do it without him and he was okay with that. For the first time since the day he was born, Steven Loomis was completely aware and completely at peace with what he was and what he was meant to do. It had taken discovering there was another human subspecies, but it had finally happened. Someday he would talk to Dr. Scoma about it to understand it better. But for right now, he understood everything he needed to understand.

A week later Felix Garcia was leafing through the latest garbage that some of his junior writers had turned in when one of his more promising young reporters came to his door almost out of breath, "Hey chief, have you checked the wires?"

Felix put down the pages he'd been reviewing to look at the guy, "No, what about the wires?"

The kid could not contain himself, "Oh, my God, you won't believe it! It's all over the news, Twitter, everywhere."

Rather than ask another question Felix turned on his computer and pulled up the latest headlines, and there it was, larger than life. He felt as though he had been kicked in the gut. He pushed everything on his desk aside and pulled the article up from the beginning:

Daphne Shuster, API: New York

*I*n what seems to be a tragic end to what has been called the most remarkable legal case in history, the Loomis family appears to have perished in an airplane accident over the Atlantic. Steven Loomis was charged with the first-degree murder of Donald Riche, a man suspected of kidnapping and killing Tracy Loomis and nine other girls. After a jury trial that was covered globally had gone on for more than three months, the case was resolved when Loomis and his legal team came to an agreement with David Neall, the district attorney, and Bart Logan and Melanie Farris, the two deputy DAs that handled the case. Loomis was given two years in prison, but was released after only 14 months. The flight plan filed by the pilot of the private Gulfstream 5 jet showed the plane scheduled to touch down in Paris, France to refuel and then on to Denmark. The plane, owned by GIC, the company that Steven Loomis worked for, was said to be CEO Art Goodman's, CEO *private airplane. Mr. Goodman could not be reached for comment. The company has put out a statement saying, 'We will use every resource available and we will provide assistance to any agency to find the family. The GIC family is absolutely heartbroken at what appears to be a tragic accident.' According to FAA documents now under review by the National Transportation Safety Board, the plane seemed to have no issues for three and a half hours as it made its way over the Atlantic. Then, at 2:00 AM New York time, the plane began to lose altitude, which prompted an immediate check-in with air traffic control. When traffic control could not get a response all the way through when the plane dropped under coverage of the air traffic control satellite and radar, they began to vector the Coast Guard and any other nearby vessels in the direction of the flight. So far, no survivors and no wreckage has been located on the surface. Survival experts explained that even if one of the passengers were to make it through a crash alive, the Atlantic Ocean would probably induce hypothermia within a few minutes. All agencies involved in the search have committed to continue the search throughout the night and for as long as it is necessary to find out what happened. His wife Beth, his daughter Bethany, his son Chris, and his in-laws, Tom and Lucy Delaney, accompanied Steven Loomis.*

Robert Grady walked through the precinct with a spring in his step. He had all his mail under his arms and was whistling and had a nice tan. It was his first day back from his weeklong vacation, so he was as light as a feather. He walked into his office, spilled all his mail, opened his blinds and stood with his hands on his hips, smiling at the city. He then heard a soft knock on his door and turned back to see Mark Mullins, and his smile disappeared. Mark Mullins looked truly like someone who was absolutely miserable. He looked at Grady and did not even ask about the vacation.

He got right down to it, "Have you seen the paper?"

Grady, frowning now, shook his head, "I just got here, Mark, what's the deal?"

Mullins stepped up and threw the newspaper folded over on Grady's desk. Grady walked over, picked up the paper, read it for five seconds and sat down heavily in his chair. He looked at Mullins whose look said everything he needed to know. Grady said nothing, nodded and went to look out the window. Mullins knew to just let him deal with it on his own. After about five minutes of trying to process the information, Grady just glanced at the mail spilled on his desk and he was going to move on when he saw the corner of a postcard. He picked it up and looked at it, it was a postcard from Coronado, California. He frowned and picked it up. It had no writing on it, just the postcard from Coronado with a picture of the Hotel Del Coronado on it. The postmark was two days ago and it had been sent from Dallas, Texas. Grady frowned truly wondering what the hell that was all about. He shrugged, tossed the postcard on his desk and was about to grab the paper again when his eyes flew open. He looked at the postmark date on the card again, and a thin, knowing smile appeared on his face. Coronado was where the Navy SEALs began their training.

He shook his head, walked over to look out the window and under his breath said to himself, "Well played, Loomis, well played."

He threw the postcard in the trash, grabbed his other mail and started going through it with a different kind of smile on his face.

Thousands of miles away, in the mountains of Colorado, someone else was reading the headlines of the Loomis air tragedy. Unlike detective Grady, this individual did not need a postcard to have a sly grin appear on his face. Nigel Barlow threw the newspaper, along with the pile of papers related to the story that was in the folder he had had developed by his people, on a table and walked over to his massive window with the breathtaking view of the Rockies. There was absolutely nothing in the story or any of the information developed by his people in the FAA, NTSB, Coast Guard, FBI, none of them, that gave a hint of anything other than exactly what it appeared to the world, a tragic and heartbreaking accident. Still, the man stood looking at the view with a smile on his face and a sense of satisfaction, excitement and curiosity driving his contentment. Whatever else Steven Loomis was, he was not dead, nor was his family. He was also every bit the formidable opponent Barlow had anticipated, but Barlow had not quite anticipated the level of support and the depth of the resources Steven Loomis had access to. It was invariably Art Goodman who was behind the resources and the support Loomis was getting. And those resources were not to be trifled with or be underestimated. He was going to have to reconsider what he had planned to do regarding Steven Loomis. For the time being, he did not care where the man or his family were, and while for others that may cause unease or anger, for Barlow it only made the game more challenging, and in the end, when the enterprise began to bear fruit, more satisfying.

He smiled one last, broad smile as he looked at the mountains. As he turned away from the window, he also spoke to himself, "And so the game begins, Mr. Loomis, so the game begins."

Five days later, a limousine showed up at the safe house in Manhattan to pick up what looked to be a polished, well-dressed socialite on his way to a family reunion in the Hamptons. The driver, Terrence Hill, had seen thousands like him, all with that pompous, entitled look that said 'I am better than you.' The guy was on time at least, and when Terrence went to try to pick up his bags, the man picked up two himself. Terrence also had to admit that the guy didn't look at him as if he was some bug to be careful of. He was easygoing and had a pleasant way about him. Maybe not all of these upper-class, pencil necks were assholes. When they got on the way to the private terminal at Teterboro, Terrence also noticed that the guy was not immediately on his cell phone, texting or talking to someone, he just looked out the window in contemplation. Terrence tried to start a conversation with him, something he rarely, if ever, did, "So, where are you headed today?"

The man smiled and looked at Terrence through the rearview mirror, "I'm headed to San Diego."

Terrence smiled back, "I'm from Cali, man! Are you going for business or just for pleasure?"

The man again looked at the rearview mirror, "I'm moving there, actually. All of my things are already there, now all that's left to move is myself."

Terrence nodded, "I hear you, brother, moving's a pain in the ass. Where in San Diego are you moving to?"

He responded, "To Coronado, a small condo."

Terrence smiled wide, "Niiice! You'll enjoy the town. Lots of great places to eat, not the tourist crap, nice seafood, small hole-in-the-walls. Have you ever been to Coronado, Miisterrrr ...ah... Sebastian...?"

Terrence was looking for the paperwork with the guy's last name on it, but before he could find it the man answered, "I have been there, many times and it's Hunter, Sebastian Hunter. Actually, it's Hunter, just Hunter."

Terrence smiled, "I like that, man. Hunter, just Hunter."

The sense of irony he felt when he heard his new name was not lost on him. His legend was Sebastian Hunter, academic, researcher and writer. But as far as he was concerned, he was indeed just Hunter.

Epilogue

Almost on the opposite side of the world, in a suburb of Auckland, New Zealand, a young family was playing on the front yard of their home. The two girls, roughly five and six years old, were swinging on a swing set with their father pushing both of them while their mother was trimming some rose bushes. As they'd spent their afternoon just enjoying the sun, they also watched as the new family next door was getting their furniture delivered. From what they were able to tell, they had one girl about eight years old, a little boy of about three, and it appeared that their grandparents also lived with the family, which in New Zealand was nothing out of the ordinary. The lady of the house was a good-looking woman of about 40, who had been managing the furniture delivery all day. During a break, she came over to the fence and introduced herself as Mary Donner, her father and mother were Richard and Donna Freeman, and her children were Christian and Bethany Donner. After a few minutes of small talk, weather, prices at the grocery store, other neighbors, Mary excused herself to keep making sure the furniture got delivered and placed where it needed to be placed. When Liz Brunell told her husband about the family next door, she told him she could tell Mary had gone through some difficult times, but was a sincere, decent and open woman that she felt she could build a friendship with. She also told her husband, Norman, that she thought he might want to reach out to Mary's father, Richard, who while obviously older than Norman, seemed quite fit and quite active. Liz's assessment of her neighbors would prove to be dead-on, at least for the first four and a half years of their friendship. Whatever Liz and Norman Brunell had thought could be the evolution of their friendship and how it would play out, could not have possibly anticipated what would eventually come to their peaceful, beautiful neighborhood. But for now, it was simply two families meeting each other and forming what would indeed be a tight friendship.

www.ingramcontent.com/pod-product-compliance
Lightning Source LLC
Chambersburg PA
CBHW030938140726
R18570700001B/R185707PG47905CBX00005B/9